BETWEEN THE RAINDROPS by Mary Lynn Baxter

He flipped on the lamp, hoping to dispel the image of Beth Loring's beautiful face.

Nothing doing. His vision of her was as clear as ever.

Dammit, Weston! Have you lost your mind? She's an assignment, and that's all! Forget that and you are in deep trouble.

MOMENTARY MARRIAGE by Annette Broadrick

"Don't you want to get into something more comfortable first?" he asked.

She sighed and closed her eyes.

"Come on. I'll help you. You'll rest much better if—"

Lauren's eyes popped open, and she slapped his hand away from her belt. "What do you think you're doing?"

"Helping my *wife*—" he emphasized the word "—get more comfortable."

THE ICE CREAM MAN by Kathleen Korbel

Jenny had been watching how the muscles on his legs shifted, how his faded jeans hugged his hips. They fascinated Jenny.

They didn't fascinate her half as much as what she saw when Nick got to the street. Reaching back to pull a bandanna out of his rear jeans pocket, he revealed what his bandanna had hidden. A beeper.

Why would an ice cream man need a beeper?

It wasn't fair. The one breath of fresh air in her claustrophobic existence, and she was going to have to report him to the police.

MARY LYNN BAXTER

Award-winning author Mary Lynn Baxter knew books would occupy an important place in her life long before she began to write them. After graduating from college with a degree in Library Science, Mary Lynn became a school librarian before opening the D&B Bookstore in her hometown of Lufkin, Texas, where she and her husband, Leonard, own a small farm and share a passion for gardening. She has written twenty novels, a number of which have been on the Waldenbooks bestseller list. In 1985 she won a Waldenbooks award for her top-selling novel *Everything But Time*.

ANNETTE BROADRICK

believes in romance and the magic of life. Since 1984, when her first book was published, Annette has shared her view of life and love with readers all over the world. In addition to being nominated by *Romantic Times* as one of the best new authors of that year, she has also won the *Romantic Times* Reviewers' Choice Award for *Heat of the Night, Mystery Lover* and *Irresistible;* the *Romantic Times* WISH Award for her heroes in *Strange Enchantment* and *Marriage Texas Style!;* and the *Romantic Times* Lifetime Achievement Awards for Series Romance and Series Romantic Fantasy.

KATHLEEN KORBEL

lives in St. Louis with her husband and two children. She devotes her time to enjoying her family, writing, avoiding anyone who tries to explain the intricacies of the computer and searching for the fabled housecleaning fairies. She's had her best luck with her writing—for which she's garnered the *Romantic Times* award for Best New Category Author of 1987, and the Romance Writers of America RITA awards for Best Romantic Suspense and Best Long Category Romance—and her family, without whom she couldn't have managed any of the other. She hasn't given up on those fairies, though.

UNDERCOVER
Lovers

MARY LYNN BAXTER
ANNETTE BROADRICK
KATHLEEN KORBEL

Silhouette Books

Published by Silhouette Books
America's Publisher of Contemporary Romance

SILHOUETTE BOOKS

by Request—Undercover Lovers

Copyright © 1994 by Harlequin Enterprises B.V.

ISBN 0-373-20102-8

The publisher acknowledges the copyright holders of the individual works as follows:

BETWEEN THE RAINDROPS
Copyright © 1987 by Mary Lynn Baxter

MOMENTARY MARRIAGE
Copyright © 1988 by Annette Broadrick

THE ICE CREAM MAN
Copyright © 1989 by Eileen Dreyer

This edition published by arrangement with Harlequin Enterprises B. V.

® and TM are trademarks of Harlequin Enterprises B.V., used under license. Trademarks indicated with ® are registered in the United States Patent and Trademark Office, the Canadian Trade Marks Office and in other countries.

Printed in U.S.A.

CONTENTS

A Note from Mary Lynn Baxter

Dear Reader,

Between the Raindrops was my twelfth book for Silhouette and turned out to be one of my favorites.

I've always been fascinated with people who do undercover work, such as private detectives, because they are oftentimes hired to find someone else's secret.

In this particular book, the reverse is true. The hero, Cole Weston, has the secret, a secret he isn't willing to share with the heroine, Beth Loring.

Another reason this book is special is the setting. Nacogdoches, Texas, in the heart of the piney woods, is the oldest town in Texas and only twenty miles from where I grew up. I'm partial to this part of the country, of course, with its lush pine forests, huge oak trees and abundance of flowers.

But most of all I enjoyed writing this book because it allowed me to tell the story of two strong but vulnerable people who eventually found true happiness between the raindrops in their lives.

Mary Lynn Baxter

BETWEEN THE RAINDROPS

Mary Lynn Baxter

To Larre', Sandy and AKA—thanks, ladies!

Prologue

The second the tall, broad-shouldered man crossed the threshold into the luxurious office, the foul aroma of cigarette smoke slapped him in the face.

"Damn, why the hell don't you quit smoking those cancer sticks?" he asked.

"Huh," the older man camped behind the desk snorted, "the same reason you don't, I reckon."

Having no suitable comeback, the younger man tossed a manila folder on the desk.

The man latched onto it like a lifeline. "So you found her?"

"Did you doubt it?"

"Well, come on, tell me. Where is she?"

"Twenty miles away. In Nacogdoches."

A fisted hand pounded the desk. "You mean my granddaughter's that close?"

"That's exactly what I'm telling you. However, circumstances have changed somewhat. The child's adoptive father is deceased and his wife is rearing her alone."

For a moment there was silence in the room while the silver-haired man seemed to digest what he had been told. "Mmm, that should make it easier for you."

"Hey, I've done my part. Now it's up to your lawyer."

"That, my boy, is where you're wrong," he said emphatically. "I want *you* to make our case airtight. I want you to prove this woman an unfit mother. Get to know her, find her soft spots, her vulnerability."

"Whoa, wait just a damned minute. You know I don't handle that type of case personally."

A bushy white eyebrow tilted. "But for me you would—right?"

A harsh sigh vibrated around the room. "Dammit, man, you sure know how to exact your pound of flesh."

"Ah, it'll be a piece of cake, you'll see. If we have to, we'll offer her cash. That gets 'em every time."

The young man pondered that as he stroked the back of his neck with his fingers. When he spoke his voice was as hard as nails. "If I agree, this makes us even."

Without waiting for an answer, he squared his shoulders, turned and walked calmly, coolly to the door and closed it firmly behind him.

Chapter One

"**W**hat!"

The shriek ripped through Beth Loring's lips, leaving her mouth open in stunned disbelief.

Her attorney, Giles Renfro, winced against the painful outburst. "Beth, please, this isn't easy for me, either."

"You . . . you can't be serious," she stammered. It was absurd! Impossible! Megan was hers. No one was going to take her baby away from her.

Suddenly the room spun like a Ferris wheel. Black dots danced before her eyes.

Renfro made a hasty move toward her. "For chrissakes, Beth, don't faint on me now."

It was the touch of his cold fingers on her wrist that brought Beth back to reality. After what seemed like aeons, his square face came back into focus.

"Please," she whispered at last, "just give me a few minutes and I'll be all right."

Giles looked anything but convinced, taking in the pallor of her porcelain skin. Nevertheless he let go of her hand and, after peering closely at her for another moment, backed away and headed straight for the small bar in the corner of the office.

Only part of Beth's brain was aware that he was busy popping the top on a bottle, while the other was chanting, *It's just a dream. You'll wake up any second now and find you've had a nightmare.*

"Here, drink this."

Beth blinked before reaching out and accepting the glass. Although her hand trembled violently, she managed to raise it to her lips. Once the fiery liquid reached her stomach, Beth knew she had made a mistake; her insides rebelled. With a savage shake of her head, she thrust the glass at Giles and clutched at her stomach.

"Sorry," Giles muttered gruffly, setting the glass aside. "I thought a little shot of bourbon might make you feel better."

Beth stood erect, her eyes somewhat less glazed. "The only way you could make me feel better is to tell me this is all a bad dream."

Renfro shook his head and sat down on one corner of the desk, his arms folded. The light from above played off the bald spot on the top of his head.

"I wish I could," he said. "But it's a fact, and you have no choice but to face it. Megan's grandparents want custody of her, and the way I see it, they're prepared to go to any lengths to do just that."

Each word was like a dagger piercing Beth's heart. "But...how can they...? I mean..." She shuddered, her eyes wide and panic-stricken. "Megan's mine. When Lee and I adopted her, you...you assured us that the adoption was ironclad, that everything was done by the book. That she was ours for life."

Renfro tugged at his mustache before wetting his lips. "And I stand by that today, but that doesn't keep Dexter Manly from trying."

Words failed Beth. It was only after she swallowed hard that she was able to speak. "You mean *the* Dexter Manly, the oil magnate?"

"I'm afraid it's one and the same."

"Oh, my God. If only we'd known." Beth's voice was barely audible as she sagged against the wall, knowing that if she ventured a step, her legs would buckle beneath her.

"What difference would that have made?" Renfro demanded bluntly. "You know you would've taken Meg no matter who the parents were. It's just a damned shame this all had to come about. It makes me madder than hell when the code of silence on private adoptions is broken," he added, talking more to himself than to Beth.

"You're right, it wouldn't have made any difference," Beth whispered at last.

"Anyway, Manly's daughter was Megan's mother."

Beth felt a numbing, icy chill spread into her chest. Her palms sweated. Her heartbeat accelerated. She began shaking all over. This could not be happening. It simply could not be happening.

Beth's state of mind was not lost on Renfro. "For God's sake, Beth, sit down," he urged, gesturing toward the deep cushioned chair on his right.

Ignoring his sympathetic command, Beth whispered, "Could he really get her? Is...that possible?" Her eyes, huge with fear, clung to Renfro's face.

He thought for a moment. "Anything's possible, but..."

"No!" Beth screamed, tears spilling down her cheeks. "I won't let him take my baby. Megan's *mine*," she added on a broken sob.

"Shh," Renfro began awkwardly, turning away from the pain mirrored on her face. "I promise I'll do everything in my power to see that Megan is never taken from you, but we might just have to fight it out in court. I'll warn you now."

Knowing that she wasn't capable of standing up a second longer, Beth stumbled toward the chair and fell into it. With trembling fingers, she then dug into her purse for a Kleenex.

Renfro eased himself into the chair next to Beth and reached for her hand. "The worst is yet to come I'm afraid." He paused, as though reluctant to continue. "I figure Manly's plan of action will be to prove you an unfit mother, to show that because you work, you are unable to properly care for Megan. And to add insult to injury, he'll try to dig up something from your past, something unsavory, that will hopefully strengthen his case."

Beth felt a tight squeeze in the area of her heart. Would the fact that she'd lied on the adoption papers increase the chance of having Meg whisked away from her? No, she quickly told herself. That night so long ago was past history. But what if the Manlys' lawyer...

"Oh, Giles," she cried, "what am I going to do? If only Lee were here."

"But he's not, Beth," Renfro pointed out gently. "He's dead, and you have to come to terms with that."

"Oh, I've come to terms with it, all right," she said bitterly, "but it doesn't make it any easier."

"I know," Renfro responded, the same gentle edge to his voice.

Beth sniffed back a sob. "And if Lee were still alive, Dexter Manly wouldn't dare try anything like this. It's...it's because I'm a widow...."

Renfro shook his head. "Don't think that for a minute. You'll only be deluding yourself if you do. That man would take on the devil himself in order to get what he wants."

"But I still don't understand why he didn't keep Megan when she was born."

"It's simple, really, a story you've heard at least a thousand times. Young woman gets pregnant and goes home to her parents. In this case Daddy was most unforgiving, and it was apparently only after she agreed to give the baby up for adoption that he agreed to help her. Oh, yes, and the fact that the baby's father was dead was in the daughter's favor. They sent her to live with an aunt, and it was through the aunt and Manly's lawyer that the adoption was carried out."

Renfro paused and stood up. When he spoke again, his voice was grim. "The daughter, however, never recovered from giving her baby away and as a result took her life."

Beth's hand flew to her mouth. "Oh, no," she gasped.

"My thoughts exactly," Renfro added. "But in any event, Dexter Manly was able to use his influence and wealth to find Meg's whereabouts, and because of his guilt, he wants to compensate by getting the baby back and rearing it—he and his wife, that is."

Beth scooted to the edge of the chair, all the while grasping at Giles's fingers. "Please . . . you can't let them take Megan."

He pried her fingers loose and patted them. "I've already told you I'll do my best. Just trust me and try not to worry. Everything's going to be all right. You'll see."

A short time later, Beth was anything but reassured as she backed out of the parking garage and nosed her car into the busy intersection. Her head was pounding and her eyes felt like they were full of sand. She was nearly crazy with worry.

Blinking against the bright sunlight, she slipped her sunglasses over the bridge of her nose and tried to calm the irregular beating of her heart.

"What now?" she agonized aloud.

Her first impulse was to go to the nursery, pick up Megan and go straight home and lock the doors. The two of them against the world, she thought illogically. But that was impossible, and besides it would accomplish nothing. As Giles had pointed out, she had to face the fact that losing her two-year-old daughter was a real possibility.

Oblivious of the gorgeous fall morning, she automatically headed her car in the direction of her boutique, The In-Look.

It was all Beth could do just to see the road ahead. Hot tears marred her vision as she turned onto North Street and headed toward the Stephen F. Austin University campus. As she braked at the first red light, she could see the sign of the boutique. Knowing that her best friend and partner, Jenny Davis, would not be there yet, Beth saw it as a refuge. She needed some time alone to get her raw emotions under control.

She and Jenny were fortunate to have found a prime location near the college. The students were their best customers. With the recent addition of a small, exclusive line of furs, however, the boutique was beginning to cater to the older, wealthier women in town.

Beth had moved to this quaint East Texas town of Nacogdoches from Tyler and had started to work immediately as a secretary in the dean's office. It was while working there that she met and married Lee Loring, a professor at the college.

She had always yearned for a home and family of her own, and when Lee asked her to marry him, she said yes, even though what she felt for him was not a wild passionate love. He had been several years older than she, and afterward he never forgave himself for marrying Beth, especially when he learned he could not father a child.

Still, it had been a happy marriage, and adopting Meg was the bond that had keep them together. Then a year ago he had died. With the insurance money left to her, Beth had gone into partnership with Jenny.

Now, as she maneuvered the car into her parking place in the rear of the store and switched off the ignition, there was a lump lodged in her throat like a tumor. The gravity of the situation was increasing with each passing moment. How on earth would she survive if she lost Megan? Megan was her life. All she'd ever wanted was to provide her daughter with the love and security she herself had never had.

Suddenly she went rigid while the blood drummed in her ears and a sizzling anger began to build inside her. She would fight Dexter Manly, fight him with everything she had. Fair, dirty— it didn't matter, just as long as she won in the end. But to do that she would have to depend on someone other than herself, and that someone was Giles Renfro. It would be terribly difficult; she feared dependency. She had learned at an early age, the hard way, that when it came down to it, she could count on no one but herself.

Not this time, however. Not only was she at her attorney's mercy, she was also being forced to take on a whole new personality, one of a fighter. But fight she would if it meant keeping Megan.

This self-imposed vow firm in her heart, Beth got out of the car and made her way inside the boutique. It was after flipping on the lights in the back office that she paused and looked around. Next to Megan, the boutique came first. She adored the cheery atmosphere, the smell of new clothes, the bounce of the plush carpet as she padded from dressing room to dressing room, her arms filled with clothes for prospective customers.

It was through the boutique that Beth planned to provide her daughter with love and security. She hated leaving Megan at the nursery, but for the time being she had no choice. Only now, she hoped it wouldn't all be in vain.

Shaking herself mentally, Beth discarded her bulky sweater. Feeling secure that she would have at least another thirty minutes in which to remove the tear stains from her face, she crossed to the coffee bar, where she scooped out some grounds.

The Mr. Coffee had just begun to swish and gurgle, when Beth heard the back door open and shut. The knowledge that Beth was no longer alone had barely registered when Jenny stormed through the office, tossing her jacket across the top of her desk.

Beth had always disliked tagging people, but with Jenny it was justified. Jenny Davis was a bundle of nerves; she ran entirely on nervous energy. Short and thin with pixielike features and flashing blue eyes, she made Beth tired just being in the same room with her. Maybe that was why they got along so well—they were exact opposites.

"Geez, Beth, you look like a Mack truck ran you down and then backed over you."

Beth chewed on her lower lip and turned her back on her friend, her shoulders beginning to shake.

"Hey, hey," Jenny exclaimed, closing the distance between them. "What's wrong?"

"Oh, Jenny," Beth cried, "I've..." Beth fought for control, unable to go on.

Jenny stared in astonishment. She was seeing a side of Beth that she rarely ever glimpsed. It disturbed her. For the most part, Beth was unflappable. Her every action, no matter how small, how unimportant, was feminine, precise. It had been like that as long as Jenny could remember. It was as if Beth had been born into a state of grace, blessed with gentleness, brains and looks—the complete package.

They had been friends since Beth had come to Nacogdoches, and Jenny didn't think she'd ever met another human being as unified as Beth, as complete. Until now, that is. Even when Lee had died, Jenny hadn't seen the panicked look in Beth's eyes.

"For heaven's sakes, Beth," Jenny demanded after a moment of strained silence, "spit it out. Tell me what has you so upset."

Beth groped for Jenny's hands and squeezed them tightly. As though a dam had suddenly broken inside her, Beth poured out, in agonizing detail, everything Giles had told her.

Another silence fell over the room, before Jenny exploded, "Why... why that no good, sorry bastard! He oughta be horsewhipped. Just who does he think he is?" she continued to rant, turning to the coffeepot as though she needed something to do with her hands. She poured two cups of the steaming liquid.

Beth locked a hand around the cup that Jenny gave her and eased down into her desk chair. "He's Dexter Manly—that's who," she countered, her lower lip unsteady.

"Well, don't you worry, honey," Jenny said confidently. "The way I see it, you've got the best lawyer in town and Manly doesn't have a snowball's chance in hell of taking Meg away from you, regardless of how much money he has."

Beth set her cup down and massaged the area above her eyes. "That's what I keep telling myself, but..." She hesitated. "If only Lee hadn't died... if only the boutique were doing better so I could stay home with Megan," she ended on a wail.

Jenny stiffened suddenly, as though Beth had touched on a raw nerve. "You know, in time the shop *will* show a profit," Jenny declared. "It's just that right now, everything we make has to go back into the till to keep the door open. Just give it more time." Even though her voice held a firm note of reassurance, Beth couldn't help but notice that Jenny refrained from looking at her.

Beth sensed something was bothering her friend and had been for some time. At the moment Beth was too preoccupied with her own problems to encourage Jenny to confide in her.

When they had gone into business together, they'd agreed that Jenny would take care of the bookkeeping and Beth would take care of selecting and buying the merchandise. So far the arrangement had worked fine. Yet Beth could not understand why the business was not showing a profit. But when she questioned Jenny, as now, she was told she was being too impatient. Still Beth could not help but wonder....

Jenny gently disengaged her hands, drawing Beth back to the moment at hand. "Come on," she pleaded, "let's finish our coffee and get to work. That's the best tonic I know for broken hearts.''

Beth couldn't have agreed more, only for her it didn't pan out quite like that. Oh, she worked all right, worked until she thought she would drop, but through it all, she could not rid herself of the fear that somehow Manly and company would find a way to take Megan away from her.

"Well?"

"Well, what?" Cole Weston demanded innocently as he rested his tall frame against the corner fireplace in the den of the Manlys' hilltop mansion. His decision to stop by the house had been a spur of the moment one. However, with Dexter barking at him like a dog fighting over a bone, Cole knew he had made a mistake, especially as he had nothing of importance to report.

"Don't you play innocent with me, boy," Dexter ordered, treading farther into the room and not stopping until he reached the fireplace. There he grabbed the poker and thrust it into the burning logs, bringing new life to them, causing them to hiss and crackle.

Cole remained undaunted, merely watching as his friend and mentor went about his task. In his late fifties, Dexter Manly was a commanding presence. Tall, vigorous, he was endowed with a mop of thick silver hair and large features. Everything about him was oversized—large blue eyes, large uneven nose, wide mouth and a big booming voice.

As though aware of Cole's scrutiny, Dexter whipped his head around. "Let's stop fencing. How 'bout it?" he said laconically, his eyes narrowing under shaggy brows. "Have you got the goods on her yet?"

Cole straightened to full height and stared at Dexter as if he'd sprouted two heads. "What the hell! I've only been living next door to her for three days. Gimme a break, will ya?"

Dexter also raised himself up, meeting Cole eye to eye. "Three days, huh. Well, to my way of thinking that's plenty of time to come up with something, especially as you're supposed to be the best damn private detective in the state of Texas."

And according to most people he was.

Cole's career had begun as a student at a local high school in Houston, when on his newspaper route he'd stumbled upon a robbery and aided police. At eighteen, he became the youngest patrolman ever hired in Texas. His career was cut short by the Vietnam War. When he got out of the service, he decided to go back to school. As a means of working his way through college, he became Dexter Manly's bodyguard.

They took an instant liking to each other, and it was a friendship that held through the years, long after Cole had opened his own private detective firm. The years since had been good to Cole. He was the proud owner of a five-thousand-square-foot Houston home filled with the most advanced spy gadgetry available. He also owned a private jet and a three-hundred-acre ranch between Nacogdoches and Lufkin. He had worked on thousands of cases, but now he concentrated mostly on murders and kidnappings, taking cases around the world.

Cole Weston had posed as a doctor, chased cars for miles and staked out houses for days at a time. He'd been locked in car trunks and had been pushed off a cliff.

He'd had a contract out on his life, been shot in the hip with a .22 caliber gun and been stabbed three times.

But he loved his work and wouldn't think of doing anything else. He was the best at what he did. His work was his life. He had never entertained the idea of marriage—and now that he was thirty-eight, he considered himself too old—because he did not think it fair to subject a woman or child to his life-style. Not that he didn't like women. Quite the contrary. In the social circles of Houston he was known as a playboy.

He was adventurous as well as flamboyant, but one need not be fooled by that outer shell. Underneath was a strong, determined, oftentimes ruthless man who was dedicated to his job to the exclusion of all else. He was fond of saying, "I'll keep working until they shoot me down, bury me or put me in a wheelchair like Ironside."

Cole had balked at personally handling the case for his old friend, but because Dexter was adamant, he'd agreed. After all, it was Dexter who had set him up in business, believed in him when no one else had.

Once he'd yielded to Dexter's pressure things had rolled along smoothly. In fact, Cole had found it to be much easier than expected. Beth Loring lived in a fairly new suburban neighborhood, with several houses sitting vacant just waiting to be sold or rented. As luck would have it, a vacant home was on the left side of hers.

Cole had rented it for six months, moved in and sent Dexter the bill.

Now, as Cole watched his friend try to get control of his volatile temper, he stepped back and almost smiled. "Just take it easy, okay? These things take time, you know. And you want it to be done right, don't you?"

"Hell, you know I do." Dexter's tone was crisp as he dropped the fireplace tool back in place with a clatter. "It's just that I'm so eager to see my granddaughter. And of course, Eleanor—"

"Did someone call my name?"

Both men swung around at the sound of the third voice. Standing in the doorway was a tall, regal, middle-aged woman. Her fine-honed features were remarkably free of lines and her figure was as trim as a girl's. Only her strong brown eyes, rimmed by dark circles, betrayed fatigue and tension.

For a second Cole thought he saw Dexter's eyes soften. Then Dexter spoke and the illusion was shattered. "You're just in time to hear Cole's report," Dexter said sarcastically. "Which adds up to zero, I might add."

Cole grinned, refusing to rise to the bait. He knew Dexter like a book; his bark was much worse than his bite. That aside, Cole had never been intimidated by him and he wasn't about to start now.

"Hello, Eleanor," Cole said softly, having developed a deep affection for this genteel lady, who in his estimation was endowed with saintly qualities to have lived with Dexter Manly for thirty-five years.

Crossing to her, Cole leaned over and grazed her cool, scented cheek with his lips.

Eleanor hugged him briefly before stepping back and looking up at him with troubled eyes. "When—when do you think we'll have enough evidence to go to court?"

Cole sighed, turning toward Dexter, who was watching him like a hawk. "Not for some time, I'm afraid," he said gently, knowing how difficult this was for Eleanor, because the custody idea was Dexter's, not hers. "As I was telling Dexter, these things take time."

Eleanor slipped her hands into the pocket of her raspberry wool dress, walked to the fireplace and backed against its warmth. "I just pray it's not going to be too long and drawn out." Her eyes were still leveled on Cole. "I don't think I can stand—"

"Eleanor," Dexter cut in, "don't start harping on that again. You have no choice but to stand it."

Eleanor visibly flinched against her husband's harsh words. "I . . . know, but . . . I can't help but think of . . . Mrs. Loring."

"Hellfire, woman!" Dexter roared. "What about us? Megan's our granddaughter."

"It's too bad you didn't think of that when you forced our daughter to give her up," Eleanor retaliated fiercely.

Following Eleanor's words, a charged silence filled the room.

As for Cole, he'd seen and heard enough. If he stayed another second, he'd punch Dexter in the nose, taking great pleasure in watching his body hit the floor. Even though he cared deeply for this man, he knew Dexter could be a bastard at times.

"Look," Cole began uncomfortably, speaking to them both, "there's nothing to be gained from rehashing the past. When I come up with something concrete, you'll be the first to know."

With that, Cole turned and made his way toward the door. Once outside, he breathed deeply of the cool fresh air. Had he made a grave mistake in committing himself to this case?

His shoulders were slumped as he trudged to the car.

The late afternoon sunlight was fast losing its punch when Beth walked into the house, Megan by her side, her fingers clinging to Beth's.

It had been nearly a week since Beth's fateful meeting with Giles Renfro and every waking moment had been filled with fear, fear that if she let her daughter out of her sight she would never see her again. She had no choice except to carry on with her usual routine, though her heart was not in it. She had worked, but she couldn't wait to pick Megan up at the nursery and get home. This afternoon was no exception.

Beth gazed down at the top of her daughter's mop of golden curls, her eyes filled with unsuppressed emotion. "Well, puddin', it's great to be home. Your mommie's one tired lady."

Ignoring Beth, Megan untangled her fingers and took off toward the patio door, her chubby legs churning like a tiny locomotive.

"C'mon Mommie, c'mon," Megan urged.

Beth laughed and shook her head. "Not now, darling. Let Mommie fix herself a cup of coffee and then we'll see about going outside."

Megan threw her a toothy grin and Beth's heart turned over. "How would you like a cookie and a cup of milk?"

Not waiting for an answer, Beth dumped her purse and other paraphernalia on the buffet and followed Megan into the den, where she lifted Meg into her arms, only to pause suddenly. Something caught her eye. On closer observation, she saw that it was her new neighbor, chopping wood in his backyard. She shifted again, bringing him into full view.

The afternoon was warm and he wasn't wearing a shirt. From where Beth stood, she could see it hanging close by on a tree limb, flapping in the breeze. For a moment, she was mesmerized by the way his muscles bunched together under the heavy swing of the ax. Sweat was glistening like dewdrops on his skin and she could not help but admire his body. Who was he? she asked herself. What did he do for a living? This was not the first time she'd noticed him. Every morning since he'd moved in, she'd seen him jogging down the tree-lined sidewalk about the time she was dressing Megan.

Megan, wiggling in her arms, brought her out of her musings. "All right, wiggle worm, let's go have our treat."

Minutes later found Megan in her high chair, munching on an Oreo cookie, with the majority of it smeared across her cheeks. Beth was sipping on a cup of instant coffee, but not before she had gone to her room and slipped into a jogging outfit.

She was content just to sit and look at her daughter, marveling anew at how perfect she was. And to make her that much prouder, everyone seemed to think Megan looked exactly like her. Of course, Beth could not see the resemblance, other than the fact that Megan had her color of hair.

Megan's head was crowned with an abundance of golden curls, a perfect foil for the dark brown eyes, the tiny rosebud mouth and the creamy skin the color of magnolia blossoms. No doubt about it: Megan Loring was a little beauty. And she was hers, Beth told herself with fierce pride, only to suddenly experience a cold chill around her heart. *Not for long, if Dexter Manly had his way,* an inner voice taunted.

"No!" Beth yelped, drawing Megan's attention. Megan's eyes were on her, round and questioning.

Forcing herself to relax, she smiled at Meg.

"Down, Mommie. Peeze."

"Not until after I've cleaned you up, you little pig."

Once Meg's face was shining, devoid of chocolate and the milk mustache, Beth lifted her out of her chair onto the floor. Megan again made a beeline for the patio door.

"Outside," she said.

"Oh, all right, you win," Beth said with a smile, tossing the dirty washcloth in the sink. "but we can't stay outside long. It'll be dark soon."

By the time Beth had put on Megan's lightweight sweater, Megan was pounding her fists on the glass door. Still hunkered down in front of her, Beth gave her daughter a bear hug before standing up and sliding back the door.

A ball was lodged between the edge of the concrete patio and the grass. Megan scurried toward it and picked it up, while Beth looked up at the sky, thinking that it had been a long time since she'd seen such a perfect evening. She breathed deeply of the fresh, invigorating air.

"Roll Mommie the ball," Beth encouraged, easing herself down onto the grass Indian-style, all the while conscious that her neighbor had stopped chopping wood and was watching their every move.

Megan's gleeful laughter rivaled the rustle of the leaves as she and Beth rolled the ball between them.

"Here it comes," Beth called. "Grab it."

But Megan's short legs couldn't quite reach it and the ball took an unexpected turn, landing in the neighbor's yard. Before Beth could scramble to her feet, Megan was toddling after it.

"Megan, come back!" Beth shouted.

Megan paid no attention to Beth's cry. By the time Beth crossed the property line, her daughter was face to face with the stranger.

"Man," Megan said in a confiding, purring voice.

"No, Megan!" Beth was horrified.

"Up," Megan said, raising her arms.

Chapter Two

Beth felt the color surge to her cheeks as she stood in stunned silence. She knew she should say something, anything, that would shatter the charged moment, but she couldn't. Like her daughter, she was held spellbound by this man's rough good looks.

His hair was the color of chestnuts, though the temples were peppered with gray, giving him a worldly, distinguished look. And his eyes reminded her of dark chocolate morsels, good enough to eat.

But Beth was not fooled. Hand in hand with those pleasant features was a determined-looking square jaw and cast-iron chin that suggested a ruthlessness that would surface if he was ever crossed. She knew the type: a diamond in the rough; a little polishing was all that was needed. No doubt there were plenty of women around to do just that, she thought scathingly. Yes, he definitely had the word *playboy* stamped all over him.

He stood well over six feet and up close his body was perfect. Her gaze clung to the whorls of hair gracing his broad chest. At least he had managed to grab his shirt and slip into it before Meg had descended on him, though he hadn't bothered to button it, Beth thought disconcertingly, wondering what it would be like to touch . . .

His sudden movement was like a dash of cold water on Beth's torrid thoughts, effectively breaking the spell. Her gaze widened as Cole stooped somewhat awkwardly and lifted the child to his shoulders. "There you are, moppet. How's that?"

Megan giggled, bouncing the heels of her shoes against his chest. "Man called me 'moppet,' Mommie. Funny name."

"Very funny. But come with Mommie now." Still mortified over the sudden chain of events, Beth could not bring herself to look at him, though she could feel his eyes boring into her. Instead she focused her attention on her daughter, trying to control the flush that heated her face.

"Want to stay with man."

"Megan . . ."

The child, obedient, yielded to pressure. Sighing, Megan said, "Moppet down, peeze."

Cole set her down with a swing that made Megan shriek with glee. "She's adorable," he said, forcing her to face him.

Cole was prepared to introduce himself, but the words froze in his throat. The striking features in front of him suddenly left him speechless. The first thing he noticed about Beth Loring was her eyes. They were enormous, a pale green, like celery, framed in thick, gold-brown eyelashes that should have been false but were her own.

Almost as though by accident, he noticed she was beautiful. A splendidly developed creature with milk-white skin and hair the color of warm honey that capped her heart-shaped face, emphasizing a broad, candid forehead, straight small nose, red mouth with deep corners and a firm, delicately squared chin. But her face was only the beginning. Her slender frame supported what appeared to be a small waist and generous breasts.

Cole was caught completely off guard. She was nothing like he expected. Of course he had seen a picture of her and had seen her from a distance, but neither prepared him for the impact of coming face to face with the flesh-and-blood Beth Loring.

Then Cole came to himself, flushed dully and slowly extended his hand. "By the way, I'm Cole Weston and you're . . . ?"

"Beth Loring." Her soft, moist lips curled ever so slightly in a half amused, half embarrassed smile as she stood with her arms crossed beneath her full breasts, which were strained against the knit top.

Cole smiled. "My pleasure, neighbor," he drawled. Then before she could respond, he dropped once again to his knees, level with Megan. "And what's your name, little lady?"

"Moppet," she said without hesitation, displaying a dimple in a winsome smile.

Cole laughed and, after tussling her curls, stood up, his attention once again focusing on Beth.

"Is she always such a flirt?"

Beth shrugged and smiled, completely baffled herself by Megan's open display of affection to this stranger. "I don't recall that ever happening before, but with Meg one never knows. . . ."

"How old is she?" Cole asked, his smile slow and lazy. His eyes seemed to stroke every inch of her face.

"Two," Beth said, taking her daughter's hand and drawing her close with a curious urgency. Her gesture did not escape Cole, who, with an unaccustomed pang of conscience, thought, *She's afraid of me, and she doesn't even know who I am.*

Clearing his throat, Cole said, "She certainly talks well for two, or at least, I think she does." He paused with a shrug. "Having never been around children, I'm certainly no judge."

"That's a surprise, considering how my daughter reacted to you." Her smile was tentative. "But, yes, I guess she is above her level. When I get home from work, my evenings are devoted to her," Beth explained. "I'm afraid it's made her rather precocious."

"And is there a. . .Mr. Loring?" Cole forced himself to ask, feeling more like a heel by the second. But dammit, wouldn't she think it odd that he wouldn't be curious about a man in her life, or the lack of one?

Beth's eyes clouded. "My . . . husband's deceased, Mr. Weston," she said.

"Sorry," Cole muttered tightly, turning away, unable to look at her.

A silence followed, with Beth asking herself why she didn't take Megan and go home. Why was she standing there making inane conversation with a man who would never be more than a passing acquaintance?

Suddenly the color in her cheeks resurfaced and her mouth thinned in irritation. So what if he had the best-looking body she'd ever seen on a man and his large hands were gentle as they'd lifted Megan, making him appear all the more masculine? Why did she care that his faded jeans, minus a belt, had slipped below his navel, drawing her eyes to...

She took a deep breath and glanced away. "Mr. Weston, I'd..."

"Make it 'Cole,'" he pressed with a wide grin, causing an unwanted flutter around a heart.

"All right, Cole," she said, still a trifle off balance. "I need to take Megan home."

"In that case, why don't I be real neighborly and walk you and moppet to the door?" he said casually.

This drew an unexpected giggle from Megan, but she didn't say anything, only watched Cole with the inquisitiveness of a child.

Beth laughed, too, her eyes seeking his. "Oh, please, I don't think that's necessary. After all, it's only a few steps."

Cole was totally captivated by the tinkling sound of her laughter, the way she looked at him as though they were really seeing each other. She was a woman he could talk to, he was sure of it. That in itself was a major feat.

The women in his life, for the most part, were brittle and false, anxious under the cleverly made-up, fixed smiles and fluttering lashes. He didn't believe they knew what they claimed to want and feared for all of them and himself, too, as it seemed some kind of zany game passed from one generation to the next.

But with this woman he felt he could move to a higher level, enter into a new game, with new rules. Yes, under different circumstances Beth Loring would have been a woman worth pursuing. It was too bad...

It was then that he noticed Beth was watching him, a puzzled expression on her face.

Cursing silently, Cole shook himself. The silence stretched. What was happening to him? Not since his high school days had he been so smitten with a pretty girl. Had he known it beforehand, had he been prepared, he would have been on guard. His contempt for involvement had equipped him to handle most attractive women with a certain apathy. But this unexpected confrontation had thrown him off balance.

"Well, it's been a pleasure...Cole," Beth began awkwardly, trying to disperse that "certain something" that simmered between them. Although she couldn't put a name to it, it was there nevertheless, and it disturbed her, making her feel raw, exposed.

Having completely recovered, Cole said, "I'll walk with you."

Beth pulled up short. "Really, that's not necessary," she said more sharply than she intended.

Cole wouldn't be put off. "I know, but I want to."

Beth shrugged, suddenly feeling out of sorts with this man. "Suit yourself."

They were almost at Beth's back door when, determined to break the uncomfortable silence, she asked, "What do you do for a living?" To her surprise, she wanted to know.

Did he hesitate, or was it just her imagination? Beth wondered, glancing sideways at him as he moved slowly and easily, matching his gait to hers and Megan's.

Then he spoke, his voice low and smooth. "I'm a factory representative, which allows me to work out of my home." The lie almost stuck in his throat, and for a reason he didn't wish to acknowledge, Cole experienced another twinge of conscience.

"Must be nice," Beth said forlornly. "I'd give anything if I could work at home."

"And you can't? Work at home, I mean."

"No way. I'm partners in a boutique and we're frantically trying to make it into a paying proposition." Realizing she was telling this stranger too much, Beth clamped her mouth shut.

Her action was not lost on Cole, but he was not ready to let her go, so, pulling a cigarette out of his pocket and slowly lighting it, he stalled for time. After all, he was doing his job, wasn't he? Finding out all he could about this woman was the name of the game, and he had to abide by the rules—didn't he?

"Cold, Mommie."

"Mommie's sorry," Beth said, leaning down and sweeping Meg up into her arms, cuddling her close, barely aware that twilight had fallen and the air was quite cold.

"Really, Mr...er...Cole, I must go in. It was nice meeting you."

Cole nodded, his face serious. "Same here."

Silence.

"Bye, man," Megan chimed in, releasing the tension and drawing a deep-throated laugh from Cole.

After ruffling Megan's curls once again, he turned his back, only to pause suddenly and twist around. "How 'bout if I call you sometime?"

Beth hesitated with one foot inside the door. "All right...I'd like that."

Beth tried to relax. This was her time. With Megan bathed and in bed, she was sitting with her feet propped up on the wicker coffee table, sipping a cup of hot tea. But she could not relax; until this thing with Megan was settled, she feared that luxury would continue to escape her.

She had literally forced herself not to pick up the phone and call her attorney, knowing that if he had anything to report, he would have called her. But it was hard to sit idle, to face each day with that threat hanging over her head. It was as though she were living on a precipice—one tiny push and she would go over that edge.

To add to her trepidation was her unwanted fascination with the man next door.

A shiver ran through her as she stood up and walked disjointedly into the kitchen, where she reached for the pot and rewarmed her now tepid cup of tea. Unconsciously she found herself migrating toward the window and cracking the shutter just enough to see the house across the way. There was a dim light coming through the draped window from what she guessed was his bedroom. Was he also unable to sleep? To her dismay, that thought sent a shaft of excitement through her.

Flushing boldly, Beth glanced at the gold watch circling her wrist and saw that it was twelve-thirty. "Damn," she muttered aloud. It was past her bedtime. But to try to go to sleep now would be futile, so she purposefully let her thoughts drift back to her neighbor.

Who was he? she asked herself again. Somehow she just couldn't picture him as a factory representative. Was he married? If so, there was no ring on his finger, but then, in this day and time that meant nothing. Still, she didn't think he was married. Divorced? More than likely. Surely a catch like Cole Weston hadn't been allowed to keep his freedom. Or had he?

One thing she did know for sure was that he was a man who would take charge, a trait she had always admired in men. And he was downright handsome, as well.

What would it be like, she fantasized, to have a strong man like him to lean on, to make the pain, the fear and the hurt disappear.

"You're a fool, Beth Loring," she said out loud. "You're missing Lee, that's all." The last thing she needed was to become involved with Cole—or any man, for that matter. No, as much as she might like to have someone special in her life, it was not to be. All her efforts must be channeled into making a good home for Meg and getting her business on its feet so that she could better fight the Manlys.

That in itself would not be easy. Having been treated as if she were an outcast, she constantly had to work on her self-esteem. Orphaned at the age of nine, she had gone to live with her aunt and uncle and two female cousins, both older than she. From the moment she had set foot under their roof, her life was comparable to that of Cinderella and the two wicked stepsisters. Her cousins got everything, while she got nothing.

Again she shivered, hating it when her thoughts turned to her past, especially when it brought to mind Giles's words about the possibility of the Manlys digging into her background. *Please, dear God,* she prayed, *don't let that one night, that one mistake, cost me my child.*

The seriousness of what had happened hit home again. No one here knew. No one could possibly know. It had been taken care of a long time ago. There was absolutely nothing to fear. The reassurance kept racing through her mind.

But the demons inside her refused to lie. Most of the time she was able to snuff out the guilt, but not now. Her emotional stability had been reduced to a thread.

With a quivering hand, she fumbled in her pocket for a Kleenex while her mind backtracked....

When Beth was fifteen, her two cousins had insisted she go with them to a party. She had been delighted, as they never included her in any of their plans. However, the moment Beth had stepped into the smoke-filled room, she knew she had made a mistake. The host was a sleazy, fat, older man who immediately yanked Beth's older cousin into his arms and began kissing her.

Then he grabbed Beth. She was both repulsed and shocked.

"No!" she cried, wildly shaking her head, fear freezing her breath.

But her struggles were to no avail. The man's alcoholic breath warmed her face while his hard lips plundered her soft ones.

Once the torment had ended, the man laughed. "Ah, come on, honey. What kinda game you playin'? Don't act the innocent with me. Now why don't you be a good girl and go take off that pretty outfit?"

At that moment she realized where she was. She had walked into a pornography party.

"No, I won't do it! You can't make me!" she screamed, edging toward the door, aware that her cousins were already parading around the room, clad only in their panties and bras.

Beth never made it to the door. A tall, bearded man jumped between her and the exit, while the fat one wrapped his hand around her arm like a vise. Beth struggled violently.

"Oh, no, you don't," Fatty warned, grabbing her by the blouse and ripping it nearly off, exposing a breast in the process.

Beth screamed, horrified, and clutched at the torn fragment of her clothes. But the man slapped her hand away, and it was then that the pictures were snapped.

She was still in a state of shock, a short time later, when the police arrived. A neighbor had called and complained about the noise. Beth, along with the others, was arrested. Several hours passed before her pompous uncle marched into the station and took them home, supposedly having gotten the charges dropped.

Yet Beth never had proof that he had done so. . . .

Following the incident, the quality of Beth's life had gone from bad to worse. The facts became twisted and she ended up being blamed for the fiasco.

As soon as she had turned eighteen, she moved to Nacogdoches, completely alienating herself from her so-called family, and even though it took years, she finally obtained a degree in marketing from Stephen F. Austin University. She pushed herself to the limit, and to those who did not know her, she appeared headstrong and stubborn, but those who were her friends knew that she was merely covering up for the lack of self-confidence, a flaw that was still very much in evidence. . . .

Suddenly Beth whimpered, the sound of her own voice bringing her back to the present. Her cheeks were wet with tears and she had no desire to move as she continued to stare out into the inky blackness. That was when she saw the light disappear in the house next door. Cole Weston again. Why couldn't she forget him, forget that he even existed? *Because you find him attractive, that's why,* she admitted honestly.

Again, nothing could ever come of this fascination. As it was, she had more on her plate than she could digest.

Why did he have to come into her life now?

The timing could not have been worse.

Cole yawned again, stretched. He silently cursed at the images of his neighbor dancing in his head.

Mustering the necessary energy, he struggled to a sitting position on the edge of the king-size bed. He reached over and flipped on the lamp, hoping to dispel the image of Beth Loring's beautiful face.

Nothing doing.

His vision of her was as clear as ever. Everything about her appealed to him: the beautiful smile, the sparkle in her unusual eyes, the perfect profile and the way the errant wisps of blond hair fluttered about her face as if they just happened that way.

Dammit, Weston! Have you lost your ever lovin' mind? She's an assignment, and that's all! Forget that and you're in deep trouble.

Still ridiculing himself, he made his way into the bathroom, where he doused his face with cold water and looked in the mirror.

He shook his head in dismay. He was not yet forty and took the best care of his health possible, working out religiously, running every day, rain or shine, and holding his intake of booze and cigarettes to a minimum. But his hair was splattered with gray and his leathery skin and eyes were edged with severe lines, a living testimony to too many late nights and too many long working hours.

Something had to give, and soon. Maybe more sleep was the answer. Once he made up his mind, he was disciplined enough to do it. That trait had been largely responsible for pulling him through more than one tight situation. He was stubborn enough not to let anything stop him from reaching his goals, which meant, in most cases, committing himself totally to his clients.

That and his craving for danger and excitement.

To the men he'd fought with in Vietnam, he seemed daring to the point of recklessness, the type who got a thrill out of living on the edge. With women it was the same. The moment was all that counted.

Only Reynolds, his friend in the army, understood him, understood that he had to have complete freedom.

"You keep having to prove that boundaries are not for you," Reynolds had told him. "You'd rather die than have to live within them."

Cole had given his friend credit for seeing a side of him that very few people ever saw.

Reared by a father who drank too much—his mother had died as the result of his birth—he had been on his own since before he was seventeen. His father's sister had pitched in during those formative years and helped with his upbringing, providing his only stability.

Although his father had long since died, he'd left his mark. Cole was positive his father had always held it against him for not dying instead of his mother. The fact that Cole had not

wanted to stay in South Texas and farm his father's rice fields
had been the proverbial straw that broke the camel's back.

As far as Cole was concerned, that was all history, never to
be revived.

He turned on the faucets, climbed into the shower stall and
let the hot water cascade over him, as if the steamy spray could
wash away the mental and physical scars.

The damage was indelible; the majority of it came with the
territory. Cops, private eyes, servicemen—cut from the same
bolt of cloth—were society's cleanup crew, sifting through the
rubble of human meanness. None of them remained immune
for long.

Especially not him, especially not while he was involved in a
case that he wouldn't ordinarily touch with a ten-foot pole.

Cole twisted, and the hot, needlelike spray danced over his
neck and shoulders. He knew he should call Dexter and at least
let him know that he had made contact with Beth Loring, but
his gut instinct told him that to do so would merely add to his
problems.

He was one to listen to his gut instinct. It was telling him that
involving himself with Beth would be the same as holding a
lighted stick of dynamite in his hand and watching it explode.

He guessed the only thing he'd ever feared in his life was
getting too close to anyone; his line of work was not conducive
to family life. All he wanted was the freedom to do his job so
that he could retire on his ranch and live the life of ease.

After drying himself, he slipped into his sweatshirt and made
his way back into the bedroom. There he began his morning
ritual of stretching, pulling, twisting, limbering up his taut
muscles.

Finally he was ready to run, and he felt damn good. So what
if he was living in a rented house with rented furniture, forced
into a situation not to his liking? After all, he *was* indebted to
Manly. He could handle it. Life was good, and he wasn't about
to let a woman with celery-colored eyes mess up his play-
house.

He had to play the game and he would play it like a pro. That
was the way it would be.

* * *

In spite of her sleepless night, Beth was up and dressed on time the next morning, looking smashing in an olive-colored sweater, glittering with the fantasy touch of gold, and matching three-quarter pants. Boots, a decorative belt and bracelets completed the outfit.

By dressing with a flair for casual elegance, Beth hoped to buoy her sagging spirits. It had worked.

Her daughter was dressed to the hilt, as well. She looked adorable, Beth thought, in a red-and-white jump suit with a red coat and cap to match, her curls peeping out the sides of the cap.

"I'm ready if you are, sweetheart," Beth said, addressing Megan, who was playing with her doll on the floor in front of the fireplace.

Megan shook her head. "Baby stay home."

Beth flinched. "Not today, but soon, I promise, soon," she whispered, more to herself than to the child, as she took Megan by the hand and led her outside.

She had buckled both Megan and herself in the car and had begun backing out of the driveway, when she suddenly slammed on the brakes.

"Damn!" she cried, her eyes glued to the rearview mirror.

Cole Weston was standing in the driveway, directly behind the car.

Chapter Three

With her heart hammering like a drum inside her chest, Beth jammed a finger down on the automatic window button. As soon as the buzzing stopped, she stuck her head through the opening and shouted, "Are you crazy? I almost ran over you!"

Nonchalantly Cole ambled around the rear of the Pontiac and, stepping to the window, leaned over and peered inside. "Sorry, I didn't mean to scare you," he said with a grin.

"Well, you did," Beth snapped, thinking he didn't look sorry at all.

He was close enough that she smelled simultaneously his warm, minty breath and the pungent odor of perspiration. She caught herself leaning back out of harm's way, suddenly conscious of him in every way. He was entirely too close.

It was obvious he had been jogging. Sweat poured profusely from his face, calling attention to the tense lines around his eyes. This morning they seemed deeper, more pronounced. Or was it simply her imagination? Still, there was no mistaking the powerful width of his shoulders and the glint in his narrowed eyes.

While staring at him with a frown of disapproval, she tried to ignore the heartbeat that refused to settle back to a normal rate. She had worked hard to put thoughts of this man in cold storage and wasn't any too pleased with his unexpected appearance.

"Hi, man," Megan was saying, flashing him a toothy grin, vying for her share of the attention, oblivious to the charged tension in the air.

"Hi yourself, moppet," Cole quipped, suddenly reaching across Beth, and in doing so, slightly grazing the breast nearest him. For a second he reeled, feeling a sensation not unlike a jolt of electricity shoot up his arm. What the hell? he cursed silently, shifting his feet uncomfortably. Had Beth felt it, too? He tried to gauge her reaction, but her attention was focused on Megan.

The moment passed as he tweaked Megan on the nose, careful not to touch Beth when he withdrew his arm. His action brought a delightful squeal from Megan, and she held out her arms to him.

Beth sat as stiff as a board, smarting from Cole's innocent touch. Or was it innocent? She couldn't be sure. A warmth continued to surround her, leaving her weak and vulnerable. Drat that man! What did he want from her? And Megan? What was there about him that enthralled her tiny daughter? Megan had taken to him like a duck to water and Beth could not figure out why. It wasn't as if Megan knew she was different, that she didn't have a daddy. She was too young to understand that. So what was it? Charisma, Beth told herself. Hadn't she herself fallen victim to that same charm?

Careful to keep her gaze averted, Beth listened a moment longer to the exchange between the two of them before asking unsteadily, "Was . . . there something you . . . wanted? I . . . we need to go. It's my morning to open up the shop," she added with an edge to her voice when he showed no signs of leaving. Even though he was no longer leaning in the window, the weight of his body was still cushioned against the car, making movement impossible.

"Actually, I stopped to invite you and Megan to dinner at my place tonight."

Beth jerked her head up and back, her burgundy-colored lips parted in astonishment.

Cole chuckled. "Shut your mouth, Beth Loring," he ordered softly.

As though programmed by the low, gravelly sound of his voice, Beth did just that.

This brought another chuckle from Cole. "Do you always comply so readily?"

Although Beth recognized the teasing glint in his eyes, she knew his request had been a serious one.

He was watching her with a curious intensity, as if he were x-raying her thoughts. "Well?"

"I . . . I don't think so," Beth said.

"Why not?" he asked bluntly.

She was momentarily caught off-balance and her eyes widened. "I . . . er . . . don't know you," she stammered, the excuse sounding lame to her own ears. To make matters worse, she knew she sounded like an old maid librarian who was afraid of getting attacked between the shelves.

Cole raised an eyebrow. "And just how well do you need to know me?"

Another leading question. Again Beth brushed it aside.

"Look, Mr.—"

"Cole."

Beth sighed in exasperation. "I . . ."

"If I promise not to bite, will you say yes?" A grin tugged at his lips, almost completely disarming her. But not quite.

Suddenly Megan laughed and began chanting, "Man bited Mommie. Man bited Mommie."

That did it. Beth could no more keep a straight face than she could fly. She looked at Cole and they burst out laughing.

With mirth still dancing in her eyes, Beth acquiesced. "Okay, neighbor, expect two for dinner."

"Good," Cole said, still grinning. "I'll expect you at seven sharp."

With that he pushed away from the car and began trotting down the sidewalk.

Shocked by what she had just done, Beth didn't know how long she sat there watching his legs churn like the blades of a well-oiled windmill.

* * *

Midway through the day, as she carted armfuls of new merchandise to their proper place on the racks and shelves, she was still feeling that same emotion. Could she plead temporary insanity? she wondered.

To make her feel worse, Megan had cried when she had left her at the nursery. It was as if she sensed Beth's trepidation. When she had gently pulled Megan's fragile arms from around her neck, it felt as though a dagger were piercing her heart. Later, when she'd called the nursery, Mrs. Nelson, the owner, had laid her fears to rest. Megan was fine, playing and scampering around like her usual self.

Though Beth was relieved on that score, she continued to rebuke herself for her foolish commitment, only to turn around and tell herself again how silly she was acting. After all, hadn't he asked her just to share a meal, not his bed? Besides, he had invited Megan, as well. What could possibly happen with her daughter underfoot?

Having at last put her mind to rest, Beth began choosing a combination of mix-and-match outfits for a college student who had expressed an interest in the new items Beth had ordered.

She had just chosen her pick of the group and was calculating their monetary value, when Jenny stuck her head around the door. "Phone for you, line one."

"Thanks," Beth tossed over her shoulder as she walked the short distance to the desk and lifted the receiver.

"Hello."

"Beth, it's Giles."

Her stomach plummeted to her toes.

When Beth remained silent, Renfro went on, "Could you come by the office this afternoon?"

"Has . . . something happened?" Beth barely recognized her own voice. She sounded like a croaking bullfrog.

A pause. "As a matter of fact, yes," Giles said uneasily.

Beth cleared her throat, hoping to get around the knot of panic lodged there. "Tell me now."

Another pause. "Beth, this is not something that should be discussed over the phone."

Beth bit down into her lower lip, feeling the taste of blood on her tongue. "Please . . . tell me now," she repeated, her voice having risen several octaves.

"All right, Beth, if that's the way you want it."

"That's the way I want it," she said without emotion, though she gripped the receiver so tightly that the circulation in her hand was threatened.

"Dammit, Beth, you'd try the patience of a saint."

"Giles!"

"Have it your own way, then," he muttered irritably. "Charles Ransome called me just a little while ago." He paused, obviously waiting for a reaction from Beth.

"Charles Ransome?"

"The Manlys' lawyer, remember?" Giles prompted.

"Oh, yes, I remember now." Beth evened out her breath.

"Well, the gist of our conversation boiled down to his wanting to see if you'd be willing to meet with Manly and bring Megan." In spite of Beth's sharp gasp, he continued, "I'm sure Manly thinks that if he sees you face to face, he can convince you—"

"You tell Mr. Manly that he can go to hell!"

"Now, Beth."

"Don't you dare 'now, Beth' me! I don't want him anywhere near me or *my* daughter, is that understood?"

"Of course you don't, but there's a better way. . . ."

The censure she detected in Renfro's tone fanned her fury. "For heaven's sakes, Giles, just whose side are you on, anyway?"

The sudden stillness on the phone was like a deafening roar.

At last Giles spoke, his tone chilly at best. "I'll pretend I didn't hear that, Beth, and since we seem to be getting nowhere with this conversation, I'll say goodbye. I'll be in touch later."

Beth stood still for a moment, listening to the empty sound of the broken circuit.

Then, with a renewed burst of energy, she slammed the receiver down on the hook in total frustration and practically fell backward in her chair.

That was where Jenny found her fifteen minutes later when she came bounding through the door.

"Beth?" she said tentatively.

Beth raised her head, taking in a wary expression on her partner's face. She tried to smile, but the gesture failed miserably.

"More bad news?"

"You might say that," Beth admitted, hearing the slight tremor in her voice. She could not afford the luxury of falling apart at the seams, no matter how much she might want to. She had Megan to think about. She had to stay strong.

Jenny closed the door and walked farther into the room. "How 'bout a cup of tea?"

Beth nodded absently.

Once the water was put on to boil, Jenny flopped down on the small couch in front of Beth's desk and looked at her with probing eyes.

"What's it all about this time?"

"Giles called."

"Your attorney?"

Beth nodded again.

"And?"

"Dexter Manly wants to meet with me . . . and Megan."

Jenny made a face. "I hope Renfro told that 'you know what' where to stick it."

A ghost of a smile softened Beth's tense lips. "Oh, Jen, I don't know what I'd do without you to give me a lift."

A sudden shadow dimmed Jenny's features. "Well, we all need a morale booster every once in a while. Myself included," she added. Then, just as quickly, her face brightened. "Seriously though, I hope you don't intend to do anything that foolish—see Manly, I mean."

"Not on your life, and I told Giles so, too."

"Sounds like you're in for the fight of your life."

"Without a doubt," Beth agreed, pinning Jenny with a determined look. "That's why we need to talk—about money."

"Oh, Beth, please, not again," Jenny cried, only to suddenly jump up at the sound of the singing kettle.

Beth waited patiently while Jenny fixed the tea. She was not going to be put off, not this time. While they waited for the liquid to cool, Beth said softly, "Jen, I need to increase my owner's withdrawal, if not permanently, at least temporarily."

When Jenny moved to interrupt, Beth held up a hand. "Hear me out, please. I need more money, and I need it now. Even though Giles hasn't said anything, I'm sure he's worried about getting paid—he's well aware of my financial situation."

Beth paused and took a swallow of her tea, then went on, "From the looks of things, this is going to be a long, drawn-out battle and I mustn't spare any expense to keep Megan." There was a desperate note in her voice that she didn't bother to hide.

"I know," Jenny wailed, leaning across the desk and clasping Beth's hands. "I know what you're going through. Believe me, I do."

Beth shook her. "No, you don't, Jen. You can't imagine until you've had a child of your own."

Jenny sighed. "You're right about that; you know I'll do anything I can to help, but as I've already told you, the business is tapped to the limit. There's no way we can take another dime from the till—and keep the doors open, that is."

"That bad, huh?" Beth responded dully.

Jenny averted her gaze. "That bad."

"But why, Jen? I just don't understand. Just lately our customers have more than tripled, especially over the past few months."

"You've seen the books," Jenny said flatly, and Beth was positive she heard a note of hostility punctuating each word.

There was a moment of uneasy silence.

Jenny was the first to break it, her voice back to normal as though she were eager to make amends. "What about the bank?"

Beth shoved a hand through her blond curls. "Don't you think I haven't tried? But I already owe them a hefty sum. The insurance money Lee left me wasn't enough to get into the business."

"Oh, Beth, I'm sorry," Jenny whispered, her face pinched.

Beth knew Jenny was close to tears. But dammit, so was she. She was fighting for her life and her daughter's, and all she seemed to be doing was going around in a vicious circle.

Jenny began to fidget. "I...guess I'd better get back out on the floor."

"Yes, I guess you'd better," Beth said tightly, still more than just a little miffed at Jenny. Once she was alone, she sat staring into space. She couldn't seem to rid herself of the feeling that something was definitely amiss. Surely Jenny wasn't lying to her. Or was she? No, that was ludicrous, Beth told herself. She had looked at the books herself. All had appeared correct and aboveboard. Yet . . .

"Beth."

The quietly spoken use of her name jolted her alert. A salesperson was standing in the doorway. "UPS just arrived with more freight. Jenny said for me to come and get you."

"I'll be there shortly," Beth answered with a tired sigh, having to dig deep just for the strength to put one foot before the other.

By seven o'clock Cole was showered and dressed, and had everything ready for his guests. He was nervous, and more than a little confused. He knew it didn't make any sense—no woman was going to have that kind of power over him—but there was something about Beth Loring that seemed to kick him straight in the gut.

Dammit, she wasn't that different from the countless others that had gone through the revolving doors of his life. Oh, maybe she was better-looking than the average and had a figure men dream of, but nothing more.

Yet if there was ever a woman that was off-limits to him, it was this one. Even if it were possible to have a relationship with her—of course it wasn't—the last thing he needed was the responsibility of a two-year-old child. No, he would simply do the job he had to do and then walk with a clear conscience and no regrets.

With that pledge uppermost in his mind minutes later, he opened the door at the sound of the first chime.

Beth stood on the porch, Megan beside her, staring at him. Beth was breathtaking in a pair of black pants, a white cowlneck sweater with dolman sleeves. And Megan was her usual enchanting self in a pink two-piece hooded jogging suit with blue piping. Her hair was drawn up in a bunch of curls on the top of her head.

"I...hope we're not late," Beth said in that neat husky voice that belonged exclusively to her.

For a moment Cole said nothing, feeling as though his tongue were made of lead. So much for good intentions, he thought wryly while trying to maintain an objective attitude, determined to stick to his guns and not take her beauty as a personal assault.

"Come in," he said, smiling, moving aside.

"Hi, man," Megan said boldly, giving him her trademark: the toothy grin.

Cole laughed and pulled on a wisp in her topknot. Then he switched to Beth. Her eyes held his for a second. They seemed to say, What's all this about? Why are you setting out to charm me—us? Cole's eyes divulged absolutely nothing.

He was having enough trouble just breathing. With her close proximity, he was acutely aware of the perfection of her breasts, the slight scent of an enticing perfume, and it was all he could do not to grab her and crush her against him. Then, accidentally, his fingers grazed her arm.

Beth smiled stiffly, her arm feeling paralyzed where he'd touched her.

"Crazy about that sweater," he said hoarsely, suddenly striving to put things on an even keel.

"Thanks," she murmured on a breathy note. "We sell tons of them at the shop."

His eyes rested on her a moment longer before shifting to Megan. "Come with me, moppet. I've got something to show you." Then he shot Beth another quick glance. "You don't mind, do you?"

"No..." Beth replied hesitantly, unable to overcome the nervousness that was pressuring her insides. She had almost called him several times during the day, even after she'd gotten home from work, to tell him she couldn't make it tonight. But, not understanding why, she'd been unable to carry through with her threat. He was no different from the countless other men who had asked her out since Lee's death. Yet he *was* different, and for a reason that she didn't care to analyze, she wanted to see him again.

Now, however, as she watched Megan trustingly slip her tiny hand into Cole's and follow him toward a bucket of toys in the corner of the room, she wasn't so sure she had made the wise decision.

He was devastating in a pair of jeans and a dark brown sweater that made his dark brown eyes that much darker and mysterious. Yes, by anyone's standards, he was a fine specimen, and it would be so easy to give in to his potent brand of charm. However, to do so would be a mistake—a dangerous mistake.

Once Megan was playing contentedly, Cole rose to his feet and faced Beth.

"You shouldn't have done that," she said.

Cole played innocent. "What?"

Beth rolled her eyes. "You know what. All those toys."

He shrugged. "No big deal."

"Well, thanks, anyway." Beth's voice was soft. "I'll see that Megan thanks you, also."

Again he shrugged, before turning his back on her to concentrate on the waning fire in the fireplace. Beth stood transfixed for a moment, finding pleasure in the way the muscles rippled in his arms and thighs, especially his thighs, as he reached for a huge log and lifted it onto the fire. She was held spellbound by the way his buttocks suddenly tightened....

Realizing where her thoughts were heading, Beth yanked her head around and began noticing her surroundings. The room was relatively empty. A leather sofa and two matching chairs sat close to the large hearth, which seemed to be the focal point. The bookcases on either side were devoid of books, but there were several exquisite wood carvings of various animals there, instead. She must remember to ask him where they came from.

Properly furnished, the room could have been a showplace with its high-beamed ceilings and its richly paneled walls, not to exclude the wall that was solid glass. Yet she knew he had just moved in, and undoubtedly it would take him a while to fix it up. Or maybe he was satisfied with it the way it was. After all, she knew absolutely nothing about him.

She felt him watching her. "I hope you like Mexican food," he said in his deep, rich baritone.

"Love it," she responded, dodging his eyes.

"Good, because it's my weakness, too. Even if it does sound like I'm patting myself on the back, I make the best enchiladas this side of the border."

She laughed a breathy little laugh, and for a moment he couldn't remember what they had been talking about. He was noticing her eyes and her mouth, when all of a sudden he remembered it was the cocktail hour. "Before we chow down, why don't you get comfortable and I'll fix you a margarita."

By the time she sat on the soft couch, he was standing at the wet bar in the opposite corner of the room.

"Please, don't make it too strong," she said.

"One weak margarita coming up."

While he was mixing the drinks, a silence fell over the room. Beth watched Megan as she played with a small doll, trying her best to take the bonnet off its head.

She couldn't help but smile, again having to quell the urge to go over and give the child a crushing hug. She was becoming paranoid, though she tried to watch herself around Megan, not wanting to communicate her fear.

Yet at this moment, transferring her gaze to Cole's rugged profile, Dexter Manly and his threat seemed a part of another lifetime. Beth was content just to look at Cole.

"Comfortable?" he asked as he strode toward her, relieved that she was smiling. Gone was the bleak, cornered look that had darkened her eyes moments before, marring their clear beauty. Without her knowledge, he'd been watching her, aware of her fear, fear that was almost tangible.

He felt a growing tightness in his throat, while silently damning both Manly and himself. He suddenly had the urge to get plastered, bombed out of his head. What a stupid idea this was, asking her to dinner. But when he sat down beside her, he had schooled his features to show none of those fierce emotions.

"I'm fine, thanks," Beth murmured, reaching out and accepting the glass of lime-colored slush. Without hesitation, she licked some of the salt from the rim, then took a swallow.

Cole watched her tongue and grew warm all over. Damn!

"Mmm, this is delicious," Beth said, taking another sip.

"Another of my specialties," he said with a smile that curved his mouth only a millisecond before vanishing.

She laughed. "For someone who doesn't like to brag, you've certainly got it down to an art."

Cole barely heard her words, her laughter having once again cut through his armor, sending a sudden tingling straight to his groin.

He covered by fumbling in his pocket for a cigarette, then lighting it, thinking, *at this rate, this is going to be one helluva long evening.*

"Care for one?" he asked at last.

"No, thanks. They're bad for you," she murmured, meeting his gaze without a flicker.

He threw back his head and laughed before reaching across to the nearest ashtray, where he ground it out. "Chalk one up to you." Then he stood. "If we don't eat soon, the enchiladas are going to be dry as a bone. So if you'll bring the drinks, I'll get Megan."

To Beth's surprise and delight, the meal went off without a hitch. For the most part, the topics of conversation were impersonal: the state of the economy, television, the movies. Cole did inquire about The In-Look, and Beth had just explained how she'd gotten started in it, when Megan claimed their attention.

She tumbled sideways in the makeshift chair Cole had put together. Without warning, she'd dropped off to sleep like a kitten.

Before Cole could move, Beth reached over and lifted the soft, unresponsive little weight in her arms, so that Megan's head rested against her breast.

Cole scrutinized them, struck by a sense of pathos; something in Beth's attitude, the child's limp form, even the bunch of curls on the top of Megan's head, gripped his heart with the oddest pang. He couldn't define his feelings; he only knew that he found something touching in the relationship between those two.

"She's had it, hasn't she?"

"Yes, as always." Beth smiled. "I have to get her up so early and then she plays her heart out at the nursery."

Cole was standing now. "Why don't you put her down on my bed?"

"That's fine," Beth said softly. "And then I'll clean up the kitchen."

"Oh, no, you won't. We'll have coffee or drinks and *I'll* clean up the kitchen later tonight."

A small frown worked its way in between her eyes. "If you're sure."

"I'm sure." Cole's voice was husky. "Let's go make Megan comfortable."

The king-size bed dominated the room. As the glow from a lamp bathed it in a muted glow, it loomed large and very personal, Beth thought. What would it be like to share this bed with Cole Weston? she wondered, feel his hard limbs entwined with her soft ones, withering beneath him. . . .

Her footsteps faltered, while her heart threatened to burst. God, what had come over her? She dared not look at Cole, mortified at her thoughts.

"Here, let me have her," Cole demanded gently, reaching for the child.

Before she thought, Beth looked up at him. He was close, close enough that she could smell his spicy cologne, feel his warm breath.

His arms fell to his sides as his eyes caught hers. Beth's lashes flickered, the lamp shining directly upon her. Cole's hands closed hard upon themselves; he was thinking how much he'd like to kiss those heavy lashes, how much he'd like to feel them against his face like the fluttering feathers of a bird's wings. He could feel them now. . . .

"Mommie!" Megan whimpered, totally shattering the moment.

Beth's gaze fell and she snuggled her daughter close. "It's all right," she cooed. "Go back to sleep."

As soon as Megan's breathing evened out, Beth leaned over and laid her on the bed, avoiding looking at Cole. After draping the edge of the bedspread over the child, she silently followed him out of the room, clenching and unclenching her fingers.

It occurred to Cole minutes later, sitting on the couch, to take it slow and easy. Beth was sitting beside him, a cushion away, half facing him, feet tucked under her hips, toying with the border on the back of the couch.

She sat withdrawn, unresponsive, like a closed invitation. He was glad. The episode in the bedroom had shaken him more than he cared to admit, and if Beth's pale face was any indication, it had shaken her, too. As far as sticking to his pledge— well, he was batting zero. He'd just have to do better.

"So what'd you think about the dinner?" he asked, almost desperately.

"Sorry," she said, a blush coloring her cheeks, "I'm not usually so ill-mannered. It was delicious. You definitely have the right to brag."

He laughed at that, a deep rich sound that poured through her like the rarest of wines. *Careful, Beth,* she warned. *This man is way out of your league. You can look, but you can't touch.*

She said nothing for a time, putting down her wineglass and fiddling with the stem. "Before I forget, I want to ask about those wood carvings on your bookshelves."

Cole's gaze followed hers. "Oh, those."

"They're beautiful."

"I made them."

"Really?" she said, awed. "You're not joking, are you?"

He chuckled. "No, I'm not joking." He got up then and sauntered across the room to the cases. He reached for the small replica of a bald eagle, and brought it back to the couch and handed it to Beth.

"Do you sell these?" she asked.

"No, I give them away. Consider this one yours."

She frowned and shook her head. "Oh, no...I couldn't."

"Yes, you can. Just consider it a gift and say thank-you."

"Thank...you," she said with a smile, looking at his mouth and crossing her legs. His mouth was so appealing. "Is this just a hobby, or what?"

"You hit the nail on the head. It's a hobby and nothing more."

"I think that's wonderful," she added, her voice taking on a warm, whimsical note. "When I was about six I used to watch my uncle work with his hands. He was talented—though not as talented as you," she added hastily. "Anyway, I remember watching him build my cousins a dollhouse, and I wanted one so badly I could taste it."

Cole knew what was coming next, and his heart wrenched, picturing her a small child yearning for something she couldn't have, but wanted so very badly.

"I never got one," Beth added sadly, her lashes veiling her eyes as she gazed down at her hands. "But I'll see that Megan has one. That was one of Lee's—" Suddenly she broke off, embarrassed by her trek into the past. She was sure he was bored.

"Was Lee your...husband?" he asked, thinking how easily the lies came to his lips, growing more and more uncomfortable with his deceit by the minute.

"Yes," Beth said simply.

"Did he make you happy?" The moment the words left his mouth, Cole could have bitten off his tongue. *Damn you, Weston! Delving into her marriage is not part of the deal!*

Before she could speak, he added tersely, "Forget I asked that, please. It's none of my damned business."

"That's...all right." Beth risked looking at him. "I don't mind." Strangely, she didn't. Overall, the years with Lee had been good ones and talking about him didn't bother her. "Yes...we were happy," she added at length, "especially after we got Megan." A pause. "She's adopted, you know."

A muscle snapped in Cole's jaw. "Well, one would never know it by looking at her or by the way you treat her."

Her mouth pinched in pain. "I love her more than life itself, and all I've ever wanted was to be a good mother to Megan and make the best home possible for her."

Every word was like a knife in Cole's heart. Feeling desperate, he said, "Well, you're doing a damn good job."

Beth hesitated. "I just hope...my best is good enough," she said in a hushed tone. Then, changing the subject for fear of saying too much again, she asked, "What about you? Any...family?"

"If you mean have I been married, the answer is no," he said brusquely.

"Why not?" she asked, intrigued.

His voice was strained. "Why? Because children, which spell responsibility, scare me. They're not conducive to my line of work. Anyway, I don't think I could stand the restriction. I guess I enjoy my freedom too much."

Beth flinched, feeling as if he'd just thrown a glass of ice water in her face. *I guess that told you!*

A heavy silence hung in the air. Neither moved. Neither spoke.

Beth stood up, blushing, as if she'd said something suddenly outrageous. She wanted to go home. Now. She shouldn't have accepted this invitation. She had known it all along, only she hadn't wanted to admit it. Now she had no choice.

"Look," she began, "it's getting late and I . . . have to go." The words came out in a rush, as if she could not check them.

"Beth, I . . ." Cole could go no further, finding his voice had shut down, while his dark eyes seemed to spring forward, searching hers.

For a moment they gazed at each other, Beth's lips parted on a terrified breath, Cole's heart beginning to pound.

In a breathless whisper, Beth said, "I'll go and wake Megan."

"Beth . . ."

"I have to go, Cole."

"No!"

With a single movement he pulled her to him, holding her fast in his arms.

"Cole . . . please!"

The words were lost as Cole's mouth, savage and tender at once, came down upon hers. He kissed her deep in her mouth, his tongue hot and probing.

Then, just as quickly as it had begun, it was over. Cole thrust her away from him.

"You're right," he said harshly. "You'd better go."

Chapter Four

Cole dreaded going back into the house. He had just walked Beth and Megan to their door and he felt a restlessness he'd never known before. Delaying the inevitable as long as possible, he remained on the porch, unconscious of the raw chill in the night air. He fished in his shirt pocket for a cigarette and, after lighting it, camped against the brick wall, a foot propped up behind him for balance. He then turned his eyes to the sky and patiently searched for the Big Dipper.

He could think of a hundred reasons he didn't want to step inside those four walls, but they all added up to the same one: *Beth*.

When he finally did go inside, he felt a piercing loneliness dividing inside him like cancer cells, striking him to the bone.

Maybe his Aunt Lillie was right, he decided. He had been too long among the downtrodden, the scum, the outlaws of society. He peered down at the carpet, rubbed the toe of his boot on the leg of his jeans, then walked deeper into the room, to the still-roaring fire.

Instead of seeing the flames, he saw Beth's face in all its vibrant beauty. He blinked several times, yet he could not dispel that image, nor could he move.

"Dammit to hell!" he cursed aloud, the sound of his own voice effectively breaking the spell.

Furious at himself for his mind's antics, he crossed to the bar and with a savage gesture opened the small fridge and jammed several cubes of ice into a glass, topping it with a splash of Scotch. After taking a swig, he went to the couch and sat down, refusing to so much as glance in the direction of the hearth.

"Weston," he spouted again, "you're turning into a basket case." Suddenly his eyes swung toward the front door, any second expecting to see the men in white come through with a net to cart him off to the funny farm. When he was reduced to talking aloud to himself, he knew he was in trouble—big trouble.

Seeking peace, he took a long pull on his drink before he let his head roll back against the cushion. But there was no rest for the weary; Beth filled his thoughts to the exclusion of all else.

Why was he so drawn to her? For the first time, he tried to analyze it. She was gentle, emotional and predictable. Predictable in that she wanted to shape her future.

While he, on the other hand, was determined, rude and oftentimes ruthless. He lived on the edge, totally unconcerned with tomorrow. In fact, he didn't want to know what was on the far horizon, nor did he always think before he acted. If he had, he'd more than likely be dead.

An even more glaring obstacle was their life-styles. Beth was a homebody who wanted a home and family. That was the last thing he wanted. It was obvious they were like oil and water and should never be mixed.

That was it! The thing that was so fascinating, so intriguing about her, was that she was his exact opposite.

In spite of the chill that had fallen over the room—the fire had died down to a few coals—sweat broke out above his brow. Realizing that he was still clinging to the glass of Scotch, he set it down with a thud on the table beside him and sighed disgustedly.

He knew he should go to bed, but he was positive peace of mind would elude him there, too. Not only was he captivated by Beth, but by her tiny daughter, as well. He guessed that was the biggest surprise of all—Cole Weston enthralled by a child. If his buddies could see him now—it was as amazing as it was miraculous. Children were as foreign to him as the planet Mars. But when Megan gave him that toothy grin, he was her slave.

And still, there was her mother....

"You just need a woman, Weston. That's what's wrong with you!" He stood up, this time comforted by the sound of his voice. With dragging footsteps, he trudged into the bedroom, where he sprawled across the bed and shut his eyes.

No quarter given. Beth's lovely face sprang up on the back of his eyelids. It was in that moment that he finally admitted he wanted her. He wanted her in every way possible. He wanted to take her hand, hold it, kiss the back of it, both hands, have them meet his hands, have their fingers meet, close together, linked.

What he wanted was to follow the line of her shoulders to her throat, to her soft, trembling mouth, from her mouth down to her breasts. He wanted to know the shape of her, feel himself buried deep inside her, feel her expand to accommodate him, hear her cries of ecstasy....

Suddenly, and with a silent expletive, Cole rolled over and sat straight up as if he'd been shot. Merciful heaven!

Why couldn't he get it through his thick skull that she was off-limits? He was here for one purpose and one purpose only, and that was to spy on Beth Loring. He winced against the unvarnished truth. But it was the truth, and he had to accept it. There was no time like the present, he told himself.

And one thing was certain: she didn't want him—he had sensed that—and he was damned if he was going to chase after her like a lovesick cow.

Feeling at long last that he was in command of the situation, Cole shifted to get better situated for the short night ahead, only to suddenly freeze as though coldcocked.

His hand touched something. Even before he reached over and switched on the bedside lamp he knew what it was. He forced himself to look down at the pillow near his hand. Lying atop it was the doll he had given Megan.

A loud groan ripped through him as he slung it across the room. He knew then what he had to do....

* * *

"Jenny, oh, my God, Jenny! What..." Beth's voice played out as she stared at her friend, stunned by her appearance.

One of Jenny's eyes was black-and-blue, while the opposite side of her face bore a welt that was equally as hideous. It was a purplish yellow in color.

"My God," Beth whispered again, moving closer.

Jenny burst into tears. "Oh, Beth," she began.

"Shh," Beth urged, placing her arms around Jenny's trembling body and holding her close.

When it seemed as if she could cry no more, Jenny pulled away, and wrapping her arms around her upper body, turned her back on Beth and walked to the window.

"Jenny... please... tell me what this is all about. Were you in an accident?"

Jenny swung around, desperation pinching her features. She raised a tissue to her nose.

"Oh, it was no accident," she said bitterly. "You can rest assured on that."

Beth's expression became more puzzled. "But I don't..." Suddenly it dawned on her, and all the color drained from her face. "You... mean... Ellis did this to you!" Her words sounded unnatural, squeaky.

Tears were once again streaming down Jenny's face. "Yes... I'm afraid... he did."

"But... but *why*?"

Ellis McCall was Jenny's fiancé, and though Beth knew they had had some troubled times, this was the first evidence of physical violence.

"Oh, Beth...please...don't ask me to explain...not now." Once again Jenny turned away.

"Oh, no, you don't!" Beth exclaimed, erasing the distance between them and spinning Jenny around to face her. "I'm not letting you cop out on me. You're beat to a pulp and you say you can't tell me why that bastard did this to you—well, forget it. I'm not buying that."

As if stalling for time, Jenny reached for the coffeepot and commenced pouring herself a cup of the hot brew, lifting questioning eyes to Beth.

"No, thanks," Beth muttered, intent on not letting her friend off the hook. If only she'd stopped long enough to encourage Jenny to talk, maybe this disaster could have been avoided. She'd known Jenny was hurting, but she'd been so wrapped up in her own problems she'd failed to heed Jenny's silent plea for help. It wasn't too late, Beth told herself dogmatically, if Jenny would listen. But when it came to Ellis McCall, she couldn't count on Jenny using good sense.

"Jenny, look at me," Beth said, following a moment of silence. "You don't have to take this, you know. Not from him, not from any man, not ever."

"If only it were that simple."

"Jenny, he hit you!"

"Don't you think I know that?" Jenny cried, sobs once more racking her body.

Beth felt awful. "I'm sorry," she said quietly, trying to stifle her own frustration. "I didn't mean to yell at you. Stop crying now and drink a little more of your coffee."

There was another silence while Jenny did just that. Beth, for the lack of something better to do, changed the filter and began making a fresh pot, finding that her own hands were far from steady.

At length Beth said, "If you won't tell me what this is all about, then will you do one thing for me—no, two things," she corrected quickly. "Will you promise me you'll give serious thought to filing charges against Ellis and then stay the hell away from him?"

Jenny's jaw dropped "What?"

Beth prayed for patience. "You heard every word I said."

"No...no, that's impossible." Jenny shook her head vehemently. "You...you don't understand. I...would never do that."

It was all Beth could do not to reach over and grab Jenny by the shoulders and shake some sense into her. But of course she didn't. Jenny needed her friendship, not her censorship. "All right, just what are you going to do?"

"Ellis...has never done anything like this before," Jenny explained. "And he promised never to do it again." She paused and blew her nose. "He's...been under a lot of strain lately."

I just bet he has. "Jenny, Jenny, that's no excuse for—"

Jenny's hand went up, halting Beth in midsentence. "I know what you're about to say and I couldn't agree more, but I love Ellis.... I have to give him another chance."

The fight went out of Beth. "Whatever you say," she said tonelessly.

"I know ... you don't like Ellis, but ..."

Beth's gaze softened. "Oh, honey, it doesn't matter what I think of him, not really. You're the one who has to put up with him, not me." Jenny was right, though; she didn't like Ellis McCall, had never liked him. In her estimation, he was a moocher who used people for his own selfish purposes. But Jenny had never been able to see that side of him.

Suddenly his image flared to mind: the medium-height frame, the longish dishwater brown hair, long aquiline nose, full red lips and a suggestion of desperation and ruin in his deep-set dark eyes. Beth didn't trust him as far as she could throw him. Now she knew she had grounds for her dislike. Any man who would hit a woman was a sorry creep.

"Would you mind if I went home for the day?" Jenny was saying.

Beth blinked, regrouping her thoughts. "By all means go. Go home and go to bed." She paused with a flimsy smile. "And if you need me, you know where I'll be."

Jenny's chin wobbled. "I ... hate to bother you with all my troubles. You have enough of your own, with Megan...."

"Forget it," Beth rushed in. "You'd do the same for me. Now go."

Beth felt as limp as a dishrag when at last she was alone. Poor Jen, she thought, but, then, there was nothing she could do, even if she wanted to. It boiled down to the fact that Jenny was not willing to help herself. Still, Beth was appalled by the whole sordid mess. What had possessed Ellis to mistreat Jenny? Even more mind-bending was Jenny's defense of him. Would it happen again?

A sudden chill darted through Beth as she sat down at her desk. What next? she asked herself, feeling tears nip at her own eyelids. Not only was she worried about Dexter Manly, but thoughts of Cole Weston and the lingering memories of that evening with him were driving her crazy, as well.

She hadn't seen him since, except at a distance. Like clockwork, he zipped past Megan's window every morning, out for his morning run.

She would catch herself shifting to the window and watching him, calling to mind those chocolate-brown eyes as they had peered into hers, taste again those firm lips that had kissed her in a way she'd never been kissed before, those tender hands that had meshed their bodies together, leaving no doubt as to his arousal....

She turned away from the window feeling weak all over. She guessed that what upset her even more was that she didn't know what would have happened if he hadn't pulled back. Would she have let him make love to her?

She was trying in earnest to corral her tormenting thoughts, when she heard a knock on the door.

"Yes?"

Jenny poked her head around the door. "Beth, Mrs. Hubbard is here for her fitting."

"Tell her I'll be right there," Beth said, pushing her troubles aside one more time.

"We have to talk."

Dexter Manly's head popped up and his eyes narrowed as they crawled up Cole's six-foot-plus frame, parked like a statue in front of his desk.

"So talk," Manly said, his facial expression undergoing a change.

Cole returned his hard look, though caught momentarily off guard by the way Dexter's heavy brows crowned his eyes and seemed to ramble like an untrimmed hedge. Why hadn't he noticed that before? If his stomach hadn't felt as though it were in a shredding machine, he might have laughed at his comic analogy.

But not this morning; laughter was the farthest thing from Cole's mind.

The silence hung like a cloud over the room as they continued to size each other up, each preparing for battle in his own way.

"Ah, hell, Cole," Dexter said at last, heaving his large body to a stance, "take off your boxing gloves for a damned minute and let's have a cup of coffee. The way I see it, it's too damned early to be out of bed, much less embroiled in such serious conversation.''

Although Cole felt himself relax somewhat, he wasn't about to give this man an inch for fear he'd take a mile—*a mile of my hide*—which he wasn't prepared to give.

"You go ahead and help yourself," Cole responded tightly. "I believe I'll pass. Thanks, anyway."

"Suit yourself." Manly's voice was gruff as he stepped over to a small but fully equipped wet bar, which housed not only the best in liquors, but a blender, ice bucket, glasses and coffee maker.

"Sure you won't change your mind?" Dexter asked.

"I'm sure." Cole's tone was brisk as he lowered himself into the nearest chair.

Manly took his time adding a generous amount of cream and sugar to his coffee, while Cole gave the rest of the room a quick survey. Although he'd been here many times, the opulence never failed to catch his fancy.

The walls were richly paneled and the floor, a highly polished parquet, was accented by an area rug. In the middle of the rug sat Manly's heavy oak desk. It was massive, stained dark in contrast to the lighter floors and walls, and polished to a sheen. On top were two phones and a personalized pen set.

Manly took a hearty sip of his coffee before returning to his desk. Instead of taking his usual seat behind it, he perched on the front corner of his desk top and looked at Cole.

"Care for a cigarette?" he offered.

"No, thanks."

He sighed. "All right, Cole, let's have it. What's on your mind?"

"I want out."

Silence.

Manly took an exaggerated drag off his newly lighted cigarette, squinting at Cole through the haze of smoke. "No way. You gave me your word and I intend to hold you to it."

"No, Dexter, read my lips. I'm through. I'm putting someone else on the case, someone that's as capable as me."

Manly leaned over onto one knee, his face only two feet from Cole's. "You do and I'll have your ass."

Cole rose from his chair, reciprocating Manly's angry stare. "Dammit, Dexter," he said, "you don't understand. And I can't explain, so you'll just have to trust me when I tell you it's for the best."

"I'm the one who says what's best," Manly bellowed, his voice shaking the room. "And I'm telling you that I don't want a bunch of peons handling this case." He paused, cramming his cigarette in the ashtray. "You're the only one who can get my granddaughter for me."

They stood, glaring at each other in a moment of highly charged silence.

"Nothing you can say will make me change my mind." The words shot out of Cole's mouth with stunning coldness.

Manly's palm slapped the desk. "We'll see about that! You owe me, and don't ever forget it!"

What little cordiality that had existed between them quickly vanished.

"And now I'm calling in the cards," Manly added quietly. Too quietly.

Cole winced as if Dexter had kicked him below the belt; as far as Cole was concerned, he had. "Dammit, you're not playing fair." Fear gripped Cole so tightly that the sweat oozing through his pores seemed congealed.

He had to get off this case or else sacrifice his principles. If he continued to be around Beth Loring, he wouldn't be responsible for his actions, but getting that across to Dexter Manly without baring his soul was a whole new ball of wax. Yet he couldn't discount his debt to Manly. Wouldn't that be sacrificing his principles, as well? Hadn't he given his word? If only he didn't feel such a deep obligation to this man. If only he'd been able to get his business started on his own.

Dexter folded his arms across his chest. "You've given me no choice, Cole. You're forcing me to play dirty." He paused, thrown off track by Cole's sudden expletive. "I don't know what brought this on, not that I give a damn, because it really doesn't matter. All that matters is that you gave me your word, and I'm holding you to it."

"Nothing like going straight for the jugular, is there?" Cole's voice was hoarse, but steady. His knuckles on the desk were white.

"You'd do the same, only worse," Dexter said roughly. "You'd tear my head off."

Seconds passed, then minutes. Still neither moved, nor spoke.

"Well?" Dexter's brassy voice invaded the silence, while his big Adam's apple worked in his throat.

"All right, Dexter, you win!" Violence burned in his voice.

On the heels of those words, Cole pivoted and tore out of the room, and didn't pause until he reached his Lincoln. It was only after he'd started the engine and pulled out onto the loop that he allowed his mind to function.

His thoughts began flying as fast as the wheels on his car. Damn! He was back to square one, exactly where he'd started. *Keep your cool, old boy.* So he'd lost a battle. So Manly had him over a barrel. So what? He'd been in worse situations, hadn't he? So how had he gotten out of them? By fighting like hell, that was how. Well, this was no different, he told himself.

He'd rise to the challenge, preserve his integrity, do the job he had agreed to do. The sooner he began digging into Beth's past, the sooner he could finish the case and get the hell out of her life.

If it wasn't already too late, he thought, feeling suddenly like a man whose life had just taken another unexpected and frightening turn.

Beth twisted the key in the ignition with all her strength. Nothing. Not even so much as a whine.

"That tears it," she hissed aloud, feeling a lone tear slide down her cheek.

What to do? she asked herself silently, gritting her teeth. As usual, she was running late, and now with the car refusing to start, she was really in a mess.

Although she was properly dressed for the cold morning in a sweater dress, boots and cape, she shivered against the cold seeping into her bones.

Thank goodness Megan wasn't with her, she thought. When she had awakened Meg to dress her, her daughter had felt a tad warm and had a drippy nose to boot. Beth had immediately called her good friend and neighbor, Mattie Engles, and asked her if she would keep Megan, not wanting to expose the other children at the nursery. Mattie had not only said yes, but had volunteered to pick up Megan when she took her husband to work.

Deciding to try one more time to start the engine, Beth pumped the accelerator and turned the key. Again nothing. The engine was still as dead as a stinking mackerel.

"Damn, damn, damn," Beth muttered under her breath, leaning across the seat and lifting her purse and briefcase. She hoped it wouldn't be too late to catch Jenny.

"Beth, open the window."

The sudden, unexpected sound of Cole's voice made her blood run hot and wild. She swung around, her breathing labored.

He was peering at her through the glass. He was dressed in his usual running garb, only this time he had a hood pulled over his head. His cheeks and chin bore a light, brown stubble, an "early Don Johnson look," she thought irritatingly. He looked so good.... It just wasn't fair.

Without intending to, Beth's eyes collided with his grin, only to watch it suddenly disappear.

Cole was quick to note the tears glistening in her eyes and the fine white line around her mouth. His heartbeat increased a notch. Megan. Where was Megan?

"What's wrong?" he demanded, concern sharpening his voice.

The warm breath fogged up the window. With an unsteady hand, Beth reached for the door handle and jerked it up. As the door unexpectedly swung open, Cole just managed to dodge it.

"For starters," she wheezed, "you almost scared me into tomorrow."

"Sorry, but I figured you heard me." After a short pause, he added, "Where's Megan?"

"At my...our neighbor behind us. She was feeling puny this morning, so I asked Mattie to watch her. It's a good thing I did, too, because my car won't budge."

Beth was looking at him carefully now, expecting any minute to feel a bout of uneasiness, especially after the way they had parted.

Her worry was in vain; Cole's expression was cool and told her nothing.

"Scoot over," he said, "and I'll see what I can do."

Under the circumstances, Beth would have preferred to get out, but as Cole didn't give her time, she was forced to comply with his arrogant request.

However, she didn't move fast enough. To her dismay, Cole sat down on the end of her cape, curtailing further movement. She sat like a statue and watched him out of the corner of her eye. He had removed his hood, leaving his hair an unruly mess. A lone strand dangled across his forehead as he continued his scrutiny of the instruments. Suddenly she had the urge to reach up and shove the stray lock back in place.

Instead she clasped her hands tightly together and turned away, but not before she saw the hard muscles in his thighs contract when he ground his shoe down on the gas pedal. A dull flush stained her cheeks.

"Now let's see what we have here," Cole mumbled, concentrating on the gadgets on the dashboard, completely ignoring her.

Well, that was just fine with her. Wasn't that what she wanted—just to be friends and nothing more? Sure it was, she told herself adamantly. But if that was true—if she really believed it—then why was she so conscious of his nearness, making it difficult for her to breathe normally?

She heard the engine turn over, but her excitement was shortlived; after one sputter, it choked itself out again. She stared at him with a frown on her face.

He shrugged and returned her stare, taking in her heightened color, thinking how fresh she looked . . . and smelled, her scent enveloping him like a web.

She wet her lips. "Do you have any idea what's wrong with it?"

Not taking his eyes off her, he said, "Could be the battery or it could be the spark plugs. . . ."

"Is that serious?"

He chuckled. "I take it you don't know much about cars."

Beth drew back and wrinkled her nose. "You're right. I know nothing. If they don't run, all I know to do is holler for help."

"Well, take my word for it, a good mechanic can fix you up."

"I'll have to take care of that later. Right now I need to make a phone call and get a ride to work."

"No need. I'll take you," he said quickly.

"Oh, no, I couldn't impose on you like that. You've already done enough." She worried her lower lip. "I'll call Jenny."

"Forget it. I'll take you. Just sit tight while I get my car. I'll only be a minute."

Giving Beth no time for a rebuttal, he got out of the car and was gone.

Beth barely had time to shift positions before he eased his Lincoln up the driveway behind her.

When she saw him reach across the seat and open the door, she scrambled out of her car and walked briskly to his, the north wind nipping at her heels.

"Brrr," she said, sinking down into the soft seat.

Cole inhaled deeply, getting another whiff of her perfume. "You got that right," he agreed on a ragged note.

Beth said nothing as she turned and stared out the window.

After a moment, Cole asked, "Why don't you put your car in the garage? I've noticed that you never do. On a cold morning like this, it would help, you know."

Beth kept her face averted. "I know, but unfortunately my garage is crammed full of... my hus—of Lee's stuff."

"I see."

No, you don't see. She wasn't sure she could even see the reasoning behind keeping Lee's things, especially the sailboat. Still, she hadn't been able to get rid of them. It was almost as if she were reluctant to close that chapter of her life. She had never felt guilty about it until this man... *Can it, Beth!*

Silence ensued as they breezed down the almost deserted streets. By the time Cole pulled up in front of The In-Look the quiet had climbed to a screaming pitch.

Beth tried to smile, but at best it was a sickly attempt. "Thanks... for the ride."

He nodded. "Think nothing of it. What time do you close the shop?"

"Around five-thirty, but—"

He cut her off. "Why don't I come back and get you?"

"Please...don't. I mean, I appreciate the offer," she amended hurriedly, her voice sounding ghostly, "but Jen will take me home."

For a moment he looked like he wanted to argue, but then the mask was back in place, his tone cool. "Whatever makes you happy."

Abruptly he got out of the car and came around to her side and opened the door. When she stepped out and stood up, she was standing so close to him she could feel the heat of his body, see the swift rise and fall of his chest....

He regarded her broodingly, as if he had something else to say, but could not find the words. Then he stepped into his car and was gone.

Beth stood stationary, wondering with a sinking feeling in her stomach how she was going to stamp out her burgeoning fascination for Cole Weston.

Chapter Five

Cole sat at his desk and waited, impatience gnawing at him. He had called his assistant, Sam Boyd, several days ago now, giving him explicit instructions as to what he wanted him to do. He'd also given him instructions to get back to him no later than this morning.

So far Cole hadn't heard a word, but he knew it would be futile to call Boyd. He was Cole's crackerjack investigator and when he had the information, Cole would hear from him. Patience, however, was not Cole's strong suit.

He pushed back his chair and, swinging his long legs out from under the desk, trudged to the window. Before adjusting the miniblinds so that he could see outside, he glanced down at his watch. Eleven o'clock. Why hadn't Sam called?

Once the blind was open, sunlight flooded the room, causing him to blink. As his eyes became attuned to the glare, his gaze settled on Beth's house.

Ah, Beth. The nemesis to his peace of mind.

Cole stirred restlessly, caught between his inclinations and his training. If only Dexter hadn't insisted on holding his feet to the fire, he'd be long gone. *Who the hell do you think you're kid-*

ding! Even if Manly had agreed to let him off the hook, he wouldn't stay away from Beth.

So where did that leave him?

He had no intention of getting involved; that determination hadn't changed. So, what if he let his attraction have free rein; could he then get her out of his system? She was like an itch that he couldn't seem to scratch; once he did, maybe it would cease to itch.

Suddenly the doorbell chimed, putting his thoughts on hold. With a muttered curse, he stormed out of the room and to the front door.

With a scowl on his face, Cole yanked it open. Sam Boyd stood on the porch, his eyebrows raised in mock fear while his arms flew halfway above his head.

"Please don't shoot," he begged. "I surrender."

"Damn you, Sam," Cole said, his lips splitting into a sheepish grin as he took in his assistant's appearance. Sam Boyd was nattily dressed in a beige blazer, gold vest, brown slacks and a dark tie over a pale yellow shirt. His oversized nose was out of sync with the rest of his lean features, and he had grown a bushy mustache to detract attention from it.

"What's the matter, Cole, did ya wake up with a burr under your butt this morning?"

Cole grinned again. "Don't I always?"

"Now that you mention it . . ."

"Hey, don't just stand there. Come on in."

Boyd gave him another wary glance before reaching for his briefcase sitting beside his right foot. "Sure it's safe?"

"Sam!"

"Okay, okay, don't get back on your high horse."

Cole stepped back and let Sam enter, then pointed down the hall. "Straight ahead and to the right is my office. Want a Coke or something?"

"Nothing for me, thanks," Sam said. "I just came from McDonald's."

Cole made a face. "One of these days, you're going to OD on that junk."

Boyd rubbed his stomach and grinned. "Oh, but what a way to go."

Cole just shook his head, falling in behind Sam. When they reached the small bedroom that Cole had turned into a make-shift office, he gestured for Sam to be seated, while he perched on the edge of the desk.

"Got what you wanted, boss," Sam began without preamble, his voice businesslike and serious. Gone was the banter of a moment before. "Or at least I think I did," he added, raising questioning eyes to Cole.

As he concentrated on what his assistant was saying, Cole tried to ignore the sudden tightening in his belly. "I was expecting you to call," he hedged, postponing what he knew was certain to be unwelcome news.

"I was going to, but I figured this was too hot to handle on the phone."

"That important, huh?" This time Cole's stomach gave a brutal twist. He winced.

Sam was looking at him rather strangely, but Cole pretended not to notice and went on, "Well, let's have it. What did you find out?"

Acting as if he had all the time in the world, Sam reached for the briefcase, and after landing it with a resounding thud on the top of the desk, he popped the latches and removed a manila folder. He held it out to Cole, who was now standing beside him.

For half a heartbeat, Cole hesitated, staring at it as though it were something evil. Then he all but snatched it from Sam's hand. "Thanks," he mumbled, rounding the edge of the desk and taking a seat behind it.

"You're welcome," Sam said with exaggerated politeness. Then added, "Is that offer of a Coke still open?"

Cole jerked his head up. "Uh . . . yeah . . . sure. The kitchen's just off the den. Can't miss it.

Sam stared at him a moment longer, then shaking his head, turned and left the room.

With a grimace, Cole dipped his head back into the contents of the file and didn't look up until he heard Sam reenter the room.

Sam stopped in his tracks. "What the hell? You're green around the gills."

Cole slammed the folder shut, his face unreadable. "Your imagination's working overtime, my friend."

Again Sam raised his arms in mock defense. "Whatever you say."

"Sorry," Cole said bleakly, standing up and walking to the window, his shoulders slumped.

"Why, I thought you'd be jumping through hoops when you looked at this report. I can just see Manly's face when you tell them this. The old man's a shoo-in to win the case now. Hot damn, it's just what the doctor ordered!"

"Yeah," Cole said in a lackluster tone, everything going dead inside him, "just what the doctor ordered."

"Beth?"

"Yes." Beth looked up at Jenny from her position on the floor. She was kneeling on one knee, nose deep in a box of invoices.

Jenny cocked her head. "There's a good-looking hunk out front asking for you."

"Me?" Beth's voice sounded foreign even to her own ears.

Jenny flashed her a knowing smile. "Yes, you," she mimicked.

"Oh" was all Beth could manage as she scrambled to an upright position, knowing beyond a shadow of a doubt who was waiting for her. But why? Hadn't she made it plain she wouldn't need his assistance in getting home?

"Been holding out on me, huh?"

In spite of Beth's efforts to keep her emotions under control, she felt her face flush with color. "It's not what you think," she snapped. "And wipe that smug smile off your face while you're at it."

Jenny's smile widened. "Aha, methinks the lady protests too loudly."

Beth was on her feet now, glaring at her friend. "Okay, you've had your fun, so lay off, okay?"

Although Jenny's face fell solemn, that same smile lingered around her mouth. "So it's no big deal. Then who is he?"

"My neighbor."

"Neighbor! I never had a neighbor that looked like *him*."

"Yes, neighbor," Beth stressed, her eyes darting toward the open door of the stockroom, which was only a short distance from the showroom floor. "Keep your voice down, for crying out loud. He'll hear you."

Jenny shrugged again, her eyes dancing. "So?"

It was Beth who smiled this time. "Oh, you! One of these days..."

"Hey, don't get me wrong." Jenny laughed. "I'm all for it. I was beginning to think it was going to take a blast of dynamite to get you interested in the opposite sex again. I think this is wonder—"

"Jen!"

At Beth's command, Jenny's mouth instantly clamped together as though she'd been programmed.

"Seriously, would you knock it off?" Beth pleaded. "Like I said, he's just a neighbor who was kind enough to bring me to work this morning after my car refused to start. You know I have to leave it parked out in the weather."

Jenny raised her eyebrows. "The plot thickens."

Beth balled a fist and pointed it at Jenny before saying, "Come on, I'll introduce you. Then I'll find out what he wants." Suddenly she halted in her tracks. "I've got it! Maybe he's here to buy something for one of his women friends."

"Yeah, and I'm Joan Collins in disguise, too."

Before she crossed the threshold, Beth threw Jenny a murderous look, thoroughly disgusted with her friend's antics.

Jenny merely smiled and followed her.

Even though his back was turned, Cole sensed Beth's approach. The moment he swung around, their eyes locked.

Beth was the first to turn away, groping for her composure while cursing the telltale warmth that stained her cheeks. God, what the sight of this man did to her equilibrium....

He was wearing a powder-blue sweater, leather jacket and a pair of snug-fitting jeans that did nothing toward calming her fluttering heart.

She saw Jenny giving him the once-over and knew she was thinking the same thing.

To break the silence, Beth drew a deep breath and took the plunge. "Jenny Davis," she said, "I'd like for you to meet my...neighbor...Cole Weston."

Cole smiled and stepped forward, extending a hand to Jenny. "A pleasure, Ms. Davis."

"Call me 'Jenny.'"

"All right, Jenny," Cole said, dropping her hand and smiling politely. Then his eyes switched to Beth's, warming considerably. "I came to get you. Are you ready?"

Beth was clearly flustered. "Uh...yes...I mean no! I thought I told you that . . . Jen would take me home."

"Oh, that's all right," Jenny chimed in, "you go ahead. Remember, I'm working late and you have to get Meg," she finished lamely.

Beth could have strangled her friend right there on the spot, but the fact that Jenny mentioned Megan was the only thing that saved her. Also, Beth conceded reluctantly, Jenny had mentioned working late. Still . . .

"Well?" Cole's low, gravelly voice sliced into the lengthening silence.

"I'll...only be a minute," Beth said, short of breath, her legs feeling like rubber as she made her way into the office. Thinking Jenny was sure to follow, she stood just inside the doorway and waited. No Jenny. *Chicken,* Beth thought when it became obvious that her friend was going to keep her distance.

While she crammed the invoices in her carryall and slipped her coat on, her mind was racing ninety miles an hour with unanswered questions. Why had he flagrantly disregarded her refusal of a ride home? More to the point, what did he want from her? It was obvious he could have any woman he wanted, so why the interest in a widow with a child? It just didn't make sense.

Of course she was flattered. Who wouldn't be? Yet she was still convinced, born of a caution founded on intuition, that to become involved with Cole Weston would be very unwise, indeed.

Jenny was nowhere to be seen when Beth rounded the corner into the front of the store. Out of the corner of her eye, she noticed the Closed sign was displayed on the front door. Then her vision was completely taken up with Cole, leaning negligently against the counter.

"Ready?" he asked, straightening up.

"If . . . you are," she said in a voice that was almost a whisper.

They were silent until Cole buckled himself in behind the steering wheel. Then he faced her and said, "Oh, by the way, I checked your car and took the liberty of getting the parts needed to fix it."

Beth was aghast.

"Did I fail to mention that I'm a pretty good backyard mechanic?"

"Yes, you did," she said succinctly.

"Well, it doesn't matter, but what does matter is that you don't have to pay anyone to work on it, not when I'm around to do it for you."

"You're a *mechanic*?"

Cole shot her a look, his dark eyes seeming a mile deep, the corners of his mouth twitching. "Well, let's just say that in a crisis I can certainly hold my own under the hood of a car."

When Beth remained silent, he went on, "I would've taken care of it today, only—" He broke off. "Only I had some work that was pressing."

At the sudden change in his tone, Beth stole a glance at him. His profile now had a grim cast to it, a perfect match for the bleakness in his voice. She had a sneaking suspicion that he was purposefully keeping his eyes averted, though why she couldn't begin to say. Trying to understand what was going through his mind would be a lesson in futility, so she turned away, mulling over a way to tell him that she didn't want him to fix her car, that she didn't want him to do anything for her. She didn't want to feel obligated.

Turning to face him again, she began tentatively, "Look, Cole, I appreciate your offer, but it's really not necessary for you to take on the responsibility of my car. There's . . . a mechanic I can call."

Cole's tone bore the height of patience, as though he were talking to Megan. "Relax, will you, and trust me. It's no big deal. By noon tomorrow, you'll have your wheels. Okay?"

Beth frowned. "If you're sure . . ."

Cole chuckled. "Did anyone ever tell you you're one hard headed lady?"

This drew a smile from Beth. "All the time."

He started to laugh, that marvelous deep-bellied hooray so infectious that Beth felt it should be banned, especially since it did strange things to her insides. Why hadn't she noticed it before? Was it because he had such a Jekyll-and-Hyde personality? One minute he wore that guarded, tense expression, then the next minute, he could easily have written the definition of charm.

She shifted in her seat and forced herself to pay attention to what he was saying. "And I'll also take you to work in the morning and Megan to the nursery."

"Oh, no, you won't," she declared, fully alert now, her tone brooking no argument. "Jenny will come after us."

Although Cole's jaw bunched perceptibly, his tone was conciliatory. "You're the boss."

"Please don't misunderstand. I didn't...don't mean to sound ungrateful, but I've...been so used to doing things on my own that it's hard to..." Her words trailed off. "What I'm trying to say is that—"

"Don't," Cole interrupted. "I know what you're trying to say and I understand."

Beth's alarm was lessening as she met his eyes briefly. "By the way, how's the little one?" he asked abruptly, changing the subject.

"Mattie said she's feeling somewhat better, but if she's not considerably better in the morning, I'm going to call my doctor. Mattie's been giving her liquid Tylenol every so often, which has kept the fever down."

"Sounds like she's in competent hands," he said, then once again changed the subject. "Are you hungry?"

Beth thought for a moment. "Now that you mention it, I am, but..."

"Good, I am, too. What d'ya say I zip through the drive-in window at Chen's and get some Chinese food to go. Then we'll pick up Megan and go to your place." He paused and glanced at Beth, as if testing her reaction. "I'll even run over to the house and snatch a bottle of wine."

"Oh, please...I don't think..."

"Your stubborn streak is showing."

"I know, but—"

"You have to eat, don't you?"

"Yes...."

He grinned, "Aw, come on, I'm only asking you to share a little dinner."

If only it were that simple, Beth thought, though his grin was fast melting her resistance. "Chinese food, it is," she said at last, thinking, *fool...fool...fool!* "But don't you ever accuse me of being stubborn again," she added on the rebound. "I think you've got the market cornered on that."

Again Cole laughed that marvelous laugh. Beth smiled; it was impossible not to.

Still chuckling, Cole said, "I've been told that a time or two."

"I just bet you have. I just bet you have."

Another silence followed as Cole steered the Lincoln off North Street and into the drive that led to the restaurant's take-out window.

Ordering was a relatively painless task as they both had similar tastes. Within minutes, they were again en route home with a sack of egg rolls, one order of vegetables with chicken and one order of vegetables with beef sitting between them.

Beth watched as Cole suddenly reached over and flipped on the radio, its stereo sounds immediately filling the air.

A sigh escaped her as she laid her head back and closed her eyes, relishing the moment, refusing to think about what she was doing and the repercussions that might follow.

"Tired?"

"Sort of," Beth murmured, feeling his eyes on her.

"Bad day, huh?"

"No, not really." Her eyes fluttered open and she turned her head toward him. "It's physical more than anything. I've been unpacking quite a bit of freight lately and the old muscles are rebelling."

"Well, we'll just have to see what we can do about that. I'm a pro at rejuvenating tired muscles."

Beth's heartbeat faltered. Just the thought of his hands on her body... "Is... there anything you *can't* do?" she asked, trying to even out her breathing.

When Cole spoke, his voice, too, seemed a little thick. "Not... when I make up my mind, there isn't."

Beth turned away, not wanting to think there was a deeper meaning behind his statement. Getting her mind back on track, she said, "I almost forgot. You need to turn left at the next street and Mattie's house is the first one on the left."

Moments later Cole braked in Mattie's driveway and went for the door handle.

"I'll get Megan," Beth said hastily, watching a question pop into his eyes. "I'll be right back," she added, and was gone before he could say anything.

Within minutes, Cole was holding the door open while Beth got in with her precious burden.

"She all right?" Cole demanded before closing the door on Beth's side.

"She's fine," Beth whispered.

Cole stayed where he was, his throat choked with sudden emotion. Megan, asleep and wrapped in a fleecy blanket, lay in the curve of Beth's arm; Beth's golden head was bent, her face absorbed as she gazed at the lovely, relaxed little form. The frosted bulb overhead burned above the seat; the mother and child were haloed in its soft light.

Mentally shaking himself, he closed the door and went around to his side, climbing in behind the wheel.

Both were silent until they drove up in Beth's driveway. Then Beth said, "If you'll reach in my purse, the key should be on top."

"Sure you don't want me to take Meg?"

Beth shook her head. "I'm afraid it'll wake her up."

Once inside, Beth still did not relinquish Megan. Instead she headed straight for the child's room, only to stop suddenly and turn around, her eyes seeking Cole.

He had just set the sack of food on the Formica-topped counter and was standing awkwardly, looking as though he were totally out of his element.

"You can come, too, if you'd like," Beth said softly.

Cole's expression was unreadable as he hastily closed the distance between them. Wordlessly he followed Beth into the baby's room, where she switched on a lamp just inside the door.

The room's decor, made up of multicolored miniblinds, a chair filled with stuffed toys and a canopied twin bed were lost on Cole. His eyes were caught up with Beth as she laid Megan on the bed. He shifted restlessly at her side, feeling like a fifth wheel.

"She's out like a light, isn't she?" he whispered, taking in the petallike tendrils surrounding Megan's tiny face.

Beth gently raised one eyebrow. "While I get out of my coat, would you begin to undress her?"

She watched him closely as he carefully, but awkwardly eased the coat off the small arms. Megan was now half-awake and patiently allowed it.

"Man, Mommie," she whispered adoringly, staring up at Cole, a small smile passing between them.

Cole suddenly caught her to him and gave her a swift hug, then released her.

Beth turned aside to fight the pressing tears. It was like stumbling unawares on someone's nakedness, she thought. Should she tell him that she'd seen him exposed, or quietly creep away and never let him guess what she'd seen? Forcing the tears back, she sighed softly and tossed her coat over the back of the chair, knowing perfectly well she would opt for the latter.

Later, when the bed was turned back, they finished undressing Megan. When the limp little arms and legs had been coaxed into miniature pajamas, Cole tucked the covers around her shoulders, trying to ignore an unsettling sensation creeping around the edges of his heart, questioning for the first time ever his choice of life-style.

"She's quite taken with you, you know," Beth murmured, reclaiming his attention.

At that precise moment, he dared not look at Beth for fear of what she might see in his face. It was as if she and this defenseless baby had dug deep inside him, found something that belonged to them in his heart. And he was urging them to take it. Crazy!

Yet back in the den, he had no choice but to face her. Whereas before they had been fully occupied, with the preparations for Megan's bedtime, now they shifted uncomfortably in an uneasy silence. The tension was plainly felt.

Beth finally broke it.

"While I see about dinner, why don't you take off your jacket and make yourself comfortable?" If her voice sounded a bit ragged around the edges, she chose to ignore it.

"I'll get a fire started, then," he said.

"That'd be nice." She threw him a brief smile over her shoulder.

They both went about their tasks thankful for something constructive to keep their hands and minds occupied.

A short time later the fire was crackling, embracing the room in a cozy glow, and they were munching on the Chinese food.

"Mmm, I'm glad you suggested this," Beth said.

Cole's eyes were warm. "No more than I." Suddenly he dropped his fork. "Damn, I clearly forgot the wine."

Beth quit chewing for a moment. "All's not lost. I think I have a bottle in the cabinet over the stove. Would you do the honors?"

It turned out to be a California wine—mellow and smooth.

"By the way, you have a nice place here," Cole said, a couple of sips under his belt. His eyes again scanned the kitchen before moving to the large den with its corner fireplace, wicker furniture and a piano gracing the far corner.

"Thanks," Beth said, chasing her food down with a sip of wine. "After…Lee died, I sold our large place and bought this. We like it. It suits us."

Cole's gaze was soft. "That, it does."

Beth lowered her eyes and stood up. "If you've finished, why don't you go into the den and take the wine? I'll dump this mess in the garbage and join you shortly." Again that odd note in her voice. Again she ignored it.

His tone was husky. "Don't be long."

Beth still had the weak trembles minutes later when she took a seat beside him on the couch, a plump cushion separating them.

They sat for a moment in silence, Cole content just to look at her. Look at the way her gold hair capped her head, bright and shiny, the way her breasts jutted against the soft material of her sweater with each breath she took and the way her green eyes were smiling at him now. She was like a chameleon: by turns determined, mysterious, childlike. . . .

Beth flushed as their eyes stayed fastened to each other for a long moment. Again it was she who broke the tension, her smile still intact, though her pulse was skyrocketing.

"Tell me...what did...what do you think about...the shop?"

Cole inhaled deeply and, leaning back, crossed his right leg over his left knee in a casual manner.

But Beth wasn't fooled. She knew he was as shaken as she by that exchange.

"I was impressed, as you knew I would be."

She warmed to his words. "Well, I am rather proud of it. But I didn't know it was that obvious."

"Hey, don't apologize," he said, reaching over and refilling their glasses. "If you've got it, flaunt it, I always say."

Beth laughed. "I'll remember that next time I feel guilty about bragging."

Suddenly Cole's face grew serious. "Speaking of The In-Look—you can tell me to mind my own business—but I'm curious if your partner makes a habit of coming to work looking like she's been in a boxing match."

Beth licked her lips and hesitated. "It's...never happened before...."

"I'm not asking you to break a confidence, of course."

Beth ran a finger across the back of the couch. "It's...not that. Actually, I don't know what happened myself."

"Well, as long as it's nothing to do with the shop."

Her eyes widened. "Not as far as I know. Or at least, I hope not. It was just a lover's tiff, I expect. She's been living with a man by the name of Ellis McCall, and for some reason, he went nuts and started pounding on her." Her voice was low. "Jenny...wouldn't tell me why. I did beg her to file charges, but of course I was just talking to hear my head rattle."

Cole said nothing, but vowed silently to run a personal check on this Ellis McCall. His intuition was sending out warning signals loud and clear.

Another moment lapsed before Beth said casually, "How 'bout your work? You've never told me exactly what you do."

Her question socked him in the gut. *Hell, you should have been expecting it,* he told himself. *This is like playing Russian roulette.* It was just a matter of time until that loaded gun was pointed at him. And even though he should have been prepared, he wasn't. But, then, one never is when a gun's at his head.

"Actually, I'm an investigator of sorts," he hedged, transferring his gaze, "for the firms that employ me. There's really no glamour to it, just a lot of hard work."

The fact that he was so evasive fueled her curiosity. "I guess it doesn't leave you with much free time for your wood-carving hobby."

"Not nearly as much as I'd like," Cole said, feeling that he was once again on safe ground.

"And you don't resent that?" Beth pressed, still unsatisfied, wanting to know more.

Cole set his glass down on the coffee table and stood up, turning his back to her, walking to the fireplace. "Sometimes. But not often. My work—it's like a hobby to me. You might even call it my mistress." He thought for a minute. "Yes, I guess I love my work—at least most of the time," he added on a sober note.

Beth's eyes narrowed. "I can see you have a different view of work than I do. Oh, don't get me wrong. I love the boutique, as you well know. But it could never take precedence over my child and my home."

"Well, if I had a ... home like this ... and a child like Megan—" He broke off, suddenly furious with himself. *That's crap, Weston, and you know it. So stop babbling like an idiot. Think before you open your mouth!*

Covering the awkward silence, Beth asked softly, "What about a ... family?"

He turned a tense, expressionless gaze on her. "There's an aunt who reared me—my mother died when I was born—and who I see occasionally. And my father's dead, but he never knew or cared if I was alive or dead," he added bitterly.

His dark brown eyes narrowed dangerously and she realized there were demons behind his calm demeanor. He was tormented by his past.

She felt sorry for him, because she could identify with those feelings of loneliness and rejection. She didn't *want* to feel sorry for him, knowing that it could only bring her misery and heartbreak. Yet there was something about him that pulled at her heartstrings, that simply wouldn't let go.

Feeling weary all of a sudden, Beth leaned back and closed her eyes.

"I need to go and let you get to sleep."

At the sound of his close, husky voice, Beth's eyes popped open. His hand was outstretched as he leaned over her.

Like a fool, she placed her hand in his and let him pull her up. When she stood facing him, he didn't drop her hand.

He took a deep breath, let it out.

A trembling started inside her. She looked down.

"Beth."

She raised her eyes and again was caught.

"One could easily drown in your eyes."

"Does that include you?"

"Yes."

Her throat closed; she couldn't speak.

"This is madness, you know."

"I . . . I know."

"What do you suggest we do?"

Before she could react, he took her in his arms and kissed her. It was a long hungry kiss that neither seemed willing to end. Cole's hands explored, pressing her body against his; her breasts against his chest were softer than he had imagined.

Now, for the first time, she felt him against her, rigid and pulsating. She was neither shocked nor disappointed by the extent. The thought had haunted her. . . .

Just as they reached that point from which there could be no retreat, Beth tore her lips and tongue away. "You're right. This *is* madness. You'd better go."

Cole fought the compulsion to grab her again. "You are absolutely right," he said, his eyes burning down into hers. "It would be insane for me to even want to stay."

Beth's lungs ached from the effort of breathing. "If you don't leave now, I might not give you a choice."

"If I don't leave now, I won't have a choice." His voice was strained, as if his throat had narrowed.

Beth reached up, took his face between her hands and planted a soft kiss on his lips. "Good night, and thanks for everything," she whispered, and opened the door.

Cole nodded mechanically, his eyes peering deeply into hers. "All right, but I'll see you tomorrow. Remember, I have a date with your car."

Chapter Six

Beth walked around the shop with a warm glow in her heart. The frightening part was that she couldn't seem to snuff it out. Sleep the night before had been virtually impossible, and it hadn't helped that Megan had also spent a restless night. She had been fretful, and Beth had spent a good part of the night shuffling back and forth between bedrooms.

But Cole had been the reason for her restlessness. She knew she was playing with fire by continuing to let him be a part of her life. It was crazy and irresponsible and unforgivable. She was complicating her life beyond any semblance of sanity. Yet she was hooked, hooked on his broad shoulders, the feel of his hard body against hers and the touch of his lips and tongue. The combination was as potent an aphrodisiac as she'd ever experienced.

As she skirted around the shop getting ready for what she hoped would be a busy day, she kept on indulging herself, letting her thoughts run wild.

She had just walked into the office, ready to tackle the stack of invoices she had neglected the night before, when the door was thrust open.

She watched as Jenny came huffing and puffing into the room, toting the ledger and checkbook that she had gotten out of the car. Without so much as a pause, Jenny said, "This seems to be your week for visitors, my friend."

"Oh?" Beth said, but her heartbeat had increased considerably. Cole. Had he already finished with the repairs on her car? What a pleasant surprise it would be to see him this early in the morning.

"It's not Cole," Jenny said, dousing Beth's hopes. "To tell the truth, I don't know who he is."

"He?"

"Yes, he. Older man. Big dude, too."

Beth was clearly puzzled. "And he wants to see me?"

Jenny shrugged. "That's what he said."

"Well, ask him to come to the office. That is, if you're going back out front."

"Sure thing," Jenny quipped as she breezed back out the door.

Beth stared into space for a moment before idly picking up a pencil and rapping it against the pad on her desk. Who could it be? she wondered, thoroughly perplexed.

She didn't have long to wait. Seconds later, Jenny once again opened the door, admitting a big burly man with features to match—a total stranger.

Standing behind the man, Jenny lifted her shoulders in another shrug, while her eyes seemed to say, "Beats me." Then she walked out and shut the door discreetly behind her.

"Beth Loring?" the man asked, coming to a halt in front of her desk.

Beth rose, not liking this man looming over her. For some unexplained reason, she felt ill at ease. "Yes," she responded cautiously, "I'm Beth Loring. And you're . . . ?"

"Dexter Manly."

If he'd said he was Al Capone, Beth couldn't have been more shocked. For a moment she thought she might faint. She gripped the edge of the desk, holding on to it for dear life while the room spun crazily before her eyes. *Dexter Manly!* Here. In the flesh. Oh, God, No! What had she done to deserve this?

He can't make me talk to him, can he? she asked herself, her stomach squeezed tight in pain.

"Mrs. Loring," he began.

Beth shook her head, backing up. "Please . . . Mr. Manly, you . . . you shouldn't be here."

"That's beside the point, Mrs. Loring," he said crisply. "I am here and I don't intend to leave until I've had my say."

Suddenly red-hot fury boiled through her. "Just who do you think you are?" she hissed, glaring at him as he calmly lowered his bulk down into the closest chair.

"I know who I am," he replied with arrogant complacency. "I'm the child's blood kin. I'm her grandfather."

Again Beth felt herself threaten to slip into that black void that seemed to be taunting her from the edge of her subconscious. How much simpler it would be, she thought, if she could give up and topple over that edge and let herself be sucked into oblivion.

But she couldn't do that. Not now, not ever. She was fighting for all that was near and dear to her. Damn him to hell! *Remember he's on the defensive, not you,* an inner voice whispered. *Loring is the name on Megan's birth certificate, not Manly. Don't let him get the upper hand. Fight him!*

Folding her arms across her chest, Beth faced him like a warrior prepared for battle, to fight to the death if need be.

"Say what you came to say and then get out of my store and out of my life. But let me warn you now, I won't tolerate any abuse from you. None whatsoever."

Manly's mouth curved in a sneer. "Believe it or not, Mrs. Loring, I didn't come here to engage in a battle of words. I came to try to talk some sense into you, to save you from future heartbreak."

Beth closed her ears. Of all the mitigated gall! This man had the arrogance of a rutting bull. For the first time in her life, she knew what it felt like to want to claw another human being's eyes out.

"Now let me tell you something, Mr. Manly," she said, not bothering to control the tremor in her voice or the fire shooting from her eyes. "Megan is mine! Neither you nor anyone else is going to take her from me. I'm not some little windup who will roll over and play dead. I'll fight you to the bitter end." In spite of her efforts to keep her voice on an even keel, she failed miserably. With each word she uttered, the pitch climbed a decibel higher.

Manly uncoiled his frame and got up, his bushy brows shadowing hostile, piercing eyes. "I can see there's no talking to you, and that's a damned shame, too, because I'm not through, and you'd do well to understand that. Megan is my flesh and blood and I intend to get her back." He paused, his eyes having grown colder. "I never lose, Mrs. Loring. You'd be wise to remember that."

When the door closed behind Manly with a dull thud, Beth felt herself shrivel up like a balloon that had suddenly been punctured. Her life's blood seemed to drain from her body.

How dared he come here! she cried silently while pounding her fists on the desk. *How dared he!*

Beth knew the first thing she should do was pick up the phone and call her lawyer, but at the moment, she was too strung out to punch the numbers. She had to get control of herself. It was imperative that she be able to think with a clear head, keep her wits about her.

The tears showed no signs of letting up as she shoved her chair back with her foot and began pacing frantically. For the longest time, she had deluded herself into thinking that things were not as bad as she'd thought, that it was ludicrous to think Manly could actually take Megan from her. Now that she came face to face with the enemy, there was no doubt that Dexter Manly was for real, and wouldn't let up until he had Megan in his clutches.

No! I won't let him do this to me!

But how was she going to stop him? Laws. There were laws, she reminded herself. Then that tiny spot of hope disappeared as though it had never existed. A man like Manly, with more money than sense, more power than a president and more influence than the pope, was above the law. Hadn't he all but told her as much?

Beth was sobbing now, and instead of getting control she was losing it, feeling herself unravel on the inside little by little.

Giles. She would go see Giles. This minute. Forget the phone. He was supposed to be the best, wasn't he? He would know what to do. It was while she was mopping up the tears that Jenny burst through the door.

"My God, Beth!" Jenny cried, taking in Beth's ravaged face.

Beth snatched up her coat and purse, barely acknowledging her friend. "That . . . man . . . was Dexter Manly."

"Oh, no," Jenny wheezed again, her eyes wide as saucers.

"I'm going to see Giles. Would you let me use your car and cover for me while I'm gone?" This last was thrown over her shoulder as she headed out the door.

Jenny pitched her the keys. "Don't worry about coming back."

It was an emotionally despondent and drained Beth Loring who sat in her den later that afternoon with a cup of coffee in her hand. She had just fed Megan a snack and, after giving her a dose of medicine, had put her down for a short nap. The baby's sniffles had turned into a cold and she wasn't feeling her usual perky self. Since Megan never stopped running and playing at the nursery, she was exhausted as well as irritable.

Beth had breathed a sigh of relief when Megan had fallen asleep. She had not been up to coping with her.

When Beth had arrived at Giles's office, she'd had to wait twenty minutes to see him. She had been ready to climb the walls. Giles's secretary had thrown her strange looks, as she'd been unable to sit still.

At last having gotten into the inner sanctum, she had blurted out all the gory details of her conversation with Manly, her words stumbling over one another. She'd had difficulty spitting them out fast enough.

Even now she could see Giles's mouth as it flapped open.

"You mean to tell me that son of a—that Dexter Manly actually came to your shop?" It was obvious he was having a tough time digesting that fact.

"That's exactly what I'm telling you, along with quoting practically verbatim every word he said."

Having calmed down somewhat, Giles fiddled with the edges of his mustache and looked as if he were deep in thought.

"What do we do now, Giles?" Beth demanded, her voice low and tense.

"For starters, I'll call Ransome, Manly's lawyer, and tell him to keep Manly away from you."

"That's all well and good, but that wasn't what I meant." She caught her lower lip between her teeth to keep it from trembling.

"Now, now," Giles soothed, "getting upset won't solve a thing, my dear. Just because Manly came to see you and threatened you, doesn't mean a thing. Nothing's changed. You still have custody of Megan, and until a judge says otherwise, there isn't one thing he can do about it but talk."

Beth's face turned ashen at the mention of the judge. "You still don't think he has a chance? I mean . . ." She faltered, unable to go on. It was as if her vocal chords refused to function any longer.

Renfro's tone was even and reassuring. "As I've told you from the beginning, there's always the chance the judge would rule against you. But the chance is slim," he added hurriedly, conscious of Beth's state of mind as well as her health, thinking that if a good hard wind came it would blow her away. "But don't you think for one minute that I don't have something up my sleeve in the event we do go to court."

A bell went off in Beth's head. She jerked her head up. "Oh, Giles, I can't stand the thought of going to court." She ran a hand tiredly over her eyes.

"I know," he said gently. "Of course, if Manly backs off, then there'll be no reason to go to court."

Beth's flame of hope died. "But he won't," she said flatly, "so we're back to square one."

Renfro scratched his bald head. "I wouldn't say that."

"Well, all I know is that I can't go through another scene with Dexter Manly and keep my sanity."

Giles Renfro's eyes suddenly grew cold as ice, something Beth had never seen before. "You won't have to. I promise you that. What I want you to promise me is that you'll try not to worry. Live normally, take one day at a time and don't instill your insecurities in Megan."

She nodded and he added, "Remember, one day at a time. . . ."

Now, as she put her tepid coffee down on the wicker table beside her, Beth forced herself to get up, feeling her bones crack. After she'd left Giles's office, and despite Jenny's objections, she had gone back to work. She couldn't stand the thought of being alone. She had needed to keep busy, to be around people. As a result, she'd worked herself into a stupor.

After giving the weary muscles on the back of her neck a quick rub, Beth made her way from the den into Megan's room. There she stood by the bed and stared down at the sleeping child.

As usual, Meg was clutching her teddy bear under her chin, her tiny rosebud mouth slightly open, allowing her to breathe easier. Beth felt her heart turn over with love and fear. She wouldn't want to live if she lost Megan.

Hot tears stung the back of her eyelids as she leaned over and put her lips against the soft dewy skin. Then she turned and stumbled out of the room. *Oh, God, give me the strength to handle this burden alone.*

It was after she had discarded her dress and slipped into a caftan that the doorbell rang. Without caring who was there, she walked to the door and flung it open.

"Beth Loring?"

"Yes."

"These are for you," a man said, and thrust a box at her.

She clutched at the doorknob with one hand, the box with the other, and watched as he sauntered down the sidewalk and hopped into a white van with the words A Touch of Love Florist painted on the side.

Still behaving as though she were in a fog, Beth stepped back slowly and closed the door. She headed for the couch, her eyes clinging to the long box. Who on earth would be sending her flowers? Immediately upon sitting down, she untied the string around the box and, tossing the lid aside, carefully eased back the green tissue paper.

"Oh, my, how lovely," she whispered aloud.

The tissue held at least two dozen long-stemmed red roses. With trembling fingers, Beth lifted the beauties out of the container and stood up, the delicious smell invading her senses.

She remained with her head buried in the blooms for several moments, and then suddenly her head came up with a start. The card. Where was the card? Her gaze lowered to the box.

With trembling fingers, she reached down and eased the small card out of the envelope and read the scrawling message: "Just being neighborly. Enjoy. Cole."

She should have known, she told herself. But, then, in defense of herself, wasn't such a gesture out of character for him?

Trembling, her mouth feeling suddenly dry as cotton, Beth once again lowered her head into the exquisite blooms, though not before a torturous expression crossed her features and the beginnings of panic coursed through her veins.

Just what do you think you're doing, Beth Loring? It was in that moment that she knew that her relationship with Cole had gotten completely out of hand. It was foolish on her part to think that she could continue to see him and not pay the penalty for such indulgence.

With a disgusted groan, she trudged into the kitchen and, after plopping the roses down, began rummaging through the cabinets for a vase large enough to hold them, all the while blinking back tears, feeling her despondency like a potent drug.

She wouldn't see him anymore. Since nothing could ever come of their relationship, what was the use of going on with this charade? Marriage and commitment were not for him, while she could not, would not, settle for anything less.

Besides, keeping her child was her top priority. She must not deviate from that goal. To do so would be a fatal error—one that she didn't intend to make.

So deep in thought was she that she couldn't identify the sound when she first heard it. Her hand stilled at the base of the vase and she cocked her head, listening. She heard it again. The doorbell. Whoever was on the other side of the door seemed hell-bent on getting her attention. The bell was pealing nonstop. She hurried her footsteps for fear the noise would wake up Megan. Any minute now she expected to hear her cry.

"Cool it, will you?" she muttered. "I'm coming, I'm coming."

This time when she yanked the door open, her heart dropped to her toes.

Cole was leaning against the post on the porch, one hand jammed in the pocket of his tight-fitting jeans and a smile on his face.

"Hiya, neighbor," he said, his gaze crawling up and down her slender frame.

Her mouth felt parched. All her joints seemed to have gone dry, as well. Raising her head to look him in the eye was a maximum effort.

His eyes grew dark as he took in the picture she made standing reed straight in a green free-flowing caftan. It matched her eyes, he thought, making her look even more enticing. He couldn't help but wonder if she had anything on under it. Suddenly he had to fight the impulse to grab her and lose himself in her body.

When she didn't return his greeting, Cole lowered thick eyelashes and went on, "Your vehicle's in tip-top shape." He took his hand out of his pocket and dangled the keys in front of her face. "In fact, it purrs like a kitten, if I do say so myself."

Damn him! Beth thought. Why did he have to look at her like that? Why did he have to be so charming, so...everything? She pushed her lower lip out slightly and drew it back in before she spoke; her voice sounded slightly warped.

"Thanks. I really appreciate you fixing it." She paused, licking her dry lips. "And I also want to thank you for the roses. They're absolutely gorgeous, but you shouldn't have sent them...."

His face went tight with lines around his mouth. "Why not?"

Again Beth licked her lips. "You...shouldn't throw your money away like that," she said for the lack of anything better to say. Why didn't he just go away and leave her alone? she cried silently. As it was, she wanted to fling her arms around his neck, bury her head against his chest and beg him to hold her.

"Why not? I've got plenty of it," he said, watching her closely, as though he sensed all was not quite right.

Beth took a deep breath to maintain control over her emotions. "That's all well and good. But that's not the point and you know it."

"Do you like the flowers?"

"Of course I like them, but—"

"Then for chrissakes," he exploded suddenly, "can't you just say thank-you and let it go at that? I just felt like sending you flowers, that's all. It's no big deal."

If it was no big deal, then why was he looking at her...as if he could eat her....

"Aren't you going to invite me in?" he asked casually, his good humor obviously restored.

Beth gave a start. *Don't you dare! Send him on his way.* "Well . . . I . . . sure, come in."

Once inside, Cole crossed to the middle of the room and then stopped and turned around. "Where's my girl?"

"Asleep," Beth said, trying to untangle her snarled emotions. *You shouldn't have let him come in.* "Meg has a minor ear infection. The doctor called in a prescription and I'm afraid it zonked her."

There was a long pause as Cole seemed to consider carefully what to say next, "Has something happened? You seem worried—" he shrugged "—or something." He shrugged again. "Distracted, maybe. I don't know."

Beth was now standing only a few feet from him. Cole closed the gap between them, his eyes delving into hers. On closer observation, he could see that tears had stained her cheeks and the corners of her eyes.

"You've been crying, haven't you?" It was a statement, not a question.

The soft, low tone of his voice was almost Beth's undoing. "Yes," she whispered, looking away, but not before she caught herself drowning in the fresh scent of his body, triggering an instant response in her, a response she couldn't control. She struggled to find her voice again. "But I'm . . . fine now."

Cole reached out and, catching her chin in a gentle grip, turned her head back around to face him, feeling his own gut wrench with apprehension. What had happened to put that stricken look in her eyes? Surely it hadn't been the flowers.

"Did something happen at work?" he asked gently, his voice thick.

Beth tried not to flinch, but when his fingers grazed her skin, it was like a jolt of electricity shooting through her. She stepped back.

Cole felt the color drain from his face; there seemed to be less blood in his veins than he had begun the afternoon with.

"Please, I appreciate your concern," she said without expression, as though talking to a stranger, "but . . ." To her dismay, hot tears filled her eyes and she couldn't go on.

Something terrible *has* happened, Cole thought. But what? Surely Manly hadn't... No. Impossible. He let that thought die because it was extremely ugly, even grotesque. As a result some of the tension slowly leaked out of him.

"Hey, I'm a good listener," he said, again reaching out and this time trapping a tear with his fingers, dying to crush her against him.

"Don't," Beth rasped sharply, jerking her head back. "Don't... please."

Cole felt a cold stone drop in his gut. But all he did was shake his head and say softly, "You don't—can't mean that."

Beth let out a ragged breath and turned away very slowly, her insides drawing themselves into small tight coils. "You and me...us...we'll never work. Anyway, there's..." Her voice played out. She took another deep breath, digging for the words to continue, but unable to find them.

Cole felt the tension come back then. It started in his shoulders, shot up his neck and fastened around his mouth. His lip felt stiff, the inside of his mouth dry.

"Go on, I'm listening," he said carefully, too carefully.

Beth straightened her shoulders in sudden defiance. "What I'm trying to say is that at this time in my life, there's no room for a...man."

Suddenly an empty silence fell between them.

"You're a liar, Beth Loring," Cole said at last, his eyes looking like year-old ice.

Her mouth sagged open. "No..." she whispered.

"Yes," Cole countered harshly. "You want a hell of a lot more than friendship from me and you damn well know it. When I touch you, your body sings a different tune...."

"Stop it! Don't say another word," she cried, her tone matching the harsh bite of his. "There's so much you...don't understand...so much I can't tell you...."

Cole said nothing, marveling at the depth of the hole he had dropped into and wondering how the hell he would ever climb out of it.

The silence grew.

They stared at each other. She could hear his breathing and her own, could feel the condensation forming in the space between them as the air from their lungs blended.

When at last he spoke, his voice sounded taut, stretched to the limit. "Please . . . Beth, don't . . . do this."

She shook her head, her face paper white. "Please . . . just go."

He wanted to say something; his brain continued to send urgent messages to his body, to his tongue, but the signals were intercepted. He forced himself to move to the door.

Beth was hardly aware when the door closed behind him. She sat by the window until the moonlight grew pale and the lawn was enveloped in long, dusky shadows. Then she went to bed, but not to sleep.

Cole's head felt as though it were the size of a bowling ball sitting on his shoulders. And his ears felt as if someone were hammering nails into them.

He rolled over in the bed, praying that it wasn't his old ear infection rearing its ugly head. He grimaced again when it suddenly hit him that he'd tried his best to consume every drop of liquor he'd had on hand the night before, though it hadn't helped. Much to his chagrin, he'd stayed stone sober and the pain around his heart remained just as biting.

A groan parted his lips and he exhaled slowly as images of Beth expanded his insides. He already missed her. That hadn't ever happened to him before and he groaned again, wondering why life always managed to turn that one last trick.

Suddenly his thoughts were mercifully caught up by the shrill ringing of the phone. He grabbed the receiver, struggling to sit up on the side of the bed.

"Yes?" His tone was clipped.

"Cole, is that you?"

It was Dexter Manly.

"Of course it's me," Cole growled. "Who else were you expecting?"

Manly obviously chose to let the sarcasm pass, because when he spoke, his voice was free of antagonism. "Can you come down to the office?" he asked.

Cole took a deep breath, let some of it out and said, "Now?"

"Yes, now."

"No, as a matter of fact, I can't. I feel like hell and I'm not even up. Can't you tell me what you want on the phone?"

"I suppose so," Dexter replied grudgingly.

"Well, then, let's have it."

Dexter cleared his throat. "Just thought you oughta know I got impatient and went to see Beth Loring yesterday and—"

"You did what?"

"Now, boy, don't you take that tone with me," Dexter began.

"Why, you bastard!"

"Now you wait just one damn minute," Dexter bellowed.

"No! You wait a minute. And you'd better be glad I'm not in your office. Otherwise I'd be stomping your ass about right now. Maybe by the time I do get there, I will have cooled off."

With that, Cole slammed the receiver back in its cradle, only to feel as if his head had shattered into tiny pieces. He was shaking all over.

Dexter talked to Beth! Even now he couldn't believe it. No wonder she had been upset. What had Dexter said to her?

Well, he damned sure meant to find out. He'd take great pleasure in following through with his threat.

But when he stood up, the room spun in giddy circles. He grabbed for the headboard. It was too late.

Miraculously he passed out before he hit the floor.

Chapter Seven

The dream went on spinning crazily, carrying him along with it. He was reliving the years in Nam. In the dream he struggled to get away from the terror, which came stealthily upon him. He knew again the conflict, the bitter, never-ending fight to live, the thunder of ripping guns, the rending of the earth and its flesh and blood. He knew he could not escape.

And the thunder!

He awoke again and this time he lay sprawled across the bed, perspiration covering his entire body. If he had not awakened, he would have had more of that dream, and it would have left him more hopelessly weak and helpless.

What had caused him to regain consciousness? His pounding head? Or the nausea teasing his insides? Then the muttering, heavy noise came again from the north. Thunder of an approaching storm. Panic overwhelmed him.

His heart began to beat as though he were running, and his head—well, he no longer even thought of it as part of his body. It ached so badly it didn't even count.

The thunder was louder now. Lightning slashed through the black heap of clouds, and then came the crash and ponderous roll of a deep sound. He trembled.

He had to get up, he told himself, to get something in his stomach. Slowly he eased himself to the side of the bed, but every muscle, every bone in his body protested, giving him the feeling of being severely drawn and quartered.

A moan tore through his stiff lips as another burst of pain seared his brain. How long had he been like this? One day, two days, longer? He had no idea. How long had it been since he'd walked out of Beth's house? It had all started then. That much he could remember.

He cradled his head in his arms, only to flinch suddenly as skin touched skin. He was burning up with fever. It was then that he knew, even in his pain-glazed mind, that he'd come down with the fever he'd contracted while in the jungle.

It had flared up only one other time since he'd come back. Then, too, he'd been plagued with those terrible dreams of slithering belly-down in the trenches with bullets zinging around his head. Somehow it all seemed related.

He tried to stand and this time he made it. But not for long, he feared. Feeling his stomach heaving, he knew that any second he was going to be violently ill.

His only hope was to breathe deeply, but even that was denied him. He could barely open his mouth. After a moment, he took a tentative step and then another. If he could just get some juice down, maybe he'd survive. Or better still, maybe he should call for help. *Think!* his pain-riddled mind screamed.

Beth. She was close. She would help him.

He rubbed his palms against his sides to rid them of their iciness and took a step toward the bedside table and the phone.

The storm was above him now, pounding and thrusting itself against the wood shingles, pelting rain down to the soaked, dark yard and against the windows. Then the room was illuminated by the flash of lightning, and the pounding thunder rolled against the house. Another burst of pain ripped through his skull.

He knew his teeth cut into his lower lip because the saltiness of blood was in his mouth. He was on the verge of losing consciousness again. He fought it, not understanding why, but something deep inside would not let him give up. He must stay on his feet, fight back to a conscious state.

He succeeded. At first only a tiny light was visible, then he made out a couple of blurry images that turned out to be furniture. Again he opened and closed his eyes; the images became clearer now.

Carefully he forced his legs to move, and somehow he managed to make it into the kitchen. Survival. That was the name of this game. Once there, he managed to get a half cup of juice down his throat, though the process was slow and excruciatingly painful.

Weak and again disoriented, he made it back to the bed and fell across it. Wind still rattled the house and rain tapped at the windows.

Beth's image finally filled his mind like a benediction and he slept.

The sky was clean, rain-washed when Beth awakened. Two robins by the window were sending their sweet songs through the hushed morning.

It was too early to get out of bed, she told herself. It was only seven o'clock, and besides, it was Saturday and she had the day off. But turning over and trying to go back to sleep would be fruitless. Already her mind was jumping around like a live wire.

After whipping back the covers, she crossed to the window and adjusted the blinds, allowing her access to the street outside, expecting any minute to see Cole trot by.

She waited, twisted her head to the right and to the left. No sign of him. "Where are you?" she murmured aloud.

She supposed he could have changed his schedule, but she doubted that. Mornings were his time and she saw no reason that he should change now. She frowned in spite of the glorious day unfolding before her eyes, suddenly furious with herself for thinking about him, much less caring where he was.

But the truth was she missed him, missed knowing that he might pop in at a moment's notice and brighten her day, missed the heady excitement of those dark eyes as they looked at her with desire, hinting at much more to come.

Suddenly she was having trouble breathing. What did this all mean? Love? Could that be it? God forbid! It was absurd to think such a thing. A sane, rational person like her didn't just fall in love with a stranger. That didn't happen, except maybe in the movies or on television.

She wanted desperately to see him again, and only after three days' time, too. She was just asking for more trouble. The trap was widening; another wrong step and this time she just might lose her soul. Dared she take the chance?

"Mommie."

It took her a minute to get her bearings and then she turned around quickly. "Good morning, love," Beth said with a smile.

Megan was coming toward her, dragging her teddy in one hand and a book in the other. Beth dropped to her knees and held out her arms. When Megan launched into them like a tiny missile, Beth almost lost her balance.

Megan giggled, bouncing in Beth's arm. "Hey, aren't you awake a little too early?" Beth asked, no longer tottering on her heels.

Megan suddenly scrambled out of her arms and stuck the book between them. "Read to baby, Mommie."

Beth laughed and hugged her again. "All right, but just one story. Mommie has a lot to do before it's time to take you to Angie's birthday party."

Mattie Engles was having a party for her three-year-old granddaughter and Megan had been invited. Beth had been reluctant to let her go, having planned to devote the entire day to Megan. But because she didn't want to hurt Mattie's feelings and because she thought it would be good for Megan, she had relented.

"Mommie come too?" Megan asked, lifting adoring eyes to Beth.

Beth gave her daughter's hand a squeeze. "Mommie'll take you, but I probably won't stay. You'll have a good time without me. There'll be lots of friends for you to play with."

Megan seemed pacified and minutes later was enthralled with the story Beth was reading to her. However, it wasn't long before Meg's eyelashes began to droop. Before Beth turned to the last page, Megan was fast asleep.

Beth put the book aside and eased off the bed, but not until she'd reached for the blanket and spread it over Megan. For a moment she stared down at the precious miracle that was hers, trying to pretend the hole in her heart did not exist.

Sighing deeply, she finally turned away and left the room, switching her mind to the thousand and one things she had to do on her day off, such as washing, cleaning and grocery shopping.

It was with a vengeance that Beth tackled the housework. But much to her chagrin, she found herself stopping at various intervals and crossing to the window, hoping to catch a glimpse of Cole.

It was only after she'd bathed and changed clothes and had gotten Megan up and dressed and to the party that she finally began to unwind. By then, though, it was after two o'clock, and she suddenly lost interest in going to the grocery store or anything else that required the least bit of effort.

It was while she was walking back from taking Megan to the party that the idea had occurred to her.

"Forget it, Beth!" she muttered under her breath.

It was such a wild and fantastic idea that she felt she had no choice but to act on it at once.

When she approached the property line between her house and Cole's, she stopped. Fiddling with the strings of her windbreaker, she squinted. As it had for the past three days, his place appeared deserted, yet his car was in the garage. It didn't make sense.

"Let it be!" she said aloud.

But that was impossible, and while silently damning herself, she began making her way toward his house, not bothering to tag her churning emotions. She stepped up to the front door and quickly shook her head with little rapid movements, almost as if she were shivering.

She pressed the doorbell and waited, keeping her mind blank, refusing to admit her insanity. She got no response, and after what seemed like aeons, but in actuality was only minutes, she shifted from one foot to the other and pressed again. Still no response.

Instinctively she placed her fingers around the doorknob and turned it slowly. To her surprise and bafflement, the door was unlocked. Feeling like an intruder, she whipped her head around, positive that every eye in the neighborhood was on her.

All was quiet; no one seemed to be paying her the least bit of attention. There was very little activity on the street.

Regaining her courage, though a knot had formed in her stomach, Beth pushed open the door and stuck her head inside. "Cole. It's me, Beth."

No answer.

"Cole," she called again, "are you here?"

Again no response.

By this time, Beth was across the threshold, standing in the gloomy shadows of the entry hall. She shivered against the sudden chill in the air and the musty smell that penetrated her nostrils.

What was going on? Something was wrong. But what? Deciding that the worst Cole could do was ask her to leave, she shut the door behind her and stared down the hall.

"Cole, can you hear me? It's Beth."

Hearing something, she paused and listened. A moan, perhaps? As she tried to identify the sound, she reached the door at the end of the hall and stopped.

Slowly, with her heart in her throat, she pushed the handle and entered the room, blinking against the brilliant shafts of sunlight coming through the open blinds. Her eyes went straight to the bed and froze.

Cole was standing by the bed, weaving like a drunk man, looking like death warmed over.

"Cole, what happened?" Beth shouted.

His face was ghostly white and damp hair clung to his forehead. Under each arm and on his chest were patches of sweat. His whole body was shaking.

He started to say something, but as he opened his mouth a wave of nausea hit him, and he threw his hand to his mouth and headed for the bathroom. With Beth watching in shock, he dropped to his knees and leaned his head over the commode. Again and again he retched, until he had the dry heaves.

Within seconds Beth was by his side, and after grabbing a towel and wetting it, she wiped his face. His body went limp, and she cradled his head in her lap.

Cole looked up at his savior. *Beth*, he mouthed, and though his eyelids were heavy, he fought to maintain consciousness.

"It's...the...fever...I got...in Nam." His eyes closed and then opened again. His voice was barely audible. "The worst...is over...I think."

"No, it's not," Beth cried, helping him to his feet. "We've got to get you to the hospital."

Cole shook his head, though it was clearly an effort. "No...please...no hospital. There's...nothing they can...do." He was out of breath. "Has...to run its course."

"Then let me call a doctor, please," Beth begged, positive he wouldn't make it through the rest of the day, much less the night, if he didn't get help.

"No..." he said with great difficulty. "Just help me back to the bed."

Beth held his body against her while they inched toward the bed. Once he was flat on his back, he moaned again. Beth thought he had passed out, but when she reached for the covers, Cole grabbed her hand.

"Please...don't...leave me."

"Don't worry," Beth whispered, tears burning her eyes, "I won't."

With her legs feeling like sponge rubber from bearing the brunt of his weight, Beth sank onto the side of the bed. She stared down at him, panic beginning to spread like quicksilver through every part of her body.

He lay motionless. Had he passed out for sure this time?

She had to help him. But how? She blinked away the tears while sinking her teeth into her lower lip. There had to be *something* she could do. If it were Megan, she would take her to the bathtub and put her in lukewarm water in order to bring the fever down.

Suddenly Beth straightened, as if a light had clicked on inside her head. Why not? If it would work for Megan, why wouldn't it work for Cole? Of course she couldn't go the whole nine yards, but she could start with his face. Then she'd see, she told herself, eyeing his fully clothed body.

It was worth a try, she told herself, determined to shake off the fear that had replaced the panic. Fear that he would die right here in front of her eyes if she didn't do something quickly.

Another moan split his lips, and he began twisting his head from side to side, his eyes squeezed tightly together.

In spite of her jellied legs, Beth jumped up and made a mad dash for the bathroom, where she turned on the faucet. While it was running, she grabbed several small towels off the shelf and chucked them into the sink.

"Oh, please, let this do some good," she cried aloud, the sound of her own voice helping to temper the burgeoning nightmare. Ignoring the tear-smudged face staring back at her in the mirror, she wrung out one towel and ran back into the bedroom.

Cole had tossed the covers off himself and was staring around the room wildly.

"Beth?" he whispered hoarsely.

She grabbed his right hand. "Shh. It's all right. I'm right here. I'm not going to leave you."

Apparently satisfied that she spoke the truth, he closed his eyes once more while Beth gently reclaimed her hand and began bathing his face with the cool, wet cloth. After a few moments, he settled down and drifted into a restless sleep.

Yet the fever raged. Just washing his face alone was not going to be enough; she saw that right away. Aspirin. Why hadn't she already thought of that?

Losing no time, Beth raced back into the bathroom and yanked open the medicine cabinet. Thank God. Glaring at her on the sparsely filled shelves was a small bottle of Bayer aspirin. She grabbed them and went back to Cole's side, but not before running into the kitchen and filling a glass with water.

After sitting back down on the bed, she placed her hand under his neck and tried to rouse him. "Cole," she whispered, "open your mouth and try to swallow these aspirins."

Cole shook his head and tried to push her hand away.

Beth inched closer, determined that he was going to take them. With a better grip on his neck, she tried again.

"Please, Cole," she cried softly, not even aware that the tears were streaming down her face. "You've got to try, or I'm going to call an ambulance and get you to the hospital."

Some of her terror must have filtered through to him, or else mention of the hospital penetrated his pain-fogged senses, because his eyes popped open.

"Time," he said thickly. "Just . . . a little more time . . . and I'll be . . . all right."

She doubted that, but at least he was rational, she thought jubilantly. That was something in itself.

Praying that the pain relievers would help, she remained by the bed and continued to bathe his face, losing count of the times she trudged back and forth to the bathroom.

It was during one of those trips that she accidentally gazed at the clock on the beside table and noticed the time. Six o'clock. She blinked. It couldn't be that late, could it? She looked at the clock again. No mistake. The dial registered six o'clock.

Megan!

"Oh, no!" she gasped.

In her concern over Cole, she had forgotten to pick Megan up at the party. What must Mattie be thinking? But more important, how could she justify forgetting her own child? A hand flew to her throat, while a whimper passed through her lips.

She had no excuse, she berated herself. Yet how could she have deserted Cole when he'd needed her? She could not have left him, she argued silently, suddenly rational again; she would do it all over again given the same circumstances.

She had to call Mattie. Sinking into the chair beside the bed, she punched out the number.

When Mattie answered, she sounded frazzled.

"Mattie, it's Beth."

Her sigh of relief rippled through the line.

Beth clutched the receiver. "Nothing's wrong, is there? I mean, nothing's happened to Megan, has it?"

"No, it's nothing like that. It's you I've been worried about." Mattie paused, clicking her teeth. "It's just that you've never gone off and left Meg this long without calling. . . ." She faltered, as if she didn't know quite what else to say.

Beth could not have felt worse. "I'm sorry, Mattie. You have every right to be upset. But if Megan's all right," she hurried on to say before she lost her nerve, "I'm going to have to beg your indulgence awhile longer."

"No problem." Mattie sounded puzzled. "But . . ."

"I'm at a...friend's. There's...a problem and I'd like to stay longer," she finished lamely, something telling her not to let Mattie know where she was.

"As I said, no problem, but in order to put your mind at rest, why don't you let Megan stay the night? Angie's still here and she'd love to have Meg stay with her."

Beth thought for a moment. She hated to impose on Mattie, but it would certainly help by giving her plenty of time to see about Cole. "If...you're sure," she said at last, reluctant to leave Megan overnight. She had never done that before.

"Of course I'm sure."

Beth sighed. "Thanks, Mattie. Now if you'll let me talk to Megan..."

When she hung up the receiver a minute later, Beth didn't feel much better, but at least Megan was happy and didn't appear upset that her mommie wasn't coming after her.

Since there was no use in crying over spilled milk, Beth turned her attention back to Cole. She felt his head; the fever raged on.

Out of her mind with worry, she racked her brain for another solution, realizing that just bathing his face was not the answer, nor were the aspirins. She knew then what she had to do; she should have done it from the start.

She stood up and peered down at him, taking in his fever-ravaged face. His eyes were sunk back in his head as far as they could go, his skin had a pale, unhealthy tint to it and his lips sported a white line around them, a testimony to his pain. Two days' dark growth of beard covering his lower jaw was the only thing that appeared natural about him.

Once again she brushed back his hair, all the while feeling as if a giant hand had a squeeze on her heart.

It wasn't that she hadn't seen a man without his clothes. She had, of course, but only her husband. The thought of taking Cole's clothes off and plastering his body with wet towels caused tremors to surge through her.

But she no longer had a choice; it was either that or the hospital. The fever had to be controlled.

Thank heavens he wasn't wearing a pullover shirt, she thought inanely as she leaned over and began unbuttoning his shirt. Once she reached the top of his jeans, she faltered. His shirttail was still tucked inside, hampering her progress. After several tugs it came loose, and she was able to complete her task.

By the time she got the shirt off him, there was a fine line of perspiration dotting her upper lip and her mouth felt as if it were full of sawdust.

For Pete's sake, Beth, get hold of yourself! There's nothing different about this man's body.

Oh, but there was, she corrected herself silently. There was no comparison between Cole's physique and Lee's. Where her husband had been a tad fleshy and hairless, Cole was just the opposite. Even in his weakened condition, his muscles were awesome, not to discount the tanned skin covered with dark, springy hair.

Suddenly she longed to run her hand through the coarse mat; all that kept her from doing so was Cole's fretful flailing of his arms. Feeling her face turn crimson, Beth grabbed his arms and pinned them down to his sides.

"Shh," she whispered. "It's . . . all right."

While her soothing voice continued to quiet him, she struggled to get herself back together. Without flinching, she then reached out and put her hand on his belt buckle.

That was as far as she got.

She couldn't go through with it, after all. Taking his shirt off was one thing, but removing his jeans and underwear was a different matter altogether.

He's sick, you idiot, she reminded herself severely. *Now's not the time to think how touching him would make you go crazy on the inside. Don't think about it!*

When she finally unbuckled his belt and pulled it through the loops, she couldn't get enough oxygen. She was having trouble swallowing, probably because there was no saliva to swallow.

Forcing her mind to go numb, she popped the snap and slowly pulled down the zipper. That done, her eyes fastened firmly on Cole. He was still asleep. Keeping her mind divorced from reality, she moved to the foot of the bed and tugged at the bottom of his jeans, keeping her eyes glued to her hands. Slowly but surely she felt the jeans clear his hips.

Once they had joined the belt and shirt on the floor, she forced herself to look up, indulging herself, letting her eyes slide over his body, only to almost stop breathing.

Suddenly an icy rush of adrenaline flooded her chest. Her pulse skyrocketed. Her scalp tingled and goose bumps pimpled her arms.

Cole lay before her like a naked god. He was beautiful. She tried not to look at the perfection of his flat stomach, the hard-toned thighs, but most of all, she tried to ignore the mastery of his manhood. . . .

Beth stood transfixed, like someone drugged. Then, giving her head a violent shake, she forced her limbs to move, and scurried back into the bathroom, where she started slinging towels under the faucet. For the next hour, she kept up a relentless pace, applying towels to his body until her own limbs were so weary she could hardly function.

Soon she was rewarded. By the time she removed the last set of cloths and had covered his body with a clean top sheet and blankets, there was a marked improvement. His fever had lessened considerably.

It was hard not to give in to tears of thanksgiving, but now was not the time for such luxury, she cautioned herself. Cole's body needed nourishment. She heated a can of chicken-and-rice soup and dragged herself back to his bedside, where she attempted to feed him.

"Cole, can you hear me?"

His eyes opened slowly. "Beth?"

The fear in his voice caused her heart to turn over. Tears rose unchallenged to her eyes. "I'm still here," she whispered. "I want you to try to eat a little of this soup."

He nodded and with her help was able to raise himself enough to swallow several spoonfuls. Then he shook his head and pushed her hand away, falling back against the pillows.

Beth didn't know how long she sat there in a trancelike state, watching him. But it wasn't long until she felt her own eyelids droop.

Suddenly she sat up, terrified, not knowing what had awakened her. When he moved convulsively once again, she knew. Cole's eyelids began to flutter. He twisted, clutched at the sheet, muttering incoherently. He was having another chill.

Without stopping to question her decision, she flung back the covers, climbed in beside him and held him, calling his name.

"Cole, it's okay. Just let me hold you." She pressed into his side, arms close around him, her hair drifting across his mouth. He didn't even know she was there.

"Damn," he said in a strangely calm voice. Then again, "Damn," and then he went limp.

Later, when she became aware of her hand on his naked back, feeling the warmth of his skin, she had to turn away. The urge to stroke the curve of his spine and the roundness of his buttocks was so strong it made her hand feel as though it were suspended from the rest of her body.

Instead she chose the less dangerous path. She slid her hand into his and left it there. When she felt his fingers interlock with hers, the healing tears flowed.

Eventually they slept.

Chapter Eight

She was so warm, so content, so unwilling to move. Her eyes opened slowly, seeking the source of that warmth. Abruptly her body stiffened. There was an arm splayed across her stomach, riding under her breasts. Her back grazed a hairy chest and her bottom curved perfectly into naked male hips. He was hot and hard.

In that instant, it all came back to her.

Horror replaced the contentment, welding her to the spot. Her eyes darted to the clock. Four o'clock. She had spent nearly the entire night in Cole's bed! How could she have done such a stupid thing? she asked herself, her thoughts turning to Megan and the possible repercussions. What if someone saw her leave Cole's house at this ungodly hour of the morning?

No matter that a sane and sensible explanation was available, fleeing a man's house like a thief in the night was just the kind of dirt Dexter Manly was hoping to find.

Careful not to disturb Cole, who was sleeping like a baby, Beth crept out of bed and tiptoed out of the house. Looking neither to the right nor left, she scurried across the yard and opened her back door. After taking a hot shower, she crawled under the covers, more exhausted than she'd ever been in her life.

Tomorrow, she told herself, would just have to take care of itself.

At eleven o'clock that same morning, Beth and her daughter were out on their deck. Megan, unusually quiet, sat on a cushion, playing with a stack of colored blocks. Beth, who had just washed her hair, was leaning over the railing to catch the sun. As she tossed the mass from side to side, a rustling sound caught her attention.

She raised her head and her heart leaped into her throat.

"Cole!"

Beth stared at him, her face framed in unruly curls, her eyes wide and startled.

Cole, too, seemed startled. He looked at her and said, "You remind me of Rapunzel."

"Do I?" Beth laughed a hyper little laugh. "I just washed it," she said, bunching the bright strands and holding them back from her face, looking, he thought, like a young girl.

"I can tell."

They had been speaking with reservation in the suddenness of this unconventional meeting. Now consciousness returned; Beth flushed at the same time Cole's color rose.

"Since you didn't get much sleep last night," he said uneasily, "I'm surprised to find you awake." His eyes drank her in, deciding she had fared much better than he'd thought. The few shadows under her eyes were barely visible and her cheeks carried a warm, healthy glow. She was dressed in a pair of jeans and a long-sleeved green shirt exactly the color of her eyes. He caught his breath just looking at her.

There was a brief silence.

When he spoke again, his voice sounded disembodied. "Actually, I came by to say thanks...for taking care of me. I'm not sure I can ever repay you."

"I don't expect you to," she said softly, a faint cloud drifting over her face. "Are you sure you should be out of bed? But, then, you don't need me to tell you what a rough time you had," she finished lamely, the details of the past night still as fresh as the morning dew.

She turned away, feeling herself grow hot all over.

"Thanks to you I'm over the worst," Cole said gently, bridging the lengthening silence.

It appeared he spoke the truth. To Beth, he looked amazingly unaffected—well, almost, she quickly amended. The grooves around his mouth were more pronounced and his color was not yet back to normal, but even those minuses failed to detract from his overall good looks. How could he have rebounded so quickly?

It was apparent he had just come from the shower; his damp hair glistened in the sunlight and he looked fresh in a yellow shirt, open at the throat, jeans and a chamois jacket that hung loosely over his belt.

"I'm glad," she whispered at last, her lips parted as she studied him blatantly. And he seemed to return that hungry appraisal as if to say, *We're not the same people, especially now that you know my body, have touched every part of it with your hands....*

The connection between them was tangible. It seemed almost to isolate them from the universe.

Beth's chest rose and fell with quickly caught breaths, and the eyes searching hers so closely made her heart race out of control. She smelled him, inhaled him, feeling again that pleasure in her veins.

"Would...you like...something to drink?" Her voice had no strength left; it was a wonder that she could make herself heard. "Hot chocolate?" she added with a nervous smile.

Suddenly two little hands appeared on the rail, followed by a mop of glossy curls. Megan, mounted on a stool, beamed at him.

"Cole?" Megan's usual wild-rose color was drained away. There were stains under her eyes and the long curling lashes.

"Not today, moppet. Cole has to work," Beth said gently.

The small face clouded; the red mouth began to quiver.

"Oh, sweetheart," Beth pleaded, "don't start again." To Cole she said, "Do come up." As he hesitated, she added, "Megan will tune up if you don't."

"We can't have that now, can we?" he said, two giant steps landing him on the deck.

"I'll get the drinks," Beth said. "I won't be a moment." She hurried indoors, returning with a tray containing three cups brimming full of liquid. She set the tray down on the patio table.

Megan had climbed onto Cole's knee.

"My, but you're getting heavy," he teased, his eyes seeking Beth's.

"You can say that again," Beth murmured. "I can barely lift her." Turning to her daughter, she said, "Megan, darling, get down, sit on your stool and drink your chocolate like a grown-up lady." Megan obeyed, carefully taking her cup of faintly-colored milk.

Cole, accepting his own cup, said quizzically, "Is this a cup of peace?"

Beth frowned. "Do you think that's necessary . . . after what . . . after last night?"

Their eyes met over the rims of their cups, hers as beautiful as springtime.

"I wasn't sure." His voice was low and intense. "Just the other night you were pushing me out of your life."

Beth flushed painfully. "Well, let's just say I changed my mind."

Suddenly and heartily, Cole laughed, his eyes crinkling at the corners like crepe paper. "If you're expecting me to take issue with that, you're wrong. I've never looked a gift horse in the mouth, and I don't intend to start now."

"Mommie, more drink, peeze."

Beth laughed and turned to Megan, thankful for the intrusion.

"Anything wrong with Your Highness today?" Cole asked soberly.

"We were naughty," Beth answered in the same tone. "Our little fingers are meddlesome and it seems we can't learn. We climbed up on the cabinet and pulled the cookie jar off the shelf, causing it to smash into a thousand pieces."

"Oh-oh." Cole's eyes drew together. "I'm sure she didn't mean to."

Beth laughed, her eyes very bright. "You sound like my daughter. That's exactly what she said: 'Mommie, Mommie, I didn't mean to.'"

Cole cocked his head and crooked a finger at Megan, beckoning her toward him. Needing no second bidding, the child, who had finished her cup of chocolate, came to stand against his chair. He smoothed the curls out of her face.

"Would a surprise make moppet feel better?" he asked.

Megan grinned and clapped her hands.

Cole then switched his attention from Megan to Beth. She was staring at him with raised eyebrows and a question in her eyes.

"Since it's such a perfect day..." He faltered, clearing his throat. "I thought you two might like to ride to the ranch with me and maybe on the way back stop by the zoo and let Megan ride the train."

Megan began jumping up and down. "Go, Mommie, peeze."

Beth was astounded and it showed. "You mean now? Today?"

"Yes, to both questions," Cole said.

Beth's eyes narrowed suspiciously. "I thought you had to work."

"Let's just say I changed my mind."

A long silence passed.

Then Beth said, "Megan, take your stool and toys to your room."

Reluctant but obedient, the child flitted away.

Beth faced Cole. "I don't know..."

He was standing now, peering down at her, only a hairbreadth away. "Please."

"Are you sure you're up to it?"

"I'm sure. Say you'll go. Please."

His softly worded plea was her undoing. "All right...just give me...us a minute," she murmured breathlessly.

Cole's chest expanded with what looked like a deliberate breath, but his face showed nothing.

"I'll be back shortly," Beth said, still sounding low on oxygen.

He nodded.

Yet Beth didn't move. They stood for another moment in awkward silence. Then Cole took her face in his hands and brushed her lips with his.

"Don't be long," he whispered.

* * *

"This belongs to you? All of this?"

"All three hundred acres, bought and paid for." The corners of Cole's mouth twitched. "Well, what d'you think?"

Beth was awestruck. "It's . . . beautiful."

Spread out before her in all their splendor were green pasturelands sectioned off by fences as far as the eye could see. Then, nestled at the top of a distant hill was a house, barely visible from the entrance to the ranch.

When Beth was getting Megan and herself ready for this spur-of-the-moment outing, she had questioned the sanity of such an adventure. But when Cole had said please in that low, throbbing tone of voice, her bones had melted right along with her resistance.

Now, as she continued to gaze about her, absorbing not only the beauty of the land but also the beauty of the day, she harbored no regrets. According to the calendar, winter had moved in and swept away fall, but this day bore no evidence of that. There was not a cloud in the sky and there was just enough nip in the air to make it perfect.

"Baby go?" Megan asked suddenly, wiggling in Beth's lap.

Cole stuck out his lower lip and laughed, but his question was directed at Beth. "Does she ever forget anything?"

Beth returned his smile. "Don't you know that most children have minds like steel traps? Or at least, this one does." She gave Megan a quick hug.

"Yes, ma'am, you're going to the zoo, but not right now," Cole explained patiently. "In a little while."

This seemed to pacify Megan and she turned her attention to the Cabbage Patch doll in her arms.

"How 'bout letting me show you the house, and then we'll take a walk around outside?"

There was such a little-boy eagerness in Cole's voice that Beth had to laugh, while thinking, what the heck, she'd already thrown caution to the wind, so why not make a day of it? Why not take the moment and run with it? Tomorrow would be soon enough to face the realities of life. *No dark shadows today.*

She looked up, her green eyes dominating her soft face. "Lead on, Mr. Weston, we're at your mercy."

Cole watched her peripherally, liking the way the light turned the white strands of her hair even whiter. She pushed the sunglasses back on her nose with a finger and held his gaze.

Clearing his throat, Cole shoved the Lincoln into gear. "Right. What the hell are we waiting for?"

The inside of the sprawling ranch house was as breathtaking as the outside. They were met at the door by a charming grayhaired woman, who, Cole told Beth, kept things going like clockwork while he was away pursuing his other interests.

Her name was Mrs. Cooper, and she greeted Beth and Megan with enthusiasm, whisking Megan away promptly, enticing her with the large aquarium in the corner of the den.

Don't worry about this little lady," Mrs. Cooper flung over her shoulder. "I'll take care of her." Megan's little fingers reached trustingly for hers.

The tour of the inside was rather quick, as Cole seemed anxious to get outside. What time Beth did have in the house, she made the most of, taking in the large airy rooms that were papered in bright patterns and that had numerous skylights. The huge den, with its stone fireplace, and highlighted by the wide expanse of glass that allowed one to view the distant woods, was perhaps her favorite room in the house.

It was a house with a soul, Cole's soul, unlike the one in town, which revealed little about the sometimes withdrawn, secretive man. Again this thought brought to mind the puzzle of what he did to command this kind of money and power. The power being in the private helicopter that sat on the pad next to the house, ready to fly at a moment's notice. She realized anew how little she knew of this man.

"Why the frown?" Cole murmured, coming to stand behind her.

Drawing a deep breath, Beth inhaled his cologne. "I didn't realize I was frowning."

"Well, you were."

Turning, she pulled off her glasses and met his intent gaze. "If you must know, I was thinking there's so much about you I don't know."

Nothing in Cole's face changed, except the dark eyes that suddenly became guarded. "Maybe that's because it's not worth knowing."

A very long pause followed.

"Why don't you let me be the judge of that?" she said, feeling her agitation drain away to a wariness and desire to find the chink in that calm facade. There must be one somewhere.

Cole smiled, but it was a small, grim smile that vanished almost immediately. "What d'you say we leave this serious talk for another time and go outside."

She shrugged. "Okay by me."

Cole stared at her for another second, then gestured for her to precede him. When they walked into the kitchen, Megan was chattering happily with Mrs. Carpenter.

"How's it coming?" Cole directed to the housekeeper, whose hands were busy stuffing a wicker basket.

"How's what coming?" Beth chimed in, eyeing the woman's handiwork with curiosity.

Cole flashed her an innocent smile. "You mean I failed to tell you that we're going on a picnic?"

"Baby go, too," Megan chanted, seemingly determined to get in her two cents' worth.

Beth's gaze sought Cole's. "No. Actually, you didn't," she said quietly.

He chuckled, looking sheepish. "Well, I guess I wanted to surprise you." A frown crimped his forehead. "It's okay, isn't it ... I mean you want to go, don't you?"

"You...you know I do," she said for his ears alone while the housekeeper and Megan were intent on their own conversation.

Her soft, raspy voice sent chills up his spine and for a moment he simply stared at her, soaking up her uncommon beauty like a sponge. Then he said, though a tad brusquely, "Let's go."

Megan took him at his word, tearing over to him. "Baby go, too," she said in her sweet voice, and once again she put out her hand to him. And a tenderness that no woman, even Beth, had ever been able to induce rose up in him for this endearing tot.

Beth didn't move, couldn't move, as she saw the tall, powerfully built man take her daughter's hand, and hope flooded through her like a shaft of light. Was it possible there was room in his life for them, after all?

"That's right, my little friend," Cole said, looking down into a face as beautifully formed as Beth's. Two perfect subjects, he thought automatically. "Wouldn't think about going without you," he added softly.

The second they walked out the door, Beth put her face up to the warmth of the sun and then turned impetuously back to Cole, a smile on her face. "It's such a glorious day."

A man could get lost in that beauty, he thought. "I agree," he said thickly, straining as though his vocal cords had lost their punch.

"Where are we going?" Beth asked as they rounded the corner of the house, her eyes looking beyond to the line of woods that bordered the fenced yard.

"To an enchanted place," he whispered conspiratorially, looking down at her breasts, making no attempt to hide his fascination.

When he looked at her like that, Beth couldn't think, couldn't talk. All she could do was feel, feel the heady warmth that flooded through her.

"I...like enchanted places," she finally said in a frail voice.

They walked in silence for a minute, the leaves stirring as the breeze rustled the trees.

Then it happened. One moment the child was skipping along in front of Beth, the next the collie bounded around from the other side of the house and, in a sudden burst of affection, knocked Megan down.

"No, Caesar!" Cole rapped out the order.

Instantly the dog backed away from Megan and trotted over to Cole.

"Oh, Meg, are you all right?" Beth cried as they both bent to pick her up and stand her on her feet.

Megan whimpered in pain, holding on to them, balancing with difficulty on one leg.

Abruptly Cole swept her up in his arms, carried her over to the nearest tree and leaned her against it. She was still whimpering, but her eyes were trusting while he gently examined the tiny limb.

Beth looked on anxiously at his side. "Cole?"

"It's very minor," he said briefly. "She must have turned her ankle slightly when Caesar sent her flying. I'll go back and get the car, and when we get down to the creek, I'll wet the towel in the basket and make a compress. In no time she'll be good as new."

"Are . . . you sure?"

"Sure, I'm sure. She'll be scampering around like nothing ever happened." He paused and wiped a tear from Megan's cheek. "Caesar apparently couldn't contain his excitement over seeing two new faces."

The child looked gravely at him as he lifted her atop his shoulders. "Bad doggie," she said.

This drew a smile from both adults. "Not really. Caesar didn't mean to hurt you. He wanted to play, but you're not quite the right size for him yet."

Megan's fingers were buried in Cole's hair. Looking down, she asked, "When I'm growed, will him be my friend?"

Cole suppressed a smile. "You betcha."

In spite of Megan's minor disaster, the afternoon was an unqualified success. Because Megan was unable to get around for a while, she commandeered Cole exclusively, and Beth sat back and listened with amusement to the odd conversation between the man and the child.

He gave her an elementary lesson in nature, telling her the names of wildflowers and trees—Megan solemnly repeating parrotlike each one. He called her attention to the birds that played hide-and-seek in the bushes, watching her as she breathlessly waited for the flash of color when he pointed out a blue bird winging its way in and out of the woods.

Soon, as Cole had promised, Megan's ankle ceased troubling her and the two of them played with Caesar until, utterly exhausted, Megan crumpled on the blanket beside Beth.

Out of the blue, Cole asked, "Do you mind if I borrow your daughter for a minute?"

She stared at him, puzzled by his strange request. He returned the look steadily, giving nothing away.

Beth bent down to Megan. "Cole wants you to go with him—all by yourself. Will you go?"

Megan didn't hesitate. "Take doggie wiff us?"

"No," Cole said. "Let's leave Caesar here with Mommie." His eyes twinkled. "It'll be just the two of us, okay?"

Megan tugged on a finger. "Me ready," she announced.

Cole stooped down and swung her high before settling her once again on top of his shoulders. The child's squeals followed her until they disappeared from sight.

Beth just shook her head and went about the task of spreading the food, and once that was done, she rested on her arm and lazily took in her surroundings. She was sure the oak trees were as tall as the sky, still breathtaking in their fall wardrobe. She gazed up at them while listening to the melodious sound of the water rippling over the rocks and pebbles in the nearby creek.

When she lowered her head, she saw Cole and Megan coming through the woods.

Cole was holding one hand behind him and Megan's with the other one. Suddenly Megan unclasped her hand and lifted her arms. Cole placed a sheaf of forget-me-nots in them.

She turned and ran toward Beth.

"Mommie—" she was panting with excitement "—for you...."

Cole reached them with another armful of forget-me-nots. "Go on," he prompted.

"'Cuz they're bootiful, just like you."

Beth sat surrounded by the flowers, unable to speak. "On closer observation, though, they're not quite as lovely as you," Cole murmured huskily, having eyes only for her.

Beth felt he had stripped away her skin, leaving her vulnerable and exposed. She turned away, grappling for something to say that would lessen the tension. "If... you two are hungry, the food is ... ready."

The lunch was devoured, with not a crumb of food left, and after they finished and cleaned up the mess, Megan's eyelids began to droop. Beth made a bed for her in the back of the car, and with a tired smile for Caesar, who seemed determined to stand watch, the child fell sound asleep.

A silence hovered; the only sounds rivaling the quiet were the sounds of nature. The woods were alive with their special kind of music and Beth was content just to sit and listen.

Cole stretched himself out beside her, and with his hands linked under his head as a pillow, he watched the clear sky and Beth. He marveled how any woman could sit so still. She didn't fidget or talk. She just sat there, with a faraway expression on her Madonna's face.

He thought about her deep integrity and her steadiness in her pain. He thought about her strength, her intellect, the compassion in her. He thought about how much he wanted to be the only man who ever touched her again. Just the thought of another's hands on her... Suddenly he had to know.

"Has there been anyone since... your husband?"

His unexpected question shocked Beth, but she tried not to let it show. She shifted and looked him in the eye. "What...do you think?" she hedged.

His mouth stretched into a grim line. "Don't play with me!" he said harshly.

She rolled away from him and turned her back, saying nothing.

"Beth... I'm sorry." His voice was taut. "It's just that..."

"What?" She rolled back over and looked up at him. He had shifted positions and now was cradling his head in the palm of his hand, peering down at her. His broad chest was close enough to touch.

With a muted groan of disgust, Cole looked away, but not before Beth saw the flicker of pain that crossed his face. Would she ever understand the different facets of this man's personality?

"Forget it," he muttered. "I... have no right."

Beth said nothing, all the while trying to stop the dull ache that had begun somewhere around her heart and was working its way through her system. Just when she thought— Oh, never mind what she thought. However, she felt compelled to answer his question.

"There's... been no one since... Lee died."

If anything, her whispered words seemed to increase the anguished look in his eyes. When his gaze returned to hers, it was written in every line of his face.

"You...didn't have to tell me, you know." His voice sounded old, as though his lungs had dust in them.

"I know," she whispered, "but I wanted you to know."

He groaned. "Dammit, Beth, I'm no good. You and Megan deserve—"

"Shh," she pleaded, reaching up and placing a finger across his lip. "Why don't you let me be the judge of that?"

Another groan tore through him as the morning sunlight pierced her blouse so that he could see clearly the way her breasts lifted with the motion of her arm.

When at last he spoke, his voice was harsh. "Please, Beth, don't make it any harder."

A minute passed. The quiet was as thick as the sunlight had been a few seconds before.

"Cole...you...me, we can't ignore this," she whispered bravely.

"You're right. I *know* you're right, but I...." Cole wanted to tell her that ties that bind were not for him, that he was a loner and could only be happy that way. He wanted to tell her that he didn't know how to love and that she should not expect anything from him. He couldn't because he wasn't sure it was true anymore. Things were so different. She was so different.

Most of all, he wanted to tell her the truth. If he could just tell her who he was and the role he was playing in her life—end the deceit once and for all—then he just might be able to... What? Love her? Marry her?

He winced inwardly, feeling as if he'd suddenly been kicked in the groin, reminding himself once again that those questions were irrelevant because she did *not* know who he was. He didn't have the guts to tell her.

Beth was content to watch him in silence. He returned her perusal with lips parted, while his eyes traveled boldly down her body without apology and with total possession.

For the longest of moments, their eyes held, mind and soul, burning away time. Beth throbbed with unfulfilled passion, folding her arms across her swollen, sensitive breasts.

"We've got to deal with this, Cole," she said softly. "Or at least I do." She meant it; she had fought her attraction for him long enough. In fact, her heart had voted yes so long ago that the vote had been tossed out. But it was her head that still fought the inevitable. He was too practiced; she would be just another notch on his belt. Yet she could no more heed that warning than she could stop breathing. To have him in her life, even on the fringe, would be a coup beyond comparison.

"I know," he replied, uneasiness in his deep voice as he continued to examine her. Weeks before he hadn't even known she existed. Now she was close to toppling his very foundations.

The same finger that had crossed his lips a moment before reached out and touched them again.

"You've got a tiny scar right here," Beth said softly.

"I know."

"A little dent."

"I . . . know."

Beth moved closer.

"Do you know what you're doing?"

She nodded wordlessly.

A groan tore through him as he drew the tip of her finger between his teeth and sucked on it. Letting her finger go, he looked into her eyes, stroked her chin ever so gently as one does a kitten, listening for her purr. From there he moved to her breasts, fondled them, cupped them in his hands until they swelled into perfection under the soft fabric of her blouse.

He kissed her then, robbing her lips of their sweetness. From that moment on, they were as one, swept away by passion.

Suddenly Cole went rigid and pushed her away, gasping for the simple right to breathe.

"Cole?" Urgently he filled her vision. Pain, like an icy finger, drew a jagged line across her heart.

"Oh, Beth . . . please . . . don't look at me like that! If I hadn't stopped . . . I wouldn't have been responsible . . ." he confessed harshly, still fighting for air.

Beth tried to swallow the lump in her throat, her eyes still glued to his face. What was wrong? her heart cried. She knew he wanted her. . . .

Then he added in a toneless voice, looking beyond her, "Anyway, Megan just woke up."

Beth closed her eyes, fighting for her composure. The moment had gone, never to be recaptured.

Chapter Nine

Beth put Megan to bed, while Cole fiddled with the fireplace. When she returned to the den, a cozy fire was crackling in the hearth and two glasses of wine were sitting on the mantel. Cole's back was to her. Yet he seemed to sense he was no longer alone, for he turned slowly around to face her.

"The fire's . . . nice," she said haltingly.

He knew she was nervous. He could see it in the way she clasped her hands together, heard it in the slight tremor in her voice.

Determined to put her at ease, because he was feeling the same way—like a lovesick teenager on his first date—he smiled and reached for the glasses of wine, holding one out to her.

Silently Beth closed the gap between them and latched onto the glass for dear life. Her warm, sweet fragrance surrounded him like a veil, invading his senses. He breathed deeply, certain he could get drunk on her smell alone.

"To us." There was a waver in his voice.

"To us," she echoed, lifting her glass to toast his.

They drank in silence, while the walls of the room seemed to shrink, locking them in.

With so much to say, they suddenly found themselves out of words.

Then Cole asked, his eyes shifting, "Have you always played the piano?"

He could almost feel her tension lessen. "No, unfortunately I haven't," she said, her eye following his to the baby grand piano.

"How old were you when you started playing?"

"Oh, after I married. Why are you so inquisitive?"

He traced the curve of one high cheekbone with his finger. "Because I'm slightly drunk on you and having trouble separating what's reality and what I feel for you."

"Well, I don't know if it helps," she whispered, "but I'm having the same problem."

"We're . . . This is crazy, you and me."

"I know."

"Would you play something for me?"

"Anything special?" she asked in a small, dazed voice.

"No," he answered, a residue of adrenaline still pulsing through his body.

She walked to the piano and started to play a romantic melody. He sipped on the wine and watched her slender fingers stroke the keys. After a moment, she was completely lost in what she was doing, having begun to sing the last words of the lyrics. She finished with a flourish.

He whistled softly. "I'm impressed."

"Then how about a reward?" She held out her empty wineglass.

He removed the glass from her hand and then slowly pulled her to her feet.

"I'm sorry, but the bar is no longer open."

Their gazes melted together.

His arms went around her, folding her into him. He inhaled the fragrance of her hair, felt the hot flush of her cheeks against his own and the fullness of her breasts. They stood together in a desperate embrace, fueled by a sensual rush that could not be denied. Their lips fused, tongues slowly exploring, discovering. Beneath his mouth and hands, she felt herself dissolving into ripples that spread wider and wider as her hips slanted toward him.

Instantly all their inhibitions vanished.

"You have no idea how I've dreamed of this moment."

His voice was the merest murmur as she rested her face against his chest.

"Me, too," she said, lifting her face up to his, her mouth seeking his again, and as if to give action to words and substance to thoughts, he felt the warm probing of her tongue. There was no brief exploration but a languorous probing, circling, then darting, as she pressed herself closer against him.

His fingers fumbled with the buttons on her blouse. He slipped them inside the lacy bra, making contact with her breast. His palm was warm on the soft roundness, causing her nipples to spring to sudden attention beneath his hand. He did not caress her, just held her while she swelled in his hand.

"Cole," she breathed, her arms tightening around his neck, pulling his head down to meet her lips. Their lips meshed again hotly and then she pulled away, taking his hand and leading him toward the bedroom, her perfume leaving the trail like footprints. He followed, his gait unsteady, his breathing shallow.

He stood mesmerized as she slipped out of her jeans and shirt, only to suddenly decide he couldn't stand not touching her. He reached past her breasts and, grasping her neck lightly, drew her to him.

She was wearing raspberry-colored silk bikini panties, and he touched them lovingly before pulling them off. Shyly, she placed her hand over her nakedness, but he tenderly removed it.

"Don't," he rasped, leaning over and placing his lips against her hand. She was warm and sweet, and he lingered there.

At last he stood and placed a hand on his belt buckle. "Help me," he pleaded.

She tugged on his zipper. "My hands won't cooperate," she said.

"Mine, neither," he replied, bending down and brushing his lips against hers. Once. Twice.

When he was able, he released her mouth and began undressing. Shortly his clothes pooled around his ankles. He was nude except for his jockey shorts, and she swallowed convulsively as she moved to the edge and thrust out her hands, urging him close.

While she delved her tongue into the hair on his belly, she tugged at his shorts. There was no doubt about his reaction; she could feel his firmness against the soft skin of her chin. She did not move away, not for a few more seconds. When she did, she took him with her onto the bed.

Their lips came together, slow and searching. Beth felt herself sink into the sensations of his mouth while his hands traced the curves of her body. Her eyes seemed to shimmer in the moonlight and her bright hair fanned on the pillow as though it belonged to the moon. It was as if her body were a mirage, except that when she reached out to touch it, it was there.

She placed her hand on his face, pulled him to her, offered the firm smoothness of her breasts to him, the rounded undersides rising in funneled peaks nibbed with tiny, roseate circles. She gasped as his lips closed over one, then the other, and he heard the half cry that followed, a sound of delicious delight. The pink tips puckered beneath the slow circling of his tongue, while their firm legs were moving against one another in a slow, rubbing motion.

He held the warm convexity of her abdomen with his hand, caressing the softness of it, and then moved down, slowly, slowly, his fingers finding the tiny opening between her thighs.

"Yes, oh, yes," she whispered, pulling at him, on fire for him.

He drifted close, then closer, and suddenly pulled away, looking down at her and smiled. He saw her question and answered it.

"Not...yet," he whispered incoherently. "It's...too soon."

It was her turn. She began to caress him with her lips and her hand, shyly at first, then as her passion grew, with more boldness. Where her hands and her lips touched him, her hair fell and formed a halo around his body.

With a groan, he rolled over her. He had to take her; the rest of the slow playing would have to wait. She was burning, ready with longing, and she opened her legs and pulled him inside her, deep into the wet, moist cavity. He filled her, her muscles tightening, clinging to him.

They moved slowly at first, until their rhythm was perfectly synchronized. Her small gasps became moans as he plunged deep inside her, filling her with emotions so powerful, so strong, that her voice rose in a long shuddering gasp and then a cry for more.

Fast inside her still, he began his movements again, wishing he could stay buried deep within her, that he could disappear completely in her passion. When at last he exploded, it was as though a charge had surged through his body. He expressed his delight with every muscle and with a deep, satisfying cry. Afterward their bodies remained together, glistening with perspiration.

He pressed his lips to her forehead, her cheeks, then her lips, soft, butterfly kisses, which she returned. With her face buried in his shoulder, their bodies were soft with fulfillment.

She lay quietly, cradled in his arms, and he listened to her breathing grow shallower and steadier. She was asleep within minutes. She slept almost unmoving, warm and soft and childlike, but the memory of her wanting, writhing body lay with him, too.

Outside, the night had fallen to blanket the house, and he felt the drowsiness steal over him. She felt good beside him. No, he corrected himself, more than good. She felt right. He moved slightly and she made a little noise of pure contentment.

Her lips were parted and her hair billowed lavishly across the pillow. He wanted to take her again, but something stopped him. Instead he feasted his eyes upon her.

He wanted to memorize her like a blind man. He wanted to be able to find his way from her throat to her knees, to the tip of her toes, and when she was away from him, in her other life, he would resurrect the memory and treasure it like the real thing.

He had, as the old adage went, been bitten bad.

Sighing, he placed his hand on her breast, left it there and closed his eyes, thinking about the word *forever* in connection with her, trying out the sound of it in his head just to see how it hit him.

To his surprise it didn't sound bad at all. What it meant exactly, what it would require of him, he did not know.

But the fact existed, changeless as eternity.

He felt her watching him.

"Hi." Cole smiled.

"Hi, yourself."

"What are you thinking?"

She brushed her lips against his ear and whispered, "In what order?"

"It doesn't matter."

She raised herself, crooked an elbow and propped her chin against her hand. "I was thinking about how right we are for all the wrong reasons."

He kissed her softly. "I'm not sure I want to know what you mean by that."

"I'm not sure I do, either," she murmured weakly.

His fingers began making circles on her hips. "What else were you thinking?"

"That . . . I'm thirsty." Her smile was sweet. "How about you?"

"Mmm." He kissed her again. "Sounds good to me."

She rose, slipped into a robe and flashed him another smile. "Don't go away."

He leaned over, reached for his pants and pulled out a cigarette. He then positioned himself against the headboard. A beam of moonlight illuminated the hollow impression where her body had been. He felt himself grow hard, wanting her again.

Noises were coming from the kitchen. She returned with a tray, two glasses and a bottle of wine.

"Something to revive you?" she asked.

"I'll take you, instead," he whispered, reaching out for her.

She grinned. "You already did."

She poured, and handed him a glass, then stretched out beside him on the bed. He lay back against the pillow, the cigarette long gone, and watched as she sipped on the wine.

She seemed lost in some distant thought. The room was silent.

"Come closer," he said at length.

"I don't think that's possible."

But she tried nevertheless, fitting against him like pieces of a perfect puzzle.

"Was it as good for you as it was for me?" he asked, his tone low and husky.

"Yes," she whispered, not meeting his eyes.

"I was afraid... I mean you were so... tight... so like a virgin...I..." He couldn't go on.

Beth felt her heart turn over. "I told you...there's been no one...since Lee."

"Thank God," he whispered, lifting her hand and turning her palm to his lips. "I wanted to be the one to reawaken you."

"Oh, Cole," she said weakly, "it was never like this with...him."

"Is it selfish of me to say I'm glad?" he asked, thick tongued.

"No."

"Beth, we have to talk."

She touched his lips with her finger, her eyes dark. "Please... not now. Earlier you said something about being glad for the moment."

"Did I say that?" He smiled.

She leaned over and kissed him on the cheek. "No, but it sounded good, anyway."

He laughed outright, his eyes twinkling menacingly. "That'll cost you," he said.

"You wouldn't!"

"Oh, wouldn't I?"

He took her glass out of her hand and, after setting it aside, gently pushed her down on the bed. Then he took the base of his half-filled glass and began drawing a pattern on her stomach, concentrating on her navel.

"Cole, no!" she cried.

He paid her no mind.

With a wicked grin, he tipped the glass slightly, filling her navel with wine. She gasped and tried to grab the glass from him. But he began to follow the trail of liquid with his tongue, and she gave up and mewed a sigh of contentment.

When he reached the end of the wine, he didn't bother to stop.

He awoke alone in a room filled with dawn's early light, feeling like a million dollars. For the first time in weeks he'd slept without dreams.

He got up, and went into the pale blue bathroom, and noticed the man's bathrobe on the hook. After fingering it and seeing the monogrammed *L*, he turned his back.

He splashed his face and ran mouthwash through his mouth before entering the kitchen dressed in his jeans and shirt, though his shirt was completely unbuttoned.

Beth turned from the stove in a terry-cloth robe and stared at him. "Dressed already?" she asked, her words spoken in gusty spurts. When she thought of what they'd done to each other...

He wanted to go over and hold her, but didn't.

"I'm dressed in honor of our first breakfast together," he said.

"Oh, I see," she responded, turning back to the stove.

"What time is it, anyway?"

She turned back around to face him. "Early—six o'clock. I...I hoped to surprise you with breakfast in bed."

"What's stopping you?"

She looked at him shyly. "Are you game?"

"What about Megan?"

"I just checked on her. She's...she's still out like a light."

He nodded, saying nothing, and closed the distance between them, pulling her into his arms. He kissed her then, feeling her moist lips opening to greet him.

When the kiss ended, he continued to hold her with her head buried in his chest, the hairs tickling her lips.

A tremor shot through her. All he had to do was simply touch her and she melted like snow in the sunshine. While she'd showered, she had felt the soreness, the stiffness of strenuous, prolonged lovemaking. Ignoring the turmoil in her head, she had stood still under the steaming water, relishing the sensation of having been physically attended to. She had been, within that moment, lost in the satisfaction of him, of his massive reality, and had experienced a thrill of resurgent desire.

The same desire that was sweeping through her now.

"Did you find everything you needed in the bathroom?" she asked, wanting to prolong the moment.

"More than I needed," he answered in a strangled tone, running his hands down the small of her back. "I know I have no right to be jealous, but there I was eyeing Lee's bathrobe."

She leaned back and gazed up at him. "Why won't you believe me when I tell you that Lee is part of another lifetime?"

"Oh, I believe you." He sighed, his arms tightening around her once again. "Most of the time, that is. It's only when I see a reminder of his presence, such as a monogrammed robe..."

"You're goofy, you know that?"

"And sinfully jealous."

"So, do you want to talk about all the robes that have ever hung behind your bathroom door?"

"Aha, methinks the lady's out for blood."

Beth started smiling.

Cole smiled back, his hands cupping her buttocks, grinding her against him.

"All this is irrelevant."

She said nothing to that.

"I read you," he said, his tone husky. "So go ahead and be as silent as you want."

Beth tried to wiggle out of his arms.

His hold merely tightened. "I know," he said, "you don't want to talk about it."

"That's right."

"So what are you doing today?"

"What did you have in mind?" she demanded, relieved that he had changed the subject.

"You and Megan spending the day with me."

"I thought you'd never ask."

He stared at her thoughtfully and said, "Suppose we come out of this thing with scars?"

Was that a warning? "Are...you willing to take the chance?"

"I'm afraid it's already gone beyond that point."

His hands were once again strumming the rounded softness of her buttocks.

"Have you...forgotten...about breakfast?" she stammered.

His eyes were glassy as he stared intently into hers. "To hell with breakfast," he ground out, pulling her into his arms.

That blissful night and morning of sweet passion set a precedent. Sharing their evenings and their beds, their lives were entangled.

Still, as much time as she spent with Cole, in many ways he remained a stranger. At times he was quiet and serious, with a brooding air about him as though something terrible were weighing on his mind. In those crazy moods, he made her feel like an outcast, as though she had no place in his private world.

Yet she kept coming back for more, stopping short of labeling what she felt for him as love. Lust was closer to it, she admitted ruefully. She knew he was smitten with her, as well, having whispered to her countless times how good she made him feel, how much he enjoyed being with her.

But love? No. That word had never crossed his lips and she doubted it ever would. Though she knew she was spinning dreams out of air, she was not ready to give him up. She even went so far as to cry on his shoulders about her problems at work, mainly the lack of cash flow.

However, the grief she was suffering over Megan could not be shared. The pain was too personal and deep-seated. She kept it buried like some hideous secret that must never surface. Surprisingly, though, she was able to function almost normally, knowing that she had Cole to thank for that. He was her mainstay during those troubled times.

That day saw no break in the pattern. It was Friday and Cole had promised to take Megan to McDonald's as soon as she got home from work, and then to a Walt Disney movie.

She smiled in anticipation as she opened the back door of the boutique, returning from a long and leisurely lunch with a buyer. The In-Look had been commissioned to put on a style-show extravaganza to launch the Women's Service League Christmas Charity Ball and it was her responsibility to coordinate it.

Looking down at her watch, she noticed it was almost closing time. She smiled again, realizing it wouldn't be long until she saw Cole.

The moment she opened the door to the office and stepped inside, her smile disappeared as rapidly as leaves in a Texas windstorm.

She stopped dead in her tracks.

Jenny was behind the desk, and in front of her, wide open, was the ledger. Sitting beside her was Ellis McCall, peering over the books as though he had every right to be there.

Beth shivered in disgust as a strand of his dirt-colored hair grazed his forehead.

Jenny looked up, her face turning pale as milk. "Oh, Beth," she said uneasily. "I...wasn't looking...er...for you back this afternoon."

"That's obvious," Beth replied, her voice thick with sarcasm.

This time Jenny's face flushed with color. "It's...not what you think. Actually..." She paused and licked her lips as though trying to come up with enough saliva to finish speaking. "I...was just doing some posting to the ledger, and Ellis...well, he's just keeping me company."

Beth boiled inwardly. "Jenny, you know I don't approve..."

Jenny cut her off at the pass. "Oh, please, Beth, I know you're upset, but please don't be." She was standing now, twisting and untwisting her hands, looking at Ellis.

Nothing has changed. She's still afraid of him, Beth thought. She could see it in her eyes, hear it in her voice. Then why doesn't she tell him to leave her alone? But more important, why was she letting him look at the boutique's records?

Because that was exactly what Ellis was doing. He had been poring over the books with an eagle eye. And Jenny had lied. Why? What possible interest could he have in the boutique's assets and liabilities? she asked herself. Unless...

No. Absolutely not. Beth dismissed the idea as preposterous. Jenny would never cheat her. Jenny was her dear friend as well as her partner. Yet there were so many unanswered questions, such as why was there never any surplus money in the till? But instinct told her Jenny could be trusted. Beth would stake her life on that. There had to be another explanation.

Before Beth could bridge the tense silence that had descended over the room, Ellis leaned back in his chair and crossed his arms behind his head. "There's no reason to get your dander up, pretty lady." Both his tone and grin were insulting.

Beth bristled inwardly, but refused to let him see just how upset she was. "My dander *is* up, as you so rudely put it, so before we both say things we might later regret, I suggest you leave."

The grin vanished from Ellis's face. "Correct me if I'm wrong," he said with lazy insolence and a touch of menace, as well, "but I don't believe you own this business outright." He nodded toward Jenny, though his eyes remained on Beth. "Jenny has an equal say about what goes on around here, and when we're married, I will, too."

"Oh, Ellis, please," Jenny pleaded, wild-eyed. "Don't cause any more trouble. Just do as Beth asked and go."

It was Jenny's turn to bear the brunt of his hostility. "Don't push me, Jenny, honey," he warned.

"Please...Ellis," Jenny said again, turning her back on him, but not before Beth saw the fear in her eyes.

Beth was also scared, but even if she had to call the police, she was determined to stand her ground.

Ellis's eyes volleyed between the two women as another silence, longer than before, fell over the room.

Then he stood up and the small half smile that appeared on his face was mean for its size. "All right," he said, his eyes centered on Beth, "I'll go now. But mark it down—you haven't seen the last of me."

With that veiled threat hanging in the air, he tromped to the door and jerked it open, only to suddenly bite out, "Who the hell are you?"

Although Cole carefully steered the Lincoln down North Street, his mind was not on his driving; it was on Beth. He never intended for their relationship to go this far, he reminded himself. What had started out as merely a harmless flirtation—even though he should have known better—had quickly blossomed out of control, leaving him facing the biggest quandary of his life.

Just the thought of waking up with her beside him every morning... the thought of his child growing inside her, drove him wild with longing. He wrapped his hand around the steering wheel in a death grip, feeling his knuckles turn white. Marriage was not likely to happen and he knew it, so what were his options?

You could tell her the truth, and then get the hell out of her life! He had tried so many times to unburden his heart, knowing what lay behind her wide sad eyes, damning himself for being a key player in that unhappiness. But as his attraction deepened, so had his deceit. Every time he opened his mouth to spill the truth, the words froze in his throat. The terror of losing her kept him quiet.

He knew that tonight, when he held her in his arms, their bodies joined as one, their cries of ecstasy filling the air, it would be no different.

The truth would again freeze in his throat.

As he parked in back of the boutique and walked inside to the office door, he took several deep, calming breaths. He then raised his hand to knock, only to have the door swing open in his face.

The words "Who the hell are you?" greeted him.

Cole took a step backward and scrutinized the speaker as if the man were a bug pinned under a microscope.

"I could ask you the same question, if I was of a mind to," Cole drawled, not the least bit intimidated by the man's angry scowl.

At the sound of Cole's voice, Beth spun around. She moved quickly to where the two men were still sizing each other up with extreme caution.

Beth tried to smile, though it was wobbly at best. "Cole, please . . . come in," she said, reaching for his hand and clinging to it.

Ellis stepped aside, making no effort to leave.

She made the introductions and felt gratified when the encounter produced two instant enemies.

Following another moment of awkward silence and after throwing Jenny a steamy glare, Ellis left the room.

"What the hell's going on?" Cole asked, his arm encircling her waist, while his eyes darted from Beth to Jenny.

Jenny's smile was nervous. "It's . . . nothing really. Ellis was just having one of his tantrums." Then turning to Beth, she added, "You're not mad at me, are you?"

"No," Beth said softly, "I'm not mad at you, just concerned."

"Don't worry, he won't hurt either of us."

"Are you sure?" Cole asked, his mouth set in a grim line.

"I'm sure," Jenny responded. "He wouldn't dare."

"I hope you're right," Beth said with a sigh, moving to stand beside Jenny. She then gave her a quick hug, determined to believe that Jenny was on the up-and-up with her. She smiled. "Cole and I have to pick up Megan. I'll see you in the morning. We'll talk then."

The moment they walked outside, Cole stopped and reached for Beth, giving her a long, hungry kiss.

She gazed up at him, starry-eyed. "What was that all about?"

"Let's just say I missed you," he said in a voice deep with emotion.

So engrossed was she in the sight, smell and touch of Cole that she didn't realize they were no longer alone.

"Beth."

Beth whipped around at the quiet use of her name. Jenny was standing in the door, gnawing on her lower lip.

"Yes?" Beth said.

"The . . . nursery called."

Beth's blood ran cold. "And?"

"There's been an . . . accident."

"Oh, no," Beth whimpered, slumping against Cole.

Chapter Ten

While the tires on Cole's Lincoln screeched against the pavement en route to the Medical Center Hospital, Beth sat in numbed shock.

She felt Cole's eyes on her, knowing he wanted to comfort her, but there were no words that could temper the fear surging through her. He seemed to sense this, and wisely held his silence.

Oh, God she prayed, *please let my baby be all right. Don't let her be seriously injured.* Beth wanted to cry—she needed to cry—but the tears would not come. They were locked in her throat, threatening to strangle her.

Her baby. Her precious Megan. Hurt. Seriously? Possibly clinging to life? The horror was almost too much to bear. If it hadn't been for Cole, she would have totally freaked out. But he had hustled her into the car and had spewed gravel everywhere in his haste to get out of the parking lot.

She must have whimpered out loud, because Cole reached over and picked up one of her cold, lifeless hands in his and gave it a comforting squeeze.

Nothing penetrated. Nothing could get through the wall of terror that consumed her every breath. Was it her fault? Somehow, somewhere in the dark recesses of her mind, she was sure that it was.

Had she been too consumed with Cole? Had she neglected Megan? Those questions ran through her mind at a grueling pace. She wouldn't deny that she had been wrapped up in Cole almost to the exclusion of all else. But she could not in all honesty accuse herself of neglecting her child, unless having to work could be defined as neglect.

She was gnawing on her lower lip, staring straight ahead when it hit her like a blow to the face. Would Meg's accident strengthen the Manlys' case against her? If Manly and his attorney could prove neglect... *Neglect. Neglect.* Once again that nasty word taunted her with a vengeance, continuing to repeat in her brain like an automatic tape that refused to shut itself off.

Beth groaned aloud, biting down harder on her lower lip, until she tasted blood on her tongue. *Don't think about that now. Tomorrow will be soon enough.*

"Easy does it, honey," Cole whispered anxiously, trying his best to keep one eye on Beth and the other on the road. "We'll soon be there, I promise."

Beth could only nod; the huge lump in her throat wouldn't allow her to say a word.

"Damn the traffic!" Cole muttered, more to himself than to her as they stopped at one red light after another.

Finally, after what seemed like an interminable length of time to Beth, but was in reality only five minutes, they were at the hospital, and with Cole's hand firmly planted under the crook of her elbow, they dashed inside the emergency room.

A nurse behind the desk greeted them. "Are you Mrs. Loring?" she asked.

Again Beth could only nod.

"Follow me please. Your daughter's in the first room on the right."

Just as they approached the closed door, Cole paused and laid a hand on Beth's arm, stopping her. "Should I...? Do you want me to wait here?"

Beth didn't hesitate. "No, please, come with me."

Her heart pounding unmercifully, she stepped into the brightly lighted room. Her mouth was dry as a bone, and her legs threatened to give way beneath her.

Megan was sitting up in the middle of the sterile bed, looking completely lost and forlorn, a bandage splayed across her forehead.

The healing release of tears spilled from Beth's eyes.

"Mommie, Mommie," Megan sobbed, holding out her arms to Beth, her tiny chin bobbing up and down.

Beth felt as though her heart would break before she reached the child. "Mommie's here, darling," she cried, her arms encircling Megan. For a moment there was silence in the room as she merely held Megan and rocked her in her arms, her face buried in the curls at Megan's neck.

Thank God she's alive, Beth thought, continuing to crush Megan against her. Her prayer had been answered, and for now that was all that mattered. Her baby was safe and in her arms.

"Mommie," Megan whispered again, only this time the fear was absent from her voice.

Relaxing her hold somewhat, Beth looked up and noticed for the first time that Mrs. Nelson, the owner of the nursery, was present, along with the nurse who had escorted them into the room. Out of the corner of her eye, Beth saw Cole leaning against the door frame. Although he said nothing his face looked as if it were made of steel.

The nurse broke the silence. "As you can see, Mrs. Loring," she pointed out, "your daughter suffered only a small gash on the head and nothing else. No broken bones or even bruises as far as we can tell. Though I'm sure she'll be sore in the morning."

"I'm thankful for that," Beth responded, taking a deep breath.

"However," the nurse went on, "Dr. Hall would like to talk to you, so if you'll excuse me, I'll get him."

Once the nurse had closed the door behind her, Beth turned to Mrs. Nelson. "What happened?" she asked, mincing no words.

The woman sighed. "They...Megan and several others were playing on the merry-go-round—closely supervised," she added hastily. "But from what I gather—I didn't actually see it my-self—Megan slipped and fell. She landed on a rock."

Beth winced, while Mrs. Nelson paused and rubbed the back of her neck with her hand, clearly showing her agitation and nervousness. "As the nurse already told you, it cut a gash in her head, and of course, as with any head wound, the blood flowed profusely, scaring the living daylights out of us. We lost no time in bringing her here." Then to clarify the "we," she added, "Miss Darnell's out in the waiting room."

"I'm not blaming you, Mrs. Nelson," Beth said, hoping to put the woman at ease. "These things happen with children. I'm just thankful it wasn't more serious."

Suddenly Megan lifted her head and touched Beth's cheek with the tiny palm of her hand.

Beth gave her undivided attention once again. "What is it? Does your head hurt?"

Megan nodded.

Relief made Beth giddy. "I know, and I'm so sorry."

"Baby's head hurted," Megan said with big, sad eyes.

Beth's eyes became shadowed. "When the doctor comes, he'll make it better."

The doctor entered then, claiming everyone's attention. He was a tall, slender man with sandy hair and twinkling brown eyes. He reached over and tousled Megan's tawny curls.

Megan shied away from him, hiding her face against Beth's breast.

Dr. Hall smiled and held out his hand. "Mrs. Loring."

Beth returned his firm handclasp with a weak smile. Then before she could get the words out of her mouth, the doctor turned to Cole and once again extended his hand.

Cole straightened and met the doctor halfway.

"I'm . . . sorry," Beth rushed to say, and quickly introduced them.

Now that Megan was safe and secure in her mother's arms, she held out a hand to Cole and grinned at him.

"Hey, moppet," he said, her small hand becoming lost in his big one. "How's my girl?"

Ignoring his question, Megan asked one of her own. "When me gets well, can I play wiff doggie?"

"You bet. First thing," Cole answered with an amused smile.

Beth's smile was an apology. "Well, now we all know what's important to my daughter," she said.

"Only goes to show you that she's going to be just fine," the doctor said, "even after the scare she gave us. But thanks to the quick action on the part of Mrs. Nelson, she's definitely on the mend. I didn't think it was necessary to take any stitches. As you can see..." He paused, focusing his attention on the child. "Megan, honey, would you let Mommie look at your sore please?" Obediently Megan raised her head, allowing Beth to check the wound.

The doctor continued, "As I was about to say, I put a butterfly bandage over it that will pull the skin together nicely, leaving no scar."

Beth voiced her concern. "You're sure there won't be a scar? Not that it's important," she added hastily, "but..."

"Of course the scar will remain for a while," he answered honestly, "but as I said, it will eventually disappear."

The color was seeping back into Beth's face. "That's good news."

"As far as I'm concerned, you can take this little lady home and put her to bed. If she gets restless during the night, just give her a teaspoon from this prescription." He passed her a signed form and turned to Megan, touching the tip of her nose. "You be a good girl, now, you hear? And do what Mommie tells you."

Megan once again hid her face against Beth's breast.

"Silly girl," Beth chastised, looking bemused. "The doctor only wants to help you."

"He... hurted me."

"If he did, it was only because he wanted to make you well," Beth said gently. "So now I want you to give Dr. Hall a hug and then we'll go home and you can get in bed with teddy and Phyllis Fanny."

The doctor raised his eyebrows. "Phyllis Fanny?"

"Her's my dolly."

"Oh, I see," the doctor said with a wide grin, taking the initiative and giving the child a hug. Mrs. Nelson followed suit, kissing Megan on the cheek and saying to Beth, "I want to say again how sorry I am...."

Beth shook her head. "That's all right," she stressed. "I understand, and I want to thank you for getting Megan here so quickly."

With a polite nod to the occupants of the room, Mrs. Nelson left the room. The nurse and doctor followed, leaving the three of them alone.

Cole, noticing the dark shadows underneath Beth's eyes and the weary droop of her shoulders, stepped closer.

"How 'bout me driving my two best girls home?" he whispered tenderly.

Cole stood erect when Beth walked into the den. As usual, a fire was popping in the fireplace, giving the room a warm glow.

"Is she asleep?"

"Yes," Beth said, reaching up to push her hair away from her face, only to pause suddenly, noticing that her hand was quivering. She dropped it to her side and rolled her fingers into a tight ball.

The minute they had gotten home, Beth had taken Megan to her room and put her to bed. Cole had hovered just inside the room, watching, nursing what felt like a chunk of lead in his gut, struck again by the pathos of seeing mother and daughter together. In that moment, he'd been forced to turn away, unable to deal with his emotions.

Those same emotions were still warring inside him when he asked, "Would you like a cup of coffee?" From where he stood, he could see the exhaustion in every line of her slender body. He moved closer, stopping just shy of touching her.

Beth lowered her eyes. "Maybe in a minute," she murmured.

"She's going to be just fine, you know."

"I know." She forced a smile.

Cole stepped behind her, placing his hands on her shoulders.

The unexpected contact caused Beth to lean forward, then tense up even more.

"Relax," he said, his voice soft, while his hands began to knead the stiff muscles on the back of her neck. "Just relax and let my fingers do the work."

For a moment, she complied with his gentle command. She wallowed in the feeling of his talented fingers, the tips reminding her of hot pokers as they dug gently into her skin. But it was impossible to relax her body when her mind was in such turmoil.

Without warning, tears flooded her eyes and spilled over onto her cheeks. Then she began to shake in earnest.

"Honey, don't," Cole pleaded, twisting her around to face him, pulling her close, his body absorbing the tremors. "Hey, everything's going to be all right."

"No!" Her cry was muffled. "You...don't understand." She couldn't tell him, couldn't tell him of the fear that held her in its clutches as her agony grew out of proportion. How was she going to keep Dexter Manly from finding out about Megan's accident?

Her panting was so loud she had to hold her breath. There wasn't a way, she told herself. With his power, nothing was sacred. In her mind's eye, she could see the judge's face glaring at her in stern disapproval before declaring her an unfit mother and turning Megan over to the hands of Dexter Manly.

Suddenly it was all too much. The weight of the past few hours came crashing down upon her like a ton of bricks. It was as though the pressure valve to her heart had finally broken.

She cried out, clutching at the front of Cole's shirt, wadding the fabric in her hands.

"Beth, please don't," Cole begged frantically, his arms threatening to squeeze the very life from her.

She cried that much harder, deep soul-wrenching sobs. "I'm ...sorry...I..." she began.

Cole was like a crazed man. "Oh, God, you don't owe me an apology," he said. "It's just that I'm afraid you'll make yourself sick."

"Oh, Cole...I'm so scared."

His gut twisted savagely with guilt. "Would...it make you feel better to talk about it?"

She couldn't seem to stop shaking; her teeth were banging together. She recognized that she was on the verge of collapse.

Cole knew it, too, and didn't waste another second before trying to head it off. "Come on," he urged, turning her in his arms so that she was mobile, "you're going to bed." When she started to protest he went on, "I'll stay with you if you want me to, and when you're ready, we'll talk."

Like a docile kitten, Beth found herself being led to the bedroom, where, with Cole's help, she removed her clothes and slipped into a gown. Every move he made was carried out with tenderness and loving care as he tried to ignore her perfect nude body, the upthrust breasts, the flat, white plane of her stomach...places that his lips had tasted....

Seconds later she was lying on her side in the bed, facing Cole, who had stretched out beside her.

He made it a point not to touch her, for to do so would ignite the spark of passion hovering just below the surface. If he were to take advantage of her vulnerability, he would never forgive himself.

"Cole," she whispered after a moment.

"I'm here."

"Would...would you hold me...please?"

She couldn't bear the thought of Cole being so near and her not feeling his arms around her. Regardless of how deeply she grieved over Megan, she ached for Cole, for the security he offered. She was exhausted and scared. Nothing made any sense at this moment except Cole's strong arms around her.

When Cole heard her sweetly voiced invitation, he felt he'd received manna from heaven. He'd wanted to hold her—no, ached to hold her—so much so that his arms were actually sore from being restrained.

"Oh, baby, of course I'll hold you," he whispered, shifting just enough to embrace her, handling her as if he were afraid she would break.

Beth burrowed closer, wrapping her arms as tightly as she could around him, seeking his warmth, his kindness.

It was then that she knew she loved him. She loved Cole Weston. How could that be? How had she let it slip upon her unawares? She panicked. Under no circumstances could she let him know. It must be her secret and hers alone.

Her inner battle continued to wage so furiously that it made her stir restlessly. Cole, certain that she was thinking about Megan, began smoothing her hair away from her temple, making way for the gentle touch of his lips.

"Do...you feel up to talking now?" he prodded softly.

"Are . . . you sure you want to hear my tale of woe?"

"I'm sure," he lied, not feeling up to it at all. His nerves were betraying him; he could scarcely hold himself steady.

Beth sniffed back the tears. "It's . . . not a pretty story."

I know, my darling, I know, he agonized silently.

"Go on," he encouraged softly, burying his lips in her sweet-smelling hair.

Between gulps, all the sordid facts unfolded. She repeated word for word the first conversation with her attorney, when he told her the Manlys wanted custody of Megan, as well as the conversations that followed. She also poured out the mind-boggling session with Dexter Manly. The entire time she talked, Cole stroked her hair, her back and neck, trying to soothe her tense muscles.

"Do you think he'll be able to take my baby?" she asked at length, looking up at him, as though begging for any crumb of reassurance.

His chiseled lips narrowed into a thin line. "It'll be over my dead body if he does," he muttered harshly.

Beth touched his chin. "Oh, please..." she whispered, "this isn't...your fight." Her voice broke on a sob. "But it's...nice to know you care."

Her words finished ripping his heart to shreds. For a moment, he was robbed of speech.

Beth sighed against the solid wall of his chest. "Thank you for listening," she said.

"Shh, rest now, my darling," he mouthed into the delicate folds of her ear.

An almost ethereal atmosphere seemed to steal over the room as they lay wrapped in their own circle of silence, like visions in a dream, his hands a healing balm to her overburdened heart. Soon she was unable to remain passive; her own hands started to move up and down his back.

He pulled back and gazed into her eyes. Then, with tenderness, he touched his lips to her face, her throat, sliding down her neck into the soft cleft of her breasts, back up to the trembling fullness of her lips. Their tongues intertwined with melting gentleness.

It was a slow, building passion that engulfed them.

Pulling apart, they stared at each other through the moonlight, fears unspoken, unbidden. Cole was thinking of his ever deepening deceit, while Beth was thinking how much she loved him.

Love. Even though she had faced the truth, even admitted it to herself, she still found it hard to believe. From Cole, she had learned a new definition of the word, and she couldn't deny herself the chance to love, really love, for the first time in her life.

But was it possible? she tormented herself. *Dare I trust? Dare I take the chance?* God, make it work!

"Beth." He choked on her name.

She smiled at him through her tears. "Make love to me . . . now."

"Oh, Beth, Beth, I want you so much," he whispered in agony, "but . . . there's something you must know."

"Later," she breathed. "Later."

"You don't know what you're saying," he added hoarsely, his voice having dipped an octave below its normal range. "There's . . . so much you don't know. . . . I . . ."

She placed her warm lips against his, forcing him to swallow his unspoken words. "No, please . . . not now. All I want is for you to be near me. . . ."

"Oh, yes, yes," he murmured, cradling her head in the crook of his arm and burying his lips in the hollow of her neck.

Cole wanted her so badly he hurt. She was so warm. So responsive. So alive. So precious. Her flesh trembled in his worshipful hands, delicate as dancing butterflies. He ached not just with animal lust, but with desire to possess her and to be possessed by her, to trust and be trusted, to cherish and be cherished.

Love did exist; he knew that now.

Love was indeed real.

And he had found it within her.

When had it happened? *How had it happened?* Slowly but surely, she had slipped through his defenses and become a necessary part of his life. He hadn't wanted to let her go, but he hadn't ever stopped to find out why; he had just been afraid to examine himself that close.

He couldn't deny it any longer. He loved her. He wanted her as a part of his life. A real part. A permanent part. He wanted to marry her. His pulse soared at the thought, only to suddenly take a nose dive with equal intensity. Now that he had gone and committed the unpardonable sin of falling in love, he was more frightened than he'd ever been in his life.

All the danger, the gunplay, was nothing in comparison to what was churning inside him at this very moment.

He glanced down at her while she slept peacefully by his side, her head nestled in the crook of his arm, her limbs against his.

Was it possible that she returned his love? If so, could that love survive the truth? His betrayal? His mind was in such an uproar; his thoughts refused to let him sleep.

So this was love? This torment, this uncertainty and these shifting doubts? To what purpose? Only vulnerable people got hurt, and dabbling in unnecessary emotions made one vulnerable.

So cut off the emotions.

Deaden the pain.

What could be more simple!

But when he peered down once again at Beth's lovely face, he knew why such a simple theoretical equation did not add up in practice. He was as committed to loving this woman as he was to breathing.

Even this truth could not set him free.

By morning Beth had moved to fit herself tighter against his chest. He awoke first, with the yellow fingers of dawn, and he let his eyes linger on the long, lithe beauty of her. He moved his arm and she awoke at once, deep, dreamy eyes searching for his.

"Good morning," she whispered.

"Good morning," he echoed.

Trancelike, unsmiling, they stared at each other.

She longed to add *I love you*, but did not, fear of rejection holding her tongue.

He ached to add *I love you*, but could not, knowing he wasn't worthy of her love.

Their eyes, their bodies shouted their feelings as Beth, still unsmiling, stretched her body against him, turned onto her stomach and pulled herself upward with her hands on his shoulders. Turning, she gave her right breast to his lips, and as he pulled gently on it she began to quiver, moving her legs over him, rubbing the soft, curled nap against his abdomen, feeling it come alive like a banked fire fed new coals. She slid down upon him, raised her legs, and he felt her warmth rush over him again.

With the sun peeping over the horizon, they wrapped the morning around them, as if time had no meaning.

The Manlys' house was quiet when Cole rapped his knuckles against the front door, opting to bypass the fancy doorbell only inches from his right hand.

He had known what he had to do long before he'd quietly slipped out of Beth's bed and gone home to change clothes.

Now, fresh from a shower and several cups of coffee, he prowled anxiously back and forth across the wide porch. Although it was only a few minutes after eight o'clock, he knew the Manlys would be up, more than likely having coffee in the breakfast room. He was right, as seconds later he was greeted by the housekeeper and escorted there.

Dexter's eyebrows shot up in surprise, while the paper in his hands fluttered to the floor. Eleanor, too, seemed surprised, lowering her coffee with unsteady hands.

"Well, well," Dexter said, recovering quickly, though his eyes were keen with wary speculation, "you're the last person I expected to see this morning."

Cole's face revealed nothing; he was determined to keep his cards close to his chest until he was ready to deal. "'Morning Dexter, Eleanor," he drawled.

"Sit down, sit down," Dexter exclaimed, pulling out the chair opposite him.

Cole reluctantly complied, bending his right leg and slinging it over his left knee.

"Would you care for a cup of coffee?" Eleanor asked politely, though her voice, like her hands, held a tremor.

With a forced smile Cole declined, coming straight to the point. "I came to discuss Beth and Megan."

Eleanor's hand flew to her heart. "How's . . . the child?"

For a moment Cole's expression softened. "She's fine, Eleanor, just fine."

She nodded, her eyes suddenly filling with tears.

"Well, now, isn't that a coincidence?" Dexter broke in, his voice louder than usual. "I thought I was going to have to send the police after you, boy." He paused, laughing at his own joke. "Thought maybe you'd skipped the country."

Cole refused to rise to the bait. "I want you to back off, Dexter, call the whole thing off."

Eleanor gasped and a string of obscenities flew from Dexter's lips. A chill settled over the room.

"I mean it," Cole hammered on, giving neither of them the chance of an immediate rebuttal. "You've got about as much chance as a snowball in hell of proving Beth Loring an unfit mother. I can't make it any plainer than that."

"Like hell!" Manly growled, standing up with such force that his chair crashed to the tiled floor. He glared at Cole, his bushy brows hooding his eyes. "And when did you decide to switch sides?"

Eleanor was standing, too, her eyes imploring her husband to calm down. As usual Dexter ignored her.

"It's not a matter of switching sides, Dexter," Cole said patiently, though his eyes had iced over. "It's the law. No judge in this county or Angelina is going to take Megan away from her mother."

"Then we'll just have to go elsewhere."

"Dammit, Dexter, you're not listening."

"Oh, I'm listening all right, but you're not telling me what I want to hear." He paused, his expression fierce. "Are you telling me you're through?"

A pause.

"Yes, this time I'm bowing out," Cole admitted, feeling a sudden chill, not liking the steely glint in Dexter's eyes. He was not to be trusted.

Manly scratched his head. "Well, as Yogi Berra says, 'It ain't over till it's over.' "

Cole slowly raised himself out of his chair, a muscle working in his jaw. "Oh, it's over. Make no mistake about that," he said dangerously. "It's just that you're too goddammed hardheaded to see it. The best you can hope for is that Beth will let you share in your granddaughter's life.''

"We'll see about that," Dexter said with a sneer.

"Don't push it," Cole warned quietly.

"If you've had your say, then I suggest you get the hell out of my house."

"Oh, Dexter, no!" Eleanor cried.

"Hush, Eleanor," Dexter said harshly. Then, turning to Cole he added, "How'd she do it? Did she give you what you wanted?"

Cole's eyes cut into Dexter like ice picks. This was not the man who'd given him that one chance in life. This man was a crazed stranger who no longer warranted his unyielding allegiance. "I'm going to pretend you didn't say that."

Dexter merely snorted with contempt and turned his back.

Eleanor kept her silence and wrung her hands.

Cole crossed to the door. With his hand on the knob, he turned around and said to Dexter's back, "Oh, by the way, if you ever threaten Beth again, I won't have any qualms this time about stomping your ass." He paused meaningfully. "And as you well know, I don't make threats, I make promises."

Chapter Eleven

The days clicked by in rapid succession, though Beth wished she could have stopped the clock to squeeze one more second, one more minute out of each day. But since that was not possible, she made each one count, hoarded the precious moments like a miser hoards pennies.

Cole continued to awaken her body to joys she had never known. She was strung as tightly as a high wire, responding to the sound of his voice, the slightest brush of his fingers against her arm, the touch of his hand on her breast when he took her clothes off at night. She felt vibrantly alive and her appetite for Cole was growing by leaps and bounds.

During those magical days, Thanksgiving passed without a hitch. They'd spent the day at Cole's ranch, where, with the help of his housekeeper, Beth had prepared a scrumptious meal of smoked turkey—Cole had cooked it on the smoker—with all the trimmings. A fun time was had by all and Beth had likened it to a good omen for the approaching Christmas festivities. So far she hadn't been disappointed.

Even the weather was cooperating, having turned unusually cold, with no signs of letting up. Oftentimes, late November and early December heralded many balmy, springlike days. But this year the air was crisp and invigorating, and the three of them spent a good deal of time outdoors.

Together they tracked down holly bushes, thick with bright scarlet berries. They filled basketfuls and mingled them with branches of dark, glossy leaves taken from the evergreen trees that stood on the edge of the woods. Cole's house took on a festive air as Beth, carried away in a bliss of contentment, painstakingly decorated the huge den for Christmas.

Megan also became more excited as the day drew nearer, and besides Santa Claus, the greatest thrill was yet to come: Cole had promised she could select the tree for his ranch house and decorate it as she wanted.

Now, as Beth cleared her desk after a hard day's work, following on the heels of the Christmas style show, she knew she should be tired, but she wasn't. She leaned back in her chair and smiled. Much to her delight, the show had been a huge success. As a result, new customers had poured into the shop during the day and sales had skyrocketed. She couldn't help but pat herself on the back, and Jenny, too, for a job well done.

Even so, that wasn't why she was on such a high. Cole was due back in town after having been gone for several days. Suddenly the smile disappeared from her face, leaving a frown in its wake. He had been evasive about his destination, telling her he had unfinished business that needed his attention and that he couldn't postpone the trip any longer. Ordinarily she wouldn't have thought anything about his absence, as his work often took him away for two days at a time, but never four as it had now.

Before he'd left, they had made plans to go out to dinner the day he got home. Beth had made arrangements for Mattie to keep Megan, and she was looking forward to rushing home and having a leisurely bath before Cole arrived.

That was why, when the phone jangled by her side, she almost jumped out of her skin. Her eyes dropped to her watch; it was five-thirty. Cole. It had to be Cole. Her heart raced in anticipation. The days and nights without him had been so empty, so long....

After several more rings she lifted the receiver. "Hello."

"Beth—Giles."

Disappointment, laced with fear, gripped her. "This . . . is a surprise," she stammered, her mind conjuring up all kinds of untold horrors, each one worse than the other.

"Got a minute?"

"Of course." Beth cleared her throat, forcing herself to take a deep breath.

Renfro got straight to the point. "I just hung up from talking to Charles Ransome."

"And?" The tiny word had trouble getting through her stiff lips.

"They want me to agree on a court date."

Beth doubled over, feeling as though she'd just been kicked in the stomach. "Oh, no," she whispered.

"Now take it easy. It's not as bad as it sounds."

"What . . . do you mean?"

"Well, for one thing, I wouldn't agree on the date Ransome wanted, and for another, they're hurting for information." He spoke with confidence.

Beth felt a ray of hope return. "Are you sure?"

"There's not a doubt in my mind. I got the first inkling of that when Manly went to see you—he was desperate then, or he never would've done it—and again today with Ransome. Oh, Manly's desperate, all right, even with the help of a private detective."

"Private detective!" Beth cried, feeling that ray of hope fade completely. "You mean they—Manly hired a . . . detective?"

"I'm not positive, mind you," Giles replied. "But that's usually standard operating procedure. Anyway, we don't care. Let him hire ten detectives if he wants to. It won't do him any good."

Oh, but it might, she agonized silently. A private detective. She wanted to scream, knowing that if what Giles said was true, then she could very well be in trouble. If the detective unearthed her arrest record—an investigator worth his salt would surely do so—then her past would come to light. Hot tears stung her eyes. What could she have done about it, even if she'd known? *For starters,* she told herself, *you could have leveled with Giles.*

"Beth?"

"Sorry," she said quickly, trying to shake off the sense of doom. "But when you mentioned a detective..."

"Look, don't let that worry you," he advised gently. "We're in the driver's seat. For the first time I really feel that way. Ransome knows that if they went to court tomorrow, they'd be up the proverbial creek without a paddle."

"Then why the push for a court date?" Beth asked, still unconvinced.

"They're trying to put the screws to us, to shake us up, make us think they have something."

Beth was trembling. "I...I just hope you're right."

"I know I'm right," he said flatly. "I know Ransome, slime ball that he is, and I could hear the uncertainty beneath his polished demeanor. I felt I had to tell you the latest, even though nothing came of it."

"Of course...you did."

He seemed totally confident; nevertheless Beth remained uneasy, unable to block out the fact that she had withheld information from Giles. In defense of herself, she had kept thinking it would all be over before it began.

"Promise me you won't worry," Giles was saying.

"Oh, Giles, I'm fighting for my baby," she said brokenly. "How can I not worry?"

"I know, I know," he soothed. "But we're going to lick 'em, so you just go ahead and enjoy Christmas." He paused. "Along with that new man in your life."

Beth sucked in her breath. "How did you know?"

"That's not important." Giles chuckled. "But I'm glad to see that you've joined the land of the living again."

Beth fought back the sudden urge to cry. "Giles...I don't know what I'd do without you."

"Don't mention it," he said gruffly. "I'll be in touch."

Knowing he was about to hang up, Beth said quickly, "Giles about...the money...I still don't have..."

"Beth, Beth, haven't I told you not to worry about that, either?"

"I know, but..."

"Forget the 'but' and go home to that man of yours and have a merry Christmas."

Moments later when Beth walked out the door, her head was high and her steps brisk.

There was a smile on her face.

The doorbell pealed long before Beth was ready. She had dallied too long over getting Megan to the Engleses', then she'd taken her time in the bath, filling the tub with scented bubble bath and soaking until every muscle in her body was relaxed.

Hence when she opened the door, she was wearing a long robe and nothing else.

Their eyes collided, the same melting hunger reflected in them.

"Hello," Cole said, his gaze never wavering.

Beth devoured every endearing inch of him. "Hello," she whispered.

"Did you miss me?" Cole's voice was strained. He'd warned himself to take it slow and easy. After all, he'd been away from her for four days and he didn't know if some of the magic might have disappeared. He couldn't have been more wrong. His feelings for her were stronger than ever.

Beth's insides were going haywire. "You . . . know I missed you."

That was all Cole needed to hear. He stepped farther into the room and, slamming the door behind him, hauled Beth into his arms.

She nestled against him like a homing pigeon coming to roost. For a while their hearts, beating simultaneously, were the only sounds in the room.

Then Cole pulled back and looked down at her. "Oh, Beth, Beth, you don't have any idea what you do to me," he whispered, taking her hand and laying it across his chest. "Feel my heart. It's about to pound through my skin."

"Mine, too," she whispered in return.

He reached out a finger and outlined her soft quivering lips. "Where's Megan?"

"At Mattie's."

"So we're alone?"

"We're alone."

A strange light appeared in his eyes. "Do you want to go out?"

"Not really. Do you?"

"No," he said.

There was a tiny, meaningful silence.

Then Cole slowly began to undo the loosely knotted sash at her waist. She stood helpless and watched.

"Your robe," he said inanely. "It's so soft, like your skin."

Her voice was weak with desire. "I meant to be...dressed."

"I'm glad you weren't."

With easy persuasion, the robe fell from her shoulders. Her breasts were full and lovely, the nipples erect. A finger grazed the right one, then the left. He cleared his throat. "I nearly had a wreck getting back to you."

"You...should be more careful."

"I know," he said, and kissed the right nipple.

"Cherry," she whispered. "Both of them."

His lips grazed one. "Mmm, you're right."

At last she said, "Turnabout's fair play," and started unbuttoning his shirt. Cole worked on his belt buckle. Soon his clothes were in a pile on the floor. She couldn't pull her eyes away. "You're beautiful."

"Not nearly as beautiful as you."

"Women are all right, but men—well, they're a perfect work of art." As if to prove it, she began caressing him.

"You know you're starting something you can't stop," he said through clenched teeth.

She nodded, then whispered, "I have no intention of stopping."

He sucked air into his lungs, his hand dipping to the wet softness between her legs.

Her eyes fluttered and her heart raced. "Oh, Cole...."

"The couch or the bed?" he groaned urgently.

She clung to him. "Couch now, bed later."

His lips came down on hers then, hot, frantic and hungry. He pulled her down onto the couch, and they later found themselves on the rug in front of the fireplace.

The bed was forgotten.

Cole was still lying on the carpeted floor, his arms folded beneath his head, missing Beth's warmth. He didn't have long to wait; seconds later she came back into the den, carrying two glasses of chilled wine. She knelt beside him and put one of the glasses in his outstretched hand.

Beth raised her own glass in a toast and said, "To your return."

"I'll drink to that," he said, and raised himself up so he could lean on his left arm.

"Why so pensive?" she asked, examining his body again. "You had a frown on your face that would rival Scrooge."

"I'm tired. You wore me out."

"You should've gone to bed early last night."

"I did."

"Couldn't you sleep?"

"Perfectly. But I dreamed of you."

"Is that tiring?"

"Depends," he replied with a grin. "Last night I dreamed I was chasing you over the mountains."

"Did you catch me?"

"Yes, but by then I was so tired from chasing you, I couldn't do anything about it."

"Next time I won't run so fast."

He laughed out loud, pulling her head down for a quick kiss.

After a while she said, "Seriously, what were you thinking about?"

"Actually, I was wondering if you'd heard any more from . . . your lawyer." He looked away from her and stared at the fire.

"That's mental telepathy, because Giles did call me today."

"Oh?" He couldn't mask his concern. Dammit, he'd been afraid Dexter wouldn't heed his warning. . . .

"He said that Ransome tried to ramrod him into agreeing on a court date."

Cole cursed. "How'd Renfro handle it?"

"In so many words, I think he told him to go take a flying leap off a tall building."

Cole smiled, his relief obvious. "Sounds like you're in good hands."

This time Beth frowned. "He seems good. In fact, he's so self-confident it scares me."

"Don't be. It's going to work out. You'll see."

"For the first time, I'm beginning to believe you're right. I can almost see a light at the end of that long, dark tunnel."

He looked up at her and grinned. "Not only am I self-confident, but I think I'm getting hungry."

"You want to go to dinner?"

"Later," he said.

They drove home from dinner with the stereo blaring. It was a star-studded winter's night. It seemed as if a generous deity had emptied treasures of white twinkling jewels across the sky. Cole was in awe of its beauty, though he felt the urge to belt out a carol. "It came upon a midnight clear...." He wasn't sure he had the correct words.

"You're drunk," Beth said, smiling.

"On you," he said. "Only on you."

Her head was resting against his shoulder; she was content and happy—drowsy, too.

After a short silence he asked, no longer feigning intoxication. "You never did tell me how your style show went."

Beth came fully awake and sat up. "I'm glad you mentioned that. I'm supposed to call a customer tonight and make an appointment for a special fitting in the morning. I forgot to get her unlisted phone number from my file."

He threw her a lazy grin. "Are you telling me you want to go by the shop?"

"Would you mind?"

His answer was to swing the powerful car around and head in the opposite direction. Shortly they pulled up at the rear of the building, where an outside light shone brightly.

"Why don't I come in with you?" Cole said, shoving the gearshift into park.

"Thanks, but that's not necessary. There's a light switch just inside the door." She kissed him warmly on the lips and then slipped out of the car.

He was standing outside, leaning against the door, smoking a cigarette, when the door to the shop burst open.

"Cole, come quick!"

Chapter Twelve

The boutique was a wreck. Beginning with the office, where both the desks and their drawers had been pulled out, their contents dumped on the floor. Papers lay ripped and scattered everywhere.

The telephone cord had been jerked out of the socket and cut. From the walls, the pictures of models dressed in the latest fashions had been pulled down and slashed with a knife.

In the bathroom they found the full-length mirror shattered, its spiderweb cracks stained with bright red lipstick. But the main havoc had been wreaked in the the front of the shop. Racks were turned over, clothes scattered from one end of the room to the other. What was not destroyed was gone. Large chunks of clothing from the wall racks had been removed. Even the small checkout counter was on the receiving end of this act of malicious vandalism and theft. It was turned over, with the cash register and other paraphernalia lying in a mangled mess on the carpet.

Cole had his doubts about this being an ordinary burglary. Someone was either searching for something or else was intent on terrifying both Beth and Jenny, which led him to the conclusion that it was more than likely an inside job.

"Do you have any idea who could have done this?"

Beth shook her head. She was incapable of reacting. She just stood there, in the middle of the room, surveying the damage. It was too much for her to take in at once.

At first she was just numb, but then, gradually, almost imperceptibly, she began to shake.

Cole took her in his arms and pressed her close to him. He wanted to say that everything would be all right, but there was no evidence of that, so he wisely refrained.

He had no idea how long they remained together, her head buried against his shoulder, her body trembling uncontrollably, but at last he drew apart from her, saying, "We have to call the police."

"Please . . . would you do it?"

Wordlessly Cole waded through the debris and found the phone. But it, too had been ripped from the wall.

"Damn!" Cole muttered under his breath, his lips set in a grim line and his eyes cold as ice.

"I guess that one's dead, too," Beth said.

"As a doornail," Cole said tersely. "I'll have go to the nearest pay phone and make the call. You'll have to go with me. There's no way I'm leaving you here alone."

Beth drew a shuddering breath. "You . . . you don't think . . . he'll come back, do you?"

"No," Cole ground out. "But I don't want to take any chances." His expression softened as he took in Beth's pinched features. "After we call the police we'll have to call Jenny," he added gently, still wanting to say something, anything, that would erase the terror from her face.

He personally intended to see that the son of a bitch who did this paid, not only monetarily but with his hide, as well. First thing in the morning, he intended to take matters into his own hands, police or no police. He would put a man from his office on it around the clock until the culprit was in custody. Why did Ellis McCall suddenly come to mind? he wondered. He'd checked on him, but so far, he'd come up clean. Still . . .

By the time they carefully trekked back through the rubble and made it outside to the car, hot tears filled Beth's eyes.

Frantically she brushed them aside, telling herself to get ahold of herself. When the next few hours were behind her, then and only then could she afford to give in to the luxury of tears.

The inside of the car was riddled with a terrible silence as Cole fought the traffic down North Street before pulling into a parking place in front of a busy Seven-Eleven. There was a pay phone on the outside and Cole lost no time in jerking open the door.

"I'll be right back," he said.

Beth closed her eyes, forcing herself to take long, deep breaths. Who could have done such a thing? she asked herself. And more to the point, *why* would anyone do such a thing? If robbery was the only motive, then why all the unnecessary destruction? It was almost as if the person or persons responsible had an ax to grind and took great pleasure in the destruction.

Who? Who could possibly hate her that much? Or Jenny? Jenny! As her partner's name registered, she froze. Maybe it was Jenny and not her who was being avenged. Was that possible, or was she merely grasping at straws?

Whether it was Jenny or herself who had been the drawing card, there was only one person who qualified as a prime candidate. Ellis McCall. Was he the one? Was this his way of getting even? After all, hadn't he threatened her and Jenny? Just the thought of it being him nauseated her.

Suddenly it took every ounce of fortitude just to hold on to the contents of her stomach.

It was Cole's reappearance that saved her.

"The police are on their way," he said. "But I need Jenny's phone number."

Quickly Beth rattled it off to him and then asked, "While you're at it, would you call Mattie and tell her what happened and that we'll be late getting Meg, if she doesn't mind?"

A short time later, after making the call, Cole was climbing behind the wheel. His big, brawny body filled the car to capacity, and she would have liked nothing better than to curl up beside him and pretend she was having another nightmare. But this was no nightmare; this was reality at its ugliest. If nothing else, the harsh set of Cole's jaw and the steel glint in his eyes were enough to drive that reality home.

"Jenny didn't answer," he said in a clipped tone.

Beth frowned in concern. "I wonder where she is. We have to get hold of her."

"As soon as we talk to the police, we'll go to her apartment and camp out if we have to. I'm getting bad vibes about this whole thing."

It wasn't so much what he said but the way he said it that made Beth's heart lurch. It was one thing for her to think it might be Jenny's fiancé who was responsible, but to have Cole all but confirm it was another.

"You...think this has to do with Ellis, don't you?" She had to ask, yet she dreaded hearing the answer. It was bad enough to have a stranger violate their premises, but for someone they knew to do so was like throwing gasoline on an already smoldering fire. She shivered, drawing her arms tight around her.

When at last he answered, he measured his words very carefully. "If I had to guess, I'd say Ellis McCall is the one, although there doesn't seem to be a real motive. He did threaten you and he did hurt Jenny. Any man who would put a hand to a woman would be capable of anything."

Her nails dug into her palms until she thought they would pierce the delicate skin. "I...was afraid you'd say that."

"You feel the same way, huh?"

She could only nod feeling the lump in her throat increase to the size of a goose egg.

"Well, if he's the one, I guaran-damn-tee you the bastard'll pay."

"Maybe...maybe we're both wrong. Maybe he didn't have anything to do with it, after all," she said desperately, not wanting to face the truth.

"For Jenny's sake, let's just hope you're right." He shrugged. "Anyway, we don't have anything concrete at this point. It's all speculation on our part."

A grim silence overshadowed their ride back to the boutique. When the Lincoln once again turned into the parking lot, there were two police cars waiting.

Cole sought her eyes. "Are you going to be all right?"

The sweet concern in his voice was almost Beth's undoing. But she quickly rebounded and said, "I'll be fine."

He stared at her awhile longer, then hastily got out of the car and went around to open her door. With his arm firm beneath her elbow, they made their way toward the officer standing at the back door. The officer's two companions were busy combing the area, flashing high-beamed lights.

"I'm Lieutenant Bennett." The man's voice was crisp, but polite.

Everything about him appeared ordinary. He was of ordinary height, ordinary weight, and his hair and facial features were ordinary. The only thing that wasn't ordinary was the incredible blue of his eyes, which at that moment seemed as cold as marble chips. His eyes reminded her of Cole's, she thought suddenly, when he'd talked about Ellis McCall.

A shudder went through her slender frame. Mistaking it for fright, Cole slid his arm around her waist, drawing her against his side.

Beth extended her free arm. "I'm Beth Loring, owner of the boutique and this is . . . Cole Weston." After the perfunctory handshakes were exchanged, the lieutenant got down to business.

"Let's go inside, shall we?"

Although Beth had herself under a tight rein of control, her hands were anything but steady when she dug into her pocket to retrieve the key. She handed it to Cole and he unlocked the door.

There was a brief hesitation before Beth could make herself enter the shop. A muted cry tore loose from her throat, and Cole edged closer, his warm breath tickling her ear. He whispered, "Shh, you're doing great. It won't be long now till it's over. Just remember you're not alone."

His calm words of reassurance proved to be just the tonic she needed to get her contrary limbs moving and give her the stamina needed to get through the remainder of the ordeal.

Lieutenant Bennett, after having taken a quick survey of the damage, came back to stand in front of Beth.

"Do you have any idea how much merchandise is actually missing?"

"No, not yet," she said. "All I know is that large numbers of ready-to-wear items are gone from the racks."

"What about money?"

"No money. We never leave money overnight."

"I didn't think so, but I had to ask." He paused for a minute, then pointed out, "You said, 'we.'"

"I have a partner. Her name is Jenny Davis and Cole tried to call her, but there was no answer."

Bennett fell silent, though his eyes remained fixed on Beth. "Do you have any idea who'd do a thing like this?" As was his habit, he followed a question with a question. "I guess what I'm trying to say is, have you and Ms. Davis made anyone mad lately?"

Beth and Cole looked at each other. *He wants me to tell Bennett about Ellis McCall,* she thought. *I can see it in his face. Should she implicate him?* she asked herself frantically. What if they were wrong and he wasn't involved? As Cole had said, they had no proof. Then another thought raced through her mind. Fingerprints. Wouldn't there be fingerprints? Her theory was quickly discarded. Not if the thief were wearing gloves.

"Mrs. Loring," the lieutenant pressed when the silence lengthened.

"Since Beth . . . Mrs. Loring is reluctant to tell you," Cole said, entering into the conversation for the first time, "I'll do the honors. I think you should talk to a man by the name of Ellis McCall."

Bennett's gaze transferred to Cole. A lesser man might have been intimidated by the officer's hard stare. Not Cole. He matched him look for look.

"Oh, and who might this person be?" he drawled.

"Jenny Davis's fiancé."

The lieutenant's expression didn't change. "Just why do you think he's involved?"

"I don't know that he is," Cole said, a slight edge to his voice. "But it's a start."

Bennett paused and wrote down the name, then said to Beth, "Suppose you fill me in on all the details."

Beth did most of the talking, leaving nothing out, beginning with the time she had come to the office and was confronted with Jenny's black eye and facial scrapes, to the conversation in which McCall had threatened them.

The lieutenant merely nodded when she finished and turned to answer a question from one of the other officers. It was then that Beth noted that men had moved inside and were in the process of poking around the shop.

Cole had joined them and was helping to set the clothing stands upright. She stood silently by as Bennett walked up to him and they began conversing.

Beth knew she was taking the easy way out by letting Cole take charge, but at the moment she didn't feel guilt, she felt relief. He handled crises so well, she thought as he and Bennett continued to talk in earnest. If she hadn't known better, she would have sworn that it was Cole conducting the investigation instead of the other way around.

Shortly Bennett turned back to her. "If you'll check one more time to make sure nothing else is missing, we'll call it quits for the night."

"Of . . . course," Beth murmured weakly, forcing her leaden limbs to move.

Suddenly it hit her.

The furs! She hadn't even checked to see if any or all of the furs had been stolen.

Like a streak of lightning, she tore off down the tiny hall and thrust open the door at the end. Holding on to the doorknob, she surveyed the room.

She sagged limply against the frame. Nothing seemed to be missing.

"Beth? Anything missing?"

Even before he said a word, Beth knew that Cole was behind her. Somehow he had an uncanny way of knowing when she needed him. His presence settled over her like a soothing balm. He placed an arm lightly around her shoulders.

"As far as I can tell, it's all here." She sounded dazed. "Can you believe I almost forget to check this room?"

"Yes, I can believe it," he said. "After seeing this meaningless destruction, I can believe anything." Although his voice was soft, his face bore a savage look.

"Do you think they'll find any fingerprints?"

He heaved a deep sigh. "Let us hope. They're dusting now."

"When . . . will we know?"

"Tomorrow. I just hope the son of a bitch wasn't smart enough to wear gloves."

"You and me both."

Cole gave her shoulder a squeeze. "Let's go back in the front room. I think Bennett and crew are about ready to leave."

"Are . . . we going to Jenny's?"

He looked down at her; his eyes were sunk deep. "Only if you're up to it," he said.

She tried to smile. "I'm not up to it, but I feel like I don't have any choice. Besides, I'm worried about her."

"Well, let's wrap this up with Bennett and then we'll drive by her place."

A light shone from the front room of Jenny's apartment.

"It looks like we're in luck," Cole said, killing the engine.

Beth said nothing.

For a moment, Cole's harsh breathing was the only sound in the car as he wrestled with the sanity of what they were about to do. Beth had already been through enough. But she would not rest until she had talked to Jenny. Still, he wanted to give her one more chance to change her mind.

"Are you sure this won't wait until tomorrow?"

"I'm . . . sure," she whispered.

He cursed silently, taking in her forlorn figure, completely lost in the plush cushioned seat. How much more could she take and not break?

Thank God Dexter was not a party to this.

Suddenly his mind seemed to freeze in place. Or was he?

No way, he assured himself quickly. Dexter had his moments, all right; he'd be the first to admit that. But wrecking a place for the sheer fun of it was not one of them. Doing something like that would never occur to him.

"Well, it's now or never," Cole said at last.

"Let's . . . go."

He rang the doorbell several times before receiving any response. Beth pulled her cape tight around her as the chilly night air showed no mercy.

She glanced sideways at Cole, but he appeared totally unaffected by the damp air. From the way he looked, she doubted anything would bother him. His expression indicated chill distaste. Once again she asked herself how it was possible for one man to have such opposing personalities. She could only pity the poor soul who crossed him. Her breath shook as she dragged it in. *Steady*.

"Who's there?"

Jenny's soft voice coming through the door jarred Beth back to the real world.

"Well, here goes," Cole whispered, reaching for Beth's hand and possessively folding it in his large warm one.

"It's . . . me, Beth . . . and Cole."

The door opened immediately, though it was obvious that Jenny was surprised. Her eyebrows were raised, staring at them as if they were aliens from another planet.

"I . . . gather this isn't a social call," she said, indicating with the sweep of her hand that they should come in. Then she quickly pulled her cream-colored robe closer about her.

"No, this is no social call," Beth admitted soberly.

Jenny's facial muscles stiffened. "What's . . . happened?"

Beth turned to Cole, suddenly unable to continue, looking to him again for strength and support.

Not missing her appeal for help, Cole suggested gently, "Why don't we all sit down, and then we'll talk."

Jenny's face flushed, only to turn deathly pale. "Sorry, I didn't mean to be rude, it's just that—"

"We understand," Cole interrupted, brushing aside her apology.

Jenny's gaze shifted between the two of them. "Something terrible has happened, hasn't it?"

"It's . . . the boutique. Someone . . . broke in and not only stole from us, but . . ." Again Beth faltered.

"But what?" Jenny gasped, as though she weren't sure where her next breath was coming from, or even if it was coming.

Cole said, "What Beth couldn't tell you was that whoever broke into the building not only stole merchandise but ransacked the place, as well."

If possible, Jenny's eyes grew larger and wider. "Oh, no, oh, no!" she moaned.

"Those were my sentiments exactly," Beth echoed faintly, reaching across the cushion that separated them, taking Jenny's hand in hers.

"Did you . . . call the police?" Tears were beginning to trickle down Jenny's face.

"You know we did," Cole said, keeping his tone even with an effort. "We'll know tomorrow if our thief left any fingerprints."

Jenny suddenly jumped up from the couch and walked to the nearest window.

"I . . . can't imagine who would do such a thing," she whispered, keeping her back to them, hunching her shoulders.

Beth knew what was coming next. She faced Cole, her eyes imploring him to please tread carefully; it was obvious Jenny was on edge. Was Cole right? Did she know more than she was letting on?

"Can't you?" Cole asked quietly.

Jenny whirled around, her expression guarded. "What do you mean by that?"

Cole changed his tactics. "Have you seen your fiancé lately?"

"Ellis?" The name was spoken on a mere breath.

Beth knew she was playing dumb, and by the way Cole's lips curled in disdain, he knew it, too.

"Yes, Ellis," he said, his tone brittle.

Cole's words were the trigger that set her off. Without warning, Jenny broke down and sobbed, deep wrenching sobs that doubled her over.

Before Cole could make a move toward her, Beth leapt to her feet and rushed to Jenny's side. "Don't," she pleaded, placing her arm around her friend's waist, leading her back to the couch.

Cole's face revealed a hint of anger, but he kept his silence as though convinced that Beth was much more adept at handling the situation than he was.

"Oh, Beth," Jenny said frantically, sinking her fingernails into Beth's arm, "please believe me when I tell you I don't know where Ellis is."

Although Beth flinched against the physical pain Jenny was inflicting, it was nothing compared to the mental agony Jenny was enduring. Not only was Beth concerned for Jenny, but herself, as well, though for different reasons. If the insurance payoff wasn't sufficient to cover the damages, she would be in deep trouble.

With her financial situation in such dire straits, there wasn't an extra dime to put into the business. She was going to have to borrow money to pay Giles as it was, and if he was wrong and they had to go to court, then she honestly didn't know how she was going to manage.

But now was not the time to think about that, she warned, Jenny's sobs continuing to fill her ears.

Cole reached over and tapped Jenny on the knee. For a second she responded, staring at him, ceasing to weep. "Considering Ellis's veiled threat the other day," he said, "we think he may have had a hand in this, based purely on the fact that so very little was stolen and so much destruction done."

"I can't . . . I won't believe that," she replied emphatically.

"How was he fixed for money?" Cole asked, not at all put off by her defense of her fiancé.

Jenny averted her gaze. "I'm . . . not sure."

"I don't believe that," Cole said with just the right amount of authority.

Again Beth was amazed at his ability to interrogate, as though it were something he did every day. Dismissing the thought as absurd, she concentrated on what was being said.

"Well, believe it," Jenny said sharply, though still unwilling to look either of them in the eye.

She's lying, Beth thought with a sinking feeling in the pit of her stomach, yet she couldn't quite bring herself to come right out and accuse her of it. They were both too emotionally strung out, and one wrong word or deed could be suicidal. Beth recognized that, but she wasn't sure Cole did.

"Well, I don't," Cole declared bluntly, bringing to life Beth's worst fears. "But I'm not going to pursue it any further tonight. Beth's already been through enough and I'm taking her home. Tomorrow you'll have to talk to Lieutenant Bennett and he'll be asking you the same questions, and I suggest you come up with better answers."

"It could have been any number of people," Jenny retaliated. "Just because . . . Ellis shot off his big mouth doesn't mean he would do anything like that."

Beth shook her head at Cole, thinking, *we're wasting our time. She's either scared to death or she believes what she's saying.*

The silence hanging over the room was so thick it could have been cut with a knife. Then Cole stretched out a hand to Beth, pulling her up to stand beside him. Together they faced Jenny.

It was Beth who finally spoke. "We're going now. Maybe... tomorrow you'll see things in a different light." She paused, suddenly unable to find the right words to say to her friend, who was now defensive and distrusting. "Anyway... we have our work cut out for us," she added on a deliberate note.

"I'll be there," Jenny whispered, still keeping her eyes averted.

With nothing left to be said, Beth filled the silence by making a disjointed move toward the door. Cole followed suit, reaching out to open it for her.

"Beth."

They both paused instantly, but it was Beth who whirled around, hope etched in the lines of her face. "Yes?" she said.

Jenny's chin was wobbling and tears were flowing steadily down her cheeks. "I..." she began, only to have her voice suddenly fail her.

"Go on," Beth urged softly, desperately wanting Jenny to speak her heart.

Jenny lowered her eyes. "Never... mind. I'll see... you tomorrow."

Beth wanted to scream. But she didn't. She merely turned sad eyes up to Cole and together they walked out the door and closed it firmly behind them.

It was past midnight when a sound-asleep Megan was finally picked up at the Engleses' house and put down for the rest of the night in her own bed.

When Beth had explained to Mattie in greater detail what had happened, Mattie had been appalled and had insisted that Beth let her keep Megan for the remainder of the night.

Beth had thanked her and declined, needing to have Megan close to her.

Now as she walked back into the den, having shed her clothes for a long robe, her eyes hungrily sought Cole. Her heart skipped a beat, as it did every time she saw his face.

He met her steady gaze and then they both moved at once, not stopping until they were wrapped tightly in each other's arms. Nothing was said; words were unnecessary. Cole simply held her, molding her limbs to his, blocking out of his mind the fact that she was naked beneath her caftan. Unwittingly his blood pressure elevated.

"Want me to fix you something to eat?" he suggested gruffly, loosening his arms from around her.

Beth stepped back and went to stand in front of the roaring fire. "Not now . . . I couldn't eat a thing."

"Something to drink, then?" He pushed an anxious hand through his hair and waited. She looked so fragile, like a breakable piece of glass.

She gave him a wan smile. "Now *that* I could handle. A cup of hot tea would do wonders."

"One cup of hot tea coming up."

Beth watched as he strode into the kitchen, never tiring of feasting her eyes on the slant of his muscled shoulders or the way his slacks molded his thighs and buttocks as if they were part of his skin. No matter how exhausted or worried she was, having Cole around never failed to buoy her spirits.

She eased herself down onto the couch, shoving all thoughts of the past few hours to the back of her mind, content to wait while he puttered around in the kitchen. After a moment, her head fell back against the cushions, but her thoughts refused to cooperate. The wretched condition of the store was imprinted on the back of her eyelids.

"Are you awake?" Cole's huskily drawled words caused her eyes to flutter open.

Sweeping her hair away from her face, Beth smiled her thanks. A silence followed while she sipped the tea.

"Is it okay?" he asked after a minute.

Beth smiled again and took another sip. "It's . . . delicious," she said, though in truth she barely tasted it; she was distracted, giddy with a fear that simmered right below the surface. It was impossible to concentrate too long on any one thing.

"Good. Maybe it'll put a little color back into your face."

"I . . . know I must look a mess," she whispered self-consciously.

He flicked a curl off her forehead. "You could never look a mess," he said with husky tenderness, aching to shield her from the pain and grief he knew was churning inside her.

She took another drink of her tea, while trying to quiet her racing pulse. If it were possible, she would have liked nothing better than to take Megan and run away with this man, just the three of them against the world. But that was just her fantasy. With no promises, no commitments between them, she didn't even know from one day to the next if he would be a part of her life. She had to be content with one day at a time.

"We'll start the cleanup in the morning," he said, breaking into the silence.

Beth's hands began shaking before she could set the saucer down on the coffee table. She twisted them together in her lap. "I still can't believe it happened," she said brokenly. "Someone actually ripped my place apart."

Cole's face hardened. "Don't worry," he spit out, "he'll pay. You can count on that."

"I . . . feel so violated . . . so—" she broke off with a shiver.

"And madder than hell, I hope."

Beth nodded fiercely, then asked, "You think Jenny's involved somehow, don't you?"

"Don't you?"

Beth sighed. "Yes, I do, though I think she was sincere in her defense of Ellis. There's something wrong. I just can't put my finger on it yet."

"I feel the same way, and I think it's only a matter of time till it all comes out."

"I . . . hope you're right. I don't know how much more I can take."

Cole groaned silently, knowing exactly what she meant. If only he could tell her that the nightmare with Megan was over. But he couldn't, not yet. It would be unforgivable to add false hope to her list of woes. Enough rocks had already been thrown at her.

Looking at her face, he saw that her eyes were closed, her thick lashes sweeping her cheeks like a tiny brush. He longed to lean over and touch his lips to that creamy skin. But he refrained, and instead drew a deep harsh breath and got to his feet.

He wasn't fit to touch a hair on her head.

Reacting to the sudden movement, Beth's eyes popped open.

"I'm going now," Cole said, his tone bleak, "so you can get some sleep." Extending a hand, he pulled her to her feet. They stood within a hairbreadth of each other.

With the back of his hand, Cole touched her cheek. It was warm, a little feverish. Her eyes were big, larger now in the muted firelight.

"Don't go...please," she said almost in a whisper. "I don't want to be alone."

Slowly, deliberately, she untied her robe and slid it off her shoulders, letting it fall to the floor. She held out her arms to him, her nipples pink and large against the ghostly white skin of her breast.

Cole stood transfixed, every pulse in his body throbbing, realizing in that moment he'd been granted another reprieve.

For this night, at least, she still belonged to him.

Chapter Thirteen

The following days were spent reorganizing the store. Again Cole was Beth's tower of strength. She could not have done without him. Even with both his physical and moral support, it was still a slow, painful process at best and one that she hoped never to experience again.

It took three working days just to clear the debris and put things back in their proper place.

Throughout it all, Jenny was nervous and unresponsive, which did not help the situation. Several times Beth tried to get her to open up, to talk to her, but as before, Jenny remained closemouthed. She was hurting, Beth could feel it, but there was nothing she could do if Jenny wouldn't confide in her.

Of Ellis McCall there was nothing. It was almost as if he had disappeared off the face of the earth. That was a major part of Jenny's problem, Beth thought, but there was more, much more. Beth was convinced of that. The police were also looking for Ellis to question him, although there were no clear fingerprints to bring about an arrest.

Cole remained convinced that Ellis was the guilty one, and as a result spent time down at the police department, prodding

Lieutenant Bennett to find him. If Beth thought Cole's behavior odd, she chose to ignore it, partly because she had enough to contend with without adding his actions to the list. She dismissed his diligence as his wanting to help, and let it go at that.

Then there was the damage to assess and the list for the insurance company to be made, a process that was both nerveracking and tedious, but not nearly as tedious as waiting for the insurance company to pay up so that the merchandise could be replaced.

Cole had insisted on loaning her the money, but she refused. He had been furious. Every detail of their heated exchange was imprinted on her brain. . . .

It had happened the night before last, the night they had finished getting the boutique back in order. They had been at her place, relaxing over dinner.

"You're worried about money, aren't you?" Cole asked.

"You know I am, but I'm hopeful the insurance company won't drag their heels and will pay off as they should."

He reached over and gently caressed her cheek. "I want you to listen to me," he began, his voice soft, persuasive.

Beth shook her head vigorously, knowing what was coming. "Please . . . don't," she whispered. "The answer is still no."

Cole's lips thinned. "I've never met a more hardheaded woman. Your head is as hard as a brick."

If the situation hadn't been so serious, Beth would have laughed. But it was serious, and the last thing she wanted to do was laugh. Cry, maybe, but laugh, no.

She got up from the table. "Cole, we've been over this before," she said wearily. "My answer is still the same. I won't take money from you."

"Just why the hell not?"

Because I don't know when I can pay you back and when you walk out on me, I don't want any ties. I couldn't stand it. "Because . . . I . . . It's important that I take care of this alone." Her eyes pleaded with him to understand. "It's . . . my problem and I have to handle it."

From that moment on, things were strained between them, and when she'd closed the door behind him the tears had flowed, reminding her once again just how fragile the thread was that bound them together.

The next morning he'd called and told her he was going to the ranch, making no mention of their tiff, asking her to come later and bring Megan.

Beth hadn't needed extra prodding, especially as Christmas was just around the corner, and every day Megan asked when she was going to get the Christmas tree and see the doggie. The fact that a decorated tree sat in their den made no difference to Megan; she hadn't forgotten Cole's promise.

Nor had Beth. Even though they hadn't parted on the best of terms and even though Cole hadn't mentioned wanting to see her, she couldn't wait to see him, fool that she was. One day away from him was like an eternity.

Now as Beth stopped the car at the entrance to the ranch, she rested her hands on the wheel and looked at the house. The serene atmosphere surrounding it never failed to fill her with peace and tranquillity. She couldn't help but envy Cole this wonderful hideaway.

Was there a chance she might one day share . . . ?

Cool it, Beth, she cried silently, cutting her thought off at the pass. *Just because you've fallen head over heels in love with him doesn't mean he feels the same about you. So for heaven's sakes, don't go pulling more dreams out of the air. Just take each moment you have with him and squeeze a lifetime out of it.*

"Mommie, me want to see doggie," a little aggrieved voice informed her.

"Sorry, darling," Beth muttered, bending swiftly to kiss her daughter's adorable face.

Then she started the car, all doubts vanishing, exultant at the thought of seeing Cole.

They left the car outside the gate and walked through the yard. There was no sign of life, although it was after eleven on the overcast winter morning. But Beth could see smoke coming from the chimney, and gently, carefully, without knocking, she opened the front door.

Cole lay back in one of the big chairs, obviously asleep, an unlighted cigarette resting on his chest, and she held her breath as she saw the new lines scored deeply in his face.

The collie was dozing at his feet. He raised his head and peered at them through lazy, indifferent eyes. Megan trotted across happily to pat the dog, and then, moved by one of those inexplicable impulses that manage to bring tears to one's eyes, she stood by Cole and put her little hand on his knee and patted it invitingly.

He struggled to open his eyelids, and when he fought free from sleep and Megan came into focus, the look of sweetness that came into his face, temporarily erasing the harsh lines, was such that it yanked at Beth's heartstrings.

"Hiya, moppet," Cole said, lifting Megan up and sitting her on his knee. She found the cigarette and studied it, fascinated by this strange new toy.

Over her head Cole's eyes found those of the woman still standing in the doorway, and a grave, uncertain glance passed between them.

"I . . . I brought Megan, Cole."

"What about yourself? That's just as important."

She started to tremble. "You didn't say that," she whispered.

"I was a damned fool."

Megan began to squirm in his lap. "Me pay wiff doggie."

Cole looked down at her. "Only if you promise not to pull his ears."

Megan giggled and scrambled off his lap, heading for the collie.

"Careful, Meg," Beth warned, watching as the child squatted beside the animal and tentatively placed a hand on his honey-colored coat.

Cole stood up and advanced toward Beth, drawing her attention away from Megan.

She stood as if cemented to the spot as he narrowed the distance between them. Then he reached out and slipped his hand under her hair, where he began working his thumb along her nape.

Their eyes melted into each other's.

"Am I forgiven?" he asked huskily.

The trembling inside her increased twofold. "There's nothing to forgive."

"I . . . missed you."

"Me, too," she said in a breathy gust.

He stared her mouth. "Are you all right?"

I'm fine now that I'm with you. "Tired, but fine."

"Me, too."

Her brows furrowed. "Is that why you were asleep at this time of the morning?"

"Yeah. Stayed up half the night."

"Why?"

"It's a secret," he whispered, pulling her closer.

"Oh," she whispered.

"You're beautiful." His voice had grown hoarse.

"So... are you."

He brushed her lips with his. "We're kind of sickening, aren't we?"

She smiled. "In... the worst way."

With a suppressed groan, he drew her lower lip between his teeth and began sucking on it. When he let it go, he said thickly, "It's Christmas. We'll blame it on that."

Then his mouth closed over hers.

Beth clung to him, digging her nails into his shoulders as his tongue warred hotly with hers, making her head spin crazily. With a free hand, he circled her waist and pulled her even closer. Even through the thick jeans, his desire made its presence known against her delicate skin.

The touch of tiny fingers around their legs brought them crashing back to earth.

Beth, struggling for breath, stared down into her daughter's upturned face.

"Doggie wants outside, Mommie."

As Beth strove to get her bearings, she could hardly breathe, much less speak.

Cole, too, was having difficulty in getting himself back together. But he was the first to recover.

"Come on, honey," he said to Megan, "we'll let Caesar out." After he took the child's hand, he turned back to Beth, his eyes intense, deep and smoldering, clearly telling her they had unfinished business to attend to.

All five of Beth's senses were clamoring with unfulfilled desire while she watched the two of them, the tall, hard-muscled man and the chubby, two-year-old child slowly amble toward the door, the collie matching them step for step.

When they returned a short time later, Beth had regained her composure. "Where's Mrs. Cooper?" she asked, just now missing the housekeeper.

"I gave her the weekend off," Cole said, his voice still not quite steady, thinking how delicious Beth looked and tasted.

She was wearing a pair of jeans, and her red sweater, though far from tight, nevertheless managed to show off her rounded breasts to perfection.

"What do you want to do first?" he asked at length.

"I thought we were going to chop down a Christmas tree. You promised Meg, remember?"

He laughed. "So I did, so I did."

The rest of the morning and afternoon was filled with a special kind of magic. It didn't matter that the weather was damp and chilly; Beth thought the cold made it seem more like Christmas.

Megan wanted Cole to cut down every tree they passed, until Cole laughingly called a halt and chopped down the last one Megan's short finger pointed to.

By the time Cole hauled the tree back to the house, Megan could barely contain her excitement. Once the tall cedar was standing upright in the corner of the den, Megan hindered more than helped as they all pitched in and made colored paper chains. Beth had gone into Lufkin and returned with a dozen packets of crepe paper in every color of the rainbow. That evening Megan took over the floor of the den and together she and Beth pleated, folded and creased the strips of paper that Cole had very efficiently cut and prepared.

He sat in his chair, waiting patiently for the next chain to be handed to him before fastening it onto the top of the tree. As he watched Megan concentrating earnestly, with the tip of her pink tongue protruding from the middle of her mouth, and Beth, so sweet as she patiently helped the child, his heart melted.

Coming out of his reverie, he saw Beth smiling at him.

"Penny for your thoughts."

"This is going to be the best Christmas I've ever had," he said gruffly.

Her hands stilled and her face lighted up like a candle. "Oh, Cole, I hope so. I can't begin to tell you what it means to me to be able to share this with another person. Ever since Lee died, Meg and I . . .''

She stopped, confused, thrown off balance with the mention of her husband, and looked pleadingly at him. "I'm sorry, I didn't mean . . ."

"You didn't," he said gently, defusing the tension. "I'm not jealous of him anymore," he added with a sheepish grin.

Beth felt her heart turn over. "I'm glad," she whispered.

"What about another chain in the meantime?" he asked lightly. "We're wasting time, ladies. Let's get this show on the road."

Megan giggled and the work detail was resumed until Megan fell asleep on the floor. Together Beth and Cole carried her to the spare bedroom and put her to bed.

Once they were back in the den, Beth began putting the finishing touches on the tree while Cole put a Lionel Richie album on the stereo. Then he helped her. Soon the huge tree was ablaze with twinkling lights and ornaments in addition to the homemade chains.

Beth stood back and admired her handiwork. "Well?"

"Are you by any chance fishing for a compliment?" Cole teased.

"Me? Surely you jest."

His lips twitched. "Well, I'll have to admit it's beautiful," he said, tapping her playfully on the bottom. "But the credit belongs to Megan."

She made a face at him and then watched as he ambled over to the stereo and flipped the record.

"I think I'm going to go take a shower. Cutting the tree and then stringing those lights made me feel sweaty."

"That so?" She pitched aside an empty ornament box and walked to him, putting her arms around his waist. "I happen to like the way you smell."

"Umm," he said, nuzzling his lips against her ear.

"When . . . you get out of the shower, why don't you slip into something comfortable?"

"Isn't that supposed to be my line?"

"Yes, but remember, we're at your place."

Laughter was still rumbling through him when he stepped into the shower and let the hot water pelt his body, feeling the fatigue drain out of him. He soaped his face first and then the rest of his body. He knew he had company long before he felt her hand touch his shoulder, felt a finger run down the center of his back, stopping at the crease of his buttocks, then starting around toward his front.

He raised his face to the water's stinging spray and then turned to her. She was nude; he could see the blue veins beneath her nearly translucent breasts. The nipples were pebble hard. He reached out to them.

"Uh-uh," she whispered softly, stepping behind him. "Not yet."

"Why?"

"This is my treat, that's why. Where do you want me to start?"

"I'll leave that up to you."

She latched onto the soap and began rubbing up and down his chest. Her strokes were gentle yet insistent. Once again he reached out to her.

"Please," he grated.

"Yes, now," she whispered, standing on her toes, her lips nearly touching his, her body bent to accept him.

They washed each other with care, lingering over some places longer than others. When at last he turned off the water, they were a bit glassy eyed.

There was no break in their lovemaking as they dried each other and drifted into the bedroom. As Cole pulled back the bedspread, she crawled in beside him, and he gasped with pleasure when he felt her tongue stroke him. Finally he could stand it no longer. He pulled her to him and began kissing her, slowly, deeply, as though afraid some part of her might escape his passion.

Surely there had never been such rapture from the beginning of time, and he took her with him every sweet moment of the way. It was a breathless, slow, anticipatory climb to the heavens, until they reached that final crest. Triumphantly they began the wingless flight down, gliding surely and smoothly back to earth.

It was Beth who awoke first, and it seemed that the house itself was too cramped to contain her happiness. Briefly touching Cole's dark head, she stretched, recalling in vivid detail the miracle of the night.

It was not their physical coupling she wanted to treasure, perfect though it had been, but the words that Cole had whispered. Words he'd never spoken before, and that had come, not in a fit of passion, but in measured, deliberate utterances from deep inside his soul.

Would they ever be whispered again? Oh, they had to be! They must be, she agonized. This had to be the turning point.

Suddenly the alarm went off, breaking the silence with a nagging buzz. Beth shifted with a start and her eyes opened wide, while Cole's hand frantically patted at the clock for the button. He had forgotten to shut it off. He turned toward Beth, who was propping herself up with a pillow.

"What a terrible noise," she exclaimed.

Cole chuckled. "I never hear it. I'm always awake before it goes off and hit the switch when I get up for my run."

"What happened this morning?"

"Need you ask?" he demanded huskily.

"No," she whispered, "but I'd much rather wake up to music."

Cole reached over and undraped the sheet from her bare breasts. "Music in the morning would be a perfect way to start the day. That and a little lovemaking."

Beth looked down at herself, shocked at the things Cole made her say and do. "See anything you like?" she asked, smiling.

"Well, let me see," he said, his eyes roving over her. Softly he cupped one breast in his hand and touched her nipple with his tongue. "I'm greedy. I'll settle for them both."

His lips caressed her breasts and her nape. Responsively Beth sank back into the bed, her free hand feeling the taut muscles of his abdomen. Then she drove her hand lower until she reached the hardness she had enjoyed over a good part of the night.

"Oh, yes." He sighed, easing himself over on top of her.

The unexpected ring of the phone froze them in place.

"Oh, no," she moaned.

"Oh, yes!" he said, reaching for the phone on his side of the bed.

A silence ensued while he listened, and Beth watched his face go through a series of changes: first relief, then disbelief, then regret.

When he hung up, he turned to her.

"Cole?"

"That was Lieutenant Bennett. They picked up McCall and he confessed everything."

Beth's hand flew to her mouth. "Oh, poor Jenny."

"There's more," he said quietly.

A knot of fear formed in her throat. "What?"

"Jenny's in the hospital. She . . . tried to kill herself."

"Jen, it's Beth. Can you hear me?"

For a moment, there wasn't even so much as a flicker on Jenny's waxen-colored face as Beth leaned over her. Disheartened, she lifted a lifeless hand and eased herself down into the chair beside the bed. She then lifted her eyes to Cole, who stood next to her. His face was grim.

Beth had never seen her friend look so bad. Not only was her pert face devoid of color, but the circles under her eyes were almost black and her lips were tissue-paper white.

As she clung to Jenny's hand, Beth still could not believe that Jenny had tried to take her life. Following the call from Lieutenant Bennett, the frantic trip to the hospital had reminded her of the incident with Megan. After throwing on their clothes and waking Megan, they had left immediately, and after dropping Meg by the Engleses', they made a beeline to the hospital.

Luckily the doctor had just stepped out of Jenny's room, and together she and Cole had spoken to him. He told them Jenny had swallowed a bottle of sleeping pills, apparently after learning of her fiancé's arrest. But he said he'd been able to pump her stomach, and barring any complications, she was going to be all right. He'd gone on to inform them that the maid had found her early that morning when she'd gone to clean her apartment.

But the details of what had driven Jenny to take such a drastic measure were still a mystery.

Now, as Beth reached out and smoothed the hair off Jenny's forehead, she thought she heard a slight moan.

"I think she's waking up," Beth whispered.

Cole moved closer to the bed and rested his hand on Beth's shoulder. "I believe you're right."

While they watched and waited, Beth said, "I wonder if the doctor notified her parents."

"Where do they live?"

"In Lufkin."

"Do you think maybe you oughta call them?"

A shudder went through Beth. "I probably should, only I . . . hate to have to tell them . . . what happened."

"I understand," he said heavily, giving her shoulder a comforting squeeze.

She faced him, a drawn look on her face. "Do you . . . think she did this because of Ellis's arrest?"

"That was part of it for sure, but—"

"I know," Beth cut in, "there's got to be more, as we've said all along." Suddenly tears welled up in her eyes. "If only she'd talked to me, maybe I could've headed this off."

Suddenly Jenny's eyes fluttered open and locked firmly on Beth.

"You came," she whispered pitifully.

A lone tear found its way down Beth's cheek. "Did you doubt it?"

"I . . . Yes, I did," Jenny said, running her tongue over her dry, swollen lips.

"Do . . . you feel up to talking?" Cole put in softly, still standing beside Beth.

Jenny tried to smile at Cole. "I'm glad you're here . . . with Beth."

"I wouldn't have it any other way," he replied simply.

Again Jenny licked her lips. "About . . . Ellis . . ."

"We know he's been arrested," Beth said with difficulty.

"Please . . . I want to tell you what happened . . . should have told you a long time ago." Her eyes were wide and filled with terror.

Beth tightened her grip on Jenny's hand, hoping to calm her. "I'm listening," she soothed. "Go ahead."

"First I want to tell you how sorry I am . . . Ellis tore up the shop."

"Oh, Jen, hon, you can't hold yourself responsible for Ellis's actions."

Jenny shook her head and then winced. "No...you don't understand. I am responsible," she stressed, her voice rising.

"Shh, don't upset yourself," Beth pleaded, glancing up at Cole.

He said calmly, "Just tell us what's on your mind, Jen."

His even-toned voice had the desired effect, for when Jenny continued, she was more in control. "I'm sure you didn't know, Beth, but Ellis gambled heavily."

"No. No, I didn't know," Beth answered, feeling suddenly ill.

"Well...because I thought I loved him and he loved me..." Again she paused, the tears making tracks down her face. "I... gave him money."

"Where did you get the money?" Cole inquired lightly when it was obvious that Jenny wasn't able to go on, giving her time to pull herself together again.

Jenny dabbed at the tears with the Kleenex Beth pressed into her hand. "I...took it out of...the boutique." Once the terrible words were spoken, she broke down. She cried as though her heart would break.

Only Cole's sharp intake of breath registered on Beth's shell-shocked brain, as Jenny's body continued to heave with sobs.

All that money... wasted on that scum! Beth thought.

She tried to say something, but all she could do was cling to Jenny while raw pain consumed her. Jenny's sorrow was like a sore that had suddenly erupted, spewing its poison.

At last, Jenny pulled back and then fell exhausted against the pillow, though her eyes never left Beth's face.

"Don't hate me...please," she begged. "Every time...every time I gave him money, he swore it'd be the last and that he'd pay me back. But...he just kept getting deeper and deeper in debt, and before I knew it he became desperate...and real mean. That was when he began to...hurt me." Her lower lip trembled uncontrollably.

So did Beth's as her mind worked frantically to digest Jenny's confession. "Oh, Jenny, Jenny, why didn't you tell someone?"

"I...wanted to, but I was afraid. He...kept telling me he'd hurt me again if I told anyone, especially you. After that day in the office, after you told him to leave, he went crazy...."

"That's when he broke into the shop, right?" Cole asked.

Jenny nodded mutely.

"You know the courts will show him no mercy," Cole added bluntly, testing Jenny's reaction.

Before Jenny could respond, Beth put in, her voice filled with bitterness. "I . . . hope they throw the book at him."

"Oh, they will when I get through," Jenny whispered, her voice coming alive for the first time.

"If you feel that way, why did you do this to yourself?"

Jenny bit down on her lower lip. "I . . . don't know, I honestly don't. He . . . he just kept taking and taking and there just didn't seem to be any end in sight." She paused. "When I found out he . . . destroyed the shop and knowing it was my fault . . . I couldn't handle it."

Beth couldn't speak; tears choked in her throat.

"Will . . . can you ever forgive me?" Jenny whispered.

"Oh, Jenny," Beth wailed.

Jenny clutched at Beth's hand, panic written in every line on her face. "Oh, please, say yes. I swear I'll pay every dime of the money back. And . . . and if you need any for Megan, all you have to do is ask and it's yours. I'm so sorry, so sorry," she whimpered.

"Jenny, if you keep this up you'll never get your strength back," Cole intervened softly, reaching for Beth and pulling her away from Jenny's grasping hands and arms.

When Beth started to rise, Jenny grappled for her hands again. "Please . . . tell me you forgive me!"

Beth stared down into the anxious, upturned face. "Oh, Jen," she wept, "of course I forgive you. Things will work out. I know they will. Now please close your eyes and try to get some rest."

Then with Cole's arm around her, they quietly left the room.

Chapter Fourteen

The days spilled one into another and with them came the anticipation of Christmas. Cole was determined Beth was going to enjoy the holidays, convincing her to put Jenny's treachery aside, as well as the continued threat of the looming custody battle.

They spent hours shopping, though most of their energy went into buying Megan's gifts from Santa Claus. Cole wanted to go overboard, but Beth put her foot down. In the end, he only bought her two Cabbage Patch twin dolls—a boy and a girl—to add to her collection. Beth thought they were too costly, but he insisted and she gave in good-naturedly.

His presence gave her the inner strength to endure those dark times, even though there were moments when she ached for him to tell her he loved her. Then she'd thrust that thought to the back of her mind and concentrated on her blessings.

Such as now. It was Christmas day and Santa had come and gone. Megan, exhausted from playing with her new toys, was in bed.

Beth felt Cole's eyes tracking her movement as she neatly placed the last of Megan's toys under the tree so it wouldn't look so bare.

"I don't know where you get the energy to move a muscle, much less do that," Cole said, lying on her couch, a smile on his face, patting his stomach.

She laughed. "I must say you did make a pig of yourself, especially on my chicken and dumplings."

"Not to mention that Neiman-Marcus cake." He groaned, though a smile still lurked around his lips. "But darn it, I just couldn't quit eating."

"So I noticed," Beth responded with playful sarcasm.

He cocked his head. "Are you suggesting I made a pig of myself?"

Beth feigned innocence. "Now where would you get an idea like that?"

"Well," he admitted with an impish grin, "I did kinda pig out."

Beth laughed and finished her task. That done, she turned back to Cole, her expression soft and warm. "By the way, I don't think I told you how much I appreciate the brass urn and plant you gave me."

"The moment I saw it I knew you'd like it, considering how crazy you are about plants."

"Well, you were right."

"And I in turn thank you, madam, for the engraved gold money clip."

She frowned suddenly. "Do you really like it? I . . . couldn't think of anything you didn't already have or need."

"It's perfect," he said huskily, getting up and reaching for her.

She nestled against him, feeling his breath tickle her skin.

After a moment of silence, he whispered in the folds of her ear, "I want you to come with me."

She stepped back and looked up at him. "Where to?"

"You'll see," he answered, leaning over and kissing her on the tip of her nose.

"This is not fair," Beth groaned, following his lead. "I'm not used to this cloak-and-dagger stuff."

Cole didn't say a thing, just gently propelled her in the direction of the spare bedroom.

When they were standing in front of the closed door, Cole paused. "All right, close your eyes."

"Cole!" Her tone registered her exasperation.

"Do as I tell you, woman." His eyes were dancing with merriment.

"Oh, all right," she said, shutting her eyes.

"And don't open them until I tell you to." That order was given while he opened the door and led Beth into the room. After turning on the light, he said, "Okay, you can open your eyes."

Beth blinked several times, and when she could focus, her mouth fell open. Several emotions flickered across her face: surprise, awe, and delight—sheer delight.

"Oh, Cole," she whispered, tears glistening in her eyes, "It's . . . beautiful."

Sitting in the middle of the bed was a miniature wooden dollhouse, intricately designed and carved with fine-honed skill.

"Do . . . you like it?"

Beth swung around to face him. "Like it! I love it . . . but how . . . I mean . . . I don't understand. . . ."

Cole's face was serious. "Remember when you told me about the dollhouse your uncle made for your cousins?" He paused with a smile. "Well, this one's for you . . . and Megan. Merry Christmas."

Beth swallowed against the huge lump in her throat. "Oh, Cole, I . . ."

He took her in his arms and buried her face against his chest. "Don't cry, dearest. It was meant to make you happy."

"I am happy," she wailed. "That's why I'm crying." Then raising her head, she asked, "When . . . did you make it?"

He kissed her gently. "Remember those few days I was gone? I was here working my buns off so it'd be ready for Christmas."

"How . . . how can I ever thank you enough?"

"You already have, my darling, you already have."

They made love far into the night, slow, sweet love, until they were totally exhausted and could do nothing but rest quietly in each other's arms.

Beth didn't know how long she lay there before she turned toward Cole and whispered, "Are you awake?"

"Mmm."

"Are you hungry?"

A deep chuckle rattled in his chest. "You've got to be kidding."

"No." She giggled.

"What do you suggest?" he murmured.

"How about sneaking into the kitchen and seeing what you can find."

He pulled back so he could see her face, "Me?" he croaked.

"Please . . . it's so cold."

"What do I get in return?"

"Mmm, I'll think of something."

"See that you do," he said, tossing back the covers and reaching for his jeans. He then paraded into the kitchen and brought back the small tray of snacks Beth had prepared earlier for them to munch on.

"Will this hold you awhile?"

He watched her attack the food with gusto, and got back into bed and leaned on his elbow.

"Sure you won't change your mind?" she asked.

Cole shook his head. "Gawd! That's the last thing I want." She grinned and threw a cracker at him.

His eyes narrowed. "Ah, so now you're declaring war?"

"No." This brought on a round of giggles. "Why, I wouldn't dare do such a thing." Catching him by surprise, she hit him with a cheese ball.

His gaze was steady and intimate. "You'd better think twice before raising my ire." He picked up a cracker dotted with cream cheese and menaced her with it. "Don't say I didn't warn you," he said, now sporting a leering grin. "You're in big trouble."

"I'm innocent."

"Hardly." A blob of cream cheese landed at the corner of her mouth. "My, my, my, it'd be a shame to waste that," he said, and he commenced to lick it off. She was bubbling with laughter. "You give up?" he asked.

"Only if you do."

"Never."

"Is that a promise?"

"Forever."

The laughter stopped. "What are you saying?"

Neither one moved for a minute.

"I think I'm asking you to marry me."

Her look turned wary. "But you're not sure?"

"I thought I was."

"Oh."

She was quiet for such a long time that Cole finally said, "Forget it. It was just a thought."

"Or a slip of the tongue?"

"No."

"Good," she whispered, her eyes brimming with unshed tears, "because I wasn't about to let you off the hook."

Cole's Adam's apple worked furiously. "Does...that mean you love me?"

"With all my heart."

"Oh, Beth," he grated against her lips. "Are you sure I'm not dreaming?"

She traced his unsteady lips with the tip of her finger. "If this is a dream, I never want to wake up."

The following day Beth was positive her feet never touched the ground. At work she traipsed around on a euphoric cloud. She had to keep pinching herself to make sure she wasn't dreaming.

Though she received strange looks from Jenny and the other workers, she kept her secret close to her heart, too greedy to share it. After Cole asked her again to marry him would be soon enough to shout it from the rooftops. There was no doubt in her mind that a proposal was in the offing. Just the thought of waking up every morning with Cole beside her made her giddy. To add icing to the cake, his presence would be a strong weapon against Dexter Manly. With Cole on her side, she was confident no one would be able to take Megan away from her.

Those thoughts were dancing around in her head as she opened the door to her house. It was five after five and she was late getting home.

Megan dashed in ahead of her and ran straight to her doll sitting in a chair by the fireplace.

"Me play wiff dolly."

"That's right, darling, you play with your doll while I change my clothes."

Humming, Beth slipped into jeans and a sweatshirt and then padded to the kitchen to fix Megan a snack. A minute later she was kneeling in front of the child, placing a bowl of chopped fruit in her lap.

"Here, sweetie, munch on this. Dinner's going to be late because Mommie's going to fix something special for Cole."

Megan grinned. "Cole coming."

"He sure is," Beth said, leaning over and pecking Megan on the cheek.

It was when she started to stand up that she heard the sound behind her.

She froze.

"Mommie!"

It was Megan's cry that sent her into action. Her head was halfway around when she felt a sudden, excruciating pain on the back of her neck. Then everything stopped.

There was only the dark . . . and silence.

Chapter Fifteen

"**W**hat do you mean you don't know where he is?"

Dexter Manly's secretary seemed taken aback at Cole's sharp tone and thunderous expression.

"Just...exactly that, sir," she stammered. "Mr. Manly told me he'd be out for the day and that's all I know."

Her face was colorless and her gray eyes were leery, but none of that registered on Cole. His frustration was fast reaching a feverish pitch. He glared at her while his mind was quick at work.

He had to find Dexter. Of all times for him to be out of pocket, he thought furiously. Before coming to his office, he'd gone by the house and his housekeeper had told him virtually the same thing. Then he'd asked for Eleanor. She'd proved to be a dead end, as well. According to the housekeeper, Eleanor had been out of town all week, visiting an ill sister.

How convenient, he'd told himself when he'd jumped back into his car. Not bothering to try to control his elevated blood pressure, he'd driven straight here, to Manly's office, only to fare no better.

He was become more agitated by the minute. He had to talk to Dexter today. Dexter would have to drop the case against Beth once and for all if he, Cole, made good his threat.

But there was Dexter's attorney, Charles Ransome! Why hadn't he thought of him before now? He would know what Manly's plans were. *Hell, Weston, you're really slipping!*

"Sir, if you'd like to sit down, I'm sure I can find someone to help you."

The sound of the soft voice brought Cole to a dead stop.

"Forget it!" he said, and stormed out the door.

A short time later found him more out of sorts than before. He'd run into another brick wall. Charles Ransome was also out of town. According to his secretary, he was attending a conference in Washington, D.C.

Cole was scowling when he yanked open his car door and sank down in the seat. He exhaled slowly while his head fell back against the headrest.

What now? Disappointment weighed heavily on his shoulders. He had been so in hopes of settling with Manly once and for all so he could propose to Beth that evening, finalize their plans for the future. He couldn't do that until he told her the truth—the whole bloody truth. No way was he going to take such an important step with his deceit hanging between them.

Don't panic, he told himself. *You have plenty of time.* Since she hadn't found out thus far, chances of her doing so before he could fess up were slim.

He didn't know how long he sat staring into space, but when he finally pulled away from the curb, the tightness in his gut had lessened considerably.

Beth stirred restlessly. She was dreaming. She was running but going nowhere. She knew she should try harder; it was a matter of life or death. Yet her legs refused to move. Behind her was a dark figure, no face, just a figure. It kept getting closer and closer. She tried to call for help, to reach for Megan, but her voice was frozen....

Suddenly she heard something, and was immediately jolted back to a fully conscious state. What had awakened her from her dream? Had it been her own whimper?

She moved her head, wanting to shake it, as if to clear it. But she couldn't. A sharp, blinding pain darted through her skull like an arrow. Whimpering again, she forced her eyes open, only to find herself facedown on the carpet. What on earth was she doing on the floor?

Suddenly it struck her. It was no dream. It was horrifyingly real. *The dark figure, everything!* Fear overcame her like a flash of light. *Megan!* Where was Megan?

Crawling to a sitting position, she swallowed against the blinding pain that again shot through her head, and forced herself to survey the room.

"Megan!" Had the words cleared her stiff lips?

She waited. Nothing. No Megan. The room was as silent as a tomb and just as empty.

Please let it be a dream, after all, she pleaded. But she knew it wasn't.

Beth wanted to move again, but couldn't. Her breathing was short and quivering. Hot bile had replaced the huge lump in her throat. Her baby! Someone had taken her baby! *No, not Megan! Not her! Please, not her!*

She had to get help. Cole! She had to call Cole. He would know what to do.

Then she heard something. Or was it someone? Had he come back for her? She heard the squeak of the front door. Her palms were icy cold. She held herself rigid; she could only sit there, waiting. In her state, she would never make it to the back door before she was overtaken. Fighting for control, she bit into her bottom lip and squeezed her eyelids shut.

Suddenly the door opened into the den. Beth looked up and saw the shadow of a man.

"Cole!" she cried, recognizing him immediately.

Seeing her huddled over like a question mark on the floor, he bounded across the room and hunkered down on one knee, drawing her trembling body into his arms.

"Shh, I'm here now." His eyes were wet, his chest heaving.

Beth grasped at him frantically. "Oh, Cole, Cole," she whispered. "Thank God! Thank God! Thank God!"

"Tell me!" he demanded urgently, stumbling to his feet, bringing her with him.

"It's . . . Megan," she gasped.

"What about Megan?"

"She's gone! Kidnapped! Someone...was in the house... waiting...knocked me out...took her."

Cole's face lost its color while his stomach exploded like a mine field. For a brief moment he thought he might pass out. He began to shake and beads of perspiration formed on his upper lip. His dark eyes were crazed as though he were chasing demons inside himself. He opened his mouth to speak, but no words came.

"Cole!" Her hand tightened on his arms; she was unable to comprehend the strange expression on his face.

He pushed her slightly away, and when he spoke, it seemed as if the words were dug out of him.

"I know who has Megan."

Everything went dead inside her; fear slammed against her ribs like a tidal wave.

"You...know? But I don't...understand. How could you...?" Beth was white as paper; her lips had a bluish tint and her eyes were wild.

"I'm responsible for this," he added dully. "It's all my fault."

His words hung in the air. She rotated slowly while trying to digest what he had just said. It couldn't be true, it *couldn't*. Beth felt panic rise in her throat.

"What did you say?"

Cole's face was set like stone. The stunned disbelief mirrored in her eyes and voice was ripping his guts to pieces. Her pain was his pain; her humiliation his humiliation.

The time was at hand. He had no choice now but to tell her the truth, the whole ugly truth.

Instead he longed to hold her, to comfort her, to assure her that nothing would happen to Megan. But fear had him in its clutches and wouldn't let go.

Avoiding her eyes, he forced himself to speak.

"Dexter Manly hired me to try to prove you an unfit mother for his granddaughter so that he could get custody of her." He paused. "I'm a private detective." Ignoring her stifled cry, he rushed on, "But God, Beth, you've got to believe me when I swear I had no intention of going through with it. There was no way in hell I was going to let Manly take Megan away from you. I . . ."

That was when she snapped.

"You *bastard*!" she shrieked, suddenly charging toward him. When he shot out his arms to grab her, she pulled up short, recoiling as though she couldn't bear for him to touch her.

Her next words bore this out. "Don't you dare touch me!" she screamed.

Cole reeled against her harsh words, as though she'd actually struck him. "Please . . . Beth . . . oh, God . . . you've got to believe me when I tell you that I never would've let it go that far." He was pleading now. "I . . . I love you and Megan more than life itself."

She didn't say a word, merely continued to stare at him. Pain laced with contempt slowly spread across her face.

He knew then, in that instant, that as sure as God made little green apples, she would never in a million years forgive him, no matter what he said. He had gambled and lost.

Suddenly she found her voice. "Love!" she cried. "You don't know the meaning of the word." Tears were flowing steadily down her cheeks as she glowered at him, thinking, *I was right. I never really knew him.* "How . . . could you?" she added on a high cracked note, feeling not only a fool, but cruelly betrayed, as well. *Damn him to hell!*

There was no antidote for the pain that ripped through her at that moment.

Cole took a step toward her, his face contorted in agony. He felt sick with tension. "Please . . . Beth, don't shut me out. Let me help you. Together we'll get Megan back unharmed. I promise you."

"No! Don't come near me!" Backing up and turning away, she pulled herself together and began to speak in a toneless voice that betrayed the pitiful hold she was keeping over her terror and distress.

"Go away. I don't want to see you again."

When she uttered those words, she might as well have driven steel spikes through Cole's heart. *If I stand here long enough maybe I'll bleed to death, and then it'll all be over.*

When he failed to move, she whispered again, "Go away."

Somehow Cole managed to uproot himself and trudge heavily to the door. Once there, he paused and faced Beth's rigid back.

"I'm leaving." There was no emotion in his voice; it sounded mechanical. "But I'll come back, and when I do, I'll have Megan with me."

She turned to face him. "I don't want your help. Ever. Haven't you done enough already?"

There was an instant of frozen time when he could do nothing. Then slowly he walked to the door, his shoulders slumped in defeat.

By the time he got into the car, he was shaking like a leaf in a gale. He clutched the car keys so tightly in his palm that he drew blood. For perhaps a minute after that, he was unable to get the key in the ignition.

He was alone again. Exactly as he had started. But this time there was a mark, a mark she etched indelibly on his heart. To lose her now was unbearable. He already felt empty.

Finally he got the car mobile, his shaking having turned into a hard, cold anger. Anger against the one person responsible for this latest nightmare.

Dexter Manly.

He had to move—and fast. Cole thrust the car into reverse, shot back out of the driveway, then threw the gear into drive; the tires screeched when he accelerated. As he neared a stop sign, he suddenly realized he was traveling too fast, and ground down on the brakes while sharply yanking the steering wheel to his left. Like an out-of-control race car, the rear of the Lincoln swung into the next lane. Miraculously, and only through his competent handling of the situation, did he miss careening into the car beside him.

But he scarcely noticed. His mind was in overdrive, planning how he would deal with Manly.

When he tromped down on the brakes a short time later in the Manlys' circular driveway, he tore out of the car and raced up the steps. Not bothering to announce his presence, he shoved open the door and barreled across the threshold. A highly indignant housekeeper met him in the entry hall, sparks flying from her eyes.

"Sir... Mr. Weston... wait just one second!" she spluttered indignantly, placing her more than ample figure squarely in front of him, her hands on her waist. "Just what do you think you're doing?"

Silently and with ease, Cole skirted around her, never missing a stride.

"Well, I've never..." she began, but her words were lost on Cole as he forged his way down the hall and into the den.

Dexter was alone, relaxing in his recliner, a paper spread across his lap.

"What the hell!" he growled, looking up and seeing Cole's menacing figure looming over him.

"Get up."

"What?"

"You heard me, you bastard, get up!"

Manly's mouth gaped as he stumbled to his feet and backed away.

Cole edged toward him, all the while staring him down. "If you don't tell me right this second where Megan Loring is, I'll put you in two weeks of traction. Believe me, that's no idle threat."

Manly was visibly shaking now, but his voice had lost none of its strength. "Are you crazy?"

"Now, Dexter, now!"

"You don't scare me, Weston. I'm not telling you a thing."

Cole hit him with a left hook that tilted his chin back, and followed with a right cross that knocked him against the wall. When Manly got his eyes focused, Cole jerked him up by his shirt and whispered into his terror-filled face, "If you don't come clean and tell me real quick which one of your horse's asses has Megan and where, I'm going to make a permanent hole in the middle of your face. I'm through talking."

"I don't know what you're—"

Cole drew back his hand and doubled his fist. "Don't say I didn't warn you."

"Wait! Don't!" Manly's face started to crumple like a used napkin. "I'll... tell you where she is."

"I think you made a wise decision," Cole said, the smoldering fury in his eyes overriding his calm voice. "Now suppose you start at the beginning."

Fifteen minutes later, Cole was once again behind the wheel of his car. However, before he even thought about cranking it, he reached over and unlocked the glove compartment.

When his hand closed around the hard metal object, there was a satanical gleam in his eyes. He laid it down beside him and patted it.

He had a score to settle and the .38 Special was his calling card.

Beth was out of her mind with grief and worry. There had been no word from the police concerning Megan's whereabouts and she didn't know how much longer she could endure the agony of not knowing. Just the thought of her precious baby in the hands of a stranger made her blood curdle. If anything happened to her...

The moment Cole had walked out of the house, she had run to the telephone and called Lieutenant Bennett. Luckily he'd been at the station, and shortly thereafter he and another officer had come to the house.

Beth had told them everything, watching the shock appear on Bennett's face when the name Dexter Manly had crossed her lips. After giving the house a thorough going-over, they had left. Almost immediately, having seen the police car, Mattie Engles had come over, concerned, wanting to know what had happened.

Basking between crying jags in the warmth of Mattie's strong arms, Beth had repeated the whole story. Mattie had stayed with her the entire night, offering what comfort she could. Neither one had slept a wink.

Now, however, Mattie was gone, and Beth was again pacing the floor, berating herself with every step. Why hadn't she seen it coming? Why hadn't she realized something was amiss when Dexter Manly had been so quiet? Why hadn't Giles sensed he was up to something? Overconfidence. In a nutshell. Overconfidence on both their parts. But in the end it was Megan who was paying.

Why doesn't the lieutenant call? she screamed silently. It had been over twelve hours since Megan's disappearance. Twelve long torturous hours. She had cried until there were no more tears left; her eyes were almost swollen shut and her hair hung in damp strands about her face.

But it hadn't helped. Nothing helped. Nothing would, she knew, except a call from the police saying they had found Megan.

"Please, please call," she whispered aloud, pausing at the window and looking out at the sun peeping through the clouds. How much longer could she go on like this? she wondered, closing her eyes and leaning her head against the cool window, a fresh onslaught of tears cascading down her face.

Later she had no idea what made her twist her head, but when she opened her eyes, the side of Cole's house filled her vision. Even through the tears she could see it plainly.

Cole. She hadn't dared let herself think about him and his betrayal; the pain was too deep, too severe. She'd kept thoughts of him in the dark recesses of her mind. But now, while her eyes were glued to his house, the blood in her veins seemed to freeze and something clicked inside her head. *If she wanted Megan back, she would have to depend on Cole.*

The truth was that the wheels of justice moved much too slowly for her. She knew they were doing their best, but in this case their best was not good enough.

Cole knew Dexter Manly. Cole was a private detective. Cole could work, if need be, outside the law. Cole was mean when crossed. More important than any of those, Cole adored Megan and would never knowingly let any harm come to her.

Yes, Cole was the answer. She knew that now. Had known it all along, only wouldn't admit it. How ironic, she thought, that when she thought she'd never need him again, she needed him the most. Was it too late? Had Cole taken her at her word and stayed out of it? Would her pride and heartache cost her her child's safety?

Everyone made mistakes, she told herself. No one was perfect, least of all her. She had known in her heart that all was not right with Cole, but she hadn't wanted to face the truth, afraid it would shatter her newfound happiness. It had been easier just to let it slide.

No longer. She had no choice but to take the initiative, to beg if necessary. For the first time, it dawned on her that the fear of losing her and Megan was what had kept Cole quiet.

She felt she had resolved something deep inside herself. *If only I'm not too late.*

She crossed the room and grabbed her purse and then her windbreaker. She had to find Cole. Now. Time was precious; she couldn't afford to waste another moment.

She had just reached the door, when the telephone jangled behind her.

"Damn!" she muttered, frustrated that she was stalled, yet hopeful that it was news of Megan. Whirling around, she dashed to the phone.

"Yes!" she gasped.

"Mrs. Loring, Lieutenant Bennett."

Her heart was in her mouth. "Yes?"

"Cole Weston has located your daughter. I'm on my way."

"Where? Tell me where!"

"I'll send an officer for you."

"I'll be waiting. Please . . . hurry."

Cole saw the lieutenant when he got of out his patrol car. He strode toward him.

"What d'you have?" Bennett asked, shifting a wad of tobacco from one side of his mouth to the other.

A grim-faced Cole cocked his head in the direction of a small cabin that was sitting back in a clearing just off the highway.

"They're in there," he said.

Following Manly's directions to the letter, Cole had easily spotted the hideaway. He'd hidden his car in the underbrush across the highway, not taking a chance on being spotted. Then he'd made his way cautiously through the woods, stopping several yards from the cabin. Immediately he'd begun to figure out the best way to get inside and get Megan.

The more he'd thought about it, the more his palms had sweated. What if he bungled the job? What if he couldn't subdue the slime ball without Megan getting hurt? Those questions and others had passed through his mind, and in the end he'd decided he couldn't take the chance. He'd never felt so frustrated in his life and he'd had to physically and mentally restrain himself from taking any action. Fear for Megan's safety, however, had won out, and using his car phone, he'd called Lieutenant Bennett.

Now as Cole faced Bennett, murder was in his eyes. "There's only one," he said. "Should be easy to take him out."

"I'm not sure," Bennett said. "We have to think of the child."

"Dammit, Bennett," Cold said harshly, "what do you take me for, some idiotic amateur? The safety of the child is *everything*."

Cole meant every word he said. It was also his only chance to partially redeem himself. Not just for Beth, either—it was a foregone conclusion that she was lost to him—but for himself. He wouldn't want to live if anything happened to Megan.

"I suppose you have a plan in mind," Bennett drawled.

"You're right I do and I think it'll work without a hitch, too." He paused and moved closer. "I suggest that you talk to him, keep him occupied while I go in through the back door."

Bennett lifted his cap and scratched his head. "Sounds all right, but I figure one of my men should be the one who goes in from behind."

Cole's mouth turned down at the corners and his eyes grew cold. "The only way you're going to keep me from going in that house is to shoot me on the spot."

Bennett's eyes fell under Cole's hostile gaze. "Okay, Weston," he said, "but you sure as hell better know what you're doing."

Cole was in the process of checking his gun when he heard footsteps. He looked up and saw Beth, accompanied by an officer, emerge from the woods.

She halted in her tracks a few yards from him, her gaze dipping first to the gun and then back up his face.

"Cole?" she breathed.

"I'm going in after her," he said, watching as the rest of the color left her face.

After a moment, he looked away and jammed the gun down into his holster.

"Please...bring my baby back," she whispered. "And...be careful."

Cole dared not look at her. Instead he turned and fled, sure-footed, through the woods.

Afterward Cole was still amazed at how easy it had been.

While the police talked to the goon, letting him know he was surrounded, Cole, as planned, made his way up to the windows in the rear of the house. He peered inside, and when he saw that Megan was on a cot in the small bedroom and the man was in the front room, Cole acted.

He kicked in the back door and hurled himself to the floor, all the while pointing his gun at the wild-eyed young man.

"Move and you're dead," he said with deadly calm.

The greasy-haired man trembled in his boots. "Hey, dude, don't shoot, don't shoot!"

Once Cole had him cuffed, he tore down the short hall and flung open the door to the room where Megan was. Megan, sitting in the middle of the cot, crimson cheeked, curls in sad disorder, big tears trickling down her cheeks, flung out her arms and cried.

As Cole caught her to his heart, she began to sob in earnest, lovely, relieved, luxurious sobs, as she buried her face in his neck and clung to him with loving hot hands.

Tears, irrepressible, rose in Cole's eyes. "Oh, baby, my sweetheart."

"Cole," Megan wept. "Cole. Mommie?"

"Mommie is right outside, darling."

Cole lost no time in lifting the precious child in his arms and carrying her outside.

Jubilant hollers and whistles greeted them from a distance as he headed straight toward Beth and put Megan into her arms.

"Megan—Megan!" Beth's head was bowed over the little form and Cole saw that she was crying.

"She's all right, Beth, no harm done."

Beth continued to cling to her daughter, rocking her in her arms.

Cole stood there, unable to move. He wanted to put his arms around the both of them, squeeze them close, but he dared not. Instead he chose to speak, knowing if he didn't, he might not get another chance.

The words, as if they had a will of their own, tumbled from his lips. "I . . . love you, Beth, and no matter how much I want to, I can't change what happened or my part in it. I'd give anything if I could. I just want you to know that I would have died before I'd let anything happen to Megan. I love her . . . as if she were my own."

He waited, his face pale and drawn as if he were in pain from some persistent internal injury. Was it possible that she could find it in her heart to forgive him? Or was he asking too much?

She didn't speak, didn't move. He groaned silently, feeling as if some vital fluid were leaking out of him.

It was final. He had truly lost her. He felt his knees weaken and his head grow light; something had broken apart inside him. He had to force himself to turn and put one foot before the other.

He had taken only three steps when he heard her whisper his name; the tiny sound was barely audible over the noise of the woods.

Like a dying man granted a reprieve, he spun around. It was a moment of pure joy.

"You know what's so incredible about all this," she said, "is that when I thought I hated you, I loved you the most. And nothing you or I could ever say or do would change that." She smiled through her tears. "So if you still want me . . . and Megan, we're all yours."

This was so completely unexpected that Cole had to think for a moment before he could take it in. He wanted to hold her in his arms and never let her go. But still he hesitated. "You mean you can forgive me?"

He heard the sob catch in her throat before she walked into his arms. "Oh, my darling, don't you know there's nothing to forgive?"

Epilogue

What was wrong? His chest felt heavy, restrained. Was he having another nightmare? He wanted to panic, feeling as if something wet and sticky were over his mouth. He began clawing for his next breath, only to suddenly hear a hyper giggle.

He fought to open his eyes, to get his bearings. Megan was sitting across him, her smile telling him that she was having the time of her life.

"Good morning, love," Beth whispered.

He shook his head as if to clear it, then turned his head to see her regarding him with warm amusement. She was watching Megan, enthralled, put her small hand on the powerful chest and tentatively stroke the mat of hair.

"Mommie don't got this," Megan pointed out with great interest.

"Mommie doesn't have this," Beth corrected automatically before winking at Cole. "She's all yours," she added, backing away and pulling the sheet up to her shoulders.

"You minx," Cole teased, kissing Megan and then lifting her to her feet beside the bed.

"Daddy, play wiff me some more," Megan pleaded.

Seeing Cole weakening under her daughter's soft voice and innocent eyes, Beth cut it, "Not now, sweetheart. It's not long until Papa Manly will be picking you up."

Megan danced a gig. "Daddy come, too."

Beth laughed. "Not this time. Just you and Papa and Granny Eleanor. Before I help you dress, though, Mommie wants you to pick up the new blocks Daddy bought you that you left scattered all over your room."

"Daddy help?"

Cole chuckled and threw Beth a look. "This kid of ours sure is some con artist."

"Pooh, it's you she can wrap around her little finger."

Cole chuckled and turned back to the child. "Not this time, moppet. Give Daddy a kiss and run do what Mommie told you to."

The child flung her arms around Cole's neck, and after giving him a loud smack on the cheek, she flittered away.

They waited until she was out of the room, the door closed behind her, before facing each other.

"Good morning, Mrs. Weston."

"And the top of the morning to you, Mr. Weston."

Cole's eyes were warm. "I still can't believe we're married, that I'm part of a real family."

"Want me to pinch you to prove it?"

"You might have to," he whispered, his face suddenly serious.

Beth's face sobered to match his. "I know what you mean," she said softly, "especially after what we went through."

"That's one of the reasons I love you so much," he said with tenderness. "I don't know of another soul who would have dropped charges against Dexter, much less let him see Megan." He watched her closely, while a lone finger traced a line across a bare, creamy shoulder.

Her eyes darkened. "I...just couldn't stand to see any more suffering. You and I...Megan, we had so much, and they...had so little and were so broken...." She paused and, capturing his roving hand in hers, smiled sweetly. "Anyhow, it was easy with your love to make me strong."

Two days after Megan's kidnapping, they had married. Then with Cole beside her, she had confronted Dexter, who was out of jail on bond, along with Eleanor. Dexter had immediately broken down and begged Beth to forgive him, telling her that he'd gone temporarily insane and that he never meant any harm to come to Megan, that he'd just wanted to have her with him for a while.

It was after that emotional scene that Beth had decided not to testify against Dexter at his hearing. Because of her leniency, he got off with probation. It was then that she let him become a part of Megan's life.

That had been six months ago now and she had not once regretted that decision. Every time she saw the three of them together it brought tears to her eyes. They doted on the child and she on them.

"Hey, I'm jealous."

Cole's husky voice startled her out of her reverie. "What did you say?" she asked sweetly.

His finger began wandering again. "I said I'm jealous."

"Why?"

"Because I don't have your attention."

She smiled and grabbed a handful of his chest hair. "Greed doesn't become you."

"Are you complaining?"

"Me? Complain?" Her eyes were sparkling. "Never."

His eyes seemed to devour her for a moment, and then once again his voice dropped the teasing note. "You know we've got two wonderful things to celebrate this week, don't you?"

"How could I forget," she said. "Megan becomes legally yours tomorrow and—"

"And my office officially opens here with me behind its desk."

"Oh, Cole," she cried, moving closer to him, the sheet slipping from her breasts, exposing their fullness to his eyes. He swallowed and turned away. "Are you sure that's what you want? I mean, you're so used to being in the field, where the action is."

"Shh, don't say it. Don't even think it," he said. "That was my past. You're my present. I don't want to be out of your sight any more than I have to. This way we'll be a normal family, both going to work and then coming home to each other and our child . . . and maybe someday our children," he added eagerly.

"Oh, Cole, I love you," she whispered, and kissed him, a long, hot kiss.

They lay together for a while, kissing and touching. Then she draped one leg across his hips and they began to make love languorously, without speaking.

Later she rolled on top of him, letting her full weight rest on his body. Skin to skin. He wrapped his arms around her small waist and hugged her as he thrust deep inside her. They moved in perfect harmony, their soft, low-pitched moans filling the silence.

She didn't move. She stayed on top of him. He stroked her hair. After a while she stirred and propped her elbows on his chest, staring down at him.

"Will I ever be as happy as I am this minute?" she murmured, loving him.

"Oh, my love, don't you know?" he said gently. "Our happiness is just beginning."

* * * * *

A Note from Annette Broadrick

Dear Reader,

I'm so pleased that *Momentary Marriage* has been brought back by request, because it has one of my favorite characters, Jordan Trent. Agents have always been a special kind of hero to me, and Jordan epitomizes what I like best—the tough guy who works hard to hide his vulnerabilities. Of course, he meets his match in this book, causing him to risk his heart *and* his life.

I wanted this story to reflect how some of us lock our hearts away, refusing to give them the freedom to love, in the same way that Eastern European countries were at one time locked away so that the inhabitants found it difficult to experience other cultures.

Just as all of Europe is now expanding and growing, so, I hope, is each reader as she identifies with the fears that my characters experience. The transforming power of love can heal entire countries, as well as individual hearts.

My wish is that this story might touch your heart and help in whatever healing process you might need.

With best wishes and
fondest regards,

Annette Broadrick

MOMENTARY MARRIAGE

Annette Broadrick

This book is dedicated to the many friends I've made
at the Lake of the Ozarks. You have welcomed me
into your homes and hearts as though I were
part of the family.

Thank you, dear friends. You are part
of my heart, also.

One

As he rapidly strode down the long hallway to Mallory's office, Jordan Trent watched, with a certain amount of grim humor, a couple of staff members as they scattered before him like quail in the presence of a hunting dog. Mallory had gone too far this time. Jordan intended to tell him exactly what he thought of him and his damned emergencies. Jordan was sick to death of the constant pressure and unremitting tension of his job. He had needed every minute of his vacation, something that Mallory didn't seem to understand.

How dare Mallory pull this latest stunt! Jordan fully intended that someone would pay for this. From the reactions of those with whom he'd come into contact since he'd arrived at the office, it was obvious to Jordan that his mood had communicated itself to those around him.

He barely slowed his pace when he reached the correct office. Grabbing the knob of the unmarked door, Jordan thrust the door open and walked in without bothering to knock. James Mallory glanced up without surprise from the papers he was holding. In fact, Mallory's expression showed no emotion at all.

Jordan hadn't expected anything else.

Mallory never gave his thoughts away and as far as Jordan could prove, Mallory didn't possess any emotions.

Without waiting for an invitation, Jordan sank into the well-padded chair in front of the scarred desk and said, "This had better be good," in a menacing tone.

Mallory leaned back in his chair and met the implacable gaze of the man across the desk from him. "So how was your vacation, J.D.?"

"Funny you should ask. What the hell was so all-fired important that it couldn't have waited another week?"

Mallory studied the younger man in silence for a few minutes. "Somehow I thought having time off would help to sweeten your disposition." He shrugged. "I can't really expect to be right a hundred percent of the time, I suppose."

"I don't need your harassment, Mallory. Why did you level your artillery at me?"

Mallory raised his bushy brows slightly. "Artillery?"

"You know damned well what I mean. Telling the local police I was wanted back in the States!"

"You are," Mallory responded mildly.

"Your implication was that I am highly dangerous."

"You are," he added with a nod.

"And that I am wanted by the government...'you are,'" he mimicked along with Mallory as the other man agreed with the statement. "Dammit, Mallory! Your so-called sense of humor definitely needs an adjustment or two."

"Are you saying I ruined your image on, uh—what's the name of that island you were visiting?"

"It doesn't matter. I suddenly found myself persona non grata and was asked to leave. Immediately."

Mallory shrugged. "You ignored my messages."

"Why shouldn't I have? This was my first vacation in five years. Five years, Mallory. I know damned well I'm not the only operative you've got working for you. So why me?"

"I need your special skills on this one."

"What special skills? My rare ability to keep myself from getting killed?"

Mallory nodded. "There is that. Plus you have the unusual ability of always getting what you're after. We need that little extra boost on this one, I'm afraid."

"I'm touched, Mallory. I really am. How long have I worked for you now? Eight—ten years? And I do believe I've just heard the first compliment you've ever paid—to me or to anyone. Do you suppose you could repeat it for taping? You know, as a little token to remind me of you in the unlikely event I should ever allow your presence to slip from my mind."

Mallory leaned back in his chair and put his feet up on the desk. He stared at the younger man for a moment with pursed lips. "Of course," he admitted wryly, "you do have a way of ignoring all the procedural guidelines that have been handed down from above, which has created something of a furor from time to time."

"So fire me," Jordan suggested in a hard tone.

"You're too eager," Mallory pointed out quietly.

"You're right about that. I'm too old for this kind of life, Mallory. I've been telling you that for the past two years."

"So you have. But you don't really mean it and we both know it. You thrive on living on the edge, surviving by your wits and instincts." He paused and lit a cigarette. "Face it, J.D.," he said, exhaling a lungful of smoke, "You'd be bored with any other life."

Jordan waved the smoke away in disgust. "Thank you, Dr. Mallory. And how much do I owe you for this vocational counseling session?"

Mallory allowed himself a small smile. "Just one of the fringe benefits around here. I don't even require a fee."

"Good thing. Do you have any idea what my plane fare to get halfway around the world from you set me back? And it still wasn't far enough!"

"I'll see that you're reimbursed."

Mallory's quiet tone caused Jordan to study him for a moment in silence. "This deal must really be important," Jordan finally said. "I've never seen you willing to part with any cash before."

Mallory met his gaze with an implacable expression. "I really need you on this one."

"Which one is that—?"

"Does the name Trevor Monroe mean anything to you?"

"Of course. He's the U.S. senator from Virginia."

"And heads up the Senate Overseas Intelligence Committee."

"Are we being investigated?" Jordan asked facetiously. "Again?"

"No. We've been given permission to pull out all the stops on this one."

"I'm afraid to even ask," Jordan said slowly. He hadn't heard that tone of voice from Mallory before. Whatever it was that was in the works, it was serious.

"The senator's wife has been having some health problems. He decided to take her to see a specialist in Vienna. Very few people knew about this trip, for obvious reasons. The senator is in a very sensitive position with our government."

"So what does he want—surveillance? A guard? Should I pretend to be his wife's brother?"

"Too bad we didn't think of that earlier. You see, Frances Monroe disappeared two days ago while en route to the doctor's clinic for tests."

Jordan immediately understood the implications: holding a member of a government official's family automatically insured that official's full cooperation.

"Do they have any idea who did it?"

"None. We've kept it quiet and no one has come forward claiming responsibility."

"Where's the leak in security?"

Mallory realized that Jordan had already dismissed his ire at his forced return. Jordan recognized that the government had a serious problem that could reach catastrophic proportions if not handled properly.

"We're working on it. In the meantime, it's an all-out hunt to find Mrs. Monroe."

"Where do I come in?"

"We think she was taken behind the iron curtain—either into Czechoslovakia or Hungary. You know that area better than anyone we have and you've got contacts there. We're counting on you to get her out."

"You never ask for much, do you, Mallory?" Jordan asked, disgust evident in his tone. He shook his head and stretched his legs out in front of him, crossing them at the ankles.

"I know you prefer to work alone—" Mallory began.

"*Insist* on working alone," Jordan inserted smoothly, studying the shine of his shoes with considerable interest.

"Yes. Well, whatever. This is going to take two of you."

Jordan straightened slightly, his gaze lifting slowly until it met Mallory's eyes. "No exceptions, Mallory."

"I can understand your feelings, J.D. Particularly after what happened in Istanbul last year."

"My so-called backup almost got me killed."

"An unfortunate incident."

"It would have been even more unfortunate...at least to me...if he'd succeeded."

"You have no need to worry about loyalty this time. Your assistant can be counted on to be there for you."

"Thanks, but I'm not interested." Jordan kept his eyes trained on the man who was nominally his boss, wishing he could gain some insight into the man's thinking processes.

After the incident in Istanbul, Jordan had tried to get Mallory to fire him—right after Mallory had tossed Jordan's written resignation into the wastebasket with no more than a glance.

At that meeting, Jordan had learned a great deal about the agency for which he worked. His was a lifetime job. Unfortunately, the statistics for his line of work didn't give him too many years to worry about.

"Why don't you let me catch a flight to Vienna this evening, Mallory, and we'll see what I can come up with? If I need reinforcement, believe me, I'll contact you immediately."

"It isn't that simple."

"I never pretended it would be simple. But if you want me to meet with my contacts, I need to do it alone."

"That's all right, she won't be—"

"She? What are you talking about, *she*, Mallory? We don't have any female operatives."

"Lauren isn't exactly an operative, although she does work in one of the departments here."

Jordan stood and began to pace back and forth between the desk and the window. "Are you out of your mind, Mallory? You expect me to take an amateur with me?"

"Lauren is in our cryptology department. She's a very bright lady—a mathematical whiz that we recruited right out of college. She's also multilingual."

Jordan, his hands on his hips, stopped pacing and glared at Mallory. "I don't care if she pole vaults, sings "God Bless America" while standing on her head and placed in the Olympics, I don't want her."

"You have no choice. The senator insists we have a woman there for his wife. He feels his wife will need that added emotional support."

Jordan began pacing again. "I don't believe this. I simply don't believe it. You want me to perform a damn miracle and now you throw in a sizable handicap and tell me I have no choice."

Mallory didn't look at Jordan. Instead he leaned over and punched a button on his phone. When a disembodied voice answered, he said, "Please ask Ms. Mackenzie to come in." He brought his feet down from the desk and folded his hands in front of him.

"Why would an untrained woman want to get involved in this situation, Mallory? We don't have any idea what we're going to find over there. Just give me a chance to check things out—"

"We don't have time," Mallory stated in a firm tone. "You and Lauren are booked on an evening flight. Her passport states that she is your wife."

Jordan felt as though he'd either lost his hearing or his sanity. He wasn't sure which loss would be easier to accept. "My wife?" he repeated, almost in a whisper.

Mallory nodded. "There're fewer complications that way."

Jordan walked over to the window and adjusted the blind so that he could peer out. Yes, the familiar landscape reassured him that most of his senses were still functioning adequately. He glanced over his shoulder. "I don't know the first thing about wives or having one. I certainly don't see how having a strange woman along as a wife would make things less complicated."

"Because you're going to have to spend all your time together, except when you need to reach your contacts. Then Lauren will be the typical American wife who enjoys shopping while her husband is busy with business."

"How is it you make your explanations sound so reasonable when I know that the whole scheme is totally insane?"

There was a knock on the door. Instead of answering Jordan, Mallory raised his voice slightly and said, "Come in."

Jordan watched from his position by the window as a young woman opened the door and walked into the room. Then he realized the whole thing must be a joke. She looked like a caricature of a prim, brainy, introverted and totally repressed professional woman. No one dressed that way any more.

Granted Jordan didn't know all that much about women's styles, either in hairdos or business suits, but this woman gave the impression that she was interested in neither. She wore a two-piece suit that effectively concealed her figure. She could be Twiggy-thin or in the late stages of a pregnancy, for all he could tell by the clothes she wore. Her hair was haphazardly pulled to the nape of her neck in a loose coil. Several wisps had come loose and fell in front of her ears and along her neck.

The tortoiseshell glasses and the low-heeled sensible shoes reminded Jordan of *Marian the Librarian*, a character from a play he'd seen in college.

Mallory's sense of humor had always been a little bizarre, but Jordan thought he'd carried the joke to an extreme this time, seemingly insensitive to this woman's feelings.

Jordan watched as she walked over to Mallory's desk without glancing toward the window. She spoke to Mallory in a low well-modulated voice.

"You wished to see me, Mr. Mallory?"

"Yes, Lauren. Please have a seat." He nodded to one of the chairs across from him. "I want you to meet Jordan Trent. As I've previously explained, he's the man you'll be working with."

Jordan watched as the woman slowly turned her head and looked at him. She did not change her expression. "Mr. Trent," she murmured, nodding her head toward him. Then she sat down, crossed her legs and returned her gaze to Mallory.

Jordan had never felt quite so dismissed in his life and he found the sensation somewhat unsettling. She certainly hadn't seemed impressed with the man who supposedly was going to play an important role in her life for the next few days.

Not that he could take exception to her behavior. He certainly wasn't the embodiment of any woman's secret fantasies. He faced himself daily in the mirror and knew that his harsh features, stern expression and height were more intimidating than reassuring.

"Now that you two have had an opportunity to meet," Mallory blandly stated, "I'd like to go over our plans with you."

Jordan reluctantly returned to the chair he'd occupied earlier and sat down, which placed him next to Lauren Mackenzie.

She glanced at him briefly and gave him a tentative smile. If he hadn't been watching her so closely, he would have missed it. A sudden thought flashed across his mind. *She's shy!* Was that why she wore such an effective camouflage, or had she in fact donned it for his benefit? Whatever the reason, she certainly made a statement.

"Now, then," Mallory began, glancing down at a file in front of him. "Lauren fits the same general description as Mrs. Monroe. As soon as we're through here she's going to have her hair restyled and lightened in order to more closely resemble Mrs. Monroe."

"Why?" Jordan demanded, not liking the sudden suspicion that had crossed his mind.

"Because, if you succeed in finding Mrs. Monroe in either Hungary or Czechoslovakia, she can leave the country using Lauren's passport."

"You're making a few assumptions, aren't you, Mallory?" Jordan asked. "We have no idea where we're going to find Mrs. Monroe, or what her physical condition will be." He glanced around at Lauren. "Why would you agree to voluntarily stay behind in a potentially explosive situation?"

Lauren studied the irascible man beside her with something bordering on dismay. He was nothing like the person she had pictured when Mallory had first discussed the matter with her.

Granted she rarely saw the men who reported to Mallory. She had assumed that the people working covert operations would be uniformly nondescript so that they could blend into their surroundings when necessary. There was no way this man could go anywhere unnoticed; she was confident of that.

He was several inches over six feet, with black, piercing eyes that seemed to stare a hole through her. His crisply curling hair glinted like a raven's wing in the light from the window. High cheekbones and a strong jawline completed the picture of a man no one in his right mind would choose to tangle with. He certainly wasn't the type of man who appealed to her at all.

Not that her personal preference had anything to do with the situation.

"I was told they needed someone of my general description. I was willing to help," she explained quietly.

Jordan shook his head. "You have no idea what you're getting into."

"Perhaps not. I suppose you'll have to explain it all to me as we go."

Was that sarcasm he heard in her quiet voice? He studied her more closely. Her calm, gray-eyed gaze met his without blinking.

"Do you have to wear those glasses?" Jordan asked abruptly. He was pleased to see that he had caught her off guard with his remark, then felt ashamed of himself for his reaction.

"Only for close work, Mr. Trent. However, much of what I do is close work."

"Well, you won't be doing any 'close' work on this trip. That should relieve your mind," he replied, his glance lazily going over her.

Lauren could feel the heat of temper filling her and, not for the first time, she wished that she had not inherited the temperament that seemed to plague red-haired people. His innuendo had been unnecessary and unjust. Did he think she had volunteered for the sake of spending time with him as his wife?

She reached up and pulled her glasses off. After methodically searching for the carrying case in her handbag, she placed the glasses in the case, the case in her purse, then looked at him again. "Is that better?"

Jordan found himself at a loss for words for a moment. Without the bulky frame of the glasses, he could see the beauty of her eyes. They were large and wide-set, surrounded with a dark fringe of lashes that gave her gaze a mysterious depth. Her eyes continued to meet his without flinching. He coughed and nodded. "Uh, yes. I was just wondering. I mean..." He let the words trail away uncertainly. Where had he ever gotten the idea this woman was shy? From the look in her eyes and the soft flush in her cheeks, Jordan had the distinct impression he was not on her list of favorite people.

"Do you have any questions about all of this, J.D.?" Mallory asked.

"Questions, no. However, I have several objections." He turned in his chair so that he was facing Lauren more fully. "I don't have anything against you personally and I'm certainly not trying to discriminate because of your gender. But I am concerned about taking someone into the field with me who has no training. It's too dangerous. I don't need the extra worry." He turned back to Mallory. "Can't you appease the senator some way and give me a chance to see what I can do on my own?"

"No."

The immediate answer and the implacability of the tone put an end to that particular topic. After several moments of silence, Mallory said, "Anything else?"

Jordan prided himself on thinking fast on his feet and on his ability for getting himself out of tight situations. However, at that moment, he could see no way out of his dilemma. In his frustration, he muttered, "I don't have a clue how to pretend to be a husband."

Lauren kept her expression carefully noncommittal, although she could not prevent herself from softly biting down on her bottom lip to prevent a smile.

"I'm afraid we don't have time to give you a crash course in matrimony, J.D.," Mallory said with a grin.

"It isn't funny."

"I agree. This is deadly serious. All of it. However, I know you can handle it or I wouldn't have insisted on using you on this one." Mallory stood up, a clear indication that he considered the matter closed. "Do what you always do so well, J.D. Improvise."

Two

Two

Improvise, hell! Jordan thought furiously while packing for the trip a few hours later. He should have refused flat out. The whole idea was totally ridiculous. What did Mallory think he was pulling? Trying to do a little matchmaking? Maybe he hoped to find a man for his little cryptographer.

Well, it sure as hell wasn't going to be Jordan Trent. He was a loner and always had been. His life-style suited him perfectly. Mallory had been right about that—Jordan enjoyed what he did to make a living. He liked never knowing where he'd be the next week. He preferred the excitement and danger of his present life-style to the monotony of a nine-to-five existence, a house in the suburbs, a wife and children.

So why was he upset? This was going to be a tough assignment but he already knew several people who might be able to shed some light on the mysterious disappearance of Mrs. Monroe.

Jordan forced himself to face what was really eating at him. He didn't relate well to other people. He never had. Consequently, he'd never shared long periods of time with another person, male or female. The pattern of his existence had been set early in his life.

Jordan had been eight when his mother had died of pneumonia. His grandmother, herself in ill health, had contacted his father, Morgan Trent, in Chicago and informed him for the first time of the existence of his son.

To give the man credit, Morgan Trent immediately flew to the small Southern California town where Jordan had been born and lived. There had never been a question about Jordan's paternity. At eight, Jordan hadn't understood why this stranger had appeared one day, packed all of his belongings and taken him away from everything and everyone Jordan had known.

Morgan had explained that he was Jordan's father, but it hadn't really mattered to Jordan. He had gotten along without a father for eight years. Why did he need one now? Jordan could look back later from the vantage point of his thirty-five years and better appreciate what his father had tried to do for him.

Jordan hadn't been an easy child to get to know. An only child, he'd grown up learning how to keep himself busy without needing other people. His mother had worked long hours and he'd seen very little of her. His grandmother had been there to look after him, but she had never kept very close watch over where he went and how long he was gone.

So Jordan resented the sudden restrictions placed on him by his newly acquired father and stepmother. He didn't like their rules, their big home, and the fact that everything about their life was so formal.

He'd never seen the two of them share any affection or camaraderie. There was no spontaneity in the home, just stilted efforts at conversation.

Jordan willingly escaped by going away to school. He'd continued to be a loner there as well. His life-style had made him excellent recruiting material by the time he graduated from college.

With no close ties, he could easily disappear for weeks at a time without question. He deliberately chose women friends who were not inquisitive about his work and who showed no signs of possessiveness. He'd grown used to a certain type of woman with whom he was comfortable.

He knew nothing about a woman such as Lauren Macken-zie.

Jordan glanced at his watch. He needed to pick her up within the hour. They would catch the shuttle into New York, spend the night in the air and make connections for Vienna after they landed in Frankfurt.

He realized how strange he felt to be traveling so openly on commercial airlines. His previous excursions into Europe had been through military connections. There was something to be said for military travel, but not much.

Jordan checked the tickets Mallory had given him earlier. They were traveling first class. Interesting man. Jordan just wished he knew what Mallory was up to.

Lauren Mackenzie stood in front of her bathroom mirror and tried to come to terms with her new image. Her dark au-burn hair had been lightened to a reddish blond. She had to get used to it immediately. It wouldn't help her believability if she kept doing a double take every time she caught sight of her im-age in a mirror.

The color wasn't the only thing that was different. Lauren had never given much thought to her hairstyle. She had thick, healthy hair that she'd always worn pulled away from her face. Now it was too short to be pulled back. Instead her hair feath-ered across her forehead and curled around her ears.

What a difference a haircut makes, she decided with a smile. Perhaps it paid to be cared for by professionals.

The woman who had shown her how to apply the makeup had complimented her on her glowing complexion. Since she shared the same skin tone as her mother and both her sisters, Lauren had always taken her complexion for granted. She knew that she could not tan. Instead she turned red, blistered and peeled. So while other women her age had been out by the pool or at the beach learning social repartee, Lauren had stayed in-side, alone, and read.

Oh, well, Mr. Trent didn't seem to have a great abundance of social chitchat, either, if their meeting this afternoon had been any indication.

Drat! That was another thing. She couldn't keep referring to her husband as Mr. Trent. But she didn't like J.D., which was what Mallory called him. That put her in mind of a cigar-smoking wheeler-dealer—a kingpin-type, ruler of all he surveyed.

She'd seen his name on the passports they were given: Jordan Daniel Trent. She wondered if anyone called him Jordan? Daniel? Dan? Jordie? She shuddered at the thought of his reaction if anyone used that diminutive on him.

Glancing at her watch, Lauren hurriedly finished touching up her makeup and returned to her bedroom and the open suitcase on the bed. She couldn't get over the number of outfits they'd provided for her. The woman in charge of preparing her for the trip explained that everything had to look as though she and Jordan were typical American tourists, which meant they had money to afford a trip to Europe.

Lauren picked up the small pile of satin and lace that represented the colorful nightgowns she was expected to wear. Surely not in front of him? No one had said anything about their pretending to be married once they were alone in their hotel rooms. What if there was only one room?

She turned and hurriedly dug through one of her drawers. She'd take one of her own gowns just in case. Actually it was more of a nightshirt. Her sister had given it to her several years ago and it was faded, but the picture on it was still discernible. A familiar figure from the daily comics was sitting on her bed and speaking into a phone, saying, "I'm afraid I'm going to be late to work this morning. My hair won't start."

Meg had decided Lauren needed a little humor in her life. *Never more than right at this moment,* she thought, trying not to panic.

The doorbell rang and startled, she jumped several inches. *So much for nerves of steel,* she decided. Here she was doing the most adventurous thing in her life and she was determined not to be intimidated by the great unknown waiting for her out there. She'd never traveled overseas; in fact, her only vacations had been with her family.

What would her mom and dad think if they knew that she was going to be traveling with a man, pretending to be his wife? Who was she kidding? She knew exactly what they'd think. And who wouldn't?

She could just hear Meg and Amy now, teasing her about her extensive experience with men.

The doorbell rang again and Lauren rushed to the front door. Checking to make sure it was Mr. Trent—oops, uh, Jordan—she quickly unchained the door and opened it.

The clothes he was wearing were totally different from the casual attire he'd had on in the office earlier. The silvery gray suit emphasized his tanned skin and black eyes and hair. If he'd seemed imposing earlier, he looked downright intimidating now.

Lauren stepped back and motioned vaguely. "Come in," she said, pleased with the casual tone of her voice.

Jordan stepped inside so that Lauren could close the door, but he didn't take his eyes off her.

"What have they done to you?" he asked, his eyes narrowing slightly.

Now what? He didn't have to make his aversion to her quite so clear this early in their association. What did he think she would do, attack him at the first opportunity?

"Mr. Mallory told you that I would be made up to look like Frances Monroe."

"Does she dress like that?" he asked, a note of disbelief evident in his voice.

Lauren glanced down at the dress she had chosen to travel in. She'd been told it was wrinkle resistant, could be hand washed and dried quickly—all excellent attributes for a traveling outfit. Her chin came up. "What's wrong with the way I'm dressed?" she asked in an ominous tone.

Jordan realized, too late, that she was misjudging his reaction. The dark green dress did a creditable job of showing him that here was one woman who did not suffer from any figure flaws whatsoever. On the contrary. She would probably create a minor riot on a beach, if the curves shown to great advantage by the clinging dress were any indication of what lay underneath.

"Nothing. Not a thing. It just surprised me, that's all. I assumed that Mrs. Monroe was an older woman. That dress doesn't look...I mean—" Damn. He was getting himself in deeper with every utterance.

"Mrs. Monroe is in her mid-thirties, I believe."

"How old are you?"

"I don't see that my age has anything to do with this. I'm twenty-five."

"Oh. When I saw you earlier I thought you were—" Whoa. If you have any instincts for survival, you won't finish that statement, Trent, he thought.

"You thought I was—?" she repeated with unfeigned interest in her eyes.

"Uh, well, from what Mallory had told me, I just assumed that you were, uh, older."

"I see." She started toward the bedroom to get her suitcase, but paused in the doorway and looked back at him. "What difference does it make?"

"None," he assured her hastily. "None whatsoever!" Jordan watched her as she disappeared into the other room. Well, they were off to a flying start. He'd barely prevented himself from insulting her before they'd even left town.

Or at least he assumed she would feel insulted. How did a woman who looked like Lauren Mackenzie feel about herself? And what had been the purpose of that masquerade in the office? Come to think of it, he could see how her attractiveness might create a certain amount of distraction in the men who worked alongside her. Of course, it didn't affect him at all.

She reappeared in the doorway carrying her suitcase.

"Is that all you're taking?"

"I was told to travel as lightly as possible."

"Oh."

"Why?"

"I don't know. I just thought that women had to have a lot of luggage. At least the ones I've seen always travel with a half-dozen bags or so."

Lauren approached him and set the suitcase at his feet. "I think we should get something straight at the very beginning of our association, Mr. Trent. I do not appreciate being compared to all the other women in your life. By the same token, I will refrain from drawing any comparisons between you and the men that I happen to know."

Her cool tone and haughty manner incensed him. All he was trying to do was make small talk to break the ice. Instead the icicles rapidly forming from their conversation could almost be seen.

"Don't call me Mr. Trent, Lauren. I know all of this is new to you, but I'd appreciate your giving me a slim chance of pulling this charade off without your blowing our cover at the first opportunity."

She nodded. "Certainly. What shall I call you?"

He glanced at her in surprise. Didn't she even remember his name? He shrugged. "My friends call me Jordan."

"Aahhh. Your friends. I'm relieved to know you have some. Mr. Mallory gave me the impression you were the original lone wolf out in the wilds, working alone and preferring it that way."

"I am and I do. But contrary to what you may believe, I do happen to have acquired a few friends through the years."

Their voices had steadily become more clipped and cutting. Lauren gave him a brief flash of teeth in an effort to imitate a smile. "There's no accounting for taste, is there?" she said. "Shouldn't we be going?" she continued, glancing at her watch. "We don't want to miss our connections."

Jordan picked up her suitcase and headed toward the door. Lauren followed him, making sure the door was locked when they left the apartment.

At least I don't have to worry about accidentally endangering her on this trip, Jordan decided in the elevator. *I may end up murdering her myself before everything is over.*

By the time their plane left New York a few hours later, Lauren realized that she and Jordan had scarcely spoken to each other since leaving their apartment building.

This will never do, she thought ruefully. *The flight attendants will probably think we've had a fight before we ever started this vacation.*

She glanced at Jordan out of the corner of her eye. He had taken off his suit coat, loosened his tie, and seemed to be engrossed in a newspaper an attendant had handed to him. She stared unseeingly down at the magazine in her hands. Shouldn't they be talking, making plans, getting acquainted? Something?

Clearing her throat, Lauren said in a low voice, "Don't you think it would help if we shared some of our past history with each other? Just in case we're in a situation where it might be needed?''

Jordan slowly turned his gaze to her, his black eyes unreadable. She had a point—one he should already have thought of. Jordan couldn't understand his emotional reactions around this woman. His brain seemed to have taken a backseat to his feelings, which could get them both killed.

He nodded. ''Why don't you start?'' he suggested.

Feeling more than a little frustrated with his obvious reluctance to be the first to open up, Lauren began, ''I was born and spent the first twenty-one years of my life in Pennsylvania. My parents still live in Reading. I have two sisters—I'm the one in the middle.'' She paused, trying to think of a way to summarize what was important in her life. ''I'm very close to all my family. We try to get together as often as possible. My older sister is married; my younger one is in college.''

''What are their names?'' Jordan asked, surprised that he wanted to know more, that he was attempting to visualize her growing up.

Lauren raised her brows slightly. ''Meg—Margaret—is the older one. She never answers to anything but Meg. And Amy is the youngest.''

''Are they anything like you?''

''In looks? Disposition?'' She shrugged slightly when he remained silent. ''I suppose, a little in both. We seem to have inherited our dad's Scots temper along with the tinge of red in his hair.''

''Are all of them mathematical geniuses?''

Lauren found herself studying his expression, trying to find any sarcasm in that question. She was surprised to see genuine interest. A movement behind his head caught her eye and she glanced up in time to see the smiling attendant pass by. Perhaps she had noticed their earlier silence and had decided they were now making up.

Perhaps they were.

''We all have an aptitude for figures. Meg put hers to use with her music. She plays several instruments quite well.'' She thought for a moment. ''I don't know about Amy. She's the dreamy one, always floating around with her head in the clouds.''

"Whereas you are logical and practical," he said with a slow smile that Lauren found rather endearing. It gave him a touch of vulnerability that she would not have guessed he harbored behind that stone-faced facade of his.

"I try, but sometimes my temper runs away with me." Impulsively she touched his arm that rested between them. "I'm sorry for my earlier remarks to you. I'm not usually that way with people I've just met. Somehow you managed to get under my skin."

His smile widened into a grin. "As long as we're talking about apologies, I owe you a couple myself. There was no reason to take out my frustration on you because of this assignment."

They sat there in silence for a few moments, studying each other.

"To tell you the truth," Lauren admitted after a while, "I did feel as though I'd been rather thrust upon you."

"For good reason. You were. I should be used to being overruled by now, though. Our working system certainly isn't set up as a democracy—the one man, one vote system. Whatever Mallory says goes."

"That didn't seem to stop you from trying to change his mind."

"That's because once in a while I've had success in convincing him that my plan is more workable."

Lauren shifted the magazine in her lap and the light caused a glint on her hand. Jordan reached over and took her left hand in his. A brilliant solitaire diamond sparkled on her ring finger, next to a gold band.

"Where did these come from?" he asked quietly.

Lauren grinned. "Why, darling, how could you have forgotten giving them to me on the most joyous occasion of my life!" She fluttered her lashes at him and gave him such a simpering smile that he began to laugh.

The change in him so astounded Lauren that she could only stare. Gone was the harsh-faced man she had met earlier in the day. Jordan's well-shaped mouth caught her attention, his white teeth a sharp contrast to his tanned face. His eyes sparkled and, for the first time, Lauren discovered how very attractive dark eyes could be. She was fascinated by this further glimpse of the man with whom she traveled.

"Now then," she said with a smile, "What about you? Any sisters? Brothers? Where did you grow up?"

The sudden cessation of all expression on his face stunned her. In less than a second he returned to being the cold, aloof man she'd met earlier.

As though reading from a prepared script, Jordan said, "I was born in California, moved to Chicago when I was eight, spent most of my growing-up years in boarding schools in New England."

"Oh." She hesitated for a moment, then asked, "Are your parents still alive?"

"My father is. My mom died when I was a child."

"Oh," she repeated, unsure of what to say. His voice betrayed no emotion. "So you're an only child?"

He nodded.

Lauren felt a chill surround her and she shivered slightly.

"Are you cold?" he asked, reaching overhead and turning the nozzle until there was no more air coming down on her.

"Thank you," she said softly.

"Would you like a pillow and blanket? We've got a long night ahead of us. I could use some sleep, myself. I seem to have spent the past forty-eight hours in the air." Jordan signaled the attendant who promptly provided them with the requested items.

"Jordan?" Lauren asked after they got settled in.

"Hmmm?"

"How long have we been married?" she asked softly.

He turned his head so that he was staring into her eyes, only a few inches away.

"I don't know. How long would you like to have been married?"

"Maybe three years? That would give us time to be used to each other, don't you think?"

"I have no idea. Three years is as good a time period as any, I suppose."

"Do we have any children?"

"No!" he answered abruptly.

"You don't want them?"

"Why are you asking all of these ridiculous questions, Lauren? How I feel about children is irrelevant to what we're doing!"

"Not necessarily. That would be something we would have talked about by now."

He sighed. "I'm beginning to see why you make a good cryptographer. You have to know all the answers, don't you?"

"Not all the time, no. But I do enjoy the challenge of working out a puzzle."

"Well, you can go to sleep now. Once we complete this little affair, I'll drop out of your life as quickly as I appeared. I'm not a puzzle that you have to figure out."

As Lauren pounded her pillow and built her nest against the bulkhead of the plane, she thought about Jordan's remarks. No doubt he was right. They weren't going to be together long enough for her to need to understand the type of person he was. However, Lauren had a strong hunch that she would be compelled to figure out what events in his life had made the man she saw today. The more she talked with him, the more protective layers she found wrapped around him.

Lauren closed her eyes and sighed. For some reason that she couldn't quite fathom, she wanted to get back in touch with the laughing man she'd caught a glimpse of earlier.

She knew that her insatiable curiosity had once again taken over and she wouldn't rest until she solved the intricate puzzle known as Jordan Trent.

Three

They arrived in Frankfurt, Germany, in time for breakfast before catching their flight to Vienna.

Lauren didn't feel as though she'd slept at all. Somehow she must have. Otherwise she wouldn't have awakened in the morning light to find her head resting on Jordan's chest and his arms wrapped securely around her.

When had that happened?

As soon as she had shifted he'd immediately opened his eyes, fully alert. Lauren had never seen reflexes so finely tuned. She'd mumbled an apology for disturbing him and had gone to the restroom. The image she saw there dismayed her and she went to work to overcome the slept-in look she wore. After combing her hair and freshening her makeup, Lauren forced herself to return to her seat and the man waiting there for her.

Jordan excused himself without further comment and Lauren gave a quick sigh of relief. She needed the few minutes of privacy. Glancing at her watch, she knew they would be landing soon and the charade would begin in earnest. They would have to go through customs.

By the time they were seated and being waited on in the airport restaurant, Lauren had managed to calm down a little. The landing and going through customs hadn't been as bad as she had expected.

"How are you feeling?" Jordan asked, sipping his second cup of coffee.

"Much better than I was earlier. I don't know why I was so nervous. Customs wasn't so bad."

"Not this time, no. Every country has its own idiosyncrasies. And if we do go into Hungary or Czechoslovakia you'll find an entirely different attitude from the one we just encountered."

"Do you really think we'll go there?"

"I sincerely hope not, but I won't know until I've made a few contacts." He paused, looking around. "Which reminds me," he said in a lower voice. "From now on, even when you think we're alone, don't discuss what we're doing, okay?"

She nodded.

"Just remember that we're married and on vacation. Try to get into the part."

"I don't mind the vacation. The married part has me a little concerned."

His mouth twitched slightly. "Oh, really? You've managed to hide it well up until now."

"Yes, well, now that the time has come that I'm closer to sharing a room with you—"

"I know. But that can't be helped. Mallory was right. We need to stay as close to each other as possible. I'll have to leave you for short periods of time, but otherwise, we're going to be bosom buddies for the next few days."

Lauren noticed that his gaze idly dropped to her chest when he made his last remark and she could feel herself flushing. Damn him, anyway. Wasn't the situation awkward enough without his making innuendos?

"I should hope we'll at least have separate beds," she said, trying for a casual tone.

"Why? Do you pull covers?"

She just stared at him without replying.

His eyes narrowed slightly. "Don't tell me you've never shared a man's bed before."

Lauren could feel her face flushing with embarrassment.

Jordan lifted his hand to his forehead and groaned. "No, Mallory. No, you didn't do this to me!" He dropped his hand and glared at her. "Whatever possessed you to agree to be married to me when you've obviously had no experience?"

Lauren drew herself up and glared at him. "If I had been told I needed bedroom experience, believe me, I would never have consented to the plan. I was told they needed my help because of my resemblance to Mrs. Monroe. There was never any discussion about how you and I would conduct ourselves!"

"I see," he said, amused at her indignation.

"If you need a woman, I'm sure you can find one elsewhere," she pointed out with prim dignity.

"Yes, that's true. Of course, I'm going to be fairly busy for the next few days so I probably won't be able to devote any of my time to the hunt." He made a barely perceptible shrug of feigned nonchalance. "However, I'll do my damnedest to contain my animal lusts." He could no longer conceal his smile. "Admittedly it will be tough for me since your luscious innocence will be around to tantalize me."

Jordan realized when he heard his words that he wasn't really jesting. Not that he had any intention of making love to her. Hell, he didn't even particularly like her, and despite some widely held beliefs of the general public regarding men in his occupation, he didn't go in for casual sex with anyone.

And he certainly did not intend to start something with a twenty-five year old virgin.

"I hope you're gaining some sort of amusement out of baiting me, Mr. —" He held up his hand suddenly and she amended her words. "—Jordan. I'm not in the least affected by your crude comments."

Her high color contradicted her lofty remarks, but he thought it best not to point that out. He was already in enough hot water. He didn't know why he enjoyed teasing her so much. Probably because she took the bait so easily.

Suddenly Jordan felt ashamed of himself. Here was a woman who was obviously out of her familiar milieu and handling herself very well. It must have taken a great deal of courage for her to agree to come on this trip with a complete stranger, a man who had made no effort to make the situation any easier.

But he'd be damned if he would apologize! He hadn't re-cruited her for this assignment. If she couldn't say no, that was her problem.

A sudden vision of them in bed together flashed before his mind. He had a hunch she would certainly know how to say no if he tried anything at that time!

Noting that she was finished eating, he said, "Are you ready?"

"Yes," she answered in a clipped voice.

Sighing, he stood and held out his hand. "My mother never did manage to teach me many manners, Lauren, but I am sorry if my teasing offended you."

Staring up at him, she slowly got to her feet and placed her hand in his. She wrinkled her nose and smiled. "I should be used to being teased by now. My whole family is made up of notorious teases." Gently withdrawing her hand, she said, "I just don't know you well enough to know how to take what you say. But I'll learn."

They were silent while he paid for their meal. Walking down the concourse toward their gate, Jordan said, "You don't have to worry about my making overtures toward you, Lauren. I would never take advantage of the situation."

She kept her head down for a moment, then glanced up un-til she met his gaze. "Thank you, Jordan," she said formally. "I appreciate your reassurance. And I want you to have my re-assurance," she went on in a solemn voice, "that I will re-strain my lusts as well so you will have nothing to worry about either."

Startled by her words, Jordan threw back his head and laughed, a full-throated, amused sound that caused more than one person to glance around at them. He threw his arm around her shoulders and hugged her to his side for a moment, then let go. Still laughing, he held out his hand for a handshake. "That's a real worry off my mind, Lauren, let me tell you. I'm relieved to know I'll be safe with you. Let's shake on it."

Once again Lauren had found the man she'd been shown a glimpse of earlier. She wondered how she could encourage that man to show up more often. She found him practically irresis-tible.

* * *

By the time they arrived at the hotel where they would be staying in Vienna, Lauren no longer cared who might end up sharing a bed with her. She cared only about finding a place to stretch out for a few hours. Her last full night's rest was a dim memory in her mind.

She knew she hadn't slept much since she'd been approached to make this trip. On more than one occasion she had suddenly decided to back out of the commitment. Only her strong sense of fair play and the idea that she would be able to help in a time of crisis had kept her going.

Now she was too tired to think about anything. She allowed Jordan to guide her in the right direction at the right time. Lauren was barely aware of anything by the time they reached the room.

"You're in luck, it seems. We won't have to fight over the covers tonight, anyway."

Lauren looked toward the beds that were side by side. She let her purse strap slide off her shoulder and as she watched the purse hit the floor she had no thought of trying to stop it.

Jordan walked over to her and lifted her chin so that he could look into her face. "You're exhausted, aren't you?"

Forcing her heavy eyelids open, Lauren noted with disgust that Jordan looked fresh and ready to go.

"Never mind. Why don't you stretch out for a while? I need to go out, anyway."

Lauren sank down on the side of the bed without saying a word.

"Don't you want to get into something more comfortable first?" he asked as she began to lower herself onto the pillow.

She closed her eyes with a sigh and groaned slightly.

He grinned and sat down beside her, slipping off her shoes. "Come on. I'll help you. You'll rest much better if—"

Lauren's eyes popped open and she slapped his hand away from her belt. "What do you think you're doing?"

"Helping my *wife*—" he emphasized the word, "—get more comfortable. Really, dear, you're certainly cranky when you're tired." There was a definite gleam in his black eyes.

Lauren was too exhausted to argue. Besides, he was right—about everything. Forcing herself into a sitting position, she began to unfasten her dress. Then she paused. "Am I expected to furnish your viewing entertainment while we're here?" she demanded to know.

He grinned and got to his feet. "Not at the moment, I'm afraid. I have to get going. I'll be late for my appointment."

"What—?" Lauren started to say when he suddenly leaned over and kissed her hard on the mouth. She was too startled to resist. By the time he pulled away from her, she could only stare at him in bemusement. Nuzzling her ear, he whispered, "You're going to have to go along with me, Lauren. Just trust that I know what I'm talking about. We can't afford to take any chances. Do you understand?"

She nodded and he straightened. "I'll see you later, darling," he said, then picked up the room key and left. She was still staring at the door when he opened it a few seconds later. "Don't go eat without me. I'll be back as soon as I can, okay?"

Lauren nodded her head like a puppet might, her movement jerky.

"Good girl," he said with a grin and closed the door once again. This time it stayed shut.

The kiss they had shared had shot a burst of adrenaline throughout her system and Lauren slid off the bed. She still felt as tired as ever, but decided to take a shower before going to sleep. By the time she returned to the bedroom she was pleasantly relaxed. Tucking her terry-cloth robe around her, she crawled under the covers and fell asleep, content to face whatever else the future had in store for her after some much needed rest.

A key turning in a lock awakened her sometime later and Lauren drowsily opened her eyes. For a moment she couldn't place where she was. In the deepening shadows of evening, the room seemed totally unfamiliar. Then the door opened and Jordan came in.

Lauren sat up in bed and switched on the lamp beside her.

"Hello," Jordan said. "Looks as though you managed to get some rest." He felt pleased that his tone sounded so casual. She looked so appealing sitting there, bathed in the soft light, her hair tousled and her eyes startled. He'd caught his breath at the first sight of her. Her gleaming skin seemed to call out to him, begging to be caressed. Except he knew better.

"I must have," she said, sounding confused. "What time is it?"

"Time for something to eat. How does that appeal to you?"

"Very much."

He opened his suitcase and sorted through it. "I'll take a quick shower, and then we'll see what we can find."

Lauren watched him disappear into the bathroom. After the door closed, she quickly left the bed and went to the closet where she had hung the clothes she'd brought with her. Dressing as though for a fire drill, Lauren was ready in moments. She took a little more time with her hair and makeup, but was still ready when he came out of the bathroom sometime later.

He'd chosen casual clothes that went along with the holiday spirit of their trip. The pull-over shirt fit his broad shoulders and chest very well. She hadn't been aware of his build until now.

Staying in good physical condition was no doubt part of his curriculum. Lauren just wished she wasn't so aware of him as a man. She was afraid her thoughts must be written on her face and she busied herself searching inside her purse.

"Have you misplaced something?" he asked, watching her.

"Oh, uh, no. I just wanted to make sure I had everything," she explained a little breathlessly.

"Ready?"

"Yes."

They were quiet until they reached the street. Jordan guided her to a car parked by the curb.

"Where did you get this?" she asked, surprised when he opened the door and motioned for her to get in.

"I wanted to feel a little less hampered in my movements, so I rented a car. Besides, we needed a place where we could talk."

As he drove through the streets of Vienna, Jordan explained, "You may think it silly, but I want us to assume that everywhere we go our conversation is being monitored, even in our room."

"Is that why—?"

"I kissed you this afternoon?" he ended for her. "Yes. We need to be aware of where we are and what we're attempting to do."

"Were you able to get any information this afternoon about Mrs. Monroe?"

"Some, which is another reason for the car. We're going to Brno in the morning."

"Where's that?"

"In Czechoslovakia."

"Is that where she is?"

"There's a strong possibility. Enough to check out the lead."

"Then your friends were able to help."

"Hardly friends, innocent. Some people would sell their mother if the price was right."

"Oh."

"Sorry if I disillusioned you about human nature," he said after several minutes of silence.

"It isn't that, exactly. I was just thinking how much I take my family and my life-style for granted. Nothing very exciting has ever really happened in our lives. We've just gone through life accepting our homes and jobs and friends without question. I've never really thought about how other people live."

"You'll find the same types all over the world, Lauren. In my profession, I happen to deal with a different type of human being than you've ever had occasion to meet." He muttered something under his breath and she looked around at him, noting his grim profile.

"What did you say?"

"I just said I hope you don't have to meet them. But under the circumstances I don't see how I can protect you from the possibility."

She smiled. "I'm a grown woman, you know. I don't need protecting."

"Hang on to that thought, honey. You're probably going to need it."

The restaurant they chose was quiet. They were early for the dinner hour, which was fine with Lauren. It gave her a chance to get used to being in a new place without feeling that everyone knew she was a foreigner.

"Have you been in touch with Mr. Mallory?" she asked over dessert.

"Indirectly."

"Have they received any more news regarding the lady in question?"

"No."

"Oh. Then no one has any idea who might be responsible," she said in a low voice.

"I don't want to start naming names at the moment, but I have some strong ideas. Let's just say the sooner we find her, the better off she'll be."

Lauren shuddered at his grim tone and the look on his face. Here was one man she would definitely not want as an enemy.

How about as a lover? a small voice seemed to whisper inside her head. The thought shocked her. Lauren didn't think of men in that context. The few with whom she had made friends were casual acquaintances, usually with romantic ties to someone else.

When it came right down to it, she really didn't know much about men, she decided. Fathers don't count. She smiled at the thought.

"I would love to know what's going on in that pretty head of yours," Jordan said softly, watching the changing expressions on her candlelit face.

When the color rose to her cheeks, he grinned. "I bet they're worth a great deal more than a penny."

"I doubt that," she said, trying not to stammer. "Actually I was thinking about my parents," she said, only stretching the truth slightly. "I'm going to find it very difficult not telling them about my visit to Europe once I get home."

"It would be a little difficult to explain, wouldn't it?"

"Yes. Mr. Mallory told me to tell everyone I was going to California for some additional training."

"Makes sense, I suppose. One of his most adhered to policies is the 'need-to-know' one. Less chance of a slipup somewhere."

"Yes, he explained that to me. I understand the reasons," she said, glancing around the luxurious restaurant ruefully.

"Well, maybe you can come back some other time," he suggested.

"Somehow I doubt it."

"Insist on spending your honeymoon in Vienna," he said facetiously.

She stared at the way the candlelight was reflected in his eyes and suddenly realized that despite the less than auspicious start of their relationship, she would never think of Vienna without remembering Jordan Trent.

Glancing down at the expensive tablecloth in front of her, she absently reached for her coffee.

"Lauren?"

His low tone made her look up at him, startled.

"I'm sorry. Did I touch a sore point with you? I seem to have a real knack for offending you without knowing exactly how."

"You didn't offend me."

"But something about a honeymoon in Europe did."

She shook her head. "No, not really. I was just thinking how remote the possibility would be, that's all."

"Why?"

She shrugged. "I'm just one of those people who will stay single all her life."

He muttered a word that was unprintable but succinct. She met his gaze in surprise at his quietly spoken vehemence.

"I take it some idiot broke your heart and you're determined never to trust another man."

Her sudden peal of laughter startled him. It was the first time he'd seen her genuinely amused. He found her adorable. Baffling, but adorable.

"You couldn't be more wrong," she finally managed to say.

"Oh?"

"Look at me. I'm not the type of woman men go for, surely you recognize that."

Jordan had a sudden image of Lauren the first time he saw her—glasses, boxy suit, low-heeled shoes, careless hairdo and he almost flinched at his remembered reaction to her. How could he have missed the beauty of her eyes that reminded him of the soft mist of early dawn, or the velvety softness of her cheek that caused his hand to itch from wanting to touch it. And that figure. Were all men blind? Then he remembered her deliberate camouflage.

Lauren Mackenzie was like a hidden treasure that had suddenly been exposed to light. She glittered and gleamed with newness, wholesomeness, vitality. Would he ever forget her sense of humor?

"It depends on the man," he said slowly, carefully thinking through what he wanted to say. "A man of discernment would recognize what a prize you are, Lauren. You have a great deal to offer the man lucky enough to win your love."

He sounded very sincere, yet the words seemed so peculiar coming from him. They reminded her of some of the heart-to-heart talks she'd had with her father.

That was it. He was trying to be reassuring and kind, which rather surprised her. Kindness certainly hadn't seemed to be one of his character traits.

She smiled. "I'm not sure what to say. You've quite taken my breath away with your lovely words." Her tone was teasing but her eyes reflected her vulnerability.

No longer able to resist the temptation, Jordan reached across the small table and brushed his knuckles against her cheek. He'd been right. Her skin felt like velvet. He could feel himself reacting to the touch and he hastily lowered his hand.

"Are you ready to go?" he asked briskly, glancing around the room.

The sudden mood transition caused a small ache to appear somewhere in the region of Lauren's heart. What had she expected, anyway? He was still doing his best to pretend a husbandly affection. She needed to remember that their time together was a charade and temporary. Sort of a momentary marriage that would end as soon as their mission was completed.

Four

Lauren noticed that Jordan had very little to say on the return trip to their hotel. Of course he could be tired, since he hadn't had the benefit of the nap she had enjoyed.

When they arrived, he escorted her in silence through the lobby, into the elevator and down the hallway to their room. Only when they reached their door did she sense a change in him.

"What is it?" she said, almost whispering in the quietness of the hallway.

Without saying a word he motioned for her to stand to the side of him. He inserted the key and turned the knob, shoving the door open without entering.

When nothing happened, he flicked on the light and glanced around the room, then relaxed.

"What is it?" she repeated, ashamed to hear the slight tremble in her voice.

He shook his head and chuckled. "Paranoia setting in." He waved to their beds, which had been turned down for them. "Obviously the maid has been here since we left."

"How did you know someone had been in the room?" she asked, looking around uncertainly.

"I knew," he said in a flat tone of voice. "Look, I'm going to have to leave you again. There was someone waiting downstairs I need to see."

She didn't know whether that was true or not, but it didn't matter.

"You'll be all right alone?" he asked.

"Of course."

He nodded, walked into the bathroom and looked around, returned to the bedroom, checked under the beds and inside the closet. "I'll see you later."

Lauren began to prepare for bed in a thoughtful mood. Deciding to relax in a steaming bath, she carried her nightclothes into the bathroom with her and closed the door.

She had just seen another side of Jordan's personality, one that frightened her with its intensity. The professional had peered out at her and she began to have some inkling why Mr. Mallory had insisted on sending him to Europe.

By the time Lauren completed her bath, she was pleasantly drowsy. Pleased that she had bought a book at the airport in New York, she began to read, unaware that she was listening for his footstep outside the door.

Eventually her fatigue overcame her and she closed the book, turned off the light and wiggled down under the covers. If this was an example of marriage, Lauren decided sleepily, she would do just as well to continue to live alone.

Lauren woke up sometime during the night and realized that Jordan had returned while she slept. She saw his reassuring bulk in the bed beside her. He was so close she could have reached out and touched his back as he lay turned away from her.

How amazing! She felt protected immediately, knowing he was nearby. Shifting to find a more comfortable position, she drifted off to sleep once again.

Jordan knew that Lauren had awakened, but he didn't move. He'd awakened instantly at the subtle change in her breathing. It was a habit he couldn't seem to break, nor did he want to. His skill at being aware of someone else in a room had come into play more than once in his career. It was second nature to him now.

Lauren hadn't stirred when he'd come in earlier. He'd undressed in the bathroom, realizing that he'd have to sleep in his briefs. He was certain that Lauren wouldn't appreciate waking up to his nude body come morning.

The man he'd seen loitering outside the hotel when they'd returned had given him some valuable information—if it could be believed. Jordan felt the man was more trustworthy than some he'd dealt with in the past. The man felt that Jordan had once saved his life.

Jordan's memory was a little hazy about the matter but he was willing to accept the man's help, whatever his reasons.

Now, at least, he had been given a possible address where Mrs. Monroe might be. Jordan didn't want to think about her state of mind or physical condition. There was nothing he could do about that. He would find her, then make any necessary decisions.

He caught the sound of Lauren's regular breathing once more and he relaxed. Turning onto his back he lay there, staring up at the darkened ceiling. This was a new experience for him, lying next to a warm, desirable woman and not touching her.

Jordan found it disconcerting how much he did want to touch her. The quick kiss they had shared that afternoon had unnerved him more than he had wanted to admit at the time. Her lips had been so soft and giving. It had taken a great deal of willpower to end the kiss and pull away from her. He'd already made a promise to her and he intended to keep it.

He just wished he didn't find her quite so attractive.

The sound of a shattering explosion that seemed to be right there in their room caused immediate reactions in both Lauren and Jordan. Lauren screamed. Jordan was on his feet, pistol in hand, checking the room and eventually looking out their window down at the street.

Lauren threw herself out of the bed and ran to where he stood. "What was that?" she cried, trembling violently.

Absently placing his free arm around her shoulders, he pulled her close to his almost-bare body. "An explosion of some kind," he muttered in an absent tone, continuing to watch as people began to gather from all directions. He tried to make out what the shouts were but the sounds weren't clear enough.

Lauren suddenly realized she was pressed tightly to a well-built, unadorned male. Her thigh-length nightshirt prevented most of her from touching him directly, but she could feel the hair on his thigh brushing against her.

"Well," she said shakily, trying to move away from his firm grip without success, "I didn't think it was your travel alarm." Now that she realized she hadn't been a part of the explosion, Lauren tried to calm down, but her heart wasn't having any part of the calming exercise. Not as long as she was so intimately clutched to the tall male holding her. Then her eyes focused on his other hand.

"Where did you get that?" she asked, nodding toward the pistol.

"I brought it with me," he said, still watching the street.

"Isn't that illegal?"

"Not necessarily."

"You didn't declare it."

"No."

"Then it was illegal."

"Only if you get caught."

"An interesting use of logic," she managed to say. When he didn't seem to have any intention of letting her go, she asked, a little breathless from trying to talk calmly when she felt anything but calm, "Would you kindly let me go?"

He looked down at her in surprise as though amazed to find her tucked so closely next to him. He also realized that neither of them had many clothes on. Jordan stepped away from her as though she had suddenly scorched his fingers.

"Hey, lady," he spread his hand out as if to reassure her, "you're the one who ran to me, remember?"

"I know. I wasn't accusing you of anything." She paused. "I really was afraid."

"So was I," he said, walking over to his side of the bed and picking up the pair of pants he'd left there. Placing the gun on the table, he stepped into the pants, zipped them, then turned around and faced her.

"I didn't think people like you were ever afraid of anything," she said.

"People like me," he repeated in a steady voice, "are just as human as the rest of you. We have thoughts and feelings. We feel pain when we get hurt, bleed like any mortal being."

They stood looking at each other and Lauren didn't know what to say. Whether it was because of the unorthodox way they'd been awakened, or the early hour, she didn't know. But something had changed between them. There was a tension that hadn't been there before. She didn't understand it—where it came from, or why it was there—but she could sense its presence as though another person had entered the room and joined them.

Lauren padded quietly over to him and placed her hands on his bare chest. "I didn't mean to imply that I think of you as something less than human."

"Didn't you?"

She shook her head. His face was hard and without expression, but somewhere in his eyes a small flash of pain—of vulnerability—seemed to appear momentarily, then was gone. She would never have seen it if she hadn't been so close to him.

Never before had Lauren felt such a need to comfort someone. She forgot that this man was fiercely independent, a loner who fought his own battles and invariably won. What she had seen was a glimpse of the small boy who had learned a harsh lesson at a very early age: life didn't always guarantee a happy ending.

Going up on tiptoe, Lauren placed her lips softly against his, wanting him to know that she cared, that she was in no way judging him or his life-style. She slipped her hands up so that they encircled his neck.

Totally bemused by her uncharacteristic actions, Jordan was at a loss as to how to respond to her. What in the hell did she think she was doing, anyway? Did she believe a kiss would make everything all right—like a child who thinks that mommy can kiss it and make it better?

Whatever her motives, he could not remain unaffected by her closeness. His arms closed around her and he responded to her with an urgency that surprised them both. He took over the kiss, showing her how, teaching her to open her mouth for him.

He felt, more than heard, the soft gasp she gave but he was too much involved with the scent and taste of her to acknowledge her surprise. She felt wonderful in his arms.

His hands roamed restlessly up and down her spine as his mouth explored hers. When he was forced to draw away for breath, he continued to kiss her cheeks, her eyes, the soft hollow of her neck, then he returned his mouth to hers, having missed its soft sweetness. He felt the tiny quivering of her lower lip as he took possession once more.

Without conscious thought of the implications of what he was doing, Jordan swept Lauren up and placed her on his bed, following her down without ever losing contact with her.

Lauren had never before felt such a swirl of emotions. She'd had no idea a kiss could cause such a violent reaction within her body. Her legs were trembling so that her knees had almost given way by the time he lifted her in his arms.

She'd had no idea that a man's hands could evoke so many sensations. His touch set off tiny electrical sparks beneath her skin as though small units of energy were being snapped on after lying dormant for the past twenty-five years. Her body seemed to understand what was happening and was responding to him.

Lauren lightly traced the musculature of his back and shoulders, intrigued with the interplay of smooth skin and taut muscles beneath her fingers. They found the slight indentation of his spine that created an alluring path for her fingers to follow down his back until they reached the waistline of his trousers. Undeterred, she followed a path around to his stomach. His involuntary movement, flinching at her touch, caused her to pause.

"Don't stop," he managed to mutter in her ear. "I'm just very, very sensitive in that area." He followed his words with like action, running his hand along her thigh and under her short gown until he found the sensitive skin around her navel.

Oh, yes! Now she understood just how sensitive skin could be to a touch. And such a light touch, as well. How strange. And how wonderful.

Growing bolder she explored his chest, enjoying the feel of the mat of hair that covered it, as black and as curly as the hair on his head. He was such a wonderful example of virile manhood. Lauren had never known anyone even remotely like him.

When he tugged on her gown she immediately raised her arms so that he could pull the garment over her head. Tossing the gown on the floor and removing the pants he'd put on earlier, Jordan turned back to her, pulling her closer to him. Her eyes were closed, her expression dreamy. They lay on the rumpled sheets, his thigh between hers, his arm beneath her shoulders. All he could do was to drink in the sight of her ivory-colored skin, highlighted by the dim glow of the early morning dawn from the window.

Gently he touched the rose-colored tip of her breast with his finger and watched as she caught her breath. God, she was lovely, so lovely, so desirable. And he wanted her very, very much.

Jordan leaned over and with his tongue lightly traced a circle around the rosy tip. Lauren gave a soft sigh and placed her hands in his hair, holding him close to her. Encouraged, he continued to explore, enjoying the moment, helpless to prevent what was happening between them.

Time lost all meaning as they learned how to please each other. There was no doubt in Jordan's mind that Lauren was totally untutored. Nor was there any doubt but that she was quite willing for him to show her what she had been unaware of all these years.

Jordan didn't question why a woman who had held herself aloof from other men would be willing to give herself to him. At the moment it was enough that they were together.

He was in no hurry to consummate their lovemaking. He wanted her to enjoy it and he refused to rush, which was why they were both still wearing their briefs when there was a sudden pounding on the door.

They sprang apart as though a sudden shower of ice water had hit them.

"Who is it?" Jordan roared, ready to kill whoever it was that had interrupted them at that moment.

In heavily accented English a man said, "I am from the police and wish to speak with you, Mr. Trent."

They gazed at each other, Lauren with horrified dismay, and Jordan with a great deal of disgust. Whatever the police wanted, it was certain to delay their plans for leaving the country later that morning.

"Just a moment, please," he said, getting up and pulling on his pants. As he walked by her bed, he reached down and picked up the terry cloth robe that had fallen off during the night. "Let's don't give them any more than their hearts can stand this early in the morning, honey."

Glancing around the room, he saw his pistol still lying on the table beside his bed. In a few swift movements he grabbed it and, reaching into his suitcase, moved something in the bottom of the case and placed the gun there.

Lauren had never experienced such a confusion of emotions in her life. She pulled on the robe and hastily tied the sash, then watched the door apprehensively as Jordan walked over to it.

After offering identification, two plainclothesmen stepped inside the room.

"I'm sorry to awaken you so early, Mr. Trent," the spokesman began. "However, we didn't think it possible that anyone could have slept through the explosion."

"We weren't asleep, exactly," Jordan said, glancing over at his bed, which showed definite signs of double occupancy. Lauren could not remember ever having been so embarrassed in her life.

"Ah, yes, of course," the policeman said with a polite smile. "We are quite sorry to interrupt you and your wife."

"What seems to be the problem?" Jordan asked, motioning to the small grouping of chairs and sinking down on the side of Lauren's bed. She continued to stand by the side of his bed, restlessly twisting the sash of her robe.

"I'm afraid that the explosion caused some damage to the car you rented yesterday."

"I see. What was the explosion? Do you know?"

"It is under investigation, of course. A car bomb. Luckily no one was killed. However, there was considerable damage to nearby cars and buildings."

"Do you have incidents like this often?"

The man shrugged. "What is often? Once is too often as far as I'm concerned."

"Of course you're right. We're from Chicago and can certainly understand some of the problems the police have to deal with."

The man nodded. "If you would like, we could see what can be done about getting you another car. Were you planning to spend a few days here in Vienna before continuing your travels?"

The seemingly innocent question set off an alarm in Jordan's head. There was nothing to prevent a local policeman from working with others whose political beliefs were different from those held in his own country.

Jordan forced himself to smile and say, "Yes, we're hoping to stay about a week. Of course we do intend to explore the countryside, see some of the beautiful sights that Austria has to offer."

"Good. That is very good. We are just so sorry that your first night here must be so violent."

Jordan shrugged. "Let's hope the rest of our stay is more peaceful."

The two policemen stood and walked to the door. Jordan followed them.

Once again, the spokesman said, "Please accept our apologies—for the damage to the car and for our untimely intrusion." His eyes flickered to Lauren without expression, then back to Jordan.

Jordan opened the door for them, exchanging the usual pleasantries about the remainder of their visit. When he finally closed and locked the door, he heard Lauren move behind him.

Without saying a word he took her hand and led her into the bathroom. Reaching into the tub he turned on the water, then turned back to her and drew her close to him.

"There's a better than usual chance that this room has surveillance equipment in it. I don't know if we're being watched because of the timing of our arrival and the bombing, but it's obvious we've been checked out by the local authorities. Someone may suspect why we're here." He silently added that if the latter were the case, Jordan and Lauren didn't have a hope in hell of succeeding with their plan.

"What do we do now?" she whispered, her face without color.

Jordan wished he could suggest that they continue where they'd left off—but he knew better—for several reasons. One, the mood was gone—their possible danger now occupied their thoughts. Two, Jordan wasn't at all sure that he could handle having a relationship, however temporary, with Lauren Mackenzie. He'd never reacted to a woman before the way he did to her.

Of course he found her physically attractive, but there was so much more than that as he'd discovered this morning. He felt so protective of her. He admired her, not only for her beauty, but for her intelligence, her wit and her ability to immediately grasp a situation.

She was nothing like the women he was ordinarily involved with. And more importantly, he knew that he was the first man she'd been with.

Whatever possessed her to come to him so willingly? What did she expect from him? Whatever it was, he couldn't give it to her. Their lives were poles apart. They had nothing in common. And once they got through the next few days, they would never see each other again.

It was up to him to maintain some sort of control while they were together. That was going to add another burden to an already tough assignment.

He reached over and turned off the water. "How does breakfast sound?" he asked in a cheerful voice that sounded loud in the small bathroom.

She tried to respond to his light note with a smile, but it was hard won. "Sounds good," she said.

He leaned over and kissed the tip of her nose. "Good girl," he whispered, then straightened. "If you'll excuse me, I'll get shaved so we can go downstairs."

She nodded, still obedient to his remarks, and left the room.

When Jordan closed the door he leaned against it and sighed.

He wished he understood what was happening to him. No woman had ever affected him like this before. He didn't like it. He didn't like it at all.

Five

Lauren entered the bedroom, feeling dazed. So many things had happened in such a short period of time.

Her serene, orderly existence had exploded much like the bomb that had gone off earlier that morning. Lauren sank down on the edge of the bed and stared unseeingly at the wall.

Until now her life had been governed by her logical thinking processes. What had happened to her?

Lauren Mackenzie had grown up being treated as someone different from her peers by her teachers and classmates. What came easy for her, others found difficult to do. By the time she had finished high school Lauren had accepted that although the males she knew might be friendly to her, especially when they needed help with their homework, she wasn't the type of woman men found attractive.

Of course her parents had tried to reassure her on this point, but Lauren's logical mind continued to collect evidence to support her theory all during college. By the time she had accepted the offer made by the agency a few years ago, Lauren had resigned herself to her permanently single state and had dismissed the matter from her mind. Since there was nothing she could do about being who she was, she forgot about it. She dressed for comfort, not style, and she made friends with people who interested her, rather than with those who could advance her career.

Lauren had been surprised when Mr. Mallory approached her and asked for her help. She'd been even more surprised when he'd explained what he wanted her to do. He wanted her to pretend to be somebody's wife?

How laughable! Lauren had never even been on a date. When Mr. Mallory began to describe Jordan Trent to her, the unreality of the situation intensified. She wouldn't have been at all surprised to find a giant S on Jordan's undershirt. Mallory had convinced her that Jordan was the best operative they had and that he could be counted on to successfully conclude the assignment.

The next shock was meeting Jordan Trent and facing his anger over her role in the assignment. She'd never been exposed to a man of his nature who made his living in such a manner. She'd been in awe of him until he'd provoked her anger.

What she hadn't expected to find was his sense of humor. Even more of a shock to her was the vulnerability she had glimpsed in him.

As soon as she'd seen the sensitivity he kept so carefully hidden from the world she was able to relate to him. Both of them had learned to function well in their own fields, without allowing those around them ever to get to know the real person hiding his and her thoughts and feelings from the world.

Lauren had instinctively reached out to that person in Jordan that morning in an attempt to let him know that she understood. His physical response and her shattering reaction to him had created more of a shock to her system than the bomb exploding or the police pounding on their door.

He'd been physically attracted to her, of that she had no doubt. He'd been tender and gentle and yet his touch had forcibly shown Lauren an undeveloped side of her nature. She had never felt that way before. How extraordinary and totally out of character.

She felt as though she'd been at a masquerade party and, when Jordan admitted to being afraid, he had removed his mask for her. For the first time she recognized that they were more alike than she could possibly have imagined. She had found her other half.

So this is what it feels like, she thought, glancing down at the pillow she and Jordan had shared such a short time ago.

She suddenly remembered a scene from her childhood. She'd been sitting watching her mother prepare several varieties of cookies for the school bake sale. And the young Lauren had asked, "How long did you know Dad before you knew you were in love with him?"

Hilary Mackenzie had smiled the smile that always meant she was thinking of her husband. "Not nearly as long as it took him to recognize what he was feeling," she replied.

"How did the two of you meet?"

"Your father was working with a group of men who went from farm to farm helping with the hay harvest. They arrived one day to go to work on my father's farm."

The young Lauren sighed. "And it was love at first sight, I bet."

"Hardly. I thought he was the most obnoxious man I'd ever met. I'd just turned sixteen, you understand, and was extremely aware of my own dignity, which your father insisted on poking fun at."

"That sounds like Daddy, all right."

"Yes. He's always been a terrible tease. I felt he must have decided he had a special calling to make my life miserable, because he certainly made a career of it that summer." Hilary shook her head, remembering.

"So when did you change?"

Her mother was quiet for a moment, gazing out the window, not seeing anything but her memories. "Even now I can remember the exact moment when I knew that I loved Matt Mackenzie. The sun was setting and the men were walking in from the fields, all hot and dirty. The other men were ahead of him so that when I saw him he was alone, walking that winding path up toward the house, the sun behind him. He was little more than a silhouette." Her mother glanced down at the bowl of dough before her as though wondering where it had come from.

"I knew it was him by the way he walked," she continued. "The way he held his head, so proud and arrogant like, so full of himself as I always tell him. The sun seemed to make his hair shine even brighter red than usual, almost like a halo.''

Hilary looked over at her daughter with a sheepish expression on her face. ''I can't explain it, even now, but somehow, seeing him coming toward me I just knew that I loved him. That I'd always love him, no matter what.''

''Then what happened?'' Lauren had asked eagerly.

''Nothing.''

''Oh, Mama, don't say that. Of course something happened. You married him, didn't you?''

Hilary smiled. ''Not that summer, I didn't; you can be sure of that.''

''Did you tell him how you felt?''

''I didn't have to. I guess he saw the change in me. Where once I got angry at his teasing, after that I'd just laugh. I started talking with him more, rather than avoiding him. I began to ask questions about him because I was interested.''

''And then?''

''And then summer was over and he was gone—back to college in Pennsylvania.''

''So how did the two of you ever get together?''

''He started writing to me and I answered him. Then, during spring break, he came out to Nebraska to see me and I knew that I was more than just a friend to him, but I didn't really know how he felt.''

''Did he tell you?''

''Are you kidding? Matt would never be serious long enough to tell me how he really felt. I guess men sometimes have trouble finding the words to express how they feel.''

''So when did he propose?''

''He didn't.''

''Mother!'' Lauren could well recall her shock.

''He started writing letters with little phrases like 'after we're married—' or 'we'll have to name our firstborn Margaret Ann after my maternal grandmother' or 'I hope you won't mind living in Pennsylvania. It looks like I've found a pretty good job here as soon as I graduate.' ''

Lauren began to laugh. ''That sounds just like him.''

Hilary nodded. "Yes. When he wrote and asked me if I had any objections to getting married in June after he graduated, I told him no, I had no objections at all."

"Did he ever tell you he loved you?"

Hilary smiled that special smile. "He never had to tell me, sweetheart. He showed it in every way that counts."

"He really does show it, doesn't he, Mama?"

Hilary nodded. "He really does."

Staring at a pillow on a rumpled bed in Vienna, Austria, Lauren recalled that conversation with her mother as though she'd just had it.

How do you know when you're in love?

She had known without a doubt. When she saw that flash of vulnerability in Jordan's eyes, every irritating thought she'd ever had about him had seemed to disappear. She knew that she loved him, would always love him and without consciously deciding, she had offered herself to him free of reservation.

What must he have thought of her? she wondered, turning to the closet and reaching for something to wear. After all of her silly remarks about sharing a room with him, the first time she had the opportunity she threw herself at him.

She knew that he wasn't the type of man who would turn down such an offer. He couldn't fake his obvious response to her. Even in her innocence she recognized it.

The question was, what was she going to do now? She certainly couldn't expect Jordan to fall in love with her just because she wanted things to work out that way. Lauren was too much of a realist to even consider the possibility.

They had nothing in common. Even though Lauren had never really expected to marry, there had been times when she had yearned for a child or two to care for—who would share with her the abundant love she had.

Jordan had made it clear how he felt about children. His lifestyle wasn't conducive to a quiet home life filled with the laughter of children and the chores associated with a home. Somehow she couldn't picture Jordan mowing a lawn or trimming a hedge or tinkering with a bicycle.

Lauren should feel relieved that the interruption had come when it did. But instead she felt robbed. She forced herself to face the fact that if she could have nothing more than these few days with Jordan Trent, she wanted them with a ferocity that surprised her.

Logically and rationally her decision made no sense whatsoever. But then love could never be explained away, either logically or rationally.

She heard the door to the bathroom open and caught a whiff of Jordan's aftershave. She would never smell that well-known brand again that she wouldn't be reminded of him.

He walked out and stopped just inside the bedroom. She still wore her robe. "Sorry I took so long," he said, rubbing his jaw slowly.

She forced herself to smile lightly. "No problem. I'll hurry," she said, matching her steps to her words as she went by him.

He stopped her by placing his hand lightly on her arm. "Lauren?"

She met his eyes squarely. "Yes?"

"About what happened earlier . . ."

"Yes?"

Damn, he wished she wouldn't look at him with that clear-eyed gaze that seemed to look deep inside of him. "I'm sorry. I didn't mean to take advantage of—"

"You didn't," she said quickly, interrupting him. "If you'll recall, I'm the one who started it. I guess you'll have trouble trusting me again, huh?" she asked.

She wasn't angry! He couldn't believe it. In fact, she was teasing him. Here he'd spent all this time wrestling with his conscience, determined to make the right decision for everyone concerned, and she was treating the whole thing as though it didn't matter.

"Something like that," he said slowly, watching her closely.

"I'm sorry if it embarrassed you," she said quietly.

"Embarrassed me! Of course not. It's just that this situation is a little unusual. We have to think about—" He stopped himself and glanced around, suddenly remembering that he had to be careful what he said. He shrugged. "Go ahead. We can talk later."

She walked into the bathroom and turned to shut the door. "There's really nothing to talk about, is there? Nothing really happened."

Jordan watched the door close before turning to his suitcase. *Oh, yeah, Miss Innocence? That's what you think,* he grumbled to himself.

Before, he'd only had his imagination to fuel the flames she seemed to ignite inside him. Now he knew exactly what was underneath those attractive dresses she wore.

What he couldn't understand was what a woman like Lauren Mackenzie was doing unattached. If he were the settling down kind, she'd be the first— But that way of thinking was a waste of energy. He wasn't the settling down type. And she deserved better than he could offer.

Jordan found a shirt and socks and put on his shoes, then waited for her to reappear.

It was almost like being married.

When they entered the lobby there were people milling around, all talking excitedly. A cordon of uniformed policemen watched as a crew cleared the debris of glass and other building materials from around the entrance to the hotel.

Jordan guided Lauren into the dining area of the hotel where they were served breakfast.

After the waiter left, Lauren asked, "What do we do now?"

Jordan enjoyed his first sip of coffee before answering her. "I need to get another car and then you, my dear, will start earning your keep on this trip."

Her eyes widened slightly, unsure of his meaning. Whether he was teasing her or not she was ready to do whatever she could.

"All right," she said with a nod.

He grinned. "Shouldn't you ask what it is first?"

"I don't have to," she replied calmly.

Her calm acceptance, which showed a great deal of trust in him, almost unnerved him.

"I haven't had any trouble so far since I speak German," he began, "and I know a smattering of many of the languages in Europe. But to get detailed information, I'll need your help once we get into Czechoslovakia."

She smiled. "All right."

"Do you know the Slavic languages spoken there?"

"I've studied them, yes. I haven't had much practice in recent years, but I'm sure they will come back."

"Fine."

Within the hour they were on their way north to Brno, Czechoslovakia.

Jordan had kept their room in Vienna, and casually dropped the information that they would be exploring the countryside and might end up staying at some village inn somewhere. They repacked so that they could share Jordan's suitcase. Lauren had been shaken by the intimacy of their apparel resting so cozily together and had to remind herself that appearances meant a great deal in a situation such as theirs.

Lauren discovered that she enjoyed the drive through the peaceful countryside. Jordan shared with her some of the experiences he had had while working in Europe. He also gave her tips on what to expect behind the iron curtain, how to behave, and instructions in case of an unexpected crisis.

"I know someone to contact in Brno, which helps. He seems able to keep his finger on the pulse of the city. Nothing happens that he doesn't know about. If Frances Monroe was taken there, he'll know."

The closer they drew to the border, the quieter they became. There was only so much rehearsing they could do. Now was the time to start acting for all they were worth.

Lauren discovered that she was comfortable pretending to be Jordan's wife. She loved him and she could pretend for the next little while that the relationship was real.

Jordan wished he were going in alone. There were too many unknowns in the situation.

Mallory had been wise to suggest they stay with their real names and backgrounds. Jordan had posed as a sales representative from Chicago, Illinois for so many years that he found it easy to fall back into that role.

Now he and his wife were in Europe on vacation. He intended to mention that they had some friends in Chicago who had relatives living in Brno, in case anyone asked. Otherwise, they were just visiting a town known for its manufacturing business. What better place for a sales rep to want to visit?

Crossing the border took a little time. Their car and suitcase were minutely inspected. Passports were scrutinized and the papers on the car were carefully read. Eventually they were allowed to go on their way.

"I think it helped that you knew their language," Jordan remarked as they drove away. "Claiming that you had a grandmother born in Pizen helped."

"It was true," she said quietly.

He glanced around in surprise. "Why hadn't you told me before?"

"It never occurred to me," she admitted.

"And what other fascinating background have you yet to reveal to your husband?" he asked with a grin.

"Nothing of any interest, I'm sure."

Jordan thought about that as they continued their journey. She was wrong. He found everything about her interesting. Lauren was such an unusual blend of innocence and sophistication, intelligence and naïveté, that he never knew what to expect from her next.

His traitorous mind reverted to the early morning hours and once again Jordan experienced what it felt like to hold her, kiss and caress her. She'd been untutored but very responsive and he discovered that his willpower where she was concerned seemed to be slipping badly.

They checked into a hotel that was considerably different in atmosphere from Vienna. They were greeted with suspicion and almost open disdain.

By the time they reached their room, Lauren could no longer control her trembling.

Jordan locked the door behind the man who had escorted them to their room, then turned to Lauren. She was looking around the room as though trying to see the surveillance equipment. He smiled. She was very brave in so many ways. Perhaps it was the nonactivity of the ride that had given her too much time to think about what they would be dealing with in an iron curtain country.

"Well, my dear," he said in a hearty voice, "We're finally here. Aren't you glad we came?"

She looked around at him as though he'd lost his mind.

He walked over and put his arms around her. He could feel how stiff she was. He mouthed the words "answer me."

"Oh, yes, darling. Of course I'm glad. Just a little tired after the drive, that's all."

"Don't you want to explore the city with me, since we're here?"

She knew they had to start looking as quickly as possible. Lauren forced herself to smile. "Sounds like fun."

He smiled and pantomimed the words "good girl," then leaned down and kissed her. He'd meant it to be a reassuring kind of kiss—one that a father, brother or uncle could have given her.

However, when she responded without any restraint, Jordan forgot all his pure motives—the multitude of pep talks he'd given himself—and accepted her wholehearted cooperation by indulging in a thorough exploration of Lauren's delectable mouth.

His tongue invaded and was greeted eagerly by hers in a love play that was intensely provocative. When he finally paused for much-needed air they were both breathing hard, trying to get their bearings.

"Are you trying to distract me?" he muttered in a barely audible tone.

She grinned. "If I am, how am I doing?"

"You're asking for trouble, you know that, don't you?"

"And if I am?"

He heard the flippancy in her tone and saw the vulnerability in her eyes. Could it be possible? Was she falling for him? Dear Lord, he didn't need that. Especially now, not when they were in such a risky situation. There was no denying there was something between them. Something that would have to be worked out. Jordan knew that he wasn't going to be able to walk away from this woman and forget her.

But now wasn't the time to deal with the potentially explosive response they were having toward each other.

Jordan hugged her to him. "I didn't drive all this way to spend all our time in bed," he said in a mock-ferocious tone for the benefit of anyone who might be listening. He rubbed his knuckles along her cheek, loving the velvety softness, wishing he could touch her all over, from her ears to her toes, exploring, initiating, loving her.

Loving her? Where had that idea come from? Love was such a myth and yet, Jordan couldn't identify the strong emotion that had sprung up within him since he'd been with Lauren. He'd never felt anything like it before. As much as he wanted to make love to her he was much more concerned about her safety. He wanted to protect her from all harm.

"Let's go," he said gruffly, taking her hand and leading her from the room.

They spent the afternoon as typical tourists. They found some people who were willing to chat with them, which gave Lauren a chance to brush up on the language. Jordan watched with pride as Lauren's friendliness won over the suspicious natures of the strangers. From what Jordan could make out, she talked to them about her grandmother, mentioned some of the songs she'd been taught to sing as a child, did a few dance steps and before long was involved in a laughing discussion of the different cultures.

After some involved tracking, they also managed to locate the man who might be able to help them. When they finally found him, he was in a small room behind a local shop. He stood when Jordan walked in and then grabbed Jordan around the shoulders, hugging him tightly.

"It is good to see you once again, Jordan," he said in fluent English.

"It's good to see you, too, Stefan," Jordan replied. He'd had his arm around Lauren's waist when they came in, but had dropped it when Stefan greeted him so exuberantly. Now he turned to Lauren and, taking her hand, drew her forward. "I'd like you to meet my wife, Lauren."

Stefan laughed. "But of course, my friend. You would only have such a beautiful woman as your wife, would you not? I am so very pleased to meet you." He stuck out his hand and she grasped it gently. "Aahhh. You are very shy, I can tell."

Lauren could feel her cheeks burning and heard Jordan laugh. "There are times when she isn't so shy, Stefan," he said with a grin.

He'd almost sounded like a husband, Lauren thought with a sense of wonder. That tone of possessive pride had sounded authentic.

"Sit down, sit, both of you," Stefan exclaimed. "I must apologize for meeting you like this, but you see, I must be very careful who I am seen talking to."

"Thank you for going to all the trouble to arrange this," Jordan replied. "I appreciate it."

"I had no choice because I wanted very much to see you once again and know that things are well for you." He glanced at Lauren with a smile. "I'm pleased that you are so obviously happy." Stefan sat opposite them with a bright expression. Then the smile faded. "But you are here for more than a friendly visit, I know."

"I'm afraid so, Stefan. Have you heard anything about the disappearance of an American woman in Vienna a few days ago?"

Stefan studied the floor for a few moments of silence, then glanced up. "A nice looking woman, tall, slender, with reddish-colored hair?"

"You've seen her?" Jordan demanded eagerly.

"No, but I have heard of something that did not ring exactly true."

"What?"

"There is a story circulating about a woman who had been traveling and became ill. She was taken to a private clinic on the outskirts of town, but none of the regular employees has been allowed to care for her. She has her own nurse and doctor."

"That could be her," Jordan said thoughtfully. "Is there any way we can get in to see her?"

"We?"

"I would need to take Lauren with me."

"I see. Well, of course I can't say without doing some checking. No doubt it would be difficult, but perhaps not impossible."

Jordan laughed. "With you, Stefan, nothing is ever impossible."

"You are too kind, my friend. Give me some time and I will get back in touch with you."

"Where can I meet you?"

"I'll leave a message here at the shop by noon tomorrow. We'll see what we can do."

Jordan's frown of concentration on the way back to the hotel kept Lauren silent. He pulled up in front of a shop that sold hats, gloves and scarves and said, "Wait here. I won't be but a few minutes."

He was as good as his word. When he returned he handed her a package.

"What is this?"

"A hat with a wide brim. You'll need to wear it if we get to go into the clinic."

"You've come up with a plan, haven't you?" she asked quietly.

"I'm still debating it, but it may work." He hadn't started the car. Instead he sat gripping the wheel tightly and staring down the street. Lauren studied his grim profile.

"Tell me," she prodded.

He looked over at her and sighed. "God, I hate to get you involved in this."

"I'm already involved. You know that."

"Yes."

"So what do you have in mind?"

"I can't risk removing Mrs. Monroe—if it is Mrs. Monroe—from the clinic without causing all kinds of disturbances. The minute she's gone they'll be watching the borders for her."

Lauren nodded, understanding what he was having trouble putting into words.

"So I'll be there in her place," she said calmly.

"It's the only thing I've come up with so far, but it needs some work."

"I think it's excellent. She can leave as me. The two of you can check out of the hotel and drive back across at your leisure. If my hair and makeup is as accurate as Mr. Mallory planned, there should be no problem at all recrossing the border."

"Yes, that's what Mallory was counting on. But it leaves you in the hands of whoever kidnapped Frances Monroe."

"I know," she said quietly.

"I'm not sure I can do that."

"You don't have any choice. After all, that was the whole idea of my coming with you."

Jordan let go of the steering wheel and pounded his fist softly against it. "I don't like it."

"I'm not all that thrilled myself, you know."

"I'll talk to Stefan tomorrow, see if he has any other ideas."

"Perhaps he could help me leave the clinic later."

"As soon as I can get Mrs. Monroe to safety, I'll be back."

"But you can't. You'll be endangering—"

"The hell I can't. If I leave you, I'll damned well be back to get you."

"But we can't cross the border—"

"Not legally, but we can get across."

"Jordan, I'm sure Mr. Mallory wouldn't want you risking—"

"I don't really care what Mallory wants at this point. He's the one who recruited you for this little drama. He can accept the fact that it won't be over until you're home safely where you belong."

Lauren studied him thoughtfully. Of course she was scared. Why shouldn't she be? She had known that what she would be doing would be dangerous. As soon as they had suggested that she might be substituted for Frances Monroe, Lauren knew that she might be discovered and arrested as a spy.

There was no reason to consider that aspect of the situation. Not yet. Surely among the three of them they could devise a workable scenario with the least amount of risk for everyone concerned.

She could feel Jordan's anger and frustration radiating from him, but it was different from the day in Mr. Mallory's office. He was concerned for her because he cared about her. She understood very well. Thinking of all the dangers inherent in his crossing the border with a substitute wife caused her mind to flinch from the possibility of failure.

Jordan started the car and they drove back to the hotel in silence.

Six

They ate at the hotel in an almost empty dining room. Neither of them had much to say. Their minds were on what they might be facing the next day and they knew the discussion was over for now.

By the time they returned to the room, it was dark. Without saying anything, Lauren reached into their shared suitcase for her gown and realized that she had brought one of the silk and lace ones that were part of her role. She shrugged. When she'd packed, she'd been thinking about how things would appear at customs, not about how she'd feel actually wearing the gown. She hadn't even brought her robe.

She walked into the bathroom and filled the tub with water, grateful for the steam that told her it was hot. Shedding her clothes she gingerly crawled into the warm water and sank down with a satisfied sigh.

What a day she'd had. She'd been awakened by an explosion; then she had participated in an emotional upheaval that had destroyed all the preconceived ideas she'd had about men and sex and her own involvement in intimacies before marriage.

She continued to enumerate the events of her day in her mind: a trip behind the iron curtain, a meeting with Stefan and a plan that might mean she'd never see her homeland again. *Don't think that way!* she scolded herself. The plan would work because they would make it work. Depending on how closely she resembled Frances Monroe, it was possible Lauren could continue the charade for days.

Then what?

Jordan would be back to get her.

She smiled at the thought. She knew he would help her. Lauren had complete trust in him.

By the time she was out of the tub, Lauren felt relaxed and rested, all the minor aches and pains of travel having disappeared. After slipping on the gown she moved to the mirror and began to brush her hair.

Suddenly Lauren stopped. Her hand clenched the brush in midair, her gaze fixed on the woman in the mirror. The gown was mostly satin and it clung to her figure like a second skin. She could see the indentation of her waist just below her ribs and above her hip bones. There was even a shadow where her navel was.

She might as well be nude. In fact, her breasts were exposed through the fine lace that formed thin straps and widened slightly into two strips to her waist. She was expected to share a bed with Jordan Trent undressed like this?

She grinned. He wouldn't stand a chance.

Whatever happened tomorrow, she had tonight and she fully intended to share it with Jordan. Ever since the abrupt interruption of their lovemaking that morning the tension between them had been almost visible. Surely he didn't expect to share that bed with her and sleep! Not after this morning.

Lauren opened the door and walked out of the bathroom.

A small lamp by the bed was the room's only illumination. Jordan stood in a darkened corner staring out the window. When she walked into the room he didn't look around and from the expression on his face, his thoughts were far from pleasant.

"Jordan?"

He glanced around and suddenly straightened, his eyes locking on her as though he had no control over them.

"Yes?" he asked gruffly.

"I'm sorry for taking so long in the tub." She walked over to where he stood, the soft light now at her back.

He watched her approach him and knew there was no way he was going to be able to resist her tonight. No way. He was too worried, too fearful for her. And now she appeared in a gown he'd never seen before.

What had happened to the demure nightshirt she'd had on the night before?

Not that it would have influenced his reaction to her now, even if she wore sackcloth.

He cleared his throat. "No problem," he muttered, side-stepping her and going into the other room. He firmly closed the door—but not before she saw the hot desire burning in his eyes and the way his body reacted to the sight of her.

She'd learned a great deal about him this morning. Lauren intended to learn even more before the night was over.

When Jordan stepped out of the bathroom after a long, invigorating shower, the bedroom yielded no light to guide him to bed. Only a faint glow from the two windows enabled him to cautiously move to where he thought the bed was.

He'd been wishing he'd brought something to sleep in. At the time he'd packed, he'd been too angry to think of all of the ramifications of traveling with a woman who was supposed to be his wife. Therefore, the only things he had to wear were dress trousers and a pair of his jeans. Neither were appropriate. Both would be damned uncomfortable.

He touched the side of the bed with his leg. Carefully feeling along the edge he came to the bedside table located near the headboard. Jordan gingerly lowered himself on the side of the bed. So far, so good. Maybe she was already asleep. He forced himself to quieten his own breathing and listen. As he gradually calmed himself he located her soft breathing nearby. If its rapid rate was any indication, she was far from asleep.

What, after all, had he expected?

At least the night before they'd had separate beds, even though they'd been within touching distance of each other. Tonight there was no pretense. They needed to sleep as a married couple. Unseen ears would be alert to anything unusual.

Besides, there wasn't even a comfortable chair in the room, much less a couch. He refused to consider trying to sleep on the floor.

Carefully lifting the covers, Jordan crawled in, making sure he kept a solid distance between himself and the center of the bed. It was going to be a long night, but he needed as much sleep as possible. Forcing himself to relax, Jordan stretched out over the length of the bed.

"Jordan, darling?"

Her sudden remark in the darkened room almost caused him to spring straight up in the bed. It was soft and seductive and from the endearment she had added, Lauren obviously knew there might be listeners.

"Hmmm?" he responded warily. What was she up to?

"I never did ask you. Do you mind if this one turns out to be a girl?"

An electrified silence filled the room after her question. He whipped his head around on the pillow but couldn't see anything but a faint silhouette of her body.

"What?" he asked in a strangled voice.

"You know, the baby," she said in a tone that told him she was smiling. "I know we didn't plan on starting our family this soon, but you aren't sorry now that this one's on the way...are you?" she asked wistfully.

"Uh, Lauren—"

He felt her shift in the bed. Her foot slid along his ankle and rubbed against his arch. Jordan almost jackknifed out of the bed at her touch. "What are you doing!" he demanded in a harsh whisper.

"Oh, I'm sorry, love. Am I crowding you? This is considerably smaller than our bed back home, isn't it?" she said. "But then we never have taken up much room when we're together." She edged closer so that her hair brushed against his shoulder. "I hope he looks like you," she added.

"Who?"

"The baby. If it's a boy I'd like to name him after you. I hope his hair is black and curly like yours, and that he has large black eyes and your mischievous grin."

"Mischievous—" Jordan broke off at the thought of Lauren having his baby. For a moment he could see the infant she was describing as clearly as if it were there in the room with them: the black curly hair, the smile. Only the eyes were gray, wide pools of early morning mist staring back at him.

Then a little girl joined the baby. She had curls, too, but hers were a sandy red, almost carrot topped, her eyes a deep brown. She held up her hands to him as though expecting him to take her.

Jordan shook his head, blinking several times. Was he losing his mind? Was the stress too much? He'd been right. He was too old for this sort of life. He needed to be put away in some peaceful sanitarium somewhere—

"Or would you rather we name him after your father?"

Without conscious thought, Jordan responded. "No. I don't want to name him after my father." His voice sounded harsh in the quiet room and he tried to cover his reaction. "How about naming him after your father?" When he heard himself speak, only then did Jordan face the fact that he was going along with her idiotic game.

"Matthew Mackenzie Trent. It does have a nice ring to it, doesn't it?" she said with a certain amount of pride.

Jordan grinned. She certainly sounded like a proud mama introducing her son to an adoring audience. He shifted by turning over on his side and felt her from his shoulder down to his toes. Casually sliding his knee across her, he let his hand drop lightly on her chest, cupping her breast.

"What about our daughter?" he asked, while beginning to nibble on her exposed ear. Jordan could feel her heart racing in her chest. Surprised that she could sound so casually sleepy with a heart pounding like a steam engine, Jordan wondered just how far she intended to carry out her little game.

"Our daughter?" she repeated, ending on a breathless note.

"Umhmmm . . ." he replied, planting a row of kisses down her neck and lightly touching the pulsing beat at the base of her throat with his tongue. "Just in case it's a girl."

"Oh! Well, uh, I'm not sure."

"She'll probably have your color hair and your large eyes that seem to fill a man with all kinds of ideas—"

"They do? I mean—"

"Oh, yes. If we weren't already married I definitely would have been irritated at the way some of those men were looking at you today."

"But I—"

He cut off whatever she was going to say by the simple means of placing his mouth over hers. She tried to move away only to find herself held firmly by his arm and leg across her.

Not that Lauren wanted to move away. Not exactly, anyway. She just hadn't expected him to pounce quite so suddenly. She'd been lying there thinking about how little they could talk about in the room. One thought had led to another and she had decided to tease him. Just a little. But he'd turned it back on her without effort.

Funny, but she could see both a baby boy and a little girl. They were happy children, laughing, filled with love—and she felt such a fierce tug of joy that she turned toward him, holding him close. He'd probably only meant the kiss to shut her up, but now that she was where she'd wanted to be all along . . .

Jordan felt her resistance fade away and she flowed against him. Her breasts nudged his chest and she shifted her leg so that she sandwiched his knee between her thighs.

All of his good intentions deserted him at that moment. He certainly wasn't a saint, even though he'd tried to be one. And Lauren wasn't helping him at all. If he didn't know better, he'd swear she was intent on seducing him.

He leaned up on his elbow and looked down at her shadowy face. With a wicked smile he exaggerated a yawn and said, "Well, darlin', it's been a long day. Guess we should try to get some rest. You especially need to take good care of yourself," he added. At the same time he began to slide first one of her gown straps off her shoulder, then the other.

Lauren made a strangled sound that was something between a cough and a gasp. Jordan continued to tug at her gown until it was around her waist. "Goodnight," he said just before he began to kiss her.

His kisses were filled with passion and determination. There was no doubt in either of their minds that this time he would make love to her and that she would not discourage him.

Ever conscious of their need to be quiet, Jordan's silent lovemaking touched Lauren with his gentleness. While his hands softly brushed the silk and lace down off her body until the gown lay around her feet, his mouth continued to explore her. Her silky skin drew him on to touch and taste her. At one point he was aware that she put her fist to her mouth rather than allow a moan to escape.

She had tantalized and teased him, even if it hadn't been intentional. Now there was no turning back. Before morning, Lauren Mackenzie would better understand the intimate relationship between a man and a woman.

Lauren began to imitate what Jordan was doing, with remarkable results. When she brushed her hand across his abdomen, his stomach muscles rippled with reaction. She came into contact with the waist line of his briefs and, following his example, began to slide them down his muscular thighs and calves.

Moving very slowly so that the bed barely shifted, Jordan rolled over until he was on top of Lauren. She felt his weight pressing her down for a brief moment, then he rested on his forearms. "Am I too heavy?" he whispered almost inaudibly in her ear. She shook her head in answer.

He found her mouth once more, teasing her with nibbling little kisses across her bottom lip, tracing the line of her upper lip with his tongue, until his actions got to both of them. Suddenly penetrating her mouth with his tongue, he began to show her what he intended to do with her, his lazy strokes allowing her an opportunity to draw away if she wished.

Instead Lauren pulled him closer, shifting slightly to accommodate his weight. By the time he rose slightly above her, they were both trembling with need and desire. Lauren had never guessed that lovemaking could be so beautiful, such a luscious sharing of another person. She knew that she would be forever thankful that she had found Jordan and had the opportunity to get to know him. Having him show her the mysterious art of lovemaking seemed to be what she had waited for all her life.

Jordan lowered himself with slow deliberation until she fully sheathed him. How had he ever lived this long without experiencing such an awe-inspiring sensation of oneness with another person? He held her close to him without moving, savoring the delightful intensity of the moment.

Lauren smiled into the darkness, clutching him to her, her head sheltered in his shoulder. This was wonderful. She had expected pain, or at the very least discomfort. Instead she was astonished at his patience in seeking entrance, moving so slowly that he gave her body an opportunity to adjust to him.

His exaggeratedly slow movements were extremely erotic for them both. Constantly aware of a certain lack of privacy, Jordan was determined to give her pleasure without feeling that others were getting a vicarious thrill from their lovemaking.

The silence of the room lay unbroken except for an occasional sigh or the soft sound of a sheet being shifted, all of which could be explained as the sounds made by restless people trying to sleep in a new bed in a strange country.

Lauren felt as though something deep inside of her was becoming unraveled; the more it loosened and moved the more tense she became. Her body felt as though it were on the brink of exploding; tiny fingers of bright lights and colors seemed to shimmer in the darkness. Abruptly a shower of fireworks appeared to burst all around her, filling the room with radiance and joy, hope and love.

She buried her head deeply into his chest and held on. Jordan gave one strong surge of movement that seemed to set off a shudder that raced from his head down to his toes. Lauren felt his arms quivering, then he lowered himself helplessly to the bed beside her, his breathing harsh.

Pulling her to him he held her as though he never intended to let her go. She was content to fall asleep that way.

Sometime during the night Lauren awoke to the most marvelous sensations. Jordan still held her in his arms while he touched her delicately with his hands and mouth.

His lovemaking seemed to be a part of her dreamlike state and she responded to him mindlessly, knowing that their time together would end in a few hours.

The next time she awakened, Jordan was saying in a normal speaking voice, "Time to get up, darling, if we're going to get any sight-seeing done."

Lauren blinked open her eyes, squinting in the harsh light. She managed to focus on Jordan who stood by the side of the bed. The shock of seeing him standing there nude woke her quicker than a pail of ice water dumped on the bed.

She let out a gasp and pulled up the covers to her shoulders.

It was one thing to make passionate love to a man in the dark. It was something else to see that man in all of his natural splendor. Then she realized he was totally unconcerned with his lack of adornment.

"I thought it might save us some time if we showered together," he said nonchalantly, with a decidedly wicked look in his eyes.

"Oh, but, I, uh—"

He began a steady pressure, pulling the sheet from her nerveless fingers. "Come on, honey. We need to get a move on." Reaching down he grasped her hands and pulled her to her feet, glancing down at her with a smile. He began to walk her to the bathroom. "How did you sleep last night, dear?"

"Oh! Well, I didn't seem to—"

"I know. A strange bed and all. It's hard to get enough rest when you travel. I've spent so many years on the road that I've grown used to it."

Lauren had never known that she was capable of blushing all over. One glance into the mirror of the bathroom convinced her it was possible. Her face blushed an even brighter shade of red when she discovered that he wasn't unaffected by her.

He leaned over and kissed her under the ear, then slid his arms around her. They both stood facing the mirror. His expression reflected his amusement at her embarrassment.

"If you think I'm about to apologize for what happened last night, you're in for quite a shock," he said in a low voice.

She shook her head but somehow couldn't find her voice. Pulling her under the steady stream of water with him, he systematically soaped her entire body with loving caresses until Lauren forgot about her embarrassment. Now she could study the body that she'd only explored by touch last night. She had to admit there was something to be said for the braille method of learning, but she enjoyed being able to see him as well.

Lauren's body seemed to have learned some amazing responses to him in a very short while. Either that, or he knew what buttons to push to cause a strong reaction from deep within her.

When he lifted her, coaxing her to wrap her legs around his waist, she gasped out loud.

"Am I hurting you?" he asked, a slight frown pulling his brows together.

She shook her head.

"You can talk to me, you know. We've got the water running."

Lauren was too stunned by feeling to be able to think of anything to say. "Isn't this going to hurt your back?" she finally managed to gasp.

He kissed her—a long, drugging, possessive kiss that wiped the question from her mind. When he finally raised his head she felt so weak she could barely hold on to him.

"Are you going to give me a rubdown if I do hurt my back?" he asked in a mischievous tone of voice. "If so, it might be worth it."

She could no longer concentrate on his teasing. Lauren arched her back and let out a small cry and felt as though she were melting.

Jordan gave a convulsive movement, clasping her so close she could hardly get her breath. After a few moments he slowly lowered her to her feet.

"Wow!" he managed to say when he could catch his breath.

"Wow? What's that supposed to mean?"

"Wow! You're a pretty potent bathing partner."

She grinned, suddenly feeling extremely pleased with herself. Jordan acted as though she'd known what she was doing to him, when all the time she'd been following his lead.

Gingerly crawling out of the shower, she discovered that her knees were shaking so hard she could hardly stand. "I'm not so sure that was a good idea," she said huskily.

Leaving the water running, Jordan was out of the shower with his arms around her asking, "What's wrong? I did hurt you, didn't I? Damn!"

She shook her head. "I just didn't have any idea—How could I have known—" She glanced into the mirror and saw his anxious expression. "I'm all right, really," she said, managing to put a little stiffening into her knees. "I didn't mean to scare you."

"Oh, Lauren," he said, burying his face in her hair. "I would never want to hurt you."

"I know," she responded softly. If she got hurt over this relationship, she would have no one but herself to blame. She'd made the decision and she wasn't sorry. Now they had to get on with why they were there.

Reaching for a towel, she said, "Shouldn't you turn off the water before someone checks to see if we have a leak in this room?"

Jordan nodded without saying anything. He just released her and leaned into the shower and turned off the water.

"So what's on the agenda today?" she asked in a casual voice.

He followed her into the bedroom and they began to dress. Lauren couldn't keep her eyes off him, but she tried very hard not to stare.

"You remember the little curio shop we found yesterday?" he asked and she knew he was talking about the place where they'd met Stefan.

"Oh, yes."

"I keep thinking about that chess set I saw in there, with all the hand carved pieces. That would be a great gift for your dad, don't you think?" ·

She grinned. "Absolutely." *If my dad knew anything about chess, that is.* "I'm pleased you thought of him," she added.

He walked over and adjusted the collar of her dress, then allowed his hand to slide slowly down to her waist, then back up. "Oh, I always think of your family. They're great people. Did you remember to buy postcards to send to Meg and Amy?"

Lauren gave him a sharp look and caught the teasing glint in his eye. "Well, I thought you'd prefer to wait until we get to France to purchase those. You know how my sisters are."

His brows shot up and she flashed him a very innocent look.

Jordan glanced at his watch. "I suppose we should get going. We overslept a little this morning."

"Oh, well, what difference does it make, anyway? We're on vacation." She picked up her purse and the hat he'd bought her the day before.

"Glad you reminded me. I keep trying to keep some sort of schedule."

* * *

Stefan had a message waiting for them when they arrived at the little shop. They were to meet him at three o'clock by a well-known landmark of the city. Jordan suggested lunch, since they weren't sure when they might get another opportunity to eat.

He kept studying her during their meal until she became self-conscious. "What's the matter, do I have dirt on my face?"

If anything, Jordan's expression merely became more intent. "No. You've just surprised me, that's all," he finally said, slowly taking a bite of his neglected meal.

"You didn't realize how aggressive I was going to be, perhaps?" She tried for flippancy but from his expression, he wasn't buying it.

"I'd like to understand why," he said thoughtfully, as though repeating something that had run through his head several times.

"Why?" she repeated hesitantly.

"Why me? Why now? Why wait this long in your life and then make such a decision?"

"Are you saying I should have sat down and figured all of this out on a logical basis before making love to you?"

"I'm saying," he repeated in a patiently level tone, "that you acted totally out of character and you know it."

"You don't know my character all that well, obviously."

"I know I was the first man you'd ever been with."

"My inexperience showed, huh? And here I thought I learned so quickly."

"And you aren't fooling me for a minute, Lauren. From everything I've discovered about you, I know you to be a strong, independent woman who doesn't do anything on impulse."

"You've got to be kidding. This whole trip is an impulse. What if I just said that I was tired of my old life-style and wanted a change of pace?"

"Why me?"

She couldn't bring herself to carry on the brittle comments any longer; couldn't force herself to say, "Because you were available."

Playing for time, she took a sip from her glass, then set it down in front of her. Raising her chin slightly, she met his intent gaze. "Maybe I fell in love with you."

She watched him flinch as though she'd slapped him and knew she shouldn't be surprised. What had she expected, anyway?

"You know there's no future in it," he said quietly.

"I know."

"My life-style is—"

"I'm quite aware of your life-style. Please don't draw me any pictures, okay?"

"I took advantage of the situation after I told you—"

"Why do you have to take all the credit? I managed to take a few advantages myself, you know."

He shook his head, not at all pleased with the way the conversation was going. Wouldn't she take anything seriously?

Of course she didn't love him. What a joke. She didn't even like him. And who could blame her, the way he'd treated her from the very beginning. And yet there was something— something between them that showered sparks all around whenever they were near each other. Even after the past several hours of making love to her, Jordan recognized that he wanted her again. What was it about her that affected him so?

He wished to hell he knew.

Glancing at his watch he said, "We've got to go." Jordan signaled the waiter and when he'd brought their check, quickly paid the bill. Then he took Lauren's hand and they walked out of the restaurant together, that peculiar radiance that lovers seem to reflect obvious to everyone who glanced their way.

Seven

They circled the park twice like a couple enjoying the view and the day. Jordan teased her, whispering in her ear and making her blush, meanwhile unobtrusively watching for Stefan. Even so, he didn't recognize him.

An elderly man with a slight limp, using a cane, nodded as they passed him. It took Jordan a few seconds to remember when he'd last seen that old man. He began to laugh.

"What's so funny?"

"I forgot about Stefan's love for disguises."

She glanced around the park. "Where is he?"

"Never mind. We'll find a bench and sit down in a moment. I'm sure he'll join us."

After fifteen minutes or so, they were joined on the park bench by the same elderly man who nodded to them once again. Jordan continued to look and speak to Lauren; however his speech was directed past her shoulder. "You could have at least warned me this was going to be a costume party."

"No problem," the man muttered, as though talking to himself. "Thought you'd recognize the outfit."

"Any word?"

"Yes. The information we have is correct."

"Can we get in there?"

The old man fished into his pocket and pulled out a small bag of peanuts. He tossed one on the ground and watched a squirrel scurry from a nearby tree, grab the nut and race back to safety.

"It will be a little risky, but yes."

"How?"

Jordan continued to smile and play with the curl in front of Lauren's ear, but his eyes were watching the man nearby.

"I have made arrangements for the nurse to meet with her lover for a few minutes around five o'clock. That is still during visiting hours. You and your wife will go as visitors, mingling until you get inside. I've drawn a map which is inside the newspaper lying here beside me. Once in the clinic you will need to slip into the other wing. Her room is marked. You won't have long."

"What sort of condition is she in?"

"They couldn't give me anything on that."

"If I leave Lauren there until I can get the woman out of the country, how much protection can you give Lauren?"

"Whatever is necessary."

Jordan realized he'd been barely breathing until that last remark. Even so, their plan might not work. But if they could get to Mrs. Monroe, they'd have more information and a better chance of deciding what to do.

"Will we see you?"

"I'll be there, but you won't see me," Stefan said to a scampering squirrel.

Jordan leaned over and kissed Lauren. "We'll be there at five," he said as he pulled away from her. He picked up the paper and stuck it under his arm in an absent manner. Taking her hand, he pulled her to her feet, for all the world like a lover who was anxious to find someplace private.

Neither of them looked back at the elderly man who continued to sit and toss peanuts at the squirrels.

Jordan was pleased to see enough people going in and out of the clinic that he and Lauren could easily blend into the crowd.

He'd had Lauren wear the hat he'd purchased the day before, just in case. It completely shadowed her face.

Once inside, they followed the hallway until it turned. Then they found the stairwell and went up two flights, down another hallway until they reached the end. Praying that Stefan's plan still worked, Jordan tried the door on room 301. It opened. He peered inside. The drapes were drawn and it was shadowy but he could faintly see a woman in the only bed in the room.

Tugging at Lauren's hand, he pulled her inside and closed the door. Walking quietly over to the bed, he said, "Mrs. Monroe?"

The woman's head turned toward him.

"Are you Frances Monroe?"

She licked her lips and nodded. "Yes," she tried to say, as though unused to talking. "Who are you?" she managed to whisper, her voice breaking.

Jordan reached for her hand lying on the cover. "Your husband sent me, Mrs. Monroe. I'm going to get you out of here."

"Trevor?" Her voice grew stronger and she struggled to sit up. "Trevor's here? Oh, thank God. This nightmare's over."

"Shhhh, we don't have much time and we're going to need your help."

She nodded her head. "Yes. Whatever. Just tell me."

"Can you walk all right?"

"I'm not sure. They've been keeping me so doped up. I seem to have lost track of the days. They've been running together." Her voice became stronger. "Of course I can walk. I'll do whatever I have to."

Jordan patted her hand and spoke to Lauren. "Quick. Get out of that dress and hat." Then to Mrs. Monroe he explained, "Lauren is going to stay here in your place for a few hours. Just long enough to get you out of the country."

"But they'll see her and know—"

"Not as long as the room stays dark. If they turn on a light she can protest." He spoke as much for Lauren as for Frances Monroe.

Lauren realized that the moment of truth had arrived. It was time to do what she had to do, regardless of how frightened she was. Getting Mrs. Monroe safely back was the only thing that counted now. She stripped down to her panties and bra, then looked at Jordan inquiringly.

"Mrs. Monroe, I'm going to turn my back while you slip out of that gown and into these clothes, okay?" he asked gently.

Frances nodded. He could see that her hands were trembling so much that she would have trouble dressing herself. Fortunately Lauren stepped forward and began to help her.

When Frances stood up, Lauren was grateful to see that they were of a similar height and build. Thank God they'd gotten that much of the situation right. She couldn't see Frances's hair color, but the length was similar to hers.

"What color are your eyes?" Lauren asked.

Puzzled, the woman said, "Blue. Why?"

"Mine are gray. That's close enough."

"What do you mean?"

"You're going to be using my passport to get out of here."

"But how will you get out?" Frances asked, alarmed by the suddenness of what was happening.

Jordan spoke from across the room. "I should have you with your husband in a few hours, Mrs. Monroe. Then I'm coming back for Lauren."

Lauren hurriedly pulled Frances's gown over her head and slipped into the bed. Frances placed Lauren's hat on her head. "You can turn around now," Frances said. When he did, she said, "I never even asked your name."

"Jordan. Jordan Trent. I'm a great admirer of your husband, Mrs. Monroe. He doesn't need this kind of pressure on him."

She nodded. "I know. I've been so worried for him. There was no way to get word to him."

"Have they treated you all right?"

"Yes. I've only seen three people. The two men who stopped the car there in Vienna, and then the woman who stays here with me. How did you know she'd be gone?"

"We hoped. Look, we've got to go." He glanced over at Lauren who had stretched out on the bed in the same pose they'd found Frances Monroe in. He leaned over and gave her a hard kiss. "Don't worry. I'll be back soon."

She nodded. "I know."

Opening the door slightly, Jordan peered out. "Ready?" he asked, glancing back at Frances.

She nodded and followed him out of the room.

Lauren lay there forcing herself to take deep breaths. She needed to stay calm. Stefan was somewhere nearby. He would protect her. And before long, Jordan would be back for her.

She had to believe that. She couldn't afford to think of the many possibilities that could change all of their plans.

By the time they reached the main floor, Frances was shaking so hard she could hardly walk. "I'm sorry," she gasped. "But I've been in bed for days. I hadn't realized how weak I'd become."

Jordan wrapped his arm around her waist. "We're fine. Pretend you're overcome with grief. Keep your head down and we'll walk slowly to the car."

"Then what do we do?"

"Go back to the hotel, pack and get out of here."

He nodded to several people who passed them, looking at Frances's lowered head in concern.

"You're doing just fine," he murmured. "Don't be surprised when I call you Lauren."

"She's very brave to be doing this."

"Yes, she is."

"How fortunate that we could exchange clothes," she said breathlessly, "although I'm having a little trouble keeping the shoes on."

He grinned. "That's better than if they were too small."

He felt more than heard her slight chuckle. "Yes."

Their murmured conversation got them past the lobby and outside the front door. Both of them took a deep breath.

"I've had no idea where I was."

"Don't you remember coming here?"

"It was night. And I was so frightened. I was so afraid they were going to try to hurt Trevor through me."

An amazing woman, Jordan acknowledged to himself. How many women in her position would have been worrying over their husband?

Lauren would, if she were placed in a similar position.

He wasn't sure where the thought had come from, but recognized the truth of it. The similarity between the two women was more than superficial.

Frances dozed during the trip to the hotel and apologized when he woke her up after they'd arrived. "I can't seem to stay awake."

"Don't worry about it. You're doing fine." He helped her out of the car and into the hotel. He took her immediately to the room. Once inside, he said, "Why don't you lie down, darling, and see if that helps?" When she glanced up at him with a startled expression, he placed his finger to his lips, lifted the hat off her head and motioned for her to lie down.

Glancing around the room Frances nodded and laid down.

Jordan picked up the phone and rang the front desk. When someone answered, he said, "This is Jordan Trent. I'm afraid my wife must have eaten something that didn't agree with her. She's decided she wants to go back to Vienna tonight rather than to continue our sight-seeing. I'd appreciate it if you'd have our bill ready in a few minutes." He listened to an explanation. "Of course I understand. No. There's no problem. I'm sure it's nothing serious. Yes. We've had a very pleasant stay."

As soon as he hung up, Jordan went into the bathroom and quickly gathered up their toiletry articles.

When he walked back into the room he noticed that Frances had closed her eyes once again. In the clear light coming from the window he could see that she was a very nice-looking woman. The dress, indeed, looked like one she might have chosen. Her fair skin and goldish-red hair were remarkably similar to Lauren's, but she didn't affect him in the same way.

How strange. They were enough alike to pass as sisters, and yet one of them increased his pulse rate just by being in the same room with him, and the other one had no effect on him whatsoever.

What was it that caused the chemistry between people? He'd never had a reaction to a woman such as he did to Lauren. He didn't understand it at all.

At the moment he didn't have time to seek any answers, either. He tossed the items from the bathroom into the suitcase and closed it.

After he double-checked the room to be sure he'd packed all of their belongings, he walked over to the bed. "Lauren?"

Frances's eyes flew open at the sound of his voice. "Oh! I did it again."

"No problem." He helped her off the bed, picked up the suitcase and escorted her downstairs.

They were headed for the Austrian border within the hour. "I can't believe how easily you've managed all of this," Frances commented after they'd been traveling for several miles.

"It's part of my job," he said with a smile.

"What is that? Rescuing kidnap victims?"

"Among other things."

"Where is Trevor? Will he be in Vienna?"

"I'm taking you to an American military base. He intended to wait there until you were located."

"He never went home?"

Jordan glanced over at her out of the corner of his eye. "What do you think?"

She smiled. "Knowing Trevor, I'm surprised he didn't come after me himself."

"I'm sure he wanted to, but no one wanted to take any chances. Actually, I believe that's what your kidnappers hoped would happen."

"What do you mean?"

"Well, I've been putting some things together. We didn't have much problem locating you. It was as though you were supposed to be found."

"Then you think they would have let me go if I'd just asked?"

"Oh, no. The only reason there's been no alarm so far is because they're still confident they're holding you." *I hope*, he added silently.

"How much longer until the border?"

"Not much longer." He explained the procedure at the border and suggested she wear the hat and work hard at looking relaxed.

"If I were any more relaxed, I'd slither off the seat," she said with a grin. "My head is swimming and I feel as though I've been on a drunken spree for days."

"When was the last time they gave you something?"

"I don't remember. I had no concept of time while I was there."

"Did it seem to be given on some sort of schedule or whenever you appeared to need it?"

"I'm not sure. I tried to be very cooperative and quiet. I didn't want to give them any excuse to use force."

A very wise lady, Jordan thought to himself.

Crossing the border between Czechoslovakia and Austria was almost anticlimactic. The car and luggage were carefully scrutinized, their passports studied, but eventually they were allowed to pass.

They had driven several miles in silence before Jordan became aware of Frances Monroe's quiet sobs. He pulled over by the side of the road and stopped.

She glanced over at him, wiping her eyes. "I'm sorry," she gulped, trying to get her breath. "I know I'm being such a baby... but I was so scared and then—" she drew another ragged breath "—when I realized we'd made it... that we're actually free, I—" She started sobbing once again.

"Mrs. Monroe, you have my permission to kick, scream and cry. You've been extremely brave about all of this, and your reaction now is not only normal, but very healthy."

He reached into his pocket and drew out a clean handkerchief, handing it to her. Then he started down the road once again.

By the time Frances Monroe reached the American base where her husband anxiously waited for her, all trace of her earlier bout of tears was gone. She looked calm and in full control of herself. The tranquilizing effects of the medicine had also disappeared. Jordan was almost amused at her jaunty step when they walked down the hallway to the area assigned to Senator Monroe.

Jordan felt very blessed to have witnessed the look on Trevor Monroe's face when he caught a glimpse of his wife for the first time in over a week. He jumped to his feet and rushed toward her. "Fran! Oh, God! I can't believe it! You're actually here!" He picked her up and swung her around, then hastily placed her back on her feet. "Are you all right, darling? My

God! I've been out of my mind. I didn't know—If only I'd been with you—"

She hugged him, laughing at his practically incoherent remarks. "I'm fine, just fine. In fact, I've had a marvelous rest for the last few days in this really fancy home. They treated me like a princess." She smiled at his look of disbelief. "Really." She placed her hand over her heart. "Would I lie to you?" she asked.

"If you thought you'd get away with it, yes!" he said emphatically. He glanced over at Jordan for the first time, as though only now becoming aware that Frances was not alone.

"Are you Trent?" the senator asked, walking over with his hand out.

"Yes," Jordan replied, taking the proffered hand.

Trevor Monroe nodded. "Mallory said you could pull it off. Damned if he wasn't right." He shook Jordan's hand. "You definitely deserve a raise out of this one, and I'll strongly recommend it."

"Actually, an uninterrupted vacation would be a really nice gesture."

Trevor smiled, the strain of the past few days seeming to drain away from his face. "That's right. Mallory said something about his best man being on vacation. I guess that was my fault, because I demanded the best."

Jordan shrugged. "I was glad to be of some assistance."

The senator spun around and went back to his wife. "We need to get you to the hospital and make sure you're okay. Then there are several people who will want to talk to you about what happened."

"I believe it's called 'debriefing,' isn't it?" she asked with an innocent expression on her face, unable to completely disguise her grin at his take-charge attitude.

"We'll need you, too, Trent. We've got to let them know that they can't get away with this."

"Sorry," Jordan replied, without a trace of sincerity in his voice. "Another time, perhaps. I have a little more work to do before this matter is completely cleared up."

"What do you mean?" the senator demanded to know.

"He left his wife, darling, in order to bring me across the border."

"Your wife!"

"Lauren Mackenzie," Jordan said. "She's the lady who volunteered to take your wife's place, if necessary. In the end, that plan seemed to be the most expedient one to follow."

"I didn't realize the two of you were married . . ."

"According to our passports, we are. As you know, it's a federal offense to falsify any information on a passport."

"So it is," the senator murmured.

"I've got to get back to her tonight, if possible."

Trevor Monroe glanced at his watch. "As late as it is, you'd be better off getting some rest before going back."

"I know, but I can't spare the time. I'm sure that nice, long vacation I'm going to get will cure all my problems in a few days," he said, and walked out of the room.

He heard the senator's laugh, pleased to know that at least one person was satisfied with the progress so far.

Jordan had a gnawing sense that he needed to get back to Lauren as quickly as possible.

Eight

Lauren lost track of time as she lay in the darkened room. She tried to keep her mind blank. There was nothing to fear. Stefan was nearby. He would not let anything happen to her. She trusted Stefan because Jordan trusted Stefan. There was no reason to panic. Everything was working exactly as planned.

When the door opened she had to force herself to keep her eyes closed and her head turned away. Lauren deliberately drew small, even breaths and waited.

The room filled with light and she realized the bedside lamp had been turned on. She threw her arm over her face and muttered, "The light's so bright."

A woman answered her in Czech to the effect that Lauren would have to get used to the light because the newcomer didn't intend to sit there in the dark!

The stranger's tone of voice had been pleasant and Lauren realized that the nurse was used to not being understood by her captive patient. Perhaps Lauren's knowledge of the language would help her if things didn't continue to progress as planned.

As her eyes adjusted to the light Lauren peered from beneath her bent arm at the woman sitting nearby. She was built like a wrestler. No wonder Mrs. Monroe hadn't made any effort to get away from here.

Lauren wasn't sure what she was going to do when she had to remove her arm. Seen up close, she bore little facial resemblance to the senator's wife. Then what would happen?

She'd rather not think about it.

Deciding that she'd better move before her arm fell off from the strained position, she turned her back to her captor and stared at the wall.

Oh, Jordan, I hope you've managed to get her away from here. We make a great team, darling, don't you think so?

Of course he didn't think so. Except for their rather passionately compatible interlude in bed, she was certain that Jordan Trent had little use for her.

She wondered when it would occur to him that they had taken no precautions during their night and morning together.

Lauren had been aware of the lack of protection at that time. The thought had given her hope that perhaps she'd become pregnant. She was fully aware of the many reasons why Jordan would never be a permanent part of her life; knew she had no choice but to accept that her time with him was limited. Having his baby would help to ease her loss.

She would still have a part of him in the years to come, someone to love and cherish when she no longer had Jordan.

Lauren knew that her family would be horrified, as strictly as she'd been brought up. And she really couldn't blame them. She could almost see the sad expression in her father's eyes. Perhaps she could make them understand. She loved Jordan. And because she loved him, she wanted his child.

It wasn't as though she didn't make enough money to care for a child. Other single parents managed. So could she.

There was a tap on the door and she almost leaped out of her skin at the sudden intrusion into the silence of the room.

The woman called out, "Who is it?" in her native language.

A man's voice answered, "Anton."

She told him to come in. A low-voiced conference took place by the door and Lauren strained her ears to hear what they were saying. A couple of names were mentioned, as well as places. She committed them to memory while she continued to listen.

There seemed to be some change of plans afoot. They intended to move her first thing in the morning. Oh dear God! What if Jordan couldn't locate her when he returned?

Don't panic, she reminded herself. *Stefan is here,* she repeated several times. Everything is under control. All I need to do is to lie quietly, pretend to be drugged, and wait.

Lauren had never been too good at waiting. She hadn't realized how nerve-racking it would be to lie there so close to Frances's captors and wait to be disclosed as an imposter.

That line of thinking would quickly reduce her to hysteria and she forced herself to think of Jordan and the night before.

That line of thinking would raise her blood pressure to dangerous levels. What she needed to do was think of something peaceful, soothing—the sounds of a babbling brook, a soft breeze sifting through the trees, the murmuring of...

Lauren fell asleep.

Jordan's return to Czechoslovakia was not through normal routes. He was pleased to see that his contacts near the border were still in place, busily making money smuggling people and goods back and forth.

By the time he left the small cottage hidden deep in the woods, near the border but well within the boundary of Czechoslovakia, even Jordan's mother wouldn't have recognized him.

His clothes were those of a common laborer and not too clean. He wore a cloth cap pulled low over his eyes. The man who had given him a lift into town gave him instructions.

"You must be back by nightfall or I can't guarantee your chances of getting across."

"I'll do what I can, Franz. I'll have a woman with me."

"Bah! Why waste so much time and go to such trouble for a woman? It would be easier to find another one."

Jordan laughed. "An interesting philosophy, but one I'm afraid I don't share."

"Women are all the same."

"You know, Franz, I have to admit that I used to feel the same way, until recently. Very recently. That's when I discovered that I could be wrong."

"Never. They cannot be trusted."

"Well, I'd trust this one with my life."

"Obviously. You're risking your life for her."

"She did the same thing for me."

"But for different reasons, you can be sure."

"What do you mean?"

"Women are devious creatures. They never say what they mean nor mean what they say."

Jordan realized he'd never be able to sway Franz from his way of thinking. Why should he try? What amazed him was how much his own way of thinking had changed since meeting Lauren.

Had he once sounded so idiotic, tagging half the human race with silly labels? How easy that was, to place names on others who are different from us in order to feel superior. He shook his head. Had he become so opinionated that others saw and heard another Franz in him? It was something to think about.

Jordan closed his eyes for a moment. They burned from lack of sleep. It was almost dawn and he was still several hours away from Brno. He had to contact Stefan. Hopefully he'd managed to get Lauren out of that room before anyone discovered the switch.

Somehow he was afraid it wouldn't be that easy.

A harsh voice spoke nearby and Lauren woke with a jerk. "Here is your food. Eat," she was told in a gruff voice. The words were supposedly English but so heavily accented as to be unrecognizable. It was only when she saw the food on a tray that she understood what had been said.

Keeping her head down, she pushed herself up on the pillow and reached for the fork.

When Lauren glanced up, she noticed with relief that the woman had already turned her back to her and sat back down with her needlework.

Lauren couldn't believe she'd been there this long and had not been discovered. But then no one had expected a switch. The plan had been brilliantly audacious. Removing Mrs. Monroe without substituting someone else would have immediately set off an alert. The longer she stayed there undetected, the better chance Jordan had of getting Frances Monroe to safety.

Lauren wondered how long it would take.

She ate as much of the food as she could, then once again turned her back and pretended to be asleep. She prayed they wouldn't bother her anymore that night.

When the light finally went out, Lauren had lost all track of time. She heard the rustling of clothes as the other woman undressed. Since there was no other bed in the room, she assumed her guardian must be sleeping on the couch across the room.

They had talked about moving her in the morning. Would Jordan be too late getting there to find her?

It was almost ten o'clock in the morning when Jordan reached Brno. He'd made good time. Franz had left him at a warehouse near the border where he'd hitched a ride with a truck driver who was making a delivery to Brno.

Franz had slipped the man some money, explaining that Jordan was too stupid to understand much of what was said to him. Jordan was pleased that he had managed to understand most of what had been said. At least the trucker wouldn't be expecting much conversation.

As soon as he was dropped off he headed for the curio shop to find Stefan. When he got there Jordan discovered that no one had seen Stefan since the day before.

Jordan didn't like the sound of that at all. He started following the route of his original contacts, working through them patiently to discover where Stefan could be found. He didn't want to blow everything wide open by showing up at the clinic dressed the way he was. No one would expect him to be visiting patients looking like that.

A hand clamped over Lauren's mouth, hard, so that she could barely breathe. She tried to struggle but her hands were easily caught and held.

The room was pitch-black. She felt as though she were in a deep well with no way out and had a horrible feeling that she was going to suffocate without ever seeing the light of day again.

Something moved by her ear and a voice whispered, "Stefan."

She relaxed, finally understanding, and the hand was immediately removed. Strong arms lifted her effortlessly from the bed and she placed her arms around Stefan's neck. He seemed to be able to see in the dark because he strode across the room and opened the door without making a sound.

The hall was dimly lit and she looked at the man who carried her. It *was* Stefan, thank God. He smiled at her while he strode down the hallway to the stairway she and Jordan had used earlier. This time he took her all the way to the basement.

"I can walk, you know," she managed to whisper as he trotted down the steps as though she were weightless.

"I didn't bring any shoes for you," he said in a low voice. "We can't afford the delay of your trying to go barefoot."

"Oh."

When Stefan opened the door into the basement, she flinched at the sudden bright light. Hiding her head against his shoulder, she waited while he hurried through the corridor and at last reached an exit.

Outside the sky was still black.

"What time is it?" she asked.

"It's almost dawn."

"Have you heard from Jordan?"

"No. But that isn't unusual. He will be in touch as soon as he can."

"Where are you taking me?"

"Out into the countryside where you will be safe."

Lauren wondered if she would ever feel safe again.

They seemed to drive for hours through dense forest. Lauren soon became lost. If anyone had been following them, they, too, would have become lost.

When Stefan pulled into the driveway of a small cottage, the sun had been up for several hours. "Where are we?" Lauren asked, glancing around.

Stefan looked pleased. "This is my home, Mrs. Trent," he said with a smile. "Come. I will introduce you to my Ana. Then I must get back to Brno and meet Jordan when he arrives."

"Does he know where you live?"

"No. Both Jordan and I have become domesticated since last we worked together. It is good that our wives get this opportunity to meet."

Lauren saw no point in trying to explain the situation. Since Jordan had introduced her as his wife, she supposed she shouldn't say anything to cause anyone to doubt him.

When Stefan came around the car and lifted her out, Lauren became aware of how she was dressed. The thin cotton gown fell to her knees in a nondescript fashion. And she was barefoot! How would Stefan ever explain this to his wife?

She needn't have worried. The young woman who met them at the door was filled with concern and bustled around making Lauren feel welcomed and comfortable.

Stefan explained that Ana would need to find Lauren something to wear and that he would be back as soon as he could return with her husband.

Both the women nodded and he left.

As soon as Ana discovered that Lauren could speak her language she happily chattered to her, showing her skirts and blouses and having her try on shoes. Within a very short while Lauren felt as though she'd made a friend.

By the time Stefan found Jordan, Jordan had spent several lifetimes, at least he was sure it had been that long, looking for Stefan.

"Where have you been!" he demanded as soon as Stefan appeared.

Jordan had ended up going back to the curio shop and waiting in the back room, knowing that sooner or later Stefan would come looking for him.

"Getting your wife to safety," he said mildly.

Jordan sat down suddenly and just looked at his friend for a moment. "Is she okay?"

"She's fine."

"Did they recognize her?"

"No, although we cut it a little close, my friend. They were planning to move her this morning."

"Where?" Jordan asked, getting to his feet with renewed energy.

Stefan relayed the information Lauren had passed on to him during their drive.

"That's the best lead we've gotten as to who's behind all of this." He looked around the room. "Can you take me to her?"

Stefan laughed. "I was only waiting for you to ask. After all, maybe you grow tired of this wife of yours, huh? Could be you aren't so very anxious to see her again?"

"Very funny, Stefan. Let's go," he said, starting for the door.

"No. Not together. You must go back to the park and wait for me there." He described the car he was driving. "I will pick you up once I am sure no one is watching you."

"Of course you're right. I'm getting careless."

"No. You are a man in love. I recognize the symptoms, since I suffer from them myself."

"You? What are you talking about?"

"I left your very beautiful wife with my lovely wife, Ana. They will be telling each other all of our secrets if we do not get back there soon, eh?" He clapped Jordan on the back. "Now go. I will find you."

Jordan went over to the park, realizing that he hadn't eaten for the past twenty-four hours. Now that he knew Lauren was safe, he had relaxed enough to notice.

He never wanted to go through anything like these past few hours again. He couldn't remember ever having been quite so apprehensive about anything before.

Whenever he'd been in a dangerous situation, he'd known that he would do his best to get himself out of it. And if his best wasn't good enough, only he would suffer the consequences.

This assignment had been different. He'd never before felt such a strong sense of responsibility. If anything had happened to Lauren—   Yes, Jordan? an inner voice asked. What then? The pain that shot through him must have had something to do with hunger. He'd known other operatives who hadn't come back from assignments. And Lauren had known what she was getting into, hadn't she?

And if you'd lost her? What then?

Jordan faced the fact that nothing in his life would ever have been the same.

Lauren was special. She was his. She had given herself to him, a beautiful giving, just as he had given himself to her. He was no longer a loner, needing no one. For the first time since he'd lost his mother, Jordan admitted that he needed someone—a very special someone.

He saw Stefan's car approaching. He started walking as though to cross the street. At the last moment, he swerved and crawled into the car.

"Well?" he asked.

"No tails that I can see."

"How about you?"

"Who, me?" Stefan asked with an innocent grin. "Now who would want to watch me?"

"Probably every official in the country, if they had any sense."

"Ah, but there you have it, my friend. They find me a pitiful specimen and not worth the time it would take to keep an eye on me."

"Hah. Little do they know."

They smiled at each other and rode along in silence. By the time Stefan turned onto the road out of town Jordan was asleep.

Lauren heard the car drive up and peered through the window. It was Stefan and he had someone with him! Eagerly she ran to the door and threw it open, only to come to a stumbling halt. The man who got out of the car was unshaven and his clothes looked as though he'd worn them for weeks without cleaning them. The dilapidated cap pulled down low over his eyes made him look as if he made his living mugging unsuspecting passersby in dark alleyways.

Then Stefan said something and laughed, pointing to Lauren.

The man with him looked up and grinned. Lauren would recognize that smile anywhere, in any disguise.

"Jordan!" she cried joyously and ran toward him.

He met her halfway, grabbing her and holding her close. God, she felt so good, right there in his arms where she belonged.

"You okay?" he asked in a gruff voice.

"Of course I'm okay. You never doubted that, did you?" she asked, looking up at him, her arms around his neck.

He'd never seen that look on her face before. There was no worry or strain, just sheer happiness radiating from her. Because of him? Jordan felt humbled by the thought. Was it possible that he was that important to her?

"Oh, Lauren," he muttered, then pulled her to him in a searing kiss.

He didn't know how long they stood there in front of the small cottage. He never wanted to let her go. Stefan finally came up and clapped him on the back. "Come inside, my friend. Perhaps you would like something to eat. For myself, I'm starved."

Jordan reluctantly removed his arms from around her and they walked into the house together.

Stefan proudly introduced Ana and then Ana and Lauren pointed out the choice of clothes Lauren had made and the men agreed she would do very well as Jordan's wife dressed as she was.

"When are we leaving?" Lauren asked a little later, after they had finished eating. She looked at first one man, then the other.

Stefan looked at the deep lines of weariness in his friend's face and answered for him. "I think you will both be safe to stay here tonight. I will help you get to the border tomorrow."

"But Franz told me to be back tonight."

"What's one more night, my friend? Franz is an old woman, always worrying about everything. He enjoys being in control. It makes him feel very important."

Now that he had finally stopped long enough to eat and relax, Jordan felt as though he could go to sleep sitting in the chair.

"You're probably right, Stefan. Anyway, I'm so tired, I'm punchy. If you don't mind, we'll stay here and head back tomorrow."

Ana hopped up, saying, "I have already prepared the guest room, just in case you would stay. Come, Lauren, I will find you a gown to sleep in."

Lauren gazed uncertainly at Jordan. Wasn't he going to tell them the truth? He glanced up and saw her worried expression, not understanding its cause. "What's wrong?" he asked. "Don't you want to stay?"

"It's not that—" she began, her face flushing, and Jordan suddenly remembered. He'd gotten so used to thinking of her as his wife that he'd actually forgotten it was all part of the charade.

As far as that went, there was no reason to make any explanations at this point. He smiled at her reassuringly. "I promise not to pull covers," he said with a grin. "And I'll do my best to keep you warm."

Stefan's laugh made her cheeks turn even rosier and Lauren turned away to follow Ana into the other room.

"Lauren?" Jordan said softly.

She turned around and looked at him.

"I'm only teasing you."

"I know."

"You probably won't even know I'm there. I'm so tired I'm not sure I'll be able to stumble to the bedroom."

She smiled, then glanced at Stefan. "Sounds like a tremendous number of excuses, doesn't it? Do you suppose he's trying to get out of performing his husbandly duties?"

Stefan nodded emphatically. "That it does, Lauren. That it does."

Jordan slowly stood and stretched, his arms high over his head. With a slow wink at Stefan, he said, "I said I was tired, Lauren, not dead," and began to stalk her with a deliberate tread.

Nine

Lauren turned and fled down the hallway, the sound of the men's laughter ringing in her ears. She almost ran into Ana who was coming out of her bedroom.

"Oh, I'm sorry," Ana said.

"It wasn't your fault. I was trying to get away from their teasing."

"Oh, that Stefan. He enjoys making jokes."

"Yes, so does Jordan. No wonder they are such good friends."

"I am very glad to be able to meet Jordan Trent. Stefan speaks of him often. He says that once Jordan saved his life. He will never forget that. Ever."

"Yes, I know that feeling."

Ana looked down at the garment she was holding and thrust it out to Lauren. "Here. This should be warm enough for you tonight."

Remembering Jordan's comment about keeping her warm, Lauren refused to meet Ana's eyes. "Thank you." She took the nightgown and then on impulse hugged the other woman. "You've been so kind," she said, tears filling her eyes.

Ana patted her cheek. "You are a very easy person to be kind to, Lauren. I am so glad we were able to meet."

"So am I."

Lauren smiled at the other woman, then went into the bedroom across the hallway.

Lauren had carefully folded the borrowed clothes that she would have to wear tomorrow and was reaching for the borrowed gown when the door behind her opened and she heard Jordan say, "You don't have to wear that on my account, you know."

Out of a lifelong habit of modesty, Lauren held the gown up to her and turned around to face him.

He'd obviously showered and shaved, and was wearing only the pants he'd had on earlier.

"I'm so glad you made it all right," she said, her heart overflowing with gratitude to be with him once again.

He slowly walked over to her and gently removed the gown from her hands. "I'm so glad that you're glad. I wouldn't have blamed you if you'd wished all sorts of ills on me."

"Don't say that, Jordan. You've never done anything that I haven't wanted you to do."

He lightly drew a line from her chin, down her throat and between her breasts. "Even now?"

"Especially now," she said with a small smile.

"You're insatiable, woman," he said with a pleased grin.

"And you're exhausted," she said with an understanding look. The dark shadows under his eyes were more noticeable now that she was closer to him.

"Never that exhausted, love," he whispered, picking her up and placing her on the bed. Then he reached over and turned out the light.

They were wakened early the next morning by Stefan's pounding on their door. "All right, you two. If you intend to catch a ride into Brno with me, you'd better hurry. I'm leaving in ten minutes."

Lauren sat up, horrified to discover that they had both overslept. She glanced at Jordan. He hadn't moved from his position on his stomach, his pillow half-covering his head.

"Jordan?"

"Mmmmph?"

"Did you hear Stefan? He said—"

With his head still under the pillow Jordan muttered, "Of course I heard Stefan. How could anyone possibly sleep through that?"

"Oh. Well, you didn't move and I thought—"

"I didn't move because I'm convinced my body will shatter into a dozen pieces if I dare wiggle even a toe."

She leaned over him with a worried expression. "Oh, Jordan, what's wrong? Did you get hurt? Last night you seemed to be—"

"Last night I must have thought I was some damned teenager, showing off," he muttered, then groaned as he slowly rolled over.

She quickly stifled a giggle when she realized he was all right.

And he was certainly all right, having proven that quite satisfactorily on more than one occasion the night before. Making love in the privacy of a bedroom with thick walls had been a new and enjoyable experience for her. Lauren had a hunch that making love with Jordan at any time, anywhere, and under most any condition she could think of would be a new and enjoyable experience for her.

"We need to get up."

"I know," he said, continuing to lie on his back with his arms outspread and his eyes closed. The dark shadows were gone from beneath his eyes and the lines of strain had disappeared as well. Amazing what a good night's rest would do for a person, she decided with a smile.

Lauren's education had been extensively broadened the night before. One of the things she had learned was a certain area along Jordan's abdomen where he was quite ticklish. Accidently discovered, the small but vital area now gave Lauren a certain feeling of power over the man lying so relaxed beside her.

Testing her new theory she leaned over and very lightly touched his lower abdomen with her tongue. In an astonishingly short time Jordan was on his feet staring at her in indignation. "That's not fair and you know it!"

She climbed out of bed and quickly began to put on the clothes she'd tidily folded the night before. "We can't miss our ride, can we, Jordan?'' she asked with her brows slightly arched.

He stalked around the bed and grabbed her. "I happen to know some rather ticklish places on you, too, you know," he said ominously.

She nodded. "I know."

"But I would never stoop so low as to take advantage of such intimate knowledge."

"Me, either."

"Like hell."

Her saucy smile was too endearing to ignore. He laughed and grabbed her to him. Giving her a hearty kiss, he said, "Just wait. I'll get even."

She slipped her shoes on and opened the door enough to get out. Then she stuck her head back in and said, "I can hardly wait."

Stefan waited with good-natured impatience while they quickly drank some coffee and buttered some breakfast rolls to take with them. Then they were on their way.

The men sat up front and discussed the best way to get back to the border from Brno. Lauren listened with half a mind. The day was so beautiful. It was hard to imagine that anything bad would happen anywhere at any time on such a day as this.

She was in love and all was right with her world. Lauren studied the back of Jordan's head while he, unaware of her gaze, talked with Stefan. She loved the shape of his ears and the way his hair curled along the nape of his neck. How could she ever have thought this man looked harsh and intimidating?

Well, perhaps he was intimidating. But not to her. Never to her. She loved to watch his expression change whenever he caught sight of her. She'd never seen him look at anyone else that way. She wondered if he was aware of how differently he treated her.

Was it their lovemaking that had changed him? Did all men automatically treat a woman they'd gone to bed with differently? She wished she knew more about men, and more about how they thought. It wasn't something she'd feel comfortable discussing with her father.

There was a possibility that Jordan was falling in love with her, though, wasn't there? His tenderness toward her, his protectiveness, his gentleness, his inability to be near her without reaching out to touch her cheek. All of those things must mean that he considered her someone special in his life.

But did it mean that she would see him again once they returned to the States? Even working for the same agency they'd never had any reason to come into contact before. Of course now they knew each other. Maybe when he was in the office he'd stop in to see her, maybe ask her out to dinner, and then—

Then what, silly? What are all these daydreams about, anyway? she thought impatiently. Do you think this man would really change his entire way of life in order to make you a part of it?

I can dream, can't I?

Of course you can dream, as long as you don't get your dreams confused with reality.

In that case, she would create her own reality. Lauren closed her eyes and began to picture a little girl with reddish-blond hair and big brown eyes, and an infant boy with black curly hair and gray eyes.

By the time they reached the outskirts of Brno the men had decided that Jordan and Lauren should wait until midafternoon to head for the border. They wouldn't be able to cross until late that night anyway, and they had better opportunities for concealment there in Brno.

In the meantime Stefan would try to find out what had happened at the clinic once it had been discovered that Lauren was gone.

The day seemed to creep by while they waited in a warehouse in the manufacturing district. They'd arranged a ride with another truck driver who knew Stefan and agreed that he could use the extra cash for his family.

Jordan didn't want to take any chances on being seen by someone who might have noticed them earlier in their roles as tourists, so they waited in the privacy of the warehouse.

Lauren discovered that Jordan was no longer as reticent about his early life as he'd been at first. He seemed willing enough to answer her questions and seemed to gain some amount of relief in sharing the trauma of losing his mother and being thrust into an entirely different environment.

She, in turn, shared much of her early, more happy, childhood with him, even to telling the story of how her parents met.

"You'd like my parents, I think," she said at one point.

"Ah, but would they like me, that is the question."

"Why wouldn't they like you?" she demanded, the light of fanaticism shining in her eyes.

He grinned at her vehemence. "Oh, I don't know. There's something about trying to explain how I make my living."

"You're a sales rep from Chicago," she promptly retorted.

"Is that what you'd tell them?" he asked, surprised.

"Of course. That's what you tell everyone, isn't it?"

"Well, yes."

"Isn't that what your father thinks you do?"

"Yes."

"Well, then," she said, as though the matter were settled.

Perhaps it was.

The trucker showed up with sandwiches for them, and the news that he needed to leave in order to get back home at a decent hour.

Since they were definitely traveling light, Jordan and Lauren had no trouble getting ready to leave. She glanced back at the cavernous building with affection. This was the place where Jordan had shared some of his most intimate feelings. She had a hunch he'd never done that before, with anyone.

It was almost like discovering that the man she loved was a virgin. He'd saved his most intimate thoughts and emotions for her. She smiled at the whimsical thought.

It was dark by the time they reached the turnoff to Franz's hut. Jordan paid the driver and they stood watching the man as he turned around and went back the way they had come.

"Where to now?" she asked, looking around.

"The first of many long walks, I'm afraid. I hope you're up to it."

"Don't worry about me. I'm fine."

"Glad to hear it. Now I can devote my energies to more weighty concerns."

She grinned at him, pleased that he was in such a good mood.

Later she was glad Jordan was in a good mood because Franz certainly wasn't.

"I waited up all night for you. Didn't I tell you that you must be back last night?"

"Yes, you mentioned it," Jordan said politely. "And I tried, but it was impossible. So here we are."

"Yes. And what am I supposed to do with you, just tell me that?"

"Help us across the border."

"Yes. That would have been an easy enough task last night because the guard that substitutes at the crossing on Wednesday night has learned to look the other way when there are those who wish to travel quickly between the two countries."

"I see," Jordan said slowly.

"It will be another week before he will be substituting for the other man's night off."

"We can't wait that long."

"Of course you can't. It would be too dangerous for all of us."

"We'll just have to take our chances."

"And get yourselves killed."

"Believe me, I intend to avoid that possibility with every ounce of energy I have."

Franz shook his head and got up from the table. "Crazy Americans and their women," he muttered in a foreboding voice, walking over to the stove.

"What are we going to do?" Lauren asked Jordan in a low voice.

"I'm inclined to agree with Stefan about Franz. He enjoys being the voice of doom. The border along here is sketchily covered because there are no towns on either side for many miles. One guard has to patrol long stretches. We'll just watch and wait for our chance."

She nodded. The sooner they left this unpleasant man's house, the better. He had barely spoken to her, ignoring her as though she were some pet Jordan had brought in with him, one whom Franz wasn't sure he wanted in his house!

They waited a couple of hours and then followed Franz into the woods behind his hut. Lauren was glad he seemed to know where he was going. There seemed to be no trail to follow and the undergrowth was thick and, at some points, impenetrable.

They seemed to have walked for miles when Franz raised his hand, motioning for them to keep silent. Since no one had said anything for hours, Lauren thought he was being unnecessarily dramatic.

With sign language he pointed out the sentry outpost, the barbed wire that ran in parallel strips a few hundred yards apart. In the moonlight, the strip of ground between the wires appeared to be a barren, no-man's-land. There were no trees or shrubs to use as cover. They would be totally exposed from the time they left the wooded area where they now stood until they managed to get through both sets of heavily wired fences. The woods began on the far side of the second fence.

Lauren watched as Jordan signed back. The two men shook hands and Franz walked away in the direction he had come.

Jordan came over and knelt down beside her where she rested against a tree. "Okay, love, we're on our own now and—"

He'd just lost her attention to anything he might have to say after the unaccustomed endearment. Then she forced herself to concentrate on his low-voiced instructions.

"I want you to try to get as much rest as you can. I'm going to watch and try to figure out the pattern this sentry uses. Once I figure out his routine, we'll slip past him as soon as he returns to the other side. You understand?"

She nodded.

Jordan gazed into her eyes and felt as though he were drowning in their depths. The darkness in the woods could not eliminate the glow in her eyes. He ran his hand along the nape of her neck and massaged her tense neck and shoulder muscles for a few minutes. Her sigh was almost soundless.

He leaned over and kissed her softly. "Get some sleep. We've got a long hike still ahead of us. But at least it will be in Austrian countryside."

Lauren thought it would be impossible to fall asleep in the middle of the woods, but she stretched out on the soft needles and the next thing she knew Jordan was shaking her shoulder, his hand lightly covering her mouth. When she opened her eyes he lifted his hand. Leaning over, he whispered in her ear, "We're going to cross in another few minutes. He's due down here any time. As soon as he turns away we're going to cross."

"But what if he decides to turn around?"

"Pray that he doesn't, that's all. We need all the time we can get before he turns to face this section again. Okay?"

She nodded her head. It had to be okay. They had no choice.

Lauren watched as the guard came toward them. The moonlight was so bright that he seemed to be in a spotlight as he moved along. The contrast between the moonlight and the shadows from the woods gave them excellent cover. They waited while he walked past them for several hundred yards.

He turned and slowly began his trek back toward the sentry box. He'd seemed to be only a few short yards away when Jordan breathed into her ear the word, "Now!"

Taking her hand he began to run. Lauren had never moved so fast in her life. She didn't think her feet ever touched the ground. Then he was pushing her down to the ground while he rapidly worked wire cutters along the bottom of the fence.

He helped her wiggle through, then followed her. He took her hand once more as they raced across the brightly lit area between the fences. Lauren kept waiting to hear a yell but everything was eerily still in the moonlight. The landscape seemed unreal; it was as though they were surrounded by a backdrop for some theatrical performance.

Once again they followed the previous procedure: she lay still while he used the wire cutters.

Then all hell broke loose. There was a shout, then more shouts. Dogs began to bark, a siren went off and searchlights pinned them to the ground.

"What the hell!" Jordan exclaimed, still working frantically. Lifting the fence he shoved her under, yelling "Run! Get to the shelter of the trees. I'm right behind you."

She did what she was told. Lauren was almost to the safety of the trees when she heard the ominous sound of automatic weapons being fired. She spun around and saw Jordan racing toward her, yelling for her to keep going. Then, as though in slow motion, she saw him stumble and slowly spin before falling limply to the ground.

He didn't move.

Ten

Lauren screamed, "Jordan!" and, oblivious to the steady staccato of gunfire, ran back to him. "Jordan!" she cried again, frantically wiping the tears from her eyes so that she could see him.

The searchlights went off and the sirens were stopped midblast, leaving a deafening silence in their place. Lauren looked around and realized that they had made it. They were in Austria. But Jordan— She had to see where he'd been hit. She had to get him to a hospital. He was hurt but he was going to be all right. He had to be all right.

He lay on his side, his head shadowed. She felt along his back and her hand came away wet and sticky. "Oh, Jordan," she sobbed.

Jordan groaned, the sweetest sound she'd ever heard.

"Jordan?"

"Run, Lauren, you've got to run," he muttered.

"Oh, darling. We don't have to run. We made it. We're safe. Oh, God, please let him be all right," she whispered.

"Leave me, Lauren. Find a house and explain, someone will take you in."

"You're damn right they will, but I'm not leaving you, Jordan Trent. You're coming with me if I have to carry you every foot of the way."

"Funny," he murmured, "never heard you curse before."

"I never had a good enough reason to before." She got up on her knees. "Help me, darling, please. Please try to stand."

She didn't know how long it took her to get him to his feet. Lauren was so afraid that he was going to black out on her. Then what would she do?

She wouldn't think about it.

Slowly she began to edge him through the woods, wondering where to go and how long he could keep moving. It took all of her strength to hold him upright.

"Don't do this to yourself, Lauren," he managed to say. "I'll make it. I'm too tough to quit now."

"You'd better be, you arrogant macho male. I want you to show me what you've got. Show me that indomitable will, that refusal to give up. I dare you!" Tears still streamed down her face and she forced herself to continue forward, one slow step at a time, guiding him.

When she first saw the light shining through the trees, she thought she was imagining it. Would a house be this close to the border? Then she realized it was moving.

"Help!" she hollered. "Please, will you help us?"

The answering shout was the most welcome thing she had ever heard. Three men approached them warily.

"My husband's been shot. We're Americans. Can you help get him to the hospital?"

Her words, spoken in German, seemed to galvanize them into action. Two of the men stepped forward just in time to catch Jordan as he toppled over.

Jordan kept having the craziest dreams. He and Lauren were on the beach of Santiago Island in the South Seas. The warm breeze felt so good against his hot skin. Every once in a while he and Lauren would run out into the water of the lagoon that was protected from the heavy ocean waves by a coral reef near the point.

The cool water took away the feeling of heat and he would surface in time to see Lauren's eyes, her beautiful, misty-gray eyes, looking at him with a worried expression.

"Your eyes are so beautiful," he whispered, only to discover that his mouth was so dry he could barely speak.

"Hush, darling, don't waste your energy talking," Lauren said anxiously.

"I'm so thirsty," he tried to say, but somehow his mouth wouldn't work right.

Lauren seemed to know because she slipped a couple of slivers of ice in his mouth.

"The water feels great, doesn't it?" he asked.

"Whatever you say. Please try to rest. You're going to be fine."

Of course he was going to be fine. Why shouldn't he be fine? He had a lovely wife and two adorable children. Or did he? Of course he did. "Matthew Mackenzie Trent," Jordan stated in a clear, concise voice.

Oh dear Lord, please let him be all right. He's hallucinating or something. Let his mind be all right. He's running such a terribly high fever. Please take care of him for me.

Jordan seemed to relax and fall back into a restless sleep and Lauren sat back down in the chair where she'd kept a vigil for the past three days.

They were at an American base somewhere in Germany. She had called Mallory and he'd set some powerful wheels in motion. Within hours after Jordan's arrival at the local hospital, Mallory himself had arrived and supervised Jordan's transfer.

They'd had to operate to remove the bullet lodged in his back. The doctor said it was a miracle that it had missed so many vital organs as well as the spinal column.

Mallory had already heard from Frances and Trevor Monroe and was quite pleased with the way Jordan had handled everything.

"He's going to make it, you know," Mallory had assured her that morning. "That man's too damned stubborn to die."

"I know," she said.

"Are you ready to go home?"

"You mean now?"

"I mean whenever you're ready. Your assignment has been officially terminated. You did an outstanding job, Lauren."

"Thank you, sir."

"Now, about going home—"

"What about Jordan?"

"What about him?"

"When will he be able to go home?"

"The surgeon hasn't said."

"Then if it's all right with you, sir, I'll wait until we can go home at the same time." She struggled to try to find the right words. "You see, we started this together. I think we should finish it together."

"I see," Mallory said thoughtfully. "That's very professional of you, looking at it like that. From the way he behaved in the beginning, I somehow had the feeling you would be eager to get away from him."

"Oh, no, sir. Jordan and I became friends."

"Friends, huh?" Mallory studied her for a few minutes in silence. "A man can't have too many friends, can he?"

She smiled. "I think we'll be able to return home no later than next week, sir. If that's all right."

"I suppose it will have to be," he said drily.

Now Lauren studied the sleeping man who lay so quietly. She'd already discovered that whenever he became restless she could calm him by talking to him.

Tonight had been the first time he'd done much talking. Unfortunately it hadn't made much sense. Why had he said Matthew Mackenzie Trent with such obvious pride? Did he somehow think they were back in Brno, making silly conversation to entertain whoever might be listening to them?

"Run, Lauren! For God's sake, run!"

His sudden shout startled her and she quickly stood up. The floor nurses must have heard him as well. They came racing into the room.

"I think he's reliving the time he was shot," she whispered to them. Meanwhile she continued to stroke his hand, something she'd found calmed him.

"As long as we're here, I think we should check his bandages." As gently as possible they rolled him onto his side and checked for seepage.

"He's healing nicely," the nurse in charge said with a smile. "I know you must be relieved, Mrs. Trent."

"Oh! I'm—I, uh—Yes, I'm extremely pleased," she finally managed to say.

However, it was another week before the surgeon arranged to have him flown by military transport back to the States. Lauren wasn't exactly sure what strings Mallory pulled, but he arranged for her to fly back with Jordan.

"Where are we?" Jordan asked in a faint voice.

"Walter Reed Hospital," Lauren said with a smile.

"How did I get here?"

"You were flown in from Germany."

"Germany? We were supposed to be in Austria."

She smiled at the querulous tone of his voice. That told her, like nothing else, that he was beginning to feel better.

"We were in Austria. Then you were flown to Germany, where they took a bullet out of your back; then you were flown here."

"Oh." He was quiet for several minutes. Finally he asked, "What are you doing here?"

"Protecting the nurses from you," she said with a grin.

"What's that supposed to mean?"

"That you can be a real pain at times."

"Tell me something I don't know."

She studied him for a moment in silence, then softly said, "You can be a real love at times."

"Oh, yeah? Says who?"

"Says me."

"So what do you know?"

"I know that I'm very glad to see you feeling better."

He squeezed her hand. "I'm glad to be feeling better, too. I was getting a little tired of fading in and out. Although some of my dreams were pretty nice, at that."

"Hmmm. What kind of dreams, or should I ask?"

"Well, since you were in them, I suppose you have a certain right to know."

She could feel the heat in her cheeks at his teasing.

"You and I were on Santiago Island together."

"Where's that?"

"That's the island where I was trying to take a long overdue vacation when Mallory insisted I had to come back to work."

"As soon as you're feeling better, I'm sure you can go back."

"I just might do that. Catch up on my fishing, my reading, my sleep." He interrupted his list. "That's a laugh, isn't it? That's all I've done is sleep lately. They keep me so doped up."

"Helps your body heal faster when you're relaxed."

"Lauren?"

"Hmmm?"

"I never thanked you for saving my life."

"Don't be silly. I didn't save you from anything."

"I distinctly remember a lecture about my arrogant, macho attitude."

"You remember my saying that?"

"It rang in my ears for days afterwards."

"I was scared. I thought you were going to die."

"So did I." His voice showed no sign of amusement.

"Thank you for risking your life by coming back in to get me," she said.

"That was part of my job."

"Oh."

"I couldn't have just left you over there, you know."

"I guess not."

Jordan took her hand and laced his fingers through it. "You are one very special lady, you know that, don't you?"

"Not really."

"I will never forget you," he said softly.

But you intend to try, Lauren realized with a certainty that flashed the words across her mind.

Fighting to keep her composure she said, "I will never forget you, either."

"I'm sure you won't. I'll always remind you of the worst nightmare of your life."

"No," she said, shaking her head.

He smiled. "I can't imagine why you've been hanging around this hospital so much. Every time I wake up, you're here."

And you don't want me here, but don't want to hurt my feelings by asking me to leave.

"I was just making sure you were doing all right, that's all. Actually, Mr. Mallory expects me to come back to work as soon as possible."

"He would," Jordan muttered.

Lauren knew that if she didn't get out of there she would burst into tears. What had she expected, his undying gratitude? A proposal of marriage, for heaven's sake? "Can I bring you anything?" she asked brightly.

Jordan studied her face, her wonderful, dear face. How had he ever managed without her in his life? He could hardly wait until he was on his feet so that he could tell her. There was so much he had to say; they had so many plans to make.

After all, he wasn't getting any younger. They needed to get started on that family they talked about. He smiled at the thought.

"I can't think of anything right now, but thanks," he said, wishing he was strong enough to hold her and kiss her. Damn! He was as weak as a three-day-old kitten, and just about as useless.

"Well, then if you don't mind, I think I'll go." She pointed to the buzzer that was pinned to the bed. "If you want the nurse, you just touch that button."

"Fine. Thanks." He watched as she began to edge toward the door.

"Lauren?"

"Yes?"

"Don't I even get a farewell kiss?"

She closed her eyes for two heartbeats, then forced them open. "Of course." Walking over to him, she leaned down and pressed her lips softly against his.

She smelled so fresh, like springtime. He touched the curl in front of her ear. "I'll see you later," he said.

She nodded, unable to say another word.

He watched her walk out of the room, then began his impatient wait for her to return.

She never did.

Eleven

Jordan strode down the hallway toward Mallory's office and noticed that, once again, staff members were scattering before him. He shook his head. Some things changed; other things always seemed to remain the same.

He opened the door to Mallory's office and strode in. Mallory was on the phone.

Jordan sat down a little carefully. The doctor had been furious with him for insisting on leaving. But he'd been in that damned hospital for three weeks. What the hell did they expect?

Mallory lifted a brow at him to acknowledge his presence, but otherwise ignored Jordan. Jordan wished he could wave a magic wand and make Mallory himself disappear. Looking around the room, Jordan realized that nothing had changed since the day two months ago when he'd walked in there and had his life turned upside down, inside out and scattered all over the floor.

He didn't seem to know how to put all the pieces together because one very vital piece was missing. Lauren.

Mallory hung up the phone and asked, "What are you doing out of the hospital?"

"I got sick of the nurses."

"No worse than they were sick of you, believe me. I understand they were having to give combat pay to the nurses who were assigned to your room."

"Very funny. Now where is she?"

Mallory glanced around the room as though expecting someone to suddenly materialize.

"Who?"

"Don't give me that, Mallory. What have you done with Lauren Mackenzie?"

Mallory leaned back in his chair and placed his feet on his desk. Then he took his time lighting a cigarette. "She has taken a leave of absence."

"Damn it, Mallory," Jordan said leaning forward, then suddenly wincing. "I know she's taken a leave of absence, even though I had to get out of the hospital and do some sleuthing to discover that information. She has also sublet her apartment. So where is she?"

Mallory studied the other man, noticing the pallor in his face and the strain in his expression. The recent ordeal had certainly taken its toll. There was a fine tremor in Jordan's hands, but none in his voice. Of course he'd had a great deal of practice exercising his voice by barking at the nurses.

"Maybe she went back to Pennsylvania."

"Maybe? Don't you know?"

"I don't generally keep tabs on all the employees in this building, J.D."

"Since when? You seem to know every move I make, sometimes before I make it. Are you finally admitting your mental telepathy abilities have failed?"

"Why do you want to find Lauren? Everything wrapped up nicely in that deal."

"Because we have some unfinished business to take care of."

Mallory made a steeple of his fingers and rested his chin on them. "I wasn't aware of any unfinished business."

"Will wonders never cease? The man is a mere mortal after all."

"What unfinished business?"

"It isn't really any of your concern, Mallory, but when has that ever stopped you?" Jordan stood with slow, precise movements and wandered over to the window. Summer had arrived while he wasn't looking. Several things had happened while he wasn't looking, as a matter of fact; one of them being that he'd lost his heart. "I need to find Lauren so that we can get married."

"Aaahhh," Mallory said using a tone of enlightenment. "So Lauren has agreed to marry you."

"I didn't say that. But she will, if I can just find her."

Mallory didn't bother hiding his smile since Jordan's back was to him. "You've never lacked confidence, I'll give you that," he said.

"That's what you think."

"So. You and Lauren are getting married. How is that going to affect your job?"

Jordan glanced over his shoulder. "How do you think?"

"I think it's time you learned how the world looks from behind this desk," Mallory said quietly.

That drew Jordan back toward the other man. "What are you talking about?"

"I've been waiting for the right time to turn this job over to you. You've got the best, or at least the most devious, mind around. With you plotting covert activities, our respected enemies will never know what to expect next."

"You're serious."

"Never more serious in my life."

Jordan glanced around the room again. "What do you intend to do?"

"Oh, I won't be far. They're pushing me upstairs, with a big thanks to you and the way you handled that last matter. You made everyone in the department look good."

"We had some lucky breaks—the biggest ones being that no one recognized Mrs. Monroe or noticed the switch before we had a chance to get Lauren out of there."

"Has anyone told you what was behind the kidnapping?"

"No."

"A group of would-be saviors of mankind had decided to force some changes on the western world. Frances Monroe was only the first of many such planned hostages. They were preparing a similar kidnapping in Moscow."

"Moscow! You mean a Communist captive?"

"Yep. As a matter of fact, they were close to grabbing the Premier's wife."

"My God! They were out of their minds."

"What they're trying to do is to stop world war. They just had a rather bizarre way of going about it."

Jordan shook his head. Then he began to think of what he would do, or not do, if someone was holding Lauren as prisoner. The way he felt about her, he would do whatever he had to do to keep her safe and . . .

Maybe their idea wasn't so crazy after all. But he was glad he'd been able to stop it from going any farther.

"You changed the subject, Mallory. I want to know where she is."

"Employees' records are confidential, J.D. You know that."

Jordan repeated a colorful display of obscenities for Mallory, concluding with exactly what he could do with his confidentiality.

"Why would any woman in her right mind want to marry you, J.D.?" he asked, shaking his head ruefully.

Mallory had just verbalized the question that had haunted Jordan for weeks, ever since he realized that Lauren wasn't coming back to the hospital.

What had he ever done to show her how he felt about her? That she was the most important person in the world to him? That he wasn't really sure how he would manage if she wasn't a part of his life?

The thought of never seeing Lauren again frightened him like nothing else had in his life.

"I want the opportunity to discuss the matter with her," he finally said.

Mallory shrugged, then reached into his top desk drawer and took out a pad of paper. Ripping off the top sheet, he handed it to Jordan.

"You had that all the time!" Jordan said, his voice rising. "And you intended to give it to me all along!"

"Actually, I'd been waiting for you to ask for it politely; perhaps add a please, maybe a thank you." He put his cigarette out in an overflowing ashtray. "Unfortunately being in love didn't help your disposition any more than your vacation did."

Jordan studied the older man for a moment in silence. "When did you know?" he asked.

"By the time you walked out of this office the day you met her."

"You're crazy. I didn't even like her."

"There was too much friction and smoke not to burst into flame sooner or later. It was only a matter of time."

He looked at his boss with suspicion. "Did you set me up?"

"Who, me? Hell, no. I just needed someone to put at this desk and knew you'd have to really want to give up fieldwork in order to consider it."

"So Lauren was to help sweeten the pie?"

Mallory allowed himself a small smile. "Do I look like a matchmaker?"

"You look like the most devious man I've ever known. Funny you should admire that trait in me."

"It takes one to know one, I suppose." He drew his feet off the desk and stood up. Nodding toward the slip of paper Mallory said, "You got what you came for, so why don't you get out of here and let me get some work done."

Jordan folded the paper as though it were a map to priceless treasure. As far as he was concerned, it was. He was already out the door when he heard Mallory call his name. Jordan stuck his head back in.

"Yes?"

"You've got two months vacation waiting for you, and the Santiago Island police have discovered they merely misunderstood my earlier message. You are wanted by the government because you're extremely valuable to us. I'm sure you will find that they'll treat you with utmost respect and awe if you should decide to return."

Jordan grinned. "Thanks."

Mallory reached for his pack of cigarettes. "The least I could do," he muttered.

Jordan closed the door and went whistling down the hallway. Several people stopped and stared. They had never seen Jordan Trent in such a good mood.

* * *

Jordan spotted the street sign up ahead with a sense of satisfaction. The sign reflected the same name as the one scribbled on the paper he'd been carefully guarding. He turned at the corner. The homes had been built during another era. They were set back from the street with shade trees dotting expansive lawns. Most of the homes had inviting porches built in front, with chairs and porch swings waiting to be enjoyed.

This was the street where Lauren had been brought up. It could have been the back lot of Universal Studios. He expected to see James Stewart come walking out of one of the houses any minute, waving goodbye to Donna Reed and patting a golden retriever on the head.

Jordan could almost feel the friendliness of the people, something that was lacking in the neighborhood where he'd been brought up in Chicago. Watching the house numbers, he spotted hers three houses away.

His heart was pounding so hard in his chest that he was having trouble breathing. He could feel a cold sweat pop out on his forehead. This was ridiculous. He kept more calm when he was working than he was now.

Jordan had just realized, now that he'd found Lauren, that he didn't know what to say. What if she didn't want to see him? What if she had actually been hiding from him? Why else had she requested a leave of absence?

What was he doing in Reading, Pennsylvania?

The answer to that was simple: being a coward. *Where's all that damn courage you rely on so heavily?* he demanded to know, but got no answer.

Pulling up in front of the house, he stared at it intently. There were two stories and a dormer window that indicated a good-size attic. Cheerfully painted shutters decorated the windows. Roses bloomed along the front walk. Any minute he expected to see Judy Garland dance out onto the front porch singing "Meet Me in St. Louis."

He was cracking up. The strain of the past several weeks had been too much for him. Forcing himself to remove the keys from the ignition, Jordan slowly climbed out of the car and began the long walk toward the house.

The garage was in back. He had no idea if anyone was at home or not. By this time he wasn't sure that he cared. Maybe this wasn't the best way to handle things. A phone call might be more practical—maybe set up a time when they could meet. He ignored his cravenness and continued the long walk.

Until now, he'd been able to live with the hope of convincing Lauren that she would do well to marry him. Soon he would have to face the reality of what she thought of the idea.

He wasn't at all sure he could deal with that reality.

Stepping up on the porch, he walked over to the door and rang the doorbell. The wooden door was open so someone must be there. Sure enough, he heard a rattling of papers and footsteps coming toward him. He couldn't see anything inside the house because of the bright sunshine outside.

A man appeared in the doorway. He looked to be in his early fifties—tall and in good shape as though he took care of himself. His hair was a sandy red with a thick smattering of gray around his ears.

"Hello," the man said cordially. "May I help you?"

"Uh, yes." He waited a beat too long and added, "Please. I, uh, was looking for Lauren Mackenzie and was told that she was at this address."

The man stepped out onto the porch with Jordan, a forgotten paper clutched in his hand. The cordiality seemed to have slipped from his face unnoticed. He studied Jordan from the top of his head to the toes of his well-polished shoes. Jordan watched the man's jaw tighten as though he had clenched his teeth.

"You must be Jordan Trent," he said in a flat voice.

So much for impressing potential relatives.

Well, what the hell. Jordan grinned and stuck out his hand. "And you must be Matthew Mackenzie, the man my first son's going to be named after."

Matt looked at the hand held out to him and saw the capable strength there, as well as the hard austerity in the face and eyes that had seen too much of the wrong things of this world. Slowly changing the paper to his other hand Matt took the proffered hand and said, "In that case, perhaps you'd better come in."

Matt held the door open and Jordan stepped inside, feeling as though eyes were suddenly boring holes into his back.

The home exuded love, happiness and hospitality to such an extent that Jordan felt he could reach out and touch it. No wonder Lauren was the kind of woman she was—generously giving, warmhearted, and so wonderfully loving.

Jordan stood in the middle of the wide hallway and looked around. "Is Lauren here?"

"No."

The short word seemed to catch him in the midriff, winding him.

"Come on in and sit down," Matt said, waving to a front parlor that looked well lived in.

Jordan sat down across from the chair that had been occupied earlier by Lauren's father. Reading glasses lay nearby, as well as a tall glass of iced tea.

"May I get you something to drink?" Matt asked politely, noticing the direction of Jordan's eyes. The man certainly didn't miss much.

"No, thank you." Jordan waited until Matt sat down. "How did you know who I was?" he asked bluntly.

Matt tilted his head, still studying Jordan as though he were a microscopic specimen under a magnifying glass. "Lauren mentioned meeting a man of your description while she was in California a few weeks ago."

"I see." He looked around the room, trying to ignore the intent stare. Forcing his gaze back to the man across from him, he said, "What else did she have to say about me?"

"Very little."

"And from that you've decided you don't like me," Jordan stated flatly.

"I have no idea what I think about you personally. All I know is that when Lauren came home she was not the same person we've known for the past twenty-five years. Something had changed her. From the way her voice and facial expressions changed whenever she mentioned your name, I have a strong hunch that you had something to do with that change."

Jordan wished he could look on that information as positive, but it was too equivocal.

"I would really like to see your daughter, Mr. Mackenzie," Jordan said in a husky voice.

"Why?"

"I want to marry her," he stated baldly.

"Why?" Matt asked once more.

"Why?" Jordan repeated, puzzled. The answer seemed obvious. "Because I can't even think about a future that doesn't include her in it." His answer was as honest as he knew how to make it.

Matt's face seemed to soften for a moment. "You seem to have all the right answers. Does Lauren know how you feel?"

"I have no idea. That's why I'm here. I tried to contact her at work, but they said she—"

"Yes. She's taken a leave of absence."

"Is there something wrong? Has she been ill or something?"

He heard voices coming from the back of the house and glanced around. Feminine voices carrying on an animated conversation came closer down the hallway toward them. Jordan got to his feet because he recognized one of those voices. He would have recognized it anywhere, speaking any language.

Lauren and a woman who was obviously her mother appeared in the widely arched doorway. Lauren said, "We found your very favorite dessert at the bakery, Dad. So you can forget about your waistline for one evening and—"

Her eyes rested on the man standing there gazing at her; the man she had never expected to see again. Lauren looked shocked, as though an apparition had appeared suddenly before her.

Her dad rose and began to say, "Lauren—" at the same time she whispered "Jordan!" and crumpled into a faint.

Twelve

Jordan was at her side in two long strides and had scooped her up and laid her on a nearby sofa before either parent moved.

Unusually quick reflexes, Matt decided, watching the younger man.

Whatever reactions Jordan had expected from Lauren, swooning at his feet hadn't been one of them. Lauren was too strong a person, she'd been too willing to accept everything that happened and deal with it to let his sudden appearance shock her so. Unless there was something wrong with her.

"What's wrong with her?" His question echoed his thoughts. From his position beside her on the couch, he glanced around at her parents' stricken faces.

"She's fainted," her father offered. "She's been doing a lot of that lately. Takes after her mother in that respect, I'm afraid."

Her mother said, "I'll go get some water for her."

After her mother left, Jordan looked up at the older man. "What's causing her to faint? Has she been to the doctor?" he demanded as though he had every right to know.

"Yes. As a matter of fact, Lauren went to the doctor earlier this week, after we insisted. The doctor explained that she has a slight case of pregnancy she's going to have to work through, but he expects her to recover in seven months or so."

"Lauren's pregnant," Jordan repeated in a hollow voice.

No wonder Matthew Mackenzie had treated him like a suspect in a rape case. As far as he knew, Jordan was. What in the world had Lauren told them?

He felt her stir beside him. "Lauren? Are you all right, love? Did you bump your head when you fell?" he asked, gently stroking the hair away from her forehead.

Her eyes fluttered open and she stared up at the familiar face so close to hers.

"I thought I was imagining you," she said faintly.

He took her hand in his and gently squeezed. "Oh, I'm real all right."

"How's your back? Did the doctor say—"

"The doctor said a lot of things, but what does he know? Why did you leave?"

She continued to take in the familiar planes and hollows of his beloved face. "You didn't need me anymore so I—"

"I'll always need you, love. I thought you knew that."

Her eyes darted past him to where her father stood, watching the scene thoughtfully. Her mother came hurrying into the room. "Oh, Lauren, you gave us such a fright. Of all the silly things to pass on to one of my daughters, fainting at the drop of a hat everytime I was—"

"Mother! Uh, I'd like you to meet Jordan Trent. Jordan, this is my mother, Hilary Mackenzie."

Jordan refused to let go of Lauren's hand. He nodded his head and smiled at the worried-looking woman.

"Oh!" Hilary exclaimed, "so *you're* Jordan!" as though putting all the pieces together.

"Mother? Don't you need to start dinner? I know Dad must be starving."

Her mother smiled at her daughter's agitation. It would take a crowbar to separate that young man from Lauren; Hilary had no trouble seeing that. Whatever the problem that had occurred between them, there was obviously no lack of love there.

Of course she had recognized Lauren's symptoms as soon as Lauren had arrived home, long before the idea of an unexpected pregnancy had occurred to the rest of the members of the family circle. Lauren was in love. There was no mistaking it. But Lauren hadn't wanted to talk about him so Hilary had known they must have had a spat of some sort.

She leaned over and patted her daughter's cheek. "Of course, darling. I'll get started right away." She glanced at Jordan with a twinkle in her eye, exchanged a meaningful glance with Matt and said to Jordan, "Of course you're planning to stay here with us, aren't you, Jordan? There's no reason to look for a room when we have this large house."

Lauren pushed herself to a sitting position, saying, "Mother, we have no idea why Jordan is even here. There's no reason to suppose he wants to stay over—"

"I'd be delighted to accept your hospitality, Mrs. Mackenzie," he said, smoothly interrupting Lauren's protests. "I was hoping to be able to spend some time talking to Lauren."

"I'm sure you could use some help in the kitchen," Matt said to Hilary, gently steering her to the door. "We can always get acquainted with Jordan over dinner."

After the two departed, the room seemed to fill with unspoken words and emotions. Jordan studied Lauren's pale skin. She wasn't taking care of herself. If anything happened to her he didn't know how he could ever bear it.

Without saying a word he pulled her into his arms and held her tightly against him. There was nothing sexual about the embrace. He just needed to have her close to him. God, but he'd missed her so much.

"What are you doing here?" she finally managed to say.

"I came to find you."

"Why?"

Now that he'd met Matt Mackenzie, Jordan could better understand where Lauren had gotten her habit of plain speaking.

"Because it's hard to carry on a marriage long-distance."

"That's finished now."

"Not according to our government."

"But Mallory said—"

"Despite what Mallory would like to have all of us think, Mallory does not control all parts of the government."

"I know that, but—"

"You have a passport that clearly states you are my wife."

"Yes, I know, but Mallory said it was all right to—"

"To falsify records? Shame on Mallory, misleading you that way. You've committed a serious crime, you know."

She looked at him warily. "Want to put that into the plural? Illegally exiting a country isn't considered a misdemeanor, you know."

"Well, I'm willing to do whatever I can to save your good name."

"What are you talking about?"

"I want that passport to be accurate, Lauren. Marry me."

"Why?"

"Damn it! Why do you ask so many questions?" He stood and began to pace the floor, which reminded her very much of the day they had first met. Yes, this was the Jordan Trent she remembered. Lauren dropped her head to hide her smile.

"Why does any man ask a woman to marry him? Because I want you to be my wife, the mother of my children. I want to wake up every morning knowing that you're there beside me. I want to go to sleep every night with my arms around you!" He was almost shouting at her, he was so frustrated.

Lauren bit her bottom lip, hard, to keep from laughing out loud. Never had she heard of such an unromantic proposal in all her life, which was why she believed he was sincere. If Jordan Trent had approached her with suave, polished phrases she'd have been suspicious of his motives.

Here was the man she'd fallen in love with: arrogant, impatient, hot-tempered—"Jordan?"

He spun around and faced her, legs braced, hands on his hips. "What?" He almost flinched at the harshness he heard in his tone. He knew he wasn't handling this right, but damn, she could be the most mulish...stubborn...adorable woman....
"I'm sorry, Lauren," he said in a lower voice. "I didn't mean to yell at you."

"May I have that in writing, please?" she asked with a smile. "I have a feeling that's the first apology you've ever made."

How could he resist her? He sank down on the sofa beside her once more, this time pulling her into his lap. "You're going to marry me, aren't you?" he asked softly, then kissed her before she had an opportunity to reply.

His dreams in the hospital had been filled with her, his feverish brain capturing her time and again to soothe him until he was able to hold her once more. No dream could compare with the reality.

"Oh, darlin', I've missed you so damned much. Please don't ever do this to me again."

"What did I do?"

"Disappear. I'm going to be very possessive of you until I can believe my luck in finding you again. I'll be afraid to blink for fear I'll wake up and you'll be gone."

"I didn't mean to upset you by leaving."

"You did an excellent job of it."

"I thought it was better this way."

"For whom?"

"For both of us. After all, your life-style is so different. You never know where you're going to be from one week to the next—"

"Oh, yes, I do. Sitting behind Mallory's desk."

She leaned back in his arms and stared at him in shock. "What happened to Mallory?"

Jordan laughed. "Why? Did you think I did something to him?"

"No, seriously."

"Seriously, Mallory has been promoted. Therefore, so have I."

"But do you want to work behind a desk?"

"And spend my evenings with you? You're damned right. I'll never be much use around a house, but since I've touched very little of a very large salary over the years, we can always hire someone to keep the house repaired, do yard work and—"

Lauren stopped his speech by leaning over and kissing him gently on the mouth. That got his undivided attention. When at last she drew away from him, she said with amusement, "Just as long as you don't decide to hire someone to take your place in my bed."

"Then you're going to marry me?" he asked, afraid to allow himself to believe that despite everything, she was willing to take him on as a husband.

"Mallory's the one who first mentioned that you always got what you go after. I have a feeling I wouldn't have a prayer if I tried to resist."

The smile he gave her lit up the room. She was touched. He had absolutely no idea how she felt about him. Of course she'd never put it into words. She hadn't felt it necessary, any more than she felt the need to force him to admit that he loved her.

She might never hear him say it, but she didn't care. He had showed her in every way he was capable of demonstrating his feelings.

"When would you like to get married?" she asked, still sitting in his lap, her arms around his neck.

"Tomorrow."

"I'm not sure I could manage that."

"Well, the thing is, Mallory's finally going to let me have my vacation and I thought that Santiago Island might make a great place for a honeymoon. We could stay there until we get bored, then decide what we want to do next."

"Besides, you need to finish recuperating."

"I'm already feeling a hundred percent better." He glanced toward the open doorway. "By the way, what did you tell your dad about me? He mentioned that you told him we met in California."

"Since that's where I'm supposed to have been, where else would I have met you?"

"He treated me like a professional seducer of innocent maidens."

Lauren's cheeks turned a rosy hue. "Fathers are kinda like that," she murmured. "Protective of their daughters."

Jordan saw the little red-headed girl in his mind once again, and knew that he would be just as bad, if not worse.

"I'm sorry if I've ever caused you any pain, Lauren. I've never wanted to hurt you."

"You haven't. Not really. It's just that I could never see how we could work it out so we could spend our lives together."

"But we can. And we have." He waited for her to tell him about the pregnancy. He didn't want her to know that he already knew. He didn't want to take any chances on her thinking that was the reason he'd proposed. Her dad had known differently. Jordan had announced his intentions before he'd ever learned about her condition.

Nuzzling her neck, he asked, "Are you planning to go back to work?"

She became still in his arms and he waited, nibbling on her earlobe. "Would you like me to?"

He smiled, but she couldn't see his amusement. "I want you to do whatever you want to do, darlin'." He waited, almost holding his breath.

"Well, I'm not really sure what to do at the moment."

"Then let's play it by ear, okay? Just know that whatever you decide is fine with me."

He could feel her slowly relaxing against him. So she wasn't ready to tell him. It made no difference to him. Jordan was rather pleased with the timing of everything. If she weren't already pregnant she might have insisted that they wait and get to know each other better. Or she might have decided that she didn't want to marry him at all.

The first thing he intended to do upon the arrival of his son or daughter was to thank him or her for helping him accomplish the most important assignment of his career.

Epilogue

Sparkling white sand glinted like diamonds in the sunlight. Turquoise-blue water looked so artificial that Lauren was convinced the natives must sneak out at night after all the tourists were asleep and pour bluing into the lagoon.

They had been on the island for three wonderful days and exciting nights. Jordan had insisted that she keep a strong sun block on her skin. He loved the ivory tone and wanted nothing to harm it. Consequently, they only swam early in the morning and in the late evening, after the sun's rays had lessened.

Now they were stretched out side by side in the shade of their palm-thatched porch, lazily watching the soft rhythm of the waves and the swaying palm trees.

"This is a far cry from Czechoslovakia," Lauren murmured as though to herself.

They shared a double lounger. Jordan opened one eye and looked over at her skimpily-clad body. He was glad he'd been able to rent this small cabana away from everything else on the island. Initially he'd wanted the privacy for resting when he'd been here on his own. Now he wanted the privacy to keep everyone from enjoying his wife's rather delectable form, particularly in the evening when he coaxed her to go skinny-dipping with him.

"Oh, I don't know," he said, lazily dropping his hand onto her bare midriff. "I've noticed that there are some basic similarities."

"Such as?"

"We seem to spend a great deal of our time in bed together."

"Well, that beats getting shot at."

"I'm glad you think so. Otherwise I might have worried about my technique."

The sound she made could only be likened to a rather ladylike snort. "You're too arrogant to worry over anything you do. You think you're perfect."

"Hardly."

"I have to admit you manage to come very close at times."

He turned over and kissed her along the edge of her bikini top. "For instance?"

"If you think I'm going to lie here extolling your virtues and give you more reason to be obnoxiously arrogant, you're crazy."

"That's what I love about you, woman—all of those affectionate endearments that just roll off your lips." His hand slid beneath the thin top and he cupped her full breast, gently rubbing his thumb over the nipple. Did she think he hadn't noticed that her breasts had become fuller in the last several weeks?

She took a quick breath at his touch and he hid his smile by nudging the offending cloth out of the way and placing his lips around the tip of her breast.

Lauren ran her hands through his hair, holding him close. She had never imagined that her life could turn out so perfectly. Jordan seemed to be content just being with her. The tense professional had disappeared. In his place a teasing, boyish, passionate man had appeared. She loved his playful mood. In fact she loved everything about him . . . his openness with her, his complete honesty . . . which was why she was having such a tough time figuring out how to tell him that she was pregnant.

It wasn't the sort of thing she could drop into a casual conversation. Not that she had meant to keep the news a secret from him, not after he'd shown up at her parents' home.

Before then there had been some poignant discussions with her mother and dad who had felt he had a right to know about the baby. She hadn't seen it that way. He'd already made it clear how he felt about children, and his professional life was totally incompatible with any normal family life.

His unexpected appearance had changed all of that. He'd obviously come looking for her in order to demand that she marry him. She grinned at the thought. Never once had he asked her how she felt about getting married. He'd been just like her father, taking it for granted.

Lauren's thoughts scattered into fragments of disconnected images as Jordan finished removing her top and reached down to slide his hand inside the bottom half. He gently rubbed her skin so that all she could think about was Jordan and how he made her feel.

He never seemed to get enough of touching her, even when he had no intention of making love to her. Wherever they were, whatever they did, he either held her hand or touched her arm or kept his hand on the small of her back.

Lauren had discovered a definite indication in herself that touching him could become addictive as well. He had turned a deep golden brown since they'd arrived on the beach. And why not? He spent most of his time in the sun while insisting she stay protected from the harsh rays. The swimsuit he wore did absolutely nothing to conceal his masculinity. If anything it emphasized how well endowed he was.

His mouth gently pressed kisses across her stomach, down and across her abdomen, down and down—"Jordan!" she gasped.

"I know, love. Just relax and let me love you." He had taken all kinds of liberties with her, teaching her variations of lovemaking that had sent her spiraling over the edge time and again and he'd discovered several ways to make her wild with passion. He seemed to enjoy bringing out that fierce response in her.

Lauren couldn't lie still. She wanted to touch him, to love him, to express to him all that she couldn't find the words to say. By the time he stretched out over her she was sobbing with the need to love him.

He took her in one powerful surge, lifting her so that her thighs locked tightly around him. She clung to him, wordlessly pleading for release, her soft, incoherent moans and gasps sending him into an orbit of pleasure, knowing that he was able to give her so much pleasure in return.

They were oblivious to the day, the glistening sand, the turquoise-blue water, the swaying palm trees. The view was wasted but neither one cared.

Jordan kept the pace relentlessly rhythmical until Lauren cried out, her voice sounding like one of the gulls that visited their stretch of beach from time to time. Only then did he allow himself his own release. He gave one final, convulsive lunge, grasping her so closely that she could barely get her breath.

She didn't care.

He rolled, carrying her with him so that their positions were reversed on the wide lounger. She lay limply sprawled across his body, her head pillowed on his chest. His lungs still labored to get enough oxygen to his body.

"Jordan?" He felt her tense slightly.

"Hmmmm," he responded drowsily.

"You know, we haven't been using anything to prevent a pregnancy..."

He tried not to make any moves that would alert her to his reaction to the conversation.

"That's true," he said lazily, running his hand through her hair.

"You once said you didn't want children," she tentatively offered.

"I did? Must have been out of my mind. I love children. We've got to have at least two, one of each." He could feel her body began to relax once again.

"I'd like that," she said softly. After a few minutes of silence she said, "Of course you probably aren't all that anxious to start on a family right away..." she trailed off, wishing she knew how to just starkly tell him that, like it or not, he was going to be a father in a little more than six months! Lauren had never before considered herself a coward. But she was. Oh, yes, indeed. And she was proving it with every evasion she uttered.

Jordan could feel her apprehension and wished he knew how to help her. At this point in their relationship it wouldn't help her to know that he'd discovered her condition after she'd fainted. Someday...maybe...he might tell her. But for the time being he'd made Matt Mackenzie swear to secrecy.

"Oh, I don't know," he said. "I'm not getting any younger. I think it would be rather nice to have our children early, give them a chance to have as young parents as possible and—"

"Oh, Jordan, do you really mean that?" she asked, raising her head and looking at him for the first time in several minutes.

"Yes, darling. I really mean it. I love you and I'll love our children. You are the world to me."

Tears glistened in her eyes. "That's the first time you've ever told me you love me, did you know that?"

He raised his head slightly and kissed her swollen, well-loved mouth. "I've told you I loved you with everything I've done and said since I first met you. I just didn't know it at the time."

He waited expectantly, aware of her search for the words to tell him about the baby. He had so many questions he wanted to ask about the whole birthing process.

Would she want him with her at the time of birth? If not, he'd just have to spend the next few months convincing her that he was just as indispensable at the delivery as he was at the conception. He smiled, already knowing what she would have to say about his arrogance.

"Uh, Jordan, I think there's something you should know," Lauren began with a tentative smile.

* * * * *

A Note from Kathleen Korbel

Dear Reader,

I remember very well when I sat down to write *The Ice Cream Man*. We had been having a really bad year in my house. My husband found himself commuting to work from St. Louis to Flint, Michigan, for four months while he was looking for a new job here, and I was taking care of his ill mother and my own two children, who were convinced we were going to end up divorced and living on the streets.

So *The Ice Cream Man* fulfilled several functions for me. It was kind of a gift, a lighter, more cozy book than I'd ever done, with my first real cast of eccentrics. It was my way of preserving some of the more memorable moments of the lives of my children, who bear a striking resemblance to Emma and Kevin in the book. And it was, simply, my tribute to single mothers everywhere.

I had tasted what it was like to be a single mother, during which time I had to make budgets stretch, hugs stretch farther, homework make sense (there were also some memorable notes from math teachers when I attempted this), and try to hold a house together by myself. The only way I got through it was knowing that at a given time, I would have help. My husband would be home for good. I might still be eating tuna noodle casserole every night, but my children wouldn't have only me to come to for their affection and support and discipline. It's a heavy burden to bear, and I realized how beautifully most women do it when they have no choice and no end in sight. So, for all those single mothers everywhere who give their children so very much, *The Ice Cream Man* is my small gift to you. I hope it makes you smile.

Kathleen Korbel

THE ICE CREAM MAN

Kathleen Korbel

To Kate,
the real Queen of the World.
And to Kevin,
whose dreams span galaxies.
You're *my* babies.

And to Detective John, for the help.
Thanks.

Chapter 1

No full-grown woman with two children had any business falling in love with the ice cream man. As she waited out on the sweltering street, her hand in that of her tiny daughter's, Jenny Lake kept reminding herself of that. She was a responsible adult. Responsible adults did not drool over good physiques.

The longer she stood out under a July sun in a line of giggling, preening teenage girls, though, the less she seemed to care. For some reason, in this summer of her thirtieth year, when she never seemed able to concentrate beyond the next bill, the next crisis or the newest flood of tears, Jenny was suddenly struck by a whimsy she couldn't explain. She found herself mesmerized by a good set of buns and a tattoo.

Well, she had to admit with a secret smile as she lifted damp black hair from her neck, it was more than just that.

"What can I get for you?" he asked, leveling the most mesmerizing set of whiskey-brown eyes she'd ever seen on her.

Jenny just stared. All she could think of was the movie *Picnic*. The dangerous, mysterious man coming to town. If the man in the movie had looked anything like this guy, she would have been just as foolish as the heroine.

"Mommy?"

She might have been tempted to run away or commit a crime or sacrifice her virtue. . . .

"Mom?"

Distracted, Jenny looked down to find a set of very reproachful blue eyes leveled her way. "Bombpops, Mom. You're forgetting again."

Jenny had to grin. "Thanks, Em. I'll do better next time." She allowed one last errant thought to pass before getting down to business; she wondered once again whether fairies had, indeed, changed her three-and-a-half-year-old baby girl for a forty-year-old midget from the royal family. There should be some law against a child being more composed than her mother.

"Bombpops, please," Jenny said, lifting rueful eyes back to the ice cream man. "Two."

"What about Kevin?" Emma piped up with a tug on Jenny's hand.

"Three," Jenny immediately amended. She'd be hearing about this for hours.

"Two-twenty-five," the man answered, already bent over his freezer.

He didn't belong here, Jenny thought suddenly. He didn't look right. It wasn't the white T-shirt and low-slung jeans. Those fit. They fit too well, for several uncomfortably obvious reasons. So did the anchor and snake on his arm, wrapped around the blue *Semper Fi* proclamation. Even the way he'd pulled his dark brown hair back into a short tail made him look suspect, slightly shady. His face was angular, dark, with those hot, liquid eyes that bored holes through a person's best reserve. But it wasn't that.

Jenny thought about it as she dug into her own shorts for the change and handed it over. Maybe it was the fact that his face, for all its youth, looked too experienced. She had trouble believing he was on the shy side of thirty. And his eyes, for all their steely indifference, looked too intelligent. Maybe it was the silly fact that he didn't smell like a man who would abdicate his future to a bell and a white truck. For all his casual disregard for appearance, he was just a little too carefully put together.

Dumb reasons, for sure. Certainly nothing even the eminently practical Emma would consider. But one thing Jenny was beginning to realize as she found herself staring now at the long, graceful fingers that were lifting bombpops out to her, was that for some reason when it came to this particular ice cream man, common sense was failing her.

Then he smiled, a grudging flash of warmth that transformed the truculence into shy sincerity, and Jenny was snagged for good.

"Mom."

Jenny was busy smiling back, and didn't hear Emma's tolerant tone of voice.

"Mo-ther." Make that disgust. The thin, reedy little voice hit two distinctive notes. "C'n have my ice cream now?"

Startled again, suddenly wondering why the air actually seemed cool beyond the scope of that man's eyes, Jenny slipped an already dripping bar into her daughter's hands.

"Let's go, honey, before Kevin's melts all over the street."

Emma wasn't quite ready to complete the transaction. Tilting her very blond head to the side, she bestowed an eminently arch look on her mother. "You forgot to say thank you," she reproached.

Jenny couldn't help but laugh. Turning a sheepish smile on the man, she shrugged. "There should be some law about your children being older than you. Thank you for the ice cream."

When he answered, it seemed that he meant it. "My pleasure."

Jenny turned back then to her house. Fifteen minutes later when she should have been paying bills, she found herself staring out the front window. There at the end of the block was the white van painted in lurid Popsicles and Drumsticks. And there alongside it was the almost constant swarm of teen and pre-teen girls.

And there was Jenny, seated at her desk, tapping her pen against her teeth and thinking of tattoos.

"I'm telling you it's not natural."

Poring through her cupboards in search of something better than macaroni and cheese for dinner, Jenny wished Barb would go on home. She decided against answering her ebullient neighbor, knowing from experience that the bright, perky blonde would continue on her own without any help.

"He showed up five days ago," Barb went on, just as Jenny had anticipated. "And since then this neighborhood has started to look like a cheerleaders' convention. Not to mention the fact that certain mothers I know of have been seen combing their hair before heading out for ice cream."

Jenny wondered if Barb knew that she was one of them. The new ice cream man had apparently been the talk of the few mothers who had the chance to spend summers home in the neighborhood. It was something different than *Sesame Street* and baseball, after all. And he was *so* good-looking. Being one of the working mothers, Jenny had missed most of the speculation. Being Barb's next-door neighbor, she unfortunately got it all secondhand. In detail. With enthusiasm.

"I think Donahue was right," Barb announced with great meaning.

Finally giving up on nutrition and settling for ease, Jenny ripped open the box of macaroni and set to work. "About what?"

"Oh, Jenny, not macaroni again. Why don't I send over some of the coq au vin I have? There's plenty. I was just planning on freezing some, anyway."

Jenny almost flinched. Being a divorced, underpaid working mother was hard enough. Being a divorced, underpaid working mother who lived next to the Perfect Woman was, at times, unbearable. If Barb weren't so damned sincere and nice, Jenny could find herself easily hating her.

"Thanks anyway, Barb. The kids aren't much for wine cooking. Besides, I'd hate to take food from Bill and Buffy." Jenny winced again. She did it every time she said the names Barb, Bill and Buffy Bailey. A television commercial for suburbia: surgically trimmed lawn, Christmas lights in the shape of a manger scene and trash-can lids that fit. The real life Ken and Barbie. And they lived next door to the Divorcée from Hell.

"Do you think he could be dealing drugs?" Barb asked suddenly.

Still caught in that vision of the perfect father, Jenny almost fell over. "Bill?" she squeaked. The man who if he'd been a dog would have been a golden retriever? Impossible.

Evidently Barb thought so, too. She giggled with delight, not just at the horror in Jenny's eyes but the question.

"Of course not," she said. "I'm talking about the ice cream man. I saw it on Donahue last week."

"The ice cream man?"

Barb nodded, her perfect curls not moving an inch. "Selling drugs. Evidently that's the latest thing. They get a beeper and a gun and cruise the neighborhoods selling cocaine." Taking a sip of the instant iced tea Jenny had offered, Barb pondered her own question. "The parents didn't even know it until a man ordered the triple-flavor Popsicle and got a packet of white powder instead."

Jenny went on stirring noodles. "I wonder what he would have gotten if he'd ordered a Drumstick."

"I'm serious," her friend insisted, finally getting to her feet. "You know, you could leave sun tea out while you're at work. It's cheaper than instant. We think we should go to the police."

Jenny had to smile, not just at the sincere concern on the blonde's face but the way she dispensed little household hints in the middle of discussions on neighborhood safety. "And do what? Report a man for being too good-looking? Do me a favor and invite me to the lineup."

"You don't believe me."

Jenny wanted very much to sigh. There was so much on her mind. They were trying to take her hours away at the store, and the Jerk was still holding out child support. She had to get the car fixed, Kevin was working up to a first-class case of rebellion and she hadn't had more than four hours' sleep in the last six nights because Emma had been having nightmares again. It was so difficult to worry about an ice cream man being devious just because he happened to have dimples.

He did, too, Jenny thought with unaccustomed pleasure. Big ones on either side of his mouth that stretched into the most delightful gullies when he smiled.

It was the smile that did it. That shy flash of sincerity she'd only seen once. Somehow she couldn't equate that smile with a drug dealer.

"Jenny?"

Jenny turned to find a frown on Barb's face.

"Are you all right?" she asked. "You weren't paying attention."

Jenny was embarrassed. She couldn't believe she'd drifted off into the Fantasy Zone again. In all her thirty years she'd never gotten lost like this—well, at least not in the last fifteen years or so—but especially since she'd had the kids. She didn't have time for fantasy. After the Jerk, she didn't much have the inclination, either.

Men were men. They were childish and selfish and never seemed to be around when you needed them. And then they slipped your dreams into their pockets and walked out the door.

Fantasies were for the girls who still giggled out there on the street in the afternoon. Jenny had reality.

"I'm sorry, Barb," she apologized with a rueful smile, thinking again how she was glad to have the blonde around. Maybe that little nuclear family next door wasn't quite real, but it sure looked inviting from where she sat. "I'm just tired. It's been a long day."

Barb flashed one of those prom-queen smiles that made Jen think of TV evangelists. "It's okay, Jen. I understand. You get to bed early tonight, and everything will look better tomorrow."

"Especially if I get some mail from the Jerk."

Another smile, brighter. "I'm taking Buffy to the park tomorrow. I'll pick Kevin and Emma up, too. Okay? It'll give you a little time when you get back from work to be alone."

Jen immediately felt worse. Why did she call this woman a Barbie doll when she always came through?

Because she was tired and frustrated and broke and envious. She wanted to be a professional mother, too. She wanted to be able to sit at home and rock babies and play Chutes and Ladders. She wanted to bake cookies for the block instead of selling them for a grocery store. She wanted to be able to smile and mean it.

"Thanks, Barb. Then I'll take…Buffy overnight Friday. Let you and Bill have some time alone."

Barb just nodded with another smile that was even sweeter. "I'll let you know what the officer says."

"Oh, wait a couple of days on that," Jen suggested, unsure why she was so hesitant. "Let's just see what he does first. I'm not really sure I want the esteemed St. Anthony police swarming through the streets."

"You'll sing a different tune when Kevin comes home on drugs."

Fine. Something else she hadn't thought to worry about yet. Kevin was six. "I'll buy their ice cream for them until we decide."

It's a sacrifice, she couldn't help thinking with a silly urge to giggle as she rooted around the fridge for enough milk and margarine to finish dinner. *But for my children, I'll face that very good-looking man and take whatever he dishes out.*

With her luck, it would be snow cones.

There was a crash from the playroom and both women turned toward the shrill protests that set up.

"Emma!"

"Kevin!"

"You're looking at me! Mo-o-m, Emma won't stop looking at me!"

"I thought it was too quiet," Jenny moaned.

"I'll see you tomorrow," Barb promised, heading for the back door. "Do you want me to mail these?" she asked, motioning to the small pile of envelopes on the side of the table. "You know, the police have said not to leave bills in the mailboxes. Somebody's stealing them."

Jenny swooped up the envelopes with a tight smile. "If somebody would like my electric bill, they're more than welcome to it."

"I'm going anyway…" Barb hinted, hand on the back door.

"Thanks, but no," Jen said, stuffing the envelopes into her purse. "I'll get them in on my way to work in the morning."

Barb left and Jenny headed in to break up the impending free-for-all. By the time she made it back from drying tears and cleaning up the over-ended rubber-tree plant, the macaroni had burned to the bottom of the pan and she had to start over. And, she thought, holding the blackened pot under running water, she had to deal with all those envelopes.

During the next couple of days Jenny did her best to follow Barb's instructions. When she drove by the ice cream truck she thought of cocaine. When her children begged for something cold and melting she marched out with them and tried her best to consider the purveyor a criminal.

Under other circumstances, it would have been easy. He was a central-casting dream for the part of a Miami drug runner, especially with the just-too-long hair he still wore pulled into that tail. He was a little too good-looking in a dark way, his nose bent just enough and a scar interrupting the straight line of his left eyebrow.

He was lean and graceful and quiet. Jenny could easily see him sneaking down an alley with a switchblade in his hand or imagine him lying in wait with an Uzi.

But that was the problem. Any other time of her life she would have walked right into Barb's spotless oak-and-gingham kitchen and demanded a march to the police. For some reason this summer, the idea of this dark man in her well-mannered neighborhood disturbed her in different ways. Like an exotic bird set loose in a pigeon coop, he enticed. He intrigued. Instead of shoving him away, Jenny wanted to draw him closer.

Idiot, she thought as she pulled the chugging compact into her driveway. You're just a victim of stress. You're caught in a whirlpool that's sucking you straight to the bottom, and he's like a gull soaring in the wind. That's the only reason he's interesting. He's everything you're not.

He's free. He doesn't have too many bills and not enough money. He doesn't have children who can't understand that mom can't be everything to everyone a hundred percent of the time. He doesn't have too much to do and too little time and never, never any time alone.

He drives an ice cream truck in the summer and eats his lunch listening to rock and roll.

And he's at my front door.

Jenny almost put her nose through the windshield. The vehicle jarred to a shuddering stop when she forgot to take it out of gear. What the heck was he doing there, sitting on the porch swing with the broken slat as if he were waiting for her to come home?

"Can I help you?" she asked too tentatively when she finally thought to officially turn off the ignition and step from the car.

With a languid grace that threatened to steal her breath, he unwound himself and got to his feet. There was a rip in the knee of his jeans, and he had a bandanna hanging out of the back pocket. There were sweat stains on his shirt and pearls of moisture on his upper lip. Jenny couldn't seem to take her eyes from them.

"I hope you don't mind," he apologized, strolling up. "I've tried everybody on the block, and nobody's home. I thought I'd just sit for a minute until the next car showed up."

Automatically Jenny looked over toward the white colonial where Barb lived, but she remembered that it was story hour over at the library. Barb never let Buffy miss any kind of educational entertainment, and she'd taken Kevin and Emma, as well. The rest of the neighborhood slept peacefully in the noon heat, hidden behind fully grown trees and carefully pruned hedges. Jenny had chosen her neighborhood for its privacy. Now that she stood in her driveway with a suspicious stranger and realized that even her neighbor two houses down couldn't see her, she wondered at her decision.

By the time she turned back to her surprise visitor, he'd reached the far back door and was opening it.

"Can I help you with your groceries?"

"Uh...what did you need?" Jenny was getting a little nervous. How did you politely say no thanks to a dope dealer to keep him out of your house? How did you draw attention to yourself when the retirees were all asleep and most of the mothers at work?

He straightened up, bag already in arm, and smiled. Again Jenny was caught by some quick hesitation that robbed the action of its glibness. She *wanted* to believe in him.

"I'm sorry," he shrugged. "The truck broke down. I need to get another fan belt over here before I lose a couple of tons of red food coloring and sugar water. Would you mind if I use your phone?"

"The phone." Surely there should be something more intelligent to say. Surely she shouldn't be standing across the car from him as if he were the Boston Strangler.

But what if he were?

This time he gave her a lopsided grin. "I can wait on the porch if you want," he offered, "if you'd call. It's just that Marco doesn't speak English."

Immediately Jenny waved the offer aside. It was silly. She'd seen this man dish out ice cream for a week now. He'd been so good with the kids, so patient with the painfully tongue-tied girls. It wasn't exactly a recommendation for the Nobel Peace Prize, but she could at least let him use her phone.

"Of course you can call. Where did you leave the truck?"

"Over on St. Vincent. It died right in front of somebody's driveway, but of course they weren't home."

Jenny leaned in for the other bag of groceries and led the way toward the porch, much too aware that he was following close behind.

"The name's Nick," he said with a little nod that would have been a handshake. "Nick Barnett."

"Uh, Jenny Lake." She smiled tentatively as she mounted the porch. Even the shade by the swing was a relief after the steam bath out on her driveway. The air-conditioning in the car had gasped its last in June, and Jenny didn't even have the money to call the dealership, much less let them get their hands under her hood. She was hot and sweaty and flushed, her hair hanging in limp ringlets around her face. She'd come home from work like this every day for the last four weeks and not thought anything about it. Today she wanted to hide.

"You work for Bennet's?" Nick asked, motioning to the cheap brown uniform that made Jenny look like an escapee from the orphanage. It had been designed by the polyester-clad wife of the food-store-chain president.

"During the summer," she acknowledged, her groceries balanced on a hip as she dug for her keys. Before she knew it,

Nick relieved her of the bag. His hand brushed her hip and set up an odd static dance that startled her. "Thanks," Jenny murmured. She looked into his eyes and then glanced nervously away. "I teach—fifth-grade math."

He chuckled, completely at ease. "A better man than I, Gunga Din."

The door swung open and Jenny led the way in, the air-conditioning hitting her like a cold shower. She couldn't help the delighted sigh that escaped.

"Watch out for debris," she warned, weaving her own way through the litter on the floor. It never seemed to get cleaned up anymore before it was there again. There were two loads of laundry waiting to be folded on the dining-room table and a week's worth of unread newspapers piled by the couch. And the playroom was worse.

Alongside her, Nick was trying his best to balance the groceries and miss the odd roller skate and doll part on his way through to the kitchen.

"God," he breathed in a voice that sent the most pleasant shivers up Jenny's back. "I'd forgotten what cool felt like. You really have a nice house."

Jenny took a vague look around. "Somewhere under all this. Thanks." It was the only thing the Jerk hadn't been able to avoid. He'd kept up the payments on the upwardly mobile house he'd demanded. It was just up to Jenny to heat and cool it, to supply water and upkeep and taxes, and even that was enough to almost kill her.

Everybody saw the two-story modern and thought she'd made it through the divorce with luck. They didn't see how ratty the carpet was getting, or how many times she'd stitched up the armchair and hung pictures over the peeling wallpaper. She wished he would have left her with an apartment instead.

They reached the kitchen, which she hadn't had a chance to clean before going into work that morning, and Nick made enough room on the table to be able to set down the bags.

"There's the phone," Jenny instructed unnecessarily as she began unpacking cereal and crackers. "Would you like some iced tea?"

"Oh, yeah," Nick agreed with enthusiasm as he settled his slim hip onto the edge of her kitchen table and picked up the receiver. "It's hot out there."

How did one bring up the subject? Jenny wondered as she pulled out the instant tea and headed for the sink. Just how does one go about asking an obviously intelligent man how he got himself stuck serving ice cream for the summer? Do you have prospects? Is this what you wanted to be all your life? Or is it just a convenient cover for nefarious activities?

Behind her he was speaking what seemed like Italian into the phone, laughing with a gravelly delight that surprised her. His voice was more animated on the phone than she'd heard it in a week.

Of course, how intense can somebody get about bombpops and soft swirls? Not as intense as about a fan belt, evidently. Jenny heard him hang up just about the time she stirred the tea into being and turned to hand it to him.

He was still smiling, as if savoring a private joke or a special friend. Jenny handed over the glass.

"Marco," he explained, seeing her interest. "He's quite a character. Seems I interrupted a nooner."

"A . . . oh."

"His wife's a nurse. She works nights." His smile grew almost piratical. "And right now she doesn't like me very much. Marco will be over in a few minutes."

Jenny couldn't help but watch as he tipped his head back and drained the tea in one, long drink. Sweat beaded along his throat and trickled down toward his T-shirt. His hair was damp and curling. Jenny felt the heat stir in her as well, even though she was cooler than she had been all day.

Suddenly his eyes were open, and they were on her. "Thanks," he said, his expression oddly reticent. "That really hit the spot."

So do you, Jenny couldn't help but think. Embarrassed, she turned back to her groceries.

"It's Marco's truck," he explained, almost as if reading her mind. "Usually his kid Tony rides it, but he's down with strep throat or something. I'm fillin' in."

Jenny couldn't help but look up. "Then you usually don't—"

"Drive an ice cream truck for a living?" His abrupt laugh contained enough disbelief to certify the question silly for reasons patently obvious to only Nick. "Nah. Marco needed help, and I wasn't doin' anything right now. I'm in between sessions. School."

"You teach, too?"

He shook his head. "I learn." It seemed that he wasn't in the mood for elucidation. He set the tea glass down and straightened. "Thanks for the tea. And thanks for letting me use the phone. I didn't tell you, but the old lady across the street slammed the door in my face when I asked her."

Jenny had to grin. "Mrs. Warner slams the door in everybody's face. She thinks the Commies are coming over the hill." As a matter of fact, she'd also have those beady eyes glued to Jenny's front door wondering just what Jenny and Nick were doing in there. Jenny didn't know whether she felt irritated or amused. She did know that she was sorely tempted to keep Nick inside on some pretext just to see what kind of rise she could get out of Mrs. Warner. The old lady lived for this kind of intrigue.

Jenny and the ice cream man. Wouldn't that be the gossip of the year around here?

"Uh . . . Jenny?"

Startled, she snapped back to attention. Lord, it was getting worse. Must be the summer of her discontent, she thought with a wry smile as she apologized.

"I was just thinking what conclusions Mrs. Warner was jumping to this very minute," she told him with a quick shake of the head and a wide grin to negate the import. "Ten more minutes with the door closed, and she'll have either the police or the priest out on my porch."

He didn't seem quite as amused. He didn't do anything so obvious as look around for escape routes, but suddenly Nick was perceptibly cooler.

"Marco will be waiting at the wagon," he demurred. "I'd better be getting back."

Worried about your reputation? Jenny wanted to ask. She didn't. She walked him back to the front door, all the while thinking that for being as sweaty as he obviously was, he shouldn't have smelled quite so good. He smelled musky and dark, like a stormy night, with just enough tang to betray the lightning in those clouds. He shouldn't have looked quite so good, either. Ah, if she were only one of those giggling girls.

He turned on her porch and delivered a final grin, cocky and masculine as hell. Jenny knew it was as much for Mrs. Warner's benefit as hers. "You should think about getting new fuel injectors on your car. Yours aren't gonna last long." And then he was loping down her lawn.

Jenny couldn't manage more than a scowl. "You wouldn't fill in as a mechanic, too, would you?"

Almost to the sidewalk, Nick turned. "See me after Tony gets over his strep throat."

Feeling Mrs. Warner's hot eyes on her even through the hedges, Jenny couldn't help but smile. She smiled until Nick turned back toward the street. Then, suddenly, her smile died.

To be perfectly honest, she had been watching how the muscles on his legs shifted, how snugly his faded jeans hugged his hips. That bandanna hanging out of his back pocket swayed just a little as he walked. His loose-jointed gait was strangely out of place here in the carefully manicured streets of suburbia. It fascinated Jenny.

It didn't fascinate Jenny half as much as what she saw when Nick got to the street. Reaching back to pull the bandanna to wipe the sweat that had already gathered on his forehead, he revealed what the bandanna had hidden. A beeper. Small, square, brown, like the one the Jerk had always worn when they'd been out—just in case he'd needed to be reached.

But why would an ice cream man need to be reached? Jenny had trouble believing there were ice cream emergencies, and she doubted he wore it just in case registration opened early for a favorite class. Her heart was doing a fast slide when the situation grew worse.

Nick had no sooner reached the pavement when a long, white Caddy slid to a stop next to him. Jenny stayed at her door, watching. Could this be Marco? She didn't think ice cream dealers made that kind of money. Maybe he had a fleet of trucks and sold franchises across the country.

Out on the street, Nick stuffed the bandanna away and looked around. Jenny made it a point to close the door, and then sidled over to watch out the corner of her front window.

He was bent over the passenger door, talking rapidly, reaching into a front pocket to pass something in through the window, all the while with an eye out to the sleeping neighborhood. Jenny didn't realize that she was chewing on her thumb as she watched. She held her breath. Maybe Marco was rich enough to buy a Cadillac, but she didn't know many Italians who were black.

She didn't want to see this. She hadn't realized until now how much her funny little fantasy had meant to her. No matter their conception or import, fantasies weren't meant to die.

Nick stuffed what looked like money into his pocket and straightened, and the car slid away. Jenny and Mrs. Warner both saw it from opposite sides of the street, with polar reactions. Then, just as Nick was about to continue his walk up the street, a truck rattled into view. No logo, very little original paint, and driving, a big, burly, curly-haired man Jenny could hear laugh from inside her house. The truck pulled to a stop and Nick climbed in, laughing back.

Jenny turned away from the window. It wasn't fair. The one bright point of color in her summer, the breath of fresh air in her claustrophobic existence, and she was going to have to report him to the police.

Chapter 2

Nick Barnes had had better days. He was hot and bored and filled for a lifetime with snotty noses and whining, grasping little kids. He was beginning to dream of grape Popsicles at night, and already had the sneaking suspicion that red food dye didn't come out of white T-shirts. And on top of that, if he didn't see some action, he wasn't going to be off these damn streets anytime before he earned his first pacemaker. All in all, he'd rather spend time in the joint.

To make matters worse, just when he'd finally found something worth hanging around for, he'd had that taken away from him, too. As he watched Marco work on the overheated truck engine, Nick found himself pouting like a four-year-old over a dented fire truck.

"You can't be serious," he snarled, taking a long drag from a cigarette.

"*Paisan*, you think they send me all the way out here to pull your chain?"

"They put me out here in the first place, didn't they?"

Chuckling, Marco lifted his head from where he was considering the state of several fan belts. "Next time don't be so anxious to stand up for your ideals."

"Ideals, hell," Nick retorted, cigarette smoke curling about his head as if it were coming from his ears. "I didn't like the bastard." Taking another drag, he couldn't help a satisfied grin as he met his friend's jolly eyes across the opened hood. "Especially when he told me I couldn't ticket him because he was the police chief's brother."

Reaching over to steal Nick's cigarette for a taste, Marco shook his head in affable commiseration. "Next time such a dangerous mood takes you, remember how hot it was out here."

"It's not the heat that's bothering me."

"Remember *all* the children."

Nick leaned against the truck, looking down toward the cedar-shingled roof he could barely see through the trees. "It's not that, either."

Marco laughed so hard his head almost collided with the truck hood.

"All right," Nick admitted ruefully, casting another disgruntled glance toward the new rainbow on his shirt from the kid who just wouldn't wait until the truck had been fixed for his bombpop fix, and then had poked Nick with his prize. "It *is* that. Among other things."

Still chuckling, Marco shook his head back in among the cylinders and hoses. "You are not Captain Kangaroo, my friend."

"Captain Kangaroo only had to deal with a farmer and a moose, not this bunch of terrorists. Who says she's the suspect?"

Marco didn't seem in the least fazed by Nick's abrupt change of subject. "Tip came in sometime yesterday. Captain McGrady, your good friend, came into the squad room this morning with it."

"You mean Captain McGrady who consigned me to this Devil's Island?"

"I mean Captain McGrady who kept you from spending the rest of your career cleaning holding cells after you call the chief of police's brother a drunken, maggot-infested excuse for dog meat."

Nick grinned at nothing. "I was being polite."

Still caressing the engine with knowing hands, Marco smiled to himself. "She has twice been seen in the morning checking mailboxes. One of those mailboxes subsequently lost a check to the phone company. She is a divorced lady with two children, not enough money and an ex-husband who seems hesitant to rectify the situation. Enough, the good captain believes, to cast suspicion."

Shaking his head, Nick ground what was left of his cigarette beneath his heel. Damn. Didn't it just figure? The one person he'd found in this desert with a little life in her, and she's his primary suspect. He pulled out his bandanna again and wiped the sweat from the back of his neck, only to think of how her hair had looked, that dusty black, as if light failed to find it, disheveled and damp, curling around her neck like it was begging to be touched. And those eyes. Green, like cat's eyes.

He hadn't meant to pick her house to answer the beeper call. He'd just been hot and tired and ticked off because of the old broad across the street. He'd decided that that porch swing looked pretty damned inviting. So he'd sat, and he'd waited, knowing full well that whatever McGrady had wanted would wait until one of the denizens of this landscaped wasteland came home.

Divorced, her ringless hands had said. Skittish, her eyes had warned. Lonely and frustrated, telegraphed from every movement of her body. And with kids to boot. Even that little blond one, that little girl with the solemn blue eyes. They were still kids, and Marco had been right about that.

If there was one thing Nick wasn't, it was a kid person. He knew damned well that that was why McGrady had made him pull this little detail. Penance. Punishment for tilting at the powers that be. A gentle reminder in the idiom of police bureaucracy that he'd screwed up.

Marco had been right. Next time he'd be scrubbing toilets. But right now being imprisoned in a hot, cramped ice cream truck and surrounded by hordes of impatient, bored, shrilling kids was the equivalent of anything the Viet Cong had dished out to wash brains.

He gave in. He quit. He'd drive right by the damn police chief's brother's house and spray paint "I'm Sorry" on the garage if it could get him out of here.

Except for one thing . . .

"So I'm supposed to catch her pulling bills out of boxes and stuffing them into her purse, huh? Do they have any leads on a partner?" Nick considered another cigarette and then discarded the idea. It was hot enough without it. He hadn't known any place that could be as hot as St. Louis in the summer or as cold as St. Louis in the winter, which was why when he pulled undercover he did it in offices. He'd lost his knack for the streets.

"McGrady didn't say. Maybe he wants you to find out."

Nick snorted, his eyes back to that house, to the memory of cool, cluttered rooms and the smell of oranges. Damn. He didn't like setting up somebody he liked.

"And I'm smack dab in the middle of St. Anthony here," he groused. "Aren't I?"

"Your captain would rather not inform the local gendarmes," Marco informed him. "He assured me that you'll be in and out before they ever know you were here."

Nick snorted again.

The County of St. Louis, for which Nick worked, had jurisdiction within its sprawling borders, even though it was made up of a crazy quilt of local municipalities that guarded their own autonomy with zeal. Technically speaking, Nick didn't have to let the authorities of the newest of these municipalities know that he was operating in their bailiwick. In real life, that didn't always make for the best bedmates.

He knew most cops in the county. But never having worked in the southwest side of St. Louis, a good fifteen miles from his offices in Clayton, he didn't know a soul. A solidly suburban, middle-class haven of lawn services and private schools, this just wasn't his neck of the woods. Until Nick had been forced to shave his mustache and grow his hair just a little too long, his beat had been the high rises of Clayton and West County where white-collar crime was at its best.

This little caper had started with a few bounced checks. Then utility bills had gone unpaid, and an affidavit of forgery was delivered to the Special Investigations offices in Clayton. A team was working the county, but they were concentrating mostly in the five square miles of interconnecting neighborhoods Nick was patrolling in his van. One person simply pulled bills from mailboxes where lazy citizens left them for mailmen, and then got signatures and bank information from the checks. Then, using stolen checks acquired from the partner, they wrote third-party checks to the mailbox victim, endorsing them with the victim's own bank account number and forged signature. Cashed at that same bank, the checks were always cleared as long as the victim had enough money in his account to cover them. It was when the bank called the victim about bounced checks that the pattern began to appear and the affidavits roll in.

And now Marco was telling Nick that the most likely suspect for the person filching those payments and then pulling her chugging, sputtering automobile into a drive-up window to cash bogus checks was the woman he'd shared disturbing glances with over a handful of bombpops. The one he'd run to help like an overage high schooler, and who had made him want to smile with her disconcerted blush at his appearance.

So not only was Nick stuck on a creaky life raft amid a sea of kids with not even the questionable talents of the local cops to fend off sharks, he was doing it just so he could snap the cuffs on Jenny Lake. Giving in with another snort of frustration, Nick pulled the cigarettes back out. He'd definitely had better days.

Jenny couldn't really say that her first encounter with the police left her encouraged. She was seated alongside Lauren Sellers on Barb's plastic-covered early colonial couch balancing a glass of fresh brewed herb sun tea and watching as the representative of St. Anthony's finest scribbled in his notebook. Alongside Barb sat Lucy Sperring, Mrs. Warner's sister and representative at the little meeting. The four waited as the detective made up his mind.

He didn't look impressed. Come to think of it, he didn't look impressive, either. A tall man, he had the shape of one of those toys that kept rolling back up when you hit it. He wore a polyester suit that looked like it had been cut from the same bolt of cloth as Jenny's work uniform, and his mousy brown hair probably could have stood a wash. He had a too-red nose and the bored, patronizing eyes of a petty bureaucrat. Even Barb looked a bit disconcerted by him. Lauren, as usual, kept her thoughts to herself.

"So you think he's dealing drugs because he has a beeper and talks to black people," the man said with the same tone of voice Jenny's mother had used to use in talking about Jenny's imaginary playmates.

"Don't forget the ponytail," Miss Lucy chirped, bobbing her small gray head. "He has a ponytail."

Only Miss Lucy failed to see the disdain in the man's small eyes. "Oh, yeah," he nodded, scribbling. "I forgot about that ponytail."

It was up to Jenny to defend her call. "I would just feel happier if you would check it out," she said with a tight smile. "I realize that all we have are a series of inconsistencies, but there are a lot of teenagers around that truck every day, and I'd hate to think that we're letting anything slip by."

He nodded, shut the book with the information the women had imparted safely tucked inside and lurched to his feet. Jenny fully expected him to sway like the plastic clown she'd once vented her frustrations on. His expression certainly matched.

"Well, ladies," he said with bluff heartiness. "You just leave this all to me. I'll check this Nick Barnett out and get back to you. I appreciate your coming to me with the report."

"Anything we should do in the meantime?" Barb asked, getting to her feet, as well.

"No, young lady." He was, at best, five years their senior. "You just leave everything to me."

"Seems to me," Jenny mused as she watched the policeman walk toward his battered sedan, "that that was what my obstetrician told me when I delivered Kevin. I told him I'd be happy to, but that *I* was the one having the labor pains."

Barb giggled and turned to clean out the newly filled ashtray on her oak coffee table. "Did your obstetrician dress as dreadfully as Detective Richards?"

Jenny thought about it. "His tailor probably just cost more. He had that same wonderful color sense."

Barb nodded with an impish grin. "In that case, I hope you found another obstetrician."

Jenny raised an eyebrow in amused surprise. "Sure. But how easy can it be to get another policeman?"

"We don't need another policeman," Barb decided, straightening to her full five feet and including all the women present in her statement. "We have us. We'll keep an eye on Nick Barnett. You and I and the other mothers on the block."

Jenny couldn't help but think of the sight of him balanced on the edge of her kitchen table. She couldn't keep her mind from that tantalizing rip in his jeans.

"An excellent idea," Lucy offered from her perch on the chair. "We'll see more in this neighborhood than the police ever will." The wry smile that lit her gray, birdlike features betrayed the fact that it was her sister who would do most of the watching. Miss Lucy, as she was known, was the popular one in that household, always there if help was needed, always invited to coffee and chat. It was Ethel Warner, though, who always knew more than seemed possible when just seen from her six-by-four-foot front window.

It seemed to be the signal for general support. Taking a long sip of tea from behind a meticulously manicured hand, Lauren gave her nod of approval. "I'll have Todd check with his little friends," she offered. "Warn them about this man and get information at the same time. And, of course, you can keep an eye on him, Jenny."

It took a moment for Jenny to respond. She'd often wondered how Lauren had ended up in their neighborhood. Devotedly upscale in style and appetite, Lauren spent the better part of her days doing fashionable charity work and hobnobbing in the more acceptable areas of town. She wore her heavy gold jewelry like badges, and her designer outfits like Emma her imaginary gowns. Her son Todd, just turned sixteen, was reputed to be the biggest threat to teenage virtue since rock and roll.

As to her reference to Nick, she really hadn't meant to be mean-spirited. She just saw Jenny as *divorced*, which was somehow alien and a little unsettling. Lauren obviously believed the old, she must be hungry, so she's after my husband, adage. Jenny hadn't seen fit to tell Lauren that her husband was a carbon of the Jerk, and therefore the second safest man in the country.

Jenny saw the other two women go still at the implied insult. She smiled. "Okay," she agreed with a slow nod, her mind still recalling the sudden flash of white teeth and wide-open humor Lauren would never get to see. "I guess I could keep my eyes on him."

Conflicting emotions skittered over Barb's bright features like fast-moving clouds. Jenny came back from her personal viewing just in time to catch the concern.

"Just my eyes," she assured her friend with a rueful grin. "My emotional bank account is too paltry to afford somebody like him, thanks."

"He sells drugs," Barb reminded her.

Jenny lifted a finger. "We think. Innocent until proven guilty, remember?"

Now Barb shook her head. "Only when it comes to the law. Not when it comes to my child."

For that Jenny couldn't even think of a good comeback. She'd spent too much of herself protecting her children from no more than their father's indifference to argue with that.

Just to make Jenny feel worse for fantasizing about someone who could put the Jerk in the minor leagues of sin, Emma chose that moment to grow bored with the coloring books Jenny had supplied to keep her occupied during the meeting.

"Mommy?"

Jenny automatically crouched to Emma's height, filling her sight with the sweet beauty of her little girl. "Yes, baby." She was amazed, as she was every time she looked at her children that they had been created from her gene pool. They were too beautiful. Too intelligent by halves.

Emma came to a halt right before her. "Mom," she objected with a frown. "I'm not a baby." At three and a half, it was an important point to the little girl.

Jenny could hardly argue with her. In her soft pink-and-white sundress and sandals, Emma was neater and better put together than Jenny. Emma had been dressing herself since she was just three, and coordinating her own outfits for the last two months.

Still, Jenny smiled. "But you're *my* baby," she said, reaching up to sweep a blond bang back from the little forehead.

Huge blue eyes still reproached her. With a sigh though, Emma accepted her mother's illogic. "I'm going to the Pink House, okay?"

Jenny nodded. "Okay. Have fun, and remember to clean up before you come home."

Jenny got another scowl. "Mo-o-m. Wanna come?"

"I'm afraid not right now, honey. I'm busy with Aunt Barb."

Emma nodded and headed off. The little girl had disappeared once again into the back room before Miss Lucy spoke up.

"The pink house?"

Still smiling, Jenny got to her feet. "The Pink House," she nodded with a rueful shrug. "Most little girls Emma's age have imaginary playmates. My daughter has an imaginary condo. With a hundred rooms where she has parties."

None of the three could quite decide how to react. Barb only came up with a quiet, "Oh."

Jenny laughed. "Yeah. Oh. Who says God has no sense of humor? He gave me Princess Di's kid by mistake."

Twenty minutes later, when Jenny had finished helping Barb clean up the evidence of Detective Richards's visit and been filled in on the rest of the neighborhood news, she headed in to break up the intergalactic war in Barb's playroom.

"Just a minute, Mom," Kevin objected without looking from the television screen. "I'm on the third warp zone and only have three mushroom men left."

Jenny couldn't help but scowl at the bright figures that beeped and twiddled across the screen as Kevin rolled the joystick. "Far be it from me to keep you from saving the world. We have to get home, though."

Kevin didn't even hear her. With a face that was a heartbreaking carbon of his father's and a knack for turning anything in the house into a strategic weapon, Kevin was all boy. Freckles and pug nose and chestnut hair that had been buzzed for the summer. And his best friend was still Buffy, who had yet to figure out why girls and boys couldn't be friends. She whooped when Kevin exploded something on the screen and pounded him on the back. Kevin grinned like a pirate.

Jenny decided to leave him to his mushroom men, at least this once. Especially since it would be a cold day in August around here before she could afford a similar treat for their own house. Looking around for her other bookend, she saw crayons and a Barbie coloring book open but no Emma.

"Kevin," she said, looking around yet again, as if she could have missed her behind the potted fig or something. "Where's your sister?"

He couldn't afford more than a shrug. Bemused, Jenny turned away. She wondered where Emma had holed up.

"Hello."

Engrossed in the copy of *U.S. News* he hid beneath a *Mad* magazine cover, Nick heard the piping little voice and looked up. Then he looked down.

She stood alone alongside the driver's side of the truck, clad in a pink dress, black velvet purse and a blanket. The blanket had been pinned around her neck and trailed behind the high heels that hung off the ends of little feet. The purse swung from a bent arm. She peered up at him with huge blue eyes that looked for all the world like she was expecting obeisance. Nick stifled his first impulse to laugh.

"Can I help you?" he asked, unconsciously formal as he leaned over toward her.

With a regal poise, she nodded her head. She even lifted a hand in a very royal little wave. "I," she said in arch tones, her words carefully enunciated, "am the Queen of the World."

Nick tried his best to hide a grin. Damn if this little kid couldn't almost convince him. "Pleased to meet you, Queen," he said, laying down the magazine and leaning an arm on the window. "I bet that's an interesting job."

Another nod, just as slow, just as regal. "Yes. This cape is heavy, though."

Nick found himself rubbing a hand over his face to keep from betraying his growing amusement. "Yeah, I can see that.

You might try a towel instead. Be Queen of North America or something."

She actually looked like she was considering it. "Queens like ice cream, you know."

Nick nodded, unable anymore to contain the smile. "They do, huh?"

"Yes." She spent a moment scanning the side of the truck. If he hadn't known better, Nick could almost have believed she could read the damn thing. She wasn't like any other kid he'd met in this purgatory. Come to think of it, she wasn't like any other person he'd met.

"Uh, what's your favorite flavor?"

More consideration. "Blue."

Opening the door and stepping down, Nick tried to think what flavor that would be. "Blue."

"Yes. Popsicles. I'd like a blue one, please."

Now, that made more sense. There was just one other thing. "Do you have any money, Queen?"

Suddenly a little girl's giggle broke through all the solemnity. "Of course, silly. I have thirty dollars."

Nick was still too new to three-year-old math to understand. "Thirty what?" he demanded, leaning over again. He could see her tiny hand clenched before her like one of the magi carrying a gift. "Where did you get thirty dollars?"

The little girl looked at him as if he were very slow. "The Pink House, of course."

Nick felt more confused than ever. McGrady didn't say that this job should come with an interpreter.

"The Pink House."

"Where I have parties. And a hundred jewelry boxes."

Nick was rubbing his face again. "Where's your mother, Queen?"

"Busy."

"Oh. Uh, can I see your thirty dollars?"

He should have known. When the little girl reached up and opened her fingers, Nick saw the three pennies nestled inside and sighed.

"Uh, kid, you wouldn't—" One look at the earnest little face showed that this, indeed, was the extent of her outlay. Nick vacillated. He could just see what the crew back at the station would have to say about this. He couldn't help it. Giving in, he gravely accepted the three pennies and walked back to swing open the doors for a blue Popsicle.

"What's your name, Queen?" he asked as he handed it over.

That seemed to break through the little girl's reserve. For the first time she looked unsure. "I'm not supposed to talk to strangers."

"But I—" Never mind. He shook his head, completely left behind. He couldn't really argue with her on that one. Just because he was the ice cream man didn't mean he was a good guy. It didn't even mean he liked kids, he thought with a private grin.

He was leaning against the back of the truck watching the little girl peel the wrapper from her treat when he heard the footsteps. He wasn't that surprised when he looked up to see that it was her mother.

Today she wore khaki shorts and a pink T-shirt. Nick could develop a real fondness for pink T-shirts. Especially if they looked like that. She was running, her brows drawn with worry, her hair tumbled again so that it looked like she was always dragging her hands through it. Nick guessed she was about five-four, with pale, freckled skin that dewed up like a peach in the heat. His tongue itched for the taste of it.

"Hey, Queen," Nick whispered in warning. "I think you're about to do time in the Tower."

"What are you doing here, young lady?" Jenny demanded, coming to a stop in front of her daughter.

Emma looked singularly unruffled. "The man gave me my sicle."

"You're not supposed to get sicles from 'the man' by yourself, Emma," she chastised. "Now, you get on home. We have some serious talking to do."

Still maintaining that regal bearing, Emma turned up to find Nick watching her with a delighted grin. "Excuse me," she said.

"Yes, Your Highness."

She giggled again, delivering a killer smile beneath a coyly tilted head. Nick wondered where the hell she'd learned that.

"Thank you, man."

"You're welcome, Queen."

"Mom," she piped up, turning up to Jenny. "Is it okay if I tell him my name's Emma?"

Jenny dispatched a look that betrayed as much amusement as exasperation. "Yes, Emma. I guess you can."

With that, Emma turned for the royal proclamation. "My name," she announced, "is Emma."

"My name's Nick," Nick said just as formally. "It's been a pleasure."

Without further ado, Emma tottered off down the street on her heels, Popsicle clutched in her hand, blanket trailing in the dust, purse swinging with her unsteady gait. Left behind, Jenny could do no more than shake her head.

"I'm sorry," she apologized, motioning to the sandwich Nick had been working on when Emma had interrupted.

"No problem," he assured her with a wave of his hand. "I've never served royalty before."

Jenny chuckled, a pleasant throaty sound. "Don't encourage her. Next thing I know she's going to be assessing taxes. Did she have money?"

With a nod that was just as sincere as Emma's, Nick plucked up Emma's booty. "Thirty dollars."

Jenny started. Then she saw the copper in Nick's palm and grinned. "Put it on my tab. I'm sure once Kevin finds out Emma got a Popsicle and he didn't, we'll be back."

"Don't worry about it," Nick said with a wave of the hand. "I think Marco can stand it."

She should really do something about that poker face, Nick thought. The mention of Marco sent clouds scurrying over the bright, pert features. It made Nick wonder what was wrong.

He could smell oranges again. Tart, fresh, mouth-watering. Just like Jenny Lake. Jenny Lake, his prime suspect.

Nick guessed that a cloud or two passed over his own features.

"How's that car of yours?" he asked, needing some kind of way in, unhappy with himself for using it. "Did you get the fuel injectors fixed?"

Again the cloud, the hint of unease beneath those bright, open green eyes. "Oh, uh . . . I'm waiting for a check to come in pretty soon. That'll cover the car, thanks."

"Alimony's comin' through, huh?"

At that, she did a credible imitation of his snort of disbelief. "When pigs fly," she retorted. "No, this is . . . something else. Thanks again, though."

And before he could get off another shot, she was headed back down the street.

Nick watched from where he stood at the back of the truck, cataloguing the various reasons he shouldn't be appreciating her retreating view so much. She was a suspect. She was a divorcée with kids. She had black hair. His thing had always been blondes.

She had the greatest little tush since Marcia Sternberger in junior high.

And then, just as he was going to pull back where he belonged, Nick saw her run up to the little queen and sweep her up in her arms. Even from where he stood, almost a block away he could hear the unbridled delight in her husky laughter counterpoint the shrill giggles of the little girl. The two continued down the street wrapped around each other and telling each other secrets, and suddenly Nick was assailed by a sense of loss he couldn't explain. He just knew that he didn't want to bust Jenny Lake. He wanted to make her laugh like that, too.

He wanted what he couldn't have, which was the story of his life. With a sigh that sounded much too final, Nick pushed himself from the back of his truck and went back to business.

Chapter 3

"Do you know how tired I am of hearing this song and dance?"

At that, it was all Jenny could do to keep her temper. "Do you know how tired I am of singing it?" This was the worst part of a divorce, the constant begging. Please, honey, just a few dollars for shoes, for dentists, for school. Please help me out.

"I told you before. My cash flow is a problem right now. I'll have a check to you the beginning of September."

Sell some of Amber Jean's jewelry, Jenny thought with justifiable spite. "I have school expenses in August, and the car's about to go out. It needs fuel injectors. And Kevin wants to play soccer like his daddy. Only it'll cost us $38 to join."

"In September."

She'd been hearing next month for the last six. "Sign-up is in two weeks. Please help me out on this."

The acid roiled in her stomach; the shame of it reddened her face. There was nothing Jenny hated more than these much-too-regular phone calls. Nothing except denying her children.

"All right. I'll try. Now, stay off my back."

"Mom, ask him about the video game."

Startled, Jenny turned to find Kevin at her elbow. "Not now, Kev. Want to talk to your dad?"

"Jenny, I really am in a hurry here. I have an appointment."

Jenny felt renewed resentment for her son. God, she was tired of seeing his eyes light up only to die again.

"Say hi and then goodbye," she told Kevin with a grin. "Dad's gotta run."

Kevin barely got that out before handing the phone back to her. "Did you ask?"

"No," she told him, hanging it up and pulling her tough, independent son into her arms. "I didn't. I didn't have time for anything but the necessities. We'll have to wait a while longer, hon."

"But you promised."

Jenny sighed. "I promised I'd try, Kev. Now, if memory serves me, you were in the middle of cleaning your room before dinner."

"Aw, Mom . . ."

It was as easy as that . . . sometimes. Jenny laughed and rumpled his hair. "No more excuses, bud. You're growing enough mold in there to supply a hospital. Go on."

The huge kiss Jenny planted on Kevin's cheek only intensified his heartfelt scowl. He was well on the way to whining when he was interrupted by the clang-clang, clang-clang call of the migrating refrigerated truck. Immediately his head came up and his eyes grew wide. Pleading, begging, throwing himself on his mother's mercy.

"Please, Mom," he groaned as if she'd just grabbed his last canteen of water on the Mojave.

"Kevin, you've had ice cream every day this week."

He gathered every ounce of pathos he could muster. "Ple-e-e-a-s-e."

With a sigh of capitulation, Jenny let him go and pulled herself to her feet. "Don't give me Bambi eyes. I can't take it. Get some ice cream. Get a Ferrari, I don't care. Just don't give me Bambi eyes."

The supplication on his face dissolved into giggles as he hopped to his feet. "Works every time."

"Don't be so sure. There's more to life than ice cream."

Like money, she thought, checking her cookie jar for loose change, and I don't have any. There was enough for a couple of "sicles," and that was it. She wasn't getting paid until Monday, and she had to still get through the weekend. Macaroni and cheese time, again, she thought with a sigh.

Oh well, today there was ice cream.

Clang-clang, clang-clang.

"Mo-o-o-o-o-m!"

"Yes, Emma," Jenny answered with a grin as she followed the herd to the door, not even wanting to admit to herself that it was her treat, too. "I know. Let's go get ice cream."

By the time Nick pulled to a stop there was already a swarm of girls waiting by the curb. He gave a couple extra tugs on the bell and shut off the engine, sighing at the crescendo of giggles that met his arrival.

He wasn't going to last much longer on this detail. It was getting more difficult every day to put up with the cloying, giggling attention of so many self-conscious teens. That was almost worse than the little kids. At least they just whined. The girls flirted. And they flirted with an enthusiasm and expertise Nick had sure never noticed during his own high-school days.

It was easy with the little kids. When they got too obnoxious, you treated them like cats. You pulled them off your pant leg and shooed them in the right direction. If he tried that with this bunch, he could end up behind his own bars.

He wanted to tell them to all go home and wash their faces and trade in the miniskirts for baggy jeans. He wanted to tell them that growing up wasn't as much fun as they thought, that they should enjoy the safe years they had while they were still tucked securely away in their comfortable, reliable houses.

But he didn't. He got out of the truck and tried his best to smile and tease and play his part.

"Yo, Mr. Ice Cream Man."

Nick looked up to see a male head in that female crowd. Oh, yeah. Todd. The neighborhood lothario, out, he guessed, to treat his herd of fillies. Tall, too good-looking for his own good and very, very into latest fashion with a spike cut and a tiny gold stud in his left ear. Nick refrained from grinning. Surely he hadn't been so patently obvious when he'd been that age. Surely he'd never even been that age.

"Yo, Todd. What'll it be?"

Nick swung the door open and basked in the escaping chill. God, he was hot and tired.

"Hey, dude, whatever these ladies would like. I'm buying."

Nick wondered how long it would be before Todd tried that line out at the local bars. All the same, he acquiesced with a nod. At least if Todd were keeping them busy they wouldn't brush up so close to him or give him the honey-I'd-like-to eye flutters.

Nick was in the middle of counting change for Todd's conspicuously presented twenty when he happened to look up and see Jenny. She was standing in the street across from her house, almost hidden from his sight by the overgrown bushes and trees between. Nick handed off the change, his eyes still down the street, and didn't notice Todd's attention follow.

A mailbox. She was standing by a mailbox which wasn't hers. Nick couldn't see what she was doing. She was in between him and the box. But she was looking around her as if she didn't want anyone to see what she was about. And her two kids were coming his way at full tilt.

Damn. He didn't want to see this. He'd spent the entire night before trying to sleep through some pretty vivid dreams about her, dreams that weren't made any more comfortable by the cold shower he'd finally gotten up to take.

"Oh, yeah," Todd breathed with assured delight. "Jenny Lake."

Startled, Nick looked over, managing a dry appraisal just in time to miss Todd's keen eye. "Know her well, do you?"

Todd flashed a big grin. "Hey, like, not well enough, ya know? I, like, have this thing about older women."

"To-o-o-dd," one of the girls objected.

"Oh, man, Lacey," he objected with raised hands. "I'm kiddin', okay?"

He waited for no more than another man-to-man leer with Nick before herding his fan club away.

Nick's attention was already back down the street. So, he had Jenny at the mailbox looking nervous, and he had a possible informer, depending on how much he wanted to trust Todd around her. He should have felt better.

The problem was, he didn't feel better. He felt like he was slipping down that damn slippery slope, his perspective lost to a set of bright, teeming, wounded green eyes. And if he had any sense, he was going to go back in and ask McGrady to take him off the case.

Watching that little blonde run for him and knowing that her mother wasn't far behind, though, Nick knew he wouldn't do that.

"Well, if it isn't Queen Emma," Nick greeted her.

Emma pulled up before him with a smile that was suddenly shy. "Hi, Mr. Nick," she greeted him, head down, hair falling into her eyes.

"So how's the world today, Queen?"

"I'm not queen anymore," she said. "I'm a taxi driver."

It was all Nick could do to keep from laughing all over again. Now that Todd and the cheerleaders had dispersed, he was back to regular business, and he had to admit he was relieved. He was uncomfortable with all that, and he didn't want to have to deal with it in front of Jenny. Hell, he was having trouble dealing with *Jenny* in front of Jenny.

"A taxi driver," he said, nodding sagely, his eye on Jenny as she turned toward the truck and followed her children around the corner. "I bet that's exciting." Where would you hide an envelope in shorts that short? he wondered. Maybe inside that crisp cotton camp shirt, nestled safely in her bra.

"I charge a thousand dollars a ride," Emma informed him, bringing him back with a start. "Except for Mom and Grandma. They're free. It's so I can pay for my Pink House. Would you like to see it?"

It took Nick a moment to connect Emma's statements. "Sure. Where is it?"

"Emma," Kevin broke in, exasperated by the wait for his ice cream.

Nick immediately looked up. "Hey, Kevin, how's things?"

"Great," Kevin assured him. "Can I have my Drumstick? *Ninja Turtles* is on, and I have to watch before Mom finds out."

Nick nodded, turning to the truck. "Good cartoon. I know. I'm a connoisseur. Ever watch The Roadrunner?"

"Aw, sure." Kevin accepted his Drumstick with a look that betrayed the fact that six-year-olds didn't believe adults really watched cartoons. "My favorite's Johnny Death, though."

Nick just shook his head. "No finesse. Now, you want class, you turn on some of the older cartoons. Sylvester and Twee-tie, Bugs Bunny and the good old Roadrunner. My favorite was still the time the Roadrunner dropped the safe on Wile E. Coyote's head." With a conspiratorial grin, Nick slowly shook his head in appreciation. "Pancake city."

He saw Kevin waver and then fall, his eyes lighting like a pi-rate, and knew he had an ally.

"Nick?" Emma piped up, impatient with sharing her new friend.

"Yeah, Emma. Let's see. I bet you want a bombpop, right?"

"Yes, please. Are you coming to dinner to see my Pink House?"

Nick handed over her ice cream with a frown. "I don't know. Am I?"

"Tonight," she nodded with a perfectly sincere face. "My mom said so."

Nick took another look up to where Jenny ambled nearer, still out of earshot, and found himself smiling almost as broadly as Kevin. "She did, huh? Well, I guess I'll just have to come then. You tell her I'll bring the wine."

It was worse than macaroni and cheese. It was tuna-noodle casserole. Jenny hated it, the kids hated it and the cat hated it. But it was all she had left in the house, and they were just go-ing to have to choke some down. At least she'd found a can of mandarin oranges for dessert, which would go a long way to appeasing the kids' palates.

It didn't appease her sense of outrage or her frustration. By this time of her life she should have been able to attain some kind of stability: a home, a husband, a growing family. Jenny had always wanted to fill her rooms with children and nurture that special, loving madness that comes only with big families. She had it with hers, all seven siblings. She'd grown from child to teen to woman anticipating the same thing—a big, close family that could fend off any of the world's disasters.

Jenny hadn't wanted a huge house or a membership to the country club. She'd wanted family. She'd wanted simplicity, certainty in her life. What she'd gotten was a bad sitcom.

Her husband, that bright child of charm and drive, had grown into a superficial man of drive and drive. He'd left Jenny in the dust when he'd decided that the giggly secretary at work with the assets that bounced would fit his upwardly mobile lifestyle better than a Phi Beta Kappa who thought that there was more to life than being an arm ornament at social functions. So the Jerk and Amber Jean lived in the upper reaches of Ladue, with a pool, a membership to the country club and a lot of superficial friends. And Jenny was left to struggle alone on a too-small paycheck, child support that never seemed to be available and even less attention from her children's father.

And tuna-noodle casserole for dinner.

"I bet *Amber Jean*'s not having tuna-noodle casserole for dinner." She sighed, pushing damp hair from her forehead as she slammed the oven door. Even potato chips crushed on the top hadn't incited any wild interest in the dish from the kids. She couldn't blame them. Godiva chocolates crushed on the top wouldn't have made her want to eat the damn thing.

"What is she having?" Emma asked, as always too handy with an ear when Jenny didn't want her to be.

Jenny turned to see Emma decked out in her best dress, a little green-and-white pinafore her grandma had gotten for her. "Honey, why are you so dressed up?"

Emma blinked up at Jenny as if her mother needed to think more. "For dinner."

Instinctively, Jenny crouched to her daughter's level. "Emma," she objected as evenly as she could, "you don't usually come out of your room for tuna-noodle casserole, much less dress up."

"Of course I do," Emma smiled grandly. "When Nick comes to dinner."

"Nick?" It took Jenny a moment. She had to get through imaginary playmates before she attached the new name. "Oh, Nick. He's coming to dinner tonight?"

Emma nodded. "I invited him."

"I see. Do I have to set an extra plate?"

Now Jenny could tell that her daughter thought her extremely silly. "Of course."

Jenny just nodded. Taking a quick look down at the paint-spattered shirt and cutoffs she sported, she thought that this was just the night she'd like to entertain a handsome man with a tattoo. Maybe he'd come in his good white T-shirt and they could compare ponytails. Or maybe she'd ask him to pop the hood of her compact.

Suddenly Jenny found herself wishing for more than another night alone with bedtime stories and overdue bills. But Jenny knew what good that kind of wishing did. Abruptly she regained her feet and turned back to her dinner. "Well, go ahead," she said lightly. "Just make sure he washes his hands before he eats."

"My face, too?"

Jenny almost burned her hand on the oven when she whipped around.

He didn't have on his best white T-shirt. He had on an oversized linen jacket and pleated pants and a mock turtleneck. And he'd taken out the ponytail. Suddenly Jenny couldn't think of anything to say. Nick was leaning in her kitchen doorway, one hand resting high against the door frame, the other holding a wine bottle. And he was smiling that cocky, crooked grin again that told her just how much he liked to catch her off guard.

"Oh, my God..."

Pulling himself up straight, he extended the wine bottle. "Emma said that you'd invited me. She wanted me to see her pink house." He took a moment to scan the cluttered kitchen before returning his regard to Jenny. "It doesn't look pink to me. But then, I'm not a kid. Does that make a difference?"

For a moment all Jenny could do was stand and stare. This might just come under the heading of worst nightmare in her life. She had the feeling it was even going to beat out the time she got the hem of her dress caught in her panty hose at a formal party and walked around with her underwear showing for ten minutes.

No, this was definitely worse. She'd realized how good-looking Nick was. It was, after all, hard to miss in those tight jeans and negligible shirts. The first time she'd seen him walk, she'd realized he was sexy. What she hadn't realized until now was how classy he was. Tonight he looked like a completely different person, a powerbroker or an actor on hiatus. Definitely dangerous. And he carried the style of the outfit with an easy grace that threatened to take Jenny's breath away.

Damn. And she looked like she'd just been rat-hunting in the attic.

Jenny made an abortive reach for the bottle and then changed her mind, wondering if she had to invite him to stay if she accepted the wine. She ended up with her hands in her cut-off pockets. "I guess you haven't figured out yet that Emma has a rather formidable imagination," she said, trying in vain to pull her eyes from the way that just-too-long chestnut hair framed the angles of his face. God, it made her hungry.

He just shrugged. "Beats reality all to hell." Then he set the bottle on the kitchen table and turned back to Jenny with a grin. "Hey, Kevin!" he yelled. "Come in here a minute!"

Nick did something Jenny hadn't accomplished since Kevin had turned three. He got him unpeeled from the TV with one shout. Jenny found herself staring again.

"I think your mom doesn't trust me," he told the little boy with a smile that betrayed just what kind of silly women mothers could be. "So I figured I'd let you frisk me for weapons. Make her feel a little better, ya know?"

"Why doesn't *she* frisk you?" Kevin asked.

Nick's answer had to wait for the lightning that sparked between his eyes and Jenny's. His was deliberate, taunting, testing. Hers was an uncomfortable surprise, sizzling all the way to her toes.

Nick ended up holding his hands out to his sides in a classic position. "I think she thinks I'd feel better if a guy did it."

Kevin shrugged, but performed the service anyway with a professional air that told Jenny he'd been watching too many police shows.

"He's clean," he pronounced finally. Jenny groaned.

"See?" Nick countered, hands still up, that cocky grin back on his face. "No knives, no guns. No loaded weapons of any kind."

Jenny almost laughed. She knew better than that. She'd seen the fit of those jeans. Just the thought sent her whirling back to the sink, a blush suffusing her face. She didn't need this. Not now. Not ever. Not when this guy was supposed to be the new neighborhood drug dealer. Not even if he weren't, she knew.

The Jerk had taken his mid-life crisis right over to old Amber Jean. Jenny wasn't going to make the same mistake and drop hers in the lap of Mr. Softy.

"I'm not going to bite," he said softly from just behind her.

Jenny whirled again, this time backed right up against the sink. Nick stood no more than two feet away, and his aftershave preceded him. It was that tang, the one that smelled too much like lightning, that tickled her nose and crept in beneath her good sense.

And his eyes. Those eyes the color of brandy, laced with sunshine and nightfall. Those eyes that seemed to melt right through her.

At least Kevin had escaped back to the tube. Jenny was having enough trouble without having to worry about his much too inquisitive little ears.

"Do you really think this is a good idea?" she demanded, trying her best to assume the pose of an outraged mother.

"What's wrong with it?" Nick asked. "Emma invited me to dinner. I accepted. I promise never to come between you and the telephone so you can dial for help if necessary. If you'd like, I'll even call Mrs. Warner across the street to let her know I'm here. That way we'll have a witness to everything."

"Why?" Jenny asked.

He shrugged, that self-assured gleam back in his eyes. "So you stop looking like I'm going to murder you all in your beds and run off with the silver."

Jenny shook her head. "Not that why. Why go to all this trouble?"

This time when Nick smiled, Jenny saw the assurance slip a little. There was just enough surprise beneath to convince her he was telling the truth.

"Because I haven't liked anything about this job except for you. I've been watching for you every day, you know."

"No," she admitted, wondering if she should tell him the same. "I didn't."

He nodded. "You think I eat my lunch up at the corner because I like warm soda and hot vinyl seats? You usually get home from the store right about one, and I like to watch you walk into the house."

Jenny wasn't sure just how she was supposed to react to this. "I don't think I want to hear that."

Nick shrugged. "It's true."

"It's ... *weird*."

That made him laugh, and that did even more damage to Jenny's self-control. It was that raspy laugh, the one she thought was reserved for his good friends. Its sound settled in her chest and warmed her where she'd been cold for so long.

"No," he finally disagreed, his eyes holding hers with purpose as he lifted a hand to brush the tangle of hair back from her forehead. "It would be weird if I *didn't* stop to watch you."

Jenny saw his hand approach, felt the brush of his fingers, as sweetly coarse as the sound of his laughter, and couldn't seem to find her objections. She couldn't even seem to locate her suspicion that this man was doing something illicit. She just knew that he incited something in her she thought had been mortally wounded too long ago. That gull she'd watched so far over her head now dipped lower, almost close enough for her to touch, its cry the taste of freedom, of the open sky and the sun. As much as she wanted to be frightened by it, Jenny couldn't be.

"I wanted to be able to talk to you without feeling like I had a telescope at my back," Nick admitted. "I wanted to prove to you that I'm more than just what you see out there every day. And," he added with a sudden grin, "I wanted to see what a real home-cooked meal could taste like. I've been eating bachelor food for too long."

It was Jenny's turn to laugh. Looking up at him with eyes that sparkled with wry humor, she gave in. "Well, you sure came on the right night for that." Only her own little devil kept her from elucidating. Instead, she took him by the shoulders and turned him toward the playroom. "You go on out and watch TV with the kids while I change. After all, if Emma wore her best dress for you, I should be able to at least get out of this stuff. You can baby-sit while I shower."

That goading grin firmly back in place, Nick turned his head back toward her. "I'm a great back scrubber."

This time Jenny gave him a good nudge in the right direction. "I believe Emma's your date this evening. You can have a sparkling conversation with her over drinks while I change. Apple juice for her, beer in the fridge for you if you'd like. I'll be back."

By the time Jenny got back, she felt cleaner if not any less confused. She'd just invited a possible drug dealer to her house for dinner, and she hadn't even told the police about it. She didn't even want to. In fact, she'd gone to the trouble of pulling on the only pair of stockings she'd worn since church last Sunday just to look good for him. A dependable peach-jersey shirtwaist had been called into service, and she'd even gone to the extent of adding a little makeup for good measure.

Nobody would believe it. Jenny hadn't so much as dated since her divorce two years ago. Her family, especially her two sisters, had gone to great and tortuous lengths to rectify the situation, but Jenny had been adamant. She'd also been pretty bitter, but that had to be normal. Especially after the Jerk came to her in Emma's hospital room, while the child was battling with a surprise bout of pneumonia, to tell her that he'd been sleeping with his secretary and suddenly found himself more enamored of *her* back rubs than Jenny's demands for participation.

Since that day Jenny had learned all there was to learn about putting on a brave front and putting off prying questions. She'd also discovered a lot too much about court systems, especially ones presided over by judges who'd just had their own wives take them to the cleaners. And she knew about the tight little fraternity of lawyers that played racquetball together and dealt deals that only excluded ex-wives with children to try and raise.

Jenny had precious little trust left for anyone but those sharing her own gene pool. To put some of that rare commodity into a man who was being investigated by the local police didn't seem terribly sound, even to Jenny. But she had a gut feeling that they were all wrong about Nick. She just couldn't get past the fact that he had a smile that seemed to surprise emotions in him that he didn't even recognize. Honest emotions. And that had been something, she'd realized two children too late, that the Jerk had never had.

Or, she thought with a wry smile as she reached the bottom steps and headed into the playroom, it could be a matter of hormones. Maybe hers were finally just rising from the dead.

They were certainly setting up quite a clamor in her every time Nick looked her way with that lazy, assessing look of his. She felt tingles in places she'd forgotten she had. She found herself overcome with the desire to comb her hair and straighten her clothes, just like all the little girls who lined the streets waiting for the ice cream man to appear. Now that he was here in the house, she felt the first stirrings of anticipation, a feeling that seemed for all the world like the first breezes of a hurricane.

It felt so good. It felt *too* good, after all this time.

But if it were only that, she wouldn't let Nick into her home. Jenny had fought too long and too hard for her children to let anything or anyone jeopardize them—even a man she felt attracted to.

Especially a man she felt attracted to. She'd already seen what a disappearing father could do to a child. She wasn't about to watch it happen again.

Which was why, she supposed, she was so surprised to find Emma chatting so comfortably with Nick. Nick, of course, looked a little more than bewildered, but that was normal when faced with an alien being like Emma. One had to get used to her gradually, kind of like non-euclidian geometry.

What surprised Jenny was that Emma had her hand in Nick's. Emma didn't take to people. She saw it as her karma to rule them. Familiarity only bred contempt. Emma even held her grandparents at a proper distance, bestowing kisses rather than slobbering and hugging like most three-year-olds. She'd been three before she'd even let Barb give her a hug. Emma just wasn't like that.

And here she was looking up at Nick as if he occupied the throne on the other side of hers. Jenny couldn't quite take it in.

Maybe her instincts, rusty as they undoubtedly were, were right. Maybe this guy wasn't the criminal she'd helped paint him out to be. Maybe he was just a student who was finishing school a little later than most and driving an ice cream van for a friend. Jenny found that in that moment she wanted more than anything else in the world to believe it.

Jenny made it a point to use the dining-room table, centerpiece and all, but in the end there was only so much she could do to make tuna-noodle casserole look palatable. She stood looking down on her table and found herself wishing once again for something intangible. Something . . . more than just subsisting for the rest of her life.

That was where Nick found her, still looking down at the sparsity of food on the table, running her finger absently over the sleek teak of the Danish table, her eyes just a little distant and sad, her hair tumbled around her head like smoke and the dress poured over her sweet figure like honey.

Nick was surprised by the pang of longing the sight set up in him. He saw the empty place in this room, in this home where this bright young woman held her family together by her fingernails. He saw the patches and the twelve-year-old car in the driveway, and heard her shove that all aside with a challenge. He also saw more security, more love here than in even the best, most prosperous places he'd inhabited on his way to adulthood, and missed it all over again for never having had it.

"I hope the wine's appropriate," he said, stepping in.

Jenny looked up, and Nick saw her quickly shunt her frustration aside. She straightened with a grin and tilted her head just a little. "I'm not sure. Just what wine goes with tuna-noodle casserole?"

Nick knew she couldn't miss his instinctive reaction. His heart hit bottom almost as fast as his stomach. He wasn't sure what he'd been anticipating, pot roast, maybe even meat loaf.

But not tuna-noodle casserole. Of all the gastronomic nightmares from hell, that was it.

With the greatest of efforts, he offered a smile. He guessed he shouldn't have been surprised when she laughed back.

"You asked for it, pal," she goaded with great delight. "Next time Emma invites you over, make sure you ask what's on the menu first."

"Oh, don't get me wrong," he instinctively apologized, stepping closer so that he could catch the elusive citrus in her perfume. "I mean, I really..." In the end, though, his voice faltered over so bald a lie.

"Hate tuna-noodle casserole," she finished for him, still grinning. "Don't feel like the Lone Ranger. So do we. Unfortunately, that's what's in Mother Hubbard's cupboard. Next time, get yourself invited over to Barb and Bill's next door. Now, she can cook. She personally knows thirty-seven different things to do with a duck."

Nick couldn't help laughing at the wicked glint in Jenny's eye. He couldn't imagine what she'd say about him behind his back. "I guess when it's a choice between food and company, I choose the company every time."

Jenny's grin just broadened. "Fool."

Nick challenged her eye-to-eye, his own smile infected by her sharp humor, his taste heightened by the sight of her wrapped in that peach dress. It softened her, highlighted the outrageous green of her eyes, the curious black of her hair. "I'd rather not know how to do *three* things with a duck, if it's all the same to you," he said more quietly. "Ducks aren't my style."

Jenny became very still, the smile still hovering deliciously. "She's also very good with chickens."

"Are you trying to tell me you can't cook?"

Jenny motioned to the table. "You're looking at my ability to stretch out a meal on a shoestring budget."

Nick felt a flash of discomfort from her words. He'd nudged just a little too far. Maybe because he understood their import better than she thought. Maybe because he'd seen the ache in her eyes as she'd looked down on the meager fare. He didn't want to hurt her any more than she already had been.

"Jenny, I didn't mean to imply anything."

Jenny looked up at Nick in surprise. He leaned against the dining-room doorway, beer still in hand, for all intents and purposes still exuding that same flirting sensuality that had taken discussions of poultry to such new and interesting heights. But she heard the caution in his voice. The sudden sincerity that gave her back her distance if she needed it, and afforded privacy and respect. All in one sentence. He left her breathless.

"Nick," she said, her eyes sharp and bright, wanting least of all that he should be uncomfortable in her house after he'd brought such surprising life back into it. "My situation is hardly secret. My mother sends care packages, my sister sends hand-me-downs. Barb sends leftovers. The old ladies across the street send the lawn service. I think that's just because they can't abide the sight of grass tall enough to lose small animals in, but there you are. I've been divorced for two years, and I've been paddling like hell to stay upstream the whole time. So trust me, there isn't anything you could say that could insult me." She had already turned away to introduce her corkscrew to Nick's wine when the afterthought hit her. "Unless, of course, you called me a lawyer. *That* would insult me."

From behind her she heard Nick take a drink of beer. "I take it you don't get along with lawyers?"

"Euphemistically speaking. Right now I'm on Shakespeare's side."

"Shakespeare."

"Uh-huh." She screwed the implement in, thinking how symbolic the act was and grinning. "'The first thing we do,'" she quoted with a flourish of the free cork, "'let's kill all the lawyers.' I always did like Shakespeare's sense of priorities."

Jenny looked over to see that Nick wasn't quite sure how to take her spiel.

"Well," he said with a half grin. "I guess that means a long-term relationship is out of the question."

She was still feeling reckless enough to be his straight man. Wine bottle in hand, she shrugged. "Why? You're an ice cream dealer."

"An ice cream dealer on his way through law school."

Jenny didn't know whether to laugh or cry. Didn't it just figure? The first man she'd let in her house with the exception of the refrigerator repairman and he turns out to be one of *them*. Well, after all, it was only par for the way her life was going. Next he'd tell her that he knew the Jerk, and oh, he respected him so much for his talents in corporate law. And then she'd have to hit him.

"You're right," she said instead, bending over to pour the wine into the two crystal glasses she'd pulled from her long-unused set. "I've used up my lifetime allotment of lawyers."

Nick didn't move. "Do I leave now?"

Jenny looked up and smiled, wishing she really felt like it. "And miss a dinner like this? You'd never forgive yourself. I'm just afraid that I can't invite you back again."

And that, she thought with a feeling in her too much like shattering glass, was that.

Chapter 4

"**Y**ou have to invite him back."

Jenny sat quite still in Barb's blue-flowered armchair and balanced a glass of tea on her lap. She would have definitely preferred to throw it, but this was, after all, Barb's house. It wouldn't go unnoticed as long as it would at her own. The meeting today, called on such quick notice, only included Barb and herself. And, of course, the ubiquitous Detective Richards.

"Don't be ridiculous," she snapped at the offending party. "I told you it would be . . . unwise. Besides, I really don't think he's who we think he is."

Detective Richards did a neat trick with his left eyebrow that packed all his disdain for housewives into it. "Oh?" he asked. "That's a pretty sudden turnaround for you, isn't it, Mrs. Lake? What changed your mind all of a sudden?"

"I've been talking to him, Detective."

"And I've been researching him. Just like you ladies asked. And I've found that Nick Barnett does not exist. Not at the License Bureau, not in any of the local schools, not even in the Marines."

"He had a tattoo," Jenny retorted, knowing how perilous her footing was even as she defended Nick. "Not dog tags."

"Well, he's gotta be drivin' that truck on something more than a tattoo, lady. And it ain't in our computers."

"Which means what?" Barb asked from her corner of the couch.

"Which means that Barnett seems to be an alias. And since you were so anxious to find out if he's sellin' drugs—which, by the way, are on the uprise in the area, just like you thought—I figured you'd like to help us find out what his real name is. Or what he's up to on that truck."

Jenny leveled a freezing glare at the detective, who this very minute looked like he had her in the pincers. "By inviting him over."

Richards gave her an elaborate shrug. "Well, you did it once."

Jenny opened her mouth to explain, once again, and then realized that a concept like Emma just wouldn't register on the good man. "And I told him I wouldn't do it again. What's he going to think when I change my mind?"

"That you got the hots for him, probably. Which is fine, 'cause maybe you can find something out about him."

Jenny set her tea on the table, putting it just out of her reach so that it wouldn't be such a temptation. "Why don't *you* talk to him, Detective Richards?"

"Because," he said as if he were explaining to a very small child. "I don't want one penny-ante drug dealer. I want his supplier. If I can get you to loosen him up, I might come up with something. Besides, I bet he'd be a lot happier talkin' to you."

"Shouldn't this be handed over to the county narcotics bureau?" Barb asked diffidently.

That seemed to be something the detective definitely didn't want to hear. "We don't need them pokin' their busy noses in down here. I'm on line with a guy from DEA who's investigating the rash of ice-cream-truck traffickers, and he assures me this is the way to go." Lowering the level of his tea with a long, loud gulp, Richards seemed to take the time to dredge up a modicum of tact. "Look, ladies, this is a hard neighborhood to stake out. The guy's got a run of about five miles, and all of it's heavily wooded. There aren't all that many responsible adults home during the day to help us keep an eye out for him. It just makes it a lot easier on us if we have a contact already set up."

"He's not dealing drugs," Jenny insisted.

"He's doin' somethin'," Richards retorted. "And we gotta find out what."

Rustling in her chair just enough to betray her agitation, Barb finally put in her vote. "Jenny—"

Jenny didn't even need to look over to read it. She'd known what the outcome of this little chat would be from the moment Richards had brought up Nick's name. She was going to let Nick right back into her house. She was going to encourage it. And she was going to suffer for it.

"All right," she sighed, feeling the weight of her words settle on her like a sentence even as she tried to think of a way to lighten the impact on Nick. "But you owe me a lot of coq au vin for this, Barb."

"And don't try and warn him, or say somethin' like, 'So, why are you usin' a fake name?'" Richards said. "You do that and he disappears before we can find out anything."

She hadn't even thought of that, but it was the best option of all.

Except that she wouldn't do it.

"Nice to see you could take time away from the high life to visit your friends."

Nick gave the dispatcher a grin and headed toward his office. He hadn't been in for about a week, but of course everybody knew what he was doing. His continuous run-ins with McGrady were the stuff of legend around here.

"Hey, Barnes," one of the bomb-and-arson guys greeted him. "What's new on *Sesame Street*?"

"Big yellow bird shoots frog. Film at eleven."

The Special Investigation office was grouped with the other detective bases, so that Nick worked a particleboard wall away from the guys in narcotics, burglary and bomb-and-arson. Greetings floated in from each of the different branches as Nick made his way into the cubbyhole that housed him along with four other special investigation detectives.

"Like the outfit, Nick. Makes you look ten years younger."

"After this, wanna pull some undercover time in school?"

"High school?"

"Grade school!"

Nick curled his lip in response. He'd never been terribly thrilled with his face. Too off-center-looking for the places he usually had to work. The fact that nobody was questioning his place on the ice cream truck proved it. He wanted his mustache back.

His attitude slid further when he opened his door. A bell jangled, and the anticipation could be heard in every laugh along the hall. He looked up. A bell from an ice cream truck. Wonderful. It looked like nobody was going to let him off easily.

And then there was the box of crayons and coloring book on his desk. Much as he didn't want to, Nick found himself grinning. It was good to be home.

"Baker," he said, sitting down and pulling out one of the crayons. "What do you have so far on the Lake woman?"

Baker, a short, sharp woman of thirty with a military taste in clothing and a buzzed blond cut strode over and handed him the file. "I missed you, too, honey," she retorted with a dry, toothy smile that portended more to come.

Nick just stuck the crayon behind his ear and set to work.

Jenny Lake, the file reported, thirty years old, graduate of St. Mary Magdalen School, Nerinx Hall High School, St. Louis University with B.A. in mathematics and education, Phi Beta Kappa, graduated magna cum laude, went to work teaching at West Vine Elementary School to put husband through law school at Washington University. Three pregnancies, two live births, Kevin Barton Lake, Jr. and Emma Louise. Divorced two years. Husband remarried to Amber Jean Wilson (*Amber Jean?* he thought. Sounded like a cheerleader.) Present address 12 Summerset, Ladue. Pays child support in amount of $250/month, in arrears six months (*Two-hundred-fifty? Who was he kidding? That was highway robbery. And the bastard couldn't even get that in on time. Probably in too deep to his pool service.*) To support herself, Jennifer Lake taught fifth-grade mathematics at Mary Mother of Eternal Patience and rang up groceries at Bennet's during the summer.

"Who can blame her for trying to make ends meet?" Baker had been reading over his shoulder.

"Yeah," Nick retorted. "All you divorced women stick together."

"Nobody else is gonna do it."

"Tell you what," he suggested, opening his drawer for a notepad. Instead he found a family of Smurfs, two teething rings and a box of animal crackers. This time he allowed a laugh.

"Hey, you guys, this is great!" he yelled for the benefit of every listening ear. "You gave up all your toys just for me! I especially like your teething rings, Washington!" Washington had just gotten his first set of dentures. The laughter rippled all the way down the hall. Nick broke open the box of crackers and shared them with Baker, who had perched on the side of his desk. "Now, find out the make and model on the car this Lake guy drives. And the license."

"Why? He's not stealing out of mailboxes."

Shrugging, Nick jotted the information down in brick red and replaced the crayon. "Because I don't like the bastard."

Nick's words brought a big smile to the policewoman's face. "I love to hear you say that."

Nick just smiled back. "I'm sure he's doing *something* wrong out there."

Baker tapped the file. "What about her?"

Looking back down at the evidence of Jenny's need, Nick still found himself shaking his head. "I don't think so. She just doesn't look like she's bringing in any extra income. All the same, I'll keep hunting."

"Yeah," Baker retorted in a too-knowing voice as she headed down to the computer. "Right."

The dry tone of that voice made Nick lift his head. There was no way Baker could have known. He hadn't even been in the office since he'd met Jenny. Her reaction was just typical sarcasm. Even so, it unsettled him.

It struck too close to the truth. Nick *was* interested in more than just the case here. He hadn't lied to Jenny when he'd told her she was the high point of his job. He did position the truck just so he could watch her walk up to her porch while he munched on peanut-butter-and-jelly.

And he was getting in too deep for his own good. He should walk in to McGrady right now, beg forgiveness and ask off the case. Maybe he should even tell the truth, that he was fantasizing too much about the suspect, making himself too comfortable in her house and actually talking to her kids.

And maybe McGrady would bust a gut laughing.

Everybody in the place knew about Nick's solitary nature. He lived alone because that's the way he preferred it. He socialized only a little, and that with other cops. And as for women, he hadn't been able to find one without an overactive biological clock. And as everybody within shouting distance of McGrady's office knew since Nick had been assigned to this case, Nick didn't like kids.

He had no patience for them. They were noisy and troublesome, and he'd never seen the good side of them growing up. Of course, that was the wonder of the foster-care system, that it popped you out without a secure base or a real regard for another human being, but what the hell. He'd made it through, escaped to the Marines and made it a point not to look back.

Except for odd little moments, like when he'd been invited in on family prayers over at the Lakes'. Jenny had looked at him when he'd suddenly gotten up and stalked out, but she hadn't asked. Nick had taken himself back to the kitchen and the last dose of wine, seeking some kind of antidote to all the love and support in that little pink-and-white room of Emma's.

God, the woman had no husband, she had no money and she was pulling enough hours between her kids and work to lay out a drill instructor. And she knelt on that floor and thanked God for what she had, and meant it. She'd taken the time to tell her kids that because they had each other, they didn't need anything else. *And meant it!* All the screwed-up families in the world, and he had to stumble onto the real thing.

Nick slapped the file shut and got to his feet. He popped a cookie into his mouth. Looked around for some coffee. He'd been closing his eyes to that particular void too long to give in to it now. Nick Barnes was a survivor. He didn't need that homey garbage, with little blond girls asking you how elephants dance, and bright-eyed boys comparing cartoon preferences with you. He didn't need the scent of oranges waking him in the dark. What he needed was some coffee.

In the end, he knew he'd go back. He didn't think Jenny was the thief, and if he weren't around to find the real one the department would just as easily tap-dance all over her in hobnail boots. And she deserved better than that.

What he deserved was a shrink.

"Don't you think you should dress up a little?"

Jenny looked down at her uniform and then back up at Lauren, who was assessing her with a definitely uncomfortable eye.

"What would you like," Jenny retorted. "A bikini and gold body paint?"

Lauren fluttered a distressed hand, setting up a jangle among her bracelets. "No, of course not. It's just...do you really think he'll be attracted by that outfit?"

Jenny couldn't help but laugh. She was standing with Lauren and Barb in the Bailey kitchen planning the Barnett Assault, as Jenny had taken to calling it—more to keep the considerable butterflies at bay, than for any better reason. She'd just pulled six hours at the store and was sporting a throbbing headache. She'd locked her keys in her car and had then fried when she'd finally gotten inside. She hadn't had lunch. And she hadn't even faced her children yet. She might as well deal with Nick now, while she was still too uncomfortable to care.

"Lauren," she said. "You're talking like I'm preparing for an espionage assignment or something. I'm going to ask him to help fix my car. I really don't think silver lamé is appropriate for that, do you?"

Barb grinned, but Lauren was taking her part of this seriously. "Of course not, Jens. But, well, I'm afraid that your uniform just isn't...well, becoming."

Jenny grinned. "Well, if worse comes to worst, I'll pull one of the shoulders down real low and sing to him."

Barb burst out into giggles. "That would send him screaming in the other direction, Jen."

Jenny offered a heartfelt scowl. "Thanks for the support, hon. After all, this was *your* idea." Just because she couldn't hit a note in a bucket with a barrel of double-ought shot, it wasn't something Jenny considered a laughing matter. Especially when everybody laughed.

Barb giggled again. "I'm just trying to offer constructive criticism."

"Wonderful," Jenny retorted. "So far, the only instructions I've gotten for this caper are take off my uniform and don't sing. That kind of leaves me a lot of leeway, doesn't it?"

Lauren finally worked up the enthusiasm to grin along. "We're right here behind you, Jens. Go out and get him."

Jenny just shook her head, foregoing the urge to tell Lauren that she really hated Lauren's idea of a nickname. "Richards was right. I am the only man for this job."

Lauren got in her last shot. "In that uniform, you *look* like the only man for the job."

"You're just jealous because you have to wear that heavy new tennis bracelet and I don't," Jenny retorted with an easy grin.

Lauren never knew just how to take Jenny. She lifted the offending arm, an arc of diamonds glittering in the sun that streamed through Barb's spotless windows and then, uncertain, glanced up at Jenny.

"It's beautiful," Jen assured her. "But it just wouldn't go with this smashing brown polyester. You might as well be the one to wear it."

Lauren smiled. "A girl should be able to treat herself now and again, don't you think?"

"Lauren," Jenny retorted, "Häagen-Dazs is a treat. *That* is an orgy."

"Speaking of which," Barb interrupted, eyes on the bracelet. "That ice cream truck isn't going to sit there all afternoon."

Even Lauren laughed. "Jens is a bad influence on you, Babs."

Jenny didn't think that either woman saw her wince.

Jenny was all set to follow Lauren out of the house when Barb surprised her by pulling her aside. "You really seemed convinced that he's not guilty," she said, the gravity in her voice matching the concern in her eyes. Barb wasn't one to pry, but she knew better than most what was going on where. "Why?"

For a moment, all Jenny could do was look out onto the peaceful shade of Barb's yard. The neighborhood was quiet at this time of day, when the heat took over and even bored the birds to silence. The trees rustled listlessly in the breeze and set the shadows to a slow dance.

Jenny couldn't help but think of how much the peace of this neighborhood meant to her. The huge old trees, the deep lawns and constant neighbors. She didn't want anything to happen that would hurt it.

And then she thought of the raw pain she'd surprised in Nick's eyes the night before when he'd stumbled from Emma's room. He'd avoided facing her, but what she'd seen had reminded her of a little boy looking into the lighted rooms of a warm, noisy house on a cold night and knowing he didn't belong. How could a man break her heart without so much as a word?

Still feeling the chill even in the summer wind, Jenny shook her head. "Because Emma likes him, Barb."

It actually took Barb a moment to answer. "Emma?" Her surprise couldn't have been greater if Jenny had said that the Queen of England danced topless.

Jenny nodded, her smile as good as a shrug. "Had him upstairs introducing him to all her animals. She even held his hand."

Still Barb faltered. "Emma?"

Emma didn't even let the Jerk hold her hand, which said quite a bit about Emma's discriminating taste in people. Those great blue eyes of hers saw more than most adults. Those patient little ears heard what Jenny swore hadn't been said. And Emma, who held most of the world at arm's length, had a spe-

cial affinity for life's casualties. A silent pat to trembling hands,
a smile to bravely passive faces.

And she'd found Nick.

"Emma likes him," Jenny said again in some wonder. "And
I like him." This time she did shrug. "But then, at one time I
liked the Jerk."

"It's not the same, at all," Barb insisted, instinctively defending her friend.

Jenny grinned. "You're right, there. I can't see the Jerk
sporting a Marine Corps tattoo on any part of his body. Nor,
come to think of it, would I want to see it if he did. Now, on the
other hand, Nick . . ."

"Is up there eating his lunch," Barb interrupted with a tolerant smile. "The perfect time to discuss cars, if I'm not mis-
taken."

"I know," Jenny retorted, with an upraised hand. "'Jenny,
act your age.' That does get boring after a while, though,
doesn't it, Barb?"

Wrong person to ask. Barb couldn't imagine any reason to
prevent one from accepting her responsibilities. Jenny just
laughed and offered a conciliatory pat on the arm and acted on
Barb's suggestion. She walked out the door.

Jenny started down the street with at least a modicum of
purpose. She wanted to find out one way or another just what
Nick Barnett was up to. She wanted to get Detective Richards
out of her hair. She wanted to get this conversation over with
and rediscover the joys of air-conditioning and aspirin.

She'd made it about four houses down when she noticed the
envelopes sticking out of the mailbox. They distracted her.

"Damn!" she sighed, heading in that direction with a look
over her shoulder to make sure she wasn't in Mrs. Warner's line
of sight. The trees effectively shaded her. Opening the box a
little, she checked the contents. "Aw, now why don't they listen to advice and mail these?" she whined, taking another look
around and shoving the envelopes into her pocket. "They're
just asking for trouble." Turning back to her original purpose, she gave her head one last shake and rubbed at the growing throb at her temples. "Not to mention somebody else I
know."

* * *

Nick had spent the last few hours convincing himself that this was the only thing he could do. He'd debated the fact that he was too involved and countered it with the obvious answer that it was better to have somebody who cared investigating Jenny than somebody who didn't.

He challenged the wisdom of trying to get back in her good graces after she'd all but thrown him out the night before. He'd even considered telling her that he was really resigning from law school. Instead he was going into a really respectable field. Teaching or accounting or... oh, hell, the priesthood.

No, he'd decided with the first wry smile of the battle. You can only strain credibility so far. Besides, that wouldn't allow for any unforeseen opportunities in the emotional expression department. Just in case any came up.

So here he was girding his loins, so to speak, sweating more from the turmoil of what he had to do than from the hundred-degree temperatures, and suddenly Jenny was walking his way. Alone. Smiling.

So, just what was wrong with this picture?

"Hi," she greeted him, bobbing her head almost shyly, the sunlight making her squint a little.

Grinding out his cigarette and setting down his can, Nick nodded back. "Hi. Thanks again for dinner last night."

"Oh." Again that little bob sent her hair trembling about her head. "Don't think anything of it. It wasn't like I cooked real food or anything."

There was a moment of silence, taut, brittle, as if each of them was waiting for the other to speak. Not knowing quite what else to do, Nick opened his door and slid out. He felt absurdly like a high-school boy meeting his date at the drive-in.

"Popsicle?" he asked, heading toward the back of the truck.

Envelopes. There were three envelopes in her pocket. His heart faltered. His eyes strayed. He couldn't see more than a first name on the return addresses, but that was Frank. Unless Jenny had some bigger secrets than even the police department knew about, she wasn't a Frank. Nick wanted to throw something.

"Actually," Jenny said, sounding terribly stiff. "I was going to ask for a . . . favor."

Nick turned to face her, his surprise showing. Did this mean he didn't have to pretend to be a priest?

"A favor?" he countered as easily as he could, especially downwind of that perfume. "What kind? Does Emma need to run a tab? Financial crisis in the kingdom?"

"Don't encourage her," Jenny warned with a grin. "No, it's not Emma. It's . . . well, it's my car. You said you thought the fuel injectors were going bad."

Leaning against the back of the truck, Nick frowned in bemusement. "Yeah. One of these days you're gonna be driving home from Bennet's and they're just gonna quit on you. Why?"

"Would you have a set of metric tools?" she asked. "The car needs to be fixed and I'd give it a shot, but I don't have anything metric to my name except a prescription for ampicillin."

Nick couldn't help but betray his surprise. "Fix the car? You know how?"

"I know how to do a lot of things," Jenny assured him, with more pique than pride. "A repairman charges forty dollars just to ring your doorbell."

There was a whole new understanding of Jenny in Nick's expression. "I hear ya. When do you want to do it?"

Jenny shrugged. "As soon as possible. I, uh, can't afford to be without a car. Especially with school coming up soon."

"Well, sure. But . . . do you mind my asking what changed your mind? About having me around."

He saw that he'd hit a live nerve. Again, that poor poker face, the emotions skittering over her face faster than cloud reflections on a lake. Frustration, resentment, anger, discomfort. She turned her head, just a little, as if it could better hide the truth behind her answer. But when it came, she had the guts to give it all.

"Sure. I had an unproductive session with the Jerk yesterday. The funds I'm short of aren't coming, from him or anyplace else right now. It doesn't mean I've changed my mind. It means that I'm using you. The pay is beer and chili."

"The jerk?"

She flashed him a quick, wry grin absolutely devoid of guilt. "The lovely ex-Mr. Jennifer Lake. Don't ever tell my children I call him that. But it helps stoke the fires of self-righteous indignation a little when I need the energy to do things like fix my own car."

For a moment Nick just looked at her. She looked so independent, so self-sustaining, with that challenging fire in her eyes. He could only imagine the price she'd paid for that strength. No apologies, no retreats. She did what she had to for herself and her children. And if that meant robbing from mailboxes, Nick wasn't sure she'd apologize for that, either.

"Beer and chili, huh?"

"All you can eat."

"Deal. How 'bout Sunday? I'm off."

"Sunday it is." For a moment, it seemed that Jenny deflated a little. "Thanks, Nick. I really appreciate the help."

Nick took a second to run an appraising eye over the pink, flushed cheeks, the wide, sparking green eyes, the full, brassy mouth. Even in that androgynous lump of material they called a uniform she had the ability to raise his blood pressure twenty degrees. When he finally answered, it was a smile free of all the tortuous deliberations he'd gotten snagged in earlier in the day.

"My pleasure," he assured her, and realized that he meant it.

It wasn't until Jenny was halfway down the street that Nick realized he'd forgotten to ask about the envelopes.

A sainthood, Lord, for the man who invented air-conditioning, Jenny thought. And a severe talking-to to the God who thought up children.

"Mom!"

"Mom!"

"Mom!"

"I've changed my name," Jenny informed them both as they danced impatiently by her elevated feet. She'd stretched out in the playroom, trembling with effort, exhausted with heat, crabby with headache. And there, like little human magnets, they'd found her. "Until you guess it, I'm not answering."

"Aw, c'mon, Mom."

"You heard me." She didn't even bother to open her eyes. She did purse her lips, though, and both of them fought to get the first kiss.

"Bill?"

"Wilma?"

"Eleanor?"

"Ralph?"

"Ralph?" Jenny retorted, eyes opening, body refusing to move no matter what she commanded. "You guessed! What can I do for you?"

Kevin beat Emma to the punch by a nose. "Mrs. Warner has my ball," he said, his face a struggle between distress and outrage. "The soccer ball Dad got me for my birthday."

The soccer ball Mom got him and put Dad's name on, when it looked as if he wasn't going to remember again. "Kicked it in her yard, huh?"

Outrage won out. Nothing provoked indignation like older women who didn't understand the vagaries of soccer. "I didn't mean to, but Buffy and Dustin were blocking the other side of the goal."

"Wasn't Miss Lucy there?" Jenny asked, carefully closing her eyes against the light, her arm around Kevin's waist as he stood alongside the couch.

"No. I think she was out walking. Mrs. Warner said we couldn't have it back again. She said she was tired of picking it out of the ivy."

"Okay," Jenny sighed. "I'll see what I can do. A little later."

"Mom, now," he whined. "She might throw it into the fire or something."

"I don't think so, honey. Now, go on out for a while so Mom can get rid of this headache."

"But I don't have a ball!"

"Go do something..." Her abstracted search for inspiration was interrupted by the front doorbell. "Go answer the door. That'll keep you busy. If they want money, tell 'em I already gave."

Both kids pounded down the hallway through to the foyer to win first place at the door. The sound of their race echoed through the rooms and reverberated through Jenny's skull. She groaned.

Then she heard the excited babble, which meant that it wasn't Barb, and it wasn't the Jerk, and it wasn't the mailman.

The mailman. Oh, God, she had to remember to get those envelopes taken care of again. They weren't something that could just lie around the house for days. And then she'd have to put a stop to it.

Jenny was giving serious consideration to getting an eye open for the surprise visitor when she realized she didn't need to. She smelled him.

Her heart stumbled. Butterflies swarmed in her stomach, and her headache set up a fresh pounding. Nighttime and lightning. Leather and denim. Danger and attraction.

Nick.

"I thought we said Sunday," she said without opening her eyes.

It wasn't hard to hear the humor in his voice. "How'd you know it was me?"

"I'm a mother," Jenny assured him. "I know everything."

That got a laugh out of him. Jenny wished she felt as jolly.

"Are you okay?" he asked, suddenly sounding serious.

"Fine. I've been cooking a headache all day, and it's finally well done."

"Anything I can do?"

Jenny still didn't get her eyes open. He was nice enough just on the other senses without facing all that light yet. "Wanna go over and beat up an old lady for me?"

There was a polite pause. "What?"

Jenny managed to get her eyes open and grinned. He did look just the least bit confused. "On the other hand, you'd scare the hell out of her if you just showed up on her doorstep." It was something about the glisten of sweat on his throat, the hair falling into his eyes and the indecent fit of those faded, ripped jeans. And he had a Deadhead shirt on. That clinched it. He was scaring the hell out of her, too. "Mrs. Warner took Kevin's ball and he wants retribution."

Nick took a quick look over his shoulder, as if he could really see the house. "The neighborhood FBI? *That* Mrs. Warner?"

"The chief of police's aunt. That Mrs. Warner."

She heard the hesitation in his voice. "Oh, brass, huh? Well, that'll cost you extra. What do you want, your basic roughing up or a little arm-twisting for good measure?"

"Arm-twisting!" Kevin piped up with relish. "Make her stop taking my ball."

Jenny afforded herself another groan. "Thank you, Nick. I'll send him to you when he needs bail money."

Nick stood by the foyer wondering what he should do now. Jenny really did look pale, her face drawn from the artillery attack going on in her head. He had the urge to go over to her, to take her hand and run a soothing hand over her cheek. It amazed him how suddenly protective he felt of this woman who wouldn't allow anyone to protect her.

"Why don't you guys go on outside for a while?" he said to the two little ones who flanked him. "Let your mom get some rest."

"Don't be worried, Nick," Emma said with a patient mother's smile. "Mommy does this sometimes. Then she takes a nap and gets better. We're used to it."

Nick still wasn't really sure how to answer that kid. Especially when she sounded older than he did. "Yeah, well, thanks. Now, go on out."

He really thought his idea was an inspiration until Kevin slammed the door on his way out. Nick winced. Jenny winced.

"Did you take aspirin or anything?" he asked, heading into the playroom.

"I'm just going there now," she assured him without moving a muscle.

"Where?" he asked. "I can get them."

"Kitchen." He didn't say anything, but she answered him anyway. "I figured I'd save time by keeping them in the place that causes the most headaches."

"Right next to the tuna, right?"

That got a smile out of her. "You're catching on."

Nick should have been relieved at the chance he'd been given to check out her place. For some reason he felt like a heel. It didn't keep him from sorting through the piles of paper on the kitchen table when he went in search of aspirin and water.

The kitchen wasn't as messy as it had been the first time he'd been through. This time he took a moment to notice the refrigerator art, construction-paper flags and little handprints, imaginative renderings of warplanes and big, scrawling figures that probably only meant something to three-year-olds and their mothers. Nick wondered how the hell she got the fridge door open without knocking half that stuff off.

And then there was the collection of jelly glasses and mismatched Tupperware that took up her shelves. Nothing matched in this house—not towels or plates or silverware. It was as if she replaced things as they broke, never having enough money to invest in a whole new set. There was *Sesame Street* dinnerware and *Star Wars* glasses, and a sign over the kitchen sink that proclaimed, "Children need love. Especially when they don't deserve it."

Nick found himself smiling. A pragmatist, this woman. An idealist who lived in the real world. She had sun-catchers in the window that spilled jewels over the walls, and a collection of tiny frogs in a shadow box on the wall. Suddenly Nick wished somebody he'd lived with had had enough whimsy to collect frogs. He wished he'd been hung in a mother's art gallery, his work collected in a huge box to be preserved for the day he'd moved away. When Nick had moved out, he had gone with a driver's license and a high-school diploma, and that was it.

Suddenly he was shaking himself again, fighting the pull of this house, this family. He had to find out about the forgery and then get the hell out.

Picking the aspirin bottle off the windowsill and filling a glass with water, Nick took another moment to sort through bills and school notices and snapshots without any luck.

No envelopes. No evidence. Just a very attractive lady stretched out on the couch rubbing her head and a quiet, cool house. Nick walked back in, gave Jenny the aspirin and settled himself on the edge of the glass-and-teak coffee table well within the perfume perimeter.

Working her way up to a sitting position, Jenny popped the tablets in and swallowed with a huge grimace. It was only then that she was able to get her eyes open and focus on her benefactor, only to find him no more than a foot away. Her eyes just a little too wide, she flashed a tired grin.

"Thanks. Again. I appreciate it."

Feeling suddenly foolish, Nick shrugged. "Anytime."

"You never told me."

"Told you what?"

"Why you came over."

"Oh." He flashed her a sheepish grin. "Sunday. What time?"

Jenny grinned back. "Would two be okay?"

"Sure." He didn't think about what he did next, he just acted. "Why don't you get some sleep?" he asked, his words unaccountably quiet, his hand up to brush her hair back from her forehead in a way that would have reminded anyone else of a parent comforting a sick child. "You look like you could use it."

Jenny's answering smile faltered a little. Her eyes grew wide with his touch. "A rank play for sympathy," she assured him in a curiously small voice. "My mother used to call me Sarah Bernhardt."

Still Nick hesitated, uncomfortable with staying, unwilling to go. He'd liked that touch of her, the silk of her hair, the velvet of her skin. He liked making her smile, especially that hesitant, sweet smile that said she was feeling more than she wanted. Nick could have stayed all day and coaxed that smile out of her. He could have even seen his way to stroking his hand across her forehead, her cheek, her hair, soothing, quieting.

But he knew better. That just invited involvement, and that wasn't possible. For more than one reason, the main one being Frank, whoever he was.

Or was the real reason the false security he felt with this woman? Nick knew better than to trust that. He'd been proven wrong too many times.

She was forging checks. It was his job to find out how. That was all. And when this was over, he'd go back to his apartment in Clayton and reclaim his solitary life. And by God, he'd like it. Because right now, Nick couldn't see how he could do any different.

"Young man! Young man, let her go!"

Nick turned to the sound of the quavering voice, wondering what the hell was up now. He didn't get as far as his feet. He didn't even see the intruder. What he did see was the afternoon paper as it slammed into his head.

Chapter 5

"Miss Lucy, no!"

"Hey, lady!"

Nick and Jenny collided on the way up. Nick had his arms up trying to ward off the flurry of slaps he was getting with the business section and sidestep enough to get over the table and at his attacker. He only succeeded in knocking Jenny back down.

"You get away from her, do you hear me?"

Nick got a quick impression of wrinkles and gray hair and a big straw hat with a wilted flower on the crown. And gloves. Good God, he was being whaled by Grandma Walton. He was never going to hear the end of this down at the department.

"Miss Lucy," Jenny objected, shoving her way back up again. "It's all right. Nick was getting me some aspirin. It's all right!"

The old lady didn't hear in time. Nick had just made it around the table when she came out of a backswing with a huge purse Nick swore was carrying bricks. It caught him square in the side of the head and sent him reeling.

Suddenly, though, as if she were on a three-second delay, she gaped. The paper dropped, her hand flew to her mouth, and Nick came to an uncertain halt.

"Oh, dear," she stammered, her watery blue eyes lifting way up to Nick's face. She couldn't have topped five feet, dressed in organdy and thick shoes. She looked like somebody Nick would find in Shaw's garden sniffing the roses and talking to the birds. "Oh, dear, dear, dear."

"Nick? Are you okay?" Jenny asked, a hand to his arm.

Nick realized that he must have looked a little wild, because when he turned to answer her Jenny was fighting a huge grin.

"Couldn't you have a German shepherd, like everyone else?" he demanded, rubbing at the side of his nose where the purse's zipper had left a new crease.

Jenny stifled a laugh and gave him a pat. "I'm sorry, Nick. I haven't introduced you. This is Miss Lucy Sperring. She's Mrs. Warner's sister from across the street. Miss Lucy, this is Nick Barnett, the ice cream man."

"Oh, it's a pleasure," Miss Lucy piped up as if the introduction weren't at all out of the ordinary, a hand demurely extended, the purse back over her arm.

Not knowing quite what else to do, Nick shook hands.

"It's just that the children said that you'd thrown them out and, well, you were bent over Jenny like that..."

Jenny leaned over as if she were sharing a secret between girls. "My virtue is safe, Miss Lucy. My paper?"

"Oh, yes, dear. I thought I'd drop in with it. Especially..."

"Yes, Miss Lucy."

"Well, dear, then I'll drop dear little Barbara hers. Good day." Resettling her purse and giving a proper little tug on her gloves, Miss Lucy shot Nick a smile straight out of a Tennessee Williams play. "And you must stop in and visit with us, Mr. Barnett. We do so enjoy company."

Jenny shot Nick a warning glance. When Miss Lucy had cleared the room on her way out the door, Jenny allowed in a straight voice, "Set foot in that yard and Mrs. Warner will have the police helicopter circling."

"That's what I thought." Nick couldn't quite pull his gaze from the empty door where Miss Lucy's presence still remained like a well-mannered ghost. "She's the ball warden's sister?"

Standing alongside, Jenny considered the same view. "Amazing, isn't it? Like having the Queen Mum and J. Edgar Hoover sharing the same train berth."

Nick just shook his head. "Lady, you got some neighborhood."

"They take care of me," Jenny defended them.

"Yeah," Nick retorted, rubbing at the side of his head where the memory of something very solid inside that purse still lingered. "I know."

Jenny chuckled. "I'm sorry. Really. I'm used to Miss Lucy just walking in. She does it to everybody. She's harmless."

"She's an ozone commando."

"Broaden your horizons a little, Nick. You might get to enjoy it a little."

"Anybody else I should know about?"

Easing back down on the couch, Jenny propped her feet on the coffee table and thought about it. "Well, Mr. Ventimiglia writes letters to the president and Libby Vilhels balances crystals on her forehead looking for enlightenment. And Bill Hobbs on the corner is trying to make *The Guinness Book of Records* for having the most ailments in one body."

Almost by unspoken consent, Nick joined her on the couch, propping his feet alongside hers, a hand still testing the sore spot at the side of his head. "A fairly normal bunch for south county."

"Don't be smug," she retorted, leaning her head back against the couch. "Where do you live that the people are so different?"

"Clayton."

Jenny snorted. "Of course. The center of the universe."

"I live in an unair-conditioned efficiency off Skinker, so I can be close to school. Is that a crime?"

"I bet people balance crystals on their forehead in Clayton, too."

"They don't carry plates and napkins out to get Popsicles."

Now Jenny laughed, eyes closed, comfortably quiet, headache subsiding. She sat alongside Nick as if it were the most natural thing to do, and she didn't know how to stop it.

"Don't make fun of Barb," she asked. "She's six of the most sincere people on the face of the earth."

"She's gonna be buried in a Tupperware container."

That took care of the subsiding headache. It flared when Jenny started laughing again. "Stop that," she begged, giving him a smack. "Now I'm not going to be able to look in her cabinets without thinking of somebody burping the lid over her."

"I bet she's got a kid named Muffy."

"Buffy."

Now he was laughing. "And a golden retriever?"

"And a compact station wagon."

"You were right," he admitted, leaning back next to her. "I should have gone over there for dinner."

Half an hour later Kevin ran into the house with the ball he'd sweet-talked out of Miss Lucy to find his mom and Nick asleep side-by-side on the couch. With a disgusted scowl, he intercepted Emma and took her up to his room to play.

At first Jenny thought it was the alarm. It was six-thirty and she had to get the kids up for school. She sighed and stretched and tried to reach over to shut it off. That was when she realized she was on the couch.

The phone. It wasn't the alarm she heard but the phone, relentlessly ringing out in the kitchen. Jenny opened her eyes and realized two things simultaneously. She'd been asleep for at least an hour, and Nick was still asleep next to her.

Sitting up, she looked over at him, stretched out in an identical position, head against the cushions, feet up on the coffee table, one arm on the couch back, the other over his stomach. His chest rose and fell in an even, deep rhythm. His eyes were closed and his face so relaxed Jenny wondered if she'd been wrong about his age. He looked curiously young in the half-light in the playroom, his hair tousled over his forehead and his mouth open just a little as he gently snored. He looked vulnerable, and that was something Jenny had never thought she'd say about Nick Barnett.

She was just sitting there staring, wondering at the urge to reach out to him, the sweet ache in her chest at the sight of him, when the phone finally stopped ringing. Jenny looked up, surprised by the silence, completely unnerved by the fact that she'd been comfortable enough with Nick to fall asleep alongside him. Stunned by the fact that he'd been comfortable enough with her to do the same.

What made it worse was that looking at him now made her realize just how tired he'd looked before. He must have been putting in long hours to fall asleep on a stranger's couch in the middle of the afternoon.

"Is Mr. Nick coming to dinner?"

Jenny looked up to find Emma in the doorway, the cat clutched in her arms and dressed in Cabbage Patch clothes.

"No, sweetheart. I don't think he could survive it twice. He just fell asleep."

"Kevin said we should be quiet so you wouldn't be crabby."

Edging off the couch, Jenny held out her arms. The little girl trotted over and snuggled into Jenny's embrace.

"Well, thank you both. I'm feeling all better now."

"Did Mr. Nick have a headache, too?"

"I wouldn't be surprised after Miss Lucy got through with him. Now, why don't we be quiet for him so he's not crabby, huh?"

Emma took a moment to consider the sleeping man on her couch. "He doesn't do this a lot, does he?"

Surprised, Jenny looked from her daughter to the sleeping man. "No," she admitted softly, more troubled than she could say by Emma's observation. "I don't think he does."

It wasn't the phone that got her attention this time but a knock at the back door. Hopping to her feet, Jenny tugged Emma after her. She wasn't exactly sure what she should do about waking Nick up. He might have something to do, somewhere to go. But looking down at him now, so quiet and peaceful, she couldn't bring herself to wake him.

She should have known it was Barb. By the time Jen got to the door, the blonde was peering in through the curtains with the kind of look that preceded the calling of police.

"Hi, Barb," Jenny greeted her. "Aren't you supposed to be cooking something?"

Barb didn't consider the situation a laughing matter. Still looking carefully around as if expecting a sudden rush from a weapon-wielding intruder, she stepped into the kitchen, her arms loaded with food containers. She must have decided that she needed a plausible excuse to visit.

"Are you all right?" she asked, setting the booty down on the countertop by the sink. "You didn't answer your phone."

Jenny couldn't help but grin. "I take it Miss Lucy told you about my surprise visitor."

Barb shot Jenny a meaningful look. "The ice cream truck's been in front of your house for over an hour."

Jenny gave in to a groan. So much for the neighborhood network. By dark the word would be around that Jenny was doing unspeakable things with the ice cream man. She wondered whether Lauren would be relieved that Jenny was interested in somebody other than her husband or outraged at Jenny's aberrant behavior.

"Who's called you so far?"

Now Barb offered her own version of a sheepish smile. "Mrs. Warner, Mr. Ventimiglia and Patsy Deaver. It's turning into a great story."

"Did you tell them I was working undercover?"

Bad choice of words. Jenny could see the double entendre strike home and fight for expression in Barb's carefully controlled face.

"The question came up."

Jenny afforded herself a grimace. "Go see for yourself what happened. He's in the playroom. Want some tea or something?"

Now Barb allowed just the least bit of doubt. Jenny could see the suspicion flick across the blonde's mind that Jenny had somehow done the man in and left him in with the *TV Guide*.

"He fell asleep," Jenny offered with barely controlled humor.

"He was crabby," Emma added with a knowing nod from her perch on a chair. The cat now sat in her lap.

Barb actually crept in through the French doors and stood there, looking down as if watching a sleeping lion. The expression on her face mirrored all her distrust, distress and uncertainty. Jenny grinned at her and turned to clean off the table for dinner.

Barb walked back into the kitchen to find Jenny frowning at an envelope she held in her hand.

"He doesn't look quite as dangerous lying on the couch," Barb admitted, looking at the envelope, then Jenny. "What's wrong?"

Jenny shook her head. "I've been looking for this for three days, and I just found it right on top of a pile of mail on the table. Lord," she sighed in exasperation, "if I were organized, I'd be dangerous."

Barb was still Barb. "You have a lot on your mind," she assured Jenny with a passing hand on the shoulder. "You do have room on your wall here for a mail organizer, though. You can get them at the crafts store. Did you find anything out?"

Jenny had to suppress a grin at the sudden, conspiratorial hush in Barb's voice. Excitement was a rare commodity in St. Anthony. It seemed that when it struck it even had the ability to infect Barb.

"No," Jenny answered in a voice just as hushed and then turned to the fridge for something to drink. Soda, she thought, with lots of chemicals and preservatives. Just the kind of thing that made old Barb wince. "How 'bout a soda, Barb? Diet, of course."

"No, thanks," Barb demurred, her expression just as carefully noncommittal as Jenny had anticipated.

"Spot says she would like a soda for us," Emma piped up, lifting the placid tabby she'd named herself. Spot was evidently getting weary of looking like a furry kindergartner. Her tail was beginning to switch.

"Tell Spot that she's not old enough for soda," Jenny answered, popping the can and taking a long swig. "And tell her also, please, not to wear my lipstick anymore."

"But she wants to look lovely."

"She's lovely already, Emma. She has to stay out of my things, please."

Emma exhibited one of her patented pouts. "Okay," she acquiesced and headed out.

It didn't occur to Jenny that the little girl was headed back toward the playroom. She had dinner to cook and about a week's worth of laundry to catch up on and Kevin to talk to. And that didn't even take into account the situation that placed Barb in her kitchen and a near stranger asleep on her couch.

In point of fact, Nick was no longer asleep. He hadn't been since the cat had run up his chest. For a long moment he sat straight up on the couch, trying to understand what the hell had happened. Somehow he'd ended up sound asleep on Jenny's couch with her daughter curled up alongside him and a cat now staring malevolently at him from atop the television. A cat in a dress. Nick shook his head.

He remembered stopping in the house to get a line on those checks. He remembered the sight of Jenny lying on the couch, eyes closed, looking as fragile and vulnerable as a tropical flower in winter. And he remembered Miss Lucy.

Had she knocked him out? He couldn't really remember. The side of his head sure ached, but he didn't have the queasy, concussed feeling. He looked down at Emma, thinking maybe to ask, but she was engrossed in the letter P, her eyes already glazed by the bright, flickering television. Since it was a cinch the cat wasn't going to tell him, the only option was to look for other life.

Rubbing ruefully at the tender ache in his left temple, Nick lurched to his feet and headed toward the sound of the voices. Maybe Jenny would explain.

One look at the two in the kitchen brought it all back. He'd been talking. Sitting alongside Jenny as if he belonged there, talking about her neighbors. And then, as subtly as nightfall, the two of them had drifted to silence, to easy comfort side-by-side. To sleep.

Nick couldn't believe it. He couldn't imagine it. He wished suddenly, with a yearning that surprised him, that he'd woken up before she had.

Barb noticed him first. Jenny had her back to the playroom door as she retold Miss Lucy's surprise attack.

"I'll tell you something, Barb," she was saying, using the soda can for punctuation. "That old lady has a mean swing on her. I thought Nick was going to be down for the count . . . Barb?"

But Barb's attention had drifted, her eyes widening as they focused beyond Jenny's shoulder. Curious, Jenny turned to look. Then she found herself staring, too.

No wonder Barb had been distracted. Nick stood in the doorway, looking rumpled and a little disoriented. He was running his hands through his hair as he stretched out the worst of the kinks, and his eyes still had that soft, sleepy look about them. Jenny couldn't help the smile that crept all the way up from her toes. It was all she could do to keep from saying, "Aaaw."

"Hi," she greeted him, not realizing how soft her voice sounded. She didn't see Barb transfer her wondering look to Jenny.

Nick smiled back, his eyes a little sheepish as he leaned a hip against the doorway. "I seem to have made myself right at home. I'm sorry."

Jenny just shrugged. "Hard for me to kick you out since I was asleep, too."

"How's the headache?"

"Well," she admitted. "That one's gone, but we might just have another one brewing. Barb just showed up to tell me that the neighborhood grapevine is all a-twitter about your van being here so long."

Nick had a very impressive scowl. When Jenny saw it she realized how Miss Lucy could have felt the need to defend her. His presence in the neighborhood probably had those two old ladies locking up everything but their police scanner.

The problem was that to Jenny his scowl just made him look more enticing. There was such a dark set to his features, a hidden place that added shadows and meaning to his reactions. She wanted to know what that was. She wanted to know why Emma had realized that he wasn't the kind of man who relaxed enough to fall asleep around other people.

"And don't say typical south county," she warned, keeping her tone deliberately light. "Gossip is part of the human condition everywhere."

"Thanks for the sociology lecture," he groused, pushing away from the door and approaching. "I'll bear it in mind when I punch out that old guy with all the diseases for calling you loose."

Jenny flashed him a wry grin. "And they said chivalry was dead."

When Nick smiled back, it was with a sensual promise that left Jenny's knees weak. "Thanks for the couch. See you Sunday?"

Jenny nodded. "Sure." Silver-tongued devil, she thought in despair. The man was making her into an idiot.

"By the way," he added when he came alongside Barb, who was just as suspiciously quiet as Jenny. "Do you always dress your animals?"

Jenny responded with a slow, dry smile. "Don't you?"

She could hear Nick's chuckle all the way down the driveway.

"What are you going to do about him?" Barb asked, the hush in her voice more wonder than conspiracy.

"Enjoy him," Jenny answered automatically. When she saw the stunned distress on Barb's face, she offered a smile and a pat on the arm. "Calm down, Barb. I'm talking basic fantasy here. Do you know what kind of school he goes to?"

Barb seemed unable to do more than shake her head.

"Law school." Jenny waited for the understanding to dawn, and behind it the relief. Then she nodded. "That's the problem with having been married to the Jerk," she said. "I can only think with my hormones so long before reality interferes. Even if Nick isn't a drug dealer. Even if he's selling ice cream to support his work for Mother Teresa, he's still going to be a lawyer. I've danced that tune one time too many. I'll watch this one from the wings."

Barb smiled. "I think I'm glad."

Finishing off her can of soda, Jenny tossed it in the trash and turned to her neighbor with a piratical grin. "Although, come to think of it, I would like to see Mrs. Warner's face when I started dating a man with a ponytail."

As a rule, Sunday morning at the Lakes' was a madhouse. Jenny had long spent her Saturday nights dreading the alarm clock the next morning, living for the minute she walked back in the door from church.

When she opened the door this Sunday, though, it was no relief. For the first time in days she had time to notice just how much of a mess the house was. There were toys and clothes everywhere, bits of cutout paper and stick weapons of all sizes. Not to mention the dirty dishes that lurked behind those French doors in the kitchen.

Usually Jenny had a great amount of patience for the mayhem children wrought on a house. As she stood in the front foyer on this particular day, though, she suddenly decided that it was just too much that Kevin had draped kite string all throughout the playroom to make an "art project."

"It's cleaning time," she announced, bringing both children to a stunned halt.

"What?"

"This house is a mess," Jenny told them, hands on hips for extra emphasis. "We're cleaning it up. Right now."

Tilting his head to the side in an expression of supreme distaste, Kevin considered her. "Who's coming over?"

"Nobody," Jenny answered automatically. "Do we need somebody to come over to clean the house?"

"Usually."

"Don't be a snot. Just get started dismantling your spiderweb."

He gave it one more shot. "Are you *sure* nobody's coming over?"

Jenny just glared. It was enough to get Kevin moving.

Somebody coming over, she thought with a scowl as she headed up for her room to change. Where did I get such smart alecks? You'd think a woman didn't have a right to a clean house.

For some reason she didn't notice that her room wasn't much better than the rest of the house. She'd long since gotten used to filling the other side of the king-size bed with clothes to be folded or projects or books she was working on in bed. It seemed to keep it warmer that way. This week's work included preparations for school. Her clean clothes lay folded over the bench at the bed's foot and her dresser was piled with clutter.

Jenny slipped out of her church dress and stood in bra and panties looking for something to wear. Of course, there was somebody coming over today, but that wouldn't put her in such a cleaning frenzy. After all, she wasn't doing anything but keeping an eye on him for the police, getting license plates or something for Detective Richards. It wasn't as if she were trying to seduce him.

No, she thought, picking through a pile of shorts and jeans, I'm not doing anything special—but all the same, that just doesn't look right. That doesn't fit right. That makes me look fat. But it doesn't make any difference. After all, it's only Nick coming over.

Unable to resist, she took a quick look up at the mirror.

There she was, stretch marks, love handles and all. Well, not exactly a lot of stretch marks, just a few silvery threads creeping up the side of her belly that were her children's gift to her. And, well, the love handles weren't as bad as they used to be. Just enough to keep her from being too skinny.

She still had good breasts, she thought, doing her best to make her assessment objectively. Even after nursing the babies, she was still firm and full. And when she took the trouble anymore to wear her good underwear, the lace and satin that had once seemed so important, she could compete with the best of them.

The only reason she was wearing lace and satin today was because it had felt so nice beneath her dress. Even so, she didn't change it when she slipped on her slacks.

If she'd really thought about it at all, she would have admitted that ecru slacks and a pink sweater weren't the things to fix a car in but, well, she always had time to change. Casting a quick glance at the clock, Jenny found that the minute hand had only inched forward a couple of numbers. She still had plenty of time to get finished before Nick showed up. Hours. Months. Years. Too much time, and not nearly enough.

Not that it made any difference.

Cursing, Nick threw another shirt into the corner. He knew he was just going to have to come home later and clean it up, but the growing pile gave him some satisfaction.

Surely a cop should have something better to put on. After all, he spent most of his time in the high-rent district. A person would think he'd have something appropriate to put on for an afternoon in suburbia.

Undercover, of course. On the job.

All the same, if he drew too much attention to himself he couldn't blend into the neighborhood enough to see who else might be slipping envelopes out of mailboxes. He couldn't get the chance to ask Jenny what she was doing with Frank's mail in her pocket.

So far, there hadn't been any action on a victim with the first name of Frank, which relieved Nick. Baker was going through Jenny's bank-account figures to see if there was any unaccounted-for money coming in, and they were waiting for her credit-card statements to verify overspending. Which meant that Nick didn't have much time to try and ferret out somebody else.

He still couldn't believe that Jenny had offered him the perfect opportunity to spend time at her house, especially after he'd gone to such lengths to try and come up with something himself. If he was lucky, he could stretch out the afternoon to late evening. Between fuel injectors, beer, chili, talking, he figured he could get her pretty relaxed.

For the case. So he could collar whoever was doing this and get the hell off dingdong duty.

Even so, he couldn't figure out what to wear. He didn't want to go back in his workday outfit. Those jeans were becoming his trademark. On the other hand, it was counterproductive to try and fix an engine in an Armani suit.

Damn, the apartment was hot today. He was sweating and it wasn't even much past noon. It would be hard to get Jenny to relax if he couldn't. Not like the other day. Standing before his closet in his briefs, Nick found himself shaking his head. He was still baffled. Uneasy. He couldn't figure how he'd come to fall asleep on Jenny Lake's couch. What's more, he couldn't understand how she'd managed to treat the whole thing as if it were normal.

Nick Barnes didn't fall asleep on the job. He certainly didn't fall asleep in front of strangers. That left you open somehow. Vulnerable to attack. And Nick had never to his knowledge let his guard down enough to be in that kind of danger. He just figured, standing there looking through clothes that suddenly looked ill-fitting and strange, that the tight discomfort in his chest was from the heat, from the pressure of the job, from having to go back to that five-by-five icebox on wheels in the morning.

That tight ache in his gut at the sight of windblown black hair and huge green eyes was one thing. The constricting emptiness in his chest at the idea of never getting the chance to fall asleep on Jenny's couch again was quite another. Nick didn't allow that kind of thing.

He only ached to get out of that apartment and on with the job.

Looking over the shirt he held out before him, he shook his head and threw it in the corner.

Nick pulled into Jenny's drive on the stroke of two. The neighborhood was quiet, with only a few kids skateboarding down the block and Todd entertaining a knot of teens by his car. Nick had waved as he'd driven by, and Todd had waved back, signaling his approval of Nick's vintage GTO.

His own car, Nick noticed, was a late-model Firebird. Red hot and bad, the stamp of an overprivileged suburban youth. Nick had seen the boy's father laboring over the surgically manicured lawn and the guy didn't look quite as nonchalant as his freewheeling son. Maybe the gift of expensive new cars wasn't as easy for the old man as the son would believe.

There were a lot of secrets behind those fancy doors; a lot of problems that never came to light until the lawyer or the police showed up. Nick figured that Jenny was probably more in the majority with her money problems than either she or the brass over in Clayton thought. It was just a matter of finding out if it was Mr. Sellers or Mrs. Bailey or maybe Mr. Hobbs, with all those medical bills to pay, who was sneaking envelopes out of boxes.

Or, like McGrady thought, Jenny.

The compact wasn't in the driveway when Nick pulled up. He decided Jenny must have left it in the garage overnight. Pulling out the bag he'd decided to carry his work clothes in, he opened the door and stepped out.

Across the street, a curtain slid back from the window. Nick saw it and grimaced. Well, he thought as he mounted the steps to Jenny's porch, can't have everything. He guessed he should have known he wasn't going to have a nice, comfortable afternoon with Jenny without an audience.

At least the old battle-ax wouldn't get in the front door for a helping of chili. The last thing he needed was a confrontation with the police chief's aunt. He couldn't even imagine what they could do to pay him back that would be worse than what he was doing now.

Nick opened the screen door and balanced it against his hip. It sounded awfully quiet around here. Usually Jenny's kids came barreling out of that door at the vaguest sign of life. Nick raised his hand to knock and prepared himself for anything.

Well, almost anything.

Before his hand even hit the door, it swung open. A good thirty people crowded into the foyer with balloons and party hats. The minute they saw sunlight, they began jumping up and down.

"Surprise!"

Chapter 6

Swinging the car around the corner, Jenny checked her watch again. Damn. It was already ten after two. She just couldn't believe she had a sister-in-law who insisted on running out of gas within twenty minutes of the time Nick was supposed to show up. A sister-in-law who was also pregnant, which made turning down the mercy mission nigh unto criminal.

Of course Kate had been penitent. And of course she'd had to make it a point to notice that Jenny was wearing makeup and nice slacks. The kids had just egged her on by mentioning the housecleaning binge.

So, now Jenny was ten minutes late, and Nick was probably sitting out on the porch getting hot and crabby. Kate was on her way back to her house in the city, filled with gasoline and gossip. Sometimes Jenny couldn't believe how screwed up her life could get.

His car was in the driveway. At least, she guessed it was his car. It looked like something he'd drive, an old '68 midnight-blue Goat that had been painted and shined to a gleam. A lot of power under an understated hood.

Jenny caught herself grinning. Kind of like its owner, she couldn't help but think. Pulling up behind his car, she switched hers off and waited for it to stop chugging. And then she went about looking for Nick.

He wasn't on the porch swing, waiting in that languid slouch that had taken her breath that first day. He wasn't pacing the yard, and he didn't have a key to her house. She could always ask Mrs. Warner where he went, but Jenny wasn't really sure she had the patience today to put up with all that disapproval. She just hoped Nick hadn't gone across to ask after her. Mrs. Warner would just as soon lock him up in the basement as say hello. Then nobody would see him again, Mrs. Warner would have all the ice cream she wanted and her nephew, the police chief, would end up dragging her away.

"Mom, are we going in?"

Jenny shook her head. Too much Stephen King, she decided, and opened the doors.

She couldn't see a note on the front door. She didn't see any sign at all that Nick had been there—except for his car. Maybe she should go across and see if Mrs. Warner was fixing any extra lunches. . . .

Jenny had her key out and aimed at the door when suddenly it opened. She jumped back. Emma shrieked. The crowd in Jenny's foyer yelled surprise. Caught right in the center, Nick just lifted his beer can in salute.

"You didn't tell me it was your birthday."

"You knew!" Kate accused the minute she showed up.

Still struggling with the frustration of wanting to kill her family for being so thoughtful, Jenny could do no more than shake her head. "No, I didn't. Trust me."

She already had a party hat on, and had been handed a rum-and-Coke by her brother Tim. The house echoed with the tumult of twelve Gardner grandchildren and the babble of seven Gardner siblings plus spouses as they finished setting up the party they'd brought along with them. Squeezed in among all the relatives and looking for all the world like a man caught in a crowded elevator with a lot of strangers, Nick sipped at his beer and flinched at the noise.

"You did, too, know!" Kate insisted, her voice rising accordingly. "You were dressed up and your house was clean."

"So what?"

Now more than one of her family scowled. "So when was the last time that happened?"

Joey and Claire had made it a point to come in from out of town for her birthday. Jenny really appreciated all the care that had gone into their surprise. She just wished they'd done it on a different day. Or better yet, that they hadn't done it at all.

Thirty. She hadn't really thought she'd react so badly to it but she was. She didn't want to face the passing years anymore. Their scope had grown too limited of late. And here was her family rubbing her face in it.

On the other hand, she had to admit that she was getting more than a kick out of watching her brothers' reactions to Nick. He'd worn his hair back again, and with the polo shirt he wore the Marine tattoo was amply visible. Jenny's brothers were all religiously white-collar and obsessively protective. It didn't take much to know that Nick wasn't exactly what they wanted to see show up at Jenny's house.

The women, on the other hand, reacted more to the scar at Nick's eyebrow, his out-of-line nose and the biceps that sported that tattoo.

"So," Joey said, throwing an arm around Nick's shoulder. "Are you dating our little girl here?"

His little girl was four years older than he.

"He's fixing my car," Jenny spoke up. Poor Nick was looking more and more bemused all the time.

"Fixing your car?" Tim demanded. "Why didn't you ask us?"

"Because the last time one of you clowns tried to fix my car, it ended up in the shop for two weeks."

"Do you play whiffle ball?" Joey asked Nick.

Jenny groaned.

Nick stared at Joey as if his hair were on fire. "Whiffle ball?"

"Family tradition," Joey assured him. "On birthdays."

The other boys nodded right alongside.

"We're gonna go out and play later. Wanna come on out?"

"Yeah," Nick shrugged, still unsure. "Sure."

"This is a special game," Joey continued, taking another long drink of beer without taking his eyes off Nick. "For Jenny's thirtieth birthday. We figure we'd better let her play before she's too old to lift a bat."

Jenny answered instinctively. "Eat snakes, Joey."

"Just trying to make your friend at home, Jen."

"Eat *big* snakes."

Jenny knew better than to explain. She'd been through this too many times already. The famous Gardner manhood-and-patriotism test. Anybody who seriously dated one of the Gardner girls had first had to pass the whiffle-ball test, the theory being if they could handle a bat they could be trusted to handle a sister. She just took a long drink of her rum-and-Coke.

"Feel free to run for your life," she grinned limply. "Nothing is more terrifying than a Gardner-clan rally in full swing."

"No," Nick said with a private sparkle in his eye that more than one of the Gardners caught, "I think I'll stay for cake and ice cream."

"Busman's holiday," she warned.

Joey had just detached himself to get another beer. Hearing that, he turned. "What do you mean?"

Jen took great pleasure in telling him. "Nick is the ice cream man in the neighborhood."

Jenny wasn't the only one to laugh at Joey's stunned reaction.

Actually, Jenny had to admit that the party went off better than she'd feared. She loved her family, and usually couldn't wait to get together with them. They were a noisy bunch, preferring to express their love in a bickering, challenging fashion some people wouldn't recognize. She even liked the four in-laws in the bunch, three wives and one husband. All had ended up passing the whiffle-ball challenge and now played mean family sports up at the Michigan cottage where the family vacationed every year. Usually Jenny couldn't ask any more than having her family around her again.

Today, all she'd wanted was Nick.

At first she'd been really worried how he'd deal with all the nonsense. Joey's challenge was just the beginning of the outrageous ribbing, and Jenny was afraid Nick wouldn't know how to take it. She'd been relieved to see him hold his own with that dry, quiet humor of his catching everybody off guard.

Of course it hadn't hurt at all when Emma had trotted into the kitchen where everyone was gathered to take Nick by the hand to introduce him to her cousins. The astonishment among the gathered family had been genuine and heartfelt. When all the questioning gazes turned on Jenny for suitable explanation, all she'd been able to do was shrug.

Ah, and then there was the whiffle-ball game. Jenny had had a sneaking suspicion all along that those biceps and triceps weren't just there for decoration. The first time Nick stepped up to bat she had her proof. Joey lofted the ball in over the plate and then hit the dirt when it almost took his head off on the return trip.

Jenny knew for a fact that she wasn't the only woman on the street, much less the family, who stopped whatever she was doing when Nick stepped up to bat. He had such a nice stance, loose and fluid, with those arms and shoulders rippling and that little tush wiggling as he set up. She saw Claire smile more than once, and Kate, swollen with her third child, rolled her eyes from the sidelines.

By the time she snuck away from the party to quiet her newest niece up in her bedroom, Jenny had to admit that she felt happier than she had in months. Her house was noisy and full. Her family was home. And Nick had gotten a grand slam off Joey and ended up sharing a beer and views on the Cardinals. There was a symmetry to her day that had been missing for too long—even if it had to happen on her thirtieth birthday.

The telegram came amid the horseshoe tournament. All of the Gardners were in the backyard laying down bets, and Jenny had disappeared somewhere. Since Nick had been corralled by Emma to "see something" (her cat riding in the handlebar basket of her tricycle out in the front yard), he was the one who ended up with the job of handing Jenny her message.

He made a quick recon of the backyard, only to see that the competition had gotten fierce. Two of the men were pitching, and three were wrestling by the swing set. The women were taking bets on both ventures. No Jenny. When asked for ideas, Kevin just shrugged.

"Probably playing with babies," he said and headed back out, purloined cookie in hand.

Nick was sure that answer made sense to someone. He hadn't seen any babies, but then that wasn't something Nick watched out for as a rule. He took another quick look around the first floor just to find kid debris and diaper bags, and decided it was time to breach the second floor.

He climbed the first step shaking his head. Nobody at work would believe this day. Nick Barnes surrounded by kids— screaming, shrilling, laughing, fighting kids. Nick Barnes stuck smack in the middle of suburbia's answer to the storming of the Bastille. Nick Barnes not scratching and kicking to get free.

To be honest, he kind of liked Jenny's family. They acted a lot like the cops he knew, carefully cloaking their camaraderie beneath some of the most elaborate insults he'd ever heard. Outrageous to a fault and protective as hell. He could just imagine what Jenny had gone through when she was dating.

He could imagine, having heard the way they tap-danced around the subject of her ex-husband, what she'd gone through with her divorce.

They were a family that had judged him quickly and then cavalierly set their judgment aside and welcomed him like a sibling within the space of a well-hit whiffle ball.

He shook his head again and found himself amazed when he realized he was smiling.

Nick found her in the first room he searched. It must have been her room, all feminine clutter and refrigerator art, the big four-poster bed covered in a peach, gray and black comforter as thick as snowfall and the bedside table topped with books and stuffed toys and clumsy art projects.

She sat before the window, a nimbus of sunlight outlining her and turning her hair to smoke. Curled into an old rocker, she gently rocked back and forth, her head down, her finger caught in the hand of the tiny baby nestled in her lap, her eyes wide as she talked to the child. Entire conversations, as if the baby were answering, her own reactions magnified on her mobile features. Her smile was a radiant one, as if the sunlight suffused her as well, her eyes liquid and soft looking down on the child.

Nick saw her and stopped. A great silence filled him. There was nothing more one could add to the scene, the perfection as rare as a madonna by a master. And then he noticed what could kill him.

That face, so exquisitely beautiful as she smiled and sang down to the baby, that face that radiated a joy Nick had never known, had tears streaming unchecked down it.

Struck, shaken, he stood without moving, unable to take his eyes from her, unable to break the fearful spell she was weaving. And then, just as Nick was going to leave—to run—she looked up.

"Sometimes," she admitted in a voice that spoke of cherished secrets and wonders, "I forget just what I have."

Maybe it was the way the light glinted off those tears, but Nick thought that her smile had a hollow edge to it, a place missing. She smiled for what she dreamed as much as for what she had, he thought. And that was why she refused to apologize for the tears.

The baby reached again for her, a blind, uncoordinated movement with hands so small they seemed unreal. Nick saw her turn back, instinctively feeling the communication and returning her attention to the bundle in her lap.

"A . . . telegram," he offered diffidently, feeling the usurper in this woman's room, this place of motherhood and belonging. "It just came."

Jenny's head came up, fear briefly flaring. Old superstitions reared and died. Just as quickly she rose to her feet, carrying the baby with her as easily as if it had been a part of her, and approached Nick.

He handed the telegram to her. She responded by handing Nick the baby.

"Don't..." But before he could protest, a set of wide, unfocused blue eyes were turned his way and that tiny, insistent hand was seeking him out.

Nick looked up, instantly panicked, searching for help. Guidance. Deliverance. Jenny was already tearing into her message.

What did you do with a kid this small? he wondered, turning his attention back to the weight that seemed so ungainly in his hands. What if he dropped it or hurt it? Weren't you supposed to hold its head some kind of way? Couldn't you break its neck or something? And they had that soft spot. If you touched it wrong, the kid could die. Quickly he looked around for someplace to set it, thinking that ten pounds had never felt so heavy. He wasn't sure where Jenny had found it, but there wasn't any sign of where to put it back.

When she laughed, he jumped. She looked up, quickly brushing leftover tears away with the back of her hand and brandishing the telegram.

"Could a person have better parents?" she demanded with glee, the momentary loss polished over with her news. "'Jenny,'" she read. "'Stop. You're getting older and we're not. Stop. We love you almost enough to come home for your birthday. Stop. Love. Stop. Mom and Dad.' What warmth, what sincerity."

"Come home?" Nick echoed, holding the baby out a little as if in offering. Jenny didn't seem to notice.

"They're in Beijing," she acknowledged. "Isn't that neat?"

"Sure. Now, will you...uh..."

With another laugh that looked suspiciously superior, Jenny took the baby back and fitted it against her hip like a tight end running back a football. Nick looked at it and wondered just how women managed to do that without dropping the kid. And how the kid managed to look so comfortable. Jenny started swaying back and forth and the baby cooed.

"Not familiar with the equipment?" she asked, that laughter still lingering in her eyes in a way that lightened her whole face. She didn't seem to think she needed to explain the swaying. Nick wondered if she even knew she was doing it.

He shrugged his answer, trying to find something to do with his hands now that he had nothing to fill them. "It's not really my line of work."

"I think that's what you call an understatement, Nick," she grinned. "You looked suspiciously like a whore in church standing there with that baby." For a moment she studied him, indecipherable emotions skittering across the soft fields of her eyes. Then it seemed to Nick that she actually braced herself, even though her smile was brighter than ever. "Just what are you doing on an ice cream truck?" she demanded, finally slowing to a stop.

"I told you," he answered, trying his best to sound sincere. "Marco needed some help. And... well, I like kids a lot, ya know?"

Now the smile looked suspiciously self-satisfied. "Yeah, and I like tuna-noodle casserole."

He was getting all set to protest, wanting to say something complimentary about the baby that even now was wriggling unnoticed in Jenny's grip, when he saw that it wouldn't do any good. Kind of like telling God you believed in him with your fingers crossed. She had him pegged.

"All right," he admitted, eyes briefly down as he searched desperately for plan B. "I owed him some money. I was available and he decided it would be really funny to watch me out on that wagon with *all those kids*." Well, stick as close to the truth as you can. At least he could give that lie some weight.

Still supremely delighted, Jenny nodded. "Well, if it makes you feel any better, you're handling it like a pro."

Feeling absurdly complimented, Nick gave her a stiff little bow in return. "Thank you."

Finally tiring of all the adult conversation, the baby voiced an opinion of her own. Jenny moved with fluid comfort and swung the baby neatly up into her arms.

"This is Amanda Jane," she said, her eyes on the baby's, her finger stroking the dewy cheek. "Tim and Nancy's little girl. Doesn't she look just like Tim?"

Nick actually looked, but came to his usual conclusion. "She looks like a baby."

Jenny offered a scowl. "Romantic. Well, I'd better take her to her mom. She's ready to eat, and I'm afraid all I can offer is a dry well."

Flashing Nick a more distant smile, she shoved the telegram in a pocket and headed for the stairs. Before Nick turned, he got a look at the other corner of her room and bit back a grin, his attention suddenly stolen away from kids. As a cop, he lived for evidence, and he'd just spotted some that belied a lot of Jenny's breezy nonchalance. There, by the closet, was a pile of discarded blouses.

Claire didn't look in the least bit happy. With an apron tied around her khaki-silk jumpsuit she was washing up the barbe-cue dishes and sharing the leftovers with Jenny, a custom kept since childhood when the two of them had been sole executors of kitchen detail.

"I can't believe you allow him in the house," she snapped, her voice quiet just in case the men out in the driveway would hear them. The fuel injectors were in the process of being re-placed, all her brothers kibitzing.

Taking a deep breath, Jenny took stock of her younger sis-ter. Taller than Jen, slim and professional-looking, the real working woman. The redhead in the crowd, Claire had spent a nervous few years wondering whether her brothers were telling the truth when they told her she was adopted. Claire was the rebel, the one who couldn't tolerate being compared to Jenny, who had made it her life's work to be different than the older, resented, revered sister.

And now that sister had betrayed a sacred trust by rebelling herself.

"He owns a suit," Jenny countered, wondering at the out-rage in Claire's eyes. Claire hadn't liked the Jerk any better.

"He sells drugs," Claire snapped, shoving a dish into the rack with enough force to set the glasses to tinkling.

Taking a quick look to make sure they didn't have any eavesdroppers, Jenny leaned against the counter and faced her sister. "Who've you been talking to? Mrs. Warner?"

Claire couldn't keep the betrayal from her mirror-green eyes. "I haven't paid attention to Mrs. Warner since she told me she thought Tim was working for the KGB. I was talking to Barb."

Jenny's heart sank. Barb. The woman whose word didn't need a Bible. She wondered if Claire would ever believe her now.

"He isn't."

Her frustration bubbling over, Claire came to a halt and faced Jenny's challenge. "Then who is he? And why is he selling ice cream when he goes to law school?" That sent her off on another tirade. "*Law school*, for God's sake. Don't you learn your lessons?"

"Claire," Jenny said in a carefully controlled voice, holding her sister's hot gaze with deliberate eyes. "He's here so I can help find out if he's legitimate. He's here because the police asked me to invite him over. I agreed. But since I've gotten to know him I've decided to help prove that he's innocent."

"Innocent."

Jenny nodded. "I don't think it's possible. Not Nick."

One hand resting on a slim hip, Claire glared. "That's what they said about Ted Bundy, baby. How can you take that kind of a chance around my godchild?"

Now Jenny's eyes sparked a little on their own. "Around *my* children, Claire. Do you really think I'd hurt them?"

For a minute the challenge was fought in silence. Neither woman had practice backing down. Neither could have loved the other more. Laughter drifted in from the front, the men's having the ring of dirty jokes and locker rooms, children's squealing with excitement. In the living room Amanda Jane was mewling to her mother for more lunch and outside one of the neighborhood jocks was revving an engine. In the kitchen, the wall clock ticked.

It was finally Claire who backed down. "No," she admitted with a hesitant grin. "You're the official poster child for

Mother's Day. That's why I couldn't understand it when Barb admitted what you were doing.''

Jenny nodded, not expecting apology or explanation, just glad for the returned equilibrium. Along with the excitement in her family, came the fights. All that energy, all that emotion, all those opinions. Fights flared and then died as fast as sun storms, but they bothered Jenny more than they did most.

"Besides," Jenny offered with a wry grin of her own. "You said it. He's in law school." She was turning away when a thought came to her and she gave her sister one last glance. "Although I would buy tickets to watch him swing a bat."

Claire's answering laugh assured her that in at least that they were both agreed. Taking one final moment before returning to the dishes, Claire bobbed her head just a little, her way of emphasizing a sensitive point.

"I just wanted to be sure you hadn't—" even in the silence of the kitchen she faltered "—sold out."

Her arms full of bowls to be washed, Jenny smiled for her sister, knowing what her answer meant. Knowing now how worried Claire had been. "I'd love to be married again, Sassy," she admitted, deliberately using the name the family had long ago pinned on their individualist. "I'd dearly adore to have more babies and stay home and knit." She saw Claire's inadvertent wince and her smile broadened. "But all I *need* is enough money to take care of my children. If I could get the Jerk to come through, I'd spend the rest of my life working overtime and be thankful for small favors. I'm not the kind of girl to court a man for his stability."

"At least not anymore," Claire agreed, her eyes purposefully swinging out toward the party in the driveway.

Jenny laughed. She couldn't wait to see what kind of man Claire finally settled on. If she didn't miss her bet, Claire would be more surprised than she.

"Want to come test out your high-performance vehicle?" Nick asked only minutes later, appearing at the door in his favorite Deadhead T-shirt and jeans. He was wiping the grease from his hands and brushing the perspiration from his forehead with his forearm, one foot into the house, one hip holding the door open.

Jenny saw Claire inadvertently stiffen and smiled. "You mean one of my brothers hasn't electrocuted himself on the car yet?"

"You can't electrocute yourself on a car engine," Nick assured her dryly.

Jenny shook her head. "They could." Quickly drying her hands on the apron Claire still wore, she followed him out the door.

Night again, even while the sun was shining. Jenny could smell it as she followed Nick, and it made her want to curl up and purr. As a matter of fact, she was enjoying everything about this walk down the drive. The view was fine, the scent and sound of his swinging walk, the one that still seemed so alien to the sidewalks and zoysia around here. He walked more like one of the Jets from *West Side Story*, loose and agile as if watching for trouble, as if ready for anything.

The only thing waiting for him were her brothers, leaning over the hood of the compact and looking like a high-school shop class. Jenny had to admit that she hadn't seen anything to match it in a long time. She hadn't had as much fun as she had this afternoon, licking barbecue sauce from her fingers and sharing a beer with Nick as he argued baseball and local politics.

This was the real world, she thought. Beer and chicken and diaper bags in the living room. Whiffle-ball games in the street with a family that yelled and fought and laughed all in one breath. A man who looked like sin and didn't know how to talk down to a three-year-old. Jenny didn't know what the Jerk thought he could get out of that fancy address in Ladue, but she bet he never sat in a lawn chair in his backyard and bet on how many times he could throw popcorn up and get it in his mouth.

And the more she thought about it, the more she realized that she was the lucky one, after all.

She should have known it couldn't last. There was just something about her luck that prevented her from holding onto an optimistic mood for more than twenty minutes without disillusionment.

It wasn't the ride in the car. That went well. Jenny drove, and every one of her brothers did their best to pack in along with Nick to make sure that the two of them didn't do anything suspect on the ride. They ended up looking like one of those circus acts, the kind with all the clowns piling out of the little fire engine. Jenny laughed so hard that she killed the car three times at a stoplight. And of course, heard about it from not only the brat pack in the back but from Nick, who had proved an uncanny knack for meeting her family word-for-word in the insult-and-tease category.

By the time the car was officially pronounced fit and the families began gathering their paraphernalia to leave, Jenny had almost managed to forget that the electric bill still waited to be paid, that she had to get up at four in the morning to go into work, and that she'd vowed never to develop an interest in Nick because of his law-school aspirations.

That seemed to be the mistake. Because when she and Nick stood by Tom's car wishing him and Diane a safe trip home, Tom suddenly reached into the glove compartment.

"Oh, hey, Nick, I forgot to give you this."

When he turned back to them, he held a card between his fingers like a conjurer. Tom was the entrepreneur in the family, the one who kept his finger on financial pulses and prided himself on his money-making acumen.

"Like I said," he was telling Nick, who accepted the card. "This guy has done well by me. Sharp mind, quick on the move when you need it. He'll start you at any level you want and grow with you."

"Thanks," Nick acknowledged with a nod and a quick shake of the hand. "I appreciate the help."

Tom just shrugged with that big, hungry smile of his. "You'll need a place to squirrel away those fat fees when you start getting them, counselor."

Nick nodded, a little smile lighting his features. "Your next arrest is on the house. Just try and wait until I get out in June."

Jenny barely heard the rest of the salutations. She stood on the sticky asphalt of her driveway feeling the heat take her in waves, fighting the sudden nausea that swept her.

Counselor. All those fat fees.

She wanted to run. She wanted to shut the door and never come out, hide herself again in the mountain of minutiae it took to raise children so that she couldn't possibly have the energy to look at another man.

She just couldn't go through this again. She couldn't watch another man suck her dry and then pitch her on the trash pile.

Suddenly she didn't care that Nick was holding Emma's hand, or that he played the best game of whiffle ball the family had ever been witness to. She just wanted him gone before he hurt her. Before he hurt Kevin and Emma.

Standing out there with Kevin and Emma and Nick, looking for the world like a real family waving relatives goodbye, Jenny couldn't help but think that she had actually been lulled into envisioning something this domestic. She should have known better. She'd been the only one fending for her family for two years and that just wasn't going to change.

At least, not with Nick it wasn't.

Chapter 7

"**W**e have a new victim!"

Printout held high, Baker charged into the office sounding more like a game-show host than a civil servant.

"And who is the lucky contestant?" Nick asked, secretly dreading that his first name would be Frank.

Coming to a halt before Nick's desk, Baker took a moment to officially read the name.

"Mr. Melvin Waterson," she announced. "And he promises never to leave his mail in the box again."

Nick plucked the paper from her hand and read the details for himself. "What a good boy. Too bad he didn't think of this before they cashed four hundred dollars' worth of checks against his account."

Grinning with anticipation, Baker leaned close. "I saw McGrady in the building," she warned. "I imagine he's going to tell you to step up the investigation."

"I step any higher," Nick retorted without looking up, "I'm gonna look like the Rockettes. Which reminds me—" his smile was purely lascivious "—get out your steno pad, little girl, and prepare to sit on my lap. We have some work to do."

Baker gave him the glare he deserved. "Don't practice for that fancy law office on my time, chump."

Nick grinned. "Just think," he taunted her. "This time next year, that'll be *Mister* Chump."

She grinned right back. "A pleasure."

Finding the top of Nick's desk more comfortable than any of the chairs, Baker crossed her legs and handed Nick the file she'd compiled on Jenny.

"What are your thoughts?" Nick asked, paging through bank and credit-card statements.

Baker never batted an eye. "That all men are slime."

Nick slowly scanned numbers, knowing how much it cost to live in St. Louis County and seeing what Jenny brought home. She was definitely walking a delicate balance here. He also spotted something else amid the charge accounts, and checked again. "Have we learned anything about this particular slime?" he asked.

Baker had been saving her best smile for this answer. "That he has a nasty speeding habit. In a red Porsche, of all things."

Nick clucked. "So easy to spot."

Baker nodded. "Patrol said to say thank you. They haven't had so much fun in ages. They especially enjoyed the useless threats."

"How many?"

"Four, to be exact."

Now Nick smiled. "He should be sufficiently softened up for a little soul-saving message in another week or so. Don't you think?"

"If he's not broke."

"He'd better not be. He owes his wife a lot of money. And he's about to find out that he's gonna owe her more."

"Barnes," Baker said with just enough caution to tell Nick she meant it. "I really appreciate the blow you're striking for divorced mothers everywhere."

"But?"

"Do you think you should be doing it for her?"

Nick looked up to see the carefully camouflaged concern in Baker's eyes. They had been partners for almost two years, wasting hours on stakeouts, tap-dancing through undercover operations and just slogging through paperwork. Baker knew him. She was the best friend he had. Nick figured that the least she deserved was an honest explanation.

"All right, Chris," he conceded, setting the file down before her. "I don't want it to be Jenny. I've developed a soft spot for her and that oddball little family of hers. I don't want to pull the rug out from under her feet when I see how hard she's working to keep it there."

"What else?" Baker demanded. Leaning forward she tapped the bank statements with a polished nail. "She's living right at the limit, Nick. She's been putting money into her checking account that doesn't correspond with paychecks. Usually in amounts of about a hundred dollars or so; and if you'll look close, she shoved another two hundred in just yesterday. It's not lottery winnings, and she doesn't belong to any office pools. Where's it coming from?"

"I'll find out," Nick promised, looking back down at the evidence Baker had so painstakingly compiled. "I have a gut feeling on this one, Baker."

"Are you sure you're not thinking lower than that?"

Nick's head came up. He saw that his partner's concern was honest, a cop's concern for his objectivity. And well she should have been concerned, he couldn't help but think. He wasn't objective. Hadn't been since that moment when he'd found Jenny in the rocking chair.

He'd spent the last two nights tossing and turning, waking from vague dreams that had wandered through long, empty hallways and cold rooms. Looking, walking, never knowing just what he wanted but knowing that he couldn't find it.

He'd spent yesterday compiling snapshots of neighborhood joggers, strollers, visitors—anyone who would have the same chance Jenny had at the mailboxes.

He sat here now trying his best to deny the evidence Baker had brought him, trying to find some way to prove that no matter what, Jenny wasn't the one he was after. If Frank had been the victim this time he might have wavered, maybe crumbled in his conviction. But Frank was safe. Jenny was safe. And Nick still walked silent halls in his dreams, looking for the way out.

"We only have one person's word that she saw Jenny at a mailbox," he argued, his voice sharper than he'd intended.

Baker wasn't one to back down. Especially to Nick. It was what made them such good partners. "And a disaster of a bank statement, three credit cards bobbing right up at the limit and no foreseeable help from the ex-husband." Leaning very close now, Baker faced him nose-to-nose, her chocolate eyes sincere. "I think it stinks, too, Barnes. But if she's doing it, she's gonna be collared."

Nick nodded. "If she's doing it, Baker, I'll snap on the cuffs myself. But until then, I'm not counting out any of the other people I see wander around that neighborhood. Now, are you gonna help me or not?"

Straightening, Baker offered him a bright smile that betrayed why so many of the cops jostled for first place in her line of suitors. "My pleasure, *Mister* Chump."

"Don't you realize that this is illegal?" Jenny demanded. "We could both go to jail."

She was seated at her kitchen table, a stack of envelopes piled before her. She tapped at them with a finger, trying her best to keep her temper. This was all getting to be too much. If she didn't stop it right now, somebody could get into real trouble. She was just amazed that old Mrs. Warner hadn't caught on a long time ago, with that eagle eye of hers always focused out the front window.

"They really wouldn't put us in jail," Kevin argued without much conviction. "Would they?"

Jenny looked at her son, who wore a smart-alecky grin tugging at the corners of his mouth, and she wanted to scream. That was just the way the Jerk had looked when she'd told him she knew he was cheating on his law-school exams. Nothing could really happen to me, he was saying. I'm above all that. I'm too handsome, too popular, too charismatic. For the Jerk, it was still working. The last thing Jenny wanted for Kevin was to develop that kind of attitude.

It was time for some real threats here.

"Kevin," she said, struggling to keep her voice even. "You have been taking people's mail out of their mailboxes. That is

a crime. They put people in jail for that. The police are looking for someone right now who's doing that kind of thing, and
when they catch them, they're going to put them in jail. Would
you *like* jail?"

Wrong tack. He screwed up his face as if she'd just asked him
to kiss a girl. "No."

She nodded, lifting the envelopes she'd pulled out from under his bed. "Well, then, this time you can put them back."

"Aw, Mom," he whined, squirming in his seat. "I was
playing mailman. I needed some letters to deliver to Buffy."

Jenny supposed she should have been thankful. At least he
didn't want to play doctor with Buffy. That would probably
come later.

"That's why God invented paper and pencil, darling," she
said instead. "You make your own envelopes. Now, after
you've put these back," she went on, "you can sit in your room
for half an hour or so and think about how you're not getting
television today or tomorrow, and that if I catch you doing this
again you won't see a lit screen until you take computer class in
high school. Do I make myself clear?"

Now came Kevin's version of the pout. "Dad wouldn't make
me do that."

Two, three, four, five . . . Dad wouldn't come to any of his
soccer games, either, but Kevin managed to conveniently forget that at moments like this.

"I asked you a question," Jenny said with great restraint.

He hung his head, knowing how very much Jenny hated the
TV time he put in, and how close he usually skated to losing it
anyway. "Yeah."

"Pardon?"

"Yes, ma'am."

Doing her best to keep the smile off her face, Jenny handed
over the evidence. Kevin walked to the door as if the guillotine
waited on the other side.

Jenny probably would have gone easier on him if she felt
better. But today she was making yet another stand at the lawyer's office, trying to get services she couldn't immediately pay
for. She figured that if she could get Mr. Whittier to get the Jerk
to cough up a little more money, she could pay *him* off as well

as her charge accounts. She might even have enough left for school clothes for herself.

She had to admit that the birthday party had been a more generous gesture than she'd imagined. After everyone had taken off she had found several packets of money in her purse from brothers and sisters who knew of her pride, her need to stand on her own feet, but her need nonetheless. The total had reached a little over two hundred dollars, with some gift certificates thrown in from Kate who had insisted that Jenny be prevented from spending all her birthday money on something practical.

So she'd managed to pay off her electric bill, after all, and had treated herself to a baby-sitter, a walk in the mall and the first nice new purse she'd bought in two years. It had been the best present of all.

The problem was, of course, that she was stuffing her purse in preparation to go see Mr. Whittier, and confrontations about the Jerk just gave her indignation.

Suddenly unsure again, Jenny checked her watch. She had time. She didn't have to be in Clayton until three. Still the butterflies collected, unwanted companions, her little reminders of all the times she'd faced humiliation in lawyers' offices over the last two years. She'd rather go to the dentist and have all her teeth pulled. It felt better.

When the doorbell rang, Jenny pounced on it. Anything to take her mind from her impending appointment. Her heels clacking on the foyer parquet, she straightened the skirt she'd donned for the meeting and wondered who wanted her.

Kevin hadn't been outside very long. She hoped Frank Patterson hadn't caught him slipping his overdue mail in his box and was even now standing on the porch holding her recalcitrant son by one ear. She couldn't have had such luck.

It wasn't Frank. It was Nick.

It seemed to Jenny that he swept all the summer heat in before him. She didn't remember it being quite so stifling outside, so that just the touch of the humid air took her breath. She didn't remember enjoying the feel of it so much, either.

"After Sunday, I figured you'd stay as far away from here as you could," Jenny said, suddenly at a loss.

Nick smiled, shoving his hands into his back pockets and making Jenny think of a truant teenager. A sexy truant teenager. He'd worn another old T-shirt today, this one boasting the original Rolling Stones logo, and another pair of impossibly erotic jeans, the glint of the gold belt buckle pulling her eyes in objectionable directions.

"Takes more than a little whiffle ball to scare me away," he assured her.

Jenny looked up to see a wry glint in those whiskied eyes. She saw the sum of the hours they'd shared, the simple pleasures of an afternoon barbecue, and it warmed her even more. Why couldn't she keep her mind on the fact that this man was climbing onto the Jerk Express? All she could seem to concentrate on was the attraction that warmed those incredible eyes, the seductive smell of him, the way he stood with one leg up on the doorsill like he owned the place.

"How's the car running?" he asked, bringing her abruptly back.

"Oh, fine," Jenny said with a distracted nod. "Just fine. Thanks." She was letting the summer in, the air-conditioning out. She was flushed and hot and had to get ready to face the lions, and still she didn't want to move.

Nick was nodding, his eyes never straying from hers, his smile at once suggestive and sweet. Jenny couldn't pull her eyes away, either. His dimples were back, and suddenly her tongue was restless against the roof of her mouth.

"I was on my way back home and I thought I'd check in," he was saying with a quick nod over his shoulder. The white truck waited at the curb. Several teens had gathered, and the activity was drawing attention from across the street.

"Looks like you've brought your business with you," Jenny offered diffidently, hand still on the door, undecided, increasingly uncomfortable.

Nick took a look and grimaced. "Pied Piper, that's me," he acknowledged dryly.

"The teens have really started coming out of the woodwork," she offered, an eye to the back of his head before he turned back to her, her expression torn. She didn't want to ask. Didn't want the answer. And yet he was turning back to her.

"I have the only game in town," he grinned, and her heart sank.

Unable anymore to meet that inviting gaze, she let her own slide away. That was when she noticed the activity behind the tall fence across the street. Mrs. Warner was stirring. It wasn't a good sign. She never ventured from behind that fence without a complaint.

"Biddy at six o'clock," Jenny warned.

Nick swung around again. "My cue to leave. I don't think she wants a Popsicle." Turning back to Jenny, he leveled one of those hesitant smiles on her that threatened her pulse rate. "Before I go, I'll get my payment."

Jenny blinked. "Payment?"

He nodded. "I never got that chili."

Jenny scowled. "You did load up on chicken and potato salad like the famine was coming."

Nick lifted an excepting finger. "But no chili. The offer was for beer and chili."

Out of nowhere, a short, freckled missile shot through the door, sending Nick stumbling to the side.

"Hi, Mom. Hi, Nick." And Kevin was clattering up the stairs before Jenny could greet or recriminate.

Nick looked a little like he'd just been hit by a car. Jenny eased up for a laugh.

"The best way to avoid further punishment is to be unavailable for it," she explained. "A wonderful diversionary tactic."

Nick couldn't help casting a nervous look up the stairs, obviously wondering when the return trip was planned. "Okay. Well, about that chili."

"Mrs. Warner has met the teens and they are hers," Jenny warned, not sure what he was going to say but sure she didn't want to hear it.

Nick turned to see the little knot disperse and Mrs. Warner cast her cold eyes toward his own backside. "Then I'll just make the date. Since you won't have the time to turn me down, that'll be that."

Now it was Jenny's turn to blink. "Date?"

Nick swung back on her, eyes bright, smile broad and certain. "Dinner. I decided that since I didn't get my chili, and I didn't get you a birthday present, I could take care of both problems with one invitation. Friday night, seven o'clock. I'll be here."

"Friday?" she objected, desperately digging for an excuse. "Oh, no, I—"

"Don't have anything to do." He flashed a triumphant smile. "I checked your calendar. The only excuse I'll accept is a note from a doctor stating that both kids have bubonic plague."

Mrs. Warner had reached the sidewalk, her short, plump stride purposeful. Nick cast one last look her way and leveled a parting grin Jenny's way. "Dress up. This is going to be the best damn chili in town."

"But, Nick...!"

She didn't have the chance. Before Jenny could object, he was loping back down the lawn, nodding a greeting to the blustering Mrs. Warner and flashing by her before she could get a single warning off.

Suddenly as Jenny watched, the truck screeched off, bells tinkling like a runaway sleigh, Mrs. Warner staring after empty space, her face still screwed up in righteous indignation. The old lady had barely had time to consider turning her wrath in Jenny's direction before the door to the cedar-sided two-story home shut firmly and the bolt could be heard sliding home.

All in all, Jenny had to admit she had a lot to be grateful to Nick for. After all, she'd spent the last two hours so addled by his sudden invitation that she'd made it clear through her appointment with Mr. Whittier without once wanting to throw up. Even when he insisted that the court schedule was just too tight to expect action anytime soon, that the original financial arrangement was almost impossible to break, that the idea of penalizing the Jerk for potential income was still too alien to conservative St. Louis to consider. Then he'd patted her hand as if she were a six-year-old in the big, fatherly lawyer's office and told her that she could take all the time she needed to pay him off. Especially since he hadn't managed to get her enough money to live on, much less pay off her lawyer.

But now she found herself firmly wedged into rush-hour traffic in downtown Clayton, the near hundred-degree heat and humidity making a joke of her makeup and hairstyle, the sun glinting brutally off the glass-and-steel buildings, the other cars and her own hood. The traffic was moving in spastic fits and starts, and with her windows down in lieu of air-conditioning, Jenny was the beneficiary of clouds of bus exhaust.

Now, she felt as if she were going to throw up.

She was going to have to pay off Mr. Whittier. Then somehow she was going to have to find another lawyer. This was absurd. She knew better than to think that she had no recourse against an ex-husband who refused to live up to his responsibilities just because he was such good friends with the legal community in town.

The Jerk had his office right here in Clayton, a cool, gray-and-mauve haven up about fifteen floors. He was probably looking down at the rusted roof of her car right now and laughing. Try and beat the system, Jenny, he'd said when it had all begun. I'll have you for breakfast. And he had. He'd played the judge like a symphony and walked out with everything but the furniture.

There just had to be something she could do.

That was when she decided that God really had a warped sense of humor. Jenny was in the middle of figuring out ways of breaking through the Fortress Lake when the car died. Again. It happened in the heat. Evidently the manufacturers just weren't used to constant hundred-degree temperatures. It was the only problem she'd had with the car, the heat. Unfortunately, this time she couldn't get it started again.

She tried everything, waiting, pumping the gas, not pumping the gas, cursing, checking fuses, even praying. No one seemed to be home. The rather long line of people behind her wanted to get home, though, and they communicated that with her in no uncertain terms. So when she finally unsnapped her belt and slammed the door open, there was a crowd of people ready and willing to help push her out of the way.

And that was when she looked up.

Somehow, she had managed to kill the car right in front of the Jerk's building. Leaning in to pull out her brand-new purse,

Jenny shut the door without enough force to do damage to locks. She pushed her hair out of her eyes and picked her sticky silk blouse away from her stickier torso. Other than stepping into traffic and flagging down a car phone, she had no other option but to step into the building and ask for help.

She'd rather land facedown in a bucket of mud. Unfortunately, she had a baby-sitter who had to get to her job at the movie theater, two small children waiting for dinner and about forty cents in her purse. Letting loose with several choice expletives that caused a few heads to turn out on that shimmering, stifling street, she stalked into the building.

Inside the cool marble-and-glass foyer, the guard lifted his head. His thin white eyebrows quirked. "Can I help you?"

Just the sudden blast of climate control sapped some of Jenny's rage. "My car died. May I use a phone?"

He inclined his head and lifted the receiver. "Who can I get you?"

"A man named Nick Barnett," she snarled. "He's the one who fixed it."

Now the muscles on either side of his mouth twitched. "Number?"

For a moment Jenny just stared at him. She came to a stop, her shoulders sagging as the realization hit her more forcefully than it should have.

Number. She didn't know. She'd invited Nick into her home, shared enough chemistry to satisfy a college course and been caught anticipating a dinner date with him, and she didn't so much as know his phone number.

For some reason, the realization stunned her. She suddenly felt as if she'd lost her footing. How could she feel as if she knew him so well, when she didn't even have enough of his trust to know his phone number? The only thing she knew was that he lived off Skinker somewhere.

And that Detective Richards claimed that Nick Barnett didn't exist.

If it was possible, Jenny felt even worse.

"Never mind," she smiled limply, dropping her purse and running a hand through her hair. "I have brothers."

"Yes, ma'am."

Fifteen minutes later she had to admit defeat. There was no one available to help. Her baby-sitter was getting frantic, and Jenny had run out of options.

"All right," she announced, pulling out her driver's license. "I didn't want to do this, but I'm Mrs. Lake. I need to see Mr. Lake. The Wellerby, Cline, Phillips and Phillips law offices."

The guard's face was a study in composure. "Of course."

The Jerk's secretary didn't have quite as much facial control as she considered the disheveled state of her surprise guest.

"Mrs. Lake?" she echoed, trying to keep the disbelief polite. "Excuse me, but I've met Mrs. Lake."

Her head pounding again and her stomach roiling with the fact that she had to ask the Jerk for help to his face, Jenny took another swipe at her hair and flashed the probable third Mrs. Lake a chilly smile. "The ex-Mrs. Lake."

"Oh," said the carbon copy of Amber Jean, with a smile that betrayed a lot of orthodonture. "Of course. I didn't think you were Amber."

Jenny stiffened. "Bite your tongue."

"Was he expecting you?"

Now Jenny's smile broadened with some relish. "Oh, I don't think so."

He wasn't. Cushioned behind a desk that cost more than her kitchen appliances, and privileged to a view that encompassed every square inch of office space in downtown Clayton, the Jerk took Jenny's surprise appearance badly.

"Your timing stinks, Jenny."

Jenny did her best to maintain control. There was something about that razor-sharp Brooks Brothers suit and salon hairstyle, the manicure and matching tie and handkerchief that grated on her.

"So does the car you left me with," she retorted, dropping into one of the plush leather chairs he kept for paying customers before he could object. "If you'll take a close look out your west window, you'll see it parked at the front of the building. Well, parked isn't really a good description. I guess lying inert would be better."

He couldn't keep his eyes from where he just knew she was getting sweat stains on his good furniture. "Get to the point."

"A sign from God, dear," Jenny smiled. "It seems he wanted me to see you today. He killed my car in front of your building."

"Well, get one of your hundred brothers to come pick you up."

"No one's available."

"Get a cab."

Now she counted for control. "I have forty cents in my purse. Cab drivers resent being asked to drive twelve miles for forty cents." Another sweep through her hair, another deep, controlling breath as she fought amid her discomforts for tact. "I'm sorry. I really don't want to be here, either. I need some help getting home, and I didn't know what else to do."

He began to pace. "Jenny, why don't you ever take care of things?"

Jenny stared. "I've been trying," she retorted, her voice carefully quiet. "Even an automobile has a life expectancy."

He didn't seem to be listening. Still measuring the thick, gray carpet in his Italian loafers, he addressed the view. "All I wanted was a new life. Some peace, some support. And you keep turning up, dragging me back. Dragging me down."

"Please . . ."

"I suppose you want a new car," he snapped. "Or maybe a chauffeur."

"I need enough money to get home."

"Why should I, dammit?" he demanded, turning on her then, his face a mask of fury. "Why should I forever be giving you more? You got the house, Jenny. You got *my* house. I worked for that house. It was my goal, the symbol of everything I fought for, that first step up. You *know* what it meant to me. And you grabbed it, lock, stock and alarm system." Working himself up to a fine state of indignation, he ended up leaning over her. "Well, what else do you want, dammit? My law license?"

For a minute Jenny could only stare at him. Who said divorce got easier with the passing months? It had been a long time since she'd seen him this worked up. If he wasn't careful, he was going to be cleaning off his shoes. Her stomach couldn't take much more.

There were so many ways she wanted to answer him. She wanted to ask him why the hair-pulling routine when he was in the process of putting in a new sauna. She wanted to tell him that what she wanted was some return on all the years she'd busted her own buns to get him that damn law license. But by now Jenny knew how well this man listened. He'd already turned away, stalking over to watch Clayton empty out on a Wednesday night.

"All I want," she said as deliberately as she could, her hands clenched atop the soft linen roses on her skirt, "is enough money to take care of our children."

He whirled on her. "Don't give me that, now. Those kids were your idea, not mine. I'm tired of you trying to make me feel guilty for something that isn't my fault."

Even after all this time, it hurt. Jenny gave in to a little rancor. "I forgot. You weren't even in the neighborhood when either of them was conceived." Emma, who had his blue eyes. Kevin who had his heartbreaking smile.

"I gave in," he retorted. "You know that. You wanted them, I let you because it seemed to make you happy. But nothing really made you happy, did it, Jen? You just wanted more."

"I just wanted more from you," she answered, suddenly exhausted, suddenly tired of the recriminations, the endless, pointless bitterness. She just wanted to go home. Heaving herself to her feet, she picked up her purse.

Behind her, the secretary slipped into the door. "Mr. Welerby is waiting for that report, Mr. Lake."

He whirled on her. "I know that, dammit! Why don't you explain to him that I couldn't finish it because *you* keep letting every passing pedestrian into the office!"

The secretary looked stricken. Jenny felt guilty, and then hated herself for it. For always feeling guilty when he was the one who was the jerk. She lifted a hand to the girl in silent apology and headed for the door.

"Jenny!"

Sighing, she turned. He was bent over his desk rifling through a drawer. "Here," he barked, pulling something out. "Take it. Just take it and go. I'll get a way home. And this is the last time."

Suddenly Jenny was catching a set of Porsche keys. She stared from them to the Jerk and back again. "I don't want your Porsche."

"No," he retorted, ignoring the secretary who still hovered in the door. "You want my butt. Don't dent the car, and for God's sake don't lose it. I want it back by Monday at the latest."

Which meant that he and Amber Jean had bought yet another car. It was a cinch he wasn't going to let the little woman drive him to work each day to appease his ex. When she followed the secretary out into the anteroom Jenny lifted the keys for her to see. "Just in case he tries to claim it's stolen."

She looked stunned. "He wouldn't."

Jenny grimaced. "He did. Twice."

She was going to enjoy the ride in that damned Porsche if it killed her.

And then she was going to deal with Nick Barnett.

Chapter 8

"I'm not going out with him, and that's final."

Detective Richards didn't seem impressed. "It's your neighborhood, lady," he shrugged, draining yet another glass of Barb's tea in a gulp that sent a good proportion sliding down his chin.

Today, he was wearing food on his tie and enough oil in his hair to service the entire U.S. fast-food industry. Jenny wanted to throw him out. But before she let that decision reach her lips, she saw Barb frown.

The blonde didn't say anything. She knew it was Jenny's decision. She also knew what Jenny was risking in continuing with the venture, more than Detective Richards could ever understand or appreciate.

His way of looking at it was that Jenny was getting a free meal and maybe a quick cuddle. Barb had been there when Jenny had reached home from the Jerk's office two days earlier, sobbing with frustration and impotence. She'd cushioned the rage and given Jenny room to defuse before facing her children again. But she had also just heard the detective's update on Nick, and it worried her even more than Jenny's state of mind.

First, his car. Richards had traced it to Marco Manetti Food Industries, a number that seemed serviced by no more than an answering machine. The address given was a blind, a room with a set of connecting phone systems to reroute calls. Manetti, an immigrant who owned everything from food stalls down at Soulard Market to mushroom caves in southern Illinois, was harder to catch than the Pope on a quick trip.

Second, the school. Washington University still couldn't cough up any Nick Barnett.

And third, the point that seemed to satisfy the detective the most. Three days before, two fourteen-year-olds had been busted for possession of cocaine, both with home addresses not more than six blocks away. Both stolidly contesting that they got the stuff through a friend who bought from a third party, somebody they claimed had been working the neighborhood during the summer. So far the friend had been unavailable. The family had taken him to Europe for a week or so, therefore preventing the fingering of the third party.

But who was new to the neighborhood this summer, the detective had asked with a sly smile. And who had access, and mobility and opportunity?

"Listen," Richards said, wiping the tea away just before it sank into a once-white collar. "I'm not gonna wire you or nothin'. All I want is a phone number. An address. See if he'll take you home."

Immediately Jenny stiffened again.

Richards lifted a hand. "Okay, okay. See if he'll tell you more about this apartment of his. Anything. Find out how he affords that fancy school he says he goes to."

Jenny paced the room to work off her temper. She ended up by the front window where she had a great view of the red Porsche sitting in her driveway. It was a great car, shiny and fast and seductive, with seats that caressed you like a lover. And it was only going to be hers for another few days—until her own was repaired or until the Jerk demeaned himself by stopping by and picking it up.

Well, why not enjoy it as much as she could while she had it? She was sure going to resent having the old car back with its hot, worn seats and loose clutch. She'd miss the fun, the adventure. Probably resent never being able to afford something as beautiful as the Porsche as long as she lived.

But for three more days, it was still all hers.

Well, why the hell not?

This time there was a note on the front door. Taped at what must have been Jenny's eye level, it read that she had to run the kids to her sister's because of a baby-sitting crisis and to just go on in.

Nick took a quick look around, unable to believe that Jenny would leave an invitation like that on her front door. Surely she didn't mean that the house was open to anyone who walked through the neighborhood.

She did. When he tested the doorknob, it turned smoothly. Nick took another quick look. The last thing he needed when he had the opportunity of a lifetime was for that old bat across the street to call the cops on him.

He saw Todd's mother—Lauren, he thought her name was—pulling into their drive in a very shiny BMW. Then there was that Hobbs guy, the one with the diseases. He was out with a small, yapping dog that was decorating other people's lawns. Nick had been amazed when he'd seen the guy for the first time. He'd expected a retiree, one of those guys who delighted in regaling audiences with his surgery stories. This guy wasn't more than fifty, a skinny little thing with a melancholy look like he thought he was Lord Byron composing poetry or something. His wife looked just like him, except she had the shrill voice in the family. Probably handy for yelling at inattentive doctors.

Nick shook his head with a wry grin. Ah, humanity. Anybody in the damn neighborhood could be filching those checks. Come to think of it, anybody in the neighborhood could belong to that latest satanic cult they'd unearthed. Cultivated lawns and nice cars didn't necessarily spell civilization.

Well, at least the dragon across the street seemed to be sleeping. Her curtains didn't do so much as flutter when he tested the knob again, so he slipped into the house.

Cool. Comfortable. Nick took a deep, slow breath, savoring that elusive smell of summer and citrus groves, and looked around.

Nobody could accuse Jenny of repressing her kids for the sake of a clean house. Evidence of that lay scattered everywhere, from books to planes to sticks wrapped together in a form familiar to anyone with male hormones. Nick grinned. She probably didn't let the kid have guns, so Kevin just invented them. Nick remembered when he'd made his first tommy gun out of Legos. Now, he supposed kids made Uzis and lasers, but basics just didn't change.

Walking through, he picked up a scarf that lay draped over the oak banister. Silk, smooth, a dusty rose color that he'd seen on her the other day. It smelled like her. He thought it probably felt like her, too. Walking on into the house, Nick ran a thumb over the silk and anticipated.

Restaurants. It had been what had been missing on those charge slips. In reviewing Jenny's file, Nick had run a finger down every charge he could find, and not one of the listings had been for food. She'd charged gas and house supplies and school clothes for the kids. There had been a charge from a doctor's office and the vet. Nowhere on the four-month listing did Nick see anything that hinted that Jenny Lake took herself out for an evening away. From what showed up on her file, she worked, took care of her children and juggled finances.

The invitation to dinner had been a means to soften her up and to gather more of the information that McGrady seemed so sure would lead back to Jenny. In reality, Nick could have done it any number of ways, but it had just seemed too unfair that when Jenny's husband was on a first-name basis with the maître d' at Anthony's Jenny couldn't dress up for anything more impressive than McDonald's.

Besides, he wanted to spend an evening with her away from the prying eyes of neighbors.

Walking through to the living room, Nick caught his reflection in the hall mirror. He hoped he looked more appropriate for his mission tonight. After all, he'd pulled out his best yuppie camouflage, a gray-linen suit with pleated pants, white shirt and bright aqua tie with gold-bar tie clasp. His hair was still too long for the image, but he'd tried to brush it back out of the way so that it wasn't so noticeable. Still a little too fast for this neighborhood, but closer than the Grateful Dead T-shirts, he was sure.

He just wished he could enjoy the evening without having to let work interfere. He wished he could sit in the quiet comfort of her house instead of taking advantage of the chance to search. Taking a moment to size up the sleek lines of the bright blue Danish modern furniture in the living room, he chose the window desk as his next target.

Nick was rifling through the bills when he saw the lights swing into the driveway. Scooting just out of visual range, he quickly reassembled the pile. That was when he saw the cards. With an eye to Jenny's approach, he flipped a few open.

Birthday cards. Obviously left after the party the other day. *We won't take it back, so have fun. Buy something for yourself with it. You can't spend gift certificates on the mortgage.*

Nick couldn't help but smile. So, the two-hundred-dollar deposit was explained. Her family had stuffed money into her hands for her birthday, and Jenny had let them. He could just imagine how hard it was for her to do that, but he also knew how much she'd needed to. His bet was that most of it had gone to the gas company, anyhow.

By the time Jenny opened the door, Nick was comfortably seated on the couch flipping through *Sesame Street* magazine.

"I'm sorry I'm late again," she called on the way in. The door slammed shut behind her and her shoes clacked against the parquet flooring.

Nick looked up with a smile. When he caught sight of Jenny, he froze.

Jenny came to her own shuddering stop.

Nick's magazine slid to his lap, forgotten. He couldn't take his eyes from where Jenny stood staring at him. She was in a dress, soft wrinkled silk the same color as his tie. It still floated in the aftermath of her rush, skimming her hips and swirling around her legs. It was a simple dress, a shirtwaist with an ecru belt and gold buckle pulling the billowy silk in at the waist, so that the dress hinted rather than outlined, flirted rather than seduced. On Jenny, it took Nick's breath away.

He got to his feet, Jenny's eyes following him up. Her expression must have matched his, and it made him smile.

Holding his arms out in diffident display, he shrugged. "I figured that I'd show you the other side of Nick Barnett."

Jenny's smile was hesitant, as if caught between attraction and flight. "I'm not sure any of the neighbors would recognize you." Her voice was as breathy as her smile.

"You look...wonderful," he finally admitted, wishing suddenly that he hadn't suggested this. Just the sight of her, eyes wide and glistening, hair tumbled around her face like a wind-ragged cloud, hand caught at her throat, sent his objectivity toppling.

He wasn't going to get off this case intact. He finally, certainly, inevitably admitted that he would do his best to take this woman up to that soft, tumbled bed of hers and make love to her.

And what was worse, he saw the realization flare in her eyes, as well.

"It's Kate's dress," she demurred, hand straying over material Nick desperately wanted to test. "She let me borrow it since she can't wear it for a while longer."

Nick had to think Jenny had more practice averting temptation than he—or maybe she'd had more reason to. The heat had no more than flashed in that emerald green before she offered him a quirky smile and motioned to the two objects he'd left behind him on the couch.

"Uh, is there something I should know about what you play with while other adults aren't around?"

Startled, Nick looked around. He'd forgotten. Lying alongside the magazine he'd just dropped was the silk scarf from the banister. The silk that had run through his fingers much as her dress would...as her skin would, with a soft sibilance that beckoned, tempted, seduced.

Pulling away from the image with a start, Nick turned back to her with a grin he hoped like hell looked sheepish. "I was hoping I could find something to talk to Emma about."

Jenny arched an eyebrow. "The magazine or the scarf?"

Nick shrugged, finally admitting the truth. "I could smell your scent on the scarf."

Jenny didn't seem to know what to do with that information. Ducking her head a little, she looked around as if seeking escape. "How about a drink before we go?" she asked, shoving her hands into her skirt pockets. "It'll give me a chance to settle down after the police."

Immediately Nick stiffened. "The police?"

With a shrug that was equal parts consternation and allowance, Jenny led the way into the kitchen, sure Nick would follow. "The reason I'm late was that I got stopped again. I guess the police have some fascination with red Porsches. I've been driving this one for two days and have been stopped three times. I haven't had a ticket, just warnings. For being . . . red."

Nick almost gulped. "A red Porsche?"

Flashing a wry grin over her shoulder, Jenny flipped on lights and opened the refrigerator. "The Jerk's. The compact died right in front of his office building Wednesday when I went to see my lawyer. I ended up having to drive his car home. Beer? Bourbon?"

"Beer. The compact? The compact died?"

Jenny handed him a beer. "You're forgiven. It seems that the fuel injectors were just the tip of the iceberg. Once those were fixed and the pressure increased all along the line, a lot of other little things went wrong. The car dealership was thrilled to see me."

Nick was feeling progressively worse. He had to get hold of Baker and call off the dogs. "How long are you going to be driving the . . . uh, Porsche?"

Taking a sip of a wine cooler, Jenny sighed. "Only until Monday. That's when the Jerk comes to pick it up." With a feral smile, she tilted her head a little. "I think he doesn't want us seen in his neighborhood."

Nick scowled. "His loss."

Jenny grinned back. She was leaning against the sink, bottle in hand. "That's what I keep saying. But then, I don't think I'd like his neighborhood, either. I don't think anybody up there'd recognize reality if it ran over them with a truck."

Taking a pull of his own beer, Nick settled a hip on the kitchen table, perfectly at ease with the unique seating arrangement. "You know, maybe I'd like to be here Monday when he shows up. I'd kind of like to see what kind of a man could give this up." He swept the bottle in an arc, encompassing the house in his statement. "This is just the kind of house I'd like when I get out. I think I could really bust my butt for it."

Nick didn't really think of just what in the house provoked the sentiment. Not the architecture. He wasn't the kind of person to notice architecture. He couldn't tell Doric from derrick.

It wasn't the neighborhood. He wasn't heavily into suburbia, especially after working the yuppie detail all these years. He just knew that this house felt like home. There was a peace that filled it that had nothing to do with noise, a comfort that couldn't be equated with furniture.

Looking around in the soft shadows, Nick nodded. He didn't examine his statement more than the feeling of satisfaction it gave him. When he turned for Jenny's reaction, though, he was brought up short. She was staring at him as if he'd slapped her.

"Jenny?" Nick pushed away from the table.

Before he could reach her, Jenny visibly shook herself. "The Jerk didn't give it up," she said with a faint smile that spoke volumes. "He fought tooth-and-nail for it."

Nick didn't know how to answer. He had the feeling that the two of them were referring to two completely different things. He just didn't know how to explain what he meant. He didn't know if he could explain even if he knew how. That was the kind of thing Nick didn't share.

Giving up, he finished off his beer and set it down. "Does Italian sound okay to you?" he asked, facing Jenny but avoiding her. "I made reservations, but I can change them."

Her eyes more troubled than she knew, Jenny nodded. "Italian's fine."

Italian could mean anything in St. Louis. For a city founded by the French and Spanish, it had a preponderance of restaurants specializing in Italian cuisine. Nick had picked Ruggeri's, a small, neighborhood restaurant located in the south end of the Hill, the mecca of Italian culture in town. Tucked into a basement, you entered the place by going down stone steps and passing beneath exposed brick and pipe.

Ruggeri's wasn't the fanciest place in town, by far. It wasn't the largest or smallest. But it packed a lot of flavor into its claustrophobic little rooms. Books and antiques lined the bare brick walls. Formica tables scraped uneven floors, patrons ducked low ceilings and the phone was wedged in between two supporting beams.

The Jerk would have never been caught dead in a place like this. The maître d' didn't ignore patrons and the waiters didn't sneer. The minute Jenny stepped through the door, she decided she liked Nick's taste a lot better.

Just that thought resurrected her anxiety.

"When do they bring out the chili?" she asked with a grin that belied the clammy fear that had suddenly bloomed.

Nick refused to rise to the bait. "One excuse is as good as another."

They were shown to a little table back in the Pipe Room. Nick held Jenny's chair and then slid in across from her. Jenny saw him unbutton his suit to get comfortable and found the panic taking over. The room was too close, Nick too handsome, the situation too suddenly threatening. Scraping her chair back as the waitress showed up, Jenny shot to her feet.

"Excuse me," she stammered, hoping Nick didn't hear the sudden crescendo of her heart. "I'll . . . uh, be back."

"That way," the waitress offered with a vague wave of the hand.

Jenny interpreted correctly.

It was so stupid. There wasn't a reason in the world she should be having an anxiety reaction. Just because this was the first time she'd been out on a date in about ten years. Just because she hadn't even had the luxury to go out to a restaurant since the divorce. She had no business having sweaty hands and a racing pulse. She shouldn't be trembling like a virgin on the verge of a swoon. Even so, when she looked in the little bathroom mirror what she saw was a woman a little too wild-eyed for her taste.

And she still had to go back out there and get Nick to cough up an identity.

What was it that had her so excited, so upset? Was it the duplicity or the adventure? Was she more afraid of him or more attracted to him? She certainly hadn't expected him to look quite so good in a suit. She guessed she hadn't expected more than the turtleneck he'd worn before. In that tailored gray linen, he looked like a powerbroker. It fit him better than the T-shirts and jeans, somehow. She could so easily see him treading the boardrooms of multinational corporations that the ice cream truck seemed the fantasy.

That made her realize her first impression had been right. He didn't belong on that ice cream truck. He wasn't the same kind of person as Marco Manetti. He had too much grace, too much power leashed behind those tawny eyes and quirked grin. Nick Barnett was a puzzle wrapped in an enigma, and if Detective Richards was right that all had to do with high-level drugs. If Jenny was right, it had to do with law school.

She didn't see that it was much of a choice. On the other hand, it had been a long time since she'd been alone to dinner with a handsome man. Taking a few deep breaths to settle the terror that still tasted too much like exhilaration, Jenny washed the stale perspiration from her hands and set her shoulders before opening the door again.

"Everything all right?" Nick asked, sincere concern in the honeyed depths of his eyes.

He stood to help Jenny back in her chair, and she had to keep from looking around for the gag. It had been a long time since a man had done that for her.

"Everything's fine," she admitted, looking down at the table and then forcing herself to have the courage to face him. "I just had a sudden case of cold feet. It's been a . . . well, a long time since I've been out."

"On a date?" Nick finished for her, that damn smile tugging at his mouth.

Jenny wanted to sigh. She wanted to taste that smile. "On a date." She grimaced with the admission. "Sounds archaic, doesn't it?"

"Not at all. It sounds about right." Leaning closer, he took hold of her hand. "Is there anything I can do to make it easier for you? Sign a prenuptial agreement or something?"

Jenny fought the sudden suffocation just the touch of his hand incited. His fingers were so warm, so solid. So gentle as they wrapped unconsciously around hers. This was wrong. She had to keep her head. And she damn well couldn't do it when her heartbeat skipped every time she came in contact with the man.

"Give me your phone number," she blurted out.

Nick stiffened. Jenny faltered. Her heart slipped again, knocking against her ribs at the sudden caution in Nick's eyes. She'd had to ask the question. She just didn't want to have it answered.

"My phone number?" he asked, an eyebrow cocked.

She dipped her head, filling her eyes with the sight of empty table and chianti bottle. "I was going to call you when the car died. I mean, you fixed it...you know. But I didn't know your number. You'd never told me. And, well, then when I got home I checked." Jenny lifted her eyes and skirted his, her chest still too filled with dread to allow a good breath, her eyes wide. "Your number isn't in the phone book."

His nod was a slow one. His hand loosened around hers. "I know."

Finally drawing enough breath, Jenny tilted her head. "What is it about me you don't trust, Nick?"

"Lasagna?"

Both of them started. The waitress, a middle-aged motherly type was poised with pad and pencil, doing her best to intimate that this was the optimum time for them to order. Jenny shot Nick a look and pulled her hand away.

"Five-five-five, two-two-eight-nine," Nick said, his eyes still on Jenny.

She looked up in time to see the smile, that soft, little-boy look of satisfaction.

"Thanks, honey." The waitress grinned dryly. "I'll call tomorrow after work. But right now I'd prefer an order."

"Do you have chili?" Jenny asked, smiling back at Nick.

The waitress wasn't exactly sure how to take that. "Not even if he gave me his address and measurements," she assured them.

"I keep feeling like I've forgotten something," Jenny admitted later. They had long since finished dinner, and had progressed to drinks down in the Grand Hall at Union Station.

Seated in the wing chair alongside her, Nick balanced the balloon glass of cognac against his crossed leg and smiled. "You're just not used to going anywhere by yourself."

Jenny chuckled. "I'm not used to being wined and dined. This is wonderful, Nick. Thanks."

Across the floor, a tuxedoed man was playing Gershwin on the baby grand. Glasses clinked and conversation floated through the barrel-ceilinged art-nouveau room. Wrapped in the green wing chair and pleasantly warmed by alcohol and companionship, Jenny couldn't remember another evening as pleasant, or another date so solicitous and fun.

Nick had drawn her life from her, laughing at her family anecdotes and companionably discussing everything from literature to sports. It wasn't lost on Jenny that she hadn't learned anything about his past, or that his opinions didn't always mesh with the image he portrayed. Ambitious types didn't usually quote the romantic poets. Ponytailed rock fans didn't rattle off baseball stats like an announcer. Somehow she had to find out more than his phone number and taste in clothes. Somehow, the enticing pieces of Nick Barnett had to fit into a whole.

"Your entire neighborhood's going to be at your door when they find out you've gone out with the ice cream man," Nick warned with a wry smile.

More than you know, Jenny thought with a stifled scowl. "It would almost be worth it to stay out until dawn just to see Mrs. Warner lose sleep."

Nick's answering smile held more than conspiracy. "It could be arranged."

When Jenny met his gaze, she felt those whiskey eyes consume her. They dipped into her, breaching the chill around her heart, stealing into the depths of her resistance and sapping it. For long moments Jenny could do no more than face him, emerald eyes wide and wary, fingers wrapped tightly enough around her own wine glass to soak in the chill. Suddenly she couldn't remember what she'd originally come here for.

"Not unless you're talking about all-night bowling or breakfast at Uncle Bill's Pancake House," she countered, her voice unaccountably hushed.

Nick lifted an eyebrow in an elegant shrug, his own thumb stroking the smooth glass. "I'm just as happy sitting here talking."

No, you're not, she thought with sudden insight. There's too much heat in those eyes, too much tension in the muscles along your jaw. It should have stunned her, frightened her to know that Nick wanted her. Jenny tried her hardest to make it so.

In the end, all she could feel was the first stirring of anticipation, curling around in her belly like smoke, slipping out into her veins and infecting her limbs.

She wanted him, too. She wanted to find that hot, empty apartment of his and see how the sweat tasted on him as he took her on a hardwood floor. She wanted to watch those eyes take light and hear him gasp her name. She wanted to know that she really infected his dreams the way he did hers.

Desperate to push the mutinous yearning aside, Jenny turned her gaze to the pale gold liquid in her glass and the arsenal of questions she'd never gotten around to asking. Anything, anything but what she was contemplating, because it was the surest route to disaster.

Maybe it was a good thing she hadn't been away from the children in a long time. At least they kept her grounded. It became too easy somehow to ignore consequence and responsibility seated in an echoing room with whispering waitresses and standards drifting from the piano.

"You never mentioned, Nick," she said, trying to keep her voice even and unconcerned. "Are you originally from St. Louis?"

It took a moment for him to answer. When Jenny looked up, it was to find a wry smile on his face.

"I'm proud of you," he admitted. "It took you more than three hours to ask the obligatory question."

Suddenly he had Jenny grinning, too. "Yeah, I know. And where did you go to school?"

St. Louis was often called the biggest small town in the world. Everybody knew everybody, or somebody who knew somebody else. Social life often revolved around the questions "Where did you grow up?" and "Where did you go to school?" because just those two answers clearly defined life-styles and social circles. Jenny's mother had liked the Jerk's answer to school, not so much to neighborhood. The Jerk's family, on the other hand, hadn't liked either of the answers Jenny had given.

"Sorry to disappoint you," he offered with a salute from the cognac before he took another drink. "But I've lived all over the state. I'm originally from Springfield."

"Is your family still there?"

Nick still watched his liqueur, swirling it gently in the palm of his hand. Jenny thought she saw his eyes darken, his mouth tighten. For some reason it made her go still, as if bracing for pain.

"No family," he admitted, lifting his eyes to meet hers with surprising nonchalance. "When people call me a bastard, they mean it."

Something caught in Jenny's chest, a sharp regret that seemed to echo the faint tightness in his voice. She recognized more from his offhand words than he knew, heard the emptiness behind them, the defenses built over the years. She wondered what he had felt when he'd met the mad affection of her family.

She knew better than to ask. Instead, she nodded. "Where did you meet up with Marco?"

Nick smiled, the expression in his eyes lightening noticeably. "The Mad Manetti?" he asked. "He arrested me. Four times."

Jenny faltered. "Arrested you? He was a policeman?"

"Policeman and ex-Marine D.I. The perfect combination to scare the snot out of an obnoxious fourteen-year-old on his way to grand theft auto. It was the stuff of old B movies."

A policeman. How could Detective Richards have missed that particular bit of information? Jenny couldn't understand it. Suddenly, beyond anything else she felt about Nick or the dubious mission she carried out, she felt anger. Why should she be sitting here picking Nick's brain when the purported pros couldn't track down the basics?

"But you said he didn't speak English," she objected.

Nick's smile was lazy. "A barefaced lie to get inside your house. I wanted to get to talk to you."

Jenny wanted to hear that. But at the same time she didn't. Finding her courage seeping away, she went back to studying her wine. "So," she said, "Marco was your incentive to join the Corps."

His expression betraying his well-laid caution, as if still expecting attack, Nick gave a small nod of concession. "When I was seventeen. We'd run out of foster homes, and the courts had run out of patience."

Jenny nodded back. "Nam?"

He shrugged. "If you can make it there, you can make it anywhere."

"How did you get from the Marines to law school?"

When Nick smiled now, there was serious purpose in his eyes. "Career-planning."

Suddenly Jenny thought he wanted to say more. There was a softening in his eyes, almost a yearning as he looked at her, as if wishing he could share with her. She held her breath, wanting him to. Knowing she shouldn't.

In the end, without moving, without changing the inflection in his voice, he backed down. "I had a lot of time to plan my future. A lot of reason to succeed. I decided that my best route out would be law school. I still think so."

"And nothing's going to get in your way?"

Nick shook his head, never taking his eyes from Jenny's, making sure she saw the purpose there, the drive that had brought him from the Protestant Boys' Home to Washington University Law School. "Nothing," he said. "Living well is the best revenge, they say. Well, I'm due some."

Jenny did her best to summon up some anger. At least a feeling of betrayal. Here she sat with the first man she'd let take her out in two years, and he was telling her that he'd cloned himself from the Jerk. She should have hated him, if not herself for letting her want to trust him so much.

Somehow, she couldn't do it. All she could feel at his words was regret, a bittersweet frustration that all that life locked behind those whiskey-brown eyes would stay there. He wouldn't sleep on anyone else's couch again, because even as Jenny watched he pulled back a little from her. And—she thought with more than a little remorse as she drained the wine in her glass—he would continue to do so, even as he courted her.

He would sacrifice for goals rather than people. Status rather than love. And Jenny would spend her summers listening for the bell of an ice cream truck and longing for the sight of a vulnerable, little-boy smile.

She held his hand as they strolled back down the near-empty halls of the train station, their footsteps echoing up beyond the balcony and its closed shops, their voices hushed amid the fountains and foliage. She tasted that anticipation once again when he wrapped his arm around her shoulders, the unaccustomed hunger snaking through her like a hot current. She sat alongside him on the way home watching the heat lightning flicker against a dirty night sky and ached for more time alone, more time away from the relentless morning and the return of reality. And all the while, the regret built.

When they reached Jenny's house, she found herself wandering over to where the Porsche sat, the hot red an exclamation in the shadows and silence of the late-night street. She ran a hand over its sleek contours and thought of its smooth grace and power, the escape it promised and couldn't ever really deliver. She thought of how very much she wished it were hers.

"Jenny," Nick said, his voice bemused as he walked up alongside her. "What's wrong?"

Jenny couldn't quite face him. There were tears in her eyes, and she didn't want him to get the right idea. "Oh, nothing. I just hate to give it up."

"Maybe someday you'll have one of your own."

Finally braving a look, Jenny caught a glint in the depths of his eyes that made her wonder if he knew what she'd been thinking. "Oh, I don't think so," she smiled, the yearning stifling her. "I don't seem to have that kind of luck."

She turned so quickly that Nick didn't have the chance to answer. He'd seen it. Recognized the longing in her eyes as twin to his own. His conscience clamored to tell her, to set things right before it was too late—even as his common sense told him it had been too late right from the start.

He followed her across the walk to her porch and waited as she selected keys, her fragrance drifting like a soft vapor on the late-night breeze, the tang of orange sharpening the soft bouquet of summer foliage until it swam through him. He could smell it in her hair as it trembled on the night, could almost taste it on her skin. Frustration battled with sense. Hunger clamored more loudly than duty. Nick saw her walk into her house and followed her in.

Stepping onto parquet flooring, Jenny turned.

"Nick, I—"

"Jenny, I—"

Neither managed to finish. Suddenly the door was closed and Nick had Jenny in his arms. He hadn't meant to. He'd intended to explain, to make her understand why it was he had to gain some distance from her before they were both hurt. But when she'd turned her face to him, those forest-soft eyes liquid with pain and separation, her shoulders rigid with torment, he'd surrendered.

He never gave her a chance. Once he felt that silk beneath his fingers, Nick knew he couldn't stop without the taste of her. He bent to that upturned face, dipped into the cloud of orange blossoms. Her lips were open. He could feel the soft brush of her surprise, sensed the shudder of anticipation in her. Tangling his hands in the ebony silk of her hair, he finally took the kiss that had hovered between them since the moment they'd met.

Sweet. She tasted like nectar. She stirred beneath him as he skimmed and nipped at her tender lips. Nick felt her hesitate, soften, and just as surely come to life. Her arms came up to him; her small hands wound around the back of his neck. She straightened in his arms, folding into him, taking her own taste and igniting the fire that had smoldered for so long.

Nick pulled her to him, both hands in her hair, her head back before his need, her murmurs fueling his desire. She opened her mouth to him, invited him, and the need exploded in him.

He wanted her. He wanted to fill his hands with her and make her writhe with hunger. Her body was so soft, so strong and vibrant. He could hear her humming, deep in her throat as she curled her own fingers in his hair. She met his kisses and took his bottom lip between her teeth. Nick brought his hand down along her throat and she stretched for him, arching into his touch and lifting up on her toes to better fit into his hold.

He was melting. He was burning. He couldn't satisfy himself with the honeyed taste of her, the silken feel of her. Her breasts pressed against his chest, her nipples button-hard and tantalizing. Her thighs strained against his, hot and soft, promising, enticing. He ached. He groaned. He was seconds away from lifting her into his arms and carrying her upstairs.

He never knew how he heard it.

Suddenly both of them stiffened as if they'd been shot. The doorbell rang again.

"The kids . . ." Jenny gasped, pulling away, reaching for the doorknob before thinking.

There on the other side stood the blond cheerleader from next door and her male clone. Smiling.

For a moment there was stunned silence. The two of them managed to keep their smiles, but only barely as they gazed in on the rumpled evidence of interrupted passion.

"Oh, good," Barb finally said. "Your friend is still here. Maybe he'd like to join us in our coffee-tasting."

Nick stared. The man smiled diffidently and held up a full coffeepot.

"Our . . . coffee-tasting," Jenny echoed, her face a study in control.

"Of course, silly," Barb retorted with a bright smile, opening the door for her husband. "Isn't it one o'clock? We always do this on Friday nights."

Her husband followed her in. Nick still stared. Jenny still struggled to maintain a straight face. He could read the entire situation just in the fact that she couldn't manage to look at anybody.

"Of course," she damn near giggled with a hand to the forehead in a gesture of remembering. "Our coffee-tasting." Then, turning to Nick, she grinned much too brightly. "We do this every Friday."

"At one," Barb emphasized.

Jenny looked from Barb to Nick. "At one," she echoed.

Well, she did say that her neighbors took care of her. Finding no alternative other than hauling all three into the station for criminal improvisations, Nick shrugged. "Sure. Why not?"

And so it was that fifteen minutes later he found himself not in Jenny's bed, but in her kitchen trying to keep a straight face when he was introduced to Bill and Barby Bailey.

Sometimes there was just no justice.

Chapter 9

The next time Nick kissed Jenny goodbye, it was much less disturbing. It was also witnessed by Barby and Bill, who were doing their best to camouflage the fact that they weren't used to sitting up talking until three in the morning.

Jenny should have been relieved. Her friends had, after all, come to her rescue—more than they knew. But somehow the brush of Nick's lips against hers as he swung his jacket over his shoulder and headed out was far too tantalizing. It resurrected the fear, the anticipation, the shaky challenge of attraction and responsibility.

Watching him walk into the shadows, all Jenny could think was that she wished Barb and Bill had never interfered.

Distance, she thought the next morning as she plodded along the track at the YMCA paying for her sins. That's what I need right now. A little objectivity about the fact that he pulled and pushed at the same time. About his penchant for echoing some of the Jerk's finer sentiments while melting her like a hot chocolate bar with the quick uncertainty in his eyes.

At least she wouldn't be seeing him until Monday. Maybe she could regain a little of her balance in that time. Maybe she could start sleeping again.

She should have known better.

It was all Barb's fault. It had been Barb's idea to sign the kids up for swimming lessons, and Barb who had suggested utilizing the free time and air-conditioned building to exercise. Barb craved aerobics. Jenny had settled for earphones and walking on the elevated track. So while Jenny's kids went to class, Barb walked. When Buffy went from there to gymnastics, Barb bounced up and down with twenty other women who loved to sweat.

And it was Barb who almost caused the accident.

She'd been walking ahead of Jenny—*everyone* had been walking ahead of Jenny—when she happened to take a look down at the basketball game that was forming in the gym below. Occupied by the Eagles music in her earphones, Jenny wasn't paying attention. Within three steps, Barb came to a dead stop and people threatened to pile up over her like a freeway accident.

Jenny caught hold of the rail and glared at her friend.

"Oh, my God," Barb was mouthing, carefully made-up eyes wide.

Jenny pulled off her earphones to better chastise her friend. Her first reaction was that Barb had seen someone on the gym floor with a better Lycra outfit than hers. Her second was that it was much more serious than that. Barb was speechless, and it took a lot to put her in that condition. So of course Jenny made the mistake of following her gaze.

"O-o-o-h, my God."

It wasn't Lycra, at all. It wasn't even women. It was Nick. Somehow he'd walked right out of her anxieties and onto the court below in a shirts-and-skins basketball game. On the skins team, of course.

This wasn't fair. She shouldn't have to face this so soon after last night, when the taste of Nick's kiss still lingered, when the feel of his arms had invaded her sleep and set her to tossing and muttering with frustration. She had to regain her footing, restore her good sense. And she just couldn't do that with Nick sweating six feet below.

Jenny had always known he'd had a good physique. Fact only served to amplify that impression. He had a lean line to him, with strong shoulders and those third-baseman arms. His chest glistened, the soft brown hair that fanned out curling with the sweat. Clad only in dark blue gym shorts, his tush was everything she'd imagined.

But it wasn't just the way he looked. It was the way he moved, with a ferocious grace that ate up the floor and intimidated his opponents. When Nick went up for a basket, the ball whistled on its way down. When he attacked he did so with gusto, and when he defended he smiled like a wolf. Jenny saw an appetite there, a keen competitive drive that should have set off every warning bell in her common sense. All she could think to do was sweat right along with him.

"He kissed you last night," Barb said, deaf to the impatient urgings of other joggers as they parted around the two like a river around a logjam. "Didn't he?"

Jenny could only nod, the remembered heat intense enough to stain her cheeks.

Never bothering to look away from the game, Barb just nodded back. "I thought so."

In silent assent, Jenny and Barb began walking again. Barb never said another word. Barb wouldn't. But the two of them lost a lot of the aerobic benefit of their exercise when they couldn't keep their eyes from the game.

"I didn't know you came out here."

Jenny was drinking from the water fountain. She straightened and thought to scowl. There was such a wry humor in his eyes. For the first time, she really didn't believe him.

"The kids are in swimming lessons," she explained, automatically pushing damp ringlets out of her yes. She only wished she could do something about the sweat-stained shorts and Mickey Mouse T-shirt. "So I get in my weekly allotment of torture."

Taking her place at the fountain, Nick doused his neck with water and took long, thirsty gulps. Jenny couldn't take her eyes from his throat, from the gleaming line of his arm. She hadn't been able to breathe properly since she'd spotted him down on that court, and she had a feeling it wasn't about to get better soon. He even smelled great, like soap and exercise.

It was just too soon after last night. Then again, next year would have been too soon after last night.

"You play basketball much?" she found herself asking, unconsciously wiping her hands on her shorts.

Nick straightened alongside her and toweled the water from his head and neck with his discarded shirt. Somehow the action only further threatened Jenny's respiration rate.

"Not as much as I'd like to," he admitted. "It tends to defuse a lot of my aggressive tendencies."

"You?" Jenny echoed in mock surprise. "Aggressive? I can't imagine. Although I guess the arm-wrestling challenge that you threw off to Bill last night should have been a clue."

Nick chuckled, an easy sound, and Jenny ached. "Guys like that make me nervous. They're too...perfect."

Jenny nodded, only a vestige of guilt casting her eyes briefly upward to where Barb still walked. "Imagine living next to them. I feel like the 'before' in a before-and-after poster."

She began heading down toward the window where she could watch the rest of the swimming lesson. It only seemed natural that Nick follow. Jen cast a fleeting thought to Barb, still up there pounding down her tennies. Barb would never miss her. The endorphins were due to kick in any minute now. From that point, Barb could go on for hours.

"Tell me they instigated that little rescue raid last night on their own initiative," Nick asked.

Now it was Jenny's turn to chuckle as she pulled her attention back to the present. "The imported coffee had to be a dead giveaway. I can't afford it, much less suggest it."

Nick nodded. "I thought so. How come Mrs. Warner and old Miss Lucy didn't show up, too?"

Jenny couldn't help the self-satisfied smile. "They called this morning."

Nick just groaned.

The front room was crowded when they arrived. A cluster of parents gestured through the window and another was scattered on the couches waiting out lessons. Jenny squeezed her way in to get a look at the kids and was surprised when Nick followed right behind.

Of course, she wished he hadn't made such a concerted effort. He was still hot from the game, and the humid closeness seemed to surround her. She could hear him panting a little just beyond her ear and smelled the tang of sweat. Her tongue strayed again, licking her lips when that wasn't what she wanted to taste.

"She sure has a mind of her own."

Jenny started at the wry humor in Nick's voice. Deliberately, she turned her attention to the pool, where Emma was facing off with her teacher. Standing on the tile, shivering as if she had the ague, the little girl had her hands on her hips and was shaking her head emphatically. Not hysterically. There were no tears. She just wasn't going to do what the teacher wanted.

"I've wasted more money on these damn things," Jenny mourned. "Emma just can't come to grips with the fact that someone else knows something she doesn't. About anything."

"I just thought she didn't want to go in."

Jenny chuckled. "Oh, no. She thinks the teacher's doing it wrong."

"What are you going to do when she goes to school?"

"Suffer."

They watched a moment longer, oblivious to the fact that more than one well-clad young woman was casting second and third glances Nick's way. He'd draped his shirt around his neck and bent over to get a better view of the pool.

"You followed me this morning," Jenny accused without turning away from watching Kevin belly flop from the low board. There was a noticeable dearth of heat in her voice.

Nick looked down at her. "How did you know?"

Jenny grinned, trying her best to contain the sudden flight of butterflies in her chest. "Even the most fanatic exercise addict in the place doesn't travel fifteen miles to play basketball. Although I think a lot of them wait in the lot for the building to open in the morning."

"You're not one of the chosen?" Nick asked with a dry grin.

Jenny proffered a scowl and the tail of her T-shirt for closer inspection. "I'm wearing the wrong outfit. I'm also wearing the wrong figure. Most of those women won't even let me in the same exercise class with them. I guess they think full-figure is catching."

She wasn't in the least oblivious to the assessing look Nick passed over her. If his eyes had been radioactive, she would have glowed in the dark. Jenny wasn't sure she didn't anyway.

"Man doesn't want to gnaw on a chicken bone," he drawled. "Likes a little meat."

Jenny gave him another scowl as she gestured over to the sleek line of a jogger. "You mean you don't buy *Sports Illustrated* just to see somebody like that in a swimsuit?"

Nick turned to look. "She looks like Gumby in that outfit."

Casting one last envious look at the woman who probably didn't know what the word cellulite meant, Jenny sighed. "She's probably frigid, anyway."

Nick's surprised laugh turned a few more heads. "How 'bout if I take you away from all this?"

Now Jenny blinked, not sure what he had in mind. Not sure what she had in mind if he asked. "Where?"

"Fried chicken and coleslaw. Eleven herbs and spices. Blankets, grass, trees."

"A picnic?" she demanded. "It's almost a hundred degrees out there."

Nick proffered lifted arms. "I'm dressed for it. How 'bout you?"

Jenny tilted her head to the side, hearing fast car engines and gulls. "You're crazy."

When Nick nodded this time, Jenny wanted to know why he carried so much more than agreement in his expression. "You got that right, lady. Comin' along?"

"I'm crazy enough on my own, thanks." She almost found herself running to Barb, suddenly desperate for an excuse, for some support, for some sanity. Surely Barb in her pink exercise leotard and matching bandanna wouldn't let Jenny walk off to the park with a madman. Surely she'd remind Jenny why she shouldn't keep wanting more from Nick.

But Jenny knew even as she tried to excuse herself from Nick's impulse that she wasn't going to ask Barb for help.

Okay, so he'd given up trying to glean information out of her. So he'd thrown his objectivity right out the window. Sprawled out on the handmade quilt on the grass watching Jenny share a fuzzy caterpillar with her kids, Nick couldn't really pull together any regret.

McGrady wouldn't give a damn about gut reactions. McGrady's world was built on paper. But Nick's gut had rarely gotten him into trouble, and his gut just didn't come up with Jenny as a suspect.

Of course, McGrady would point out that Nick had never gotten involved with a suspect before. McGrady was like that. Nick didn't care. He had finally stepped across that tenuous line that divided suspicion from belief. Baker would have to show him a picture of Jenny at a bank cashing those checks for him to believe she was involved.

But in the meantime, it didn't hurt to keep tabs on her.

"You never told me," Jenny said, settling back onto the quilt.

Nick looked up, enchanted by the dew of perspiration on her cheeks. He wanted to curl the damp tendrils along her temples around his finger. "Tell you what?"

Dividing her time much as a race-goer, watching Nick and the action as the kids ran back over to the playground, Jenny offered a scowl. "How you knew I'd be at the Y today."

"Barb didn't mind your running off like that?"

"Heck, no. She probably never even knew I was gone. Barb *enjoys* that stuff."

Nick just shook his head. "I just can't understand the middle-class obsession with exercise."

"Then why did you travel across town to play pickup basketball?"

Nick looked down at the sunlight in her eyes, the line of her neck and arms as she leaned back on her elbows and thought of how she'd look in a bed, waiting to be kissed. Waiting to be loved. It took him a minute to pull himself back.

"To see you. Barb said something about your schedule last night. I thought I'd give it a shot."

Pulling herself into sitting position, Jenny grabbed another piece of chicken. Her expression wasn't exactly trusting. "Barb was talking about college-prep preschools last night. I don't think I remember the YMCA fitting into that conversation."

Nick knew that she wasn't fooled. Wondered how he was going to keep tap-dancing around this acute lady. He was seriously beginning to ponder the merit of keeping up this charade.

"Mom, look at me!"

Nick looked up to see Kevin hanging upside down from the top of the jungle gym. One leg slipped and Kevin shrieked. Nick jumped. Jenny munched on her chicken leg without moving.

"Nice, Kev, but try and keep both feet up."

Nick shot her a surprised look. "He almost fell on his head."

The smile Jenny bestowed betrayed that same smug superiority mothers had for the uninitiated. "Nah. He's been doing that since he was three."

Nick shot the boy another look to see him teetering along the top of the domelike structure as if he were walking a tightrope. Suddenly Nick was entertaining visions of broken arms and emergency rooms.

Jenny grinned. "He has the balance of a cat. Besides, aghast is just the reaction he's looking for."

It took some effort, but Nick settled back and took a swig of beer. "Why do you do this?" he demanded.

"The picnic was your idea," she reminded him equably.

Nick shook his head, an eye still to where Kevin was doing daredevil acrobatics on the equipment and Emma was doing her best to imitate him. "This mother stuff. How do you survive?"

Jenny just shrugged. "Lots of practice. I had most of the responsibility for that circus that was over at the house the other day."

Nick couldn't understand. He'd had responsibility, too. It just made him want to shy away. He'd never had a childhood, he'd always said. It was always much easier to foist one foster kid off on another. So, why should he spend the rest of his life wiping runny noses and cleaning up dirty diapers? But when Jenny talked about it, she got that faraway look that had taken her when she'd had the baby in her arms. The one that made him ache in a way he'd never known a person could.

"Didn't you get your fill?" he demanded without thinking.

When Jenny looked up, Nick realized that more had escaped in his tone of voice than he'd intended. For a moment she flirted with disquiet, uncertainty. Then she simply shook her head.

"It's different when they're your own."

Nick snorted. "Yeah, I've heard that before."

He wanted nothing of this hearts-and-flowers garbage. Nick had lived reality. He knew what a load kids were. After all, he'd been such a load that Dora had dumped him on the foster-care system rather than raise him herself. Where did it say that Jenny was different?

But she was. And that crowded Nick, taking his room, stifling his breath.

"I know," Jenny agreed. "Dumb cliché. But true. As much as I wanted children, I wasn't really sure I meant it until I had Kevin. I spent my entire pregnancy wondering how the heck I could actually love a baby enough to put up with midnight feedings and toilet training. I spent my pregnancy with Emma wondering how I could possibly love a second baby as much as I had the first."

But Nick was shaking his head. "I'm sorry. I don't think I could do that."

"Be pregnant?" Jenny asked, her voice soft for the teasing light in her eyes. "I hope not."

Nick couldn't name the sudden tightness in his chest. It had to do with the fact that Jenny refused to challenge him, that she was so calm and practical, ignoring her son's more outrageous stunts even as she spouted off about love and babies.

Suddenly the humidity was too close. The sun too hot. Nick climbed to his feet, intent on movement. He didn't see the sorrow in Jenny's eyes as he tossed his empty beer can into the trash.

"Mr. Nick?"

Looking down, he came upon the upturned face of Emma, her expression intent.

"Yeah, peewee. Whatchya want?"

"Swing me, please. My mommy hasn't learned me to kick my feet."

She held up a hand. Nick looked at it as if it were a trap. As if in accepting it, enclosing its tiny warmth within his, he would be caught. You couldn't deny the certain consideration in those blue eyes, though. In the end, Emma won.

"Mr. Nick?" she asked when her hand was safely in his.

"Yeah?" He looked down again, amazed at the amount of presence in that tiny face. Her hair was in braids and she wore a jumper, with an old watch hanging from her wrist. Why should that make him hurt?

"Do you have peanuts?"

"Huh?" He dragged himself back and instinctively began to check pockets. "No, I don't think I do."

That was when he heard the rumble of Jenny's stifled chuckle. But by then it was too late. He'd walked right into it.

"Oh." Emma nodded, brows pursed. "I don't have peanuts," she announced up to him. "I'm a girl. Kevin has peanuts. He's a boy."

And with that, she led him off. And Nick had thought Jenny had had trouble controlling her laughter.

It was getting worse. The very moment Jenny should have been calling a halt to this fantasy, she was seated cross-legged on her grandmother's quilt watching her children tumbling around Nick like puppies. And she couldn't bring herself to stop it.

This was what she wanted from life: an afternoon in the park listening to the shrill laughter of her children, smiling at the bemused humor in Nick's eyes, content with the sun and the languorous hypnotism of the heat, the creak of swings and the gurgle of the fountain down in the pond where the ducks swam.

But today instead of settling her, the idyllic setting churned her up even more. She saw here a man who needed her, needed the spontaneous affection of children—a man who only grudgingly allowed his own emotions. She saw a man who could share beautiful children with her and collect a noisy, wild brood to keep their dinner table in chaos and their old age warm.

She saw a man who didn't want children. And Jenny wanted more children. She could hear the echoes of their absence as clearly as the shrill glee of the children she had, and she missed them unspeakably. Tiny babies with wide, guileless eyes, toddlers with tumbling, stumbling gaits. Children with endless questions, endless surprises and pleasures. Past and future wrapped up in the silent, sweet face of a sleeping daughter or son, cocooned in the peace of night.

Jenny couldn't bear the idea that she would spend no more early mornings with a baby in her arms, exchanging their most private secrets in the quiet hours when the world slept around them.

And the man she was falling in love with couldn't understand that.

She'd begun to suspect the night before when he'd kissed her. When she'd wanted nothing more than to be lifted to her bed and thoroughly made love to. The realization had crystallized the minute she'd seen him walk away with Emma. Jenny had walked into this situation on a whim. She was going to walk away with a broken heart.

She still didn't know who he was. Nick Barnett didn't exist, and she didn't know why. She had his phone number. She should call Detective Richards and have it traced. She should find out once and for all just what it was that Nick—or whoever he was—was hiding from her.

It wasn't drugs. Her instincts rebelled against that idea. She wouldn't allow a drug dealer to enchant her daughter. Heck, her daughter, without even knowing what a drug dealer was, wouldn't allow it.

But it was something, and Jenny should find out. Still, every time she'd walked to the phone that morning she'd faltered. Because if Nick wasn't the one who told her why he was living a dual life it didn't matter.

Jenny wanted to laugh at that thought. It didn't matter even if he did tell her. No matter how important he was becoming to her, no matter how much sleep she lost, how much she ached to see him open those very private doors to her, she already knew his stand on the two most important issues in her life. He didn't like kids and he saw success in terms of achievement.

It wouldn't be enough for Nick Barnett to sit in a park and watch his children, and it would have to be for Jenny's husband.

"You didn't warn me about her."

Looking up, Jenny tried to force the knot of tears back in her throat. Nick plopped alongside her and reached over for another beer. He was grinning, that wide, easy smile that she'd seen him save for Marco. He looked so relaxed, so much more at peace than usual. How did Jenny tell him that her children were the therapy he'd needed all along? How did she ask him to stay?

"I tried to warn you about Emma a long time ago," she reminded him, looking down at her hands. They were still shiny with leftover chicken grease. "But there's only so much people will believe." Jenny tried her best to keep her attention away from the way Nick felt next to her. A fresh breeze picked at the damp hair at her neck, but it didn't serve to cool her.

Absently tossing her chicken bone back into the box, Jenny licked the taste from her fingers, one of the decadent pleasures her mother would never have allowed. She looked up just in time to see that Nick watched.

His face grew still. His eyes darkened. Jenny pulled her wet fingers from her mouth, the air tingling against them. She could almost feel his lips around them, sucking, licking. Tantalizing.

Pulling in enough air to cool her furnace, Jenny turned her eyes away. "Would you mind my asking you a question?"

"No." His voice was husky, tight. Jenny could hear the effort of control, and it fanned the embers in her belly. Still focusing on the blue-and-white double-wedding-ring pattern of the quilt beneath her rather than the clouds that gathered overhead, Jenny shook her head.

"What was it like being a foster child?"

It evidently wasn't what Nick had expected. When Jenny lifted her gaze it was to see the pain quickly surface, the chill of alienation and instinctive distrust. She hurt for him all over again.

Finishing his beer in a long gulp, Nick made another toss. The can hit home with a clang and sank into the trash. For a long moment he watched the pond where the ducks glided in silence and a little boy fished. Jenny held her breath, uncertain why she'd asked the question, afraid of the answer.

"There are a lot of good foster homes out there," Nick offered by way of disclaimer.

An expert in patience, Jenny waited.

Nick finally shrugged, still not facing her. "I kept waiting for my mother to come take me home."

Jenny heard the weight of his childhood in those words. She ached for him, for that little boy standing so expectantly by a window—for the man who had never gotten over it. "And she never did?"

Now he shook his head. "Not Dora. She wasn't much more than a kid herself. She couldn't bear to give me up, but she couldn't stand the responsibility. I guess she thought this was the best compromise." Again, a shrug. A stiff distancing from the endless wait. The hope and disappointment. The cycle of rejection. "I stayed in about ten places, I guess. Some houses better than others. Some people really tried, but by the time I was fourteen, I guess they'd pretty much given up on me."

Jenny could almost read it in his eyes. *How much could I be worth if my own mother wouldn't even come for me?* She saw it in Kevin at times, when the Jerk forgot him, that brutal pain of disappointment. The defenses already being constructed in a six-year-old boy. What must it have been like to have nothing but that conviction?

"And then, Marco," she offered.

Nick grinned. "And then, Marco. Caught me in an alley in south St. Louis ripping off hubcaps. Manetti decided that I made a lousy crook."

A wind lifted the edge of the blanket and ruffled the lake. Jenny didn't feel it. She didn't notice the pall cast over the sun. Her attention was on Nick, on the war he waged within himself.

"Marco's still one of the only people who can put up with me," Nick said, his good humor faltering, his eyes straying, softening.

Jenny felt a cool sigh against her cheek. The trees were beginning to whisper. "Yeah," she retorted, her eyes locked uncomfortably with his. "You're such an ogre to be around."

"I've been on good behavior."

She wanted to nod. Wanted to move or speak, anything to break the sudden tension. She could feel him struggle toward a decision. His muscles quivered with tension. The dimples alongside his mouth deepened, drawn downward with the weight of his struggle.

Jenny wished she knew what it was. She wished with all her heart she knew the outcome.

"I don't suppose the kids would like it if I kissed you," he said softly, just the tone of his voice more intimate than touch.

Jenny licked her lips. "They might not even notice."

He leaned closer, his gaze straying to her lips, to the moist trail left by her tongue.

"Jenny..."

No more than a mile away, lightning split the lowering sky. Jenny jumped back. The crack of thunder thudded into her chest. Right on its heels came the shriek, and she was on her feet.

Nick followed, trembling with the effort of control. Emma was running toward them, arms out, face already tearstained, sobs racking her small body. Storms were Emma's Achilles tendon, the unexpected chaos a frightening threat to her well-ordered little world.

"Don't let them take me," the little girl begged, arms like vises around Jenny's neck.

"Did you arrange this?" Nick demanded, only half joking.

Jenny swept Emma up into her arms. "Only if you believe in divine intervention," she answered with a faltering smile. When Nick cast an uncertain look to Emma, she made a shrug. "Post-*Wizard of Oz* syndrome," she allowed. "Emma's afraid a tornado is going to take her someplace where she can't get home to me."

"Don't...let them...Mommy!"

"I won't, baby," she crooned, eyes still on the tight discomfort in Nick's expression. "I won't."

The wind erupted then, smelling of rain. More lightning shuddered. Kevin showed up on the run. Still Nick watched her with those hesitant, hungry eyes. And Jenny thought she knew exactly how he felt.

"Would you care to continue our conversation later?" she asked.

For a moment, even as the storm descended on them at record speed and Kevin bent to retrieve the remnants of their meal, Nick stood stock-still. "Yes," he said. "I would."

And then they ran.

Chapter 10

"Jenny, it's only the Jerk. Why do you want to make a good impression on him?"

Jenny never bothered to look up from where she was digging for buried treasure among the sofa cushions. "Shut up and clean, Kate," she said to her sister.

The last forty-eight hours had been among the worst of her life. From the moment she'd scrambled in out of the rain on Saturday, Jenny had lost the rest of her objectivity. The remainder of that afternoon had been spent in the house, where Nick and Kevin compared cartoons and Jenny soothed a terrified Emma. There hadn't been a chance for privacy, since the surprise thunderstorm lasted the afternoon, intensifying Emma's fear. Jenny hadn't even managed to unpeel the little girl's arms from around her neck. Of all the times for Emma to misplace her legendary self-sufficiency, it had to be the moment Jenny and Nick most needed to be alone.

Nick had had to settle for nonverbal communication, and in the eerie, flickering green light of the summer storm, it had crawled over Jenny like electricity.

He had kissed her goodbye again. This time the kids had been watching, so the two of them had kept hands to themselves and communicated every desire, every half-wished yearning through eyes and intuition. Jenny hadn't been able to sleep since.

She ached for him. She paced and fidgeted and lost track of time wondering what he was doing as she pulled the sheets back in her bed. He had no air-conditioning. Did he sleep in the nude or in shorts, the heat raising a sheen of sweat on his body? Did he put a fan in the window so that it winnowed his hair? Did he wrap himself in crisp white sheets or sleep haphazardly over the bed on his stomach, the pillow bunched up under his head?

Lying there in the dark with only the hum of appliances to keep her company and the cool wash of air-conditioning tempting her, Jenny could imagine all too painfully just how the stubble of his beard would feel against her lips. How the night-warm skin of his back would feel beneath her fingers.

It was ridiculous. She hadn't fantasized since she'd reached puberty. She hadn't awakened with the taste of frustration on her tongue and gone to bed with the ache of longing in her belly. But within a matter of weeks, Nick Barnett had planted that dreadful anticipation in her. His eyes, his cocky grin, the loose grace of his gait. The lost child in his eyes . . .

Suddenly, within the period of two, very abrupt kisses, he'd unleashed a yearning she'd never before known, a passion that frightened her. He'd made her grieve his loss before he'd even gone.

"Jenny!"

Startled, Jenny finally straightened to consider her red-faced sister. "Kate, they'll be here in a few minutes. I'm not having them think I need help."

Kate looked stunned. "But you went to your lawyer to get more money. You sat in that man's office and told him so yourself."

Pulling herself straight, Jenny gathered her frayed poise. "Yes," she admitted. "But Amber Jean wasn't with him." *And I didn't feel so lost, so set adrift and torn. I wasn't questioning my instincts.*

Kate just sighed. "Of course. It makes perfect sense."

"Why would she come here?" Jenny demanded, tossing the small stuffed dog she'd unearthed into a clothes basket full of retrieved toys. "She's never set foot in this house."

"Well, they do have to drive two cars home."

"He could have paid someone to do it. He could have paid all of south county to do it."

Without warning Kate intercepted Jenny in mid-search and grabbed her by the arms. "Jen," her sister said, eyes sincere. "I've never even seen Amber Jean provoke this kind of tantrum. What's wrong?"

"Wrong?" Jenny took a quick look around for something else to straighten, but she'd already finished it. She even had a pitcher of sun tea steeping on the windowsill in the kitchen. "Nothing's wrong."

"And I'm just a little pregnant," Kate retorted dryly. "Is it Nick? Did he hurt you?"

"Nick?" That brought Kate's eyes home, but the rest there was too uncomfortable. Her sister read her better than most. "No, Nick didn't hurt me. He's a nice guy."

Kate groaned. "Bill Bailey is a nice guy. Nick is a major fantasy."

"Nick is a guy with hang-ups just like every other man in the world."

Kate lifted an eyebrow. "Besides wanting to be a lawyer? The American Psychiatric Association still hasn't classified that a mental illness yet, you know."

"Kate," Jenny insisted, her own message intent. "The Jerk and Amber Jean are going to show up any minute now. I'd rather take care of one unpleasant conversation at a time. We can talk about Nick later."

"As long as you're still coherent."

Jenny shot her a grimace. "Nothing like a sister for undying support."

"It looks fine in here," Kate assured her, eyes sparkling. "Just keep the door to the kitchen closed so that nothing escapes."

That brought Kate an answering grin. "Snot."

Kate gave her a hug. "I do my best. I'm taking Brooke to tea. Would Emma like to come?"

Picking up the basket and following her sister out to the foyer, Jenny shook her head. "She won't leave the house yet."

"She still sees Munchkins under the rocks?"

Jenny shook her head again, long past understanding the convoluted workings of Emma's mind. "Emma's just my baby who needs her stability. And she hasn't really had much. I can hardly hold the fear of losing me against her."

Funny, it had been Nick who'd best understood. He had taken his turn with Emma, unbelievably patient when she'd insisted Jenny stay within arm's distance during the storm, spinning stories for the little girl's wide-eyed enjoyment during the lulls. Jenny was sure it was only her imagination that his fairy tales bore a striking resemblance to reworked Fitzgerald and Hemingway.

"Well, then," Kate decided, hand on the door. "We'll all four go next week. Tell the Queen to wear her best gown."

Jenny nodded. Sharing one last quick hug, Kate opened the door.

"Oh. Hello."

Jenny almost dropped the basket. She hadn't gotten the chance to change yet, and there they were, standing on her front porch, acting as if they'd just been caught necking. The new Mr. and Mrs. Lake.

Kate faltered and then smiled, all of the family's censure in her chilly green eyes. "Well, *I'll* be going."

She never even gave the two of them the chance to respond. Left behind, Jenny overcame the absurd impulse to thrust the basket of toys into Kate's hands and announce she'd been donating it to charity. She hated being caught off guard like this. Especially when Amber Jean looked as if she'd dressed for an afternoon of bridge at the country club.

"Come on in," Jenny invited. There was a new Mercedes in her driveway and enough diamonds on Amber Jean's manicured fingers to warn ships off rocks. Jenny thought she was going to be sick.

Out on the lawn, Kate was turning around, motioning down the street for Jenny's benefit. Jenny dropped the basket on the stairs so she could hold the door for her guests, and then followed Kate's attention.

The ice cream truck. It was a little late for Nick to still be around. Even so, there he was parked at the top of the street. Offering support or spying? She wished she knew, because the sight of it only served to increase the weight of the knot in her stomach. When Kate got into her car, Jenny damn near followed.

"Oh, Danish furniture," Amber was gushing in that little singsong voice of hers. "You're so brave. I wouldn't have the nerve to put it in my house."

Biting back a dozen retorts, Jenny shut the door. "Thank you."

They had both taken a seat on the couch. Suddenly Jenny wished she would have left at least one toy in the cushions. Preferably one with sharp edges. "Tea?"

"Lemon and sugar," Amber smiled brightly.

When she walked back into the living room, Jenny brought the Porsche keys with her. "I think you have a bull's-eye painted on the back of that thing," she admitted, handing them over with the Jerk's iced tea. "The police have been following me like bird dogs."

He snorted and shook his head. "They must have a quota to keep. They stopped me five times in a week."

Jenny lifted an eyebrow. "Five times. Imagine." She knew better than to think his only offense had been red paint.

For a moment there was a silence in the room. Amber Jean concentrated on her drink, her gold bracelets clinking. The Jerk concentrated on Amber Jean. Something was brewing here, and it was churning all the way to Jenny's stomach.

"Look, Jen," the Jerk finally spoke up, his tone conciliatory, his eyes straying to his new wife. "I'm sorry about how I acted the other day. It's just . . . well, I was on edge. We were waiting for Amber Jean's test to come back, after all."

Suddenly Jenny felt uncertain. No matter what she thought of her husband's new wife, she didn't wish her real harm. "Test?" she asked, turning concerned eyes on the blonde. "Are you all right?"

Amber Jean burst into bright giggles. "Oh, I'm just fine," she cooed, finding her husband's hand and squeezing it. "I'm going to have a baby."

Jenny did her best to hold on to her glass. She stared. Somewhere deep inside her, something precious shattered. "A baby?"

Suddenly the Jerk was smiling as if he'd invented the idea. He put his arm around his little blonde, looking proprietary as hell. "It's time I was a real father," he said. "Amber Jean convinced me. We have so much to offer a baby."

What about the ones you have? Jenny wanted to demand. She wanted to scream, to shriek, to rip something apart. She never got the chance.

"Mommy?"

Saved by Emma, Jenny couldn't help but think, her eyes leveled on the silly smile on Amber Jean's vapid face. Jenny wanted to get to her feet. She settled for turning to greet her child. "Amber Jean, I don't think you've ever met my daughter Emma, have you?"

Amber Jean didn't seem to appreciate the inference. She only smiled more brightly. Emma reached the doorway and Jenny prepared for introductions. Emma never gave her the chance.

"Mommy!" she shrieked suddenly, whirling to grab Jenny's pant leg. "No! Don't make me!"

Even Jenny was confused. "Emma?"

The little girl's head was buried in Jenny's lap, her body convulsed with fear. "It's her! It's her! The witch! They're going to carry me to her castle and never let me out!"

Emma did everything but climb straight up Jenny's chest. The Jerk got to his feet, furious. Jenny did her best not to laugh. Not at Emma—the little girl was sincerely terrified—but at her accusation. Jenny couldn't have put it better herself.

"Excuse me," she announced to her stunned guests. "I'll be right back."

By the time she got Emma safely settled in her room with Kevin to watch guard against invasion, Jenny returned to find her two guests growing restless.

"Look, Jen," the Jerk announced, getting to his feet. "We came here to share this with you. Amber Jean felt it was important." Amber Jean was rock-still, a brittle shock still on her features. "Because she also thought it was time we talked to you about custody of Kevin and Emma. We could—you know—take them off your hands."

Jenny had reached her chair. Halfway to sitting, she bolted upright. The other shoe had just fallen. She stiffened with outrage. She knew she'd never strike another person, because at that moment she didn't belt the Jerk right where he deserved it.

"After all," he was saying, his eyes straying after Emma. "We have a stable home. And we're moving soon, so we'll have more room. It'll be a good place for them."

"I don't think so."

He gave glare for glare. "I'm their father, Jen."

Jenny laughed. "According to Emma, you're a flying monkey."

"Jen," he retorted, straightening into his best intimidating posture, which negated his next words. "We're trying to bridge the gap here."

Jenny nodded, a stiff, jerky movement that betrayed the cost of her control. "Fine. Start by remembering your children's birthdays. Show up for a few soccer games. Then we'll see."

Amber Jean made the mistake of sighing. "But we don't have time," she objected, still trying to smile her way through with a flutter of her hand. "I thought it would be really nice to get to know Emma and Kevin, ya know? Kinda be like practice before our own little Junior came along."

That did it. The frail remnants of Jen's patience evaporated. "Buy a doll that wets. My children aren't educational toys."

Turning away from temptation, she walked to the door. By the time she held it open, her guests had gathered themselves enough to follow.

"Congratulations," she said to the blonde, her voice trembling with the effort of sincerity. "Babies are wonderful. I hope you're happy." Then she turned to her ex-husband and the shock turned to acid. "Maybe it will teach you enough responsibility to take care of your other children."

"Don't be a bitch," he snapped.

She smiled frostily. "The car is in perfect condition. Don't try and pin any dents on me. Goodbye."

For a long time after she shut the door, Jenny stood staring after it.

A baby. Amber Jean was going to have a baby. Jenny heard those echoes again, the laughter that had never reached her rooms. The children she wanted. The children she should have had. The children she never would now.

The tears formed in her chest, great greasy lumps that weighed down her heart and blocked her lungs. Hot coals that ate away at her, stealing all the fortitude she'd worked so very hard to build over the years.

A baby. Oh dear God, it wasn't fair. It just wasn't fair!

And then, bubbling out of the depths of two years of frustration, two years of loneliness and heartache and disappointment, stripping away the last of her facade, the sobs took her.

He'd watched them pull up. Field glasses did come in handy, after all. The guy had miserable taste. That blond bimbo looked like she had all the brains of a chocolate-chip cookie. Nick found himself sneering at the fact that this upscale yuppie didn't have the sense to spot class if it hit him in the face. After all, he'd tossed Jenny aside and taken up with Miss Congeniality here.

Evidently the visit didn't go well. Before Nick had even gotten a chapter of his book read the two of them shot back out the door like scalded cats, the guy scowling at his wife as if she'd personally hiked his shorts. When they spun past the ice cream truck, she looked confused and he looked mad as hell. Nick smiled. Jenny must have sent him out with his tail between his legs.

Served him right.

Nick decided to give Jenny another few minutes before he showed up. After all, he'd seen her sister point him out. He'd waved as she'd pulled past him. So Jenny knew he was here. It was just a matter of giving her some room to cool off. Lighting up a fresh cigarette, he turned back to his book.

"Mr...Nick! Mr. Nick!"

No mistaking that voice. Grinding the new cigarette back out, Nick prepared to intercept the human missile headed his way. Emma was a good half block away when he saw the distress on her tiny features.

She'd looked that way at the picnic the other day, when she thought she was going to be blown to Oz. Only there wasn't a cloud in the sky. The book slapped onto vinyl and Nick swung out of his truck on the run.

"My mommy," she sobbed, lifting easily into his arms. "The wicked witch came, and now my mommy's crying. Come help her, please, Mr. Nick. She hurted herself . . ."

He was sure the rest made sense, but Nick couldn't quite pay attention. Jenny hurt? Did that bastard do something to her? By God, he'd have the entire force down on his butt in ten minutes flat. He'd personally rearrange that smarmy, upscale face. He was running without knowing it.

Nick shouldn't have been surprised that somebody noticed him enter Jen's house. He slammed in, the door bouncing off the wall and back again. Kevin stood in the hallway, eyes focused into the living room, hands in pockets.

"I think she's mad," he said without turning away.

Nick reached his side and set Emma down. She clung to him, terrified.

"Jenny?"

She sat dead-center on her living room floor, a laundry basket next to her, the room strewn with toys. As Nick watched, she heaved yet another, a metal truck that clanged with effect against the wall. She seemed to be aiming for a little crystal object on a shelf by the fireplace, but the sobs that racked her ruined her aim.

"I can't . . . hit it!" she cried, picking up a small, stuffed dog. "I can't even break the damn thing."

"Jenny?" Carefully Nick stepped into the living room, Emma still clinging like a limpet. "You're scaring Emma."

You're scaring me.

Abruptly Jenny looked up. Her eyes were swollen and red. She fought to control the tears that still splashed on her bare arms, but it was a losing battle. Holding out her hands, she took her little girl into her hold, her grip so tight Nick wasn't sure how Emma was breathing.

"I'm...sorry," she apologized on a hiccough, still shuddering. "I'm...sorry, baby. Mommy's just having a...tantrum, okay?"

Quizzically Emma backed up. "Like Kevin?"

Jenny proffered a watery smile, her control slipping a little. "Like Kevin."

That was when Barb made it through the front door on the run.

"I'll explain later," Jenny said without looking away from the face she stroked, "but would you mind if the kids came over for a while?"

Barb looked aghast, so Nick figured this was unusual behavior for Jenny. "Of course not."

"No!" Emma protested, holding more tightly. "*She'll* come back!"

Nick was surprised by Jenny's bubbling laugh. "No she won't, Emma. I promise. Mommy will be right here. I just think tantrums should be private, okay?"

Emma edged back again. "Promise?"

Jenny nodded and hugged her daughter again. Kevin never questioned the actions, and followed Barb and Emma back out the door. He did, however, close it behind him. Nick thought he was a brighter kid than he'd given him credit for.

"Damn him," Jenny was chanting, the tears building again, her hands up to her eyes. "Damn him."

Uncertain, untried, Nick eased closer. He didn't know what to do with Jenny. The only crying women he'd ever dealt with were suspects. And they sure as hell hadn't made him feel like he had a knife in his chest. "Come on, Jen. Come sit on the couch."

"Sit?" she countered, not seeming to notice that he was the only one left with her. "I can't...sit. I can't even hit that damn shoe!"

Pulling out of her crouch, she grabbed for a block and sailed it straight to the wall, scoring a perfect hit. The little glass object shattered with a sharp tinkle and rained down on the carpet.

"Why that?" he asked when Jenny met her victory with a gulping sob.

"Because," she said, hauling herself to her feet to face him, "that was my gift for having Emma. A crystal shoe from Neiman-Marcus. The Jerk's secretary took her lunch hour to get it for me, and then signed the card."

She was pacing now, pulling her hands through her hair, distraught beyond Nick's comprehension. "What did he say to you?" he asked, following as she pushed the French doors open into the kitchen.

Jenny reached her refrigerator, where Kevin had hung a huge sign proclaiming his love for his mother, and stopped. And sobbed. "He says he's going to ask for custody. That bastard hasn't paid attention to those kids since he filed them as a tax deduction, and now he wants custody."

She was so still, so rigid. Nick kept his distance, aching to hold her. Suffering more with each of her sobs than he had in years of silence. "Why now?"

"Why?" she asked, turning, her face crumpling a little. "Because Amber Jean's pregnant, that's why. He finds religion, and now *she's* having my babies."

"You don't really want his kids, do you?"

She brushed aside the question with angry hands. "Of course not. But, dammit, I don't want her to have them either!" There was lightning in those green eyes, a fury that paled the tears, a wild frustration that was born of places Nick had never gone. "*I'm* the one who wants babies. I'm the one who was told by him that more than one was obscene. And *he's* the one having more children."

Nick didn't know what to say. He felt the whirlpool of her emotions suck him in, felt the pull of that deadly, dangerous current. He understood in ways he didn't name and yet couldn't bring himself to address them. "Jenny, don't you think this is pretty intense?"

Jenny considered him with tear-swollen eyes, quieter for her tirade, no less devastated. Nick saw the weight of years in those tears.

"I've been saving this one up," she said on a soft, sad little sigh, the energy draining away. "I've kept my cool through every court contest, through every session begging for money and excusing indifference. I've broken my damned back so my

children didn't know what a selfish bastard their father was."
Lifting her hand in a futile little gesture, Jenny shook her head.
"I've fought every damn day to survive. To somehow win
something from all this. And one toothy grin from Amber Jean
tells me I've lost. I've lost everything." She framed her words
with shaking hands. "Young tartlet gets babies. Responsible
mother gets twenty more years of frustration."

Nick watched her fold, watched the rage collapse into grief,
the dark, endless minutes of the night betray themselves in
heart-wrenching words. "And I never hold another baby in my
arms."

He couldn't stay away. Crossing the space between them, he
gathered her into his arms, tilting her head back, wanting only
to give something back, to fill those suddenly empty places in
her beautiful eyes. "Jenny, you're only thirty. Who says you
can't have more children?"

Jenny's tears slid down his hands now. Her eyes challenged
him, their light dying, the darkness all that was left of that
teeming green. "Because I won't have them alone. I'm funny
that way, Nick." She pulled away, intent on her message.
"Look around you," she said, swinging an arm to take in the
usual state of her kitchen, including in her gesture everything
Nick had been witness to. "What man is going to jump at a
chance to inherit this?"

Nick had never anticipated being asked a question like this.
He'd never in his life considered answering. But answer he did,
even as he looked around at the half-washed dishes, the crayon-
strewn table and mud-speckled floor. Even considering the ex-
tras he didn't now see. Before he realized it, he looked Jenny in
the face and admitted the truth.

"Me."

Chapter 11

Silence. Jenny heard it, full and pulsing like a tide, rushing along like seconds. She tasted the weight of it, the tension like copper, brackish on the tongue. She saw the cost of it in the astonishment that bloomed in Nick's eyes.

He wouldn't repeat it. She knew he wouldn't. Something about the startled edge to his eyes, the brittle hesitation from flight in his posture, warned her. Nick had made one admission too many and all the pounding in Jenny's chest, all the sudden hope that stretched across her like taut wire wouldn't provoke him to make a promise out of his words.

"Well, why not?" he demanded suddenly. He took her by the arms and pulled her back to him, fitting her tight against the solid length of his body. "Why wouldn't I want a life with you?"

Jenny couldn't help it. She had to break this bubble before it engulfed her. "Because you don't love me?"

When he turned his eyes on her this time, they pierced her. Honey and sunlight, sweet warmth and promise. Anticipation, hunger, trepidation. What was in her eyes, too? "But I do love you. I've been falling in love with you since the minute I first sat on your porch swing."

No.

"You don't like kids."

"You call Emma a kid?" He was smiling, a silly, crooked cant to his face that hurt her, that taunted her.

He couldn't mean it.

"Don't do this, Nick," she pleaded, struggling to get away, to find air, room, sense. She smelled him, dark and rich, like the earth. Like the fertile, fecund earth, and she wanted to lie down in it and rest. She wanted to till it, to watch it bloom in the spring and run her fingers through its cool, soft furrows.

She wanted children and he didn't.

"I mean it, Jenny."

Jenny tried to drag in a breath only to feel the solid plane of his chest against her breasts. Only to mold more closely to him, sharpening the ache to belong, to share.

"And I should just believe you," she challenged with brittle eyes, knowing he could see the war waging in her, unsure how to shield him from it—unsure how to protect herself from his sharp eyes and gentle hands. He'd made it worse, after all. He'd crystallized her ache for children when she saw his eyes, knowing how beautiful they would be on a son, knowing how she would sate herself on his smile if it appeared the first time their daughter smiled.

It was part of loving a man, wanting to see him reborn in a baby's chuckle. Wanting to see the special wonder in his eyes when he first held his child. Sharing and commitment. Two things Jenny couldn't live without in a man. Two things Nick couldn't afford in a relationship.

Instead of answering right away, he lowered his head. Gently, swiftly, like the skim of clouds over the sun, he brushed against her lips in a promise more potent than words. The ache flared in Jenny like a struck match. Pungent, searing.

"Yes," he said. "You should believe me. You know more about me than anyone. I've opened up to you, Jenny. I've never done that before. I've never told stories to little girls or had impromptu picnics in the park." Lifting his head, he captured her gaze again, the yearning melting his golden eyes. "I want to be your family."

A sob bubbled up in her, disbelief and longing. Shattered defenses struggling to hold.

"I know more about you than anyone, huh?" Jenny gathered her outrage anew, forcing it down deep where it could take root. It helped her push away from the sapping comfort of his arms. "How about your name, Nick? Do I know your name?"

For a moment Nick looked bemused. "My name," he echoed uncertainly. "What—"

"What do you think a man could be up to that he'd need an alias, Nick? Or is it really Nick? What *do* I call you?"

The light dawned. Surprise, chagrin, understanding. The sight of it brought the tears back to her eyes. Nick knew exactly what she was talking about.

"Oh, God," she moaned, absolutely still with the weight of her words. "You *do* sell drugs."

If she'd wanted a reaction, she couldn't have led with a better accusation.

Nick looked like he'd been shot. "I *what*?"

Jenny wasn't really listening. "All this time I've been defending you. I kept telling them that Emma couldn't like you if you were a drug dealer . . . that I couldn't like you . . ."

His expression had grown comical. "A drug dealer? You think I'm a drug dealer?"

"Well, why else would you wear your hair in a ponytail and ride in an ice cream truck and carry a beeper?" Jenny demanded, completely at the end of her wits.

Then Nick laughed, and she stared. "Because I'm a cop," he told her, laughing again.

Then he was pacing, walking off her kitchen with the same kind of steps that had eaten up that basketball court, his eyes darting back to Jenny again and again as she stood like stone before him.

"You are not," she accused, turning on him. "The detective would have known."

"Detective?" He came to a stop, the laughter still bright in his eyes. "What detective?"

"From St. Anthony. He's been watching you . . . well, *we've* been watching you. He thought it was easier."

Nick bent close, his face inches from Jenny's. "You've been watching me?"

Jenny's first instinct was to shy away. With an effort she held her ground, chin up. "You had a ponytail . . ."

"And a beeper." He nodded. "I know. So this clown from St. Anthony's figures you can find out about me if you invite me over. Like, maybe, to fix your car."

Still Jenny didn't flinch, even though she desperately wanted to. "Something like that."

Why should she be defending herself? He was the one who hadn't been honest, who had only opened selected doors to her. He was professing love and still Jenny only knew fragments of him, like a scattered fall of jigsaw-puzzle pieces.

She wanted to turn away. She wanted to run before he made it all worse. Wasn't her day shaping up to be bad enough without finding out things she didn't want to know?

"But what about that black man? In the Cadillac."

For a moment Nick stared, lost. Then he shook his head, grinning. "Al Washington," he said. "From Narcotics. He bought some baseball tickets from me. It was the only chance we had to meet."

"A cop?" she asked, suddenly connecting the inference. "On an ice cream wagon? What were you doing?"

His grin was knowing, anticipating. "Undercover."

He wasn't making Jenny any happier. "What are you doing in our neighborhood?"

She really should have been insulted when he kept laughing. This time he pointed a finger. "Keeping an eye on you."

Jenny jerked back. *"What?"*

"You've been making unscheduled stops at mailboxes, young lady. Suspicious ones."

Overcome with the desperate feeling that she was sinking fast, Jenny slowly nodded her head. "And checks have been disappearing from the neighborhood." The silence closed in again as she met those laughing eyes with stunned ones. "You've been watching *me*?"

"It seems," he informed her with a grin, "that we have been watching each other."

Nick came to a halt before her, careful to keep his distance, his head bent forward as if listening to her, his eyes more alive than she'd ever seen them.

Jenny couldn't deal with it. She just couldn't manage. Too much had been tossed on her plate in too short a time. Her stomach churned and her chest hurt. There were still tears on her cheeks and a strange effervescence along her skin where Nick had taken hold of her.

She still felt the acid of Amber Jean's announcement eating away at her tenuous composure, and suddenly she was having to deal with Nick. Nick who said he loved her. Who said he'd been following her to make sure she hadn't been stealing checks from mailboxes. Nick who was everything she could want in a man and nothing she could tolerate.

Tears threatened again, hot, frustrated tears that didn't know whether to escape through sobs or laughter. Jenny shook her head, not even noticing anymore that the sun had sunk and taken much of the light with it. The lights weren't even on in the kitchen, so that Nick looked like an apparition—a savory temptation sent to taunt her, a delicious seduction meant only to remind her of what she couldn't have.

Knowing no other way to deal with the unimaginable, Jenny faced it with her embattled humor.

"So, you mean to tell me," she said, hands on hips, "that all the time I've been sneaking around behind your back, you've been sneaking around behind mine?"

Nick saw something in Jenny's eyes she hadn't anticipated. Instead of laughing, he shrugged. Smiled. Walked right up and gathered her back into his arms.

"Pretty despicable, if you ask me," he said in a gentle voice.

Almost without realizing it, Jenny wrapped her own arms around his back. There was so much support there, so much more strength than she could muster right now. Giving in to temptation, she closed her eyes and nestled against his chest.

"Reprehensible."

Jenny lost sight of her troubles. For just those few moments, she sought sanctuary. The tears escaped, after all, hot and bitter, sliding down her cheeks and soaking into his shirt. He stroked her hair. She refused to look at him, to move or return his touches. He just murmured to her, crooning her name like a litany, his voice soft and soothing. He held her against the world, against selfish ex-husbands and escalating bills. He held her against the growing night, and Jenny knew finally what she had been looking for when she'd once asked the Jerk to take her into his arms.

"I'm going to have to deal with some of this soon," she sniffed, not moving.

She could hear Nick's smile in his voice. "One thing at a time, Jen."

Jenny laughed, a harsh bark. "Where do you suggest we start?"

Nick went on stroking, his hand clumsy against her hair, as if he weren't really used to the action. It made Jenny hurt even more. "My name is Nick Barnes," he said. "Everything else is the same."

She lifted her head at that, eyes still full, expression battling against the absurd exhilaration the admission gave her.

"Even your phone number?"

He smiled. "Even my phone number. Why didn't you run over to the detective and have it checked? I gave it to you three days ago."

Jenny couldn't quite face him. "I don't know," she admitted on a half sniff, her eyes on the tearstains on his best white T-shirt. "I guess I didn't want him to be right. I didn't want you to be a drug dealer like everybody thought."

"Why didn't you just ask me?"

She shrugged. "I wanted you to be the one to tell me who you really were. Something about trust." A smile wavered along her mouth then, a tenuous return to sanity. "Seems we were both having that problem, huh?"

"Believe it or not," he told her, the shadows turning his eyes to sienna, the color of hills in early spring, the texture of honey. "I wasn't the one who didn't trust you. It was my boss. He got a tip."

"From whom?"

Nick shrugged, stroking her cheek with a calloused thumb.

Jenny wanted to lean into it, give in to the tender-rough sensation of his affection. She couldn't.

She did grin, though, a hesitant offering. "I'd put my money on Mrs. Warner. She thinks *you* get off a plane from Colombia every Monday morning."

Nick lifted an eyebrow. "She'd report you? I thought she liked you."

"Duty before all," she intoned. "Her nephew would be proud of her."

Nick grimaced, not so sure.

"But if you don't like kids," Jenny persisted, "how did you end up on the ice cream truck?"

For a moment Nick did nothing but watch her, a curious smile playing about his eyes. Surprised, troubled, intrigued. Then he just shook his head. "How about if we get ourselves some drinks and sit for this? I have a feeling it's going to get complicated."

"How 'bout if we get drinks and curl into the fetal position on the floor?" Jenny countered dryly. "I won't have to move so far to start my breakdown."

She didn't have to move far. She had to wait. Jenny should have known it wouldn't have been as easy as just pouring her troubles out to Nick. She still had neighbors who had an uncanny sixth sense and Barb for impetus. She had a family with Barb's phone number and two children whom she'd terrified. And Nick, even though he protested, had a truck he had to get back to the ex-Sergeant Manetti.

And so within the period of two phone calls and a tapping on the back door from an escapee with blond hair and very worried, three-year-old eyes, Jenny did what she'd been doing for two years. She shelved the turmoil in her for later. She wiped her eyes and assured Nick she was all right. She swept Emma into her arms and agreed, for a change, to let Barb send over dinner. And when Nick left, he promised her the end of the conversation if she promised to keep his secret.

Jenny wasn't sure what she expected, either of Nick or herself. She walked through the evening as if she were underwater, instinctively doling out food, chores and kisses as she did every other day, reassuring Barb even more than her children, especially when Barb found out about the Jerk's latest calumny. And all the while Jenny waited.

She couldn't eat. There wasn't enough room in her along with all the trauma residue. Betrayal battled with astonishment, curiosity with trepidation. Hope and dejection, anger, fear, all filled her like a roiling pot of corrosive.

And to top it, like frothy icing that was much too decadent to partake of, came the escalating hum of desire. Distracting her, preoccupying her, dancing around the edges of her perception like lightning and surprising her with its sudden shock.

She'd known it all along, from the moment she'd first walked out to see that Marine Corps tattoo where usually she just saw pimples. If Jenny Lake were another person, a less responsible person, she would have done anything to bring Nick Barnett to her bed.

Barnes. Nick *Barnes*: she had to remember that.

His other name, his other identity, a mystery man with a knowing smile and an ice cream truck. A policeman who might just be in love with her.

That revelation was what had finally unleashed the desire, setting it free from the constraints she'd imposed. It had swept out from the impulses of late-night hours to daylight, to the admission that the chemistry between Jenny and Nick was all the more potent for his proclamation. If he did mean it—if he did love her—Jenny had the disturbing suspicion that he might well consume her. What unnerved her was the fact that after almost thirty years of being the responsible one, it was what she wanted.

By the time the kids were in bed, Jenny didn't have any energy left. She'd waited for Nick to come back, to explain, to elaborate. He hadn't come. She'd even gone so far as to call him, needing to at least hear him reaffirm his promise. He hadn't been home.

She'd heard nothing. And now, as the clock snuck around to ten, she found herself in her cotton nightgown sitting on the living-room couch, where the Jerk had sat that afternoon to betray her. In the living room, where Nick had found her and asked her to be his family.

Jenny stared into the shadows of the room, seeing the nicks along the wall where her frustrated throws had landed short of the crystal shoe, seeing the modern Danish furniture Amber

Jean wouldn't have had the nerve to put in her house. Seeing the mess, the evidence of active, challenging children—seeing the sum of her life.

Well, the hell with Amber Jean. No matter what she did, she was still the one who had to live with the Jerk. She had to hold up his mirrors and coo at his intelligence. No matter what she had, she didn't have Emma and Kevin. And she wasn't about to get them, no matter what Jenny had to do.

I am the lucky one, Jenny thought again, the assertion long since her litany of endurance. I'm the one with the love, with the friends and family. Even if I never have Nick, I'll survive just fine.

It should have been easier to hold back the tears.

Nick had meant to knock on the door. A bell ringing that late at night could permanently traumatize Emma, especially after the last few days that kid had spent. He wasn't even sure Jenny had waited up for him. He'd tried her number a couple of times, only to find it busy. Nosy neighbors, supportive sisters, probably. The stuff of family. The furtive dreams of a lonely child.

The street was silent tonight, the air cooler for the storm the other day, the night sky clear with a few stars braving the moonlight. Reaching the porch, Nick thought to check in the window for signs of life before knocking. There were a few lights on. Maybe Jenny would be sitting up over a cup of coffee, or munching popcorn in front of the TV.

She wasn't. Nick saw her right away, curled up on the living-room couch like a small child left behind at a party. Her eyes were closed, and her bent knees peeked out from beneath a soft yellow robe.

Waiting.

He recognized the position, the fight to hold out for the promised visit, the struggle to stay awake, to keep watch. The inexorable pull of sleep. Still she wouldn't quite give up, just in case. If he hadn't shown up, she would have awakened stiff and sore in the morning just where she was.

For a moment he vacillated. She probably needed the sleep. It had been a hell of a day for her. Should he stir everything up again or just let her sleep? Would it be better to work the rest of that poison free right now or give her a chance to get a second wind? He wished Manetti and Baker had given advice instead of sage smiles. He wished he had enough experience to know without having to ask them.

He could have stood on that porch for hours watching her sleep, sating himself on the sight of her translucent skin and parted, full lips. But he had a responsibility to her. Knowing this neighborhood, he realized, taking a quick look around, he stood out on that porch for ten more minutes and there would be police strobes waking the Baileys.

The door was unlocked. Nick shook his head. He was going to have to talk to Jenny about that. She had too much trust in her fellow man. On the other hand, he decided as he eased the door open and slipped inside, this would give him the chance to wake her the way he wanted.

Another dream. A fantasy that had been recurring ever since he'd seen that big, homey four-poster of hers upstairs. Turning in the morning sun to find that face next to him, waiting to be awakened. Waiting to smile. And he'd be the one to create it.

He could be very silent when he wanted. Jenny never twitched as he crossed the living-room rug and crouched alongside her. She never heard his soft intake of breath when he saw what he'd missed from the window.

Tears. Almost dried, enough to still make her eyes a little puffy, streaking just a little along her porcelain cheeks. She'd taken a bath. Her hair was still damp, its curls softer. Nick could smell the lemon soap and shampoo on her. It made him want to dip his face into her neck and rest in the sweet grove of her fragrance.

Nick knew better. He was beginning to know Jenny, and what she didn't need right now was to be rushed. She'd had a lot of surprises today, not many of them welcome.

Hell, *he'd* had a lot of surprises today. If he were honest about it, he'd admit he was still moving on momentum, refusing to question his statement to her. Manetti had just smiled when Nick had admitted the problem. But then, Marco always smiled. Nick hadn't found any help or hindrance. He was all alone on this one. And to be perfectly frank, he'd put off dealing with it until he'd talked to Jenny again.

Only now he wasn't so sure seeing her again was going to help. His gut was already churning. His chest tightened with that unaccustomed ache, the one that fed on her smiles and dreams that always seemed to appear around Jenny.

"Jenny?" He reached out to stroke her cheek, brushing away the tears with his thumb.

Oh, yeah, he was going to be able to make an adult decision around her. Just the feel of that velvet skin against his thumb sent shock waves through him. She was going to break his heart, and there wasn't a damn thing he could do about it.

Jenny could smell the rain. The wind. She heard her name called and smiled, because it sounded soft, like a distant gull's cry.

Then she heard it again.

She opened her eyes. Nick was there, just as she'd wanted. He'd changed, wearing jeans and T-shirt and jacket, letting his hair loose. Funny, he really looked like a drug dealer now. Unsavory and sexy as hell. Jenny thought in that half-asleep state when all emotions floated together, that she'd do something illegal for him. She'd run away with him and disgrace herself and outrage the townsfolk.

"About time you found your way back," she whispered, not moving. He was circling her cheek with his thumb, and his eyes devoured her. He was crouched down to her level so that his face was that close. Jenny saw the stubble and knew he hadn't had a better time of it than she. Absurdly, it made her feel better.

"Well," he admitted, easing into that crooked grin of his, "I figured if there was going to be any yelling and screaming, it should go on after the kids are asleep."

Jenny lifted an eyebrow. "Yelling and screaming?" she echoed. "Now, why should that happen? Are you going to tell me you lied again? Your name is really Nick Bronkowski and you have a wife and seven kids."

She shouldn't have said it. Just the words brought her abruptly upright, almost sending Nick over backwards. Jenny's breath caught in her throat, preventing her from asking the

unbearable. God, that's just what she'd need. Not just a lawyer who didn't like kids, but a married lawyer who didn't like
kids. What surprised her the most was that she hadn't wondered before.

Nick was grinning at her now. "I can see you still haven't
called Detective Richards. Thanks."

Sitting four-square on the couch, Jenny narrowed her eyes at
him. "How do you know?"

"Because he would have pulled my records and assured you
that I'm not married. Never have been—although sometimes
my partner gets just about as demanding as a wife."

Her eyes were narrowing again. "Watch the slurs, Nick."

He was still on his heels, elbows on his knees, watching her
with amused, contented eyes. "Why the tears, Jen? Did I scare
you?"

"Tears?" she countered, getting to her feet and overcoming
the urge to knock him over on his butt. "No tears. I don't cry
for anybody anymore. I gave that up a long time ago."

Nick followed to his feet and grinned down at her. "Yeah,"
he agreed with a nod and a quick swipe at some of the remain-
ing moisture on Jenny's cheek. "About six o'clock this evening."

"Believe me," she countered, trying to keep the hope from
her eyes and voice, "that *was* a long time ago."

Nick took her by the shoulders. "I know. I'm sorry. I tried
to get back sooner, but there were a few details to take care of."

Jenny tilted her head to the side, her hair brushing the yellow cotton on her shoulder. "Is it time to have that drink?"

Nick nodded and followed when she turned for the kitchen.
"What details?" she asked.

She didn't see the wolf's smile on Nick's face. "Reinstating
the watch on a certain red Porsche, for one."

Jenny whirled on him, almost slamming right into Nick's
chest. "Watch?" she demanded. "As in police?"

He nodded.

She was surprised to find herself laughing. "*You* were behind all those tickets he got?" With his smile, she shook her
head. "But why?"

"Principle."

Still Jenny didn't move. She didn't realize she'd tilted her head a little again, as if to better assess Nick and his motives. "What does principle have to do with it?"

Nick was still grinning. "You'll probably understand better when I tell you how I got stuck on the ice cream truck."

Somehow, they didn't quite get to the ice cream truck. They didn't even get to the drinks.

Jenny poured them, splashing a healthy amount of gin into each glass and sacrificing a real lime, but she never got her first taste. Something else got in the way.

Nick.

He stood right behind her as she poured, sending some of the gin dripping from the countertop and into the cat's dish. Silent, watching, waiting. And Jenny, her body suddenly much too acutely aware of what it had missed for more than two years, knew him there like a starving animal smells water.

"Maybe this isn't such a good idea," he murmured close to her neck, his breath fanning her.

Then he'd been struck by that same mysterious bolt of lightning. Jenny should have been upset. She couldn't quite admit that instead she was glad.

"What is a good idea, Nick?" she asked without turning around. The gin was oily on her fingers and she wanted to lick it like the chicken grease. She wanted Nick to lick it.

"A good idea," he answered very quietly, "is for me to get the hell out of here before I take you right here on the kitchen floor."

He surprised a little gasp from her. Jenny held on to the chilled glass, wondering how desire could so quickly explode, like a forest fire crowning with only a few words. Her hands were shaking. Her heart slid and skipped, threatening to tumble right out of her chest where her lungs suddenly weren't working. Her trembling hands began to sweat.

"Did I tell you," she said, eyes closed, "that imagination is something I value in a man?"

For a moment there was no answer. The light over the sink kept the shadows at bay. It also seemed to throw off an inordinate amount of heat. Jenny's skin was flushed, and the brush of Nick's breath against her neck raised goose bumps.

He tried one last time, his voice tight and unhappy. "My name is Nick Bronkowski and I have a wife and seven kids."

When Jenny smiled, she opened her eyes. Nick was reflected in the window, his dark head almost lost in the shadows above her. Like a dream, following her, shadowing her even in waking moments. Always there, always tempting, tormenting. Close enough to touch, never real enough to hold.

Except Nick was real. And he wanted her.

Jenny turned on him, finally allowing the tentative banners of anticipation to reach her eyes. One look at Nick very nearly took her resolve. His eyes were hot. They swept her as if unable to remain still, soaking in the sight of her, stirring the fire that glowed at their depths. Nick stood so rigidly Jenny thought a touch would break him. His mouth was set. His brow was creased. He was fighting for distance and losing.

"Did I scare *you*?" Jenny asked in a very small voice.

He never moved, either to close the distance between them or increase it. His breath was coming more quickly; his chest rose erratically. "Yes," he finally said, his voice as tortured as his eyes. "You scare the hell out of me."

She had on nothing beneath her gown. The cotton suddenly chafed her, too cool and crisp against her aching breasts, too heavy along fiery skin. Jenny thought she could feel the heat emanate from Nick like the waves from a summer street. It brought color into her cheeks and made her hands restless. It beckoned to her tongue. Jenny wanted to taste that heat, to bask in it and stoke it with flames of her own. She wanted to raise a sheen of sweat on him and lick it off.

"Jenny?"

Her own chest was rising as erratically now as the fire from Nick's eyes stole the oxygen. "Yes."

"I didn't lie. I do love you."

Jenny could hardly move her head to nod. She could hardly bring herself to speak without begging. Nick still hadn't moved, his hands rock-still by his sides, his tongue safely behind closed lips.

"I know," she finally managed. "I love you, too, Nick."

Still they stood apart, held by the ambivalences warring within them. Neither knew how to trust, neither could afford a mistake. Both knew what hunger was, how to bank it. How to control it.

But tonight, there was no control. Even Jenny who had marked every hour of the past two years with the constraint she maintained, could summon none now when she most needed it. All she could think of was that for once, for once in her responsible life, she wanted to be irresponsible. She wanted to take a chance that might not pay off. She wanted to test Nick's limits. She wanted to awaken and see him sleep alongside of her.

She wanted to be taken on her kitchen floor.

"Nick?"

"Yes?"

"Do you like your martinis dry?"

Nick frowned, never taking his eyes from hers, never breaking that precious contact. "Yes."

Now Jenny smiled, her gaze never wavering, offering delight with her desire, honesty with her decision. "Good," she nodded, lifting her hand for him to see the moisture still on her fingers. "I was wondering if you'd take care of this gin for me."

That quickly, Nick's control shattered.

Chapter 12

The tile would be cool against her back. The air-conditioning would wash her, chilling the moist skin Nick kissed. Jenny knew she would never again allow such abandon. She knew the price of it, and she wasn't prepared to pay it.

But now, now she would sing with it.

It began the minute she felt Nick's mouth close around her fingers. He took them one at a time, his eyes locked on hers, his hands wrapped around hers as if afraid she'd pull away. Jenny saw nothing but his eyes, the deliberate invitation offered there. She felt nothing but her finger, cool in the kitchen air, sliding in to meet the rasp of his tongue as he lavished over the liquor on her finger.

The sparks flared there and raced onward, anticipating his conquest, craving it. Skittering up her arm, shattering in her chest where they lodged in her breasts, tautening them impossibly, making her want to cry out with longing. Settling in her belly where they grew, crouching in her like a hot coil, glowing hotter and hotter just with the slick pressure of his lips along her finger. Just with the hold of his hands around hers.

Jenny stood with her back against the counter, her bare feet cold against the floor, her face flushed. She knew her lips had parted. Her eyes had widened, dilated. She was breathing faster to keep up with her heart. But her heart couldn't seem to keep up with Nick's eyes. He was taking her without even touching her, and Jenny groaned with it.

"Imagination, huh?" he asked, his voice no more than a harsh rasp as he ran her sensitized fingers against the bristle of his chin.

Jenny almost jumped with the fresh lightning. She couldn't seem to hold still anymore, as if movement would dispel the pressure building in her. She couldn't even answer. The uncertain wonder in her eyes must have been answer enough.

Nick smiled, a hunter's smile. A lover's smile when he suddenly knew how to best please. Without waiting for an answer, he turned away from Jenny and with one hand swept the contents of the kitchen counter onto the floor.

Jenny stared. She barely had time to react. Nick stole her momentum. He turned back to her and took her hand. "I think it's about time you got more from this kitchen than headaches," he whispered and eased her along to the empty section of counter, where it met the wall without interference from window or cabinet. Jenny wasn't sure she really wanted to test his imagination, after all. She'd never strayed this far. She never really had made love anywhere but on a bed. In the most traditional of terms.

But then Nick slipped out of his jacket and she forgot her objections. "I thought I got to do that," she objected, her voice breathy.

"Next time," he promised. "This time I want you to follow my lead."

Next time? Shouldn't she protest? Shouldn't she stop it before there was a *this* time?

His eyes still on her, Nick lifted his hands to her shoulders. "I've been waiting so long for this," he said, his hands moving to the white buttons that held her robe closed.

"You've only known me a couple of weeks."

He smiled down at her, dropping a kiss that promised so much it took Jenny's breath all over again. "But I've waited my life to meet you."

That very nearly did in Jenny's knees. Nick's fingers brushed against her, tantalizing, anticipating. She could almost feel her skin thrumming beneath them, and it unnerved her. When he reached the last button and reached back up to slip the robe from her shoulders, though, she helped him.

He mesmerized her with his eyes. He paralyzed her with his hands. Before she knew it, she was lifted onto the counter, sitting against him so that her legs wrapped him and her short cotton gown skimmed her hips.

"Nick, this is . . ."

"Fun," he assured her, a finger to her lips.

There was a ribbon at the bodice, a white ribbon that had seemed so safe and comfortable when she'd bought it. Nick reached up to pull it apart, and Jenny bit her lip. The gown fell open a little, and she knew that he could see her breasts. He still didn't take his eyes from hers. His hands strayed to her bare arm and set up fierce goose bumps. He leaned against her so that he fit neatly into the bared vee of her thighs, so she could discover his arousal. Jenny found herself wanting to wrap more closely to him, to get through the course brush of those jeans and share the heat she felt.

She found herself wanting to move again.

Nick lifted his hand and tangled his fingers into Jenny's hair. It tingled all the way to her toes. Standing so that his mouth was the same height as hers, Nick pulled her to him. His lips found hers and set to conquering. Soft, sweet, insistent, nipping and tugging at her until she brought her hands up around his shoulders. Until she tangled her own hands in his hair and kept him against her.

She felt his other hand stray, along her arm, back up her waist, at her collarbone, skimming her like a bird across bright waves. Setting up a chorus of reactions that all seemed to finally sink into her belly. Heating her until she ached for more.

He gave it. Even as he deepened his kiss, his tongue dancing along the edges of hers, even as he mingled sighs of pleasure, he slid his other hand around to ease her gown free. His hand roamed her thighs, her bottom and the tenderest skin right at the base of her spine. He groaned when she arched against him. When she let her own hand drop, he pulled free.

"Not yet," he repeated, the heat of him reflected in the languorous smoke in those whiskey-colored eyes of his. Pulling her hand to his mouth to kiss it, he brought his other hand up.

"You are so beautiful," he murmured, his eyes finally straying, finally seeing that her breasts strained against the cotton, the nipples button-hard against him. It made him smile. "So beautiful."

He watched as he brought his hand to her breast, skimming down the yellow cotton, so lightly Jenny ached to move closer. He stroked her back and cupped a breast in his hand, savoring the weight, the fullness, the delicious texture. Jenny watched him with wonder, her trepidation evaporated with just the delight in his eyes. She'd never known a moment like this, never a pride in herself like this man inspired. Never a crescendo of sensation like he provoked.

Taking her hands in his, Nick raised her arms over her head and lifted her gown away. And then, sliding his hands slowly back down her arms, caressing the underside and sliding lower, he brought them back to her breasts.

Jenny gasped. She arched in his hands, the rasp of his thumbs torture against her sensitive nipples, torment to the ache that now throbbed throughout her. She brought her hands back to his neck, to wind into his thick hair. She tested the hard line of his jaw and the taut tendons of his throat. She could smell him, dark and potent. She could hear him, the ragged catch of his breath, the brush of his hands against her skin. She could feel him, the lightning he sparked, the hunger he incited. It was becoming so hard to wait.

Nick bent to her, so that Jenny could see the top of his head, the glossy hair against her pale skin. He took her nipple in his mouth. Jenny groaned. She let her head fall back. His hand was there. His hand was everywhere. Even as he stirred the fires even higher with his mouth, nipping, laving, suckling until Jenny curled her toes against his denim-clad legs, he brought his other hand back to her thighs. Back to sate the hunger. To open her and please her and entice her.

Jenny instinctively moved against him, seeking his plunder, anxious for his company. She wanted him in her, deep where he would be safe, where she would hold him even when he was far gone from her. She felt his finger slip in to where she waited, swollen and slick for him, and shuddered.

Nick lifted his head, his hands suddenly still. "Jenny?"

Jenny answered by tugging his shirt free of his jeans. "You'd better hurry, bud," she warned breathlessly, "or I'm going to explode into a million pieces."

He took a second to make sure, his eyes dark and turbulent.

"Please, Nick," she begged, hands clutching the material at his shoulders. "Before I throw *you* on the floor."

When he smiled this time, Nick looked years younger, eons older. Jenny laughed, a tinkling sound, like a river in sunlight. Freedom. Exhilaration. Exultation.

"Then I think it's time for that bed," he whispered.

Nick couldn't believe Jenny's reaction. Straightening like he'd insulted her—or frightened her—she shook her head.

"No," she said, her eyes level, her hands against his chest. "Here. Please, Nick."

Nick could hardly argue with releasing the tension that was threatening to explode the denim stitching on his jeans. He'd known hunger in his life, but he'd never known obsession. His obsession had been born the minute he had taken Jenny into his arms.

"Why?" he asked, not wanting to hurt her in any way, unsure she really wanted what she was asking.

But when Jenny smiled, she was every siren, every seductress who had changed the course of history. "You promised imagination, remember?"

Slipping close enough to once again fill his hands with her, Nick nodded. "Yeah. Problem is that Barb and Bill Bailey'd probably catch us when I carried you out to the sandbox."

Somehow Jenny's answering smile only served to stoke the heat higher. Nick could hardly pay attention to what he was saying as it was. Leaning forward a little to brush her lips gently across his, she reached up and pulled the light chain. Instantly the kitchen fell into shadow and moonlight.

"We'll pretend," she whispered.

Nick groaned. "Come here, you," he grated and pulled her into his arms. Just as quickly he felt her stiffen and gasp.

"Cold belt buckle."

Nick silenced her chuckle with his mouth. He wrapped around her and wrapped her around him. And that way he carried her into the playroom where the moonlight streamed in the endless windows, dust motes dancing in the silence, the floor as dark as earth and as cool as water. And it was there he laid her, his nymph, amid the forest that was her imagination.

Nick straightened from her to unbuckle his jeans. He couldn't take his eyes from her, dark-eyed, her hair like smoke, her skin alabaster white in the moonlight, her nipples a tight dusky rose. God, he had never known such power. Such a delicious hurt. He wanted so much to drive her to a frenzy, to see those eyes go liquid, to see that head thrown back and that body rocking beneath him. He wanted her to cry out to him.

The floor was so cool against Jenny's back, just like she'd thought. The air swam over her like a lazy river, and Nick kept her warm with his eyes.

Jenny watched as he discarded his jeans. She did her best to wait, her body singing in clearer and clearer tones, the pleasure soaring with just the sight of Nick's lean, hardened body. She wanted this—needed it. She needed him. Holding out her arms, she welcomed him home.

She wanted him then. Nick made her wait longer. He rekindled the banked fires, his skin hot and cold at once against hers, the hair-roughened texture of his thighs agony against hers, his tongue greedy and his hands clever. He murmured to her, sighed with her own feverish exploration, nurtured her untapped passion until she danced beneath the play of his hands.

Jenny fought the precipice, waiting for him, wanting him with her. When Nick slid his hand down to test the way, she parted her thighs for him. When he stroked and tantalized, his fingers like lightning against her, she arched, whimpered, clutched at him. When he still stayed away, she took him in her own hands and guided the way.

Nick rode the crest close to the edge, sweeping along unheeded, racing, rocking with Jenny. Just the sweet dance of her hands over his skin threatened to shatter him. When she took him into her, he knew he was lost.

Nick dropped his face into Jenny's throat, soaking in her scent, the song of her cries, the delight of her soft breasts and

velvet skin. He felt her shudders grow, felt her close around him
and invite him along. The moonlight spiraled in him, swirling
and dancing, swimming into music and shattering into day. He
heard his name whispered, sung, chanted and answered with
hers. And there, finally, spent, he pulled her into his arms and
bid her sleep.

At some point the floor became too cool. Jenny was feeling
goose bumps that hadn't been there before. She didn't feel regret for what she'd done. It was just that once the hormones
had been sated, common sense tended to creep back. She was
lying naked on her playroom floor with a man, and she had two
children who could easily walk in. Not that either of them had
ever wandered in the middle of the night, but Murphy lived for
eventualities like this.

"You're shivering," Nick observed, running a languid hand
over her arm.

"The air-conditioning has made its presence known," Jenny
allowed, trying to work up the initiative to move. She didn't
want to. She'd never felt so content in her life. There was
something about this particular set of shoulders that seemed to
carry the weight of the world, something about this chest that
begged nestling. For the first time in her adult life, Jenny gave
fleeting thought to resenting the intrusion of her children.

If it weren't for them, she could easily not move for days.
And right now—except for the chilly Italian quarry tile—she
thought she could manage that quite easily.

"Feel like a shower?" Nick asked.

Jenny shook her head against his shoulder. "Not with Emma
and Kevin upstairs. No offense, but I think they'd take it wrong
if they saw Mom step out of the bathroom naked along with a
man."

Nick didn't seem too perturbed by her answer. "Okay, then
we'll just stay down here."

Jenny thought to ask what that entailed, but before she could
gather the energy Nick pulled them both up and made the move
to the couch where one of Barby's trademark afghans resided.
Nick pulled it up, slid in beneath so that they stretched out

lengthwise, Jenny rested against his back, and laid the afghan over them both.

Jenny couldn't argue with the effect. Toasty warm on both sides, decadently comfortable. Unquestionably content.

"I'm not sure we should," she demurred anyway. "The kids..."

"Can you hear them get up from here?"

"I can hear them turn over from anywhere in the house."

Nick nodded against the back of her head and tightened his arms around her. "Gives you plenty of time to slip back into your nightgown."

"And your jeans?"

"No, I think your nightgown's enough."

Jenny elbowed and met with some satisfying ribs.

Nick just chuckled. "Ease up, Jen. You were the one who wanted imagination. When was the last time you hung out with a naked guy on the couch?"

"And how do I explain the naked guy to my kids?"

"If they show up, I promise I'll make it to the sandbox before they get this far. Then we only have to worry about traumatizing Barb Bailey."

For a moment Jenny considered what Barb's reaction would be to finding a naked Nick in the backyard. Then she found herself chuckling right along with him. "Might be worth it."

He must have been a magician. Just with the contact of his hands across her belly, Nick kept her on that couch. Jenny molded into him, savoring the alien feel of his male body against her, basking in the dying embers of lovemaking.

"Where do we start?" she asked a while later, the answers now even more important.

"I think we just did," Nick said, shifting a little so he could rest his cheek against her hair.

Jenny found herself sighing with the pleasure of it. She wrapped her arms around his and rested. "That doesn't solve all problems."

"Solved mine."

Jenny's eyes were closed. She smiled anyway. "What problems do you have?" she asked.

"Well," he murmured, "I can report back to my boss that I personally searched you and found you clean."

Jenny chuckled. "And I can tell him just how thoroughly you pursued your objectives."

She could hear the grimace in Nick's voice. "Yeah, that's just what I'd need. I'd be out selling apples on the street in a week."

"I could give you a reference as an ice cream driver, if you want."

"Thanks."

"You never asked me," Jenny said, a little while later again. Time seemed to slip so easily away in this silvered darkness. Daylight floated away and left them lying together without hurry.

"Asked you what?"

"Why I was seen at those mailboxes."

"Why *were* you seen at those mailboxes?" he echoed in his best official voice. "I was just about to ask."

"Would you believe me?"

"I'd kill dragons for you."

"Next time Mrs. Warner steals Kevin's ball, I'll be in touch."

Still they lay, entwined, peaceful, holding off the world by sheer dint of their contentment.

"Mailboxes," he nudged.

"Kevin," she explained, "has decided he wants to be a mailman when he grows up. So, to that end, he's been playing mailman."

"With other people's mail?"

Jenny nodded. "With other people's mail. I figured it out when I first found Bill Hobbs's medical bills under my bed. Kevin is on parole. I'm watching for repeat offenses."

"What about other people in the neighborhood?"

Jenny thought a moment. "No. I don't think anyone else in the neighborhood wants to be a mailman when they grow up. Buffy wants to be a stockbroker, and I want to be a cowgirl."

"I'll know where to come if I get any reports of rustling."

"Who do you think it is?"

Nick shrugged, his chest rasping against the sensitive skin of her back and sending up fresh shivers. "Hell, I don't know.

The only person I'm sure it isn't is me. And that's only because I'm never far enough away from that damn truck to steal anything.''

"Except when you're here."

"What about when I'm here?"

"You had enough time to steal my good sense. I'd like to know where you put it, please. It's probably time to put it back on."

For a long moment, there was no answer. Jenny felt the atmosphere shift, sensed Nick tense almost as if he were bracing for something.

"You mean you don't think it's sensible to make love to a man on your kitchen counter?''

Jenny smiled, but already it had lost some of its glow. "I mean I don't think it's sensible to make love to a man who lives to be a lawyer."

"Because you did once and look where it got you?"

The caution in his voice took the rest of her smile. She wanted to hug her arms around her belly, to curl away from him even as she burrowed more deeply into the strength of his embrace. "Something like that," she admitted.

"You're not being very reasonable about that."

"No," she admitted. "I'm not. I'm gun-shy. Especially after the three rounds I went today."

"Not everybody's like him, Jen."

"God, I hope not."

"I'm not going to apologize for what I want," he told her. "I'm sure as hell not going to give it up. I've worked too damn hard for it."

Tears stung the back of Jenny's eyes. She knew she was a hot reactor on the subject, but Nick was becoming so important to her. Too important.

Even so, she couldn't bear to hear that hurt edge to his voice. He *had* scraped a lot harder for what he had, after all. And if a desire to be a lawyer had gotten him this far, how could she argue?

"I'm sorry," she apologized, feeling the cold seep into their little nest and hating it. "It's just hard to believe."

"What, that I want to be a lawyer?"

"That you love me."

It was enough to stop the cold. In one motion Nick had her turned around to him, so she could see his eyes, so she could believe his sincerity. "You'd better believe it, lady. I don't lie naked on couches with just anybody."

Jenny matched his winsome smile. "Well, that's the most poignant testimony I've ever heard."

"I've also been spending evenings in the law library trying to figure how to get you out of your ex-husband's clutches."

That had Jenny's full attention. "How could you do that?" she demanded, pulling all the way around so that her feet hit the floor and the afghan slipped.

Nick's eyes slid to where the moonlight washed her breasts. "What?"

His fingers seemed to want to follow. Jenny took them in hand and demanded his attention. "The Jerk," she nudged.

He smiled, easily switching positions so that Jenny's hands were in his. "Easy," he assured her, dropping kisses onto her palms. "It's just a little harder to get custody if the D.A.'s been after you." Kiss. "And since I happen to be good buddies with the guys over at the D.A.'s office, and since your ex is in arrears about six months for his ridiculous excuse for child support," kiss, "with your permission, he's going to be hearing from the law in about two days."

Jenny was finding it increasingly difficult to keep her mind on child support. Nick bent to her hands again and skimmed her now-sensitive palms with his tongue, tasting all the way to the edges of her fingers. Hands again, and he was lighting the same, furious fires. Jenny just wanted to stretch, to purr like a cat and watch him consume her, bit by delicious bit.

"I was going to wait a while," he continued, testing the insides of her wrists and making her gasp. "You know, a few tickets, a little subtle harassment.... But I figure this custody thing warrants special attention."

"But why—" he was traveling the inside of her arms, his teeth nipping at the tender flesh, his tongue leaving a trail for the cool air to find "—why didn't somebody do this before?"

Pausing only long enough to lift a self-satisfied smile at her, Nick explored her elbows. "Because," he said, "no one else has my principles."

Jenny thought she was panting. She wasn't sure. She just knew that without even being touched, her breasts felt like splintered glass, sharp slivers of heat scattering through her. "The principles that got you on the truck?"

He nodded. "I'll have to send the chief's brother a thank-you note."

The tide was rising quickly, hot, thick lava, lapping at her toes, oozing along her calves and spilling over onto her thighs. Seeping into her belly and breasts and taking her breath. Again.

She couldn't think properly. She couldn't seem to care anymore that the Jerk was a jerk. It only mattered that Nick had cared enough to help.

"You really did that?"

Nick moved around so that he sat behind her, his legs straddling her, his lips down at her throat. "Slaved day and night."

Jenny's head came back. Nick's hands were edging around her waist. His teeth were nibbling on the tender flesh along her shoulder. She thought she was going to moan.

"I guess some lawyers aren't . . . so bad."

Nick brought his hands up so that he circled her completely, held her firmly. He was working his way up to her ear and around to her breasts.

"I hear," he said, slipping his tongue into the shell of her ear and provoking gasps, "that I'm pretty good."

"You're—" Jenny responded by sliding her hand behind her and testing his response "—okay."

He laughed, but he sounded breathless. Jenny laughed back, and sounded even more breathless than he. Nick found her breasts. He filled his hands with them, and Jenny was lost.

Nick saw the daylight edging closer and wondered if he'd stayed too long. He lay curled around Jenny on the couch, her head on his shoulder, her hands around his waist. He smelled citrus and soap, lovemaking and morning, and thought that he could live like this forever. He could survive anything if he only had the chance to have this moment each day, this fragile space of peace when Jenny slept in his arms.

She was so beautiful, her eyes closed and her lashes lying like soot against her pale skin. He wanted to run his hands through her hair and kiss her awake. He wanted to make love to her again.

But he knew better. He was on her time, now. Daylight was coming and with it waited the responsibilities, the questions she hadn't asked. The questions *he* hadn't asked.

For at least that moment when the moonlight died into mauve and the birds woke in the trees, Nick could find happiness. For that moment, he could have it all.

"Jenny?"

Her face puckered a little and she nestled closer. Nick ached to love her awake.

"Come on, little girl," he coaxed, finally giving in enough to push her hair back from her forehead.

It made her smile. "I bet you're the fairy godmother, and you're going to tell me it's midnight."

He smiled back, really feeling it take root. "Well, I figured you didn't want certain elves to find you here when they came down for cereal."

Opening her eyes, she nodded. "I appreciate the forethought." For a moment Jenny just watched him, her eyes languid and dark in the half-light, like a deep spring in the woods. "Problem is, I just don't want to move."

Nick ran a finger along the tip of her nose. "See what happens when you let your imagination get out of hand?"

She stretched against him, and Nick knew what the word frustration meant. He could hardly suppress his immediate reaction, but he knew better than to think he could enjoy it. He had business to discuss with Jenny, and it wasn't the kind you could pursue with a sleek, full, warm body nestled in your arms.

"Come on," he urged, moving faster than he should have. "There's something I have to talk to you about."

Jenny obviously didn't wake as quickly as he. When Nick eased her up to a sitting position, she sat there swaying and shivering for a minute, her hair in delightful disarray, her eyes wide and soft. Nick gritted his teeth. It was only getting worse. He had to get back into his jeans before he couldn't.

"It's okay," she assured him with a vague smile. "I still respect you."

Realizing that Jenny wasn't ready to fend for herself just yet, Nick wrapped her in the afghan and turned for his jeans. He didn't miss the fact that the one thing Jenny had definitely noticed in her half-alert state was his state of full alert.

"Isn't nonverbal communication a wonderful thing?" she offered with a much too wicked grin.

"Knock it off," he warned, already yanking on what he knew would be his most uncomfortable pair of pants. "I can't make sense when you look like that. Get some clothes on."

The sound of her giggle was like bells on the wind. "I think you make perfect sense. I'm just sorry we don't have time to...pursue the subject."

The rasp of a zipper was loud in the quiet room. "Get dressed, Jen."

Jenny offered a peculiarly girlish grimace. "Fairy godmothers just aren't as much fun as they used to be."

This godmother responded by hitting her in the face with her nightgown.

"All right," Nick said a few minutes later while the coffee perked and the birds came to raucous life outside the windows. "I need to ask a big favor, Jen."

Perching on a chair opposite him, Jenny offered that sleepy half-smile that was doing such damage to his seams. "Pancakes are out of the question, Nick. I don't cook breakfast."

He scowled. "I'm serious."

"I know," she nodded, refusing to give up her smile. "You're always serious. Gives you frown lines."

For a moment he could do no more than stare at her, his head tilted in consideration. "Well, at least I know you're not crabby in the morning. You're not there, at all."

She just smiled. When the coffee gurgled its last, she got up to pour.

"Jenny, I need to maintain my cover."

He thought she'd object, that she'd anticipate what he was going to ask. Instead, unbelievably, she giggled. "Your cover," she echoed. "It sounds so desperate, like you're running guns for the Godfather or something. I guess an ice cream man was just never my idea of a dangerous situation."

He couldn't help but grin back at her lilting observation. "You've never gotten between a seven-year-old and a bomb-pop on a hot day," he retorted.

Setting his cup down, she slipped back into her chair and eased her chin down onto her hands, that smile still lighting her sleep-softened features. "You want me to help keep the God-father in the dark."

Nick was going to take a sip of coffee. With the cup halfway up, he scowled. "Something like that."

"Am I undercover, too, then?" she asked. "Do I have an alias and a secret-decoder ring?"

"Jenny."

She smiled again and finally brought herself to upright attention. Somewhere in that odd little conversation, the alert intelligence had returned to her expression, and Nick found himself missing the gamine inside.

"The least I can do for the man who has made it his mission to personally harass my ex-husband is help him catch less despicable crooks. What can I do?"

He stopped, faced her with even consideration. "Keep seeing me."

For a moment Jenny just considered him in return. "And how do you ask for dates?" she countered.

Nick shook his head a little, the coffee back on the table as he leaned closer to convince her. "It has nothing to do with last night. I need to finish this assignment, and the only way I'm going to do it is if you don't report me to your friend the detective and the neighbors."

Jenny's eyebrows lifted. "Nobody?"

"Nobody. Not even Barby and Bill Bailey. Not even your family. For the next few days until I can find something, you have to pretend that I'm still the neighborhood drug dealer."

"And keep inviting you over."

"It would give me greater mobility."

Jenny spent a moment facing her tablecloth. Her gaze shifted a little to find the papers and books Nick had swept onto her floor. Without thinking, she got up to pick them up before the kids had a chance to ask. It seemed important somehow that they didn't stumble upon the traces of her lovemaking.

"Was this what was on your mind when you showed up last night?" she asked, fighting inexplicable tears. Stupid that his question had changed the flavor of his promises. Dumb that she should be looking for hidden agendas everywhere.

But then at one time she had been too obtuse to look for hidden agendas, and they'd jumped out to bite her. Jenny didn't want that to happen again.

Bent over the cups and cookbooks she was trying to gather into her arms, she didn't hear Nick scrape his chair back. She didn't notice his approach. Suddenly he was there on the floor next to her, pulling the little pile from her arms, turning her toward him.

"I didn't come here last night for the sole purpose of convincing you," he told her, eye-to-eye, his hand on her arm, his voice intense. "I came to ask. I forgot to do it the minute I saw the tears on your cheeks." Pulling her to her feet, he set down the books and took Jenny into his arms, barring flight and doubt with just the strength of his arms. "I was as surprised as you were, Jen," he said. "I still am. But I'm not sorry. In fact—" how could a smile be so suddenly devastating? she wondered seeing his "—I'm selfish enough to admit that for the first time since I set foot on that damn ice cream wagon, I can really look forward to this assignment."

"I'm not recess," she warned, terrified by the way his eyes sapped her resolve. Exhilarated by the conviction she saw there.

"I never said you were," he countered. "All I'm asking is that the department pick up some of the expenses of this courtship. In return, we wait until I've caught the forger before you reveal my secret identity."

"If I didn't think we had real problems," she answered, "I'd say it sounded like a lot of fun."

"Problems are to be worked out," he said. "We can do that."

For a moment Jenny's challenge was a silent one. She couldn't bear to go forward, couldn't bear to slip back. "Are

you sure?'' she asked, knowing that there was no more important question in her life.

"I'm sure."

Jenny would have been a lot happier if Nick's eyes were as
convinced as his words. Even so, she could still feel the warm
musky aftertaste of love. She could still see the flashes of passion in Nick's eyes when he'd come to her last night. And she
still saw the small, lonely boy who refused to let himself believe. For that, she nodded her head.

"All right," she allowed. "I'll give it a try."

It was only later when she sat once again alone at her table
and heard the first stirrings of her children that Jenny began to
doubt her decision.

Chapter 13

It didn't take Nick much longer.

When he left Jenny's, he headed back to the station. The drive was a quiet one, the streets still empty of rush-hour traffic, the summer morning just beginning to take shape. Nick spent the drive wondering at the events of the night before. He hadn't lied to Jen. He was still amazed that either of them had shown such uncharacteristic abandon. He was awed that she had given so much, known him so well, grown so quickly comfortable with him.

Nick wasn't usually comfortable with anyone. He'd never been relaxed enough with a woman to want to wake up alongside her in the morning. Nick's idea of a relationship had always been marked by the boundaries imposed by a lifetime of distrust. If he left first, she wouldn't get a chance to.

Suddenly, all that was different. Nick was the one who wanted to stay. He wanted to walk into that tumbled, raucous house and never see sunlight again. He wanted to curl up on Jenny's couch like a contented cat and just soak in the love in her eyes. The taste of her the night before had finally convinced him of that. She had felt so right in his arms, so alive, so vital. She had felt as if she belonged there.

As Nick sped down the interstate toward Clayton, he finally admitted that for the first time in his life, he felt as if he belonged, too.

The Corps had been his home, and then the force. Manetti had been a kind of mentor, and Baker the obnoxious surrogate kid sister. The other cops had become his friends. But none of them had needed him. None of them had made him feel as if he made a big enough difference to matter a damn.

Of course, it would take something special to give him that feeling. Dora had seen to that. But finally, after thirty-five years of wandering, Nick knew what it felt like to see home. He saw it every time he looked at Jenny.

When he walked into his office, though, the silver lining showed its cloud. The room was empty for a change, the night guy evidently down exchanging outrageous propositions with the dispatcher. There was paperwork everywhere, and a couple of new files on Nick's desk. On top of the files was the box of crayons. By the lamp sat the lumpy blue figure of Papa Smurf. Without thinking, Nick walked over and picked it up.

Toys. Kids. Why did the mere thought unsettle him? Nick had to admit that he really enjoyed Emma and Kevin, but he had never been forced to be the bad guy around them. He'd never had to disappoint them or obstruct them. They were nice kids, but every time Nick thought of having kids he thought of the homes where he was raised, the kids other people imposed on him as brothers and sisters.

There had never been privacy, never any fun. Kids had been a never-ending, mind-numbing responsibility. They had never been quiet. Never friendly. Nick couldn't think of Jenny holding that newborn without picturing a ten-year-old boy having to monitor a toddler right alongside. Never an escape, never any help, never a meal or private moment without interruptions.

Never, never any freedom.

Was this something Nick could dive back into, even for Jenny? Could he assume responsibility for Emma and Kevin, overseeing homework and doling out allowances, attending Boy Scouts and father-daughter banquets? Could he anticipate children of his own and keep from resenting their intrusion in his life? Or on his relationship with Jenny?

Marriage. He'd never really considered anything else. He wanted Jenny for his own. He loved her. He thought he loved her children. But he couldn't only *think* that, if he wanted Jenny. He had to *know*. He had to find out one way or another or Jenny wouldn't so much as let him in the door.

He'd never wanted anything so much in his life. He'd never been so afraid that he couldn't get it. Flipping the Smurf over in his hands, Nick shook his head. He'd promised her he'd work through their problems. He just hoped he could.

"I think it's time to call this all to a halt."

The meeting had reconvened, all parties present. Detective Richards slouched in Barb's blue-flowered armchair, and Lauren and Miss Lucy shared the couch. Barb paced and Jenny sat swinging her leg from the other armchair. Barb had just had the floor.

Studying the beaded moisture on her glass of lemonade (freshly squeezed), Jenny fought a smile. It was obvious that Nick hadn't quite escaped unnoticed yesterday morning. Barb was appointing herself Jen's guardian in the neighborhood meeting.

"We still haven't caught the dealer," Richards allowed, his eyes considering Jenny rather than Barb.

Jenny shrugged. "I'd really hate to let somebody like that get away with it."

Barb came to an unhappy halt. "You can't allow him to keep showing up at your house like that, either, Jen. Think of what it'll do to the kids."

"He hasn't done anything to hurt the kids."

So far Lauren and Miss Lucy watched much like a tennis match. Miss Lucy had worn her best straw hat for the occasion and Lauren came decked out in her best designer sweat suit. Jenny, as ever, was in her brown polyester uniform. She could hardly wait to get back to school just for the chance to wear old dresses.

"He seems such a delightful young man," Miss Lucy offered, her gloved hands folded in her lap. "He even knows what

kind of ice cream I want before I get to his stand on my walks."
A scan of her audience didn't seem to encourage her. "Dream-
sicle," she offered with a definite nod, as if that would settle the
matter.

Then Jenny did smile. "Have you been able to connect him
to the sales in any way?" she asked the detective.

"Not yet. We still don't have that kid who's in Europe, and
nobody else claims to know anything. We've made a couple of
arrests since then, but the information's even more vague."

Jenny just nodded.

"Seems amazing to me," the detective went on, "that you've
spent so much time with him to not find anything out."

"Well, let's see," Jenny answered, eyes up. "We've discussed the state of my car, the state of the Cards, the state of the
nation and the state of ice cream."

The detective wasn't impressed. "Lady..."

Jenny faced him. "Detective, I'm not going to ask the man
to marry me just to get his phone number."

His short laugh was offensive. "I didn't say anything about
marriage..."

Jenny lifted a finger. "Say another word and you'll not only
lose my cooperation but your suspect. I'll walk right up to that
truck and tell him just who owns that blue Plymouth in the
driveway."

At least she got a smile out of Barb on that one. Jenny really didn't enjoy deceiving Barb. After all, Barb only wanted to
help. But she had to admit that the double-life situation piqued
her imagination just a little. There was something a bit heady
about playing one role for your neighbors and another in private.

"I'll make you a promise, Detective," she offered finally.
"The minute I get his phone number, I'll call. Any time, day or
night. Will that make you happy?"

Losing his patience, he shambled to his feet. "Lady, I haven't
been happy since high school. You call me when you get *anything*."

Looking up at him, Jenny just nodded. "Absolutely."

It seemed he couldn't leave without at least one moralization. "And don't let yourself forget," he added, finger pointed threateningly, "just who that is you're dealing with out there."

"Oh, I don't think there's any chance of forgetting that, Detective." God, how she wanted to be there when he found out.

"I don't like him much," Miss Lucy announced after the detective had made his exit. She was settling her purse over her arm in preparation of making her own departure. "He has no manners. At least young Nick has manners."

"Well, that's certainly a redeeming feature on a drug dealer," Lauren muttered under her breath.

Miss Lucy never heard. "Time for my stroll, my dears. Do you all have your papers?"

They answered in chorus. "Oh, yes."

"Fine," she smiled. "Fine."

She never quite remembered to say goodbye. But then, by the time she strolled out the door, she was humming "The Toreador Song" from *Carmen*. Jenny grinned. Lauren shook her head. Barb collected glasses and emptied ashtrays.

"Jenny, you can't jeopardize yourself just to spite that policeman."

Jenny couldn't help but see the real concern in Barb's eyes. "I'm not jeopardizing anybody, Barb," she insisted, not knowing what else she could say. She stood up. "You know you can trust me."

Barb came to a sudden halt, ashtray in hand, and faced Jenny. "No, I don't," she argued, sincerely upset. "Not anymore."

"Not anymore?" Lauren echoed from where she sat on the couch. "Since when?" Her head was back on a swivel between the two friends, but it seemed she couldn't see anything.

Jenny didn't waste any attention on her. "Barb..."

Barb shook her head. "You just look too...too content, all of a sudden."

"And that's wrong?"

"With Nick it is. You *know* that, Jenny." Jenny could see her reaching for logic and failing, desperate to turn Jenny away from what she thought was a course to disaster. Barb ended up just shaking her head. "You know better."

All Jenny could do was sigh, because without knowing it Barb had hit a bull's-eye. "Maybe I don't," she admitted.

There was so much she wanted to talk to Barb about. She wanted to carry on her personal debate vocally, exposing each side for flaws, like a jeweler holding a gem up to the light. She wanted to know why she was so excited and so afraid at the same time. She wanted to know why she wanted so very much to believe Nick when she should have known better, just like Barb said. But until Nick found his thief, she couldn't say anything. She couldn't do more than pretend she was falling in love with a suspected drug dealer, and in doing so, suffer the frustrated concern of her friend.

For Barb, on the other hand, it was easy. She knew Jenny had already made one mistake, just by the look in her eyes. She was terrified she was going to compound it out of loneliness and frustration and longing. And Jenny couldn't tell her she was wrong. She couldn't tell her she was wrong on any count. Because even though Nick wasn't the person Barb thought he was, he could still be as dangerous as she feared. And Jenny could still make mistakes she couldn't take back.

She just couldn't talk about them.

"I don't care if he's selling drugs to Buffy," Barb said, her eyes eloquent as she shook the glass in her hand until the ice cubes rattled. "I don't want you hurt. Call Detective Richards. Tell him you quit."

"I can't," Jen said, finally turning away because she couldn't stand the hurt in Barb's eyes any longer. "Nick's going with me to pick up the car this afternoon."

"*I'll* do it," she argued, a hand to Jen's arm.

Jen whirled on her. "No, you won't," she snapped. "Now, I have to go, Barb."

Lauren just lifted an eyebrow at the sudden lightning that sparked between the two neighbors. "I'm glad *I* don't look so content."

Nick did his very best not to say anything about the chocolate candy bar Kevin was dragging into his back seat. That upholstery was original, after all, in pristine condition. Nick had spent the last Saturday afternoon washing it down again just to make sure. And they were climbing in out of ninety-degree heat. Nick was under no illusions about what that did to chocolate.

"Finish it," Jenny snapped economically. "Seat belts."

Nick stared. Kevin immediately backed out before the candy bar got near to a seat, and swallowed the rest of the bar in a gulp and a grin. Licking his fingers absolutely clean, he crawled back in after Emma who was arranging her dress around her knees like a princess on a carriage ride. Both of the kids snapped into their seat belts without help or fuss.

Nick really wasn't going to say anything. It was obvious from the look on Jenny's face that he hadn't looked as unconcerned as he'd thought.

"I'm sure Barby has about ten different ways to get melted chocolate out of upholstery," she assured him with a grin. "But prevention is nine-tenths of the solution."

Nick didn't quite keep the response from his expression. He was surprised when Jenny grinned again.

"My house is a mess," she said. "Not dirty. There's a difference."

"One I bet Barby can't see," he retorted with a like grin.

Jenny chuckled. "Buffy lives to build forts in my playroom. She never knew all the ways you could use cookbooks and blankets before."

If only it had stayed that pleasant. Jenny relaxed in the front seat. Nick geared down through the afternoon traffic and the kids played paper, rocks, scissors in the back seat. After the upheavals in Barb's kitchen, Jenny had actually begun to ache for her days to settle into a peace as comfortable as the one in this car. She wanted to believe it could be like Nick promised, that she could talk to Nick about his day and tell him about the funny things the kids had done. She could bask in the peace, the support, the camaraderie.

Then, inevitably, paper tried to beat out scissors, and the competition in the back seat came to blows.

"She's cheating! Mom, she's cheating!"

"No, I'm not. I win . . . ow, he pushed me!"

"But she's cheating!"

Jenny heaved a sigh. She could see the sudden tension in Nick's jaw. The decibel level put Iron Maiden to shame, and it showed no promise of peace without direct intervention.

"Sit on your own sides."

"But she bit me!"

Jenny had to turn around for that. She found Kevin waving the offended finger, which he'd obviously stuck right under Emma's nose, and Emma sitting primly with that smug little cat-in-the-cream smile that said that yes, she had cheated and had bitten Kevin and expected to come out unscathed. Jenny gave her a swipe across the knees.

Tears erupted on that side of the seat, too.

"You know how I feel about biting," she warned. "Now, if you can't play together, you won't need to come out of your rooms at all when we get home." Home was a long way off, at best, and Nick's fingers were white around the steering wheel.

"I find that rock and roll helps sometimes," she offered, turning back around.

He didn't seem to hear her.

Jenny sighed and rubbed at her tightening forehead. And she'd been looking forward to spending time with Nick, even on the way to the car dealership. Somehow, she should have known this would get in the way. But then, if he wanted to see children at their worst, this was definitely the time to partake. He was certainly getting the full treatment.

Of course, once they arrived, it didn't get any better. Emma slipped and fell into the only puddle of grease on the parking lot. Kevin wasted no time delighting over it, which infuriated Emma even more. Nick grew even more quiet as Jenny shepherded her little flock into the claustrophobic waiting room, sat Emma on a plastic chair that wouldn't notice a little more grease and gave her a *Sports Illustrated* to read.

"Thank you, Nick," Jenny said, preparing to formally let him off the hook. She couldn't bear to see a grown man suffer, and he had all the earmarks. He stood against the front door like a sane man who'd wandered into the locked ward, and his forehead had tightened to headache levels. And that was making her suffer. "I'm sure you have someplace to be. We'll be fine now."

He nodded, not taking his eyes from where Kevin persisted in blaming Emma for his troubles. "When you get the car."

Jenny couldn't think of anything to do but shrug. Emma was sticking her tongue out at Kevin, who was making dive-bomber noises with a Matchbox ambulance in her general direction. It didn't take much imagination to guess what he was hoping to annihilate with his latest strategic weapon. Jenny thought the day was about as miserable as it was going to get.

By that time in her life, she should have known how stupid that kind of thinking was.

"You want me to pay how much?"

The cashier stared at her through the window with fish eyes and popped a bubble. "That's what it comes to."

Jenny took a very deep breath. "And what about the estimate I got three days ago? The one that came in two hundred fifty dollars cheaper?"

The girl, obviously not working her way through a graduate-school degree, shrugged and popped her gum. "Dunno."

Jenny leveled her best attention-getting glare. "Then find someone who does."

Another shrug brought out the mechanic, a man who reminded Jenny very much of Detective Richards on his better days. This man was wiping his hands on a grease rag and also popping gum. And smiling.

"Now, Ms. Lake," he offered, unaware that the slightly scruffy-looking man perusing his *Field and Stream* was with the customer, "you couldn't very well drive off without a working water pump."

"You didn't say anything about it on the estimate," she objected, millimeters from losing control.

He liked his shrug as much as his cashier. "Nothin' much I could do. It needed to be fixed."

Jenny felt Nick approach from behind, and knew that he was about to come to her defense. Not even bothering to look around, she raised a hand to silence him. This one was hers. She had waited a long time to have the nerve to finish this little scenario out to her satisfaction.

"I didn't ask for a water pump," she said with such deadly calm that even the kids looked up. They were well acquainted with that tone of voice. "You didn't mention a water pump in the estimate. I—am—not—paying—for a water pump."

Another shrug, this replete with regret. "I don't know about the estimate, ma'am. I just know what was fixed. And if you can't pay for it, then I can't let you have it."

Jenny's smile was not a pretty sight. "I do know about the estimate," she answered quietly. "I have it on tape. On my answering machine. Now, I'd much rather not have to involve the Better Business Bureau and the District Attorney in this little misunderstanding. I don't even want to call my lawyer. I'll either wait here until you take it back out and put in the old one, or you can include it at the original cost for my goodwill since I didn't ask for it, anyhow."

"You want me to take it out?"

She nodded. "I'll wait." Before he could answer, she turned to her children. "I'm afraid we can't go to McDonald's until this man finishes the car. It might be *hours*."

Jenny should have felt worse about what she'd programmed her children to do. The fact that she felt herself at a distinct disadvantage in situations like this propelled her to use every conceivable weapon at her disposal to help even the score. And her children were a powerful motivator.

Within moments, it was highly uncomfortable for anyone else in the tiny waiting room. Jenny had thought the noise level in the car was bad. Now, it was unbearable. And what made it worse, was that Emma was a master whiner. No sane person could stand it for more than a few moments without running screaming into the night.

And Nick, much to Jenny's surprise, joined right in, complaining about the kids and the wait he'd anticipated when he'd brought his car in and the way this company was treating this nice lady. Jenny almost laughed aloud when he stalked back out the door.

Jenny didn't know whether it was her logic or her coercion, but she had her car back in under fifteen minutes. When she saw it rattle out of the bay, she realized she should have held out for something better. Even with its new parts, it was still a bit embarrassing to drive. The windshield was cracked and what wasn't rusted was dented.

As she pulled to the edge of the parking lot, she slowed next to the midnight-blue GTO that sat there, its driver slouching alongside with an impossibly huge grin on his face.

"I say," he said in his best Etonian accent as he headed over to assess the condition of her poor, beaten-up car. "Have you been in a terrorist attack?"

"Held hostage by a greasy man with a monkey wrench," she retorted, grinning up at him.

Nick leaned down, resting an arm on the hood over her window and shaking his head at her. "I had my hand on my badge, you know."

Jenny nodded, the exhilaration of her small victory still bubbling in her. "I appreciate it, Nick. But if you'd come to my rescue, that guy would have figured he could get away with that every time a single woman came in. I had to get out of my own jam."

He was still shaking his head. "Well, he'll never make that mistake with you again."

"He'll probably never let me in his parking lot as long as I live."

She felt so flushed with her small victory. So brave and intrepid, as if she'd just won a round with the Jerk and all his lawyers. A stupid little joy, a minor daily battle. But one she'd never quite won to her satisfaction before. It was the first time she could remember having walked away from an uncomfortable situation without feeling a residue of shame and guilt for somehow not conducting it better, not having more control, not being somehow taken advantage of. That man would sure as hell know she'd been there. And she wanted to celebrate.

"I have a date tonight," she said, squinting up to where she could see a fresh sheen of sweat glisten on Nick's upper lip. "Me, some kids and a big clown with a hamburger. I'm free for dinner tomorrow night, though. Interested?"

She wanted to see the silly exhilaration echoed in his eyes. She wanted, perversely, to see pride there. It made a difference to her that Nick would celebrate her successes along with her.

Instead, she saw strain. The tension was back in his forehead, that tight line between his eyes that reflected more than glare from a summer sun. He looked up for a moment, as if assessing the traffic that whistled and rumbled past. As if consulting a calendar, checking for room, for interest. Jenny saw the way he held on to the rim of her car with a tight hand and wondered why it hurt her that he was bothered.

"How about the day after?" he countered, looking back, but not really seeing her somehow.

The kids were getting restless in the back without air-conditioning. The promise of hamburgers had not been lightly given, and they wanted payment. Suddenly Jenny felt the heat, too. She felt the humidity closing in on her, closing off her air, her room. She saw the flat glint in Nick's eyes and thought for the first time not of windows but mirrors. Closed off, separate, distant. She saw the street, the cars chasing along after the clock, the rows of shiny new cars lined up behind her. She didn't see Nick anymore.

It didn't make sense. It just hurt.

"No," she answered, not knowing why, just knowing that she had to restrain the sudden urge to beg, to plead, to grab on to him and not let go until he explained his sudden retreat. "I'm afraid I have a teacher's meeting."

"Mo-o-o-o-m!"

Nick started like he'd been slapped. "They're hungry, Jen. I'll call."

"Nick?"

He'd already straightened. Pulling his sunglasses from his pocket he slipped them on. "When you get home from dinner tonight," he said with a sudden smile that seemed to beg patience. "I'll call."

And then he was gone.

The restaurant was noisy. The kids added their own voices, jumping unnoticed in the plastic booth and chasing imaginary foes through paper mazes and slurping shakes to the very bottom of paper cups. Jenny sat alongside picking at the junk food she usually craved on a par with chocolates and good wine, and fought the urge to cry.

It didn't make any sense. He'd helped her in that garage, playing the game like one of the kids. And then, when they'd made it safely outside he'd stepped back, as if to say, that's enough. I've come too close and I don't like it there. Jenny had known he would reach that place sooner or later, but still she couldn't accept it. She couldn't understand it.

She couldn't abide by it.

She wanted Nick there. She wanted him in her house, in her arms, in her dreams. She wanted him by her side to bolster her courage and celebrate her advances, to cushion the retreats and forgive the mistakes. She wanted him to open his private doors to her, to let out the musty secrets that darkened those seductive eyes and set his brakes so quickly. She wanted him to trust her.

She wanted to be able to trust him.

She loved him. Dammit, she'd forgotten how much that hurt.

Jenny refused to answer on the first ring. Let him think that she wasn't sitting right by the phone with a gin and tonic at hand waiting for him to call. Let him think she didn't care whether she ever heard from him again or not.

What an absolutely sophomoric reaction. She *must* be in love.

"Hello?"

"I'm sorry."

Two words, and the stuffings went right out of her knees. She sank onto the playroom floor, glass in hand, nightgown cool against freshly bathed skin, floor solid and reassuring. Still she was suddenly hot.

"You're forgiven. What did you do?"

She heard a chuckle, and it raced down her spine. Jenny found that she was lying, her head propped on a throw, the glass on her stomach, her eyes closed.

"I bet you're not that lenient with your kids."

Jenny smiled to herself. "Kids need a lot more intimidation than adults. That's because, generally, they're smarter."

"They sure had me outgunned today."

Jenny did her best to hide the leap her heart took. If he couldn't take the kids today...

"Kids get noisy sometimes, Nick."

"I'm not talking about that. I'm talking about the garage. They weren't in the least surprised by what you did. Shows they were smarter than I was. I was stunned."

Pleasure seeped into her like sunlight. "Why? Because I held my own?"

"Held your own?" he countered with sincere astonishment. "You nearly showed him his head on a platter. *I* was getting ready to take out that water pump." There was the slightest of pauses, a redirection. "And here I thought you might need help."

Jenny's eyes popped open. What had she heard just then? Not just amazement. Not just the grudging admiration, or the humor. Something...deeper. Something that sounded like her own voice when she'd called out to him on that parking lot.

She was sure Nick didn't realize himself that it had slipped out. Jenny was just such an expert at need that the slightest trace of it kindled a like reaction in her. She saw the taut line of his forehead again, the rigid distance in his eyes, and thought, suddenly, of disappointment.

Disappointment? Why?

"Jenny?"

"Oh, I'm sorry. I'm here." She closed her eyes again, soaking in the sound of his voice like water, trying to see him, his face, his movements, the subtle shadings of those whiskey-brown eyes. Trying to understand what it was he'd been looking for that afternoon that he hadn't found.

"What are you wearing?"

Jenny let her own chuckle roll down the wires. "Is this turning into an obscene phone call?"

"Depends. What are you wearing?"

"Oh, just an old yellow cotton nightgown."

She actually heard a groan. The satisfaction of it settled into her toes and turned them to curling. Need again, pleasure that he'd sought her out. That he sang his desire in unsaid sentences.

"Tell me something," she said, setting her own screen to receive. "Do you have a wood floor?"

"A what? What does that matter?"

She smiled and knew that it looked wicked. It felt wicked. "Just tell me."

"Sure. Yeah, it's wood."

"Cool?"

"Yeah. I'm lying on it right now. Feels pretty good."

Jenny's eyes were closed again, the images sharp and tantalizing. She nodded, her tongue searching out the dry edges of her lips. "I know. What are you wearing?"

"Gym shorts."

It was her turn to groan. She could see it so easily. His back, so lean, so taut and smooth like the torso of a well-caressed statue, stretched out against the gleam of oak. The lamp by his window casting little pools of light like spilled milk over the floor, the rest of the room in darkness, the breeze licking hot over his chest, skimming through the glisten of sweat.

She could see him, a drink on his chest, his arm behind his head, a knee bent. She could taste the salt, could feel the sensation of marble and velvet. Just the image sent shafts of pure pleasure through her.

"Where are you?" he asked, his voice suddenly husky.

Jenny just smiled.

She could have sworn Nick heard that smile. He didn't answer, not in words. The sound of a quickly intaken breath brushed her ear almost as intimately as if he'd been lying alongside her on that cool, earthbrown floor.

He knew exactly where she was. Jenny could almost hear him construct his own images. His had the advantage, though. He'd already helped make memories on her floor. She just had anticipation to mold. Jenny wondered if it could possibly be any more evocative.

"You're making me crazy, lady," he objected harshly, giving her his answer. "And I'm not even in the same municipality."

"Feeling's mutual," she assured him, finally sipping at the gin she'd never had the chance to drink the other night. The fire slid down her throat and approached the embers fanning in her belly. "I suddenly want to see the inside of that apartment of yours very much."

"I have the most disconcerting feeling you already can."

For a moment there was silence, a silence filled with static, with the frustrations compounded by too little privacy, too many problems, too much interference.

"I'd really like to talk," Nick said softly.

Unconsciously Jenny nodded. "Me, too. I think we need it."

"Away from the kids?"

She sighed. "Away from the neighborhood."

"We could try Coral Courts."

Jenny laughed. Coral Courts was St. Louis's most notorious landmark, the first motel with hourly rates and garages to protect anonymity. Now so venerable it had been saved the wrecking ball by concerned citizens, it still carried with it the patina of lasciviousness, the distinct air of wanton abandon.

Even at age thirty, Jenny couldn't quite gather the insouciance to patronize the Courts.

"Someplace I can give the baby-sitter a phone number, if you please."

Another pause, a gathering of innuendo and promise. "How do you feel about hardwood floors?"

Now Jenny's smile was tremulous. "I've been fantasizing about them for a week."

She heard him answer, an unintelligible sound deep in his throat and knew that she'd been right. She hadn't been the only one fantasizing. She hadn't been the only one tossing and turning in the dark. The sound heightened the tension in her, the desire that sang like ship's rigging in the wind, the fear that gestated with every unsaid word, every unanswered question. The hope that refused to be quelled, even when she saw him wince at the kids or run from the commitment.

Jenny didn't know what to say to this man to convince him that he wanted to trust himself to her. She didn't know what she wanted to hear from him that would convince her she could let him in past her defenses. She felt as if she were walking a tightrope, and that far below, just in her line of vision, the net kept growing smaller. And still, when she had the chance to get off before she fell, she didn't.

"Nick?"

"I'm here."

"What were you sorry for?"

It took him a second to answer. Coming back from his own quandary, distilling his thoughts, Jenny wasn't sure. She couldn't catch that elusive need in his voice anymore.

"For letting you get away without kissing you."

"Nick..."

"Without pulling you into my arms right out on that parking lot and making you as hungry as I was."

She gave herself a second to regain equilibrium. Jenny had never known the power of mere words before. The breadth of intimation. Deliberately seeking distance from the memory of his hot hands, his cool, sweet lips that could so sap her common sense, she opened her eyes to the shadows that collected in her house. Instead of the gentle pleasure of sleeping with Nick, she thought of the grinding loneliness of sleeping alone again. "Then it really must have been something bad to drive you away."

There didn't seem to be any answer for that. Closing her eyes against the pain that bloomed in her chest, Jenny just waited. Just wondered what it would take to open those doors. She wondered if she even had the energy left to attempt it.

"Nick?" How could her voice sound so very small? How could just his silence shatter her resolve?

"Yes, Jen."

"Why a lawyer?"

A pause, the sound only of empty air between them, of distance. "Does this have anything to do with ducks?"

Jenny would have none of it. "Why did you work so hard from the very beginning to be a lawyer?"

This time his answer was too quick. A defense. A barrier long since erected. "I liked the uniform."

More. She wanted more. She wanted to know that he wouldn't pander to the Izod god. "That's enough?"

"When you're ten and you don't have a decent pair of shoes it is."

End of discussion. The sound, somehow of a latch catching. Jenny heard it as surely as if he were in the same room. Her frustration only built. Her fear. Her determination, oddly enough. They had danced so close tonight, fingers touching in delicate ritual to appease, but not sate. She wanted satisfaction. She wanted substance.

In the end, though, she knew the limits of a phone call. It was time to call retreat. "I didn't get a chance to say thank you today."

"Thank you?"

She nodded, her eyes still closed, tears stinging but refusing to fall. "Standing up to that guy was important to me. Dumb, but important. I couldn't have done it without you being there behind me. Thanks for letting me do it alone."

Nick let another silence build to the edge of tension. "You mean you've never turned a mechanic to coleslaw before?"

"Never. You gave me the courage. I was hoping you'd share the triumph with me."

She didn't know how, but the silence changed. It became more charged, more taut, as if her words had altered the texture of the future somehow. Jenny didn't even realize she was holding her breath.

"Would tomorrow be all right, after all?"

Jenny let her breath out in a small whoosh. "Tomorrow would be fine."

She hung up smiling, and wishing she knew why. If tomorrow were so fine, why was she so scared?

Maybe because for all they'd said, they hadn't really given any answers. And she was still very afraid of the answers they would ultimately have to find.

Chapter 14

"Nick, my man, you look wasted."

Without doing much to stifle a yawn, Nick set down his *U.S. News* to face his newest buddy, Todd Sellers. As ever, the teen was decked out in the latest designer labels, with his spike haircut perfectly rakish and his sockless shoes appropriately scuffed. Today, however, Todd stood without his usual crowd of followers.

Nick made it a point to look around. "A little empty out there, isn't it, Todd?"

Todd just scowled, hands jammed in pockets. "Run into a little dry spell, they fade like suntans, ya know?"

No, Nick thought, he didn't know. He really didn't care, come to think of it, except where it connected with his case. The longer he went without sleep in that oven of an apartment, the more he wanted to wrap up this farce and get on with his life.

Of course, it probably didn't help that he'd spent the last few sleepless nights doing a spot of much too intense dreaming. Even cold showers had lost their power.

It had been particularly bad last night after getting off the phone with Jenny. It had been bad *on* the phone with Jenny. He'd been lying on the floor in just his old shorts, with the window fan blowing that hot breeze across his chest imagining what she looked like. What she felt like. Anticipating what it would feel like on his floor instead of hers. He hadn't even moved for an hour after he'd hung up the phone, so acute had been the discomfort.

And then, because he knew damn well he wasn't about to get any sleep that night, either, he'd cleaned the place.

Oh, hell, he thought, resettling in the sticky seat, he was going to have to do something about the fit of these jeans.

"You okay?" Todd asked with a squint behind his designer shades.

Nick came very close to cursing. "I, uh, hurt my...back last night. Old war wound."

"Oh, yeah, really? Man, like you should be able to take care of that."

Nick lifted an eyebrow. "Some things just can't be taken care of."

Todd shook his head with a conspiratorial grin. "Can't make me believe that, man. Just takes the resources and the bread, ya know?"

"That's what it always comes down to."

Nick got a snort and a definite nod. "Ya got that right. Well, things are a little tight for me right now, but, you know, come see me when the waters flow again, okay? A man-to-man loan."

"Hey," Nick agreed more brightly. "You're on, man. I appreciate it. How 'bout an ice cream or two on the boss?"

Little Todd, Nick realized as he slowly climbed out of his truck, bore watching. Nothing like a spot of enterprise in the suburbs to brighten a boy's summer. Maybe the day wouldn't be quite so unbearable, after all.

"Is there a hurricane coming through tomorrow and nobody told me?" Jenny asked her bagger as she began ringing up yet another three-digit order.

"Looks to me like the city's havin' a gang barbecue," he retorted, shaking out his bag.

All Jenny wanted to do was get off her feet. Take a shower. Lie down on Nick's floor.

For the hundredth time that day she shook off the image. It certainly wasn't doing her any good. Every time she began to think of what waited for her beyond the day's duties, she began dropping vegetables and misreading labels.

But her feet did ache, even with the supports and nurse's shoes. And she couldn't quite get Nick's words from her mind. All his words, scattered over the last two weeks, tumbled around in her brain so that they aligned in different patterns according to her needs. He loved her, he'd love her children— their children. He couldn't commit, no matter what; it just wasn't in his nature.

He was going to be a lawyer for stability. He was going to be a lawyer to make up for every deprivation he'd had as a kid. To get even with the system.

She loved him. She was terrified of him.

Well, at least both of those were true. She did love him. She'd spent another sleepless night last night conjuring him to mind, trying somehow to bridge the gap between them with mental images, with wishes and silent urgings. Wanting him to know, somehow in the dark and private hours of dawn that she was the one he needed.

And she was terrified of him. Of everything he brought back into her life: the tumult, the trepidation, the uncertainty... the agonizing hope.

God, how she hated that the most. Treading from moment to moment as if maneuvering across thin ice, knowing it should crack, praying it wouldn't, your eyes desperately fixed on the far shore that should get closer but didn't.

Beep, beep, plunk. She was working on autopilot, skimming cans across the bar-code machine in smooth succession, balancing fruit on the scale, punching the computer like a typist in a speed contest, her movements agitated and choppy, her mind miles away.

Only three more hours.

She wasn't going to make it.

"One-hundred-forty-two dollars and fifty cents."

Across from her, the blousy woman in the tank top and tattoo looked up. "Oh, I don't got that much. You gotta do somethin'."

Jenny counted all the way up to forty before she managed to hold her retort in. She should have anticipated this. This particular customer did this as regularly as prickly heat in summer.

"I'll tell you what," the woman decided, checking her wallet again and eyeing the already packed groceries. "I don't really want none o' them oranges. And the Chocolate Gumby cereal. And..."

The bag boy dug, Jenny rerang and the lady picked the scant nutrition from her haul and put it back. Jenny didn't say a word. But, then, she hadn't said a word that morning when Barb had made a frontal assault on her, and she hadn't objected when Kate had tried flanking maneuvers, both in an attempt to dislodge Nick's position in the Lake household. Barb had been worried, so everyone had heard about it. And Jenny still had to face Barb when she went home for the kids. She was surprised the Jerk hadn't shown up, as well, the way this day was going.

She was surprised her customer, who was puffing on her cigarette and repacking her doughnuts, didn't say something about how Nick was going to be bad for her. She was probably just too busy complaining about the prices.

Jenny simply wasn't going to make it. Her time with Nick tonight was going to be too important, and everyone she'd come into contact with today was conspiring to sabotage it. She watched the tattooed lady grunt on out and wondered just what would be next.

"Jenny, you're closing. Take over line six."

Jenny tried to warn off her next customer. "I'm..."

She hadn't even noticed. So engrossed had she been in trying to maintain her patience in the face of the last straw, so exhausted by the sleepless night and overwhelming morning, she hadn't taken a moment to anticipate her next customer.

His smile forgave her.

"Do you think you could squeeze in just one more customer?"

"One more, Marge!" Jenny yelled without looking away. "He was already in line!"

Nick's grin broadened. Jenny faltered. Her pulse rate picked up abominably. Somehow she forgot how much her legs hurt, because suddenly her chest hurt worse. That damn hope again. She was so afraid of him, and all she wanted to do was stand there and stare at him.

"I'm proud of you," he was saying, his eyes crinkling with a humor that seemed oddly intense. "I saw you cringe at every double negative. You never said a word."

Jenny tried her best to find levity. "Just one reason a schoolteacher should never work in a store."

"After this summer, I feel for you."

She should be able to think of something amusing to say, something light and smart. She couldn't. Suddenly the sun was in his eyes and it was sapping her strength.

"Pasta?" she asked, reaching for the few packages he carried.

Never taking his eyes from hers, he nodded. "I thought I'd cook tonight. I'm having somebody over. Think she'll like it?"

Jenny had to run the tomato sauce over the scanner three times. Her hands were shaking. Mushrooms, green peppers, fresh garlic. Mouth-watering ingredients, startling anticipation. She couldn't drag her gaze from his either, crystal-green battling honey-brown. Dark, sensual attraction and terror.

In the next lane a toddler was screaming for candy. One of the baggers dashed off for a price check, and the doors swished open not ten feet from her. All she could hear was Nick. All she could smell in that crowded, noisy food store was Nick. And it unnerved her.

"I think she'll like it a lot."

Again he nodded, slowly, his eyes darkening. "Good. I can hardly wait to eat."

He lifted a head of lettuce for her. Jenny brushed against his hand when she accepted it and almost dropped it on the floor. "Hungry?" she asked breathlessly.

He steadied her hand with his own. "Starved."

Jenny felt his voice to the tips of her toes. The caress of his fingers followed right after, seriously damaging the support in her knees, wiping out hours of pressure on her feet. She still wanted to sit down, but now just because she wasn't quite sure she was still standing. It was that damn hope again. Slicing through her like lightning; sapping her strength, softening her voice as if the caution could better facilitate it. Hope. What a strange aphrodisiac. The most powerful she'd ever known.

"You still have three hours," she admonished them both.

Nick's grin settled in his eyes like heady, forbidden sin. "It'll give the sauce plenty of time to bubble."

Jenny couldn't do more than blink. "Oh."

She couldn't breathe. Her sensibility had just melted, and the bar coder was beeping at her.

Pulling away, she turned to her computer, slapped at some keys and came to a figure. Somehow she managed to relay it to him and exchange money without ever really facing him. She kept watching the display of disposable lighters at the edge of her counter as if waiting for revelation. She knew Nick smiled, and knew that that smile would do even more damage to her support structure.

"Well," he said, his voice low, intimate as he picked up his bags. "Thank you. I'll be able to start cooking now."

By the time Jenny shot him a startled look, he'd already walked away. That was when she noticed that the lines had grown quiet. She didn't hear the toddler anymore. Nobody was talking about prices or weather or vacations. Wondering, Jenny turned a little to see a row of faces turned to her. Turned to follow Nick out of the store.

She couldn't believe it. Every person down the line had been witness. Not necessarily to the conversation. Evidently that hadn't been the telling point. From the looks on every one of those faces, the look on hers had been blatant. She was mortified.

And Nick, with an absolutely nonchalant expression on his face, was carrying those bags right in front as he walked very carefully out the door.

"Have a little of that pasta for me, honey," the lady in the next lane sighed. "Looks spicy as hell."

Four other women nodded. Jenny had been right. She was going to die of embarrassment long before she ever got out of this store.

* * *

It had only gotten worse. When she got home Barb had greeted her with news that another neighborhood girl had been busted for drugs, not three blocks from the house, and as much as Jenny wanted to enlighten her she had to face all that concern and outrage with a quiet face. The kids had been wild, cornered in the house with a listless, lingering rain and not happy for it. And the mail had brought two overdue bill notices and a license renewal for the car.

The first warning should have reached the Jerk that morning. It said pay up or be visited by the man with the subpoenas. Jenny had decided to give him one more benefit of the doubt before hauling in the big guns. Nick hadn't agreed, but then Nick didn't have to face the Jerk on a regular basis and plead for him to visit his children.

So, she figured she'd be getting a call from the law offices of Wellerby, Cline, Phillips and Phillips anytime now. Probably from a secretary, maybe a partner. Powerful, threatening, distant, so the Jerk wouldn't have to dirty his hands with her.

Jenny stood in the shower wondering just how the heck she thought she was going to have a good time tonight.

She got out with a churning stomach to find Emma and Spot on her bed, both of them whining. And that was how she got dressed for her big night with Nick, caught between anger, frustration and guilt.

Emma didn't want her to go. "Not *again*, Mommy," she sighed with every ounce of heart-wrenching pathos in her. "You're never here with me anymore."

Fine, Jenny thought, fastening her earrings and taking another look at her dress. This should be just about enough to bring back up that fancy dinner Nick was so busy cooking.

Just the thought brought her hand to her stomach. Trying to quell butterflies. She could feel the honey-thick warmth of those eyes again, the erotic promise of his whisper. Hardwood floors and pasta dinners, and she was going to partake like a pagan at a ritual. She didn't know whether she had the courage for it.

"I'm just going to see Mr. Nick," she finally answered the accusing, instinctively manipulating eyes of her daughter. "He asked Mommy out on a date."

"A date?" Emma asked, astonished. "Again? That's a lot."

That's two, Jenny thought. Not enough to be certain and surely not enough to throw aside all her carefully compiled protections. She knew she'd likened Nick to that dangerous stranger in town, the one who seemed to consume good sense with the promise in his eyes. But Jenny wasn't the type to succumb to that kind of heat.

Was she?

"Spot doesn't want you to go," Emma tried again. "She's afraid she'll feel boring."

"Bored," Jenny immediately corrected with a smile, seeing that the cat who was so afraid of being "boring" had given up trying to get loose from the little girl and was asleep. "Have Susie play Chutes and Ladders with Spot," she suggested, sweeping the little girl into her arms and heading for the stairs. "That will keep her from being boring."

Emma nestled into Jenny's neck, cooing with contentment, which only made Jenny feel worse. Who said parents instilled guilt? she thought. Kids were the pros. Parents were just paying them back for nights like this.

The doorbell rang when Jenny was halfway down the stairs. She looked up, surprised. Susie was already ensconced in the playroom, so it must be Nick. And he was early.

Emma immediately dug in for a tighter hold. Jenny didn't bother to dislodge the girl before reaching to answer the door.

The smile she'd been working on died a painful death. It wasn't Nick. It was the Jerk. In person. In a rage.

"You want to explain this?" he demanded, waving the letter in her face.

She'd been right. The mail had been on time. Her stomach took another dive. Emma clutched tighter, whining.

"Come in, if you'd like," Jenny greeted him with a carefully even voice. "But I'd appreciate it if you'd do it civilly. Emma's having a bad day."

"Don't you—"

"She said do it civilly."

Both Jenny and the Jerk turned at the new voice. Nick had shown up, evidently right on the Jerk's heels. He was smiling now, wearing a feral expression Jenny had never seen on him before—and he was leveling it straight at her ex-husband.

"Name's Nick Barnett," he greeted him, hand out, eyes flat and hard. "I'm a friend of Jenny's."

"Mr. Nick!" Emma squealed, unpeeling herself from Jenny and outstretching her arms.

Stepping in past the Jerk, Nick obliged, which didn't do much to increase his stock with Mr. Lake.

"Why don't you have a drink in the kitchen?" the Jerk grated. "I have some business to take care of with Jenny."

"No," Nick disagreed very evenly. "You have business with me. I'm the one who sent the letter. Hey, peewee, how 'bout hoppin' off for a minute? I have to talk to your Daddy."

Emma, astute as ever, did just as Nick asked. Dispatching one final look at each adult, she skipped into the playroom to join Susie.

"In here," Nick suggested in steely tones Jenny had never heard. Suddenly he was a different man, the man he'd fought so hard to grow up to be. The man was in absolute control, and he was exerting that control. It fascinated her even as much as it frightened her.

The three of them stepped into the living room, where Jenny had only left on one light. The shadows settled into Nick's features in sharp slashes, the taut line of his jaw, the deep creases along his mouth. He was furious, and he was thinking. In that moment Jenny saw the power in him she'd only imagined before: channeled, directed, keen as a laser and just as potent.

She saw, for the first time, the cop. The lawyer. And she wasn't sure she wanted to.

"Just who the hell do you think you are?" the Jerk demanded, looking, for the first time in Jenny's memory, ineffectual against Nick's power. "This is none of your damn business."

"Whatever is between you and Jenny," Nick retorted, "is one thing. But if you're going to act like an adolescent and hurt your kids over it, then other people get involved. And I'm one of them. I just can't believe Jenny's lawyer didn't do it sooner."

"You don't have any idea what's involved!"

Now Nick smiled, and it was a terrible sight. "I know what kind of man deserts his kids. Now if I were you, I'd work this out with Jenny while I'm in talking to Kevin, or I'll make your life so miserable you won't want to get up in the morning."

Then he was gone, leaving a rip in the fabric of the pulsating silence, leaving a void in Jenny's home. Where the Jerk was an intruder here, now, Nick belonged. God, Jenny thought, it's become impossible.

"Do you really think you can parade this guy around to scare me?" her ex was demanding, almost purple with rage.

Jenny shook her head, still even more stunned than the Jerk by Nick's words. Jenny knew where they'd been born; she knew their power, their conviction, the pain of their conception. Instead of standing here with a man she no longer loved, she wanted to go to Nick and soothe the child in himself he'd exposed.

"He's the first person who's given me decent advice," Jenny said, straightening to face her husband. "You want a part in your children's lives, then, by God, deserve it. I'm tired of apologizing for you. I'm tired of denying your children because their father is too damned selfish."

"Jenny," he retorted, her challenge more important to him than its content. "You know better than to push me."

Jenny shook her head again, wondering at how little he had changed in all the years she'd known him. Unable to think of any other way to deal with him, she turned back to the front door. "You don't scare me anymore. Now, get out."

Amazingly enough, he did.

It didn't improve the condition of Jenny's stomach. She stood for a long moment by the door, trembling, fighting to stave off the tears, the confusion. The challenge between the men still remained, a residue of ash in the air, a faint throb of energy. And Jenny was so tired of the taste of that ash. She just wasn't sure she could face more.

She didn't even know Nick had returned until he laid a hand on her shoulder.

"I'm sorry."

She laughed, a short, sharp sound. "You've apologized more in the last twenty-four hours than that man did in six years of marriage."

"How 'bout we get some spaghetti, lady?"

Jenny took an uneven breath. "Nick—"

Increasing his hold, he turned her to him. "No excuses. Go tell Emma that the wicked witch's friend has disappeared, and we'll leave."

She couldn't believe it. The room looked just as she'd imagined. After coming to an uncertain stop in the doorway, Jenny took a minute to take stock. Dark wood floor, polished to a gleam, white walls with a few geometric prints. Bookshelves, filled to overflowing, and bare, minimal furniture. Space and silence, a haven in the midst of a noisy city.

The front windows were bayed out onto the tree-lined street just off the college campus. In the daylight Jenny was sure she could see the crenellated towers past the trees, but now, with the sky given to clouds and the rain slicking the streets, the world was as shadowy as the room in which she stood.

The rain spattered on the windowsill outside. A fan in the window whirred softly and another was running in the tiny white kitchen to the right. That one was blowing mouthwatering smells of oregano, basil, garlic into the living room. Jenny wished the Jerk had left her with more of an appetite.

"Take off your shoes," Nick invited, closing the door and following her in. "Pull up a floor."

Jenny couldn't help but smile. "Do you mind if I do just that?"

"Gin and tonics on the way."

She sat just outside a pool of light, reading the titles on the bookshelves. Law, well-thumbed classics, mysteries. Anything, it seemed, Nick could get his hands on. A few knickknacks, a German beer stein and an old gavel. A diploma, still closed, propping one shelf of books and a framed law-enforcement citation propping another. Shoved there as if to negate their importance, the only hints into Nick's life. No pictures, no cards, no mementos of other people in his life.

It made Jenny ache. She saw stringent self-sufficiency in this room, rigid independence. She also saw the hard-won victories of a man who refused to rely on their meaning.

She saw a man alone. A man who in thirty-five years had not learned to share his life.

"Comfortable?"

Jenny looked up to see that he'd discarded his jacket. He was in pleated wheat-colored linen slacks and a hunter green T-shirt. He looked like sin personified. Jenny reached for the glass he proffered. Ice clinked. Condensation trickled over her fingertips. She hadn't realized until now how hot the room was. Nick joined her on the floor and the temperature went up another few degrees.

"I haven't been comfortable since the first time I thought about this room," she admitted, her gaze straying down. It only led to the discovery that she hadn't been the only one in that condition.

"Isn't nonverbal communication a wonderful thing?" Nick asked with a crooked grin.

Jenny couldn't quite bring her eyes back to his. There was so much roiling around in her—so many questions needing answers, so many protests born of isolation and defense, so much yearning she hadn't even known existed until two weeks ago. "Are we going to waste more gin?" she asked instead.

Nick sighed, lifting a hand to run it along the line of her jaw. "I think so."

That got her to look up. Unfortunately, the set they bumped into were already smokey with desire. "Nick, we have to talk."

He nodded. "I know. Problem is, right now there's only one thing I can think of." His hand slid lower, along her throat where it unleashed unexpected sparks.

Jenny jumped. Caught her breath. "Nick—"

He smiled again, that crooked admission of weakness, of preoccupation. "Jenny, I can't think of a better time to talk than when you're lying in my arms. Later."

He was leaning closer, his eyes narrowing, his hand flattening against her collarbone, seeking purchase.

"The sauce—"

"Is just about to boil."

She never felt him take her drink away. She only felt his breath, soft, musky, as he bent to kiss her. She felt his hand sweeping along her arm, coaxing, teasing. She felt her heart hammer against her chest and her breasts strain against the lace of her best bra. She felt the molten hammer of his touch, the dark lightning of his soft, surprised groan when he first tasted her with his tongue. She felt him ease her back onto that cool, dark floor.

Patience had been sacrificed to sleepless nights, subtlety to passion. Jenny felt the wood against her back, felt the harsh heat of Nick atop her, the rain-cooled breeze from the fan against her suddenly damp skin, and stumbled over a fierce hunger that shattered her.

She wanted to taste him, to touch him, to drive him to a frenzy like he'd done to her. He tangled his hands in her hair and she moaned, the sensation as sharp as her desire. He dropped kisses along her face, her throat, and she arched, writhed. She clutched at the material at his shoulders and yanked it from the waistband of his slacks. Her lips skimming the freshly shaven smoothness of his chin, she reached to un-button, to seek her own purchase.

Nick could taste it on her. Desire, hunger, as harsh and sudden as his own, as consuming. She fought him tonight, dancing against him as if mere touch would not satisfy her. As if she meant to devour him whole. The ferocity of her little moans stirred him, incited him. Throbbed in him like molten iron. He gasped when she raked his chest, her fingernails sharp and chill, her fingers so deliciously soft in their wake. He bent to taste the sweat on her skin, to fill his hands with the sweet fullness of her breasts only to find them already taut for him.

He added his own groans to hers, deep throated and urgent, the throb an ache that urged unbearably. A heat that called for communion. How he wanted to sate himself with her, the soft, tender places, the dark secrets, the bold promises. He saw the wild light in those forest green eyes and wanted to follow it to his death.

The floor was already slick. Jenny felt it against her naked skin and thought that nothing could be more provocative. Nothing, maybe except the tumescent beauty of Nick's body. The light revered him, caressing the broad planes of his chest, slicing along the sharp tendons and well-defined muscles of his limbs. Kissing his face with the gentlest of fingers so that his eyes glowed and the dimple in his chin begged to be tasted.

Jenny did. She tasted that dimple and the ones on either side of his mouth when he smiled at her hunger. She drank the tang from his glowing skin and nestled against the whisper-rough hair on his chest. She gave herself up to his touch and demanded her own. The fan cooled the perspiration on her skin. The rain kept them company in that silent, hot room. The floor cradled them.

Nick spiraled in her like a tornado, hot and urgent, faster and faster until she was caught in his vortex. Gasping, writhing, the lightning taking her, shuddering through her, drawing him closer, closer. Provoking cries, pleas from them both, until Nick met her, until he drowned himself in her, dancing in that same bright, fierce wind, that same fiery sky, breaking through to the sun and finally falling again.

And in the aftermath, the rain. The breeze, humid and cool against sweat-sheened bodies. The night, quiet and dark.

"Some day," Jenny sighed as she watched her fingers winnow through the hair on Nick's chest, "I'm going to have to make love with you on a bed. Just to see what it's like."

Nick groaned. "Give me a few minutes."

Jenny chuckled, trying to understand why tears should threaten when she felt so content. Nick was stroking her hair. She could hear his heart trying to slow, felt the still-ragged slant of his breathing. He was so warm against her, so solid and strong. Lying there in the safe silence of his apartment, she should have wanted nothing more than to stay where she was. She shouldn't have still been afraid.

"I am going to have to get to that spaghetti sooner or later," he admitted with a desultory yawn.

"Later," she voted, doing her best not to tense up. If only she could hold on to this moment a little longer. This perfect little island of peace in her life.

"I did promise some conversation," he admitted, slipping his other arm beneath his head.

Jenny closed her eyes, fighting the tight stinging in her throat. "Later."

"No," he said quietly, his hand stilling against her. "I think I owe it to you to finish it now."

"Finish is such a . . . final word." Damn, those tears were closing in fast.

Was he smiling? Jenny thought she could hear it in his voice. "You wanted to know why I was sorry yesterday."

"You told me."

He shook his head. "No, I didn't. I didn't explain it. Hell, I didn't even understand it until we talked on the phone last night."

"Understand what?"

For a moment, all Jenny heard was the fizzle of rain, the whir of the fan, the swish of traffic two stories down. She kept her eyes on the line of Nick's chest, as if fortifying herself with his reality.

He was so beautiful. So gentle.

And, she knew now, so ferocious. It didn't make her feel any better.

"You surprised me yesterday. When I saw you handle that guy like a top sergeant, I thought . . . I thought you didn't need me."

Jenny went perfectly still. She couldn't quite breathe. If there was an admission she hadn't prepared herself for, that was the one. Knowing that she couldn't hide any longer, she turned in Nick's arms. She pulled herself up on an elbow and faced him. The shadows settled deeply into his eyes, protecting him, distancing him. For once, she thought it wouldn't help.

"That matters?" she asked very quietly.

His smile was wry, admitting more than any words could. "Yeah," he said. "It does." In those three words, Jenny heard the sum of all those years of disappointment. Of his fears, not meaning enough to the people he cared for. Not counting. Not existing.

That took care of the tears. They welled up and slid down Jenny's cheeks unheeded. "If I didn't need you so very much," she admitted so softly that the rain danced through her words, "I would have been able to sleep this week. Much as I'd like to say I'm a wild woman, I don't lie naked with any man on his floor just because he has an unforgettable tush."

Jenny wasn't sure, but she saw a glint in his eyes as well, as if the shadows there had collected and swollen.

"I love you, Nick," she said, a hand up to his face. "I need you. But loving and needing aren't the problem here, I think."

"You're still worried about my job?"

She shook her head, unable to express just what seeing him faced off with the Jerk had done to her that evening. "I married a man who liked the uniform. One who thrived on the control and the power."

"Who says I—?"

Jenny shot him a look.

Nick had the good sense to grin. "I am not a barracuda, Jen. I can give you references, if you want. Go talk to Manetti. Hell, I couldn't even steal hubcaps."

"Neither could the Jerk. But he's the best legal thief in the business."

He took a moment, his eyes assessing, his hand still against her back. "And just what kind of law do you think I'm going into?"

"Law is law," Jenny retorted from instinct, even knowing how unfair it sounded—how unfair it was.

"The only office I'll have in Clayton is in the County Courts Building," he said. "I've applied for the District Attorney's office, Jen."

"The . . ."

He nodded. "I'm not a policeman because I get off on badges. I like the work. Why would I spend all these years walking an undercover tightrope and then close myself into a corporate law office?"

Jenny didn't even hesitate. "Security."

He thought about it. Then he nodded a little. "Granted. Security. Success. But there is more than one kind of success."

"Are you sure?" she asked. "I saw you in there with my ex-husband tonight. No offense, Nick, but I could hardly tell you apart. Are you sure you're not telling me what I want to hear?"

"Yes."

"And my children? *All* my children? I can't back down on that, even for you. It's too important a part of my marriage."

"I got through yesterday better than I thought."

Jenny sighed. "Yesterday is one day. The Jerk told me he'd agree to children. And then he told me he'd made that promise because he thought that's what I wanted to hear. Well, I don't want you to tell me what I want to hear. I want you to tell me what you feel."

She saw her own turmoil mirrored in his eyes. "I'll try," he promised, and she knew he meant it.

"Nick," she said with a sad little shake of her head. "I'm almost nuts with this after two weeks. How much longer am I supposed to hang on before you know?"

"Jenny, that's unfair."

"Dammit, I *know* it's unfair. But I'm not talking justice here, I'm talking survival. I just can't last much longer the way it is."

Nick came up, pulled Jenny to him, held her to him as if afraid she would run before he got a chance to change her mind. "I need you, Jenny. I love you."

Jenny curled right into his lap, her face into his neck, her arms around his shoulders. She'd never felt so wonderfully alive. She'd never felt so lost and frightened. "Nick, I don't know what to do."

"Marry me."

Jenny's tears fell harder, harder than the rain, spilling down Nick's chest. "No. I can't. I just can't."

The phone shattered their little pool of silence. Nick ignored it, his head against Jenny's, his arms tight enough around her to reassure him.

It kept ringing.

"Nick—"

Abruptly he let her go. Jenny stayed where she was, huddled on the floor, just beyond the light as he stalked over to the phone. She wanted to run after him. She wanted to run away. Sobs collected in her chest and threatened to break free.

"It's for you."

Her head shot up. Quickly swiping tears away with a hand, she got to her feet. Her baby-sitters always had her number, but they rarely used it. Jenny picked them on the basis of their self-sufficiency. God, she hoped the Jerk hadn't come back and stirred up the kids.

"Susie?"

"I'm sorry, Mrs. Lake. I didn't want to bother you—"

"What's wrong, hon?"

"Kevin. I thought you'd want to know. He's upstairs throwing up. And he has a fever. I thought he was pretty crabby... Oh, no, Emma!"

The sounds were unmistakable. Jenny wanted to laugh. She wanted to scream. Of all the times for her children to come down with the flu, it had to be while she was standing naked in a man's apartment talking about their future together.

"I'll be home right away, Susie."

Nick was already pulling on his pants. "What's wrong?"

"The flu," Jenny said with a watery grin. "My children have picked this of all nights to decorate my bathrooms."

She bent to pick up her things.

"Is there anything I can do? Do you want me to stay with you when you get home?"

"No," she answered instinctively, trying to spare him the unpleasant details of her family life. She'd just pulled her dress over her head when it occurred to her. She straightened, reconsidered, nodded. Nick still looked confused.

"Yes," she changed her mind instead, and stepped into shoes. "I would like you to stay. If you want to know what it's like, this is it. You're going to get the full family treatment, Nick. You are going to participate in the Flu Follies."

Nick wasn't sure whether he'd meant the offer. By the time he followed Jenny out the door, he was sure. He hadn't.

But it was too late now.

Chapter 15

Nick had thought it was going to be bad. He had no idea.

By the time they reached Jenny's house, several bedrooms were ruined, and both kids were wailing at the tops of their lungs up in the bathroom. The baby-sitter looked as if she'd just been through an Indian uprising.

"Will you take Susie home, Nick?" Jenny asked, heading right upstairs.

Nick was more than happy to oblige.

Things weren't much better by the time he got back. He found the Lake family firmly ensconced in the main upstairs bathroom. Both Emma and Kevin were flushed and whining, their nightclothes stained and wet. Jenny was bent over them, running a bath.

"What can I...do?" Nick asked, praying she wouldn't have any suggestions. The room was already pretty piquant, and these kids looked like they weren't finished yet.

"I have to strip beds," she said without turning around. "If you'd just get them into the tub and start rinsing, it'd help. I have to get their fevers down."

Nick tried to maintain his nonchalance. "What about Tylenol?"

Jenny straightened with a scowl and pointed to the definite pink tinge on both pajama tops and bathroom wall. "That," she said evenly, "is the Tylenol."

Nick gulped. "Oh."

"Out of those clothes, my babies," she sang, dropping a kiss on each head as she scooted out of the room. "God, this house is too cold."

Nick looked from one kid to another. It wasn't as if he'd had practice in a while, and as a child he'd always been really good at being somewhere else when something like this was going on. He wasn't sure whether he should help peel those clothes, or just pick up a rag. His first thought was just to dunk them both like doughnuts and get that stuff off them.

"Mr...Nick," Emma sobbed, hands up for help. "I throwed...up."

"Yeah, peewee," he agreed, finally unbending enough to help her. "I can tell."

"I don't want to sit in there with her," Kevin whined, his eyes glassy and cross.

"Looks like that's the only option, pal," Nick said. He'd just gathered all the pajamas when Jenny swept through and collected them.

"It's not a pretty sight out there," she warned with a wry smile.

Nick scowled. "It's not a pretty sight in here."

"I'll bring up drinks."

"Jen—"

She stopped, her arms loaded with linen, completely oblivious to the fact that the sheets would soil her good dress. Nick felt like an idiot. Worse, he felt a coward. But just the smell was churning his stomach.

"I'm not...uh, good at this."

"You're a cop," she retorted, surprised somehow.

"And as a cop," he answered as evenly as possible, "I've never been stuck in a small, smelly room with *sick* kids." He invested those four letters with every nuance of the word.

Jenny's smile didn't make Nick feel much better.

"They didn't make me a mother because I aced the course in flu," she said. "If you're serious about family life, this is where it starts."

And then she left.

Cruel, Nick thought with a scowl. Heartless. Then Emma started gasping and he was in business.

Jenny returned with large gin and tonics. Nick accepted his gratefully, already tired. He had both kids in the tub, and neither of them was happy about it. Emma cried and Kevin complained in a high, tremulous voice that grated on Nick's nerves. What was worse, the only place to sit was ground zero. He had the feeling he was going to be up and down a lot.

Jenny sat on the floor by the tub.

"Not bad, Barnes," she grinned wearily. "Might make a mother out of you yet."

Nick snorted into his drink. "The night is yet young."

"I have to clean in here, too," she noted, not moving, her face already flushed. "God, I hate the smell of pine cleaner."

"Can I make a bed or something?"

Her smile was dry. "Already done. Although, you'll probably get your chance before we're finished."

Emma began whining to get out. Kevin echoed in a higher register. Nick thought their voices reverberated like a high-caliber rifle shot around the room.

"You're still sick, babies," Jenny soothed, reaching over the edge of the tub to soak a rag and squeeze water over Emma's back. That didn't make Emma any happier. "Let's get these old fevers down, honey. Then Mr. Nick'll read you a wonderful bedtime story."

Nick raised his eyebrow. Emma, however, was appeased—at least for the moment.

"I'm sorry, Nick," Jenny said a minute later, pushing her hair back from her forehead. "It's too hot in here. I turned the air-conditioning down too far."

"It's fine," he answered, beguiled by the way the humidity curled her hair. She was leaning against the wall, her arm stretched out to encourage Kevin to keep rinsing.

"You do this often?"

Jenny shot Nick a quizzical look.

He lifted the glass. "You seem so prepared."

She smiled. "Enough times in six years to know how to get through it the easiest. When Kevin used to get the croup, we'd camp out in the bathroom for two days. I had special bathroom bedrolls for us."

Nick just shook his head. "A lot goes into it, doesn't it?"

"What?"

"Motherhood. Children."

Jenny gave her own children a considering gaze that grew very soft. "Best job in the world."

"M-o-o-o-m . . . !"

Nick was up, and Jenny had Kevin out of the water in one fluid movement. They spent the next hour repeating the procedure.

The kids' fevers came down, but unfortunately the rest of the flu refused to abate. Jenny dressed Emma while Nick dressed Kevin, and then they traded for stories. Buckets were strategically placed for accidents and the bathroom given its full cleaning. Nick was all for heading back down to the playroom for some rest, but Jenny held him off.

"Let's not push our luck," she suggested. "Stay in with Emma for a bit?"

Finally, exhausted just from the calisthenics in the bathroom, Nick agreed. He took up his position on the floor at the foot of the little girl's bed and leaned against the wall. Emma slept, her blond hair wet and tousled against the pillow. Nick watched her for a while, amazed at the beauty of a sleeping child. Stunned by how small she really was. It wasn't something he thought about when Emma was awake. She always seemed so old. Such an adult. But now, asleep, her pale lashes fanned out on freckled cheeks, she looked like a tiny porcelain doll.

If only she could stay like this, he could handle her. Nick had serious reservations about whether he was really cut out for the bathroom patrol. He couldn't believe Jenny did it with such aplomb, sailing around to clean and then dispatching kisses and hugs and not seeming to notice that she was getting wet or dirty or ragged. She really didn't seem to care.

He'd never met anyone like her. Never known a hand on his forehead when he was sick, or a soothing word to help the medicine go down. Maybe most mothers were like this. Maybe he really hadn't seen life like it was. Or maybe Jenny was just special.

"Mommy?"

Nick was up in a flash. Unfortunately, his reflexes were the wrong kind. He wasn't quick enough. Jenny had been right. He was going to get his chance to change a bed tonight.

"Okay, peewee," he soothed, an uncertain hand to the little blond head. "You sit in your rocker for a minute. I'll ask Mom where to find the sheets. Deal?"

"I'm . . . I'm sorry, Mr. Nick."

"Hey—" He crouched down to smile for that tearstained little face. "Tell you what. You can take care of me when I'm sick. Then we're even. Okay?"

That seemed to appeal to her. "You'd look silly in the bath-tub."

He got back to his feet with a grin. "Don't let that get around."

He'd thought Jenny would be in with Kevin. When he stepped into the boy's room it was quiet. Kevin was curled into a fetal position, his vast collection of invasion toys cluttered over bed and floor. Jenny was nowhere to be seen.

Then he heard a funny whimpering sound, and turned back for the bathroom.

He opened the door and came to a halt.

"Oh, Jen . . ."

"And I . . . just cleaned . . . the . . . bathroom . . ."

Nick stood frozen in the doorway, unsure whether to go in or go out. She was crouched over the bowl, hair limp and face pasty. Here Nick had thought she'd been in with Kevin, when all along she'd been trying to keep this from him.

Her body convulsed again and Nick's decision was made. He crouched down next to her and pulled her hair gently back. "You're burning up," he protested, not knowing how else to tell her how much it hurt him to see her so sick. "Why didn't you say something?"

She wiped her mouth on the rag she held and shook her head. "You've been such a help with the kids. I couldn't . . . couldn't ask you to . . ."

That sentence wasn't finished, either.

Jenny couldn't believe it. Her big night. Her wonderful date, and here she was retching in the bathroom while Nick ran relay between the kids. She could hardly get her head up anymore from where she rested it against the cool tub rim. She was just so exhausted, so hot, so shaky. And Nick was still in Kevin's room changing sheets.

Well, if this night didn't cure him, nothing would. She wanted to cry. She probably would have if she'd had any moisture left in her anywhere. She felt like a squeezed lemon. She felt like stale bread—hot stale bread.

Then Nick came back. She could smell him first, cool like a summer night, his footsteps quiet and hesitant like he wasn't sure what to do with her. That was all right, she thought. She wasn't sure what to do with her anymore.

"I found your nightgown," he was saying, crouching close enough to run the back of his hand down her cheek. That felt cool, too. Cool and life-giving. Sweet. From some hidden well tears sprang up and stung her eyes. "Why don't I help you get it on and get you into bed, Jen? Maybe you'll feel better."

"I'm sorry, Nick," she apologized yet again. "This isn't fair."

"You're right," he answered with a soft grin. "It isn't. An entire pot of spaghetti sauce went to waste, I've changed more beds than a hotel maid and when I get the flu I'm going to have to let Emma take care of me. Now come on, let's get you to bed."

He lifted her. Jenny couldn't think of a sweeter thing anyone had ever done for her. He carried her into bed, and helped her get undressed and then covered her. And when he wasn't checking on the kids, he sat right by her through the night.

By the time the sun came up, Nick felt as if he'd been awake for a week. Everybody was finally asleep in the house, all foreheads reasonably cool, all stomachs quiet. To say he'd never been through anything like that in his life would have been an understatement. He'd survived a thousand firefights in Nam, drug busts, gang fights, union negotiations. In all his thirty-five years, he'd never fought a siege like the one he had last night. He hoped like hell he never would again.

Finally crawling off to the couch downstairs, he put in a couple of hours of sleep and then stumbled awake for the day.

Coffee. That sounded like a good idea. Shuffling around the kitchen in bare feet, he ran a hand through tumbled hair and brewed a pot. Looked for cream and settled for skim milk. He still hadn't eaten since last night, when he'd spent so much time testing his spaghetti sauce so that it would be just right for Jenny.

His spaghetti sauce was probably a congealed mass by now. It served him right for courting a mother. He should have just picked out a stewardess or a bank clerk like normal men. On their dates they went to the movies, maybe a club. On his, he worked the wards.

Well, he thought, pouring off a preliminary sample and adding the milk, at least it gave him a chance to finally decide. Jenny had said if he wanted to know about family life, last night would be it. Well, it was.

He'd been dumped headfirst back into the responsibility, the backbreaking work. He'd waded in tedium and fought revulsion. And somewhere in the small hours of the night, the answer to all Jenny's questions had finally come to him.

He looked up, wondering how she was doing. He wasn't about to wake her. She'd looked so exhausted lying there, her face almost translucent, her eyes huge and dark. He'd ached again, just like before. It hurt too much, sometimes, he realized. Too much to see someone you loved hurting. The flip side of living, the caring too much, the wanting too much. The ache when you couldn't do more.

He'd never known that before. He'd never been given that. He didn't know how to deal with it. Would Jenny hurt as much if he'd been the one racked like that? Yes, he realized, remembering the pain she hadn't been able to keep from her eyes when he'd told her about his childhood. She would. She'd stroke his cheek and murmur to him, straightening his sheets and aching with her eyes.

God, he thought, with a frustrated shake of the head. That was such a small thing last night. What about the big things? The big hurts and aches? How did you survive bearing that for someone else? Wishing for their pain and dying a little when you couldn't take it from them? How did you share?

Did he have the ability? Did he have the strength?

He did have the love. But, as Jenny said, was that enough? It scared the hell out of him.

Nick had begun to pace, walking through silent rooms without seeing them, picking things up, putting them down, straightening. He reached the front window and saw that unbelievably enough it was a nice day out: fresh, clear, storm-swept. Distracted, he pulled the curtains back a little.

Suddenly, his attention was completely caught. Completely, fatally caught. Not now. Aw, hell, not now!

He leaned in a little, trying to make sure, following progress, watching hands and pockets. Following the sleight of hand that made envelopes disappear from Barb Bailey's mailbox.

"Aw, dammit. Now I'll *never* get off that damn truck!"

Jenny wasn't sure what she'd expected. She knew what she'd hoped for. She'd hoped that she'd wake to find Nick right there, sitting in the rocking chair or curled up alongside her... even curled up downstairs. He wasn't. He was gone.

Making sure the kids were still asleep, she trudged downstairs. Still hoping. Still wishing for at least a note—*something* that would promise a return.

There was nothing, just cold coffee in the pot and silence. Spot rubbed up against her leg looking for food, the church bells were ringing noon Angelus. Half the day gone. Half the day left.

What for? The hope that had seen her down the steps was fading fast, folding in on itself like a dying flower. She'd made it a point to drag Nick over last night to force his hand. Well, she sure had. She'd dumped him right in the river to see if he'd swim, and it looked like he hadn't made it to the other bank.

His hand had been so cool against her cheek, though. He'd carried her into bed. No one had ever done that for her. No one but her mother had held her head when she'd been sick. How could he stay through the worst and then just take off? It didn't make any sense.

It made perfect sense. He'd reached his decision. She'd sure seen to that. Now she had to face getting through the rest of the day alone, and then the night, and then the next day. She had to survive, just as she had the last two years.

She'd thought she hadn't any tears left. Somehow they rose again, sliding down her cheeks and spilling onto the table. So what if he was going to be a lawyer? He was Nick. He was gentle and funny and pragmatic. He was the sound of gulls and fast engines, the wind in her hair and the sun in her eyes. He was freedom and security, and it didn't matter if he decided to be a bank robber, he would still be the man she loved.

Damn him. He had to listen to her and come along last night. He had to let himself be talked into the test. She could have fooled him a while longer, long enough to. . .

To what? To marry him? To have more children? To show him just what it was he'd locked himself into, just like the Jerk? She couldn't do that and she knew it. She couldn't cage him just because she couldn't bear to lose him. Better to make it a clean cut. Better to leave now.

If it was better, it should have been easier to stop the tears.

Emma and Kevin got up after a while and ambled in to sit in the playroom. Barb came over and prescribed chicken soup. Kate called and asked again about going to tea. Each asked what was wrong with Jenny, and she used the flu for an excuse. Then each asked if there was anything else to be done. Nothing, Jenny said each time. Nothing, at all.

And she sat at the table, knowing she should do something but without the energy to move. Listening to the silence in her house and hating it. Gathering her children to her for hugs and reassuring her family that everything was all right. She watched the sun slide past her kitchen window and settle against the horizon in crimson slashes. She heard the birds, the neighborhood dogs, the television, and still she couldn't quite decide to move.

She didn't want to go forward, because it would mean admitting she had to go on without Nick. She had to face that endless succession of days again, of frustrations and responsibilities, of lonely, silent nights when there was no one to share the small minutes of darkness with her, no one to create something new with.

In the end, she knew she couldn't stay where she was. She still had two children who didn't deserve to be neglected. She had a family, and she had a life. And she damn well had to get on with it.

At the time she usually began talking the kids into getting into pajamas, Jenny changed out of her nightgown. She showered and dressed and straightened up her room. She could still smell him there, so that if she closed her eyes he was still there, his eyes like gems, his voice a hush of concern.

But he wasn't there, so she went back downstairs.

And there she found him, sitting at her kitchen table.

Jenny came to a stop. For a moment she blamed it on dehydration, or residual fever. On wishful thinking. She'd spent the day mourning him and, just like a genie, he was back.

"I thought you'd taken the noon train out of town," Jenny offered hesitantly.

Nick flashed a smile that was equal parts apology and triumph. "I'm sorry I wasn't here when you woke up. How are you feeling?"

Jenny shook her head. "Confused."

"I know." Taking another assessing glance that seemed to mean something special, he launched himself to his feet. "Can we talk?"

Jenny almost found herself stepping back. She didn't want him too close. She didn't want to feel that hope resurrecting in her chest, inflating like a balloon threatening to burst free. She didn't want to be disappointed again.

But he was here. "You did a good job on Kevin and Emma," she said, still so very unnerved. "Thanks."

"Yeah," he nodded a little. "I was talking to them. They're watching TV. Want to sit in the living room? I need to talk to you before the neighborhood breaks in."

Instinctively Jenny looked around. This wasn't exactly the center of neighborhood activity. "Why?"

He flashed a sudden smile. "Explanations come with the talk."

She followed him back in, easing down onto her couch as if in a stranger's home, unsure what she wanted him to say, afraid of what he would.

For a long moment, Nick just stared at his hands. "First of all, the reason I left so abruptly. I didn't want to wake you. You'd been through . . . a lot."

Jenny couldn't help but smile. "Childbirth," she amended, "is a lot. The flu is survivable."

Nick smiled, and in it betrayed the insecurities he'd brought with him the night before. "Yeah, well, I'm not a good judge of that stuff. Anyway, the long and short of it is that our secret is out. My cover is blown."

Jenny straightened. "How?"

Another smile, this one pure satisfaction. "Case is closed, suspect apprehended."

"You're off the ice cream truck?"

This seemed to deserve a grimace. "Well, that remains to be seen."

"Why?"

"Because the suspect is the chief of police's aunt."

Jenny sat back, stunned, trying to ingest the information. "Mrs. Warner? Mrs. Warner was stealing checks?"

Nick shook his head with another wince. "Miss Lucy."

That brought Jenny to her feet. "You *arrested* Miss Lucy?"

"Sit down, Jen," Nick urged, taking her hand. When she did—albeit reluctantly—he continued. "It's not all that bad. She's turned state's evidence. Her lawn crew got her involved. Seems it's a bit more expensive to live across your street than the old ladies thought. When the 'nice young gentlemen' came to her with the idea, Miss Lucy decided to pad the Social Security a little."

Jenny couldn't get past the bald truth. "Miss *Lucy?*"

Nick grinned. "Quite a savvy old lady. She sure had me fooled. When I laid it out to the chief, he got hold of her and she admitted it right away. Said she figured nobody would arrest a nice old lady like her. They certainly wouldn't sentence her."

"They won't, will they?"

Nick shrugged. "She'll probably get a suspended sentence."

Jenny just kept shaking her head. "Miss Lucy."

Nick nodded. "She was delighted I arrested her. Said she was thrilled I wasn't a drug runner, after all."

"Well, then," she said, still trying to assimilate the easy stuff. "It's all settled."

"Not," Nick objected, "quite."

Jenny looked up. "What?"

"There *was* a drug dealer in the neighborhood. They picked him up this afternoon."

Jenny was beginning to anticipate now. "Him?"

Nick nodded. "Todd Sellers. I figured it out yesterday. We were able to link it all up. Oh, and by the way, I met your lovely Detective Richards. I'm surprised that guy can find the rest room most days."

"I bet he was thrilled when you told him."

"He did refer to the legitimacy of my birth once or twice."

"Todd," Jenny murmured, frowning. "Poor Lauren." Ideas, assistance for both households formed in her mind, and then she turned back to Nick. "Anything else?"

"Well, yes."

She sighed. "What?"

"Marry me."

This time Jenny went very still. "Pardon?"

Nick smiled then, his face lighting, his eyes bright with delight. "You have a pretty mean boot camp, lady. But I think I passed."

"You think?"

He took her hand. Jenny let him. She couldn't seem to think, to feel. To hope. Time came to a standstill and the world held its silence for the answer.

Nick looked briefly at where he held her hand, as if considering what he had. Then he returned his gaze to her. "I went back to the apartment this afternoon," he said. "After being here and then running around with all this. I thought I could use a little peace and quiet before I came back here. Know what I found?"

Jenny could do no more than shake her head.

"Emptiness. It wasn't quiet there. It was just empty. I kept waiting for the sound of your voice, for Emma and Kevin to bolt through the door." He took a breath, discovering even as he spoke. "I missed this house. Jenny, I don't know how I'll do with a big family. I've never tried it before. But I realized today that I damn well want to try. I've lived in an empty place too long. Fill my life for me."

Jenny should have grown tired of the tears. They betrayed her again, even before she could speak. "Whiffle-ball games, and all?"

"Pink houses and tuna-noodle casserole and soccer games."

"Yes," Jenny said, and thought she'd never said anything that sounded so right before. "Yes. I'll marry you."

It was summer again. The days still stretched in languid succession to a close-approaching autumn. School would start at the end of the weekend. For now, the house was filled with the noise of a family picnic. Horseshoes were being played out in the backyard and whiffle ball in the street. Amanda scooted in her walker and Jessie gurgled as he bounced on his grandmother's knee.

In the kitchen Jenny and Claire were doing dishes and sampling leftover potato salad.

"All right," Claire admitted. "You win."

Pushing wet black hair back from her forehead, Jenny turned from the sink. "Why?"

Claire delivered a sisterly glare that grudgingly admitted defeat. "You look happier than I've ever seen you in your life."

Jenny grinned. "Probably because I am."

"I have to admit he cleaned up real well, didn't he?"

Jenny took a look through to the picture of Nick and her on their wedding day. He'd pulled out what he referred to as his yuppie wardrobe, all pinstripes and power ties. She had worn an ivory dress and hat.

"Actually," she admitted, wistfully, "there are times when I miss that ponytail."

Claire rolled her eyes. "You still have the tattoo."

Jenny grinned. "Yeah. Sometimes we get in his GTO and play the rock and roll really loud, and he wears those T-shirts..."

"And those ripped jeans?"

"I saved them."

"Probably shouldn't let the D.A.'s office know about that."

"Oh, they know. He's been begging to go undercover again."

Immediately Claire bristled. "Now?"

Jenny smiled. "Back in the high rises. He's been asked to help Kevin crack an insider-trading scandal."

"Kevin? You mean the Jer—"

"The same, much to his chagrin." A partial victory there—money for the children, but no change in attention. It just didn't seem to be in her ex, especially with his new family to consider. On the other hand, a very colicky first baby had rid him of the custody notions.

They had, in the end, come to a more manageable truce.

"Where is he?"

Startled, Jenny looked up. The door slammed right behind a bear of a man. He'd been on the heels of her father, who was in the process of going for another beer.

"Hello, Marco," Jenny greeted the ice cream magnate. "I see you've met my dad."

Marco proceeded to slap her dad on the back and almost send him over on his nose. "I like your family."

"Thanks," Jenny acknowledged. "I like yours. Now, if you'll take your loud lungs out into the yard, I'll go find Nick."

"He should be out there defending the Barnes honor."

Jenny just smiled. "You know darn well where he is. Now, go on."

"You will not allow me to witness this miracle all the police bet would never happen?"

"I'll take pictures," she promised. "He might spook if someone approached too suddenly."

Marco's laugh should have awakened Miss Lucy from her nap across the street.

Jenny made sure the two men had taken their evidently in-progress discussion of city politics outside before tossing her towel at Claire. "Finish these, will you? I have to see a man."

Claire's smile gave away her affection for her new brother-in-law. "I think it's cute."

"Yeah," Jenny agreed with an even sillier grin. "So do I."

The noise receded as she climbed the stairs. It always seemed so much quieter up here. Especially late, when the kids were in bed and she and Nick lay together talking over the day. A haven. Her home had become full and noisy and safe. And finally whole.

She always knew where to find him these days. Jenny pushed the door open a little. The room was a little cleaner, the bed emptied of clutter. It was easier to do now that Jenny was just substitute teaching. Of course, Nick refused to keep his books out of the bedroom, but she didn't mind. There was something so settling about reading together.

The rocking chair was still in front of the window, right where the morning sun would find it. The morning light was long gone, but the sky glowed softly behind him, casting him in a kind of halo, a soft light of welcome.

He'd changed in the last year. Grown, she thought, into his position, into his family. His face looked more mature, more authoritative. His hair was precisely cut now, full and just beginning to gray at the temples, and he'd recovered the mustache that seemed so important to him. He wore polo shirts instead of his favorite Grateful Dead shirts, but Jenny could still see that tattoo. The wild side of him still peeked out when she wanted it to.

Today, though, there was just peace. Wonder. Nick was rocking slowly back and forth, his eyes down on the tiny bundle in his arms. Jenny watched him and fought the sting of new tears. It never failed to break her heart all over again to see this man with his tiny new daughter and see the joy in his eyes.

He knew she was there, of course.

"I thought I heard her crying."

Jenny grinned. "Amazing. Two weeks old, and she already has all your buttons pushed. This kid is going to be a pro."

"Hey," he objected, even though his eyes still held that strange peace. "Don't talk about my daughter that way. I'm just getting in my time while I can. It's only gonna be a few years before she's gone."

"I doubt it," Jenny assured him. "I have a feeling Maggie's going to be thirty before you even let her date."

"You'd better believe it."

"I'll tell Emma, too."

"Emma's *already* thirty."

"Marco needs your help at horseshoes," she said. "And Emma is waiting for you to swing her."

The plus, the special bonus Jenny couldn't have dreamed of if she'd tried. The only person more protective, more loving, more devoted to her children than she, was Nick. He was a champion Chutes-and-Ladders player, a rabid soccer fan, an attentive escort to tea. Maggie's arrival had just cemented the growing family.

"How many more do you want?" he asked again, their little game, their special bond.

"Five," Jenny answered. "To form an even number."

"Six," Nick countered. "Then we'll have a baseball team."

"Oh, I don't know," Jen demurred. "Kids are so demanding."

Slowly getting to his feet, Nick brought Maggie over to her mother. "It's different when they're yours," he informed her archly.

They stood there for a moment, together, sharing the small silence in the house, the small life they held between them.

"Thank you," Nick finally said, his eyes warmer than any summer sun.

Jenny lifted her face to bask in his gaze. "For what?" she asked, knowing. Never hearing it enough.

"For my new family," he said, motioning to include the noise still drifting up from outside. "All of it."

Jenny couldn't offer any words that would contain the love she felt for her husband. She just smiled and reached up to kiss him, their new daughter caught between them.

Nick reached out a hand to her. Jenny saw the truth in his eyes, heard the wonder in his voice, and was content.

"Thank you," he said. "For filling my life."

* * * * *